PHILIP ROTH

PHILIP ROTH

NOVELS 2001–2007

The Dying Animal
The Plot Against America
Exit Ghost

THE LIBRARY OF AMERICA

The paper used in this publication meets the
minimum requirements of the American National Standard for
Information Sciences—Permanence of Paper for Printed
Library Materials, ANSI Z39.48—1984.

Distributed to the trade in the United States
by Penguin Group (USA) Inc.
and in Canada by Penguin Books Canada Ltd.

Library of Congress Control Number: 2012904758
ISBN 978–1–59853–198–5

———

First Printing
The Library of America—236

Manufactured in the United States of America

Ross Miller
wrote the Chronology and Notes
for this volume

Contents

THE DYING ANIMAL

For N. M.

The body contains the life story just as much as the brain.

—Edna O'Brien

I KNEW her eight years ago. She was in my class. I don't teach full-time anymore, strictly speaking don't teach literature at all—for years now just the one class, a big senior seminar in critical writing called Practical Criticism. I attract a lot of female students. For two reasons. Because it's a subject with an alluring combination of intellectual glamour and journalistic glamour and because they've heard me on NPR reviewing books or seen me on Thirteen talking about culture. Over the past fifteen years, being cultural critic on the television program has made me fairly well known locally, and they're attracted to my class because of that. In the beginning, I didn't realize that talking on TV once a week for ten minutes could be so impressive as it turns out to be to these students. But they are helplessly drawn to celebrity, however inconsiderable mine may be.

Now, I'm very vulnerable to female beauty, as you know. Everybody's defenseless against something, and that's it for me. I see it and it blinds me to everything else. They come to my first class, and I know almost immediately which is the girl for me. There is a Mark Twain story in which he runs from a bull, and the bull looks up to him when he's hiding in a tree, and the bull thinks, "You are my meat, sir." Well, that "sir" is transformed into "young lady" when I see them in class. It is now eight years ago—I was already sixty-two, and the girl, who is called Consuela Castillo, was twenty-four. She is not like the rest of the class. She doesn't look like a student, at least not like an ordinary student. She's not a demi-adolescent, she's not a slouching, unkempt, "like"-ridden girl. She's well spoken, sober, her posture is perfect—she appears to know something about adult life along with how to sit, stand, and walk. As soon as you enter the class, you see that this girl either knows more or wants to. The way she dresses. It isn't exactly what's called chic, she's certainly not flamboyant, but, to begin with, she's never in jeans, pressed or unpressed. She dresses carefully, with quiet taste, in skirts, dresses, and tailored pants. Not to desensualize herself but more, it would seem, to professionalize herself, she dresses like an attractive secretary in a

5

prestigious legal firm. Like the secretary to the bank chairman. She has a cream-colored silk blouse under a tailored blue blazer with gold buttons, a brown pocketbook with the patina of expensive leather, and little ankle boots to match, and she wears a slightly stretchy gray knitted skirt that reveals her body lines as subtly as such a skirt possibly could. Her hair is done in a natural but cared-for manner. She has a pale complexion, the mouth is bowlike though the lips are full, and she has a rounded forehead, a polished forehead of a smooth Brancusi elegance. She is Cuban. Her family are prosperous Cubans living in Jersey, across the river in Bergen County. She has black, black hair, glossy but ever so slightly coarse. And she's big. She's a big woman. The silk blouse is unbuttoned to the third button, and so you see she has powerful, beautiful breasts. You see the cleavage immediately. And you see she knows it. You see, despite the decorum, the meticulousness, the cautiously soigné style—or because of them—that she's aware of herself. She comes to the first class with the jacket buttoned over her blouse, yet some five minutes into the session, she has taken it off. When I glance her way again, I see that she's put it back on. So you understand that she's aware of her power but that she isn't sure yet how to use it, what to do with it, how much she even wants it. That body is still new to her, she's still trying it out, thinking it through, a bit like a kid walking the streets with a loaded gun and deciding whether he's packing it to protect himself or to begin a life of crime.

And she's aware of something else, and this I couldn't know from the one class meeting: she finds culture important in a reverential, old-fashioned way. Not that it's something she wishes to live by. She doesn't and she couldn't—too traditionally well brought up for that—but it's important and wonderful as nothing else she knows is. She's the one who finds the Impressionists ravishing but must look long and hard—and always with a sense of nagging confoundment—at a Cubist Picasso, trying with all her might to get the idea. She stands there waiting for the surprising new sensation, the new thought, the new emotion, and when it won't come, ever, she chides herself for being inadequate and lacking . . . what? She chides herself for not even knowing what it is she lacks. Art that smacks of modernity leaves her not merely puzzled but disappointed in herself. She would love for Picasso to matter more, perhaps to transform her, but there's a scrim drawn across the proscenium of genius that obscures her vision and keeps her worshiping at a bit of a distance. She gives to art, to all of art, far more than she gets back, a sort of earnestness that isn't without its poignant appeal. A good heart, a lovely face, a gaze at once inviting and removed, gorgeous breasts, and so newly hatched as a woman that to find fragments of broken shell adhering to that ovoid forehead wouldn't have been a surprise. I saw right away that this was going to be my girl.

Now, I have one set rule of some fifteen years' standing that I never break. I don't any longer get in touch with them on a private basis until they've completed their final exam and received their grade and I am no longer officially in loco parentis. In spite of temptation—or even a clear-cut signal to begin the flirtation and make the approach—I haven't broken this rule since, back in the mid-eighties, the phone number of the sexual harassment hotline was first posted outside my office door. I don't get in touch with them any earlier so as not to run afoul of those in the university who, if they could, would seriously impede my enjoyment of life.

I teach each year for fourteen weeks, and during that time I don't have affairs with them. I play a trick instead. It's an honest trick, it's an open and above-board trick, but it is a trick nonetheless. After the final examination and once the grades are in, I throw a party in my apartment for the students. It is always a success and it is always the same. I invite them for a drink at about six o'clock. I say that from six to eight we are going to have a drink, and they always stay till two in the morning. The bravest ones, after ten o'clock, develop into lively characters and tell me what they really are interested in. In the Practical Criticism seminar there are about twenty students, sometimes as many as twenty-five, so there will be fifteen, sixteen girls and five or six boys, of whom two or three are straight. Half of this group has left the party by ten. Generally, one straight boy, maybe one gay boy, and some nine girls will stay. They're invariably the most cultivated, intelligent, and spirited of the lot. They talk about what they're reading, what they're listening to, what art shows they've seen—enthusiasms that they don't normally go on about with their elders or necessarily with their friends. They find one another in my class. And they find me. During the party they suddenly see I am a human being. I'm not their teacher, I'm not my reputation, I'm not their parent. I have a pleasant, orderly duplex apartment, they see my large library, aisles of double-faced bookshelves that house a lifetime's reading and take up almost the entire downstairs floor, they see my piano, they see my devotion to what I do, and they stay.

My funniest student one year was like the goat in the fairy tale that goes into the clock to hide. I threw the last of them out at two in the morning, and while saying good night, I missed one girl. I said, "Where is our class clown, Prospero's daughter?" "Oh, I think Miranda left," somebody said. I went back into the apartment to start cleaning the place up and I heard a door being closed upstairs. A bathroom door. And Miranda came down the stairs, laughing, radiant with a kind of goofy abandon—I'd never, till that moment, realized that she was so pretty—and she said, "Wasn't that clever of me? I've been hiding in your upstairs bathroom, and now I'm going to sleep with you."

A little thing, maybe five foot one, and she pulled off her sweater and showed me her tits, revealing the adolescent torso of an incipiently transgressive Balthus virgin, and of course we slept together. All evening long, much like a young girl escaped from the perilous melodrama of a Balthus painting into the fun of the class party, Miranda had been on all fours on the floor with her rump raised or lying helplessly prostrate on my sofa or lounging gleefully across the arms of an easy chair seemingly oblivious of the fact that with her skirt riding up her thighs and her legs undecorously parted she had the Balthusian air of being half undressed while fully clothed. Everything's hidden and nothing's concealed. Many of these girls have been having sex since they were fourteen, and by their twenties there are one or two curious to do it with a man of my years, if just the once, and eager the next day to tell all their friends, who crinkle up their faces and ask, "But what about his skin? Didn't he smell funny? What about his long white hair? What about his wattle? What about his little pot belly? Didn't you feel sick?"

Miranda told me afterward, "You must have slept with

hundreds of women. I wanted to see what it would be like." "And?" And then she said things I didn't entirely believe, but it didn't matter. She had been audacious—she had seen she could do it, game and terrified though she may have been while hiding in the bathroom. She discovered how courageous she was confronting this unfamiliar juxtaposition, that she could conquer her initial fears and any initial revulsion, and I—as regards the juxtaposition—had a wonderful time altogether. Sprawling, clowning, cavorting Miranda, posing with her underwear at her feet. Just the pleasure of looking was lovely. Though that was hardly the only reward. The decades since the sixties have done a remarkable job of completing the sexual revolution. This is a generation of astonishing fellators. There's been nothing like them ever before among their class of young women.

Consuela Castillo. I saw her and was tremendously impressed by her comportment. She knew what her body was worth. She knew what she was. She knew too she could never fit into the cultural world I lived in—culture was to bedazzle her but not something to live with. So she came to the party—beforehand I'd worried that she might not show up—and was outgoing with me there for the first time. Uncertain as to just how sober and cautious she might be, I had been careful not to reveal any special interest in her during the class meetings or on the two occasions when we met in my office to go over her papers. Nor was she, in those private meetings, anything other than subdued and respectful, taking down every word I said, no matter how unimportant. Always, in my office, she entered and exited with the tailored jacket worn over her blouse. The first time she came to see me—and we sat side by side at my desk, as directed, with the door wide open to the public corridor, all eight of our limbs, our two contrasting torsos visible to every Big Brother of a passerby (and with the window wide open as well, opened by me, flung open, for fear of her perfume)—the first time she wore elegant gray flannel cuffed pants, and the second time a black jersey skirt and black tights, but, as in class, there was always the blouse, against her white-white skin the silk blouse of one creamy shade or another unbuttoned down to the third button. At the party, however, she removed the jacket after a single glass of wine and boldly jacketless was beaming at me, offering a tantalizingly open smile. We were standing inches apart in my study, where I had been showing her a Kafka manuscript I own—three pages in Kafka's hand-writing, a speech he'd given at a retirement party for the chief of the insurance office where he was working, a gift, this 1910 manuscript, from a wealthy married woman of thirty who'd been a student-mistress some years back.

Consuela was talking excitedly about everything. Letting her hold the Kafka manuscript had thrilled her, and so every-thing was emerging at once, questions nursed by her over that whole semester while I had secretly nursed my longing. "What music do you listen to? Do you really play the piano? Do you read all day long? Do you know all the poetry on your shelves by heart?" From every question it was clear how much she marveled—her word—at what my life was, my coherent, com-posed cultural life. I asked her what she was doing, what her life was like, and she told me that after high school, she didn't start college immediately—she'd decided to become a private secretary. And that's what I'd seen right off: the decorous, loyal private secretary, the office treasure to a man of power, the head of the bank or the law firm. She truly was of a bygone era, a throwback to a more mannerly time, and I guessed that her way of thinking about herself, like her way of comporting herself, had a lot to do with her being the daughter of wealthy Cuban émigrés, rich people who'd fled the revolution.

She told me, "I didn't like being a secretary. I tried it for a couple of years, but it's a dull world, and my parents always wanted and expected me to go to college. I finally decided to study instead. I suppose I was trying to be rebellious, but that was childish and so I enrolled here. I marvel at the arts." Again "marvel," used freely and sincerely. "Yes, what do you like?" I asked. "The theater. All kinds of theater. I go to the opera. My father loves the opera and we go to the Met together. Puccini's his favorite. I always love going with him." "You love your parents." "Very much," she said. "Tell me about them." "Well, they're Cuban. Very proud. And they've done very well here. The Cubans who came here because of the revolution had a way of seeing the world so that somehow they all did extremely well. That first group, like my family, worked hard, did whatever they needed to do, did well to the point where, my grandfather used to tell us, some of them who needed public assistance when they first arrived, because they had nothing—from some of them, after a few years, the U.S. government started to receive checks paying them back. They didn't know what to do with it, my grandfather said. The first time in the history of the U.S. Treasury that they'd gotten a check back." "You love your grandfather, too. What is he like?" I asked. "Like my father—a steady person, extremely traditional, someone with an Old World view. Hard work and education first. Above everything. And like my father, very much a family man. Very religious. Though he doesn't go to church that much. Neither does my father. But my mother does. My grandmother does. My grandmother will pray the rosary every night. People bring her rosaries for presents. She has her favorites. She loves her rosary." "Do you go to church?" "When I was little. But now, no. My family is adaptable. Cubans of that generation had to be adaptable, to a degree. My family would like for us to go, my brother and me, but no, I don't." "What kind of restraints did a Cuban girl growing up in America have that wouldn't be typical of an American upbringing?" "Oh, I had a lot earlier curfew. Had to be home when all my friends were just starting to get together on a summer night. Home at eight on a summer night when I was fourteen and fifteen. But my father wasn't some frightening guy. He's just your average nice-guy dad. Except no boy was ever allowed in my room. Ever. Otherwise, when I got to be sixteen, I was treated the way my friends were being treated, in terms of curfews and stuff." "And your mother and father, when did they come here?" "In 1960. Fidel was still letting people go then. They were married in Cuba. They came to Mexico first. Then to here. I was born here, of course." "Do you think of yourself as American?" "I was born here, but, no, I'm Cuban. Very much so." "I'm surprised, Consuela. Your voice, your manner, the way you say 'stuff' and 'guy.' You're totally American to me. Why do you think of yourself as a Cuban?" "I come from a Cuban family. That's it. That's the whole story. My family has this extraordinary pride. They just love their country. It's in their hearts. It's in their blood. They were like that in Cuba." "What do they love about Cuba?" "Oh, it was so much fun. It was a society of people

that had the best of all the world. Entirely cosmopolitan, especially if you lived in Havana. And it was beautiful. And they
had all these great parties. It was a really good time." "Parties?
Tell me about the parties." "I have these pictures of my mother
at these costume balls. From the time she came out. Pictures
of her at her coming-out ball." "What did her family do?"
"Well, that's a long story." "Tell me." "Well, the first Spanish
on my grandmother's side was sent there as a general. There
was always a lot of old Spanish money. My grandmother had
tutors at home, she went to Paris at eighteen to buy dresses. In
my family, on both sides, there are Spanish titles. Some of them
are very, very old titles. Like my grandmother is a duchess—in
Spain." "And are you a duchess as well, Consuela?" "No," she
said, smiling, "just a lucky Cuban girl." "Well, you could pass
for a duchess. There must be a duchess looking like you on the
walls of the Prado. Do you know the famous painting of
Velázquez, *The Maids of Honor*? Though there the little prin-
cess is fair, is blond." "I don't think I do." "It's in Madrid. In
the Prado. I'll show it to you."

We went down the spiral steel staircase to my library stacks,
and I found a large book of Velázquez reproductions, and we
sat side by side and turned the pages for fifteen minutes, a
stirring quarter hour in which we both learned something—
she, for the first time, about Velázquez, and I, anew, about the
delightful imbecility of lust. All this talk! I show her Kafka,
Velázquez . . . why does one do this? Well, you have to do
something. These are the veils of the dance. Don't confuse it
with seduction. This is not seduction. What you're disguising
is the thing that got you there, the pure lust. The veils veil the
blind drive. Talking this talk, you have a misguided sense, as
does she, that you know what you're dealing with. But it's not
as though you're interviewing a lawyer or hiring a doctor and
that whatever's said along the way is going to change your course
of action. You know you want it and you know you're going to
do it and nothing is going to stop you. Nothing is going to be
said here that's going to change anything.

The great biological joke on people is that you are intimate
before you know anything about the other person. In the initial moment you understand everything. You are drawn to
each other's surface initially, but you also intuit the fullest di-

mension. And the attraction doesn't have to be equivalent: she's attracted to one thing, you to the other. It's surface, it's curiosity, but then, boom, the dimension. It's nice that she's from Cuba, it's nice that her grandmother was this and her grandfather was that, it's nice that I play the piano and own a Kafka manuscript, but all this is merely a detour on the way to getting where we're going. It's part of the enchantment, I suppose, but it's the part that if I could have none of, I'd feel much better. Sex is all the enchantment required. Do men find women so enchanting once the sex is taken out? Does anyone find anyone of any sex that enchanting unless they have sexual business with them? Who else are you that enchanted by? Nobody.

She thinks, I'm telling him who I am. He's interested in who I am. That is true, but I am curious about who she is because I want to fuck her. I don't need all of this great interest in Kafka and Velázquez. Having this conversation with her, I am thinking, How much more am I going to have to go through? Three hours? Four? Will I go as far as eight hours? Twenty minutes into the veiling and already I'm wondering, What does any of this have to do with her tits and her skin and how she carries herself? The French art of being flirtatious is of no interest to me. The savage urge is. No, this is not seduction. This is comedy. It is the comedy of creating a connection that is not the connection—that cannot begin to compete with the connection—created unartificially by lust. This is the instant conventionalizing, the giving us something in common on the spot, the trying to transform lust into something socially appropriate. Yet it's the radical inappropriateness that makes lust *lust*. No, this just plots the course, not forward but back to the elemental drive. Don't confuse the veiling with the business at hand. Sure, something else might develop, but that something has nothing to do with shopping for curtains and duvet covers and signing on as a member of the evolutionary team. The evolutionary system can work without me. I want to fuck this girl, and yes, I'll have to put up with some sort of veiling, but it's a means to an end. How much of this is cunning? I'd like to think that all of it is.

"Shall we go together to the theater sometime?" I asked her. "Oh, I'd love to do that," she said, and I didn't know then whether she was alone or had a boyfriend, but I didn't care, and two or three days later—this is all eight years back, in 1992 —she wrote a note saying "It was great to be invited to the party, to see your wonderful apartment, your amazing library, to hold in my own hands the handwriting of Franz Kafka. You so generously introduced me to Diego Velázquez . . ." She included her phone number along with her address, and so I called and proposed an evening out. "Why don't you join me to go to the theater? You know what my work is. I have to go to the theater almost every week, I always have two tickets, and perhaps you'd like to come."

So we had dinner together in midtown, we went to the play, it wasn't at all interesting, and I was sitting next to her, glancing at her beautiful cleavage and her beautiful body. She has a D cup, this duchess, really big, beautiful breasts, and skin of a very white color, skin that, the moment you see it, makes you want to lick it. At the theater, in the dark, the potency of her stillness was enormous. What could be more erotic in that situation than the seeming absence in the exciting woman of any erotic intention?

After the play I said we could go for a drink, but there was one disadvantage. "People recognize me because of the television and, wherever we go, the Algonquin, the Carlyle, wherever, they may interfere with our sense of privacy." She said, "I noticed people noticing us already, at the restaurant and at the theater." "Did you mind?" I asked. "I don't know if I minded. I just noticed it. I wondered if *you* minded." "There's nothing much to be done about it," I said, "it comes with the job." "I suppose," she said, "they thought I was a groupie." "You're decidedly not a groupie," I assured her. "But I'm sure that's what they thought. 'There's David Kepesh with one of his little groupies.' They're thinking I'm some silly overwhelmed girl." "And if they did think that?" I asked. "I don't know if I like that so much. I'd like to graduate college before my parents find their daughter on Page Six of the *Post*." "I don't think you're going to be on Page Six. That's not going to happen." "I truly hope not," she said. "Look, if this is what's bothering you," I said, "we can circumvent the problem by going to my place. We can go to my apartment. We can have a drink there." "Okay," she said, but only after a serious, quietly thoughtful moment, "that's probably a better idea." Not a good idea, just a better idea.

We went to my apartment and she asked me to put on some music. I generally played easy classical music for her. Haydn trios, the *Musical Offering*, dynamic movements from the Beethoven symphonies, adagio movements from Brahms. She particularly liked Beethoven's Seventh, and on succeeding evenings she sometimes would yield to the irresistible urge to stand and move her arms playfully about in the air, as though it were she and not Bernstein conducting. Watching her breasts shift beneath her blouse while she pretended, somewhat like a performing child, to lead the orchestra with her invisible baton was intensely arousing, and, for all I know, maybe there was nothing the least bit childish about it and to excite me by way of the mock conducting was why she did it. Because it couldn't have been long before it dawned on her that to continue to believe, like a youthful student, that it was the elderly teacher who was in charge did not accord with the facts. Because in sex there is no point of absolute stasis. There is no sexual equality and there can be no sexual equality, certainly not one where the allotments are equal, the male quotient and the female quotient in perfect balance. There's no way to negotiate metrically this wild thing. It's not fifty-fifty like a business transaction. It's the chaos of eros we're talking about, the radical destabilization that is its excitement. You're back in the woods with sex. You're back in the bog. What it is is trading dominance, perpetual *imbalance*. You're going to rule out dominance? You're going to rule out yielding? The dominating is the flint, it strikes the spark, it sets it going. Then what? Listen. You'll see. You'll see what dominating leads to. You'll see what yielding leads to.

I would sometimes, as I did that night, play a Dvořák string quintet for her—electrifying music, easy enough to recognize and to grasp. She liked me to play the piano, it created a romantic, seductive atmosphere that she liked, and so I did. The simpler Chopin preludes. Schubert, some of the *Moments Musicaux*. Some movements of the sonatas. Nothing too hard, but pieces I'd studied and didn't play too badly. Usually I play only for myself, even now that I'm better at it, but it was pleasant then to play for her. It was all part of the intoxication—for both of us. Playing music is very funny. Some things come readily now, but most pieces still have a stretch that's trouble for me, passages that I never bothered to solve all those years when I was playing by myself and didn't have a teacher. When I ran into a problem back then, I figured out some nutty way to solve it. Or didn't solve it—certain types of leaps, movement from one part of the keyboard to another in an intricate way, that was kind of finger-breaking. I didn't yet have a teacher when I knew Consuela, so I did all those stupid improvised things that I invented as solutions to technical problems. I'd had only a few lessons as a kid and, until I got a teacher five years ago, I was mostly self-taught. Very little training. If I had seriously had lessons, I would spend less time practicing than I do today. I get up early and spend two, if I can two and a half hours at daybreak practicing, which is about as much as one can do. Though some days when I'm working toward something, I have another session later on. I'm in good shape, but I get tired after a while. Both mentally and physically. I have a huge amount of music that I've read through. That's a technical term—it doesn't mean looking at it like you look at a book, it means at the piano. I've bought a lot of music, I have everything, piano literature, and I used to read it, and I used to play it, badly. Some passages maybe not so badly. To see how it worked and so on. It wasn't good in terms of playing, but I had some pleasure. And pleasure is our subject. How to be serious over a lifetime about one's modest, private pleasures.

The lessons were a present to myself on my sixty-fifth birthday for finally getting over Consuela. And I've made a lot of progress. I play some pretty difficult pieces. Brahms intermezzi. Schumann. A difficult Chopin prelude. I chew a bit off a very hard one, and I still don't play it well, but I work on it. When I say to my teacher in exasperation, "I can't do it right. How do you solve this problem?" she says, "Play it a thousand times." Like all enjoyable things, you see, it has unenjoyable parts to it, but my relationship to music has deepened and that's essential to my life now. It's wise to do this now. How much longer can there possibly be girls?

I can't say that my making music excited Consuela about me the way her conducting Beethoven in jest excited me about her. I still can't say that anything I ever did sexually excited Consuela about me. Which was largely why, from the evening we first went to bed eight years back, I never had a moment's peace, why, whether she realized it or not, I was all weakness and worry from then on, why I could never figure out whether the answer was to see more of her or to see less of her or to see her not at all, to give her up—to do the unthinkable and, at sixty-two, voluntarily relinquish a gorgeous girl of twenty-four who hundreds of times said to me, "I adore you," but who never, even insincerely, could bring herself to whisper, "I desire you, I want you so—I cannot live without your cock."

That was not Consuela. Yet that was why the fear of losing her to someone else never left me, why she was continually on my mind, why with her or apart from her I never felt sure of her. The obsessional side of it was awful. When you're beguiled it helps not to think too much and just to let yourself enjoy the beguilement. But I had no such pleasure: all I did was think—think, worry, and, yes, suffer. Concentrate on your pleasure, I told myself. Why but for the pleasure do I choose to live as I do, imposing as few constraints on my independence as possible? I had the one marriage, in my twenties the bad first marriage that so many have, the bad first marriage that is as bad as boot camp, but after that I was determined not to have the bad second marriage or the third and the fourth. I was determined, after that, never to live in the cage again.

That first night we were sitting on the sofa listening to Dvořák. At one point Consuela found a book that interested her—I forget which one, though I'll never forget the moment. She turned around—I was sitting where you are, at the corner of the sofa, and she was sitting there—and she twisted her torso half around, and with the book resting on the arm of the sofa, she started to read, and because of the leaning, the bending forward, under her clothing I saw her buttocks, saw the shape clearly, which was one whopping invitation. She is a tall young woman in a slightly too narrow body. It is as if the body doesn't quite fit. Not because she's too fat. But she's by no means the anorexic type. You see there female flesh, and it is good flesh, abundant—that's *why* you see it. So there she was, not openly lying across the sofa but, all the same, with her buttocks sort of half turned to me. A woman as conscious of her body as Consuela and doing that is, I concluded, inviting me to begin. The sexual instinct is still intact—none of the Cuban correctitude has interfered. In that half-turned ass, I see that nothing has gotten in the way of the pure thing. All that we'd talked about, all that I'd had to listen to about her family, none of it has interfered. She knows how to turn her ass despite all that. Turns in the primordial way. In display. And the display is perfect. It tells me that I need no longer suppress the wish to touch.

I started to caress her buttocks, and she liked it. She said, "This is a strange situation. I can never be your girlfriend. For every possible reason. You live in a different world." "Different?" I laughed. "How different?" And right there, of course, you start the lying, and you say, "Oh, it's not such a lofty place, if that's what you're imagining. It's not such a glamorous world. It's not even a world. Once a week I appear on TV. Once a week I'm on the radio. Every few weeks I appear in print in the back pages of a magazine read by twenty people at most. My program? It's a Sunday morning cultural program. Nobody watches. It's not much of a world to worry about. I can bring you into that world easily enough. Please stay with me."

She looks to be thinking about what I've said, but what sort of thinking can it be? "Okay," she says, "for now. For tonight. But I can never be your wife." "Agreed," I said, but I thought, Who was asking her to be my wife? Who raised the question? I am sixty-two and she's twenty-four. I merely touch her ass and she tells me she can't be my wife? I didn't know such girls continued to exist. She is even more traditional than I imagined. Or maybe more odd, more unusual than I imagined. As I would discover, Consuela is ordinary but without being predictable. Nothing mechanical about her behavior. She's at once specific and mysterious, and strangely full of little surprises. But, in the beginning especially, she was difficult for me to decipher, and, mistakenly—or perhaps not—I chalked that up to her Cubanness. "I love my cozy Cuban world," she told me. "I love the coziness of my family, and I can tell already that's not something you like or want. So I never can really belong to you."

This naive niceness in combination with her marvelous body was so enticing to me that I wasn't sure even then, on that first

night, that I could fuck her as though she were another cavorting Miranda. No, Consuela was not the goat in the clock. It
didn't matter what she was saying—she was so damned attractive that not only could I not resist her but I didn't see how
any other man could, and it was in that moment, caressing her
buttocks while she explained that she could not be my wife,
that my terrible jealousy was born.

The jealousy. The uncertainty. The fear of losing her, even
while on top of her. Obsessions that in all my varied experience
I had never known before. With Consuela as with no one else,
the siphoning off of confidence was almost instantaneous.

So we went to bed. It happened fast, less because of my intoxication than because of her lack of complexity. Or call it
clarity. Call it newly minted maturity, though maturity, I would
say, of a simple kind: she was in communion with that body in
the very way she wished and wasn't able to be in communion
with art. She undressed, and not only was her blouse silk but
her underwear was made of silk. She had nearly pornographic
underwear. A surprise. You know she has chosen this to please.
You know she has chosen this with a man's eye in mind, even if
a man were never to see it. You know that you have no idea
what she is, how clever she is or how stupid she is, how shallow
she is or how deep she is, how innocent she is or how guile-
ful she is, how wily, how wise, even how wicked. With a self-
contained woman of such sexual power, you have no idea and
you never will. The tangle that is her character is obscured by
her beauty. Nonetheless, I was greatly moved by seeing that
underwear. I was moved by seeing that body. "Look at you," I
said.

There are two things you notice about Consuela's body. In
the first place, the breasts. The most gorgeous breasts I have
ever seen—and I was born, remember, in 1930: I have seen
quite a few breasts by now. These were round, full, perfect.
The type with the nipple like a saucer. Not the nipple like an
udder but the big pale rosy-brown nipple that is so very stirring. The second thing was that she had sleek pubic hair.
Normally it's curly. This was like Asian hair. Sleek, lying flat,
and not much of it. The pubic hair is important because it
returns.

*

Yes, I pulled back the covers and she came into my bed, Consuela Castillo, superclassically the fertile female of our mammalian species. And already, that first time, and at only twenty-four, she was willing to sit on top of me. She wasn't sure of herself once she was there, and till I tapped her arm to get her attention and slow her down, she was obliviously over-energetic, caroming about with her eyes shut, off in a child's game of her own. It was a little like her mock conducting. I suppose she was trying to give herself over completely, but she was too young for that and, hard as she tried, that's not what she achieved. However, because she knew how alluring her breasts were and she wanted me to be able to see them at their best, she'd climbed on top of me when I asked her to. And she did something rather pornographic for a first time, and this, again to my surprise, on her own initiative—played with her breasts around my prick. Leaned forward to place my prick between her breasts, for me to see it nestling there while she pressed them together with her hands. She knew how much this vision aroused me, the skin of the one on the skin of the other. I remember I said, "Do you realize that you have the most beautiful breasts I've ever seen?" And like the efficient, thorough private secretary taking a memo, or perhaps like the well-brought-up Cuban daughter, she replied, "Yes, I know that. I see how you respond to my breasts."

But mostly, in the beginning, the lovemaking was too spirited. She was trying too hard to impress her teacher. Slow down, be with me, I said. Less energy, more comprehension. You control the event with more subtlety than that. There's much to be said for crude naturalness, but not from afar like that. When she was first sucking me, she would move her head with a relentless rat-a-tat-tat rapidity—it was impossible not to come much sooner than I wanted to, but then, the instant I began coming, she abruptly stopped and received it like an open drain. I could have been coming into a wastepaper basket. No one had ever told her not to stop working then. None of the five previous boyfriends had dared to say that to her. They were too young. They were her age. They were glad to be getting what they got.

Then something happened. The bite. The bite *back*. The biting back of life. One night Consuela moved beyond the

confines of her comforting, mannerly, habitual efficiency, progressed beyond the tutorial into the unknown adventure, and
the turbulence of the affair began for me. This is how it happened. One night when she was stretched out beneath me on
the bed, passively supine, waiting to have me separate her legs
and slide in, I instead shoved a couple of pillows back of her
head, propped up her head like that, angled it like that up
against the headboard, and with my knees planted to either
side of her and my ass centered over her, I leaned into her face
and rhythmically, without letup, I fucked her mouth. I was so
bored, you see, by the mechanical blow jobs that, to shock her,
I kept her fixed there, kept her steady by holding her hair, by
turning a twist of hair in one hand and wrapping it round my
fist like a thong, like a strap, like the reins that fasten to the bit
of a bridle.

Now, no woman really likes having her hair pulled. It's certain to turn a number of them on, but that doesn't mean they
like it. And they don't like it because there's no way of getting
around the act of domination that is going on, that must go
on, that lets them think, It's just what I imagined sex to be. It
is brutish this guy's not a brute but he's on to the brutish
ness. After I came, when I drew away, Consuela looked not
just horrified but ferocious. Yes, something is finally happening
to her. It is no longer so comfortable for her. She is no longer
practicing scales. Uncontrollably she is in motion within. I was
still above her—kneeling over her and dripping on her—we
were looking each other cold in the eye, when, after swallow-
ing hard, she snapped her teeth. Suddenly. Cruelly. At me. It
wasn't an act. It was instinctive. It was snapping her teeth by
using the full force of the masticatory muscles to violently raise
the lower jaw. It was as though she were saying, That's what I
could have done, that's what I wanted to do, and that's what
I didn't do.

At last the forthright, incisive, elemental response from the
contained classical beauty. Till then it was all controlled by nar-
cissism, by exhibitionism, and despite the energetic display, despite the audacity, it was strangely inert. I don't know whether
Consuela remembers that bite, that activating bite that freed
her from her own surveillance and inaugurated her into the
sinister dream, but I will never forget it. The full amorous

truth. The instinctual girl bursting not just the container of her vanity but the captivity of her cozy Cuban home. It was the true beginning of her mastery—the mastery into which my mastery had initiated her. I am the author of her mastery of me.

You see, I think that in me Consuela sensed a possessable version of her family's refinement, of that unrecoverable aristocratic past that is more or less a myth to her. A man of the world. A cultural authority. Her teacher. Now, most people are appalled by the vast difference in age, but it is the very thing Consuela is drawn to. The erotic oddness is all most people register, and they register it as repugnance, as repugnant farce. But the age I am has great significance for Consuela. These girls with old gents don't do it despite the age—they're drawn to the age, they do it *for* the age. Why? In Consuela's case, because the vast difference in age gives her permission to submit, I think. My age and my status give her, rationally, the license to surrender, and surrendering in bed is a not unpleasant sensation. But simultaneously, to give yourself over intimately to a much, much older man provides this sort of younger woman with authority of a kind she cannot get in a sexual arrangement with a younger man. She gets both the pleasures of submission *and* the pleasures of mastery. A boy submitting to her power, what does that amount to in a creature so patently desirable? But to have this man of the world submitting solely because of the force of her youth and her beauty? To have gained the total interest, to have become the consuming passion of a man inaccessible in every other arena, to enter a life she admires that would otherwise be closed to her—that's power, and it's the power she wants. It isn't that the dominance is being traded sequentially; it's being traded continuously. Not so much being traded as being braided. And therein lies the source not only of my obsession with her but of her counter-obsession with me. Or so I had it figured at the time, for all the good it did me in attempting to understand what she was up to and why I was getting in deeper and deeper.

No matter how much you know, no matter how much you think, no matter how much you plot and you connive and you plan, you're not superior to sex. It's a very risky game. A man wouldn't have two-thirds of the problems he has if he didn't venture off to get fucked. It's sex that disorders our normally ordered lives. I know this as well as anyone. Every last vanity will come back to mock you. Read Byron's *Don Juan*. Yet what do you do if you're sixty-two and believe you'll never have a claim on something so perfect again? What do you do if you're sixty-two and the urge to take whatever is still takable couldn't be stronger? What do you do if you're sixty-two and you realize that all those bodily parts invisible up to now (kidneys, lungs, veins, arteries, brain, intestines, prostate, heart) are about to start making themselves distressingly apparent, while the organ most conspicuous throughout your life is doomed to dwindle into insignificance?

Don't misunderstand me. It isn't that, through a Consuela, you can delude yourself into thinking that you have a last shot at your youth. You never feel the difference from youth more. In her energy, in her enthusiasm, in her youthful unknowing, in her youthful *knowing*, the difference is dramatized every moment. There's never any mistaking that it's she and not you who is twenty-four. You'd have to be a clod to feel you're young again. If you felt youthful, it would be a snap. Far from feeling youthful, you feel the poignancy of her limitless future as opposed to your own limited one, you feel even more than you ordinarily do the poignancy of every last grace that's been lost. It's like playing baseball with a bunch of twenty-year-olds. It isn't that you feel twenty because you're playing with them. You note the difference every second of the game. But at least you're not sitting on the sidelines.

Here's what happens: you feel excruciatingly how old you are, but in a new way.

Can you imagine old age? Of course you can't. I didn't. I couldn't. I had no idea what it was like. Not even a false image —no image. And nobody wants anything else. Nobody wants to face any of this before he has to. How is it all going to turn out? Obtuseness is de rigueur.

Understandably, any stage of life more advanced than one's own is unimaginable. Sometimes one is halfway through the next stage before one realizes that one has entered it. And then, earlier stages of advancement offer their compensations. And even so, the middle is daunting for many people. But the end? It is, interestingly, the first time of life that you stand entirely outside of while you're in it. Observing one's decay all the while (if one is as fortunate as I am), one has, by virtue of one's continuing vitality, considerable distance from one's decay—even feels oneself jauntily independent of it. Inevitably, yes, there is a multiplication of the signs leading to the unpleasant conclusion, and yet despite that, you stand outside. And the ferocity of the objectivity is brutal.

There's a distinction to be made between dying and death. It's not all uninterrupted dying. If one's healthy and feeling well, it's invisible dying. The end that is a certainty is not necessarily boldly announced. No, you can't understand. The only thing you understand about the old when you're not old is that they have been stamped by their time. But understanding only that freezes them in their time, and so amounts to no understanding at all. To those not yet old, being old means *you've been*. But being old also means that despite, in addition to, and in excess of your beenness, you still are. Your beenness is very much alive. You still are, and one is as haunted by the still-being and its fullness as by the having-already-been, by the pastness. Think of old age this way: it's just an everyday fact that one's life is at stake. One cannot evade knowing what shortly awaits one. The silence that will surround one forever. Otherwise it's all the same. Otherwise one is immortal for as long as one lives.

Not too many years ago, there was a ready-made way to be old, just as there was a ready-made way to be young. Neither obtains any longer. A great fight about the permissible took place here—and a great overturning. Nonetheless, should a man of seventy still be involved in the carnal aspect of the human comedy? To be unapologetically an unmonastic old man susceptible still to the humanly exciting? That is not the condition as it was once symbolized by the pipe and the rocking chair. Maybe it's still a bit of an affront to people, to fail to abide by the old clock of life. I realize that I can't count on the virtuous regard of other adults. But what can I do about the fact that, as far as I can tell, nothing, *nothing* is put to rest, however old a man may be?

She began coming to my place in a very casual manner after that bite. It was no longer a matter of evening dates and then the fucking once she realized the little it took for her to control things. She phoned and she said, "Could I come for a few hours?" and she knew I would never say no, knew that every time, to get to hear me say "Look at you" as though she were herself a Picasso, she had merely to undress and stand there. I, her teacher in Practical Criticism, the Sunday morning PBS aesthetician, New York television's reigning authority on what is the current best to see, hear, and read—I had pronounced her a great work of art, with all the magical influence of a great work of art. Not the artist but the art itself. There was nothing for her not to understand—she had only to be there, on view, and the understanding of her importance flowed from me. It was not required of her, any more than it is of a violin concerto or of the moon, that she have any sort of self-conception. That's what I was for: I was Consuela's awareness of herself. I was the cat watching the goldfish. Only it was the goldfish that had the teeth.

The jealousy. *That* poison. And unprovoked. Jealous even when she tells me she's going ice-skating with her eighteen-year-old brother. Will he be the one who steals her away? With these obsessional love affairs you are not your own confident self, not when you're in the vortex of them and not when the girl is almost a third your age. I feel anxious unless I speak to her on the phone every day, and then I feel anxious after we've spoken. Women who in the past demanded regular calls, tele-phoning back and forth like that, I'd invariably gotten rid of —and now it was I demanding it of her: the daily fix by phone. Why do I flatter her when we speak? Why don't I stop telling her how perfect she is? Why do I always feel I'm saying the wrong thing to this girl? I'm unable to make out what she makes of me, what she makes of anything, and my confusion causes me to say things that sound false or exaggerated to my ear, so I hang up full of silent resentment toward her. But when the rare day passes that I'm able to discipline myself enough not to speak to her, not to call her, not to flatter her, not to sound false, not to resent what she unknowingly does to me, it's worse. I can't stop doing anything I'm doing, and ev-erything I'm doing leaves me upset. I don't feel the authority with her that's necessary for my stability, and yet she comes to me because of that authority.

On the nights she isn't with me, I am deformed by thinking

about where she may be and what she may be up to. But then even after she has been with me for the evening and has gone home, I can't sleep. The experience of her is too strong. I sit up in bed and in the middle of the night I cry out, "Consuela Castillo, leave me alone!" That's enough, I tell myself. Get up, change the sheets, shower again, get rid of the smell of her, *and then get rid of her*. You must. It's become an endless campaign with her. Where's the fulfillment and the sense of possession? If you have her, why can't you have her? You're not getting what you want even when you're getting what you want. There is no peace in it and there can't be, because of our ages and the unavoidable poignancy. Because of our ages, I have the pleasure but I never lose the longing. Had this never happened before? No. I was never sixty-two years old before. I was no longer in that phase of my life when I thought I could do everything. Yet I remembered it clearly. You see a beautiful woman. You see her from a mile away. You go to her and say, "Who are you?" You have dinner. And so on. *That* phase, when it's worry-free. You get on the bus. A creature so gorgeous everybody is afraid to sit next to her. The seat next to the most beautiful girl in the world—and it's empty. So you take it. But now isn't then, and it'll never be calm, it'll never be peaceful. I was worried about her walking around in that blouse. Peel off her jacket, and there is the blouse. Peel off the blouse, and there is perfection. A young man will find her and take her away. And from me, who fired up her senses, who gave her her stature, who was the catalyst to her emancipation and prepared her for him.

How do I know a young man will take her away? Because I once was the young man who would have done it.

When I was younger I wasn't susceptible. Others got jealous earlier, but I was able to protect myself from that. I let them have their way, confident that I could prevail through sexual dominance. But jealousy, of course, is the trap door to the contract. Men respond to jealousy by saying, "Nobody else is going to have her. I'm going to have her—I'll marry her. I'll capture her that way. By convention." Marriage cures the jealousy. That's why many men seek it out. Because they're not sure of that other person, they get her to sign the contract: *I will not, et cetera.*

How do I capture Consuela? The thought is morally humiliating, yet there it is. I'm certainly not going to hold her by promising marriage, but how else can you hold a young woman at my age? What am I able to offer instead in this milk-and-honey society of free-market sex? And so that's when the pornography begins. The pornography of jealousy. The pornography of one's own destruction. I am rapt, I am enthralled, and yet I am enthralled *outside* the frame. What is it that puts me outside? It is age. The wound of age. Pornography in its classic form has a kick of about five or ten minutes before it becomes kind of comical. But in this pornography the images are extremely painful. Ordinary pornography is the aestheticizing of jealousy. It takes the torment out. What—why "aestheticizing"? Why not "anesthetizing"? Well, perhaps both. It's a representation, ordinary pornography. It's a fallen art form. It's not just make-believe, it's patently insincere. You want the girl in the porno film, but you're not jealous of whoever's fucking her because he becomes your surrogate. Quite amazing, but that's the power of even fallen art. He becomes a stand-in, there in your service; that removes the sting and turns it into something pleasant. Because you're an invisible accomplice in the act, ordinary pornography takes the torment out while mine keeps the torment in. In my pornography, you identify yourself not with the satiate, with the person who is getting it, but with the person not getting it, with the person losing it, with the person who has lost.

A young man will find her and take her away. I see him. I know him. I know what he is capable of doing because he is me at twenty-five, as yet without the wife and the child; he is me in the raw, before I did what everybody else did. I see him watch her crossing the broad plaza—*striding* the plaza— at Lincoln Center. He is out of sight, behind a pillar, eyeing her as I did on the evening I took her to her first Beethoven concert. She is in boots, high leather boots and a shapely short dress, a devastating young woman out in the open on a warm autumn night, unashamedly walking the streets of the world for all to covet and admire—and she's smiling. She's happy. This devastating woman is coming to meet me. Only it isn't me in the pornographic film. It's him. It's the him who was once me but is no longer. Watching him watching her, I know in detail what is going to happen next, and knowing what is going to happen next, picturing it, it is impossible to think in what you rationally construe as your own self-interest. It is impossible to think that not everybody is feeling this way about this girl because not everybody has an obsession about this girl. Instead, you can't imagine her going anywhere. You can't imagine her on the street, in a store, at a party, on the beach without that guy emerging from the shadows. The pornographic torment: watching somebody else do it who once was you.

When you finally lose a girl like Consuela, this happens to you everywhere, all the places you ever were with her. When she's gone, it's uncanny, you'll remember her there, you'll see that space empty of you but with her as she was with you but with the twenty-five-year-old boy you are no longer. You imagine her striding like that in her shapely short dress. Coming toward you. Aphrodite. Then she is past you, she's gone, and the pornography spins out of control.

I inquire (though what good can come of my knowing?) about her boyfriends, ask her to tell me how many she slept with before me and when she started and whether she's ever been with another girl or with two boys at once (or a horse, or a parrot, or a monkey), and that was when she told me that there had been only five. However attractive, however well groomed and gorgeous, she had had relatively few boyfriends for a contemporary girl. The constraining influence of the wealthy, proper Cuban background (if, that is, she is telling the truth). And the last boyfriend was a stupid fellow student who couldn't even fuck her right, who was only concentrating on coming himself. The old stupid story. Not a man who loves women.

She was inconsistent in her morality, by the way. I remember that at that time George O'Hearn, the poet, a man married to the same woman all his life, had a girlfriend in Consuela's neighborhood, and he was there, downtown, having breakfast with his girlfriend in a coffee shop, and Consuela saw him and she was upset. She recognized him from the picture on the back of a new book of his then on the table beside my bed, and she knew that I knew him. She came to me that night. "I saw your friend. He was with a girl at eight o'clock in the morning, in a restaurant, and he was kissing her—and he's married." She was so predictably platitudinous in these things while acting independently of all convention in her affair with someone thirty-eight years her senior. Inwardly uncertain and out of her depth some of the time, that had to be; nonetheless, something special was happening to her, a big, ersatz, unforeseen something that flattered her vanity and fed her confidence and, exciting as it was, didn't appear to be turning her (as it was me) inside out.

Consuela told me, during one of my interrogations, that there was a boyfriend back in high school who used to want passionately to watch her menstruate. Whenever she started to menstruate, she was to call him, and he would come right over, and she would stand there, and he would watch the blood run down her thighs and onto the floor. "You did this for him?" I asked. "Yes." "And your family, what about your traditional family? You were fifteen years old, you couldn't stay out in the summertime after eight P.M., and yet you did this? Your grandmother a duchess," I said, "in love with her rosary, and yet you did this?" "I wasn't fifteen any longer. I was sixteen by then." "Sixteen. I see. That explains it. And how often did you do this?" "Whenever I had my period. Every month," she told me. "Who was the boy? I thought a boy couldn't even be in your room. Who was he? Who *is* he?"

A socially acceptable boy. Also Cuban. Carlos Alonso. Very proper, clean-cut kid, she tells me, who picked her up at the door in a suit and a tie, never honked for her at the curb, who would come in and meet her parents and sit with them, a reserved boy from a good family highly conscious of their social status. As in her own family there is lots of respect for the father, everyone is well educated, everyone is easily bilingual, the right schools, the right country club, they read *El Diario* and the *Bergen Record*, they love Reagan, love Bush, hate Kennedy, rich New Jersey Cubans to the right of Louis XIV, and Carlos calls her up and says don't menstruate without me.

Picture it. After school, the bathroom, suburban Bergen County, and the two of them transfixed by the enigma of her discharge as though they are Adam and Eve. Because Carlos is enchanted too. He too knows she is a work of art, the lucky rare woman who is a work of art, classical art, beauty in its classical form, but alive, alive, and the aesthetic response to beauty alive is what, class? Desire. Yes, Carlos is her mirror. Men have always been her mirror. They even want to watch her menstruate. She is the female magic men cannot escape. Dressed culturally in the decorous Cuban past, but her permissions flow from her vanity. Her permissions flow from looking in the mirror and saying, "Someone else must see this."

"Call *me*," I told her, "when you begin to menstruate. I want you to come *here*. I want to watch *too*."

Too. That's how unconcealed the jealousy is, how feverish the desire is—and that's how something close to disastrous happened.

Because I was meanwhile, that year, having an affair with a very attractive, very strong, responsible woman, no disabling wounds, no vices or wild views, a scrutinizing intelligence, reliable in every way, too unironic ever to be lightly witty but a sensual, expert, and attentive lover. Carolyn Lyons. Many years earlier, back in the mid-sixties, she'd been a student of mine as well. In the intervening decades, however, neither of us had gone in search of the other, and so when we accidentally met on the street as Carolyn was walking to work one morning, we embraced and held each other as if it were a cataclysmic event like a world war (rather than her leaving for California to go to law school) that had separated us for the next twenty-four years. We each proclaimed how wonderful the other looked, laughingly recalled the mania of a night in my office when she was nineteen, said all sorts of tender things about the past, and there and then made a date for dinner the next night.

Carolyn was still beautiful, radiantly big-featured, though beneath the pale gray eyes the biggish sockets were now papery and worn, and not so much, I would think, because of her chronic insomnia but because of that compound of disappointments not uncommon to the biographies of successful professional women in their forties whose evening meals more often than not are delivered to the door of their Manhattan apartments in a plastic bag by an immigrant. And her body took up more space than it used to. Two divorces, no children, a demanding, high-paying job requiring a lot of overseas travel—all that adds up to another thirty-five pounds, and so when we went to bed, she whispered, "I'm not the same," to which I replied, "Do you think I am?" and nothing was said on that score again.

As an undergraduate, Carolyn had roomed with one of the campus firebrands, a charismatic sixties ringleader, à la Abbie Hoffman, named Janie Wyatt, a kid from Manhasset who wrote an enchanting senior thesis for me entitled "A Hundred Ways to Be Perverse in the Library." I quote the opening sentence: "The blow job in the library is the very essence of it, the sanctified transgression, the campus black mass." Janie weighed maybe a hundred pounds, no more than five feet tall, if that, a little blonde who looked as if you could pick her up and throw her around, and she was the college's dirty diva.

Carolyn back then was in awe of Janie. Carolyn used to say to me, "She has so many affairs. Simultaneously. You go to somebody's apartment, a graduate student, a young instructor, and there's Janie's underwear hanging out to dry on the handles of the shower faucets." Students who wanted sex, Carolyn would tell me, they'd be walking along the campus, they'd suddenly want sex, and they'd call her. And if she wanted it too, off they went. They'd be walking along, they'd stop in their tracks, they'd say, "I think I'm just going to call Janie," and they never made it to class. A lot of the faculty frowned at the openness of her sexual behavior and equated it with stupidity. Even some of the boys—spoke of her as a slut one moment and then went off to bed with her the next. But she was neither stupid nor a slut. Janie was someone who knew what she was doing. She stood in front of you, small as she was, with her legs slightly apart, planted, lots of freckles, blond short hair, no makeup except bright red lipstick, and her big, open confessional grin: this is what I am, this is what I do, if you don't like it, it's too bad.

How did Janie astonish me most? Many ways—in the early days of the campus revolt, there were many things to mark her as a new, noteworthy kind of creature. She astonished me, strangely, by doing something that might sound nothing like immoderate now, given the progress in boldness that women have made since, and that didn't necessarily rival the defiant flamboyance of her public stance. She astonished me most by carrying off the shyest man on the campus, our poet. The crossover between faculty and students was exciting not only for being new but for being out in the open, and accounted for more divorces than just my own. The poet was without the skills others possess in advancing their worldly interests. He marshaled his egoism for language alone. Eventually died from drink, relatively young, but, on his own in genial America, only drink could unstring this guy. Married, with two kids, bashful as could be other than up on the platform dazzlingly lecturing on poetry. To lure this man out of the shadows was unimaginable. Except to Janie. At a party. Many students, both boys and girls, wanted to be closer to him. The smart girls all had a crush on him, this romantic stranger from life, but he didn't appear to trust anybody. Until Janie went up to him at a party and took his hand and said, "Let's dance," and the next thing we knew she had him in tow. He seemed to swim right in to trusting her. Little Janie Wyatt: we're all equal, we're all free, we can land anything we want.

Janie and Carolyn, along with another three or four defiant upper-middle-class kids, comprised a clique calling itself the Gutter Girls. Well, these girls resembled nothing I'd ever known, and not because they were swathed in gypsy rags and barefoot. They detested innocence. They couldn't bear supervision. They weren't afraid of being conspicuous and they weren't afraid of being clandestine. To rebel against one's condition was everything. They and their adherents may well have been, historically, the first wave of American girls fully implicated in their own desire. No rhetoric, no ideology, just the playing field of pleasure opening out to the bold. The boldness developed as they realized what the possibilities were, when they realized they were no longer being watched, that they were no longer subservient to the old system or under any system of any kind—when they realized they could do anything.

It was an improvised revolution at first, the sixties revolution; the campus vanguard was tiny, half of one percent, maybe a percent and a half, but that didn't matter because the vibrating faction of society soon followed. Culture is always being led by its narrowest point, among the young women on this campus by Janie's Gutter Girls, the female trailblazers of a completely spontaneous sexual change. Twenty years earlier, in my college days, the campuses had been perfectly managed.

Parietal regulations. Unquestioned supervision. The authority came from a distant Kafkaesque source—"the administration"—and the language of the administration could have come from Saint Augustine. You tried to find your wily way around all this control, but until about '64, by and large everyone under surveillance was law-abiding, members in excellent standing of what Hawthorne called "the limit-loving class." Then came the long-delayed explosion, the disreputable assault on postwar normalcy and the cultural consensus. All that was unmanageable came breaking out, and the irreversible transformation of the young had begun.

Carolyn never achieved Janie's notoriety, nor did she want to. Carolyn partook of the protest, the provocation, the insolent fun but, with characteristic self-discipline, never to the point where insubordination might jeopardize her future. Carolyn as she is now in middle age—entirely of the corporate world, uncomplainingly straight—isn't a surprise to me. Giving offense in the cause of sexual license was never Carolyn's calling. Neither was wholesale waywardness. But Janie—let me digress for a moment to Janie, in her own small-time way a Consuela Castillo's Simón Bolívar. Yes, a great revolutionary leader like the South American Bolívar, whose armies destroyed the power of colonialist Spain—an insurrectionist unafraid of battling superior forces, the *libertador* pitted against the college's reigning morality who eventually swept its authority away.

Today, the carefree sexual conduct of the well-bred girls in my class is, as far as they know, warranted by the Declaration of Independence, an entitlement that requires of them little if any courage to utilize and that is in harmony with the pursuit of happiness as conceived of at Philadelphia in 1776. In fact, the uninhibited everything that the Consuelas and the Mirandas nonchalantly take for granted derives from the audacity of the shameless, subversive Janie Wyatts and the amazing victory they achieved in the sixties through the force of atrocious behavior. The coarse dimension of American life previously captured in gangster films, that's what Janie hauled on campus, because that's the intensity it took to undo the upholders of the norms. That's how you carried the quarrel to your keepers—in your ugly language rather than theirs.

Janie was born in the city, then raised in the suburbs, out on

Long Island, in Manhasset. Her mother was a schoolteacher
and commuted each day to Queens, which the family had left
for Manhasset and where the mother still taught tenth grade.
The father commuted in the other direction, the couple of
miles to Great Neck, where he was a law partner of Carolyn's
father. That's how the girls knew each other. The empty suburban house—it excites every sexual nerve in Janie's body. She
comes of sexual age when the music is changing, and so she
turns it on. She turns everything on. Janie's cunning was that
she realized, when she got there, what the suburbs were for.
She was never free in the city as a girl, never on the loose as the
boys were. But out in Manhasset she found her frontier. There
were next-door neighbors but they weren't as close as they
were in the city. She got home from school and the streets were
empty. Looked like the towns of the old Wild West. Nobody
around. Everybody gone. So till they all came home on the
train, she had a little operation, a little sideshow going. Thirty
years later, a Janie Wyatt degenerates into an Amy Fisher, slav-
ishly servicing the auto mechanic all on her own, but Janie was
bright and a born organizer—unbroken, brazen, a sassy surfer
riding the currents of change. The suburbs, where girls, safe
from the dangers of the city, didn't have to be kept under tight
wraps, where parents weren't too concerned on a moment-by-
moment basis, the suburbs were her American finishing school.
The suburbs created the agora for this education in the un-
sanctioned to flourish. The lessening of surveillance, the gradual
giving over of space to all these kids who had been endowed
by Dr. Spock with the tools of disobedience—and it flourished,
all right. It grew out of control.

That was the transformation Janie wrote about in her thesis.
That was the story she told. The Suburbs. The Pill. The Pill
that gave parity to the woman. The Music. Little Richard propelling everything. The Pelvic Backbeat. The Car. The kids
out there driving together in the Car. The Prosperity. The
Commute. The Divorce. A lot of adult distraction. The Grass.
Dope. Dr. Spock. All of that's what led to Lord of the Flies U,
which was what the Gutter Girls called our college. Janie's was
not a revolutionary cell that was blowing things up. Janie wasn't
Bernardine Dohrn or Kathy Boudin. Nor were the Betty
Friedans speaking to her. The Gutter Girls had no objection to

the social or the political argument, but that was the other side of the decade. There were two strains to the turbulence: there was the libertarianism extending orgiastic permission to the individual and opposed to the traditional interests of the community, but with it, often wedded to it, there was the communal righteousness about civil rights and against the war, the disobedience whose moral prestige devolves through Thoreau. And the two strains interconnecting made the orgy difficult to discredit.

But Janie's was a pleasure cell, not a political cell. And these pleasure cells existed not just on our campus but all over and by the thousands, tie-dyed boys and girls who didn't always smell so good engaging together in reckless behavior. Twist and shout, work it on out—that, not the "Internationale," was their anthem. Salacious, direct music to fuck to. Music to give head by, the people's bebop. Of course, music has always been useful sexually, within the prescribed limitations of the moment. Even Glenn Miller, back when in a song you still had to come at sex through a Tin Pan Alley romance, lubricated the situation as much as it could be. Then young Sinatra. Then the creamy saxophone. But the limitations on the Gutter Girls? They used the music the way they used the marijuana, as a propulsive, as the emblem of their mutiny, the provocation to erotic vandalism. In my adolescence, in the swing band era, there was just the booze to put you in the mood. For them there was an arsenal of all-out anti-inhibitors.

Having those girls in class was my education: seeing how they got themselves up, watching them jettison their manners and uncover their crudeness, listening to their music with them, smoking with them and listening to Janis Joplin, their Bessie Smith in whiteface, their shouter, their honky-tonk, stoned Judy Garland, listening with them to Jimi Hendrix, their Charlie Parker of the guitar, getting high with them and listening to Hendrix playing the guitar backwards, reversing everything, retarding the beat, accelerating the beat, and Janie chanting, as her doped-out mantra, "Hendrix and sex, Hendrix and sex," and Carolyn, as hers, "A beautiful man with a beautiful voice"—observing the swagger and appetite and excitement of the Janies who were without the biological terror of the erection, without the fear of the phallic transformation of the man.

The Janie Wyatts of the American sixties knew how to operate around engorged men. They were themselves engorged, so they knew how to transact business with them. The venturous male drive, the male initiative, wasn't a lawless action requiring denunciation and adjudication but a sexual sign that one responds to or not. To control the male impulse and report it? They were not educated in that ideological system. They were far too playful to be indoctrinated with animus and resentment and grievance from above. They were educated in the instinctual system. They weren't interested in replacing the old inhibitions and prohibitions and moral instruction with new forms of surveillance and new systems of control and a new set of orthodox beliefs. They knew where the pleasure was to be had, and they knew how to give over to desire without fear. Unafraid of the aggressive impulse, deep in the transforming fracas—and for the first time on American soil since the Pilgrim women of Plymouth Colony were cloistered by an ecclesiastical government against the corruptions of the flesh and the sinfulness of men—a generation drawing their conclusions from their cunts about the nature of experience and the delights of the world.

Isn't the bolivar the unit of currency in Venezuela? Well, under America's first woman president, I would hope the dollar will become the wyatt. Janie deserves no less. She democratized the entitlement to pleasure.

Sidelight. The English trading outpost at Merry Mount that so incensed the Plymouth Puritans—know about that? Fur-trading settlement, smaller than Plymouth, about thirty miles northwest of Plymouth. Where Quincy, Mass., is today. Men drinking, selling arms to the Indians, palling around with the Indians. Cavorting with the enemy. Copulating with Indian women, whose custom it was to assume the doggie position and to be taken from behind. A pagan hotbed in Puritan Massachusetts, where the Bible was law. Danced around a maypole in animal masks, worshiped at it every month. Hawthorne based a story on that maypole: Governor Endicott sent the Puritan militia under Miles Standish to cut it down, a pine tree festooned with colored banners and ribbons and antlers and roses and standing eighty feet tall. "Jollity and gloom were contending for an empire"—that's how Hawthorne understood it.

Merry Mount was presided over for a time by a speculator, a lawyer, a charismatic privileged character named Thomas Morton. He's a kind of forest creature out of *As You Like It*, a wild demon out of *A Midsummer Night's Dream*. Shakespeare is Morton's contemporary, born only about eleven or so years before Morton. Shakespeare is Morton's rock-and-roll. The Plymouth Puritans busted him, then the Salem Puritans busted him—put him in the stocks, fined him, imprisoned him. He eventually exiled himself to Maine, where he died in his late sixties. But he couldn't resist provoking them. He was a source of prurient fascination for the Puritans. Because if one's piety isn't absolute, it logically leads to a Morton. The Puritans were terrified that their daughters would be carried off and corrupted by this merry miscegenator out at Merry Mount. A white man, a white Indian, luring the virgins away? This was even more sinister than red Indians stealing them. Morton was going to turn their daughters into the Gutter Girls. That was the main concern other than his trading with the Indians and selling them firearms. The Puritans were frantic about the younger generation. Because once they lost their younger generation, the ahistorical experiment in dictatorial intolerance was dead. Age-old American story: save the young from sex. Yet it's always too late. Too late because they've already been born.

Twice they shipped Morton to England to be tried for disobedience, but the English ruling class and the Church of England had no use for the New England Separatists. Morton's case was thrown out of court each time, and Morton made his way back to New England. The English thought, He's right, Morton—we wouldn't want to live with him either, but he's not coercing anyone and these fucking Puritans are crazy.

In *Of Plymouth Plantation*, Governor William Bradford's book, the governor writes amply about the evils of Merry Mount, the "riotous prodigality," the "profuse excess." "They fell to great licentiousness and led a dissolute life, pouring out themselves into all profaneness." Morton's confederates he calls "mad Bacchanalians." Morton he labels "the Lord of Misrule" and the master of "a School of Atheism." Governor Bradford's a powerful ideologue. Piety knew how to write sentences in the seventeenth century. So too did impiety. Morton published a book as well, *The New English Canaan*, grounded in fascinated observation of the Indians' society— but a scurrilous book according to Bradford, because it was also about the Puritans and how they "make a great show of religion but no humanity." Morton is straightforward. Morton doesn't expurgate. You have to wait three hundred years before the voice of Thomas Morton turns up in America again, unexpurgated, as Henry Miller. The clash between Plymouth and Merry Mount, between Bradford and Morton, between rule and misrule—the colonial harbinger of the national upheaval three hundred and thirty-odd years later when Morton's America was born at last, miscegenation and all.

No, the sixties weren't aberrant. The Wyatt girl wasn't aberrant. She was a natural Mortonian in the conflict that's been ongoing from the beginning. Out in the American wildness, order will reign. The Puritans were the agents of rule and godly virtue and right reason, and on the other side was misrule. But why is it rule and misrule? Why isn't Morton the great theologian of no-rules? Why isn't Morton seen for what he is, the founding father of personal freedom? In the Puritan theocracy you were at liberty to do good; in Morton's Merry Mount you were at liberty—that was it.

And there were lots of Mortons. Mercantile adventurers without the ideology of holiness, people who didn't give a damn whether they were elect or not. They came over with Bradford on the *Mayflower*, emigrated later on other ships, but you don't hear about them at Thanksgiving, because they couldn't stand these communities of saints and believers where no deviation was allowed. Our earliest American heroes were Morton's oppressors: Endicott, Bradford, Miles Standish. Merry Mount's been expunged from the official version because it's the story not of a virtuous utopia but of a utopia of candor. Yet it's Morton whose face should be carved in Mount Rushmore. That's going to happen too, the very day they rename the dollar the wyatt.

*

My Merry Mount? Me and the sixties? Well, I took seriously the disorder of those relatively few years, and I took the word of the moment, liberation, in its fullest meaning. That's when I left my wife. To be accurate, she discovered me with the Gutter Girls and she threw me out. Now, there were others on the faculty who grew their hair long and wore the far-out clothes, but they were just on furlough. They were a mix of voyeur and day-tripper. Occasionally they ventured out, but never did more than a few go over the trench into the field of engagement. But I was determined, once I saw the disorder for what it was, to seize from the moment a rationale for myself, to undo my former allegiances and my current allegiances and not to do it on the side, not to be, as many my age were, either inferior to it or superior to it or simply titillated by it, but to follow the logic of this revolution to its conclusion, and without having become its casualty.

This required some doing. Just because there's no memorial bearing the names of those who out on the rampage came to grief doesn't mean there weren't casualties. There wasn't necessarily carnage, but there was plenty of breakage. This was not a pretty revolution taking place on the dignified theoretical plane. This was a puerile, preposterous, uncontrolled, drastic mess, the whole society in a huge brawl. Though there was comedy too. It was a revolution that at the same time was like the day after the revolution—a big idyll. People took off their underwear and walked around laughing. Often it was no more than farce, childish farce, but astonishingly far-reaching childish farce; often it was no more than a teenage power surge, the adolescence of the biggest, most powerful American generation ever coming into their hormones all at once. Yet the impact was revolutionary. Things forever changed.

One's skepticism, one's cynicism, the cultural-political good sense that normally kept one outside of mass movements, was a useful shield. I wasn't as high as everyone else, and I didn't want to be. For me the job was to detach the revolution from its immediate paraphernalia, from its pathological trappings and its rhetorical inanities and the pharmacological dynamite that made people jump out of windows, to sidestep the worst and to seize and use the idea, to say to oneself, What a chance this is, what an opportunity to live out my own revolution. Why rein myself in because of the accident of the fact that I was born in this year and not in that year?

People fifteen, twenty years younger than I, the privileged beneficiaries of the revolution, could afford to go through it unconsciously. There was this exuberant party, this squalid paradise of disarray, and, without thinking or having to think, they claimed it, and usually with all its trivia and trash. But I had to think. There I was, still in the prime of life and the country entering into this extraordinary time. Am I or am I not a candidate for this wild, sloppy, raucous repudiation, this wholesale wrecking of the inhibitive past? Can I master the discipline of freedom as opposed to the recklessness of freedom? How does one turn freedom into a system?

To find out cost plenty. I have a son of forty-two who hates me. We needn't go into that. The point is that the mob didn't come and open my cell door. The erratic mob was there, but as it happened, I had to open the door myself. Because I too was compliant and fundamentally thwarted, even if, while I was married, I was sneaking out of the house fucking whomever I could. That kind of sixties deliverance was what I'd had in mind from the beginning, but in the beginning, my beginning, there was nothing resembling a communal endorsement of anything like it, no social torrent to sweep you up and carry you along. There were only obstacles, one of which was one's civil nature, one of which was one's provincial beginnings, one of which was one's education in genteel notions of seriousness that one could not buck alone. The trajectory of my upbringing and my education was to delude me into entering a domestic vocation for which I had no tolerance. The family man, conscientious, married and with the kid—and then the revolution begins. The whole thing explodes and there are these girls all around me, and what was I to do, continue on married and having my adulteries and thinking, This is it, this is the bound way you live?

I didn't find my way because I was born in the forest and raised by wild beasts and therefore came by release naturally. I wasn't born smart about any of this. I too lacked the authority to do openly what I wanted to do. It's not the man you're sitting across from who got married in 1956. To gain a confident idea of the scope of one's autonomy you needed guidance that was nowhere to be found, not in my little world anyway, which is why marrying and having a child seemed, in '56, the natural thing even for me to do.

One wasn't an enfranchised man in the sexual realm while I was growing up. One was a second-story man. One was a thief in the sexual realm. You "copped" a feel. You stole sex. You cajoled, you begged, you flattered, you insisted—all sex had to be struggled for, against the values if not the will of the girl. The set of rules was that you had to impose your will on her. That's how she was taught to maintain the spectacle of her virtue. That an ordinary girl should volunteer, without endless importuning, to break the code and commit the sex act would have confused me. Because no one of either sex had any sense of an erotic birthright. Unknown. She might, if she fell for you, agree to a hand job—which meant essentially using your hand with hers as an insert—but that someone would consent to anything without the ritual of psychological besiegement, of unremitting, monomaniacal tenacity and exhortation, well, that was unthinkable. There was no way to get a blow job, certainly, other than by dint of superhuman perseverance. I got one in four years of college. That's all you were allowed. In the Catskill hick town where my family ran a small resort hotel and I came of age in the forties, the only way to consensual sex was either with a prostitute or with someone who'd been your girl for the better part of your life and whom everybody figured you were going to marry. And there you paid your dues because often enough you did marry her.

My parents? They were parents. I was sentimentally educated, believe me. When my father, pushed by my mother, had at last to have the discussion with me about sex, I was already sixteen, it was 1946, and I was disgusted by his way of not knowing what to tell me, this gentle soul born in a Lower East Side tenement in 1898. Mainly what he wanted to tell me was what usually emanated from the kindly Jewish father of that generation: "You're a peach, you're a plum, you can ruin your life . . ." Of course, he didn't know that I already had a venereal disease from the loose girl in town whom everyone fucked. So much for parents in those far-off days.

Look, heterosexual men going into marriage are like priests going into the Church: they take the vow of chastity, only seemingly without knowing it until three, four, five years down the line. The nature of ordinary marriage is no less suffocating to the virile heterosexual—given the sexual preferences of a virile heterosexual—than it is to the gay or the lesbian. Though now even gays want to get married. Church wedding. Two, three hundred witnesses. And wait till they see what becomes of the desire that got them into being gay in the first place. I expected more from those guys, but it turns out there's no realism in them either. Though I suppose it has to do with AIDS. The Fall and Rise of the Condom is the sexual story of the second half of the twentieth century. The condom came back. And with the condom, the return of all that got blown out in the sixties. What man can say he enjoys sex with a condom the way he does without? What's really in it for him? That's why the organs of digestion have, in our time, come to vie for supremacy as a sexual orifice. The crying need for the mucous membrane. To get rid of the condom, they have to have a steady partner, therefore they marry. The gays are militant: they want marriage and they want openly to join the army and be accepted. The two institutions I loathed. And for the same reason: regimentation.

The last person to take these matters seriously was John Milton, three hundred and fifty years ago. Ever read his tracts on divorce? In his day, made him many enemies. They're here, they're among my books, margins heavily annotated back in the sixties. "Did our Saviour open so to us this hazardous and accidental door of marriage to shut upon us like the gate of death . . . ?" No, men don't know anything—or willingly act as though they don't—about the tough, tragic side of what they're getting into. At best they stoically think, Yes, I understand that sooner or later I'm going to relinquish sex in this marriage, but it's in order to have other, more valuable things. But do they understand what they're forsaking? To be chaste, to live without sex, well, how will you take the defeats, the compromises, the frustrations? By making more money, by making all the money you can? By making all the children you can? That helps, but it's nothing like the other thing. Because the other thing is based in your physical being, in the flesh that is born and the flesh that dies. Because only when you fuck is everything that you dislike in life and everything by which you are defeated in life purely, if momentarily, revenged. Only then are you most cleanly alive and most cleanly yourself. It's not the sex that's the corruption—it's the rest. Sex isn't just friction and shallow fun. Sex is also the revenge on death. Don't forget death. Don't ever forget it. Yes, sex too is limited in its power. I know very well how limited. But tell me, what power is greater?

Anyway, Carolyn Lyons, nearly two and a half decades later and thirty-five pounds heavier. I'd loved her old size but I soon got to like the new size, with all that monumentality at the base sustaining her slender torso. I let it inspire me as though I were Gaston Lachaise. Her wide rump and heavy thighs spoke to me of all that was female in her baled. And her movement beneath me, the subtlety of her excitement, inspired another pastoral comparison: the plowing of a softly billowing field. Carolyn the undergraduate flower you pollinated, Carolyn at forty-five you farmed. The disparity in scale between the sinuous old upper half and the substantial new lower half replicated an intriguing tension in my overall perception of her. She was for me an exciting hybrid of the intelligent, tremulous, daring pioneer who couldn't stop raising her hand in class, the beautiful dissident in gypsy drag, Janie Wyatt's most sensible sidekick, who knew all the answers back in 1965, and the assertive business executive she had become in middle age, packing the potential to overpower you.

You might have expected that as time wore on and the hothouse passion of the teacher-student taboo ceased feeding into the permissible pleasures of the present moment, our meetings would run out of nostalgic appeal. But a year had passed and that hadn't happened. Because of the ease and the calm and the physical trust inherent in a resumption of play between teammates of old and because of Carolyn's realism—the sense of proportion adult indignities had predictably imposed on the romantic expectations of a highly credentialed upper-middle-class girl—I reaped rewards that it was impossible to draw from my crazy bingeing on Consuela's breasts. Our harmonious, no-nonsense evenings in bed—scheduled by cell phone, on the run, for whenever Carolyn touched down at Kennedy from one of her business trips—now provided the only point of contact with my pre-Consuela confidence. I never needed more the straightforward satiation Carolyn so dependably afforded now that she'd been tested as a woman and stoically survived. Each of us was getting exactly what we wanted. It was a joint venture, our sexual partnership, that profited us both and that was strongly colored by Carolyn's crisp executive manner. Here pleasure and equilibrium combined.

Then came the night that Consuela pulled out her tampon and stood there in my bathroom, with one knee dipping toward the other and, like Mantegna's Saint Sebastian, bleeding in a trickle down her thighs while I watched. Was it thrilling? Was I delighted? Was I mesmerized? Sure, but again I felt like a boy. I had set out to demand the most from her, and when she shamelessly obliged, I wound up again intimidating myself. There seemed nothing to be done—if I wished not to be humbled completely by her exotic matter-of-factness—except to fall to my knees to lick her clean. Which she allowed to happen without comment. Making me into a still smaller boy. One's impossible character. The stupidity of being oneself. The unavoidable comedy of being anyone at all. Each new excess weakening me further—yet what is an insatiable man to do?

The expression on her face? I was at her feet. I was on the floor. My own face was pressed to her flesh like a feeding infant's, so I could see nothing of hers. But I told you, I don't believe she was intimidated. There was no overwhelming new emotion for Consuela to deal with. Once we'd got past the preliminaries as lovers, she seemed able to assimilate easily enough whatever her nudity provoked in me. It made no sense to her that a married man like George O'Hearn should be kissing a fully clothed young woman in a public place at eight in the morning—*that* was chaos to Consuela. But this? This was just a novel divertissement. This was coming to her, the physical fate she so lightly wore. Surely the attention being accorded by the cultural authority down on his knees wasn't something that made her feel unimportant. Consuela had been alluring to boys all her life, loved by her family all her life, adored by her father all her life, so that self-possession, repose, a kind of statuesque equanimity, was instinctively the form her theatricality took. Somehow Consuela had been spared the awkwardness that is given to just about everyone.

That was a Thursday night. Friday night Carolyn came right from the airport to me, and on Saturday morning I was at the table, already over breakfast, when she marched into the kitchen from the shower wearing my terrycloth robe and holding in her hand a bloody tampon half wrapped in toilet paper. First she showed it to me and then she threw it at me. "You are fucking other women. Tell me the truth," Carolyn said, "and then I'm going. I don't like this. I had two husbands who fucked other women. I didn't like it then and I don't like it now. And least of all with you. You make the kind of connection we have—and then you do this. You have everything you want as you want it—fucking like ours outside of domesticity and outside of romance—and then you do this. There aren't many like me, David. I have an interest in what you have an interest in. I understand what's what. Harmonious hedonism. I am one in a million, idiot—so how could you possibly do this?" She spoke not angrily like a wife fortified by the ironclad historical claim but like a courtesan of renown, out of indisputable erotic superiority. She had a right to do so: most people bring to bed with them the worst of their biography—Carolyn brought only the best. No, she wasn't angry; she was humiliated and undone. Once more, her bountiful sexuality had been deemed less than enough by another unworthy, unsatisfiable man. She said, "I'm not going to quarrel with you. I want to know the truth and then you'll never see me again."

I tried to be as composed as possible, only mildly curious, when I asked, "Where did you find this?" The tampon was now on the kitchen table, lying between the butter dish and the teapot. "In the bathroom. In the trash basket." "Well, I don't know whose it is or how it got there." "Why don't you put it on your bagel and eat it?" Carolyn suggested. All I said, by way of reply, was "I would, gladly, if that would make you happy. But I don't know whose it is. I think I should know whose it is before I eat it." "I can't put up with this, David. It makes me furious." "I have a thought. I have a suggestion. My friend George," I said, "has a key to the apartment. He's won a Pulitzer, he gives readings, he teaches at the New School, he meets women, girls, he sleeps with everyone he meets, and since obviously he cannot bring them home to his wife and four children, and since to find a hotel room in New York is sometimes impossible, and since he is always short on funds anyway, and since the women are married, many of them, and he can't take them to *their* houses"—every word I spoke, true so far—"he sometimes brings them here."

Now that was not true. That was the same durable lie with which I had saved myself before when, over the years, some woman's incriminating personal belonging—though admittedly never one quite so primordial—was discovered that had been either negligently or deliberately left behind. The durable lie of the run-of-the-mill roué. Nothing to boast about there.

"So," Carolyn said, "George fucks all these women in your bed." "Not all of them. But some, yes. He uses the bed in the guest room. He is my friend. His marriage is not paradise. He reminds me of myself when I was married. George feels pure only in his transgressions. His obedient side makes him sick. How can I say no?" "You're too meticulous for that, David. You're too orderly for that. I don't believe a word you're saying. Everything in your life is just so, everything is considered, everything is deliberate—" "Well, that alone should convince you—" "Someone was here, David." "No one," I said, "not with me. I really don't know whose tampon it is." It was a fierce, tense situation, but by bluntly lying right into her face, I survived and, fortunately, she did not leave me when I needed her most. She left only later, and at my request.

Excuse me, I have to take that call. I must answer. Excuse . . .

Sorry to be away so long. It wasn't even the call I'm waiting for. Sorry to leave you alone like this, but it was my son. He phoned to tell me how insulted he still is by everything I said at our last meeting and to be sure I got the angry letter he wrote.

Look, I never thought that it would be easy for us, and for all I know he might have started hating me even without encouragement. I knew it was a difficult escape, and I knew I could take only myself over the wall. If I'd taken him, had that even been possible, it wouldn't have made sense because he was eight years old and I couldn't have lived the way I wanted to. I had to betray him, and for that I am not forgiven and never will be.

This past year he became an adulterer at the age of forty-two; ever since he's begun showing up unannounced at my door. Eleven, twelve o'clock at night, one, even two in the morning, and there he is on the intercom. "It's me. Let me up, ring me in!" He argues with his wife, storms out of the house, gets in the car, and, despite himself, he winds up here. After he'd grown up, we hardly saw each other for years on end; for months we didn't so much as speak on the phone. You can imagine my surprise at his first midnight visit. What are you here for, I ask him. He's in trouble. He's in a crisis. He's suffering. Why? He has a girlfriend. A young woman of twenty-six who recently came to work for him. He runs a little company that restores damaged works of art. That was his mother's occupation until she retired: art conservator. He went into her field after getting his Ph.D. from NYU, joined forces with her, and now the business is quite successful, with eighteen people working for him in a SoHo loft. A lot of gallery work, private collectors, auction houses, consultant to Sotheby's, and so on. Kenny's a big, good-looking man, dresses impeccably, speaks authoritatively, writes intelligently, converses easily in French and German—out in the art world he's obviously impressive. But not with me. My deficiencies are at the root of his suffering. Put him anywhere near me and the wound within begins to hemorrhage. At his work he's active, healthy, solid, not insufficient in any way, but I have only to speak and I paralyze everything strong in him. And I have merely to remain silent while *he* speaks in order to undermine everything that makes him effectual. I'm the father he can't defeat, the father in whose presence his powers are overwhelmed. Why? Perhaps because I wasn't present. I was absent and terrifying. I was absent and entirely too full of meaning. I failed him. That's sufficient reason to make a calm relationship out of the question. There's nothing in our history to impede the filial instinct to lay every impediment at the father's feet.

I am Kenny's Karamazov father, the base, the monstrous force with whom he, a saint of love, a man who must behave well all the time, feels himself wronged and parricidal, as though he were all the brothers Karamazov in one. Parents play a

legendary role in the minds of their children, and that my ordained legend has been Dostoyevskian I know from as far back
as the late seventies, when I received in the mail a copy of a
paper Kenny had written as a Princeton sophomore, an A
paper on *The Brothers Karamazov*. It wasn't hard to ascertain
the book's relevance as an exaggerated fantasy of his own
condition. Kenny was one of those overheated kids for whom
whatever he read had a personal significance that eradicated
everything else germane to literature. He was by then wholly
preoccupied with our estrangement and, inevitably, the focus
of his paper was the father. A depraved sensualist. A solitary
old lecher. An old man with his young girls. A great buffoon
who sets up a harem of loose women in his house. A father
who, you may remember, abandons his first child, ignores all
his children, "for a child," Dostoyevsky writes, "would have
gotten in the way of his debaucheries." You've not read *The
Brothers Karamazov*? But you must, if only for the amusing
portrait of the profligate wickedness of the shameful father.

Whenever Kenny would come to me distraught back in his
adolescence, it was always over the same issue. It still is: something has threatened his idea of himself as a punctiliously upright person. One way or another, I would encourage him to
modulate that idea, to temper it a bit, but suggesting that
would make him furious and he would turn around and run
back to his mother. I remember I asked him once, when he
was thirteen and starting high school and beginning to look
and sound like something more than a child, whether he would
like to stay with me for the summer in a house I'd rented up in
the Catskills, not far from my parents' hotel. It was an afternoon in May and we were at a Mets game. Another of our
painful Sundays together. He was so chagrined by the invitation that he had to rush off to vomit in the men's room at
Shea. In the old days, in the Old World, fathers used to initiate
their sons into sex by taking them to the whorehouse, and it
was as though that was what I had proposed. He vomited because if he came to be with me, one of my girls might be
around. Maybe two. Maybe more. Because in his mind my
house *was* the whorehouse. Yet his vomiting bespoke not just
revulsion with me but, even more, revulsion with his revulsion.
Why? Because of what he desperately wanted, because even

with a father with whom he's angry and disappointed, the moment together with him is so powerful and the yearning for him is so great. He was still a boy in a helpless predicament. This was before he cauterized the wound by turning himself into a prig.

In his last year of college he thought, correctly, that he might have impregnated one of his classmates. He was too alarmed at first to tell his mother, so he came to me. I assured him that if the girl actually turned out to be pregnant, he hadn't to marry her. This wasn't 1901. If she was determined to have the baby, as she was already insisting, then that was her choice, not his. Pro-choice I was, but that didn't mean pro her choice for him. I urged him to remind her as often as he could that, at the age of twenty-one and just graduating from college, he didn't want a child, couldn't support a child, didn't intend in any way to be responsible for a child. If, at twenty-one, she wanted the responsibility all on her own, that was a decision made by her for herself alone. I offered him money to pay for an abortion. I told him I was behind him and not to cave in. "But what if she won't change her mind? What," he asked me, "if she flatly refuses?" I said that if she didn't come to her senses, she would have to live with the consequences. I reminded him that nobody could make him do what he didn't want to do. I said what I wished some forceful man had said to me when I was on the brink of making *my* mistake. I said, "Living in a country like ours, whose key documents are all about emancipation, all directed at guaranteeing individual liberty, living in a free system that is basically indifferent to how you behave as long as the behavior is lawful, the misery that comes your way is most likely to be self-generated. It would be another matter if you were living in Nazi-occupied Europe or in Communist-dominated Europe or in Mao Zedong's China. There they manufacture the misery for you; you don't have to take a single wrong step in order never to want to get up in the morning. But here, free of totalitarianism, a man like you has to provide himself his own misery. You, moreover, are intelligent, articulate, good-looking, well educated— you are *made* to thrive in a country like this one. Here the only tyrant lying in wait will be convention, which is not to be taken lightly either. Read Tocqueville, if you haven't yet. He's not outdated, not on the subject of 'men being forced through the same sieve.' The point is that you shouldn't think that you miraculously have to become a beatnik or a bohemian or a hippie to elude the trammels of convention. Successfully doing so doesn't require exaggerations of conduct or oddities of dress that are alien to your temperament and your upbringing. Not at all. All you have to do, Ken, is to find your force. You have it, I know you have it—it is immobilized only by the newness of the predicament. If you want to live intelligently beyond the blackmail of the slogans and the unexamined rules, you have only to find your own . . ." Et cetera, et cetera. The Declaration of Independence. The Bill of Rights. The Gettysburg Address. The Emancipation Proclamation. The Fourteenth Amendment. All three of the Civil War amendments. I went over everything with him. I found the Tocqueville for him. I figured, he's twenty-one, at long last we can talk. I out-Poloniused Polonius. What I was telling him, after all, wasn't so far out, certainly not for 1979. Nor would it have been back when I needed it drummed into *my* head. Conceived in liberty—that's just good American common sense. But when I was finished, what did he do? He began to recount to me all her outstanding qualities. I asked, "What about *your* qualities?" But he didn't seem to hear me, just started in again to tell me how smart she was, how pretty she was, what a funny girl she was, he told me about her terrific family, and a couple months later he married her.

I know all the objections that a pure and moral young man can give to claiming personal sovereignty. I know all the admirable labels to attach to not asserting one's sovereignty. Well, Kenny's difficulty is that he must be admirable whatever the cost. He lives in fear of a woman telling him he's not. "Selfish" is the word that cripples him. You selfish bastard. He's terrified of that judgment, so that's the judgment that rules. Yes, count on Kenny for the admirable thing, whatever it may be, which is why when Todd, his oldest child, entered high school and my daughter-in-law said that they had to have more children, he became a father three more times in the next six years. At just the point when he was sick and tired of her. Because he's so admirable, he cannot leave his wife for the girlfriend, he cannot leave the girlfriend for the wife, and of course he cannot leave his young children. God knows he cannot leave his mother. The one he can leave is me. But he grew up with the list of grievances, and so, in the years immediately after the divorce, whenever I saw him I had to plead my case, at the zoo, at the movies, at the ballgame, demonstrating that I'm not what his mother says I am.

I gave it up because I *am* what she says I am. He was her creature, and by the time he went off to college, I wasn't going to contend any longer for somebody I made sick to his stomach. I gave it up because I didn't care to feign the feminine need against which Kenny has no defense. To the pathos of feminine need my son is most cruelly addicted. During those years he was alone with his mother cultivating this archaic addiction—which, by the way, in the days of the dependent woman enslaved all the best men—he and I would always spend two weeks together in the summer at my parents' little hotel. A relief for me because my parents took over. They were starved for all the family doings, and because of our history he and I couldn't begin to make a go of it. But once the grandparents were gone, once he was in graduate school, married, a father . . . Yet he always called me when one of his children was born. Kind of him, given his feelings about me. That I lost I of course knew long ago. But Kenny lost too. The consequences of my being what I am are long term. These domestic disasters are dynastic.

Though suddenly, once a month, once every six weeks, he comes to drain himself in my presence of what's poisoning him. There's fear in his eyes, there's rage in his heart, there's weariness in his voice; even his elegant clothes no longer fit. The wife is unhappy and angry about the girlfriend, the girlfriend is complaining and resentful of the wife, and the children are frightened and cry out in their sleep. As for conjugal sex, a heinous duty he stoically performs, that is beyond even his fortitude now. Arguments abound, irritable bowel syndrome abounds, placation abounds, threats abound, as do counterthreats. But when I ask, "Then why not leave?" he tells me that leaving would destroy his family. No one would survive, everybody would have a breakdown, the suffering would be too great all around. Instead, everyone must cling to everyone else.

What's implicit is how much more honorable he is than the father who walked out on him when he was eight. His life has a significance that mine does not. This is his strong suit. This is where he dominates and is superior to me.

"Kenny," I tell him, "why not finally confront your father as a reality? Confront at long last your father's prick. This is the reality of a father. We lie to a child about these things. There cannot be candor about the father's prick to a child. That many fathers cannot contain themselves in a marriage—it's just as well that's a secret from the little ones. But you are a man. You know the score. You know all these artists. You know all these dealers. You must have some idea of how adults live their lives. Is this still the biggest scandal imaginable?"

All he and I do is berate each other, though not in the established tradition. Beyond the pages of Dostoyevsky, the story is traditionally the opposite: the father's the customary constraining authority, the son is incorrigible, and the castigation flows the other way. Yet he continues to come here, and whenever he rings the bell, I let him up. "Your girlfriend is how old?" I ask. "And having an affair with a married man of forty-two, a father of four, who is her boss? So she is not such a paragon either. Only you are the paragon. You and your mother." You should hear him about this girl. A chemist who also has a degree in art history. *And* plays the oboe. Wonderful, I tell him. Even in your adultery you are better than I am. He won't even call it adultery. His adultery is different from everyone else's. It's too committed an arrangement to be called adultery. And commitment is what I lack. My adulteries weren't serious enough to suit him.

Well, that is true. I tried not to have it be serious. But for him adultery is the recruitment of the new wife. He went to meet her family. That's what he was just telling me, how he flew down with her yesterday to meet them. "You flew to Florida," I asked him, "back and forth in a day to meet her parents? But this is adultery. What do her parents have to do with it?" He tells me that at the outset, at the airport, her parents are cold and very skeptical, but by the time they all sit down together in the condo for dinner, they tell her that they love him. Love him like their own son. Everybody loves everybody. It was worth the trip. "And did you meet your girlfriend's sister and her lovely children?" I asked him. "Did you meet her brother and *his* lovely children?" Oh boy, the little prison that is his current marriage he is about to trade in for a maximum-security facility. Headed once again straight for the slammer. I tell him, "Kenny, you want license and approval both? Well, it so happens that I willingly give license and approval both." But he doesn't stop at that. It's not enough that he's got the one father in this whole big country who will endorse what he's doing and maybe even set him up with another piece of ass with a wonderful family in Florida. I must also yield to the superiority. "The oboe too," I said. "Isn't that just grand? I'm sure she writes poetry in her spare time. I'm sure her parents do too." Credentials, credentials, credentials. This one cannot fuck if he doesn't have a dominatrix over him snapping a whip. This one cannot fuck if the girl is not dressed like a chambermaid. Some can fuck only midgets, some only criminals, some only chickens. My son can fuck only a girl with the right moral credentials. Please, I tell him, it's a perversity, no better or worse than any other. Recognize it for what it is and don't feel so special.

Here. The letter he was afraid might have been lost in the mail. Dated later the very night last week that he came to see me. As though over this past year of our trading insults I haven't got ten others like it. "You're a hundred times worse than I thought." That's the beginning. That's the boilerplate. Then this. Let me read it to you. "You keep going on. I couldn't believe it. The things you said to me. You must assert yourself all the time, prove that your choice in life was the right one and mine the cowardly one, the grotesque one, the wrong one. I came to you distressed in the extreme, and the mental violence you directed at me. The sixties—he owes all that he is today to how seriously he took Janis Joplin. Without Janis Joplin never could he have emerged at the age of seventy as the very picture of a pathetic old fool. The long white pageboy of important hair, the turkey wattle half hidden behind the fancy foulard—when will you begin to rouge your cheeks, Herr von Aschenbach? What do you think you look like? Do you have any idea? All that devotion to the Higher Life. Manning the aesthetic barricades on Channel Thirteen. The single-handed battle to maintain cultural standards in a mass society.

But what about observing ordinary standards of decency? Of course you didn't have the guts to stay in academic life and be serious; you've never been serious for a day in your life. Janie Wyatt, where is *she* now? How many failed marriages? How many breakdowns? In what psychiatric hospital has she been a patient for lo these many years? These girls go to college, and they shouldn't be protected from you? You are the living argument *for* protecting them. I have two daughters, your granddaughters, and if I thought that my daughters were to go to a college and have as their teacher a man like my father . . ."

And on like that . . . until . . . let's see . . . yes, he's stronger here. "My kids are frightened and screaming because their parents are having an argument and Daddy is so angry he is leaving the house. Do you know what it's like for me with my children when I come home at night? Do you know what it's like to hear your children cry? How *could* you know? And I protected you. *I* protected *you.* I tried not to believe that Mother was right. I came to your defense, I stuck up for you. I had to, you were my father. In my mind, I tried to excuse you, I tried to understand you. But the *sixties*? That explosion of childishness, that vulgar, mindless, collective regression, and that explains everything and excuses it all? Can't you come up with any better alibi? Seducing defenseless students, pursuing one's sexual interests at the expense of everyone else—that's so very necessary, is it? No, necessity is staying in a difficult marriage and raising a little child and meeting the responsibilities of an adult. All those years I thought Mother was exaggerating. But it wasn't exaggeration. I little knew until tonight what it was that she lived through. The pain you caused her, and for what? The burden you put on her—the burden you put on *me,* on a child, to be everything in the world to his mother, and for what? So you could be 'free'? I cannot bear you. I never could."

And next month he'll be back again to tell me how he can't bear me. And the month after that. And the month after that. I didn't lose him after all. His father is finally a resource. "It's me. Let me up. Ring me in!" His situation brings him no self-irony, but I believe he gets more than he lets on. He doesn't get anything? He must. He is by no means stupid. He can't be besieged forever by his childhood drama. He is? Well, perhaps so. You're probably right. He will be raw about this for the rest of his life. One of the innumerable jokes: a man of forty-two, adjoined to the thirteen-year-old boy's existence and tormented by it still. Perhaps it's just as it was at the ballgame. He's dying to break out. He's dying to get away from his mother, he's dying to go off with his father, and all he can do is vomit his heart out.

My affair with Consuela lasted for a little more than a year and a half. Only occasionally did we ever again go out for dinner or to the theater. She was too afraid of the prying press and of winding up on Page Six, and that was fine with me, because whenever I saw her I always wanted to fuck her right away and not have first to sit through some shitty play. "You know how the media are, you know what they do to people, and if I go there with you . . ." "Fine, don't worry," I would say agreeably, "we'll just stay home." Eventually she would stay overnight, and we would have breakfast together. We saw each other once or twice a week, and, even after the incident with the tampon, Carolyn failed to discover Consuela's existence. Still, I was never at peace about Consuela; never could I forget about the five boys she had fucked before me, two of whom turned out to be brothers, one her lover at eighteen, the other when she was twenty—Cuban brothers, Bergen County's wealthy Villareal brothers, and another cause for suffering. If it weren't for the calming influence of Carolyn and our wonderful nights together, I don't know what would have happened to me.

The agitation of having Consuela—as opposed to the agitation of not having Consuela—ended only when she received her master's degree and had a party over in New Jersey at her parents' house. Of course it was as well for both of us that it ended, but it wasn't my plan to end it, and I was bereft afterward. I was depressed off and on for nearly three years. Tormented all the while I was with her, a hundred times more tormented for having lost her. It was a bad time and it wouldn't stop. George O'Hearn was an ace. He talked me through many an evening when I found myself getting too low. And I had my piano, which was what pulled me through.

I told you that over the years I bought a lot of music, the piano literature, and so I played all the time, whenever I finished my other work. I played all thirty-two Beethoven sonatas during those years, every note of them to drive Consuela out of my thoughts. Nobody should be forced to hear a tape of that playing, which doesn't exist anyway. Some passages were in tempo, but most weren't, yet on I played regardless. Freakish, but it's what I did. With keyboard music you have the feeling of reproducing what the composers were doing, and so you're in their minds to some degree. Not in the most mysterious part, where the music originates, but still, you're not merely passively absorbing an aesthetic experience. You are, in your own clumsy way, somehow producing it yourself, and this is how I tried escaping the loss of Consuela. I played the Mozart sonatas. I played Bach's piano music. I played it, I'm familiar with it, which is a different thing from playing it well. I played Elizabethan pieces by Byrd and people like that. I played Purcell. I played Scarlatti. I have all the Scarlatti sonatas, all five hundred and fifty of them. I won't say I played all of them, but I played a lot of them. Haydn's piano music. I know it cold now. Schumann. Schubert. And this, as I told you, is on the basis of very little training. But it was an awful time, a futile time, and it was either study Beethoven and enter his mind or stay in my own mind and replay all the scenes of her I could remember—replay, worst of all, the reckless thing I did by not going to her graduation party.

But, you see, I could never figure how ordinary she was. This girl who takes her tampon out for me, and then because I don't show up at her graduation party, she's finished with me? The casualness of something so powerful ending as it did is unbelievable to me. The abruptness with which it ends, I replay *that*, thinking that the secret of the abruptness is that Consuela didn't want it to go on. Why? Because she didn't desire me, never desired me, because she experimented with me, really, to see how overwhelming her breasts could be. But she herself was never getting what she wanted. She was getting that from the Villareal brothers. Of course. There they all were at the party, pressing in on her, surrounding her, dark, handsome, muscular, mannerly, young, and she realized, What am I doing with this old man? So I was right all along—and therefore it was right for it to end. She went as far as she wanted to go. All I could have done by forging ahead was to arrange more torture for myself. The smartest thing I did was not to show up there. Because I had been yielding and yielding in ways that I didn't understand. The longing never disappeared even while I had her. The primary emotion, as I've said, was longing. It's still longing. There's no relief from the longing and my sense of myself as a supplicant. There it is: you have it when you're with her and you have it when you're without her. So who ended it? Did I end it by not going to the party, or did she end it by seizing upon my not going to the party? This is the endless debate I had and why, to stop my mind from revolving around the loss of Consuela—to stop myself from falsely particularizing this one event, the party, as the clue to everything I'd mismanaged—I often had to get up in the middle of the night and play the piano until dawn.

All that had happened was that she invited me to Jersey to celebrate her getting her degree and I had to say yes, but as I was driving across the bridge, I thought, Her parents will be there, her grandparents, the Cuban relatives, all the old childhood friends will be there, those brothers will be there, and I will be introduced as the teacher who is on television. And it was just too silly after a year and a half for me to pretend I was nothing to this young woman but a kindly mentor, especially in the presence of those fucking Villareals. I was too old for this nonsense, so I stopped on the Jersey side of the bridge and phoned her and told her my car had broken down and I couldn't come. A transparent lie—I had a Porsche not two years old—and so that very night, from New Jersey, she faxed me a letter on the family fax machine, not the most explosive letter I have ever received from anyone, but nonetheless, I could never have imagined Consuela uncontrollable like this.

But I could never imagine Consuela altogether. What more didn't I know about her because of being blinded by my obsession? Shouting at me in the letter: "You're always playing the wise old man who knows everything." Shouting: "I saw you just this morning on television, playing the role of the one who always knows better, knowing what is good culture and what is bad culture, knowing what people should read and what they shouldn't read, knowing all about music and all about art, and then, to celebrate this important moment in my life, I have a party, I want to have a wonderful party, I want to have you around, you who mean everything to me, and you're not there." And I had already sent her a present, sent flowers, but she was so furious, so angry . . . "Mr. Arrogant Intellectual Critic, the great authority on everything, teaching everybody what to think and setting everyone right! *Me da asco!*"

That's how she ended it. Never before, not even affectionately, had Consuela availed herself of Spanish with me. *Me da asco.* Ordinary idiom meaning, "It makes me sick."

This is all six and a half years ago. The strange thing was that three months later I got a postcard from her, from some Third World country with a first-class resort—Belize, Honduras, some such place—and it was completely friendly. Then six months later she phoned me. She was applying for a job in advertising, the kind of job, she said, I would hate her for, but would I write a letter of recommendation anyway? As her former professor. Which I wrote. Then I got a postcard (a Modigliani nude from the Modern) saying she got the job and that she was very happy. And then nothing more from her. One night I found her name in a new Manhattan phone book, the address of an apartment her father must have bought for her on the Upper East Side. But going back was a bad idea and I didn't try.

George, for one, wouldn't let me. George O'Hearn, though fifteen years my junior, was my worldly confessor. He was the friend closest to me during the year and a half I was with Consuela, and only afterward did he tell me how concerned he'd been, how he'd kept a careful watch over me as I denuded myself of my realism, my pragmatism, my cynicism and thought of nothing but losing her. He's the one who wouldn't let me answer her postcard, which I was dying to do, which I believed I was being invited to do by the cylindrical stalk of a waist, the wide pelvic span, and the gently curving thighs, by the patch of flame that is the hair that marks the spot where she is forked—by the trademark Modigliani nude, the accessible, elongated dream girl he ritualistically painted and that Consuela had chosen to send, so immodestly, through the U.S. mail. A nude whose breasts, full and canting a bit to the side, might well have been modeled on her own. A nude represented with her eyes closed, defended, like Consuela, by nothing other than her erotic power, at once, like Consuela, elemental and elegant. A golden-skinned nude inexplicably asleep over a velvety black abyss that, in my mood, I associated with the grave. One long, undulating line, she lies there awaiting you, still as death.

George hadn't even wanted me to write the recommendation for the job. He said, "You'll always be powerless with this girl. You'll never be in charge. There's something there," George told me, "that makes you crazy and always will. If you don't cut the connection for good, in the end that something will destroy you. You're no longer merely answering a natural need with her. This is the pathology in its purest form. Look," he told me, "see it as a critic, see it from a professional point of view. You violated the law of aesthetic distance. You sentimentalized the aesthetic experience with this girl—you personalized it, you sentimentalized it, and you lost the sense of separation essential to your enjoyment. Do you know when that happened? The night she took the tampon out. The necessary aesthetic separation collapsed not while you watched her bleeding—that was all right, that was fine—but when you couldn't restrain yourself and went down on your knees. And what the hell compelled you? What lies behind the comedy of this Cuban girl taking a guy like you, the professor of desire, to the mat? Drinking her blood? I'd say that constituted the abandonment of an independent critical position, Dave. Worship me, she says, worship the mystery of the bleeding goddess, and you do it. You stop at nothing. You lick it. You consume it. You digest it. *She* penetrates *you*. What next, David? A glass of her urine? How long before you would have begged her for feces? I'm not against it because it's unhygienic. I'm not against it because it's disgusting. I'm against it because it's falling in love. The only obsession everyone wants: 'love.' People think that in falling in love they make themselves whole? The Platonic union of souls? I think otherwise. I think you're whole before you begin. And the love fractures you. You're whole, and then you're cracked open. She was a foreign body introduced into your wholeness. And for a year and a half you

struggled to incorporate it. But you'll never be whole until
you expel it. You either get rid of it or incorporate it through
self-distortion. And that's what you did and what drove you
mad."

Hard to sanction those words, and not only because of
George's mythopoeticizing turn of mind; just hard to believe
in the disastrous potential of a character so seemingly unin-
timidating as family-bound, protected, suburban Consuela.
George wouldn't let up. "Attachment is ruinous and your
enemy. Joseph Conrad: He who forms a tie is lost. That you
should sit there looking like you do is absurd. You tasted it.
Isn't that enough? Of what do you ever get more than a taste?
That's all we're given in life, that's all we're given *of* life. A
taste. There is no more."

George was right, of course, and only repeating to me what
I know. He who forms a tie *is* lost, attachment *is* my enemy, so I
employed what Casanova called "the schoolboy's remedy"—I
masturbated instead. I would imagine myself sitting at my
piano while she stood naked beside me. We had once enacted
just such a tableau in the flesh, so I was as much remembering
as imagining. I had asked her if she would take off her clothes
and let me look at her while I played the Mozart Sonata in
C Minor, and she obliged. I don't know that I played it any
better than I ordinarily did, but that was never the point. In
another recurring fantasy, I am telling her, "This is a metronome. The little light flashes and it makes a periodic noise.
That's all it does. You adjust the pace to what you want. Not
only amateurs like me but professionals, even great concert
pianists, have the problem of what's called rushing." Once
again, I envision her standing by the piano with her clothes at
her feet, as on the night when, fully dressed, I played the C
Minor Sonata, serenading her nudity with the slow movement.
(Sometimes she would come to me in a dream identified, like a
spy, only as "K. 457.") "This is a quartz metronome," I say.
"It's not the triangular-shaped thing you may have seen, with
a pendulum, where the pendulum has a little weight on it, and
the numbers are there. The numbers are the same as on a
pendulum," and when she advances to examine the dial,
her breasts pitch forward to cover my mouth and to stifle,

momentarily, the pedagogy—the pedagogy that with Consuela is my greatest power. My only power.

"They're standard numbers," I tell her. "If you turn this to sixty, the beats will be seconds. Yes, like a heartbeat. Let me feel the tap of your heartbeat through the tip of my tongue." This she allows to happen, as she lets everything between us happen —without comment, almost without complicity. I tell her, "Actually, before it was invented about 1812—the old one, that is—there are no metronome markings on music. What they did in the general treatises about tempo was to suggest that you employ the beat of the pulse as a certain kind of allegro. They'd say, 'Take your pulse and think of the tempo as that.' Let me take your pulse with the head of my prick. Sit on my prick, Consuela, and we'll play with time. Ah, it's not a fast allegro, is it? Not at all. Now, there's no Mozart piece with metronome markings, and why, why is that so? You remember when Mozart died . . ." But here I have my orgasm, the fantasy lesson is ended, and, for the moment, I am sick no longer with desire. Isn't that Yeats? "Consume my heart away; sick with desire / And fastened to a dying animal / It knows not what it is." Yeats. Yes. "Caught in that sensual music," and so on.

I played Beethoven and I masturbated. I played Mozart and I masturbated. I played Haydn, Schumann, Schubert, and masturbated with her image in mind. Because I could not forget the breasts, the ripe breasts, the nipples, and the way she could drape her breasts over my cock and fondle me like that. Another detail. A last detail and I'll stop. I am becoming a bit technical, but this is important. This was the touch that made Consuela a masterpiece of *volupté*. She's one of the few women I've known who come by pushing out the vulva, by involuntarily pushing it out like a bivalve's soft, unsegmented, bubbling-forth body. It took me by surprise the first time. You feel it and you get a sense of this other-world fauna, something from the sea. As though it were related to the oyster or the octopus or the squid, a creature from miles down and eons back. Normally you see the vagina and you can open it with your hands, but in her case it bloomed open, the cunt on its own emerging from its hiding place. The inner lips get extruded outward, swell outward, and it's very arousing, that slimy, silky swollenness, stimulating to touch and stimulating to see. The secret ecstatically exposed. Schiele would have given his eyeteeth to paint it. Picasso would have turned it into a guitar.

You can almost come by watching her come. She would turn her eyes away when it was like that for her. Her eyes turned up and you saw only the whites, and that was something to watch as well. All of her was something to watch. Whatever the agitation from the jealousy, whatever the humiliation and the endless uncertainty, I was always proud of making her come. Sometimes you don't even worry if a woman comes or not: it just happens, the woman seems to take care of it on her own and it's not your responsibility. It's not an issue with other women; the situation is enough, there's enough excitement and it's never in question. But with Consuela, yes, it was definitely a responsibility that was mine, and always, always it was a matter of pride.

I have a ridiculous forty-two-year-old son—ridiculous because he *is* my son, imprisoned in his marriage because of my escape from mine and the significance that's had for him and the protest against my personal life he's obstinately made of his own. Ridiculousness is the price he pays for having been molded too early into a Telemachus, heroic little defender of the untended mother. Yet, during my three years of off-and-on depression, I was a thousand times more ridiculous than Kenny. What do I mean by ridiculous? What is ridiculousness? Relinquishing one's freedom voluntarily—that is the definition of ridiculousness. If your freedom is taken from you by force, needless to say you're not ridiculous, except to the one who has forcibly taken it. But whoever gives his freedom away, whoever is dying to give it away, enters the realm of the ridiculous that brings the most famous of Ionesco's plays to mind and is a source of comedy throughout literature. The one who is free may be mad, stupid, repellent, in misery just because he is free, but he is not ridiculous. He has dimension as a being. I was myself ridiculous enough *with* Consuela. But during the years I was captive to the monotonous melodrama of the loss of her? My son, shaped by his contempt for my example, determined to be responsible where I was derelict, unable to free himself from anyone, beginning with me—my son may not wish to know any better, but I go about the world insisting that I do, and still the extraneous creeps in. Jealousy creeps in. Attachment creeps in. The eternal problem of attachment. No, not even fucking can stay totally pure and protected. And this is where I fail. The great propagandist for fucking and I can't do any better than Kenny. Of course there is no purity of the kind Kenny dreams of, but there is also no purity of the kind I dream of. When two dogs fuck there appears to be purity. *There*, we think, is pure fucking, among the beasts. But should we discuss it with them, we would probably find that even among dogs there are, in canine form, these crazy distortions of longing, doting, possessiveness, even of love.

This need. This derangement. Will it never stop? I don't even know after a while what I'm desperate for. Her tits? Her soul? Her youth? Her simple mind? Maybe it's worse than that—maybe now that I'm nearing death, I also long secretly not to be free.

Time passes. Time passes. I have new girlfriends. I have student girlfriends. Old girlfriends turn up from as long as twenty and thirty years back. Some are already divorced numerous times and some have been so busy establishing themselves professionally that they've not even had an opportunity to marry. The ones still on their own call me to complain about their dates. Dating is hateful, relationships are impossible, sex is a hazard. The men are narcissistic, humorless, crazy, obsessional, overbearing, crude, or they are great-looking, virile, and ruthlessly unfaithful, or they are emasculated, or they are impotent, or they are just too dumb. The twenty-odd-year-olds don't have these problems because they still have university-based friendships, and school, of course, is the great mixer, but the somewhat older women are, by their mid-thirties, so busy with their work that many of them, I discover, now resort to professional matchmakers to find men for them. And at a certain age they stop meeting new people anyway. As one of the disillusioned told me, "Who are the new people when you *do* meet them? They're the same old people in masks. There's nothing new about them at all. They're *people*."

The matchmakers range in price for what is a year's

membership, during which time a certain number of introductions are guaranteed. Some matchmakers charge a couple hundred dollars, some a couple of thousand, and one I was told about, who specializes in what she calls "quality people," arranges introductions—up to twenty-five over two years—for no less than twenty-one thousand dollars. I thought I misheard when I was told this, but, yes, twenty-one thousand bucks is the fee. Well, it's hard on women engaging in this kind of transaction in order to find a man to marry them and to father children; no wonder they turn up late at night to sit and talk to their elderly ex-teacher, and sometimes, in their loneliness, even to stay over. Recently one of them was here trying to recover from having just been dumped in mid-meal on a first date by a man she described as "an extreme-vacation type, a super-duper adventurer into hunting lions and wild surfing." "It's rough out there, David," she told me. "Because it isn't even dating, it's just *trying* to date. I've stoically accepted the matchmaking," she said, "but not even *that* works."

Elena, kindhearted Elena Hrabovsky, who's gone prematurely gray, maybe *from* the matchmaking. I said to her, "It must be a huge strain, the strangers, the silences, even the conversation," and she asked me, "Do you think it's supposed to be like this when you're as successful as I am?" Elena is an ophthalmologist, you see, up from the bottom of the working class by dint of immense fortitude. "Life baffles you," she told me, "and you become a very self-protective person and just say the hell with it. It's a great shame, but you run out of steam. Some of these men are more attractive than the average Joe. Educated. Most of them are making good livings. And I'm just never attracted to these people," she told me. "Why is it so boring to be with them? Maybe it's boring because I'm boring," she said. "Guys pick you up in nice cars. BMWs. Classical music on the way. Take you to nice little restaurants, and most of the time I sit there thinking, Please, Lord, just let me go home. I want kids, I want a family, I want a home," Elena said, "but though I have the emotional and physical wherewithal to spend six, seven, eight hours on my feet in the operating room, I don't have it anymore for this humiliation. *Some* of them find me impressive, at least." "Why shouldn't they? You're a retina specialist. You're an eye surgeon. You keep people from going blind." "I know. I mean flat-out rejection," she said, "I'm not built for that." "No one is," I told her, but that didn't seem to help. "I've given it a fair shot," she said, getting teary, "haven't I, David? Nineteen dates?" "My God," I said, "you more than have."

Elena was a mess that night. She stayed right through till dawn, when she rushed off to scrub up at the hospital. Neither of us got much sleep because I was lecturing on the necessity of her giving up on the idea of becoming coupled and because she was listening like the diligent, serious, note-taking student she'd been when we'd first met in my classroom. But whether I helped her I don't know. Elena's intelligent, tremendously capable, yet for her the desire for a child is the standard unthinking. Yes, the idea activates the propagative instinct, and that's the pathos of it, all right. But it's still part of the standard unthinking: you go on to the next step. It's so primitive for someone so accomplished. But this is the way she imagined adulthood long, long ago, before adulthood, before diseases of the retina became her life's passion.

What did I say to her? Why do you ask? You too need the lecture on the childishness of coupling? Of course it's childish. Family life is, today more than ever, when the ethos is created substantially by the children. It's even worse when there are no children around. Because the childish adult replaces the child. Coupled life and family life bring out everything that's childish in everyone involved. Why do they have to sleep night after night in the same bed? Why must they be on the phone to each other five times a day? Why are they always *with* each other? The forced deference is certainly childish. That unnatural deference. In one of the magazines, I read recently about a famous media couple married thirty-four years and the marvelous achievement of their learning to bear each other. Proudly the husband told the reporter, "My wife and I have a saying that you can tell the health of a marriage by the number of teeth marks on your tongue." I wonder, when I'm around such people, What are they being punished for? Thirty-four years. One stands in awe of the masochistic rigor required.

I have a friend in Austin, a very successful writer. Married young in the mid-1950s, then in the early seventies got divorced. Married to a decent woman with whom he produced three decent children—and he wanted out. And he didn't get out hysterically or foolishly. It was a human rights issue. Give me liberty or give me death. Well, after the divorce he went off to live alone and at liberty and he was miserable. And so within a short time he married again, a woman this time with whom he didn't plan to have any children, who already had a college-age child of her own. A married life *without* children. Well, sex had to be over in a couple of years, yet this is a man who was vigorously adulterous throughout his first marriage and focused on sex in his writing. On his own he could have begun to enjoy openly all that he finagled surreptitiously while married. Yet unsprung from his constraints, he's miserable from the first second and believes that he'll be miserable forever. He is at liberty in the face of the fullness, and he has no idea where he is. All he knows to do is to find his way back into the condition he could no longer stand, though now without the compelling logic of wanting to be married so as to have children, to raise a family, et cetera. The charm of the surreptitious? I don't disparage it. Marriage at its best is a sure-fire stimulant to the thrills of licentious subterfuge. But my friend's need was for something more basic to his safety than the adulterer's daily drama of fording a river of lies. That wasn't the kick he remarried for, even though once he was a husband again he almost immediately resumed pursuing the old delights. Part of the problem is that emancipated manhood never has had a social spokesman or an educational system. It has no social status because people don't want it to have social status. Yet this fellow's circumstances so favored living to the limit of his prerogatives, if only for the dignity of it. But deferring, deferring, deferring? Appeasing, appeasing, appeasing? Every other day dreaming of leaving? No, it's not a dignified way to be a man. Or, I told Elena, to be a woman.

Was she persuaded? I don't know. I don't think so. Aren't you? Why, why are you laughing? What's so hilarious? My didacticism? I agree: one's absurd side is never unimpressive. But what can be done about it? I'm a critic, I'm a teacher—didacticism is my destiny. Argument and counterargument is what history's made of. One either imposes one's ideas or one is imposed on. Like it or not, that's the predicament. There are always opposing forces, and so, unless one is inordinately fond of subordination, one is always at war.

Look, I'm not of this age. You can see that. You can hear that. I achieved my goal with a blunt instrument. I took a hammer to domestic life and those who stand watch over it. And to Kenny's life. That I'm still a hammerer should be no surprise. Nor is it a surprise that my insistence makes me a comic figure on the order of the village atheist to you who are of the current age and who haven't had to insist on any of this.

Now, let the laughter subside and allow teacher to finish. To be sure, if pleasure, experience, and age is a subject of interest no longer . . . It is? Then make what you'll make of me, but not till the end.

This past Christmas. Christmas 1999. I dreamt of Consuela that night. I was alone and I dreamt that something was happening to her and I thought I should call her. But when I looked in the telephone directory, she was no longer there, and because under George's tutelage I wouldn't allow myself to renew the agitation that could have destroyed me, I had never written down that Upper East Side address I'd found in the phone book years earlier, after she got her first job. Well, a week later, on New Year's Eve, I was alone in my living room, without a girl, purposely by myself that night playing my piano because I intended to ignore the millennial celebration. Providing you're not in a state of longing, living in solitude can be its own powerful pleasure, and it was that pleasure I was planning on that night. My answering machine was on, and even normally I don't pick up the receiver when the phone rings but just listen to see who it is. That night particularly I was determined to hear not one word from anyone about "Y2K," and so when the phone does ring, I go right on with my playing until I realize that it's her voice I'm hearing. "Hello, David? It's me. It's Consuela. It's a long time since we spoke, it's strange to phone you, but I want to tell you something. And I want to tell it to you myself, before you hear it from someone. Or before you hear it by surprise. I'll be phoning you again. But here's my cell phone number."

I listened to the message, frozen. I didn't pick up the

receiver, and then when I did go for it, it was too late, and I thought, Oh God, something *has* happened to her. It was because of George's death that I imagined the worst for Consuela. Yes, George died. You didn't see the obit in the *Times*? George O'Hearn died five months ago. I'm without my closest male friend. I'm now virtually without any male friend. It's a big loss, the camaraderie with George. I have colleagues, sure, people I see at work and talk to in passing, but the assumptions underlying the way they live are so antithetical to mine that it's difficult for us ever to think freely together. We have no common language about personal life. George was the whole of my male community, perhaps because the class of men we belong to is small to begin with. And a single comrade-in-arms is sufficient: one doesn't need the whole of society on one's side. I find that most other men I know—especially if they happen to have run into me with one of my young girls— either silently judge me or openly preach to me. I am "a limited man," they tell me—they who are not limited. And the preachers can get mad when I don't recognize the truth of their argument. I am "smug," they tell me—they who are not smug. The tortured ones, of course, don't want any part of me. Certainly none of the married men ever open up to me. With them there is no affinity whatsoever. Maybe they reserve their confidences for one another, though I wonder—I don't know that male solidarity extends very far these days. Their heroism is not only in stoically enduring the dailiness of their renunciations but in diligently presenting a counterfeit image of their lives. The true lives, the unhidden lives, exist for their therapists alone. I'm not contending that they're all antagonistic and wish me ill because of the way I live, but it's safe to say that I don't universally compel admiration. With George dead, my solidarity is now entirely with women like Elena who once were girlfriends. They can't offer what I had with George, but I don't appear to make an excessive demand on their tolerance.

His age? George was fifty-five. A stroke. He had a stroke. I was there when he had it. So were some eight hundred others. It was at the Ninety-second Street Y. A Saturday night in September. He was about to give a reading. I was the one at the lectern introducing him. He was sitting in a chair just offstage, in the wings, enjoying my introduction and nodding approval.

Stretched out in front of him, in his narrow mortician's suit, were those long, lean legs of his—pliable George, in his suit, was a wire coat-hanger of a hook-nosed black Irishman. Apparently he had the stroke while he was sitting there with his six books of verse stacked up in his lap, waiting to come on, in lugubrious black, and charm the bejesus out of the crowd. Because when the audience began to applaud and he went to get up, he just tumbled out of the chair and it fell on top of him. Casting his oeuvre all over the floor. The doctors never thought he'd leave the hospital. But he hung on there unconscious for a week, and then the family took him home to die.

He was mostly unconscious at home, too. His left side paralyzed. Vocal cords paralyzed. A big chunk of his brain, just blown. His son Tom's a physician, and he oversaw the dying, which required another nine days. Took him off the IV, removed the catheter, took him off everything. Whenever George opened his eyes, they propped him up and gave him water to sip and ice to suck on. Otherwise they kept him as comfortable as they could while he slipped away at an agonizingly slow pace.

Every afternoon, at the end of the day, I drove to Pelham to see him. George had sequestered the family in Pelham so that, during all those years when he was teaching at the New School, he could have a free hand in Manhattan. There were sometimes as many as five or six cars parked in the drive when I arrived. The children were there in shifts, sometimes with one or the other of the grandchildren. There was a nurse and, near the end, the hospice person. Kate, George's wife, was, of course, there round the clock. I'd go into the bedroom, where they'd installed a hospital bed, and I'd take his hand, the hand on the side where he could still feel something, and I'd sit with him for fifteen, twenty minutes, but he was always out of it. Heavy breathing. Moaning. The good leg twitching once in a while, but nothing more. Pass my hand over his hair, touch his cheek, squeeze his fingers, but no response. I sat there hoping that he might come around and recognize me, and then I drove home. Then one afternoon I showed up and they said it had happened—he was awake. Go in, go in, they said.

They had George propped up on pillows and the bed half raised. His daughter Betty was feeding him ice. She was cracking slivers of ice between her teeth and putting the broken little bits into his mouth. George was trying to chomp on them with the teeth on the side of his mouth that still worked. He looked far gone indeed, *so* thin, but his eyes were open, and there he was, employing all that remained of his concentration in order to chew that ice. Kate stood in the doorway watching him, an imposing white-haired woman nearly as tall as George, but bulkier than when I'd seen her last, and far wearier. Attractively roundish, wry, resilient, radiating a kind of stubborn heartiness—that was Kate well into her middle years. A woman never known to shrink from reality, who looked now completely worn down, as if she'd fought her last battle and lost.

Tom brought a wet washcloth from the bathroom. "Want to freshen up, Dad?" he said. "How much does he know?" I asked Tom. "How much does he understand?" "There are stretches," Tom said, "when he seems to know something. And then he doesn't." "How long has he been awake?" "About half an hour. Go over to him. Speak to him, David. He seems to enjoy the voices."

Enjoy? Strange word. But Tom, in all situations, is the jovial doctor. I came around to George's unparalyzed side while Tom was mopping his father's face with the wet washcloth. George took it from him—to everyone's surprise, reached out with his good hand, grabbed at the washcloth, got hold of it, and jammed it inside his mouth. "He's so dry," somebody said. George pushed the end of the washcloth around inside his mouth and began to suck on it. When he took it out, there was something adhering to it. Looked like a piece of his soft palate. Betty let out a gasp when she saw it there, and the hospice woman, who was in the room too, patted Betty's back and said, "It's nothing. His mouth is so dry—it's just a little flake of flesh."

His mouth was aslant, hanging open, that stricken-looking mouth of the dying, but his eyes were focused and there even appeared to be something back of them, something of George that hadn't yet given way. Like the wall left jaggedly standing after a bomb goes off. With the same angry force with which he'd grabbed the washcloth, he pulled down the sheet that was covering him and began to yank at the Velcro at the corner of his diaper, trying to pull the thing off, and revealing those sad sticks that had been his legs. When the tungsten filament inside a light bulb goes—that's what his legs reminded me of. Everything about him, everything fashioned of flesh and blood, reminded me of an inanimate something else. "No, no," Tom said, "let it be, Dad. It's fine." But George wouldn't stop. Pulling angrily, trying in vain to get out of the diaper. When that didn't work, he raised his hand and, kind of growling, pointed at Betty. "What?" she asked him. "I can't understand you. What do you want? What is it, sweetheart?" The noises he was emitting were indecipherable, but it was clear from his gestures that he wanted her to come as close as she could. When she did, he reached out, put his arm around onto her back, and pulled her forward so that he could kiss her mouth. "Oh yes, Daddy," she said, "yes, you are the best father, the very best." What was astonishing was this force welling up in him after all those days of lying there inert and emaciated, somehow hanging on while seemingly breathing his last—the considerable force with which he'd pulled Betty to him and with which he was trying to speak. Maybe, I thought, they shouldn't be letting him die. What if there's more left than they realize? What if that's what he's trying to demonstrate? What if instead of saying goodbye to them he's saying, "Don't let me go. Do everything you can to save me"?

Then George was pointing at me. "Hello, George," I said. "Hello, friend. It's David, George." And when I got close to him, he grabbed me the way he'd grabbed Betty and kissed *me* on the mouth. There was no necrotic smell, no sickish stink, no stench whatsoever: just the warm, odorless breath, the pure perfume of being, and the two parched lips. It was the first time George and I had ever kissed in our lives. Again the grunting and he was pointing now to Tom. To Tom and then to his own feet, which were uncovered at the end of the bed. When Tom, thinking George wanted the sheet pulled up over his legs, began to straighten the bedding, George grunted still louder and pointed again at his feet. "He wants you to hold them," Betty said. "One of them he can't even feel," Tom said. "Hold the other one," Betty said. "Okay, Dad, I've got it— I've got you." And Tom began patiently kneading the foot in which there was feeling.

Next George pointed to the doorway where Kate was standing, watching it all. "He wants you, Ma," Betty said. I moved aside and Kate came over and stood where I'd been, beside the bed, and George reached up for her now, and with his good arm pulled her toward him, and kissed her as forcefully as he'd kissed Betty and me. Kate kissed him back. Then they kissed again, a long kiss this time, a quite passionate kiss. Kate even closed her eyes. She's an exceedingly unsentimental, down-to-earth person, and I'd never before seen her do anything so girlish.

Meanwhile, George's good hand had moved from her back around to her right arm, and he began to fumble with the button at the wrist of her blouse. He was trying to undo it. "George," Kate whispered softly. She sounded amused. "Georgie, Georgie . . ." "Help him, Ma. He wants to open the button." Smiling at the instructions from the emotional daughter, Kate submitted and opened the button, but by then George was at the other sleeve, tugging at *that* button, so she obligingly undid it as well. And all this time he kept hungrily going for her lips. Kate caressed his ruined face, that immensely lonely, cavernous face, kissed his lips each time he offered them, and then his hand went up to the buttons at the front of her blouse and he began to fumble with those.

His plan was clear: he was trying to undress her. To undress this woman whom, as I knew, as the children surely knew, he had not touched in bed in years. Whom he barely any longer touched at all. "Let him, Ma," Betty said, and so Kate again did as her daughter told her. She reached up with her own hand and helped George undo the front of her blouse. This time when they kissed, his one good hand was grasping at the cloth of her large brassiere. But, abruptly, that was the end of it. The force went out of him just like that, and he never reached her pendulous breasts. He didn't die for another twelve hours, but when he fell back onto the pillows, his mouth agape, his eyes closed, breathing like one who's collapsed at the end of a race, we all knew that what we had witnessed was the last amazing act of George's life.

Later, when I went to the door to leave, Kate came out onto the front porch and continued with me down the drive to my car. She took my hands in hers and thanked me for coming. I said, "I was glad I was here to see all this." "Yes, that was something, wasn't it?" Kate said. And then with her weary smile she added, "I wonder who it is he thought I was."

So George was only five months gone, and when Consuela called and left her message—"I want to tell you something. And I want to tell it to you myself, before you hear it from someone"—well, as I said, I listened to the message thinking something had now happened to *her*. This kind of thing, a premonitory dream followed by its fulfillment, is uncanny enough *in* one's dreams, but in real life? I didn't know what to do. Should I call her back? I thought it over for fifteen minutes. I didn't call back because I was afraid to. Why does she phone me? What can it be? My life is untroubled and back in my hands. Have I the resilience for Consuela and her aggressive yielding? I am no longer sixty-two—I am seventy. Can I endure at this age that mania of uncertainty? Do I dare relapse into that frenzied trance? Can that possibly be good for my longevity?

I remembered how for the three years after I lost her, even when I got up in the dark to take a leak, she was all I thought about: even at four A.M., standing over the toilet seven-eighths asleep, the Kepesh one-eighth awake would begin to mutter her name. Generally when an old man pisses at night, his mind is completely blank. If he's capable of thinking of anything, it's only about getting back into bed. But not me, not then. "Consuela, Consuela, Consuela," every single time I got up to go. And she'd done this to me, mind you, without language, without cogitation, without cunning, without an ounce of malevolence, and with no regard to cause and effect. Like a great athlete or a work of idealized sculptural art or an animal glimpsed in the woods, like Michael Jordan, like a Maillol, like an owl, like a bobcat, she'd done it through the simplicity of physical splendor. There was nothing the least bit sadistic in Consuela. Not even the sadism of indifference, which often goes with that magnitude of perfection. She was too square for such cruelty and far too kind. But imagine the sport she could have made of me were she not too well reared a girl ever to exploit to the limit the Amazonian strength of her endowment; imagine if she'd had Amazonian consciousness as well and Machiavellianly grasped the impact she had. Luckily, like most people, she was not practiced in thinking things through, and though she made the whole thing between us happen, she never understood all that happened. If she did, and if, in addition, she'd had the tiniest taste for tormenting the male who's on fire, I would have been a goner, wrecked entirely by my own White Whale.

But here she was again. No, absolutely no! Never again that assault on my peace of mind!

But then I thought, She's looking for me, she needs me, and not as a lover, not as a teacher, not so as to resume our erotic tale with a new installment. So I rang her cell phone and lied and said I went to the store and just got back, and she said, "I'm in the car. I was in front of your building when I left the message." I said, "What are you doing driving around New York on New Year's Eve?" "I don't know what I'm doing," she said. "Are you crying, Consuela?" "No, not yet." And I said, "Did you ring the doorbell?" She said, "No, I didn't, because I didn't dare to." "You can always ring the bell, always. You know that. What's the matter?" "I need you now." "Then come." "Do you have time?" "I always have time for you. Come." "There's something important. I'm coming right away."

I put down the receiver and I didn't know what to expect. About twenty minutes later, a car stopped, and the moment I opened the door for her I knew something had gone wrong. Because she had a cap on her head like a fez. And that wasn't something she would wear. She has dark black hair, sleek hair that was always cared for, always washed, brushed, combed; she would see the hairdresser every two weeks. But now she was standing there with a fez on her head. She also had a stylish coat on, a belted black Persian lamb coat nearly to the floor, and when she undid the belt, I saw underneath her coat the silk shirt with the cleavage—lovely. So I embraced her and she embraced me, and she let me take her coat, and I said, "Your hat? Your fez?" and she said, "You'd better not do that. The surprise will be too great." I said, "Why?" And she said, "Because I'm very ill."

We went into the living room, and there again I embraced her, and she pushed her body to me, and you feel the tits, the beautiful tits, and you see over her shoulder the beautiful buttocks. You see the beautiful body. She's now in her thirties, thirty-two, and not less but more lovely, and the face, which seems somehow to have lengthened a bit, is far more womanly —and she's telling me, "I don't have any hair anymore. In October I was told that I've got cancer. I've got breast cancer." I said, "This is awful, this is horrible, how do you feel, how does one deal with such a thing?" Her chemotherapy had begun in early November, and quickly she'd lost her hair. She said, "I have to tell you the story," and we sat down and I said, "Tell me everything." "Well, my aunt, my mother's sister, has had breast cancer, and she was treated for it, and she lost a breast. So I knew that in my family there's danger. I always knew this, and I've always been afraid of it," and all the time she was talking, I was thinking, You, with the most gorgeous tits in the world. And she said, "One morning I was standing under the shower, and I felt something under my armpit, and I knew that this was wrong. I went to my doctor and he said it's probably nothing to worry about, and so I went to a second doctor and a third doctor, you know the story, and the third doctor said it *was* something to worry about." "And did you panic?" I asked her. "Did you panic, my lovely friend?" I was so shaken, *I* was panicking. "Yes," she said, "enormously." "At night?" "Yes, I was running around my apartment. I was completely crazy." I started to cry when I heard this, and we were embracing again, and I said, "Why didn't you call me? Why didn't you call me then?" And she said again, "I didn't dare." And I said, "Whom did you think of to call?" And she said, "My mother, of course. But I knew she'd panic too, because I'm her daughter, her one and only daughter, and because she's so emotional, and because everyone has died. David, they're all dead." "Who has died?" "My father is dead." "How?" "His plane crashed. He was on that plane to Paris. He was going for business." "Oh, no." "Yes." "And the grandfather you loved so much?" "He died. Six years ago. It began with losing him. A heart attack." "And your grandmother, with her rosaries? The grandmother who was the duchess?" "She died too. After him. She was old and she died." "Not your kid brother—?" "No, no, he's fine. But I couldn't call him, I couldn't about this. He couldn't handle this. That's when I thought of you. But I didn't know if you were alone." "That's not a problem. Promise me now one thing. If you should start to panic during the night, during the day, anytime, phone me. I'll always come. Here," I said, "write down your address. Write down all your phone numbers, work, home, everything." And I was thinking, She is dying before my eyes, she too is now dying. Instability had merely to enter her cozy Cuban family life with the predictable death of a beloved old grandfather to set rapidly in motion a cascade of misfortune culminating in cancer.

I said, "Are you afraid right now?" And she said, "Very. Very much afraid. I'm all right for two minutes, I'm thinking of something else, and then the bottom falls out of my stomach and I can't believe what's happening. It's a roller coaster, and it doesn't stop. It can't stop unless the *cancer* stops. My chances," she said, "are sixty percent to survive and forty percent to die." And then she dropped into the talk about how life is so worthwhile and how she feels sorry for her mother, above all—the banal talk that's inevitable. I wanted to do so many things, I had so many plans, and so on. She began telling me about how foolish all her little anxieties of a few months back now seemed, the worries about work and friends and clothes, and how this had put everything in perspective, and I thought, No, nothing puts anything in perspective.

I was watching her, listening to her, and when I couldn't hear any more, I said, "Do you mind if I touch your breasts?" She said, "No, go ahead." "You don't mind?" "No. I do mind kissing you, though. Because I don't want anything sexual. But I do know how much you like my breasts, so touch my breasts." So I touched them—and with trembling hands. And of course with an erection. I said, "Is it your left breast or your right breast?" and she said, "It's my right breast." So I put my hand on her right breast. There is a combination of eroticism and tenderness, and it melts you and arouses you, and that's what was happening. You get a hard-on and melt, both at the same time. So we're sitting there with her breast in my hand, and we're talking, and I said, "You don't mind?" And she said, "I even want more of you. Because I know you love my breasts." I said, "What do you want?" "I want you to feel my cancer." I said, "I'll do that. Okay. But later, we'll do that later on."

It was too soon. I wasn't ready for that. So we talked, and *she* started to cry, and I tried to comfort her, and then suddenly she stopped crying and became very energetic, very determined. She said to me, "David, I came to you, in fact, with only one request, one question." And I said, "What is it?" And she said, "After you, I never had a boyfriend or a lover who loved my body as much as you loved it." "Have you had boyfriends?"

At it again. Forget about the boyfriends. But I couldn't. "Have you, Consuela? "Yes, but not many." "Have you slept with men regularly?" "No. Not on a regular basis." "How was your job? Was there nobody at your job who fell in love with you?" "They all did." "I can understand that. But then what," I said. "Were they all gay? Didn't you meet straight men?" "I do, I did, but they're no good." "Why are they no good?" "They're just masturbating on my body." "Well, this is a pity. This is stupid. This is insane." "But you loved my body. And I was proud of it." "But you were proud of it before." "Yes and no. You've seen my body at its most glorious. So I wanted you to see it before it is ruined by what the doctors are going to do." "Stop talking that way, don't think that way. Nobody's going to ruin you. What do the doctors say they're going to do?" And she said, "I've had chemotherapy. That's why I don't take off my cap." "Of course. But where you're concerned, I can stand anything. Do whatever you want." She said, "No, I don't want to show it to you. Because a strange thing happens to your hair. After the chemotherapy, it starts to come out in handfuls. A sort of baby hair begins growing on your head. It's very strange." I asked, "Does your pubic hair disappear?" "No," she said, "it doesn't, it stays. Which is strange too." I said, "Did you ask the doctor?" "Yes," she said, "and the doctor can't explain it. She only answered, 'That's a good question.' Look at my arms," Consuela said. She has long, slender arms and that white-white skin, and the fine lovely hair on her arms was indeed still there. "Look," she said, "there's hair on my arms but not on my head." "Well," I said, "I've known bald men, so why can't I see a bald woman?" She said, "No. I don't want you to see."

Then she said, "David, may I ask you a big favor?" "Of course. Anything." "Would you mind saying goodbye to my breasts?" I said, "My dear girl, my darling girl, they're not going to demolish your body, they're not." "Well, I'm lucky that I have so much breast, but they're going to have to take out about a third. My doctor's trying everything to keep the surgery minimal. She's humane. She's wonderful. She's not a butcher. She's not a heartless machine. She's trying first to shrink the cancer with chemo. Then when they operate they can take out as little as possible." "But they can restore it, rebuild it, can't they, whatever it is they take out?" "Yes, they can put in some silicone stuff. But I don't know if I'll want it. Because this is my body and that won't be my body. That won't be anything." "And how do you want me to say goodbye? What do you want? What are you asking me, Consuela?" And at last she told me.

I got my camera, which is a Leica with a zoom lens, and she stood up. We closed the curtains, we put on all the lights, I found the right Schubert and put that on, and she didn't quite dance then, but it was, rather, an exotic, Oriental sort of movement when she started to undress. Very elegant and so vulnerable. I was sitting on the sofa, and she was standing and undressing. And the way in which she undressed and dropped each item, it was spellbinding. Mata Hari. The spy undressing for the officer. And all the time so extremely vulnerable. She took off her blouse first. Then her shoes. Extraordinary to take off her shoes then. Then she took off her bra. And it was as though a man who had undressed had forgotten to pull his socks off, which makes him look slightly ludicrous. A woman in a skirt with naked breasts is not erotic to me. The skirt somehow confuses the picture. Naked breasts with trousers is very erotic, but over just a skirt it doesn't work. You'd be better off to keep on your bra with a skirt, but a skirt alone with naked breasts is to feed somebody.

So she showed herself to me. She undressed until she had only the panties on. She said, "Could you touch my breasts?" "Is that the picture you want, my touching them?" "No, no. Touch them first." So I did. And then she said, "I want pictures facing the camera, and in profile, and then hanging over."

I took about thirty pictures of her. She chose the poses, and she wanted everything. She wanted to have her hands underneath, holding them. She wanted to be squeezing them. She wanted them from the left side, from the right side, she wanted them photographed while she was bending forward. Finally she pulled off her panties, and you could see that her pubic hair was there as it had always been, as I described it: sleek, lying flat. Asian hair. She appeared to be all at once aroused by taking off her panties and my looking at her with nothing on. That happened suddenly. You could see by her nipples that she was aroused. Though by now I no longer was. Still, I asked her, "Do you want to stay for the night? Do you want to sleep with me?" She said, "No. I don't want to sleep with you. I want to be in your arms, though." I was fully dressed, as I am now. And she was sitting on the sofa in my arms, very close to me, and then she took my wrist and she laid my hand on her armpit in order for me to feel the cancer. Felt like a stone. A stone in the armpit. Two small stones, one bigger than the other, meaning that there is a metastasis originating in her breast. But you couldn't feel it in her breast. I asked, "Why can't I feel it in your breast?" and she said, "My breasts are too big. There's too much tissue to feel it. It's deep inside the breast."

I couldn't have slept with her, not even I who'd licked the blood from her. After the years of dwelling on her, just seeing her would have been difficult enough had she shown up under normal circumstances and not in this bizarrely wretched way. So, no, I couldn't have slept with her, and yet I kept thinking about it. Because they're so beautiful, her breasts. I cannot say it often enough. It was so mean, so degrading, these breasts, her breasts—I just thought, They can't be destroyed! As I told you, I'd been masturbating over her without interruption during all the years we were apart. I have been in bed with other women, and I have thought of her, of her breasts, of what it was like with my face sinking into them. Thought of their softness, their smoothness, the way I could sense their weight, their soft weight, and this while my mouth nuzzles somebody else. But at that moment I knew hers was no longer a sexual life. What was at stake was something else.

So I said to her, "Should I go with you to the hospital? I'll do that if you want me to. I insist on doing it. You're virtually alone." She said she wanted to think about it. She said, "It's sweet of you to offer, but I don't know yet. I don't know if I'll want to see you immediately after I've been operated on." She

left about half past one; she'd arrived about eight o'clock. She
didn't ask what I was going to do with the photographs she'd
wanted me to take. She didn't ask me to send her prints. I
haven't had them developed yet. I'm curious to see them. I'll
enlarge them. I'll send her a set, of course. But I'll have to find
somebody I trust to develop them. I should long ago, with my
interests, have learned how to develop film myself, but I never
did. It would have been useful.

She should be going to the hospital any time now. I'm expecting a message from her any moment, any day. Since I saw
her three weeks ago, I haven't heard a word. Will I? Do you
think I will? She told me not to contact her. She didn't want
anything more from me—that's what she said when she left.
I've been all but keeping a vigil by the phone for fear of missing her call.

Ever since her visit, I've myself been on the phone to people
I know, to doctors I know, trying to find out about breast
cancer treatment. Because I had always understood that the
procedure for this sort of thing was surgery first and then the
chemotherapy. And that was worrying me while she was here
—I kept thinking, There's something about her case I'm failing to understand. Now I learn that giving chemo before isn't
entirely unheard of, that it's becoming the standard of care for
treatment of locally advanced breast cancer, but the question
is, apparently, is that the treatment right for her? What did she
mean about sixty percent chance of survival? Why only sixty?
Did someone tell her that or did she read it somewhere or, in
her panic, did she make it up? Or are they gambling with long-
term survival for purposes of vanity? Maybe this is merely a
response to the shock—a typical enough response at that—but
I can't stop thinking that there's something about her story,
either that she didn't tell me or that she herself hasn't been told
. . . Anyway, that was the story, as I got it, and I haven't as yet
heard any more.

She left me at about one-thirty A.M., after the New Year
reached Chicago. We had some tea. We drank a glass of wine.
Because she asked me to, I turned on the television, and we
watched the replay of the New Year beginning in Australia and
sweeping across Asia and Europe. She was slightly sentimental.

Telling stories. About her childhood. About her father taking her to the opera since she was a little girl. She told a story about a florist. "I was buying flowers on Madison Avenue with my mother last Saturday," she told me, "and the florist said, 'What a nice hat you're wearing,' and I said, 'It's there for a purpose,' and he understood, and he blushed and apologized and gave me a dozen roses for free. So there you see how people respond to a human being in distress. They don't know what to do. Nobody knows what to say or to do. So I'm very grateful to you," she said.

How did I feel? The greatest pain I felt that night was over her being alone and panicking in her bed. Panicking about death. And what will happen now? What do you think? I guess she's not going to ask me to go with her to the hospital. She was pleased that I offered to, but when the time comes, she'll go to the hospital with her mother. She may just have gone berserk New Year's Eve because she was too miserable and frightened to go to the party where she'd been invited and too miserable and frightened to be alone. I don't think she will phone me when she's in a panic. She wanted the offer, but she won't use it.

Unless I'm wrong. Unless two or three months from now she comes to me and says she wants to sleep with me. With me rather than a younger man because I'm old and far from per fect myself. With me because, though still this side of desiccation, the decomposing corpse is no longer quite so well concealed as it is with the men at my gym who managed not to be born before Roosevelt took office.

And will I be able to do it? In all my years, I've never slept with a woman who has been mutilated in this manner. I can speak only of one woman I knew some years ago, and on the way to my apartment, she said, "I have to tell you—because of an operation, I've only got one breast. So I don't want you to be shocked by it." Now, no matter how unflinching you like to think you are, if you're honest about it, the prospect of seeing a woman with one breast is not very inviting, is it? I was able to act a little surprised, but seemingly not about the one breast, and I don't think I exhibited my nervousness at trying to put her at her ease. "Oh, don't be silly, we're not going there to sleep together. We're just good friends and I think we should stay good friends." I once slept with a woman who had a dark brownish wine stain—between her breasts and partly over her breasts, a huge birthmark. This woman was also a tall woman. Six five. The only woman I've ever had to kiss by standing on my toes and craning my neck. I got a crick in the neck from kissing her. When we went to bed, she started to undress by pulling off her skirt and her panties, which women normally don't do. They usually take off the blouse first, they start to undress their upper body. But she kept on her sweater and her bra. I said, "Aren't you going to take off your bra and your sweater?" "Yes, but I don't want you to be surprised." She said, "There's something wrong with me." I smiled, tried to make light of it. "Tell me, what is wrong?" She said, "Well, there's something about my breasts that will shock you." "Oh, don't worry. Show me." And so she did. And I started overdoing things. Kissing the birthmark. Touching it. Playing with it. Being polite. Making her feel happy with it. Saying I loved it. Such things aren't easy to take in stride. But you're supposed to be able to take charge, to act unhysterically, to deal with such things with grace. Not to recoil from anything that a body must abide. That wine stain. It was tragic for her. Six foot five. Men drawn to her, as I was, by this amazing height. And with every man, the same story: "There's something wrong with me."

The photographs. I'll never forget Consuela asking me to take those pictures. To some Peeping Tom peering in from outside, it could only have looked like a scene from pornography. Yet it was as far as you could get from pornography. "Do you have your camera?" "I have my camera," I said. "Would you mind taking pictures of me? Because I want to have pictures of my body as you knew it. As you saw it. Because soon it won't be as it was. I don't know anybody else I could ask to do this. I couldn't ask this of another man. Otherwise I wouldn't have bothered you." "Yes," I told her, "we'll do this. Anything. Say what you want. Ask for whatever you want. Say everything to me." "Could you put on some music," she said, "and then get your camera?" "What music do you want?" I asked. "Schubert. Some Schubert chamber music." "Okay, okay," I said, but not, I told myself, *Death and the Maiden*.

Yet she hasn't asked me to send her a print. Remember that

Consuela is not the most brilliant girl in the world. Because then the photographs would be another story. Then there would be tactics involved. Then her strategy would be something to think about. But with Consuela, there's a semiconscious spontaneity in whatever she does, a rightness, though she may not know quite what she's doing or exactly why. Coming to me to be photographed, that's very close to nature, to an original drifting thought, to intuition, and there is no deliberate reasoning behind it. You could make up the reasoning, but Consuela wouldn't have. She feels she has to do this, she says, to document for *me*, who loved her body so much, the quality it had, how perfect it was. But there was much more to it than that.

I've noticed that most women are unsure about their bodies, even if, like her, they are altogether lovely. Not all of them know they're lovely. It takes a certain type of woman to know that. Most have complaints about something that they needn't complain about. They often want to hide their breasts. There's some shame whose source I can never fathom, and you must reassure them for a long time before they expose them with any real pleasure and take real pleasure in being looked at. Even the most fortunate of them. There are only a few who show themselves freely, and these days, because of all the polemicizing, they're often not the ones with the model of breast you would have invented yourself.

But the erotic power of Consuela's body—well, that is over. Yes, that night I'd had an erection, but I couldn't have sustained it. I'm fortunate enough to have a hard-on and the drive, but I would have been in great trouble if she had asked me to sleep with her that night. I'll be in great trouble when she asks me once she is recovered from the surgery. As she will. Because she will, won't she? Try it out first with someone familiar and someone old. For the sake of her confidence, for the sake of her pride, better with me than with Carlos Alonso or the Villareal boys. Age may not do what cancer does, but it does enough.

Part Two. She asks me three months from now, she calls me and says, "Let's get together," and then she takes her clothes off again. Is that the disaster to come?

There's a painting of Stanley Spencer's that hangs at the

Tate, a double nude portrait of Spencer and his wife in their middle forties. It is the quintessence of directness about co-habitation, about the sexes living together over time. It's in one of the Spencer books downstairs. I'll get it later. Spencer is seated, squatting, beside the recumbent wife. He is looking ruminatively down at her from close range through his wire-rimmed glasses. We, in turn, are looking at them from close range: two naked bodies right in our faces, the better for us to see how they are no longer young and attractive. Neither is happy. There is a heavy past clinging to the present. For the wife particularly, everything has begun to slacken, to thicken, and greater rigors than striating flesh are to come.

At the edge of a table, in the immediate foreground of the picture, are two pieces of meat, a large leg of lamb and a single small chop. The raw meat is rendered with physiological meticulousness, with the same uncharitable candor as the sagging breasts and the pendent, unaroused prick displayed only inches back from the uncooked food. You could be looking through the butcher's window, not just at the meat but at the sexual anatomy of the married couple. Every time I think of Consuela, I envision that raw leg of lamb shaped like a primitive club beside the blatantly exhibited bodies of this husband and wife. Its being there, so close to their mattress, becomes less and less incongruous the longer you look. There's melancholy resignation in the somewhat stunned expression of the wife, and there is that butchered hunk of meat having nothing in common with a living lamb, and, for three weeks now, ever since Consuela's visit, I can get neither image out of my mind.

We watched the New Year coming in around the world, the mass hysteria of no significance that was the millennial New Year's Eve celebration. Brilliance flaring across the time zones, and none ignited by bin Laden. Light whirling over nighttime London more spectacular than anything since the splendors of colored smoke billowed up from the Blitz. And the Eiffel Tower shooting fire, a facsimile flame-throwing weapon such as Wernher von Braun might have designed for Hitler's annihilating arsenal—the historical missile of missiles, the rocket of rockets, the bomb of bombs, with ancient Paris the launching pad and the whole of humanity the target. All evening long, on networks everywhere, the mockery of the Armageddon that we'd been awaiting in our backyard shelters since August 6, 1945. How could it not happen? Even on that very night, especially on that night, people anticipating the worst as though the evening were one long air-raid drill. The wait for the chain of horrendous Hiroshimas to link in synchronized destruction the abiding civilizations of the world. It's now or never. And it never came.

Maybe that's what everyone was celebrating—that it hadn't come, never came, that the disaster of the end will now never arrive. All the disorder is controlled disorder punctuated with intervals to sell automobiles. TV doing what it does best: the triumph of trivialization over tragedy. The Triumph of the Surface, with Barbara Walters. Rather than the destruction of the age-old cities, an international eruption of the superficial instead, a global outbreak of sentimentality such as even Americans hadn't witnessed before. From Sydney to Bethlehem to Times Square, the recirculating of clichés occurs at supersonic speeds. No bombs go off, no blood is shed—the next bang you hear will be the boom of prosperity and the explosion of markets. The slightest lucidity about the misery made ordinary by our era sedated by the grandiose stimulation of the grandest illusion. Watching this hyped-up production of staged pandemonium, I have a sense of the monied world eagerly entering the prosperous dark ages. A night of human happiness to usher in barbarism.com. To welcome appropriately the shit and the kitsch of the new millennium. A night not to remember but to forget.

Except on the sofa where I sit holding Consuela, my arms encircling her where she is naked, warming her breasts with my hands while we watch New Year's Eve arrive in Cuba. Neither of us had been expecting *that* to materialize on the screen, but there before us is Havana. From an amphitheater corralling a thousand tourists and calling itself a nightclub comes an embalmed police-state embodiment of the Caribbean hot stuff that used to draw the big spenders in the days of the Mob. The Tropicana Nightclub of the Tropicana Hotel. No Cubans to be seen other than the entertainers in no way entertaining, a lot of young people—ninety-six of them, ABC says—wearing silly white costumes and not so much dancing or singing as circling the stage howling into hand-held mikes. The showgirls look like leggy Latino West Village transvestites walking around in a huff. Atop their heads are overdeveloped lampshades—three feet high, according to ABC. Lampshades on their heads and a rippling great mane of white ruffles down their backs.

"My God," Consuela said, and she began to cry. "This," she said, and so angrily, "*this* is what he gives the world. This is what he shows them on New Year's Eve." "It *is* a bit of a grotesque farce. Maybe," I said, "it's Castro's idea of a joke."

Is it, I wonder. Is this unconscious self-satire—is Castro so out of touch—or is it intentionally satirical and consistent with his hatred of the capitalist world? Castro, so contemptuous of the Batista corruption, corruption that you would have thought to be symbolized for him by tourist nightclubs like this Tropicana, and that is his millennial offering? The pope wouldn't do this—he has great public relations. Only the old Soviet Union could have equaled the tawdriness. There are any number of things for Castro to choose from, any number of old-fashioned socialist-realism tableaux: a celebration at a sugar plantation, in a maternity ward, at a cigar factory. Happy Cuban workers smoking, happy Cuban mothers beaming, happy Cuban newborns nursing . . . but to present the crappiest sort of entertainment for tourists? Was it deliberate or stupid or was it thought to be an appropriate joke on all this hysterical celebrating over a meaningless mark on the historical grid? Whatever the motive, he will not spend a dime on it. He will not spend a minute thinking about it. Why should Castro the revolutionary care, why should anyone care, about something that gives us a sense that we're understanding something that we're not understanding? The passage of time. We're in the swim, sinking in time, until finally we drown and go. This nonevent made into a great event while Consuela is here suffering the biggest event in her life. The Big Ending, though no one knows what, if anything, is ending and certainly no one knows what is beginning. It's a wild celebration of no one knows what.

Consuela alone knows, because Consuela now knows the wound of age. Getting old is unimaginable to anyone but the aging, but that is no longer so for Consuela. She no longer measures time like the young, marking backward to when you started. Time for the young is always made up of what is past, but for Consuela time is now how much future she has left, and she doesn't believe there is any. Now she measures time counting forward, counting time by the closeness of death. The illusion has been broken, the metronomic illusion, the comforting thought that, tick tock, everything happens in its proper time. Her sense of time is now the same as mine, speeded up and more forlorn even than mine. She, in fact, has overtaken me. Because I can still tell myself, "I'm not going to die in five years, maybe not in ten years, I'm fit, I'm well, I could even live another twenty," while she . . .

The loveliest fairy tale of childhood is that everything happens in order. Your grandparents go long before your parents, and your parents go long before you. If you're lucky it can work out that way, people aging and dying in order, so that at the funeral you ease your pain by thinking that the person had a long life. It hardly makes extinction less monstrous, that thought, but it's the trick that we use to keep the metronomic illusion intact and the time torture at bay: "So-and-so lived a long time." But Consuela has not been lucky, and so beside me she sits, under the sentence of death, while the nightlong merriment unfolds on the screen, a manufactured childish hysteria about embracing the open-ended future in ways that mature adults, with their melancholy knowledge of a very limited future, cannot have. And on this insane night, no one's knowledge can be more melancholy than hers.

"Havana," she says, and she weeps more forcefully by the moment, "I thought someday I will see Havana." "You will see Havana." "I won't. Oh, David, my grandfather . . ." "Yes, what about him? Go ahead, tell me, talk." "My grandfather would be sitting in the living room . . ." "Go on." I was holding her in my arms while she began to speak about herself as she never had before, never had cause to before, as, perhaps, she'd not even known herself before. "With *The NewsHour* on, with *The MacNeil-Lehrer NewsHour* on, and," she said, through her copious tears, "he'd suddenly sigh, '*Pobre Mamá.*' Who'd died in Havana without him. Because their generation, that generation, did not leave. '*Pobre Mamá.*' '*Pobre Papá.*' They stayed behind. He would just have this sadness, this longing for them. Terrible, terrible longing. And that's what I have. But it's for myself. It's for my life. I feel myself, I feel my body with my hands, I think, This is my body! It can't go away! This can't be real! This can't be happening! How can it go away? I don't want to die! David, I'm afraid to die!" "Consuela dear, you're not going to. You're thirty-two. You're not going to die for a very long time." "I grew up as an exile. So I'm scared of everything. Did you know that about me? *I'm scared of everything.*" "Oh, no. I don't think that's so. Of everything? It may seem so tonight but not—" "It's so *always.* I didn't want my family's exile. But you grow up and you hear 'Cuba, Cuba, Cuba' all the time . . . And look! Those people! Such vulgar people! Look what he has done to Cuba! I will never see it. I'll never see the house. I'll never see their house." "Yes, you will. Once Castro is gone—" "*I'll* be gone." "You won't be gone. You'll be here. Don't panic. There is no need to panic. You're going to be fine, you're going to live—" "You want to know the picture I've had? Of there? All my life? The picture in my head of Cuba?" "Yes. Tell me. Try to calm down and tell me everything. Do you want me to turn off the TV?" "No—no. They'll show something else. They *have* to." "Tell me the picture in your head, Consuela." "Not of the beach, not that. My parents had that. My parents talked about how much fun they had there, kids running around on the beach, people sitting in lounge chairs, ordering mimosas. They would take a house out on the beach and so on, but it wasn't that memory that I had. It was something else. I've had it forever. Oh, David—they buried Cuba long before they were buried. They had to. My father, my grandfather, my grandmother, they all knew they would never go back. And they never did. And now I never will." "You will," I told her. "What is the picture you've had forever? Talk to me. Talk," I said. "I always thought I would go back. Just to see the house. That it would be there." "Is the picture in your head of the house?" I asked her. "No. It's a road. El Malecón. If you see any kind of photos of Havana, you see a picture of El Malecón, this beautiful road right by the water. They've got this wall, and in the pictures everyone sits on the wall and hangs out. Did you see *Buena Vista Social Club?*" "I did. Because of you, of course I did. I thought of you when I saw it." "Well, it's the road there," she said, "where the waves were crashing. That wall. You see it for just a moment. That's where I always thought I would be." "The road that might have been," I told her. "*Should* have been," Consuela said, and again she was weeping uncontrollably while up on the screen, beneath their lampshades (each, we learn, weighing fourteen pounds), the showgirls parade aimlessly across the stage. Yes, this is definitely Castro saying "Fuck you" to the twentieth century. Because it's the end of his adventure in history, too, of the mark he made and did not make on the score of human events. "Tell me," I said to her. "You never told me this before. You didn't talk like this eight years ago. Then you were a listener. My student. I never knew this. Go ahead. Tell me what should have been." "That wall," she said, "and me. That's all. Hanging out there and talking to people. That's it. You're by the water but you're in the city. It's a meeting spot. It's a promenade." "Well, it looked pretty rundown," I said, "in the movie." "It did. But that's not how I've seen it all my life."

And then the grief, then the weight of sadness for all that her family had lost, for her father and her grandparents dying in exile, for herself about to die in exile (and an exile she'd never before felt so cruelly), for all of the Castillos' Cuba that Castro had ruined, for everything she feared she was about to leave—all of it was so great that in my arms, for a full five minutes, Consuela went out of her mind. I saw, externalized, the terror that her body was feeling. "What is it? Consuela, what can I do for you? Tell me and I'll do it. What is it that's torturing you so?"

And here's what she told me when she was able to speak. Here, to my surprise, is what she told me tortured her most. "I always answered my parents in English. Oh, God. How I wish I had answered him more in Spanish." "Who?" "My father. He loved when I called him Papi. But after I was little, I never would. I called him Dad. I *had* to. I wanted to be an American. I did not want all their *sadness*." "Dearest Consuela, it doesn't matter now what you called him. He knew you loved him. He knew how much . . ." But there was no consoling her. I'd not heard her speak like this before, nor had I seen her behave as she did next, either. In every calm and reasonable person there is a hidden second person scared witless about death, but for someone thirty-two the time between Now and Then is ordinarily so vast, so boundless, that it's no more than maybe a couple of times a year, and then only for a moment or two and late at night, that one comes anywhere near encountering that second person and in the state of madness that is the second person's everyday life.

What she did then was to take off her hat. To throw off her hat. All this time, you see, she'd been wearing that fezlike hat, even when she was otherwise naked and I was taking the pictures of her breasts for her. But now she tore it off. With New Year's Eve abandon, tore off her funny New Year's Eve hat. First Castro's farce of a sexy stage show and now Consuela's mortality completely unveiled.

It was appalling to see her without the hat. A woman so young and beautiful with sort of feathery hair, very short, thin, colorless, meaningless hair—you'd rather have her bald after having been to the barber and been shaved than to see this idiotic fluff on her head. The transition from thinking of someone in the way you've always thought of that person—as just as alive as you are—to whatever signifies to you, as her fuzzy hairlessness did to me, that the person is close to death, is dying, I experienced at that moment not only as a shock but as a betrayal. A betrayal of Consuela for my having so rapidly absorbed the shock and made this accounting. The traumatic moment was upon us when the change occurs, when you discover that the other person's expectations can no longer resemble yours and that no matter how appropriately you may be acting and you may continue to act, he or she will leave before you do—if you're lucky, well before.

Itself. There it was. All the horror of it in that head. Consuela's head. I kissed it and kissed it. What else was there for me to do? The poison of the chemotherapy. All it had done to her body. All it had done to her mind. She's thirty-two, and she thinks she's now exiled from everything, experiencing each experience for the very last time. Only what if she isn't? What—

There! The phone! That could be—! At what time? It's two A.M. Excuse me!

It was. That was her. She called. Finally called. I have to leave. She is in a panic. She is having surgery in two weeks. She

had her last chemotherapy. She asked me to tell her about the
beauty of her body. That's why I was away so long. That's what
she wanted to hear. That's what she's been talking about for
nearly an hour. Her body. Do you think that after surgery a
man will ever love my body again? This is what she asks again
and again. You see, they've now decided to remove the entire
breast. They were planning to go underneath the breast and to
take a part of it. But now they think it's too serious for that. So
they have to remove it. Ten weeks ago they told her they
would remove only part of it, and now they tell her they are
going to remove the whole thing. Mind you, this is a breast.
It's not a small thing. This morning they told her what is going
to happen; now it's night, and she's all alone and the whole
prospect of everything . . . I have to go. She wants me there.
She wants me to sleep in the bed with her there. She has not
eaten all day. She has to eat. She has to be fed. You? Stay if you
wish. If you want to stay, if you want to leave . . . Look,
there's no time, I must run!
    "Don't."
    What?
    "Don't go."
    But I must. Someone has to be with her.
    "She'll find someone."
    She's in terror. I'm going.
    "Think about it. Think. Because if you go, you're finished."

THE PLOT AGAINST AMERICA

To S.F.R.

CONTENTS

1

*Vote for Lindbergh
or Vote for War*

FEAR PRESIDES over these memories, a perpetual fear. Of course no childhood is without its terrors, yet I wonder if I would have been a less frightened boy if Lindbergh hadn't been president or if I hadn't been the offspring of Jews.

When the first shock came in June of 1940—the nomination for the presidency of Charles A. Lindbergh, America's international aviation hero, by the Republican Convention at Philadelphia—my father was thirty-nine, an insurance agent with a grade school education, earning a little under fifty dollars a week, enough for the basic bills to be paid on time but for little more. My mother—who'd wanted to go to teachers' college but couldn't because of the expense, who'd lived at home working as an office secretary after finishing high school, who'd kept us from feeling poor during the worst of the Depression by budgeting the earnings my father turned over to her each Friday as efficiently as she ran the household—was thirty-six. My brother, Sandy, a seventh-grader with a prodigy's talent for drawing, was twelve, and I, a third-grader a term ahead of himself—and an embryonic stamp collector inspired like millions of kids by the country's foremost philatelist, President Roosevelt—was seven.

We lived in the second-floor flat of a small two-and-a-half-family house on a tree-lined street of frame wooden houses with red-brick stoops, each stoop topped with a gable roof and fronted by a tiny yard boxed in with a low-cut hedge. The Weequahic neighborhood had been built on farm lots at the undeveloped southwest edge of Newark just after World War One, some half dozen of the streets named, imperially, for victorious naval commanders in the Spanish-American War and the local movie house called, after FDR's fifth cousin—and

97

the country's twenty-sixth president—the Roosevelt. Our street, Summit Avenue, sat at the crest of the neighborhood hill, an elevation as high as any in a port city that rarely rises a hundred feet above the level of the tidal salt marsh to the city's north and east and the deep bay due east of the airport that bends around the oil tanks of the Bayonne peninsula and merges there with New York Bay to flow past the Statue of Liberty and into the Atlantic. Looking west from our bedroom's rear window we could sometimes see inland as far as the dark treeline of the Watchungs, a low-lying mountain range fringed by great estates and affluent, sparsely populated suburbs, the extreme edge of the known world—and about eight miles from our house. A block to the south was the working-class town of Hillside, whose population was predominantly Gentile. The boundary with Hillside marked the beginning of Union County, another New Jersey entirely.

We were a happy family in 1940. My parents were outgoing, hospitable people, their friends culled from among my father's associates at the office and from the women who along with my mother had helped to organize the Parent-Teacher Association at newly built Chancellor Avenue School, where my brother and I were pupils. All were Jews. The neighborhood men either were in business for themselves—the owners of the local candy store, grocery store, jewelry store, dress shop, furniture shop, service station, and delicatessen, or the proprietors of tiny industrial job shops over by the Newark-Irvington line, or self-employed plumbers, electricians, housepainters, and boilermen—or were foot-soldier salesmen like my father, out every day in the city streets and in people's houses, peddling their wares on commission. The Jewish doctors and lawyers and the successful merchants who owned big stores downtown lived in one-family houses on streets branching off the eastern slope of the Chancellor Avenue hill, closer to grassy, wooded Weequahic Park, a landscaped three hundred acres whose boating lake, golf course, and harness-racing track separated the Weequahic section from the industrial plants and shipping terminals lining Route 27 and the Pennsylvania Railroad viaduct east of that and the burgeoning airport east of that and the very edge of America east of that—the depots and docks of Newark Bay, where they unloaded cargo from around the world. At the western end of the neighborhood, the parkless end where we lived, there resided an occasional schoolteacher or pharmacist but otherwise few professionals were among our immediate neighbors and certainly none of the prosperous entrepreneurial or manufacturing families. The men worked fifty, sixty, even seventy or more hours a week; the women worked all the time, with little assistance from labor-saving devices, washing laundry, ironing shirts, mending socks, turning collars, sewing on buttons, mothproofing woolens, polishing furniture, sweeping and washing floors, washing windows, cleaning sinks, tubs, toilets, and stoves, vacuuming rugs, nursing the sick, shopping for food, cooking meals, feeding relatives, tidying closets and drawers, overseeing paint jobs and household repairs, arranging for religious observances, paying bills and keeping the family's books while simultaneously attending to their children's health, clothing, cleanliness, schooling, nutrition, conduct, birthdays, discipline, and morale. A few women labored alongside their husbands in the family-owned stores on the nearby shopping streets, assisted after school and on Saturdays by their older children, who delivered orders and tended stock and did the cleaning up.

It was work that identified and distinguished our neighbors for me far more than religion. Nobody in the neighborhood had a beard or dressed in the antiquated Old World style or wore a skullcap either outdoors or in the houses I routinely floated through with my boyhood friends. The adults were no longer observant in the outward, recognizable ways, if they were seriously observant at all, and aside from older shopkeepers like the tailor and the kosher butcher—and the ailing or decrepit grandparents living of necessity with their adult offspring —hardly anyone in the vicinity spoke with an accent. By 1940 Jewish parents and their children at the southwestern corner of New Jersey's largest city talked to one another in an American English that sounded more like the language spoken in Altoona or Binghamton than like the dialects famously spoken across the Hudson by our Jewish counterparts in the five boroughs. Hebrew lettering was stenciled on the butcher shop window and engraved on the lintels of the small neighborhood synagogues, but nowhere else (other than at the cemetery) did one's eye chance to land on the alphabet of the prayer

book rather than on the familiar letters of the native tongue
employed all the time by practically everyone for every con-
ceivable purpose, high or low. At the newsstand out front of
the corner candy store, ten times more customers bought the
Racing Form than the Yiddish daily, the *Forvertz*.

Israel didn't yet exist, six million European Jews hadn't yet
ceased to exist, and the local relevance of distant Palestine
(under British mandate since the 1918 dissolution by the victorious Allies of the last far-flung provinces of the defunct Ottoman Empire) was a mystery to me. When a stranger who did
wear a beard and who never once was seen hatless appeared
every few months after dark to ask in broken English for a
contribution toward the establishment of a Jewish national
homeland in Palestine, I, who wasn't an ignorant child, didn't
quite know what he was doing on our landing. My parents
would give me or Sandy a couple of coins to drop into his
collection box, largess, I always thought, dispensed out of
kindness so as not to hurt the feelings of a poor old man who,
from one year to the next, seemed unable to get it through his
head that we'd already had a homeland for three generations. I
pledged allegiance to the flag of our homeland every morning
at school. I sang of its marvels with my classmates at assembly
programs. I eagerly observed its national holidays, and without
giving a second thought to my affinity for the Fourth of July
fireworks or the Thanksgiving turkey or the Decoration Day
double-header. Our homeland was America.

Then the Republicans nominated Lindbergh and everything
changed.

For nearly a decade Lindbergh was as great a hero in our
neighborhood as he was everywhere else. The completion of
his thirty-three-and-a-half-hour nonstop solo flight from Long
Island to Paris in the tiny monoplane the *Spirit of St. Louis*
even happened to coincide with the day in the spring of 1927
that my mother discovered herself to be pregnant with my
older brother. As a consequence, the young aviator whose daring had thrilled America and the world and whose achievement
bespoke a future of unimaginable aeronautical progress came
to occupy a special niche in the gallery of family anecdotes that
generate a child's first cohesive mythology. The mystery of

pregnancy and the heroism of Lindbergh combined to give a distinction bordering on the divine to my very own mother, for whom nothing less than a global annunciation had accompanied the incarnation of her first child. Sandy would later record this moment with a drawing illustrating the juxtaposition of those two splendid events. In the drawing—completed at the age of nine and smacking inadvertently of Soviet poster art—Sandy envisioned her miles from our house, amid a joyous crowd on the corner of Broad and Market. A slender young woman of twenty-three with dark hair and a smile that is all robust delight, she is surprisingly on her own and wearing her floral-patterned kitchen apron at the intersection of the city's two busiest thoroughfares, one hand spread wide across the front of the apron, where the span of her hips is still deceptively girlish, while with the other she alone in the crowd is pointing skyward to the *Spirit of St. Louis*, passing visibly above downtown Newark at precisely the moment she comes to realize that, in a feat no less triumphant for a mortal than Lindbergh's, she has conceived Sanford Roth.

Sandy was four and I, Philip, wasn't yet born when in March 1932, Charles and Anne Morrow Lindbergh's own first child, a boy whose arrival twenty months earlier had been an occasion for national rejoicing, was kidnapped from his family's secluded new house in rural Hopewell, New Jersey. Some ten weeks later the decomposing body of the baby was discovered by chance in woods a few miles away. The baby had been either murdered or killed accidentally after being snatched from his crib and, in the dark, still in bedclothes, carried out a window of the second-story nursery and down a makeshift ladder to the ground while the nurse and mother were occupied in their ordinary evening activities in another part of the house. By the time the kidnapping and murder trial in Flemington, New Jersey, concluded in February 1935 with the conviction of Bruno Hauptmann—a German ex-con of thirty-five living in the Bronx with his German wife—the boldness of the world's first transatlantic solo pilot had been permeated with a pathos that transformed him into a martyred titan comparable to Lincoln.

Following the trial, the Lindberghs left America, hoping through a temporary expatriation to protect a new Lindbergh infant from harm and to recover some measure of the privacy they coveted. The family moved to a small village in England, and from there, as a private citizen, Lindbergh began taking the trips to Nazi Germany that would transform him into a villain for most American Jews. In the course of five visits, during which he was able to familiarize himself at first hand with the magnitude of the German war machine, he was ostentatiously entertained by Air Marshal Göring, he was ceremoniously decorated in the name of the Führer, and he expressed quite openly his high regard for Hitler, calling Germany the world's "most interesting nation" and its leader "a great man." And all this interest and admiration *after* Hitler's 1935 racial laws had denied Germany's Jews their civil, social, and property rights, nullified their citizenship, and forbidden intermarriage with Aryans.

By the time I began school in 1938, Lindbergh's was a name that provoked the same sort of indignation in our house as did the weekly Sunday radio broadcasts of Father Coughlin, the Detroit-area priest who edited a right-wing weekly called *Social Justice* and whose anti-Semitic virulence aroused the passions of a sizable audience during the country's hard times. It was in November 1938—the darkest, most ominous year for the Jews of Europe in eighteen centuries—that the worst pogrom in modern history, *Kristallnacht*, was instigated by the Nazis all across Germany: synagogues incinerated, the residences and businesses of Jews destroyed, and, throughout a night presaging the monstrous future, Jews by the thousands forcibly taken from their homes and transported to concentration camps. When it was suggested to Lindbergh that in response to this unprecedented savagery, perpetrated by a state on its own nativeborn, he might consider returning the gold cross decorated with four swastikas bestowed on him in behalf of the Führer by Air Marshal Göring, he declined on the grounds that for him to publicly surrender the Service Cross of the German Eagle would constitute "an unnecessary insult" to the Nazi leadership.

Lindbergh was the first famous living American whom I learned to hate—just as President Roosevelt was the first famous living American whom I was taught to love—and so his nomination by the Republicans to run against Roosevelt in

1940 assaulted, as nothing ever had before, that huge endowment of personal security that I had taken for granted as an American child of American parents in an American school in an American city in an America at peace with the world.

The only comparable threat had come some thirteen months earlier when, on the basis of consistently high sales through the worst of the Depression as an agent with the Newark office of Metropolitan Life, my father had been offered a promotion to assistant manager in charge of agents at the company's office six miles west of our house in Union, a town whose only distinction I knew of was a drive-in theater where movies were shown even when it rained, and where the company expected my father and his family to live if he took the job. As an assistant manager, my father could soon be making seventy-five dollars a week and over the coming years as much as a hundred a week, a fortune in 1939 to people with our expectations. And since there were one-family houses selling in Union for a Depression low of a few thousand dollars, he would be able to realize an ambition he had nurtured growing up penniless in a Newark tenement flat: to become an American homeowner. "Pride of ownership" was a favorite phrase of my father's, embodying an idea real as bread to a man of his background, one having to do not with social competitiveness or conspicuous consumption but with his standing as a manly provider.

The single drawback was that because Union, like Hillside, was a Gentile working-class town, my father would most likely be the only Jew in an office of some thirty-five people, my mother the only Jewish woman on our street, and Sandy and I the only Jewish kids in our school.

On the Saturday after my father was offered the promotion— a promotion that, above all, would answer a Depression family's yearning for a tiny margin of financial security—the four of us headed off after lunch to look around Union. But once we were there and driving up and down the residential streets peering out at the two-story houses—not quite identical but each, nonetheless, with a screened front porch and a mown lawn and a piece of shrubbery and a cinder drive leading to a one-car garage, very modest houses but still roomier than our two-bedroom flat and looking a lot like the little white houses in the movies about small-town salt-of-the-earth America—once we were there our innocent buoyancy about the family ascent into the home-owning class was supplanted, predictably enough, by our anxieties about the scope of Christian charity. My ordinarily energetic mother responded to my father's "What do you think, Bess?" with enthusiasm that even a child understood to be feigned. And young as I was, I was able to surmise why: because she was thinking, "Ours will be the house 'where the Jews live.' It'll be Elizabeth all over again."

Elizabeth, New Jersey, when my mother was being raised there in a flat over her father's grocery store, was an industrial port a quarter the size of Newark, dominated by the Irish working class and their politicians and the tightly knit parish life that revolved around the town's many churches, and though I never heard her complain of having been pointedly ill-treated in Elizabeth as a girl, it was not until she married and moved to Newark's new Jewish neighborhood that she discovered the confidence that led her to become first a PTA "grade mother," then a PTA vice president in charge of establishing a Kindergarten Mothers' Club, and finally the PTA president, who, after attending a conference in Trenton on infantile paralysis, proposed an annual March of Dimes dance on January 30—President Roosevelt's birthday—that was accepted by most Newark schools. In the spring of 1939 she was in her second successful year as a leader with progressive ideas—already supporting a young social studies teacher keen on bringing "visual education" into Chancellor's classrooms—and now she couldn't help but envision herself bereft of all that had been achieved by her becoming a wife and a mother on Summit Avenue. Should we have the good fortune to buy and move into a house on any of the Union streets we were seeing at their springtime best, not only would her status slip back to what it had been when she was growing up the daughter of a Jewish immigrant grocer in Irish Catholic Elizabeth, but, worse than that, Sandy and I would be obliged to relive her own circumscribed youth as a neighborhood outsider.

Despite my mother's mood, my father did everything he could to keep up our spirits, remarking on how clean and well-kept everything looked, reminding Sandy and me that living in one of these houses the two of us would no longer have to share a small bedroom and a single closet, and explaining the benefits to be derived from paying off a mortgage rather than paying rent, a lesson in elementary economics that abruptly ended when it was necessary for him to stop the car at a red light beside a parklike drinking establishment dominating one corner of the intersection. There were green picnic tables set out beneath the shade trees full with foliage, and on this sunny weekend afternoon there were waiters in braided white coats moving swiftly about, balancing trays laden with bottles and pitchers and plates, and men of every age gathered at each of the tables, smoking cigarettes and pipes and cigars and drinking deeply from tall beakers and earthenware mugs. There was music, too—an accordion being played by a stout little man in short pants and high socks who wore a hat ornamented with a long feather.

"Sons of bitches!" my father said. "Fascist bastards!" and then the light changed and we drove on in silence to look at the office building where he was about to get his chance to earn more than fifty dollars a week.

It was my brother who, when we went to bed that night, explained why my father had lost control and cursed aloud in front of his children: the homey acre of open-air merriment smack in the middle of town was called a beer garden, the beer garden had something to do with the German American Bund, the German-American Bund had something to do with Hitler, and Hitler, as I hadn't to be told, had everything to do with persecuting Jews.

The intoxicant of anti-Semitism. That's what I came to imagine them all so cheerfully drinking in their beer garden that day—like all the Nazis everywhere, downing pint after pint of anti-Semitism as though imbibing the universal remedy.

My father had to take off a morning of work to go over to the home office in New York—to the tall building whose uppermost tower was crowned with the beacon his company proudly designated "The Light That Never Fails"—and inform the superintendent of agencies that he couldn't accept the promotion he longed for.

"It's my fault," announced my mother as soon as he began to recount at the dinner table what had transpired there on the eighteenth floor of 1 Madison Avenue.

"It's nobody's fault," my father said. "I explained before I left what I was going to tell him, and I went over and I told him, and that's it. We're not moving to Union, boys. We're staying right here."

"What did he do?" my mother asked.

"He heard me out."

"And then?" she asked.

"He stood up and he shook my hand."

"He didn't say anything?"

"He said, 'Good luck, Roth.' "

"He was angry with you."

"Hatcher is a gentleman of the old school. Big six-foot goy. Looks like a movie star. Sixty years old and fit as a fiddle. These are the people who run things, Bess—they don't waste their time getting angry at someone like me."

"So now what?" she asked, implying that whatever happened as a result of his meeting with Hatcher was not going to be good and could be dire. And I thought I understood why. Apply yourself and you can do it—that was the axiom in which we had been schooled by both parents. At the dinner table, my father would reiterate to his young sons time and again, "If anybody asks 'Can you do this job? Can you handle it?' you tell 'em 'Absolutely.' By the time they find out that you can't, you'll already have learned, and the job'll be yours. And who knows, it just might turn out to be the opportunity of a lifetime." Yet over in New York he had done nothing like that.

"What did the Boss say?" she asked him. The Boss was how the four of us referred to the manager of my father's Newark office, Sam Peterfreund. In those days of unadvertised quotas to keep Jewish admissions to a minimum in colleges and professional schools and of unchallenged discrimination that denied Jews significant promotions in the big corporations and of rigid restrictions against Jewish membership in thousands of social organizations and communal institutions, Peterfreund was one of the first of the small handful of Jews ever to achieve a managerial position with Metropolitan Life. "He's the one who put you up for it," my mother said. "How must *he* feel?"

"Know what he said to me when I got back? Know what he told me about the Union office? It's full of drunks. *Famous* for drunks. Beforehand he didn't want to influence my decision.

He didn't want to stand in my way if this was what I wanted. Famous for agents who work two hours in the morning and spend the rest of their time in the tavern or worse. And I was supposed to go in there, the new Jew, the big new sheeny boss the goyim are all dying to work for, and I was supposed to go in there and pick 'em up off the barroom floor. I was supposed to go in there and remind them of their obligation to their wives and their children. Oh, how they would have loved me, boys, for doing them the favor. You can imagine what they would have called me behind my back. No, I'm better off where I am. We're all better off."

"But can the company fire you for turning them down?"

"Honey, I did what I did. That's the end of it."

But she didn't believe what he'd told her the Boss had said; she believed that he was making up what the Boss had said to get her to stop blaming herself for refusing to move her children to a Gentile town that was a haven for the German-American Bund and by doing so denying him the opportunity of *his* lifetime.

The Lindberghs returned to resume their family life in America in April 1939. Only months later, in September, having already annexed Austria and overrun Czechoslovakia, Hitler invaded and conquered Poland, and France and Great Britain responded by declaring war on Germany. Lindbergh had by then been activated as a colonel in the Army Air Corps, and he now began traveling around the country for the U.S. government, lobbying for the development of American aviation and for expanding and modernizing the air wing of the armed forces. When Hitler quickly occupied Denmark, Norway, Holland, and Belgium, and all but defeated France, and the second great European war of the century was well under way, the Air Corps colonel made himself the idol of the isolationists—and the enemy of FDR—by adding to his mission the goal of preventing America from being drawn into the war or offering any aid to the British or the French. There was already strong animosity between him and Roosevelt, but now that he was declaring openly at large public meetings and on network radio and in popular magazines that the president was misleading the country with promises of peace while secretly agitating and planning for our entry into the armed struggle, some in the Republican Party began to talk up Lindbergh as the man with the magic to beat "the warmonger in the White House" out of a third term.

The more pressure Roosevelt put on Congress to repeal the arms embargo and loosen the strictures on the country's neutrality so as to prevent the British from being defeated, the more forthright Lindbergh became, until finally he made the famous radio speech before a hall full of cheering supporters in Des Moines that named among the "most important groups who have been pressing this country toward war" a group constituting less than three percent of the population and referred to alternately as "the Jewish people" and "the Jewish race."

"No person of honesty and vision," Lindbergh said, "can look on their pro-war policy here today without seeing the dangers involved in such a policy both for us and for them." And then, with remarkable candor, he added:

> A few far-sighted Jewish people realize this and stand opposed to intervention. But the majority still do not . . . We cannot blame them for looking out for what they believe to be their own interests, but we must also look out for ours. We cannot allow the natural passions and prejudices of other peoples to lead our country to destruction.

The next day the very accusations that had elicited roars of approval from Lindbergh's Iowa audience were vigorously denounced by liberal journalists, by Roosevelt's press secretary, by Jewish agencies and organizations, even from within the Republican Party by New York's District Attorney Dewey and the Wall Street utilities lawyer Wendell Willkie, both potential presidential nominees. So severe was the criticism from Democratic cabinet members like Interior Secretary Harold Ickes that Lindbergh resigned his reserve commission as an Army colonel rather than serve under FDR as his commander in chief. But the America First Committee, the broadest-based organization leading the battle against intervention, continued to support him, and he remained the most popular proselytizer of its argument for neutrality. For many America Firsters there was no debating (even with the facts) Lindbergh's contention that the Jews' "greatest danger to this country lies in their large ownership and influence in our motion pictures, our press, our radio, and our government." When Lindbergh wrote proudly of "our inheritance of European blood," when he warned against "dilution by foreign races" and "the infiltration of inferior blood" (all phrases that turn up in diary entries from those years), he was recording personal convictions shared by a sizable portion of America First's rank-and-file membership as well as by a rabid constituency even more extensive than a Jew like my father, with his bitter hatred of anti-Semitism—or like my mother, with her deeply ingrained mistrust of Christians— could ever imagine to be flourishing all across America.

The 1940 Republican Convention. My brother and I went to sleep that night—Thursday, June 27—while the radio was on in the living room, and our father, our mother, and our older cousin Alvin sat listening together to the live coverage from Philadelphia. After six ballots, the Republicans still hadn't selected a candidate. Lindbergh's name was yet to be uttered by a single delegate, and because of an engineering conclave at a midwestern factory where he'd been advising on the design of a new fighter plane, he wasn't present or expected to be. When Sandy and I went to bed the convention remained divided among Dewey, Willkie, and two powerful Republican senators, Vandenberg of Michigan and Taft of Ohio, and it didn't look as though a backroom deal was about to be brokered anytime soon by party bigwigs like former president Hoover, who'd been ousted from office by FDR's overwhelming 1932 victory, or by Governor Alf Landon, whom FDR had defeated even more ignominiously four years later in the biggest landslide in history.
  Because it was the first muggy evening of the summer, the windows were open in every room and Sandy and I couldn't help but continue to follow from bed the proceedings being aired over our own living room radio and the radio playing in the flat downstairs and—since an alleyway only barely wide enough for a single car separated one house from the next— the radios of our neighbors to either side and across the way. As this was long before window air conditioners bested the noises of a neighborhood's tropical nights, the broadcast blanketed the block from Keer to Chancellor—a block on which

not a single Republican lived in any of the thirty-odd two-and-a-half-family houses or in the small new apartment building at the Chancellor Avenue corner. On streets like ours the Jews voted straight Democratic for as long as FDR was at the top of the ticket.

But we were two kids and fell asleep despite everything and probably wouldn't have awakened till morning had not Lindbergh—with the Republicans deadlocked on the twentieth ballot—made his unanticipated entrance onto the convention floor at 3:18 A.M. The lean, tall, handsome hero, a lithe, athletic-looking man not yet forty years old, arrived in his flying attire, having landed his own plane at the Philadelphia airport only minutes earlier, and at the sight of him, a surge of redemptive excitement brought the wilted conventioneers up onto their feet to cry "Lindy! Lindy! Lindy!" for thirty glorious minutes, and without interruption from the chair. Behind the successful execution of this spontaneous pseudo-religious drama lay the machinations of Senator Gerald P. Nye of North Dakota, a right-wing isolationist who quickly placed in nomination the name of Charles A. Lindbergh of Little Falls, Minnesota, whereupon two of the most reactionary members of Congress—Congressman Thorkelson of Montana and Congressman Mundt of South Dakota—seconded the nomination, and at precisely four A.M. on Friday, June 28, the Republican Party, by acclamation, chose as its candidate the bigot who had denounced Jews over the airwaves to a national audience as "other peoples" employing their enormous "influence . . . to lead our country to destruction," rather than truthfully acknowledging us to be a small minority of citizens vastly outnumbered by our Christian countrymen, by and large obstructed by religious prejudice from attaining public power, and surely no less loyal to the principles of American democracy than an admirer of Adolf Hitler.

"No!" was the word that awakened us, "No!" being shouted in a man's loud voice from every house on the block. It can't be. No. Not for president of the United States.

Within seconds, my brother and I were once more at the radio with the rest of the family, and nobody bothered telling us to go back to bed. Hot as it was, my decorous mother had pulled a robe over her thin nightdress—she too had been asleep and roused by the noise—and she sat now on the sofa beside my father, her fingers over her mouth as though she were trying to keep from being sick. Meanwhile my cousin Alvin, able no longer to remain in his seat, set about pacing a room eighteen-by-twelve with a force in his gait befitting an avenger out searching the city to dispose of his nemesis.

The anger that night was the real roaring forge, the furnace that takes you and twists you like steel. And it didn't subside— not while Lindbergh stood silently at the Philadelphia rostrum and heard himself being cheered once again as the nation's savior, nor when he gave the speech accepting his party's nomination and with it the mandate to keep America out of the European war. We all waited in terror to hear him repeat to the convention his malicious vilification of the Jews, but that he didn't made no difference to the mood that carried every last family on the block out into the street at nearly five in the morning. Entire families known to me previously only fully dressed in daytime clothing were wearing pajamas and night-dresses under their bathrobes and milling around in their slip-pers at dawn as if driven from their homes by an earthquake. But what shocked a child most was the anger, the anger of men whom I knew as lighthearted kibbitzers or silent, dutiful breadwinners who all day long unclogged drainpipes or ser-viced furnaces or sold apples by the pound and then in the evening looked at the paper and listened to the radio and fell asleep in the living room chair, plain people who happened to be Jews now storming about the street and cursing with no concern for propriety, abruptly thrust back into the miserable struggle from which they had believed their families extricated by the providential migration of the generation before.

I would have imagined Lindbergh's not mentioning the Jews in his acceptance speech to be a promising omen, an indication that he had been chastened by the outcry that had caused him to relinquish his Army commission or that he had changed his mind since the Des Moines speech or that he had already for-gotten about us or that secretly he knew full well that we were committed irrevocably to America—that though Ireland still mattered to the Irish and Poland to the Poles and Italy to the Italians, we retained no allegiance, sentimental or otherwise, to those Old World countries that we had never been welcome in and that we had no intention of ever returning to. If I could have thought through the meaning of the moment in so many words, this is probably what I would have been thinking. But the men out on the street thought differently. Lindbergh's not mentioning the Jews was to them a trick and no more, the initiation of a campaign of deceit intended both to shut us up and to catch us off guard. "Hitler in America!" the neighbors cried. "Fascism in America! Storm troopers in America!" After their having gone without sleep all night long, there was nothing that these bewildered elders of ours didn't think and nothing that they didn't say aloud, within our hearing, before they started to drift back to their houses (where all the radios still blared away), the men to shave and dress and grab a cup of coffee before heading for work and the women to get their children clothed and fed and ready for the day.

Roosevelt raised everyone's spirits by his robust response on learning that his opponent was to be Lindbergh rather than a senator of the stature of Taft or a prosecutor as aggressive as Dewey or a big-time lawyer as smooth and handsome as Willkie. When awakened at four A.M. to be told the news, he was said to have predicted from his White House bed, "By the time this is over, the young man will be sorry not only that he entered politics but that he ever learned to fly." Whereupon he fell immediately back into a sound sleep—or so went the story that brought us such solace the next day. Out on the street, when all anyone could think about was the menace posed to our safety by this transparently unjust affront, people had oddly forgotten about FDR and the bulwark he was against oppression. The sheer surprise of the Lindbergh nomination had activated an atavistic sense of being undefended that had more to do with Kishinev and the pogroms of 1903 than with New Jersey thirty-seven years later, and as a consequence, they had forgotten about Roosevelt's appointment to the Supreme Court of Felix Frankfurter and his selection as Treasury secretary of Henry Morgenthau, and about the close presidential adviser, financier Bernard Baruch, and about Mrs. Roosevelt and Ickes and Agriculture Secretary Wallace, all three of whom, like the president, were known to be friends of the Jews. There was Roosevelt, there was the U.S. Constitution, there was the Bill of Rights, and there were the papers, America's free press. Even the Republican *Newark Evening News* published an editorial reminding readers of the Des Moines speech and openly challenging the wisdom of Lindbergh's nomination, and *PM*, the new left-wing New York tabloid that cost a nickel and that my father had begun bringing home with him after work along with the *Newark News*—and whose slogan read, "*PM* is against people who push other people around"—leveled its assault on the Republicans in a lengthy editorial as well as in news stories and columns on virtually every one of its thirty-two pages, including anti-Lindbergh columns in the sports section by Tom Meany and Joe Cummiskey. On the front page the paper featured a large photo of Lindbergh's Nazi medal and, in its Daily Picture Magazine, where it claimed to run photographs that other papers suppressed—controversial photos of lynch mobs and chain gangs, of strikebreakers wielding clubs, of inhuman conditions in America's penitentiaries—there was page after page showing the Republican candidate touring Nazi Germany in 1938, culminating in the full-page picture of him, the notorious medal around his neck, shaking the hand of Hermann Göring, the Nazi leader second only to Hitler.

On Sunday night we waited through the lineup of comedy programs for Walter Winchell to come on at nine. And when he did and proceeded to say what we had hoped he would say just as contemptuously as we wanted him to say it, applause erupted from across the alleyway, as though the famous newsman weren't walled off in a radio studio on the far side of the great divide that was the Hudson but were here among us and fighting mad, his tie pulled down, his collar unbuttoned, his gray fedora angled back on his head, lambasting Lindbergh from a microphone atop the oilcloth covering on the kitchen table of our next-door neighbor.

It was the last night of June 1940. After a warm day, it had grown cool enough to sit comfortably indoors without perspiring, but when Winchell signed off at nine-fifteen, our parents were moved to go outside for the four of us to take in the lovely evening together. We were just going to walk to the corner and back—after which my brother and I would go to sleep—but it was nearly midnight before we got to bed and by then sleep was out of the question for kids so overcome by their parents' excitement. Because Winchell's fearless bellicosity had propelled all of our neighbors outdoors as well, what had begun for us as a cheerful little evening stroll ended as an impromptu block party for everyone. The men dragged beach chairs from the garages and unfolded them at the foot of the alleyways, the women carried pitchers of lemonade from the houses, the youngest of the children ran wildly from stoop to stoop, and the older ones sat laughing and talking off by themselves, and all because war had been declared on Lindbergh by America's best-known Jew after Albert Einstein.

It was Winchell, after all, whose column had famously ushered in the three dots separating—and somehow magically validating—each hot news item ever so tenuously grounded in fact, and it was Winchell who'd more or less originated the idea of firing into the face of the credulous masses buckshot pellets of insinuating gossip—ruining reputations, compromising celebrities, bestowing fame, making and breaking showbiz careers. It was his column alone that was syndicated in hundreds of papers all across the country and his Sunday-night quarter of an hour that was the country's most popular news program, the rapid-fire Winchell delivery and the pugnacious Winchell cynicism lending every scoop the sensational air of an exposé. We admired him as a fearless outsider and a cunning insider, a pal of J. Edgar Hoover, director of the FBI, as well as a neighbor of the mobster Frank Costello and a confidant of Roosevelt's inner circle, even a sometimes guest invited to the White House to amuse the president over a drink—the in-the-know street fighter and hardboiled man about town whom his enemies feared and who was on our side. Manhattan-born Walter Winschel (a.k.a. Weinschel) had transformed himself from a New York vaudeville dancer into a callow Broadway columnist earning big money by embodying the passions of the cheesiest of the new subliterate dailies, though ever since the rise of Hitler, and long before anyone else in the press had the foresight or the wrath to take them on, fascists and anti-Semites had become his number one enemy. He'd already labeled as "ratzis" the German-American Bund and hounded its leader, Fritz Kuhn, over the air and in print as a secret foreign agent, and now—after FDR's joke, the *Newark News* editorial, and the thoroughgoing denunciation by *PM*—Walter Winchell had only to disclose Lindbergh's "pro-Nazi philosophy" to his thirty million Sunday-evening listeners and to call Lindbergh's presidential candidacy the greatest threat ever to American democracy for all the Jewish families on block-long little Summit Avenue to resemble once again Americans enjoying the vitality and high spirits of a secure, free, protected citizenry instead of casting themselves about outdoors in their night-clothes like inmates escaped from a lunatic asylum.

My brother was known throughout the neighborhood for being able to draw "anything"—a bike, a tree, a dog, a chair, a cartoon character like Li'l Abner—though his interest of late was in real faces. Kids were always gathering around to watch him wherever he would park himself after school with his large spiral pad and his mechanical pencil and begin to sketch the people nearby. Inevitably the onlookers would start to shout, "Draw him, draw her, draw me," and Sandy would take up the exhortation, if only to stop them from screaming in his ear. All the while his hand was working away, he'd look up, down, up, down—and behold, there lived so-and-so on a sheet of paper. What's the trick, they all asked him, how'd you do it, as if tracing—as if outright magic—might have played some part in the feat. Sandy's answer to all this pestering was a shrug or a smile: the trick to doing it was his being the quiet, serious, unostentatious boy that he was. Compelling attention wherever he went by turning out the likenesses people requested had seemingly no effect on the impersonal element at the core of his strength, the inborn modesty that was his toughness and that he later sidestepped at his peril.

At home, he was no longer copying illustrations from *Collier's* or photos from *Look* but studying from an art manual on the figure. He'd won the book in an Arbor Day poster contest for schoolkids that had coincided with a citywide tree-planting program administered by the Department of Parks and Public Property. There'd even been a ceremony where he'd shaken the hand of a Mr. Bannwart, who was superintendent of the Bureau of Shade Trees. The design of his winning poster was based on a red two-cent stamp in my collection commemorating the sixtieth anniversary of Arbor Day. The stamp seemed to me especially beautiful because visible within each of its narrow, vertical white borders was a slender tree whose branches arched at the top to meet and form an arbor—and until the stamp became mine and I was able to examine through my magnifying glass its distinguishing marks, the meaning of "arbor" had been swallowed up in the familiar name of the holiday. (The small magnifying glass—along with an album for twenty-five hundred stamps, a stamp tweezers, a perforation gauge, gummed stamp hinges, and a black rubber dish called a watermark detector—had been a gift from my parents for my seventh birthday. For an additional ten cents they'd also bought me a small book of ninety-odd pages called *The Stamp Collector's Handbook*, where, under "How to Start a Stamp Collection," I'd read with fascination this sentence: "Old business files or private correspondence often contain stamps of discontinued issues which are of great value, so if you have any friends living in old houses who have accumulated material of this sort in their attics, try to obtain their old stamped envelopes and wrappers." We didn't have an attic, none of our friends living in flats and apartments had attics, but there'd been attics just beneath the roofs of the one-family houses in Union—from my seat in the back of the car I could see little attic windows at either end of each of the houses as we'd driven around the town on that terrible Saturday the year before, and so all I could think of when we got home in the afternoon were the old stamped envelopes and the embossed stamps on the prepaid newspaper wrappers secreted up in those attics and how I would now have no chance "to obtain" them because I was a Jew.)

The appeal of the Arbor Day commemorative stamp was greatly enhanced by its representing a human activity as opposed to a famous person's portrait or a picture of an important place—an activity, what's more, being performed by children: in the center of the stamp, a boy and a girl looking to be about ten or eleven are planting a young tree, the boy digging with a spade while the girl, supporting the trunk of the tree with one hand, holds it steadily in place over the hole. In Sandy's poster the boy and the girl are repositioned and stand on opposite sides of the tree, the boy is pictured as right-handed rather than left-handed, he wears long pants instead of knickers, and one of his feet is atop the blade pressing it into the ground. There is also a third child in Sandy's poster, a boy about my age, who is now the one wearing the knickers. He stands back and to the side of the sapling and holds ready a watering can—as I held one when I modeled for Sandy, clad in my best school knickers and high socks. Adding this child was my mother's idea, to help distinguish Sandy's artwork from that on the Arbor Day stamp—and protect him from the charge of "copying"—but also to provide the poster with a social content that implied a theme by no means common in 1940, not in poster art or anywhere else either, and that for reasons of "taste" might even have proved unacceptable to the judges.

The third child planting the tree was a Negro, and what encouraged my mother to suggest including him—aside from the desire to instill in her children the civic virtue of tolerance—was another stamp of mine, a brand-new ten-cent issue in the "educators group," five stamps that I'd purchased at the post office for a total of twenty-one cents and paid for over the month of March out of my weekly allowance of a nickel. Below the central portrait, each stamp featured a picture of a lamp that the U.S. Post Office Department identified as the "Lamp of Knowledge" but that I thought of as Aladdin's lamp because of the boy in the *Arabian Nights* with the magic lamp and the ring and the two genies who give him whatever he asks for. What I would have asked for from a genie were the most coveted of all American stamps: first, the celebrated 1918 twenty-four-cent airmail, a stamp said to be worth $3,400, where the plane pictured at the center, the Army's Flying Jenny, is inverted; and after that, the three famous stamps in the Pan-American Exposition issue of 1901 that had also been mistakenly printed with inverted centers and were worth over a thousand dollars apiece.

On the green one-cent stamp in the educators group, just above the picture of the Lamp of Knowledge, was Horace Mann; on the red two-cent, Mark Hopkins; on the purple three-cent, Charles W. Eliot; on the blue four-cent, Frances E. Willard; on the brown ten-cent was Booker T. Washington, the first Negro to appear on an American stamp. I remember that after placing the Booker T. Washington in my album and showing my mother how it completed the set of five, I had asked her, "Do you think there'll ever be a Jew on a stamp?" and she replied, "Probably—someday, yes. I hope so, anyway." In fact, another twenty-six years had to pass, and it took Einstein to do it.

Sandy saved his weekly allowance of twenty-five cents—and what change he earned shoveling snow and raking leaves and washing the family car—until he had enough to bicycle to the stationery store on Clinton Avenue that carried art supplies and, over a period of months, to buy a charcoal pencil, then sandpaper blocks to sharpen the pencil, then charcoal paper, then the little tubular metal contraption he blew into to apply the fine fixative mist that prevented the charcoal from smudging. He had big bulldog clips, a masonite board, yellow Ticonderoga pencils, erasers, sketchpads, drawing paper—equipment that he stored in a grocery carton at the bottom of our bedroom closet and that my mother, when she was cleaning, wasn't permitted to disturb. His energetic meticulousness (passed on from our mother) and his breathtaking perseverance (passed on from our father) served only to magnify my awe of an older brother who everyone agreed was intended for great things, while most boys his age didn't look as though they were intended even to eat at a table with another human being. I was then the good child, obedient both at home and at school—the willfulness largely inactive and the attack set to go off at a later date—as yet altogether too young to know the potential of a rage of one's own. And nowhere was I less intransigent than with him.

For his twelfth birthday, Sandy had gotten a large, flat black portfolio made of hard cardboard that folded along a sewn seam and was secured at the top edge with two attached lengths of ribbon that he tied in a bow in order to fasten the leaves. The portfolio measured about two feet by a foot and a half, too big to fit into the drawers of our bedroom dresser or to be stacked upright against the wall in the crowded bedroom closet he and I shared. He was allowed to store it—along with his spiral sketchpads—laid out flat beneath his bed, and in it he saved the drawings he considered his best, beginning with his compositional masterwork of 1936, the ambitious picture of our mother pointing overhead at the Paris-bound *Spirit of*

St. Louis. Sandy had several large portraits of the heroic aviator, in both pencil and charcoal, stowed away in his portfolio. They were part of a series he was assembling of prominent Americans that concentrated primarily on those living eminences most revered by our parents, such as President and Mrs. Roosevelt, New York mayor Fiorello La Guardia, United Mine Workers president John L. Lewis, and the novelist Pearl Buck, who'd won the Nobel Prize in 1938 and whose picture he copied from the jacket of one of her bestsellers. A number of drawings in the portfolio were of family members, and of those at least half were of our sole surviving grandparent, our paternal grandmother, who, on the Sundays when my uncle Monty brought her around to visit, would sometimes serve Sandy as a model. Under the sway of the word "venerable," he drew every wrinkle he could find in her face and every gnarl in her arthritic fingers while—as dutifully as she'd scrubbed floors on her knees all her life and cooked for a family of nine on a coal stove—tiny, sturdy Grandma sat in the kitchen and "posed."

We were alone together in the house only a few days after the Winchell broadcast when Sandy removed the portfolio from under his bed and carried it into the dining room. There he opened it out on the table (reserved for entertaining the Boss and celebrating special family occasions) and carefully lifted the Lindbergh portraits from the tracing paper protecting each drawing and lined them up on the tabletop. In the first, Lindbergh was wearing his leather flying cap with the loose straps dangling over each ear; in the second, the cap was partially hidden beneath large heavy goggles pushed up from his eyes and onto his forehead; in the third, he was bareheaded, nothing to mark him as an aviator other than the uncompromising gaze out to the distant horizon. To gauge the value of this man, as Sandy had rendered him, wasn't difficult. A virile hero. A courageous adventurer. A natural person of gigantic strength and rectitude combined with a powerful blandness. Anything but a frightening villain or a menace to mankind.

"He's going to be president," Sandy told me. "Alvin says Lindbergh's going to win."

He so confused and frightened me that I pretended he was making a joke and laughed.

"Alvin's going to go to Canada and join the Canadian army," he said. "He's going to fight for the British against Hitler."

"But nobody can beat Roosevelt," I said.

"Lindbergh's going to. America's going to go fascist."

Then we just stood there together under the intimidating spell of the three portraits. Never before had being seven felt like such a serious deficiency.

"Don't tell anybody I've got these," he said.

"But Mom and Dad saw them already," I said. "They've seen them all. Everybody has."

"I told them I tore them up."

There was nobody more truthful than my brother. He wasn't quiet because he was secretive and deceitful but because he never bothered to behave badly and so had nothing to hide. But now something external had transformed the meaning of these drawings, making them into what they were not, and so he'd told our parents that he'd destroyed them, making himself into what he was not.

"Suppose they find them," I said.

"How will they do that?" he asked.

"I don't know."

"Right," he said. "You don't. Just keep your little trap shut and nobody'll find anything."

I did as he told me for many reasons, one being that the third-oldest U.S. postage stamp I owned—which I couldn't possibly tear up and throw away—was a ten-cent airmail issued in 1927 to commemorate Lindbergh's transatlantic flight. It was a blue stamp, about twice as long as it was high, whose central design, a picture of the *Spirit of St. Louis* flying eastward over the ocean, had provided Sandy with the model for the plane in the drawing celebrating his conception. Adjacent to the white border at the left of the stamp is the coastline of North America, with the words "New York" jutting out into the Atlantic, and adjacent to the border at the right the coastlines of Ireland, Great Britain, and France, with the word "Paris" at the end of a dotted arc that charts the flight path between the two cities. At the top of the stamp, directly beneath the white letters that boldly spell out UNITED STATES POSTAGE are the words LINDBERGH–AIR MAIL in slightly smaller type but large enough certainly to be read by a seven-year-old with perfect vision. The stamp was already valued at twenty cents by Scott's *Standard Postage Stamp Catalogue*, and what I immediately realized was that its worth would only continue increasing (and so rapidly as to become my single most valuable possession) if Alvin was right and the worst happened.

On the sidewalk during the long vacation months we played a new game called "I Declare War," using a cheap rubber ball and a piece of chalk. With the chalk you drew a circle some five or six feet in diameter, partitioned it into as many pielike segments as there were players, and chalked into each the name of one of various foreign countries that had been in the news throughout the year. Next, each player picked "his" country and stood straddling the edge of the circle, one foot inside and one out, so that when the time came he could flee in a hurry. Meanwhile a designated player, holding the ball aloft in his hand, announced slowly, in an ominous cadence, "I—declare —war—on—" There was a suspenseful pause, and then the kid declaring war would slam the ball down, in the same instant shouting "Germany!" or "Japan!" or "Holland!" or "Italy!" or "Belgium!" or "England!" or "China!"—sometimes even shouting "America!"—and everybody would take off except the one on whom the surprise attack had been launched. His job was to catch the ball on the bounce as quickly as he could and call "Stop!" Everybody now allied against him would have to freeze in place, and the victim country would begin the counterattack, trying to eliminate one aggressor country at a time by walloping each as hard as he could with the ball, beginning by throwing at those closest to him and advancing his position with each murderous thwack.

    We played this game incessantly. Until it rained and temporarily the names of the countries were washed away, people had to either step on them or step over them when they made their way down the street. In our neighborhood there was no other graffiti to speak of in those days, just this, the remnants of the hieroglyphics of our simple street games. Harmless enough, and yet it drove some of the mothers crazy who had to hear us at it for hours on end through their open windows.

"Can't you kids do something else? Can't you find another game to play?" But we couldn't—declaring war was all we thought about too.

On July 18, 1940, the Democratic Convention meeting in Chicago overwhelmingly nominated FDR for a third term on the first ballot. We listened on the radio to his acceptance speech, delivered with the confidently intoned upper-class enunciation that, for close to eight years now, had inspired millions of ordinary families like ours to remain hopeful in the midst of hardship. There was something about the inherent decorum of the delivery that, alien though it was, not only calmed our anxiety but bestowed on our family a historical significance, authoritatively merging our lives with his as well as with that of the entire nation when he addressed us in our living room as his "fellow citizens." That Americans could choose Lindbergh—that Americans could choose *anybody*—rather than the two-term president whose voice alone conveyed mastery over the tumult of human affairs . . . well, that was unthinkable, and certainly so for a little American like me who'd never known a presidential voice other than his.

Some six weeks later, on the Saturday before Labor Day, Lindbergh surprised the country by failing to appear at the Detroit Labor Day parade, where he had been scheduled to launch his campaign with a motorcade through the working-class heartland of isolationist America (and the anti-Semitic stronghold of Father Coughlin and Henry Ford), and by arriving unannounced instead at the Long Island airfield from which his spectacular transatlantic flight had begun thirteen years before. The *Spirit of St. Louis* had been secretly trucked in under a tarp and stored overnight in a remote hangar, though by the time Lindbergh taxied the plane onto the field the next morning, every wire service in America and every radio station and newspaper in New York had a reporter on hand to witness the takeoff, westward this time across America to California rather than eastward across the Atlantic to Europe. Of course, by 1940, commercial air service had been hauling transcontinental freight, passengers, and mail for more than a decade, and doing so largely as a result of the incentive of Lindbergh's solo feat and his industrious efforts as a million-dollar-a-year consultant to the newly organized airlines. But it wasn't the wealthy advocate of commercial aviation who was launching his campaign that day, nor was it the Lindbergh who had been decorated in Berlin by the Nazis, nor the Lindbergh who, in a nationwide radio broadcast, had blamed overly influential Jews for attempting to drive the country into war, nor was it even the stoical father of the infant kidnapped and killed by Bruno Hauptmann in 1932. It was rather the unknown airmail pilot who'd dared to do what had never been done by any aviator before him, the adored Lone Eagle, boyish and unspoiled still, despite the years of phenomenal fame. On the holiday weekend that closed out the summer of 1940, Lindbergh came nowhere near besting the record time for a coast-to-coast nonstop flight that he'd himself set a decade back with an aircraft more advanced than the old *Spirit of St. Louis.* Nonetheless, when he arrived at Los Angeles Airport, a crowd consisting largely of aircraft workers—tens of thousands of them, employed by the big new manufacturers in and around L.A.—was as overcome with enthusiasm as any ever to greet him anywhere.

The Democrats called the flight a publicity gimmick stage-managed by Lindbergh's staff, when in fact the decision to fly to California had been made only hours earlier by Lindbergh alone and not by the professionals who had been assigned by the Republican Party to steer the political novice through his first political campaign and who, like everyone else, had been expecting him to turn up in Detroit.

His speech was unadorned and to the point, delivered in a high-pitched, flat, midwestern, decidedly un-Rooseveltian American voice. His flight outfit of high boots and jodhpurs and a lightweight jumper worn over a shirt and tie was a replica of the one in which he'd crossed the Atlantic, and he spoke without removing his leather headgear or flight goggles, which were pushed up onto his forehead exactly as Sandy had them positioned in the charcoal drawing hidden beneath his bed.

"My intention in running for the presidency," he told the raucous crowd, once they had stopped chanting his name, "is to preserve American democracy by preventing America from taking part in another world war. Your choice is simple. It's not between Charles A. Lindbergh and Franklin Delano Roosevelt. It's between Lindbergh and war."

That was the whole of it—forty-one words, if you included the *A* for Augustus.

After a shower and a snack and an hour's nap there at the L.A. airport, the candidate climbed back into the *Spirit of St. Louis* and flew to San Francisco. By nightfall he was in Sacramento. And wherever he landed in California that day, it was as though the country hadn't known the stock market crash and the miseries of the Depression (or the triumphs of FDR, for that matter), as though even the war he was there to prevent us from entering hadn't so much as crossed anyone's mind. Lindy flew down out of the sky in his famous plane, and it was 1927 all over again. It was Lindy all over again, straight-talking Lindy, who had never to look or to sound superior, who simply *was* superior—fearless Lindy, at once youthful and gravely mature, the rugged individualist, the legendary American man's man who gets the impossible done by relying solely on himself.

Over the next month and a half he proceeded to spend one full day in each of the forty-eight states, until in late October he made his way back to the Long Island runway from which he'd taken off on Labor Day weekend. Throughout the daylight hours he would hop from one city, town, or village to the next, landing on highways if there was no nearby airstrip and setting down and taking off from a stretch of pasture when he flew to talk with farmers and their families in the remotest of America's rural counties. His airfield remarks were broadcast over local and regional radio stations, and several times a week, from the state capital where he was spending the night, he broadcast a message to the nation. It was always succinct and went like this: To prevent a war in Europe is now too late. But it is not too late to prevent America from taking part in that war. FDR is misleading the nation. America will be carried to war by a president who falsely promises peace. The choice is simple. Vote for Lindbergh or vote for war.

As a young pilot in aviation's early, novelty days, Lindbergh, along with an older, more experienced sidekick, had entertained crowds throughout the Midwest by skydiving in a parachute or walking out parachuteless onto the plane's wing, and the Democrats were now quick to belittle his barnstorming in the *Spirit of St. Louis* by likening it to these stunts. At press conferences, Roosevelt no longer bothered to make a derisive quip when questioned by newsmen about the unorthodox Lindbergh campaign, but simply moved on to discuss Churchill's fear of an imminent German invasion of Britain or to announce that he would be asking Congress to fund the first American peacetime draft or to remind Hitler that the United States would not tolerate any interference with the transatlantic aid our merchant vessels were supplying to the British war effort. It was clear from the start that the president's campaign was to consist of remaining in the White House, where, in contrast to what Secretary Ickes labeled Lindbergh's "carnival antics," he planned to address the hazards of the international situation with all the authority at his command, working round the clock if necessary.

Twice during the state-by-state tour, Lindbergh was lost in bad weather and each time several hours passed before radio contact with him was reestablished and he was able to let the country know that all was well. But then in October, on the very day Americans were stunned to learn that in the latest of the destructive night raids on London the Germans had bombed St. Paul's Cathedral, a news flash at dinnertime reported that the *Spirit of St. Louis* had been seen to explode in the air over the Alleghenies and plummet to the earth in flames. This time it was six long hours before a second flash corrected the first with the news that it was engine trouble and not a midair explosion that had forced Lindbergh to make an emergency landing on treacherous terrain in the mountains of western Pennsylvania. Before the emendation was aired, however, our phone rang continuously—friends and relatives calling to speculate with our parents on the initial account of the fiery and probably fatal accident. In front of Sandy and me our parents said nothing to indicate relief at the prospect of Lindbergh's death, though neither did they say that they hoped it wasn't so nor were they among the jubilant when, around eleven that night, word came through that, far from having gone down in flames, the Lone Eagle had emerged safely from the undamaged plane and was waiting only for a replacement part so as to take off and resume his campaign.

*

On the October morning that Lindbergh landed at Newark Airport, among the entourage waiting to welcome him to New Jersey was Rabbi Lionel Bengelsdorf of B'nai Moshe, the first of the city's Conservative temples, organized by Polish Jews. B'nai Moshe was a few blocks from the heart of the old pushcart ghetto, still the city's poorest district though home no longer to B'nai Moshe's congregants but to a community of impoverished Negroes, recent migrants from the South. For years B'nai Moshe had been losing out in the competition for the well-to-do; by 1940, these families had either left and affiliated themselves to the congregations of B'nai Jeshurun and Oheb Shalom—each planted impressively amid the old mansions on High Street—or joined the other long-established Conservative temple, B'nai Abraham, located several miles west of where it had been originally housed in a former Baptist church and adjacent now to the homes of the Jewish doctors and lawyers living in Clinton Hill. The new B'nai Abraham was the most splendid of the city's temples, a circular building austerely designed in what was called "the Greek style" and vast enough to hold a thousand worshipers on the High Holidays. Joachim Prinz, an émigré expelled from Berlin by Hitler's Gestapo, had replaced the retiring Julius Silberfeld as the temple's rabbi the year before and was already emerging as a forceful man with a broad social outlook who offered his prosperous congregants a perspective on Jewish history marked strongly by his own recent experience at the bloody scene of the Nazi crime.

Rabbi Bengelsdorf's sermons were broadcast weekly over station WNJR to the hoi polloi he called his "radio congregation," and he was the author of several books of inspirational poetry routinely given as gifts to bar mitzvah boys and newlyweds. He'd been born in South Carolina in 1879, the son of an immigrant dry goods merchant, and whenever he addressed a Jewish audience, whether from the pulpit or over the air, his courtly southern accent, along with his sonorous cadences— and the cadences of his own multisyllabic name—left an impression of dignified profundity. On the subject, for instance, of his friendship with Rabbi Silberfeld of B'nai Abraham and Rabbi Foster of B'nai Jeshurun, he once told his radio audience, "It was fated: just as Socrates, Plato, and Aristotle belonged together in the ancient world, so we belong together in the religious world." And the homily on selflessness that he proffered to explain to radio listeners why a rabbi of his standing was content to stay on at the head of a waning congregation, he introduced by saying, "Perhaps you will be interested in my answer to questions that have been asked of me by literally thousands of people. Why do you renounce the commercial benefits of a peripatetic ministry? Why do you choose to remain in Newark, at Temple B'nai Moshe, as your only pulpit, when you have six opportunities every day to leave it for other congregations?" He had studied at the great institutions of learning in Europe as well as at American universities and was reputed to speak ten languages; to be versed in classical philosophy, theology, art history, and ancient and modern history; to never compromise on questions of principle; to never refer to notes at the lectern or on a lecture platform; to never be without a set of index cards pertaining to the topics most engaging him at the moment, to which he added new reflections and impressions every day. He was also an excellent equestrian, known to bring his horse to a halt so as to jot down a thought, employing his saddle as a makeshift desk. Early each morning, he exercised by riding out along the bridle paths of Weequahic Park, accompanied—until her death from cancer in 1936—by his wife, the heiress to Newark's wealthiest jewelry manufacturer. Her family mansion on Elizabeth Avenue, where the couple had been living just across from the park since their marriage in 1907, housed a treasury of Judaica said to be among the most valuable private collections in the world.

By 1940 Lionel Bengelsdorf claimed the longest record of service at his own temple of any rabbi in America. The newspapers referred to him as the religious leader of New Jersey Jewry and, in reporting on his numerous public appearances, invariably mentioned his "gift for oratory" along with the ten languages. In 1915, at the 250th anniversary celebration of the founding of Newark, he had sat at the side of Mayor Raymond and delivered the invocation just as he delivered invocations annually at the parades for Memorial Day and the Fourth of July: RABBI EXALTS DECLARATION OF INDEPENDENCE was a headline that appeared annually in the *Star-Ledger* every July fifth. In his sermons and talks calling "the development of American ideals" the first priority of Jews and "the Americanization of Americans" the best means to preserve our democracy against "Bolshevism, radicalism, and anarchism," he frequently quoted from Theodore Roosevelt's final message to the nation, in which the late president said, "There can be no divided allegiance here. Any man who says he is an American, but something else also, isn't an American at all. We have room for but one flag, the American flag." Rabbi Bengelsdorf had spoken on the Americanization of Americans in every Newark church and public school, before most every fraternal, civic, historical, and cultural group in the state, and news articles in the Newark papers about his speeches were datelined with the names of scores of cities around the country to which he'd been called to address conferences and conventions on that theme as well as on issues ranging from crime and the prison reform movement—"The prison reform movement is saturated with the highest ethical principles and religious ideals"— to the causes of the World War—"The war is the result of the worldly ambitions of the European peoples and their effort to reach the goals of military greatness, power, and wealth"—to the importance of day nurseries—"The nurseries are life gardens of human flowers in which each child is helped to grow in an atmosphere of joy and gladness"—to the evils of the industrial age—"We believe that the worth of the workingman is not to be computed by the material value of his production"—to the suffrage movement, whose proposal to extend to women the franchise to vote he strongly opposed, arguing that "if men are not capable of handling the business of the state, why not help them become so. No evil has ever been cured by doubling it." My uncle Monty, who hated all rabbis but had an especially venomous loathing of Bengelsdorf dating back to his childhood as a charity student in the B'nai Moshe religious school, liked to say of him, "The pompous son of a bitch knows everything— it's too bad he doesn't know anything else."

Rabbi Bengelsdorf's appearance at the airport—where, according to the caption beneath the photograph on the front page of the *Newark News*, he stood first in line to shake Lindbergh's hand when he emerged from the cockpit of the *Spirit of St. Louis*—was a source of consternation to great numbers of the city's Jews, my parents among them, as was the quotation attributed to him in the paper's account of Lindbergh's brief visit. "I am here," Rabbi Bengelsdorf told the *News*, "to crush all doubt of the unadulterated loyalty of the American Jews to the United States of America. I offer my support to the candidacy of Colonel Lindbergh because the political objectives of my people are identical with his. America is our beloved homeland. America is our only homeland. Our religion is independent of any piece of land other than this great country, to which, now as always, we commit our total devotion and allegiance as the proudest of citizens. I want Charles Lindbergh to be my president not in spite of my being a Jew but because I am a Jew—an *American* Jew."

Three days later, Bengelsdorf participated in the huge rally held at Madison Square Garden to mark the end of Lindbergh's flying tour. By then the election was but two weeks away, and though there appeared to be growing Lindbergh support among voters throughout the traditionally Democratic South, and close contests were predicted in the most conservative midwestern states, national polls showed the president comfortably ahead in the popular vote and well ahead in electoral votes. Republican Party leaders were reported to be in despair over their candidate's stubborn refusal to allow anyone other than himself to determine the strategy of his campaign, and so, to draw him out of the repetitious austerity of his interminable barnstorming and envelop him in an atmosphere more like that of the boisterous Philadelphia nominating convention, the Madison Square Garden rally was organized and broadcast nationwide on the evening of the second Monday in October.

The fifteen speakers introducing Lindbergh that night were described as "prominent Americans from all walks of life." Among them was a farm leader to talk about the harm a war would do to American farming, which was in crisis still from the First World War and the Depression; a labor leader to talk about the disaster a war would represent for American workers, whose lives would be regimented by government agencies; a manufacturer to talk about the catastrophic long-term consequences for American industry of wartime overexpansion and onerous taxation; a Protestant clergyman to talk about the brutalizing effect of modern warfare on the young men who would be doing the fighting; and a Catholic priest to talk about the inevitable deterioration of the spiritual life of a peace-loving nation like our own and the destruction of decency and kindness because of the hatred bred by war. Lastly there was a rabbi, New Jersey's Lionel Bengelsdorf, who received an especially hearty welcome from the full house of Lindbergh supporters when his turn came to take the lectern and who was there to expatiate on how Lindbergh's association with the Nazis was anything but complicitous.

"Yep," Alvin said, "they bought him. The fix is in. They slipped a gold ring through his big Jew nose, and now they can lead him anywhere."

"You don't know that," my father said, but not because he wasn't himself steamed up by Bengelsdorf's behavior. "Listen to the man," he told Alvin, "give the man a hearing. It's only fair"—words uttered largely for Sandy's benefit and mine, to keep the startling turn of events from seeming as terrible to the two of us as it did to the adults. The night before, I had fallen onto the floor in my sleep, something that hadn't happened since I'd first graduated from a crib to a bed and to prevent me from rolling out of it my parents had to set a pair of kitchen chairs at the side of the mattress. When it was assumed automatically that my falling like that after all these years could only have had to do with Lindbergh's showing up at Newark Airport, I insisted that I didn't remember a bad dream about Lindbergh, that I just remembered waking up on the floor between my brother's bed and mine, even though I happened to know that I virtually never got to sleep any longer without envisioning the Lindbergh drawings stashed away in my brother's portfolio. I kept wanting to ask Sandy if he couldn't hide them in our cellar storage bin instead of under the bed beside mine, but because I'd sworn not to speak about the drawings to anyone—and because I couldn't bring myself to part with my own Lindbergh stamp—I didn't dare to raise them as an issue, though they were indeed haunting me and rendering unapproachable the brother whose reassurance I'd never needed more.

It was a cold evening. The heat was on and the windows were closed, but even without being able to hear them you knew that radios were playing up and down the block and that families who wouldn't otherwise consider listening to a Lindbergh rally were tuned in because of the scheduled appearance there of Rabbi Bengelsdorf. Among his own congregants, a few important people had already begun to call for his resignation, if not for his immediate removal by the temple's board of trustees, while the majority continuing to support him tried to believe that their rabbi was merely exercising his democratic right of free speech and that, horrified though they were by his public endorsement of Lindbergh, to attempt to silence a conscience as renowned as his did not fall within their rights.

That night Rabbi Bengelsdorf disclosed to America what he claimed to be the true motive behind Lindbergh's personal flying missions to Germany in the 1930s. "Contrary to the propaganda disseminated by his critics," the rabbi informed us, "he did not once visit Germany as a sympathizer or a supporter of Hitler's but rather he traveled each and every time as a secret adviser to the U.S. government. Far from his betraying America, as the misguided and the ill-intentioned continue to charge, Colonel Lindbergh has almost single-handedly served to strengthen America's military preparedness by imparting his knowledge to our own military and by doing everything within his power to advance the cause of American aviation and to expand America's air defenses."

"Jesus!" cried my father. "Everybody *knows*—"

"Shhh," whispered Alvin, "shhh—let the great orator speak."

"Yes, in 1936, long before the beginning of the European hostilities, the Nazis awarded Colonel Lindbergh a medal, and, yes," continued Bengelsdorf, "yes, the colonel accepted their medal. But all the while, my friends, all the while secretly exploiting their admiration in order better to protect and preserve our democracy and to preserve our neutrality through strength."

"I cannot *believe*—" my father began.

"Try," muttered Alvin evilly.

"This is not America's war," Bengelsdorf announced, and the crowd at Madison Square Garden responded with a full minute of applause. "This," the rabbi told them, "is Europe's war." Again sustained applause. "It is one of a thousand-year-long sequence of European wars dating back to the time of

Charlemagne. It is their second devastating war in less than half a century. And can anyone forget the tragic cost to America of their last great war? Forty thousand Americans killed in action. A hundred and ninety-two thousand Americans wounded. Seventy-six thousand Americans dead of disease. Three hundred and fifty thousand Americans on disability today because of their participation in that war. And just how astronomical will the price be this time? The number of our dead—tell me, President Roosevelt, will it be merely doubled or tripled or will it perhaps be quadrupled? Tell me, Mr. President, what sort of America will the massive slaughter of innocent American boys leave in its wake? Of course, the Nazi harassment and persecution of its German Jewish population is a cause of enormous anguish to me as it is to every Jew. During the years I was studying theology with the faculties of the great German universities in Heidelberg and in Bonn, I made many distinguished friends there, great men of learning who, today, simply because they are Germans of Jewish extraction, have been dismissed from long-held scholarly positions and are being ruthlessly persecuted by the Nazi hoodlums who have taken command of their homeland. I oppose their treatment with every ounce of my strength, and so too does Colonel Lindbergh oppose their treatment. But how will this cruel fate that has befallen them in their own land be alleviated by our great country going to war with their tormentors? If anything, the predicament of *all* of Germany's Jews would only worsen immeasurably—worsen, I fear, tragically. Yes, I am a Jew, and as a Jew I feel their suffering with a familial sharpness. But I am an American citizen, my friends"—again the applause—"I am an American born and raised, and so I ask you, how would my pain be lessened if America were now to enter the war and, along with the sons of our Protestant families and the sons of our Catholic families, the sons of our Jewish families were to fight and die by the tens of thousands on a blood-soaked European battleground? How would my pain be diminished by my having to console my very own congregants—"

It was my mother, usually the least ardent member of our family, the one ordinarily quieting the rest of us when we turned demonstrative, who all at once found the sound of Bengelsdorf's southern accent so intolerable that she had to leave the room. But until he finished his speech and was loudly cheered off the stage by the Garden audience, no one else moved or said another word. I wouldn't dare to, and my brother was preoccupied—as he often was in such a setting—with sketching what we all looked like, now while listening to the radio. Alvin's was the silence of murderous loathing, and my father—divested for perhaps the first time in his life of that relentless passion he brought to the struggle against setback and disappointment—was too stirred up to speak.

Pandemonium. Unspeakable delight. Lindbergh had at last stepped onto the Garden stage, and like someone half de-mented, my father leaped from the sofa and snapped off the radio just as my mother came back into the living room and asked, "Who would like something? Alvin," she said, with tears in her eyes, "a cup of tea?"

Her job was to hold our world together as calmly and as sensibly as she could; that was what gave her life fullness and that was all she was trying to do, and yet never had any of us seen her rendered so ridiculous by this commonplace maternal ambition.

"What the hell is going on!" my father began to shout. "What the hell did he do *that* for? That stupid speech! Does he think that one single Jew is now going to go out and vote for this anti-Semite because of that stupid, lying speech? Has he completely lost his mind? What does this man think he is *doing?*"

"Koshering Lindbergh," Alvin said. "Koshering Lindbergh for the goyim."

"Koshering what?" my father said, exasperated with Alvin's seemingly speaking sarcastic nonsense at a moment of so much confusion. "Doing *what?*"

"They didn't get him up there to talk to Jews. They didn't buy him off for that. Don't you understand?" Alvin asked, fiery now with what he took to be the underlying truth. "He's up there talking to the goyim—he's giving the goyim all over the country his personal rabbi's permission to vote for Lindy on Election Day. Don't you see, Uncle Herman, what they got the great Bengelsdorf to do? He just guaranteed Roosevelt's defeat!"

*

At about two A.M. that night, while soundly asleep, I again rolled out of my bed, but this time I remembered afterward what I'd been dreaming before I hit the floor. It was a nightmare all right, and it was about my stamp collection. Something had happened to it. The design on two sets of my stamps had changed in a dreadful way without my knowing when or how. In the dream, I'd gotten the album out of my dresser drawer to take with me to my friend Earl's and I was walking with it toward his house as I'd done dozens of times before. Earl Axman was ten and in the fifth grade. He lived with his mother in the new four-story yellow-brick apartment house built three years earlier on the large empty lot near the corner of Chancellor and Summit, diagonally across from the grade school. Before that he'd lived in New York. His father was a musician with the Glen Gray Casa Loma Orchestra—Sy Axman, who played tenor saxophone beside Glen Gray's alto. Mr. Axman was divorced from Earl's mother, a theatrically good-looking blonde who'd briefly been a singer with the band before Earl was born and, according to my parents, was originally from Newark and a brunette, a Jewish girl named Louise Swig who'd gone to South Side and became famous locally in musical revues at the YMHA. Among all the boys I knew, Earl was the only child with divorced parents, and the only one whose mother wore heavy makeup and off-the-shoulder blouses and billowing ruffled skirts with a big petticoat underneath. She'd also made a record of the song "Gotta Be This or That" when she was with Glen Gray, and Earl played it for me often. I never came upon another mother like her. Earl didn't call her Ma or Mom—he called her, scandalously, Louise. She had a closet in her bedroom full of those petticoats, and when Earl and I were alone together at his house, he'd show them to me. He even let me touch one once, whispering, while I waited to decide whether to do it, "Wherever you want." Then he opened a drawer and showed me her brassieres and offered to let me touch one of those, but that I declined. I was still young enough to admire a brassiere from afar. His parents each gave him a full dollar a week to spend on stamps, and when the Casa Loma Orchestra wasn't playing in New York and was out touring, Mr. Axman sent Earl envelopes with airmail stamps postmarked from cities everywhere. There was even one from

"Honolulu, Oahu," where Earl, who wasn't above cloaking his absent father in splendor—as though to the son of an insurance agent having a saxophonist with a famous swing band for a father (and a peroxide-blond singer for a mother) weren't amazing enough—claimed that Mr. Axman had been taken to a "private home" to see the canceled two-cent Hawaiian "Missionary" stamp of 1851, issued forty-seven full years before Hawaii was annexed to the United States as a territory, an unimaginable treasure valued at $100,000 whose central design was just the numeral 2.

Earl owned the best stamp collection around. He taught me everything practical and everything esoteric that I learned as a small kid about stamps—about their history, about collecting mint versus used, about technical matters like paper, printing, color, gum, overprints, grills, and special printing, about the great forgeries and design errors—and, prodigious pedant that he was, had begun my education by telling me about the French collector Monsieur Herpin, who coined the word "philately," explaining its derivation from two Greek words, the second of which, *ateleia*, meaning freedom from tax, never quite made sense to me. And whenever we'd finished up in his kitchen with our stamps and he was momentarily done with his domineering, he'd giggle and say, "Now let's do something awful," which was how I got to see his mother's underwear.

In the dream, I was walking to Earl's with my stamp album clutched to my chest when someone shouted my name and began chasing me. I ducked into an alleyway and scurried back into one of the garages to hide and to check the album for stamps that might have come loose from their hinges when, while fleeing my pursuer, I'd stumbled and dropped the album at the very spot on the sidewalk where we regularly played "I Declare War." When I opened to my 1932 Washington Bicentennials—twelve stamps ranging in denomination from the half-cent dark brown to the ten-cent yellow—I was stunned. Washington wasn't on the stamps anymore. Unchanged at the top of each stamp—lettered in what I'd learned to recognize as white-faced roman and spaced out on either one or two lines—was the legend "United States Postage." The colors of the stamps were unchanged as well—the two-cent red, the five-cent blue, the eight-cent olive green, and so on—all the stamps were the same regulation size, and the frames for the portraits remained individually designed as they were in the original set, but instead of a different portrait of Washington on each of the twelve stamps, the portraits were now the same and no longer of Washington but of Hitler. And on the ribbon beneath each portrait, there was no longer the name "Washington" either. Whether the ribbon was curved downward as on the one-half-cent stamp and the six, or curved upward as on the four, the five, the seven, and the ten, or straight with raised ends as on the one, the one and a half, the two, the three, the eight, and the nine, the name lettered across the ribbon was "Hitler."

It was when I looked next at the album's facing page to see what, if anything, had happened to my 1934 National Parks set of ten that I fell out of the bed and woke up on the floor, this time screaming. Yosemite in California, Grand Canyon in Arizona, Mesa Verde in Colorado, Crater Lake in Oregon, Acadia in Maine, Mount Rainier in Washington, Yellowstone in Wyoming, Zion in Utah, Glacier in Montana, the Great Smoky Mountains in Tennessee—and across the face of each, across the cliffs, the woods, the rivers, the peaks, the geyser, the gorges, the granite coastline, across the deep blue water and the high waterfalls, across everything in America that was the bluest and the greenest and the whitest and to be preserved forever in these pristine reservations, was printed a black swastika.

2

Loudmouth Jew

I N JUNE 1941, just six months after Lindbergh's inauguration, our family drove the three hundred miles to Washington, D.C., to visit the historic sites and the famous government buildings. My mother had been saving in a Christmas
Club account at the Howard Savings Bank for close to two
years, a dollar a week out of the household budget to cover the
bulk of our prospective travel expenses. The trip had been
planned back when FDR was a second-term president and the
Democrats controlled both Houses, but now with the Republicans in power and the new man in the White House considered a treacherous enemy, there was a brief family discussion
about our driving north instead to see Niagara Falls and to
take the boat cruise in rain slickers through the St. Lawrence
River's Thousand Islands and then to cross over in our car into
Canada to visit Ottawa. Some among our friends and neighbors had already begun talking about leaving the country and
migrating to Canada should the Lindbergh administration
openly turn against the Jews, and so a trip to Canada would
also familiarize us with a potential haven from persecution.
Back in February, my cousin Alvin had already left for Canada
to join the Canadian armed forces, just as he said he would,
and fight on the British side against Hitler.

Till his departure Alvin had been my family's ward for close to
seven years. His late father was my father's oldest brother; he
died when Alvin was six, and Alvin's mother—a second cousin
of my mother's and the one who'd introduced my parents to
each other—died when Alvin was thirteen, and so he'd come
to live with us during the four years he attended Weequahic
High, a quick-witted boy who gambled and stole and whom
my father was dedicated to saving. Alvin was twenty-one in

1940, renting a furnished room upstairs from a Wright Street shoeshine parlor just around the corner from the produce market, and by then working almost two years for Steinheim & Sons, one of the city's two biggest Jewish construction firms —the other was run by the Rachlin brothers. Alvin got the job through the elder Steinheim, the founder of the company and an insurance customer of my father's.

Old man Steinheim, who had a heavy accent and couldn't read English but who was, in my father's words, "made of steel," still attended High Holiday services at our local synagogue. On a Yom Kippur several years back, when the old man saw my father outside the synagogue with Alvin, he mistook my cousin for my older brother and asked, "What does the boy do? Let him come over and work for us." There Abe Steinheim, who'd turned his immigrant father's little building company into a multimillion-dollar operation—though only after a major family war had put his two brothers out on the street—took a liking to solid, stocky Alvin and the cocksure way he carried himself, and instead of sticking him in the mailroom or using him as an office boy, he made Alvin his driver: to run errands, to deliver messages, to whisk him back and forth to the construction sites to check on the subcontractors (whom Abe called "the chiselers," though it was he, Alvin said, who chiseled them and took advantage of everyone). On Saturdays during the summer, Alvin drove him down to Freehold, where Abe owned half a dozen trotters that he raced at the old harness track, horses he liked to refer to as "hamburgers." "We got a hamburger running today at Freehold," and down they'd shoot in the Caddy to watch his horse lose every time. He never made any money at it, but that wasn't the idea. He raced horses on Saturdays for the Road Horse Association at the pretty trotting track in Weequahic Park, and he talked to the papers about restoring the flat track at Mount Holly, whose glory days were long past, and this was how Abe Steinheim managed to become commissioner of racing for the state of New Jersey and got a shield on his car that enabled him to drive up on the sidewalk and sound a siren and park anywhere. And it was how he became friendly with the Monmouth County officials and insinuated himself into the horsy set at the shore— Wall Township and Spring Lake goyim who would take him to their fancy clubs for lunch, where, as Abe told Alvin, "Everybody sees me and all they're doing is whispering, can't wait to whisper, 'Look at what's here,' but they don't mind drinking my booze and getting treated to great dinners and so in the end it pays off." He had his deep-sea-fishing boat docked at the Shark River Inlet and he would take them out on it and liquor them up and hire guys to catch the fish for them, so that whenever a new hotel went up anywhere from Long Branch to Point Pleasant, it was on a site the Steinheims got for next to nothing—Abe, like his father, having the great wisdom of buying things only at discount.

Every three days Alvin would drive him the four blocks from the office to 744 Broad Street for a quick trim in the lobby barber shop behind the cigar stand, where Abe Steinheim bought his Trojans and his dollar-fifty cigars. Now, 744 Broad was one of the two tallest office buildings in the state, where the National Newark and Essex Bank occupied the top twenty floors and the city's prestigious lawyers and financiers occupied the rest and where New Jersey's biggest moneymen regularly frequented the barber shop—and yet a part of Alvin's job was to call immediately beforehand to tell the barber to get ready, Abe was coming, and whoever was in the chair, to throw him out. At dinner the night that Alvin got the job, my father told us that Abe Steinheim was the most colorful, the most exciting, the greatest builder Newark had ever seen. "And a genius," my father said. "He didn't get there without being a genius. Brilliant. And a handsome man. Blond. Husky, but not fat. Always looks nice. Camelhair coats. Black-and-white shoes. Beautiful shirts. Impeccably dressed. And a beautiful wife—polished, classy, a Freilich by birth, a New York Freilich, a very wealthy woman in her own right. Abe's shrewd as they come. And the man has guts. Ask anybody in Newark: the riskiest project and Steinheim takes it on. He does buildings where no one else will take a chance. Alvin will learn from him. He'll watch him and see what it is to work round the clock for something that's yours. He could be an important inspiration in Alvin's life."

Largely so my father could keep tabs on him and my mother could know that he wasn't surviving on hotdogs alone, Alvin came to our house a couple of times a week to eat a good meal, and miraculously, instead of his getting stern lectures about honesty and responsibility and hard work at the dinner table every night—as in the days after he'd been caught with his hand in the till at the Esso station where he worked after school and, until my father prevailed on Simkowitz, the owner, to drop the charges and himself made good with the money, looked to be headed for the Rahway reformatory—Alvin conversed heatedly with my father about politics, about capitalism particularly, a system that, ever since my father had gotten him to take an interest in reading the paper and talking about the news, Alvin deplored but that my father defended, patiently reasoning with his rehabilitated nephew, and not like a member of the National Association of Manufacturers but as a devotee of Roosevelt's New Deal. He'd warn Alvin, "You don't have to tell Mr. Steinheim about Karl Marx. Because the man won't hesitate—you'll be out on your keister. Learn from him. That's why you're there. Learn from him and be respectful, and this could be the opportunity of a lifetime."

But Alvin couldn't bear Steinheim and reviled him constantly —he's a fake, he's a bully, he's a cheapskate, he's a screamer, he's a shouter, he's a swindler, he's a man without a friend in the world, people cannot stand to be anywhere near him, and I, said Alvin, have to chauffeur him around. He's cruel to his sons, is uninterested even in looking at a grandchild, and his skinny wife, who never dares to say or do anything to displease him, he humiliates whenever the mood takes him. Everybody in the family has to live in apartments in the same luxury building that Abe built on a street of big oaks and maples near Upsala College in East Orange—from dawn to dusk the sons work for him in Newark and he's screaming and yelling at them, then at night he's on the house phone with them in East Orange and he's still screaming and yelling. Money is everything, though not to buy things but so as to be able always to weather the storm: to protect his position and insure his holdings and buy anything he wants in real estate at a discount, which is how he made a killing after the crash. Money, money, money—to be in the middle of the chaos and in the middle of the deals and make all the money in the world.

"Some guy retires at the age of forty-five with five million bucks. Five million in the bank, which is as good as a zillion, and you know what Abe says?" Alvin is asking this of my twelve-year-old brother and me. Supper is over and he's with us in the bedroom—all of us lying shoeless atop the covers, Sandy on his bed, Alvin on mine, and I beside Alvin, in the crook between his strong arm and his strong chest. And it's bliss: stories about man's avarice, his zealousness, his unbounded vitality and staggering arrogance, and to tell these stories, a cousin himself unbounded, even after all my father's work, a captivating cousin still emotionally among the rawest of the raw, who at twenty-one already has to shave his black stubble twice a day in order not to look like a hardened criminal. Stories of the carnivore descendants of the giant apes who once inhabited the ancient forests and have left the trees, where all day long they nibbled on leaves, to come to Newark and work downtown.

"What does Mr. Steinheim say?" Sandy asks him.

"He says, 'The guy has five million. That's all he has. Still young and in his prime, with a chance someday to be worth fifty, sixty, maybe as much as a hundred million, and he tells me, "I'm taking it all off the table. I'm not you, Abe. I'm not hanging around for the heart attack. I have enough to call it a day and spend the rest of my life playing golf."' And what does Abe say? 'This is a man who is a total schmuck.' Every subcontractor when he comes into the office on Friday to collect money for the lumber, the glass, the brick, Abe says, 'Look, we're out of money, this is the best I can do,' and he pays them a half, a third—if he can get away with it, a quarter—and these people need the money to survive, but this is the method that Abe learned from his father. He's doing so much building that he gets away with it and nobody tries to kill him."

"*Would* somebody try to kill him?" Sandy asks.

"Yeah," Alvin says, "me."

"Tell us about the wedding anniversary," I say.

"The wedding anniversary," he repeats. "Yeah, he sang fifty songs. He hires a piano player," Alvin tells us, exactly the way he tells the tale of Abe at the piano every time I ask to hear it, "and no one gets a word in, no one knows what is going on, all the guests spend the whole night eating his food, and he is standing in his tux by the piano singing one song after another, and when they leave he's still at the piano, still singing songs, every popular song you can think of, and he doesn't even listen when they say goodbye."

"Does he scream and yell at you?" I ask Alvin.

"At me? At everybody. He screams and yells wherever he goes. I drive him to Tabatchnick's on Sunday mornings. The people are lined up to buy their bagels and lox. We walk in and he's screaming—and there's a line of six hundred people, but he's yelling, 'Abe is here!' and they move him to the front of the line. Tabatchnick comes running out of the back, they push everyone aside, and Abe must order five thousand dollars' worth of stuff, and we drive home and there is Mrs. Steinheim, who weighs ninety-two pounds and knows when to get the hell out of the way, and he phones the three sons and they're there in five seconds flat, and the four of them eat a meal for four hundred people. The one thing he spends on is food. Food and cigars. You mention Tabatchnick's, Kartzman's, he doesn't care who is there, how many people—he gets there and buys out the whole store. They eat up every single slice of everything every Sunday morning, sturgeon, herring, sable, bagels, pickles, and then I drive him over to the renting office to see how many apartments are vacant, how many are rented, how many are being fixed up. Seven days a week. Never stops. Never takes a vacation. No mañana—that's his slogan. It drives him crazy if anybody misses a minute of work. He cannot go to sleep without knowing that the next day there are more deals that will bring more money—and the whole damn thing makes me sick. The man to me is one thing only—a walking advertisement for the overthrow of capitalism."

My father called Alvin's complaints kid stuff, and to be kept to himself on the job, especially after Abe decided that he was going to send Alvin to Rutgers. You're too smart, Abe told Alvin, to be so dumb, and then something happened beyond anything that my father could realistically have hoped for. Abe gets on the phone to the president of Rutgers and starts shouting at *him*. "You're going to take this boy, where he finished in high school is not the issue, the boy is an orphan, potentially a genius, you're going to give him a full scholarship, and I'll build you a college building, the most beautiful in the world—but not so much as a shithouse goes up unless this orphan boy goes to Rutgers all expenses paid!" To Alvin he explains, "I've never liked to have a formal chauffeur who was a chauffeur who was an idiot. I like kids like you with something going for them. You're going to Rutgers, and you'll come home and drive me in the summers, and when you graduate Phi Beta Kappa, then the two of us sit down and talk."

Abe would have had Alvin beginning as a freshman in New Brunswick in September 1941 and, after four years of college, coming back as a somebody into the business, but instead, in February, Alvin left for Canada. My father was furious with him. They argued for weeks before finally, without telling us, Alvin took the express train from Newark's Penn Station straight up to Montreal. "I don't get your morality, Uncle Herman. You don't want me to be a thief but it's okay with you if I work for a thief." "Steinheim's not a thief. Steinheim's a builder. What he's doing is what they do," my father said, "what they all have to do because the building trade is a cut-throat business. But his buildings don't fall down, do they? Does he break the law, Alvin? Does he?" "No, he just screws the workingman every chance he gets. I didn't know your morality was also for that." "My morality stinks," said my father, "everybody in this city knows about my morality. But the issue isn't me. It's your future. It's going to college. A four-year free college education." "Free because he browbeats the president of Rutgers the way he browbeats the whole goddamn world." "Let the president of Rutgers worry about that! What is the matter with you? You really want to sit there and tell me that the worst human being ever born is a man who wants to make you an educated person and find you a place in his building company?" "No, no, the worst human being ever born is Hitler, and frankly I'd rather be fighting that son of a bitch than waste my time with a Jew like Steinheim, who only brings shame on the rest of us Jews by his goddamn—" "Oh, don't talk to me like a child—and the 'goddamn's I can live without too. The man doesn't bring shame on anyone. You think if you worked for an Irish builder it would be better? Try it—go work for Shanley, you'll see what a lovely fellow he is. And the Italians, would they be better, you think? Steinheim shoots his mouth off—the Italians shoot guns." "And Longy Zwillman doesn't shoot guns?" "Please, I know all about Longy—I grew up on the same street with Longy. What does any of this have to do with Rutgers?" "It has to do with *me*, Uncle Herman, and being indebted to Steinheim for the rest of my life. Isn't it enough that he has three sons that he's already destroying? Isn't it enough that they have to attend every Jewish holiday with him and every Thanksgiving with him and every New Year's Eve with him—I have to be there to be shouted at too? All of them working in the same office and living in the same building and waiting around for only one thing—to split it all up on the day he dies. I can assure you, Uncle Herman, their grief won't last long." "You're wrong. Dead wrong. There is more to these people than just money." "*You're* wrong! He holds them in his hand with the money! The man is totally berserk, and they stay and take it for fear of losing the money!" "They stay because they're a family. All families go through a lot. A family is both peace and war. We're going through a little war right now. I understand it. I accept it. But that's no reason to give up the college you missed out on and that now you can have and to run off half-cocked to fight Hitler instead." "So," said Alvin, as though at last he had the goods not only on his employer but on his family protector as well, "you're an isolationist after all. You and Bengelsdorf. Bengelsdorf, Steinheim —they make a good couple." "Of what?" my father asked sourly, having finally run out of patience. "Of Jewish fakes." "Oh," said my father, "against the Jews now too?" "Those Jews. The Jews who are a disgrace to the Jews—yes, absolutely!"

The argument went on for four consecutive nights, and then, on the fifth, a Friday, Alvin didn't report to eat, though the idea had been to keep him showing up regularly for dinner until my father wore him down and the boy came to his senses—the boy whom my father had single-handedly changed from a callow good-for-nothing into the family's conscience.

The next morning we learned from Billy Steinheim, who was closest to Alvin of any of the sons and concerned enough about him to telephone us first thing Saturday, that after having received his Friday pay packet Alvin had thrown the keys to the Caddy in Billy's father's face and walked out, and when my father rushed off in our car to Wright Street to talk to Alvin in his room and get the whole story and gauge just how much damage he had done to his chances, the shoeshine parlor proprietor who was Alvin's landlord told him that the tenant had paid the rent and packed his things and was off to fight against the very worst human being ever born. Given the magnitude of Alvin's seething, no one less nefarious would do.

The November election hadn't even been close. Lindbergh got fifty-seven percent of the popular vote and, in an electoral sweep, carried forty-six states, losing only FDR's home state of New York and, by a mere two thousand votes, Maryland, where the large population of federal office workers had voted overwhelmingly for Roosevelt while the president was able to retain —as he could nowhere else below the Mason-Dixon Line—the loyalty of nearly half the Democrats' old southern constituency. Though on the morning after the election disbelief prevailed, especially among the pollsters, by the day after that everybody seemed to understand everything, and the radio commentators and the news columnists made it sound as if Roosevelt's defeat had been preordained. What had happened, they explained, was that Americans had shown themselves unwilling to break the tradition of the two-term presidency that George Washington had instituted and that no president before Roosevelt had dared to challenge. Moreover, in the aftermath of the Depression, the resurgent confidence of young and old alike had been quickened by Lindbergh's relative youth and by the graceful athleticism that contrasted so starkly with the serious physical impediments under which FDR labored as a polio victim. And there was the wonder of aviation and the new way of life it promised: Lindbergh, already the record-breaking master of long-distance flight, could knowledgeably lead his countrymen into the unknown of the aeronautical future while assuring them, by his strait-laced, old-fashioned demeanor, that modern engineering achievements need not erode the values of the past. It turned out, the experts concluded, that twentieth-century Americans, weary of confronting a new crisis in every decade, were starving for normalcy, and what Charles A. Lindbergh represented was normalcy raised to heroic proportions, a decent man with an honest face and an undistinguished voice who had resoundingly demonstrated to the entire planet the courage to take charge and the fortitude to shape history and, of course, the power to transcend personal tragedy. If Lindbergh promised no war, then there would be no war—for the great majority it was as simple as that.

Even worse for us than the election were the weeks following the inauguration, when the new American president traveled to Iceland to meet personally with Adolf Hitler and after two days of "cordial" talks to sign "an understanding" guaranteeing peaceful relations between Germany and the United States. There were demonstrations against the Iceland Understanding in a dozen American cities, and impassioned speeches on the floor of the House and the Senate by Democratic congressmen who'd survived the Republican landslide and who condemned Lindbergh for dealing with a murderous fascist tyrant as his equal and for accepting as their meeting place an island kingdom whose historic allegiance was to a democratic monarchy whose conquest the Nazis had already achieved—a national tragedy for Denmark, plainly deplorable to the people and their king, but one that Lindbergh's Reykjavík visit appeared tacitly to condone.

When the president returned from Iceland to Washington—a flight formation of ten large Navy patrol planes escorting the new two-engine Lockheed Interceptor that he himself piloted home—his address to the nation was a mere five sentences long. "It is now guaranteed that this great country will take no part in the war in Europe." That was how the historic message began, and this is how it was elaborated and concluded: "We will join no warring party anywhere on this globe. At the same time we will continue to arm America and to train our young men in the armed forces in the use of the most advanced military technology. The key to our invulnerability is the development of American aviation, including rocket technology. This will make our continental borders unassailable to attack from without while maintaining our strict neutrality."

Ten days later the president signed the Hawaii Understanding in Honolulu with Prince Fumimaro Konoye, premier of the Japanese imperial government, and Foreign Minister Matsuoka. As emissaries of Emperor Hirohito, the two had already signed a triple alliance with the Germans and the Italians in Berlin in September of 1940, the Japanese endorsing the "new order in Europe" established under the leadership of Italy and Germany, who in turn endorsed the "New Order in Greater

East Asia" established by Japan. The three countries further pledged to support one another militarily should any of them be attacked by a nation not engaged in the European or Sino-Japanese war. Like the Iceland Understanding, the Hawaii Understanding made the United States a party in all but name to the Axis triple alliance by extending American recognition to Japan's sovereignty in East Asia and guaranteeing that the United States would not oppose Japanese expansion on the Asian continent, including annexation of the Netherlands Indies and French Indochina. Japan pledged to recognize U.S. sovereignty on its own continent, to respect the political independence of the American commonwealth of the Philippines—scheduled to be enacted in 1946—and to accept the American territories of Hawaii, Guam, and Midway as permanent U.S. possessions in the Pacific.

In the aftermath of the Understandings, Americans everywhere went about declaiming, No war, no young men fighting and dying ever again! Lindbergh can deal with Hitler, they said, Hitler respects him because he's Lindbergh. Mussolini and Hirohito respect him because he's Lindbergh. The only ones against him, the people said, are the Jews. And certainly that was true in America. All the Jews could do was worry. Our elders on the street speculated incessantly about what they would do to us and whom we could rely on to protect us and how we might protect ourselves. The younger kids like me came home from school frightened and bewildered and even in tears because of what the older boys had been telling one another about what Lindbergh had said about us to Hitler and what Hitler had said about us to Lindbergh during their meals together in Iceland. One reason my parents decided to keep to our long-laid plans to visit Washington was to convince Sandy and me—whether or not they themselves believed it—that nothing had changed other than that FDR was no longer in office. America wasn't a fascist country and wasn't going to be, regardless of what Alvin had predicted. There was a new president and a new Congress but each was bound to follow the law as set down in the Constitution. They were Republican, they were isolationist, and among them, yes, there were anti-Semites—as indeed there were among the southerners in FDR's own party—but that was a long way from their being

Nazis. Besides, one had only to listen on Sunday nights to Winchell lashing out at the new president and "his friend Joe Goebbels" or hear him listing the sites under consideration by the Department of the Interior for building concentration camps—sites mainly located in Montana, the home state of Lindbergh's "national unity" vice president, the isolationist Democrat Burton K. Wheeler—to be assured of the fervor with which the new administration was being scrutinized by favorite reporters of my father's, like Winchell and Dorothy Thompson and Quentin Reynolds and William L. Shirer, and, of course, by the staff of *PM*. Even I now took my turn with *PM* when my father brought it home at night, and not just to read the comic strip *Barnaby* or to flip through the pages of photographs but to have in my hands documentary proof that, despite the incredible speed with which our status as Americans appeared to be altering, we were still living in a free country.

After Lindbergh was sworn into office on January 20, 1941, FDR returned with his family to their estate at Hyde Park, New York, and hadn't been seen or heard from since. Because it was as a boy in the Hyde Park house that he had first become interested in collecting stamps—when his mother, as the story went, had passed on to him her own childhood albums—I imagined him there spending all of his time arranging the hundreds of specimens that he had accumulated during his eight years in the White House. As every collector knew, no president before him had ever commissioned his postmaster general to issue so many new stamps, nor had there been another American president so intimately involved with the Post Office Department. Practically my first goal when I got my album was to accumulate all the stamps that I knew FDR had a hand in designing or had personally suggested, beginning with the 1936 three-cent Susan B. Anthony stamp commemorating the sixteenth anniversary of the women's suffrage amendment and the 1937 five-cent Virginia Dare stamp marking the birth at Roanoke three hundred and fifty years earlier of the first English child born in America. The 1934 three-cent Mother's Day stamp designed originally by FDR—and displaying in the left-hand corner the legend "In Memory and in Honor of the Mothers of America" and to the right of center the artist Whistler's celebrated portrait of his mother—was given to me in a block of four by my own mother to help get my collection going. She'd also contributed to my purchasing the seven commemorative stamps Roosevelt had approved in his first year as president, which I wanted because prominently displayed on five of them was "1933," the year I was born.

Before we went to Washington, I asked permission to take my stamp album on the trip. Out of fear that I would lose it and be heartbroken afterward, my mother at first said no but then allowed herself to be won over when I insisted on the necessity of at least having with me my president stamps—the sixteen, that is, that I owned of the 1938 set that progressed sequentially and by denomination from George Washington to Calvin Coolidge. The 1922 Arlington National Cemetery stamp and the 1923 Lincoln Memorial and Capitol Buildings stamps were far too expensive for my budget, but I nonetheless offered as another reason for taking my collection along that the three famous sites were clearly pictured in black and white on the album page reserved for them. In fact, I was afraid to leave the album at home in our empty flat because of the nightmare I'd had, afraid that either because I'd done nothing about removing the ten-cent Lindbergh airmail stamp from my collection or because Sandy had lied to our parents and his Lindbergh drawings remained intact under his bed—or because of the one filial betrayal conspiring with the other—a malignant transformation would occur in my absence, causing my unguarded Washingtons to turn into Hitlers, and swastikas to be imprinted on my National Parks.

Immediately upon entering Washington, we made a wrong turn in the heavy traffic, and while my mother was trying to read the road map and direct my father to our hotel, there appeared before us the biggest white thing I had ever seen. Atop an incline at the end of the street stood the U.S. Capitol, the broad stairs sweeping upward to the colonnade and capped by the elaborate three-tiered dome. Inadvertently, we had driven right to the very heart of American history, and whether we knew it in so many words, it was American history, delineated in its most inspirational form, that we were counting on to protect us against Lindbergh.

"Look!" my mother said, turning to Sandy and me in the back seat. "Isn't it thrilling?"

The answer, of course, was yes, but Sandy appeared to have fallen into a patriotic stupor, and I took my cue from him and let silence register my awe as well.

Just then a motorcycle policeman pulled alongside us. "What's up, Jersey?" he called through the open window.

"We're looking for our hotel," answered my father. "What's it called, Bess?"

My mother, enthralled only a moment earlier by the dwarfing majesty of the Capitol, immediately went pale, and her voice was so feeble when she tried to speak that she couldn't be heard above the traffic.

"Gotta get you folks out of here," the cop shouted. "Speak up, missus."

"The Douglas Hotel!" It was my brother eagerly calling out to him and trying to get a good look at the motorcycle. "On K Street, Officer."

"Attaboy," and he raised his arm in the air, signaling the cars behind us to stop and for ours to follow him as he made a U-turn and started in the opposite direction up Pennsylvania Avenue.

Laughing, my father said, "We're getting the royal treatment."

"But how do you know where he's taking us?" my mother asked. "Herman, what's happening?"

With the cop out front, we were headed past one big federal building after another when Sandy excitedly pointed toward a rolling lawn just to our left. "Up there!" he shouted. "The White House!" whereupon my mother began to cry.

"It isn't," she tried to explain just before we reached the hotel and the cop waved goodbye and roared away, "it isn't like living in a normal country anymore. I'm terribly sorry, children—please forgive me." But then she began to cry again.

In a little room at the rear of the Douglas there was a double bed for my parents and cots for my brother and me, and no sooner had my father tipped the bellhop who'd unlocked our door and set our bags down inside the room than our mother was her old self—or pretended as much by arranging the contents of our suitcases in the dresser and noting appreciatively that the drawers were freshly laid with lining paper.

We'd been on the road since leaving home at four in the morning and it was after one in the afternoon when we got back down to the street to look for a place to have lunch. The car was parked across from the hotel, and standing beside it was a sharp-faced little man in a double-breasted gray suit who doffed his hat and said, "My name is Taylor, folks. I am a professional guide to the nation's capital. If you don't want to be wasting time, you might want to hire someone like me. I'll drive for you so you don't get lost, I'll take you to the sights, tell you all there is to know, I'll wait and pick you up, I'll make sure you eat where the price is right and the food is tasty, and all it will cost, using your own automobile, is nine dollars a day. Here's my authorization," he said, and he unfolded a document of several pages to show to my father. "Issued by the Chamber of Commerce," he explained. "Verlin M. Taylor, sir, official D.C. guide since 1937. January 5, 1937, to be exact—the very day the Seventy-fifth U.S. Congress convened."

The two shook hands, and in his insurance man's best businesslike manner my father flipped through the guide's papers before handing them back to him. "Looks good to me," my father said, "but I don't think nine bucks a day is in the cards, Mr. Taylor, not for this family anyway."

"I appreciate that. But on your own, sir, you doing the driving and not knowing your way around and then trying to find a parking space in this city—well, you and the family won't see a half of what you'll be able to see with me, and you won't enjoy it anywhere near as much either. Why, I could drive you to a nice place to have your lunch, wait for you with the car, and then we can start right off with the Washington Monument. After that, down the Mall to the Lincoln Memorial. Washington and Lincoln. Our two greatest presidents—that's how I always like to begin. You know that Washington never did live in Washington. President Washington chose the site, he signed the bill making it the permanent seat of the government, but it was his successor, John Adams, who was the first president to move into the White House in 1800. November 1, to be exact. His wife, Abigail, joined him there two weeks later. Among the many interesting curios in the White House, there is still a celery glass owned by John and Abigail Adams."

"Well, that's something that I did not know," my father

replied, "but let me take this up with my wife." Quietly he asked her, "Can we afford this? He sure knows his oats." Our mother whispered, "But who sent him? How did he spot our car?" "That's his job, Bess—to find who's the tourists. That's how the man makes a living." My brother and I were huddled up beside them, hoping our mother would shut up and that the easy-talking guide with the pointy face and the short legs would be hired for the duration.

"What do you want?" my father said, turning to Sandy and me.

"Well, if it costs too much . . . ," Sandy began.

"Forget the cost," my father replied. "Do you like this guy or not?"

"He's a character, Dad," Sandy whispered. "He looks like one of those duck decoys. I like when he says 'to be exact.' "

"Bess," my father said, "the man is a bona fide guide to Washington, D.C. Don't believe he's ever cracked a smile but he's an alert little guy and he couldn't be more polite. Let me see if he'll take seven bucks." Here he stepped away from us, walked up to the guide, they spoke seriously for a few minutes and then, the deal struck, the two again shook hands, and my father said aloud, "Okay, let's eat!" as always teeming with energy even when there was nothing to do.

It was hard to say what was most unbelievable: my being out of New Jersey for the first time in my life, my being three hundred miles from home in the nation's capital, or our family's being chauffeured in our own automobile by a stranger called by the same surname as the twelfth president of the United States, whose profile adorned the twelve-cent red-violet stamp in the album in my lap, hinged between the blue eleven-cent Polk and the green thirteen-cent Fillmore.

"Washington," Mr. Taylor was telling us, "is divided into four sections: northwest, northeast, southeast, and southwest. With some few exceptions, the streets running north and south are numbered and the streets running east and west are lettered. Of all the existing capitals in the Western world, this city alone was developed solely to provide a home for the national government. That is what makes it different not only from London and Paris but from our own New York and Chicago."

"Did you hear that?" my father asked, looking over his

shoulder at Sandy and me. "Did you hear that, Bess, what Mr. Taylor said about why Washington is so special?"

"Yes," she said, and took my hand in hers to assure herself by assuring me that everything was now going to be all right. But I had only my one concern from the time we entered Washington until we left—preserving my stamp collection from harm.

The cafeteria where Mr. Taylor dropped us off was clean and cheap and the food as good as he'd said it would be, and when we finished our meal and headed for the street, there was our car pulling up to double-park out front. "What timing!" my father cried.

"Over the years," Mr. Taylor said, "you learn to estimate how long it takes a family to eat their lunch. Was that okay, Mrs. Roth?" he asked our mother. "Everything to your taste?"

"Very nice, thank you."

"So's everybody ready for the Washington Monument," he said, and off we drove. "You know, of course, who the monument commemorates—our first president, and in the opinion of most, our best president alongside President Lincoln."

"I'd include FDR in that list, you know. A great man, and the people of this country turned him out of office," my father said. "And just look what we got instead."

Mr. Taylor listened courteously but offered no response. "Now," he resumed, "you've all seen photos of the Washington Monument. But they don't always communicate just how impressive it is. At five hundred fifty-five feet, five and one-eighth inches above ground, it is the tallest masonry structure in the world. The new electric elevator will carry you to the top in one and a quarter minutes. Otherwise you can take a winding staircase of eight hundred and ninety-three steps to the top by foot. The view from up there has a radius of some fifteen to twenty miles. It's worth a look. There—see it?" he said. "Straight ahead."

Minutes later Mr. Taylor found a parking spot on the monument grounds and, when we left the car, trotted bandy-legged alongside us, explaining, "The monument was cleaned just a few years back for the first time. Just imagine that for a cleaning job, Mrs. Roth. They used water mixed with sand and steel-bristled brushes. Took five months and cost a hundred thousand dollars."

"Under FDR?" my father asked.

"I believe so, yes."

"And do people know?" my father asked. "Do people care? No. They want an airmail pilot running the country instead. And that's not the worst of it."

Mr. Taylor remained outside while we entered the monument. At the elevator, our mother, who again had taken hold of my hand, drew close to our father and whispered, "You mustn't talk like that."

"Like what?"

"About Lindbergh."

"That? That's just expressing my opinion."

"But you don't know who this man *is*."

"I sure do. He's an authorized guide with the documents to prove it. This is the Washington Monument, Bess, and you're telling me to keep my thoughts to myself as though the Washington Monument is situated in Berlin."

His speaking so bluntly distressed her even more, especially as the others waiting for the elevator could overhear our conversation. Turning to another of the fathers, who was standing alongside his wife and two kids, my father asked him, "Where you folks from? We're from Jersey." "Maine," the man replied. "Hear that?" my father said to my brother and me. Altogether some twenty children and adults entered the elevator, filling it up about halfway, and as the car rose through the housing of iron pillars, my father used the minute and a quarter it took to get to the top to ask the remaining families where each was from.

Mr. Taylor was waiting outside when we finished our tour. He asked Sandy and me to describe what we'd seen from the windows five hundred feet up and then he guided us on a quick walking tour around the exterior of the monument, recounting the fitful history of its construction. Next he took some pictures of the family with our Brownie box camera; then my father, over Mr. Taylor's objections, insisted on taking a picture of him with my mother, Sandy, and me with the Washington Monument as the background, and finally we got into our car and, with Mr. Taylor again at the wheel, started down the Mall for the Lincoln Memorial.

This time, while he parked, Mr. Taylor warned us that the Lincoln Memorial was like no other edifice anywhere in the world and that we should prepare ourselves to be over-whelmed. Then he accompanied us from the parking area to the great pillared building with the wide marble stairs that led us up past the columns to the hall's interior and the raised statue of Lincoln in his capacious throne of thrones, the sculpted face looking to me like the most hallowed possible amalgamation—the face of God and the face of America all in one.

Gravely my father said, "And they shot him, the dirty dogs."

The four of us stood directly at the base of the statue, which was lit so as to make everything about Abraham Lincoln seem colossally grand. What ordinarily passed for great just paled away, and there was no defense, for either an adult or a child, against the solemn atmosphere of hyperbole.

"When you think of what this country does to its greatest presidents . . ."

"Herman," my mother pleaded, "don't start."

"I'm not starting anything. This was a great tragedy. Isn't that right, boys? The assassination of Lincoln?"

Mr. Taylor came over and quietly told us, "Tomorrow we'll go to Ford's Theatre, where he was shot, and across the street to the Petersen House, to see where he died."

"I was saying, Mr. Taylor, it is the damnedest thing what this country does to its great men."

"Thank goodness we have President Lindbergh," said the voice of a woman just a few feet away. She was elderly and she was standing apart, by herself, consulting a guidebook, and her remark seemed spoken to no one and yet prompted some-how by her overhearing my father.

"Compare Lincoln to Lindbergh? Boy oh boy," my father moaned.

In fact the elderly lady was not alone but with a group of tourists, among whom was a man of about my father's age who might have been her son.

"Something bothering you?" he asked my father, assertively stepping in our direction.

"Not me," my father told him.

"Something bothering you about what the lady just said?"

"No, sir. Free country."

The stranger took a long, gaping look at my father, then my mother, then Sandy, then me. And what did he see? A trim, neatly muscled, broad-chested man five feet nine inches tall, handsome in a minor key, with soft grayish-green eyes and thinning brown hair clipped close at the temples and presenting his two ears to the world a little more comically than was necessary. The woman was slender but strong and she was tidily dressed, with a lock of her wavy dark hair over one eyebrow and roundish cheeks a little rouged and a prominent nose and chunky arms and shapely legs and slim hips and the lively eyes of a girl half her age. In both adults a surfeit of prudence and a surfeit of energy, and with the couple two boys still pretty much all soft surfaces, young children of youthful parents, keenly attentive and in good health and incorrigible only in their optimism.

And the conclusion the stranger drew from his observations he demonstrated with a mocking movement of the head. Then, hissing noisily so as to mislead no one about his assessment of us, he returned to the elderly lady and their sightseeing party, walking slowly off with a rolling gait that seemed, along with the silhouette of his broad back, intended to register a warning. It was from there that we heard him refer to my father as "a loudmouth Jew," followed a moment later by the elderly lady declaring, "I'd give anything to slap his face."

Mr. Taylor led us quickly away to a smaller hall just off the main chamber where there was a tablet inscribed with the Gettysburg Address and a mural whose theme was the Emancipation.

"To hear words like that in a place like this," said my father, his choked voice quivering with indignation. "In a shrine to a man like this!"

Meanwhile Mr. Taylor, pointing to the painting, said, "See there? An angel of truth is freeing a slave."

But my father could see nothing. "You think you'd hear that here if Roosevelt was president? People wouldn't dare, they wouldn't dream, in Roosevelt's day . . . ," my father said. "But now that our great ally is Adolf Hitler, now that the best friend of the president of the United States is Adolf Hitler—

why, now they think they can get away with anything. It's disgraceful. It starts with the White House . . ."

Whom was he talking to other than me? My brother was trailing after Mr. Taylor, asking about the mural, and my mother was trying to prevent herself from saying or doing anything, struggling against the very emotions that had overpowered her earlier in the car—and back then without anything like this much justification.

"Read that," my father said, alluding to the tablet bearing the Gettysburg Address. "Just read it. 'All men are created equal.'"

"Herman," gasped my mother, "I can't go on with this."

We came back out into the daylight and gathered together on the top step. The tall shaft of the Washington Monument was a half mile away, at the other end of the reflecting pool that lay at the base of the terraced approach to the Lincoln Memorial. There were elm trees planted all around. It was the most beautiful panorama I'd ever seen, a patriotic paradise, the American Garden of Eden spread before us, and we stood huddled together there, the family expelled.

"Listen," my father said, pulling my brother and me close to him, "I think it's time we all had a nap. It's been a long day for everybody. I say we go back to the hotel and get some rest for an hour or two. What do you say, Mr. Taylor?"

"Up to you, Mr. Roth. After supper I thought the family might enjoy a tour in the car of Washington by night, with the famous monuments all lit up."

"Now you're talkin'," my father told him. "Sound good, Bess?" But my mother wasn't so easy to cheer up as Sandy and I. "Honey," my father told her, "we ran into a screwball. Two screwballs. We might have gone up to Canada and run into somebody just as bad. We're not going to let that ruin our trip. Let's have a nice rest, all of us, and Mr. Taylor will wait for us, and we'll go on from there. Look," he then said, with a sweep of his outstretched arm. "This is something every American should see. Turn around, boys. Take one last look at Abraham Lincoln."

We did as he instructed but it was impossible any longer to feel the raptures of patriotism turning me inside out. As we began the long descent down the marble staircase, I heard some kids behind us asking their parents, "Is that really him? Is he buried there under all that stuff?" My mother was directly beside me on the stairs, trying to act like someone whose panic wasn't running wild within her, and suddenly I felt that it had fallen to me to hold her together, to become all at once a courageous new creature with something of Lincoln himself clinging to him. But all I could do when she offered me a hand was to take it and clutch it like the unripened being I was, a boy whose stamp collection still represented nine-tenths of his knowledge of the world.

In the car, Mr. Taylor plotted the rest of our day. We'd go back to the hotel, nap, and at quarter to six he'd come to pick us up and drive us to dinner. We could return to the cafeteria near Union Station where we'd had our lunch, or he could recommend a couple of other popular-priced restaurants whose quality he could vouch for. And after dinner, he'd take us on the tour of Washington by night.

"Nothing fazes you, does it, Mr. Taylor?" my father said.

He replied only with a noncommittal nod.

"Where you from?" my father asked him.

"Indiana, Mr. Roth."

"Indiana. Imagine that, boys. And what's your hometown out there?" my father asked him.

"Didn't have one. My father's a mechanic. Fixed farm machinery. Moved all the time."

"Well," said my father, for reasons that can't have been clear to Mr. Taylor, "I take my hat off to you, sir. You should be proud of yourself."

Again, Mr. Taylor gave only a nod: he was a no-nonsense man in a tight suit and with something decidedly military about his efficiency and his bearing—like a hidden person, except there was nothing to hide, everything impersonal about him being plainly visible. Voluble talking about Washington, D.C., close-mouthed about everything else.

When we got back to the hotel, Mr. Taylor parked the car and accompanied us in as though he were not just our guide but our chaperone, and a good thing it was, because inside the lobby of the small hotel we discovered our four suitcases standing beside the front desk.

The new man at the desk introduced himself as the manager.

When my father asked what our bags were doing downstairs, the manager said, "Folks, I have to apologize. Had to pack these up for you. Our afternoon clerk made a mistake. The room he gave you was being held for another family. Here's your deposit." And he handed my father an envelope containing a ten-dollar bill.

"But my wife wrote you people. You wrote us back. We had a reservation months ago. That's why we sent the deposit. Bess, where's the copies of the letters?"

She pointed to the bags.

"Sir," said the manager, "the room is occupied and there are no vacancies. We will not charge you for what use you all made of the room today or for the bar of soap that is missing."

"Missing?" Just the word to send him right off the rails. "Are you saying we *stole* it?"

"No, sir, I am not. Perhaps one of the children took the soap as a souvenir. No harm done. We're not going to haggle about something so small or start looking through their pockets for the soap."

"What is the meaning of this!" my father demanded to know, and under the manager's nose pounded his fist on the front desk.

"Mr. Roth, if you're going to make a scene here . . ."

"Yes," my father said, "I am going to make a scene till I find out what's up with that room!"

"Well, then," replied the manager, "I have no choice but to phone the police."

Here my mother—who was holding my brother and me around the shoulders, shielding us alongside her and at a safe distance from the desk—called my father's name, trying to prevent him from going further. But it was too late for that. It always had been. Never could he have consented to quietly occupying the place that the manager wished to assign him.

"This is that goddamn Lindbergh!" my father said. "All you little fascists are in the saddle now!"

"Shall I call the District police, sir, or will you take your bags and your family and leave immediately?"

"Call the police," my father replied. "You do that."

There were now five or six guests aside from us in the lobby.

They'd entered while the argument was under way and they were lingering to find out what was going to come of it.

It was then that Mr. Taylor stepped up to my father's side and said, "Mr. Roth, you are perfectly in the right, but the police are the wrong solution."

"No, that is the *right* solution. Call the police," my father repeated to the manager. "There are laws in this country against people like you."

The manager reached for the phone, and while he dialed, Mr. Taylor went over to our bags, swept up two in either hand, and carried them out of the hotel.

My mother said, "Herman, it's over. Mr. Taylor took the bags."

"No, Bess," he said bitterly. "I've had enough of their guff. I want to talk to the police."

Mr. Taylor reentered the lobby on the run and without stopping bore down on the desk, where the manager was completing his call. In a lowered voice, he spoke only to my father. "There is a nice hotel not very far away. I telephoned them from the booth outside. They have a room for you. It's a nice hotel on a nice street. Let's drive over there and get the family registered."

"Thank you, Mr. Taylor. But right now we are waiting for the police. I want them to remind this man of the words in the Gettysburg Address that I read carved up there just today."

The people watching all smiled at one another when my father mentioned the Gettysburg Address.

I whispered to my brother, "What happened?"

"Anti-Semitism," he whispered back.

From where we were standing we saw the two policemen when they arrived on their motorcycles. We watched them cut their engines and come into the hotel. One of them stationed himself just inside the door, where he could keep an eye on everybody while the other approached the front desk and beckoned the manager over to where the two of them could speak confidentially.

"Officer—" my father said.

The policeman spun around and said, "I can attend to only one party to a dispute at a time, sir," and resumed talking with the manager, his chin cupped thoughtfully in one hand.

My father turned to us. "Got to be done, boys." To my mother he said, "There's nothing to worry about."

Having finished his discussion with the manager, the policeman now came around to talk to my father. He didn't smile as he had intermittently while standing and listening to the manager, but he spoke nonetheless without a trace of anger and in a tone that seemed friendly at first. "What's the problem, Roth?"

"We sent a deposit for a room at this hotel for three nights. We received a letter confirming everything. My wife has the paperwork in our bags. We get here today, we register, we occupy the room and unpack, we go out to sightsee, and when we come back we're evicted because the room was reserved for somebody else."

"And the problem?" the cop asked.

"We're a family of four, Officer. We drove all the way from New Jersey. You can't just throw us into the street."

"But," said the cop, "if somebody else reserves a room—"

"But there is nobody else! And if there was, why should we take a back seat to them?"

"But the manager returned your deposit. He even packed up your belongings for you."

"Officer, you're not understanding me. Why should our reservation take a back seat to theirs? I was with my family at the Lincoln Memorial. They have the Gettysburg Address up on the wall. You know what the words are that are written there? 'All men are created equal.' "

"But that doesn't mean all hotel reservations are created equal."

The policeman's voice carried to the bystanders at the edge of the lobby; unable any longer to control themselves, some of them laughed aloud.

My mother left Sandy and me standing alone in order to step forward now and intervene. She had been waiting for a moment when she wouldn't make things worse, and, despite her rapid breathing, seemed to believe this was it. "Dear, let's just go," she beseeched my father. "Mr. Taylor found us a room nearby."

"No!" my father cried, and he threw off the hand with which

she had tried to snatch his arm. "This policeman knows why we were evicted. He knows, the manager knows, everybody in this lobby knows."

"I think you ought to listen to your wife," the cop said. "I think you ought to do what she tells you, Roth. Leave the premises." Jerking his head in the direction of the door, he said, "And before you wear out my patience."

There was more resistance in my father, but there was still some sanity in him as well, and he was able to understand that his argument had run out of interest to anyone other than himself. We left the hotel with everybody watching us. The only one to speak was the other cop. From where he'd stationed himself just beside the potted plant in the entranceway, he nodded amiably and, as we approached, put a hand out to muss my hair. "How you doin', young fella?" "Good," I replied. "Whattaya got there?" "My stamps," I said, but just kept going before he could ask to see my collection and I had to show it to him to avoid arrest.

Mr. Taylor was waiting on the sidewalk outside. My father said to him, "That has never happened to me before in my life. I'm out among people all the time, people from all backgrounds, from all walks of life, and never . . ."

"The Douglas has changed hands," Mr. Taylor said. "This is a new ownership."

"But we had friends who stayed there and were a hundred percent satisfied," my mother told him.

"Well, Mrs. Roth, it's changed hands. But I've got you a room at the Evergreen, and everything is going to work out fine."

Just then there was the loud roar of a low-flying plane passing over Washington. Down the street where some people were out walking, they stopped and one of the men raised his arms to the sky, as though, in June, it had begun to snow.

Sandy, who could recognize just about anything flying from its silhouette, knowledgeable Sandy pointed and cried, "It's the Lockheed Interceptor!"

"It's President Lindbergh," Mr. Taylor explained. "Every afternoon about this time he takes a little spin along the Potomac. Flies up to the Alleghenies, then down along the Blue Ridge Mountains, and on out to the Chesapeake Bay. People look forward to it."

"It's the world's fastest plane," my brother said. "The Germans' Messerschmitt 110 flies three hundred and sixty-five miles an hour—the Interceptor flies five hundred miles an hour. It can outmaneuver any fighter in the world."

We all watched along with Sandy, who was unable to conceal his enchantment with the very Interceptor that the president had flown to and from Iceland for his meeting with Hitler. The plane climbed steeply with tremendous force before disappearing into the sky. Down the street, the people out walking burst into applause, somebody shouted "Hurray for Lindy!" and then they continued on their way.

At the Evergreen, my mother and father slept together in one single bed and Sandy and I in the other. Twin beds were the best Mr. Taylor had been able to locate on such short notice, but after what had happened at the Douglas nobody complained—either that the beds weren't exactly made for rest or that the room was smaller even than our first accommodations or that the matchbox bathroom, heavily doused though it was with disinfectant, didn't smell right—especially as we were welcomed graciously when we arrived by a cheerful woman at the front desk and our suitcases stacked on a dolly by an elderly Negro in a bellhop's uniform, a lanky man the woman called Edward B., who upon unlocking the door to the ground-floor room at the nether end of an airshaft, humorously announced, "The Evergreen Hotel welcomes the Roth family to the nation's capital!" and ushered us in as though the dimly lit crypt were a boudoir at the Ritz. My brother hadn't stopped staring at Edward B. from the time he loaded our luggage, and the next morning, before anyone else was awake, he stealthily dressed, grabbed his sketchpad, and raced to the lobby to draw him. As it happened, a different Negro bellhop was on duty, one not picturesquely grooved and crannied quite like Edward B., though from an artistic point of view no less of a find—very dark with strongly African facial features of a kind Sandy had never before gotten to draw from anything other than a photo in a back issue of *National Geographic*.

We spent most of the morning with Mr. Taylor showing us around the Capitol and Congress, and later the Supreme Court and the Library of Congress. Mr. Taylor knew the height of every dome and the dimensions of every lobby and the geographic origins of all the marble flooring and the names of the subjects and the events commemorated in every painting and mural in every government building we entered. "You are something," my father told him. "A small-town boy from Indiana. You should be on *Information Please*."

After lunch, we drove south along the Potomac into Virginia to tour Mount Vernon. "Of course, Richmond, Virginia," Mr. Taylor explained, "was the capital of the eleven southern states that left the Union to form the Confederate States of America. Many of the great battles of the Civil War were fought in Virginia. Some twenty miles due west is the Manassas National Battlefield Park. The park includes both battlefields where the Confederates routed the Union forces near the little stream of Bull Run, first under General P.G.T. Beauregard and General J. E. Johnston in July 1861, and then under General Robert E. Lee and General Stonewall Jackson in August 1862. General Lee was in command of the Army of Virginia, and the president of the Confederacy, who governed from Richmond, was Jefferson Davis, if you remember your history. To the southwest a hundred and twenty-five miles from here is Appomattox, Virginia. You know what happened in the courthouse there in April 1865. April 9, to be exact. General Lee surrendered to General U. S. Grant, thus ending the Civil War. And you all know what happened to Lincoln six days later: he was shot."

"Those dirty dogs," my father said again.

"Well, there it is," said Mr. Taylor, just as Washington's house came into view.

"Oh, it's so beautiful," my mother said. "Look at the porch. Look at the tall windows. Children, this isn't a replica—this is the real house where George Washington lived."

"And his wife, Martha," Mr. Taylor reminded her, "and his two stepchildren, whom the general doted on."

"Did he?" my mother asked. "I didn't know that. My younger son has Martha Washington on a stamp," she told him. "Show Mr. Taylor your stamp," and I immediately found it, the brown 1938 one-and-a-half-cent stamp that pictured the first president's wife in profile, her hair covered with what my mother had identified for me, when I first got the stamp, as something between a bonnet and a snood.

"Yep, that's her all right," said Mr. Taylor. "And she is also, as I'm sure you know, on a four-cent nineteen hundred and twenty-three and on an eight-cent nineteen hundred and two. And that nineteen hundred and two stamp, Mrs. Roth, that is the first stamp ever to show an American woman."

"Did you know that?" my mother asked me.

"Yes," I said, and for me all the complications of our being a Jewish family in Lindbergh's Washington simply vanished and I felt the way I felt in school when, at the start of an assembly program, you rose to your feet and sang the national anthem, giving it everything you had.

"She was a great companion to General Washington," Mr. Taylor told us. "Martha Dandridge was her maiden name. The widow of Colonel Daniel Parke Custis. Her two children were Patsy and John Parke Custis. She brought to her marriage to Washington one of the largest fortunes in Virginia."

"That's what I always tell my boys," my father said, laughing as we hadn't heard him laugh all day. "Marry like President Washington. It's as easy to love 'em rich as poor."

The visit to Mount Vernon was the happiest time we had on that trip, perhaps because of the beauty of the grounds and the gardens and the trees and of the house, commandingly situated on a bluff overlooking the Potomac; perhaps because of the unusualness to us of the furnishings, the decoration, and the wallpaper—wallpaper about which Mr. Taylor knew a million things; perhaps because we got to see from only a few feet away the four-poster bed in which Washington slept, the desk where he wrote, the swords that he wore, and the books that he owned and read; or perhaps just because we were fifteen miles from Washington, D.C., and from Lindbergh's spirit hovering over everything.

Mount Vernon was open until four-thirty, so we had plenty of time to see all the rooms and the outbuildings and to wander the grounds and then to visit the souvenir shop, where I succumbed to the temptation of a letter opener that was a four-inch pewter replica of a Revolutionary musket and bayonet. I bought it with twelve of the fifteen cents I'd been saving for our visit the next day to the stamp division of the Bureau of Engraving and Printing, while Sandy prudently bought with his savings an illustrated history of Washington's life, a book whose pictures he could use to suggest more portraits for the patriotic series stored in the portfolio under his bed.

It was the end of the day and we were off to have a drink in the cafeteria just as a low-flying plane in the distance came zooming our way. As the roar grew louder, people shouted, "It's the president! It's Lindy!" Men, women, and children all ran out onto the great front lawn and began to wave at the approaching plane, which as it crossed over the Potomac tipped its wings. "Hurray!" people shouted. "Hurray for Lindy!" It was the same Lockheed fighter we'd seen in the air over the city the previous afternoon, and we had no choice but to stand there like patriots and watch with the rest of them as it banked and flew back over George Washington's home before it turned to follow the Potomac north.

"It wasn't him—it was her!" Someone claiming to have been able to see into the cockpit had begun to spread word that the pilot of the Interceptor was the president's wife. And it could have been true. Lindbergh had taught her to fly when she was still his young bride and she'd often flown alongside him on his air trips, and so now people began telling their children that it was Anne Morrow Lindbergh whom they'd just seen flying over Mount Vernon, a historical event they would never forget. By then her audacity as a pilot of the most advanced American aircraft, combined with her demure manner as a well-bred daughter of the privileged classes and her literary gifts as the author of two published books of lyric poetry, had established her in all the polls as the nation's most admired woman.

So our perfect outing was ruined—and not so much because a recreational flight piloted by one or another of the Lindberghs happened by chance to have passed over our heads for the second day in a row but because of what the stunt, as my father called it, had inspired in everyone except us. "We knew things were bad," my father told the friends he immediately sat down to phone when we got home, "but not like this. You had to be there to see what it looked like. They live in a dream, and we live in a nightmare."

It was the most eloquent line I'd ever heard him speak, and arguably distinguished by more precision than any ever written by Lindbergh's wife.

Mr. Taylor drove us back to the Evergreen so we could wash up and rest, and promptly at five forty-five returned to drive us to the inexpensive cafeteria near the railroad station; we'd all meet up afterward, he said, to start the night tour of Washington postponed from the day before.

"Why don't you come along tonight?" my father said to him. "It must get lonely eating by yourself all the time."

"I wouldn't want to invade your privacy, Mr. Roth."

"Listen here, you're a wonderful guide, and we would enjoy it. Treat's on us."

The cafeteria was even more popular at night than it was during the day, every chair occupied and customers standing in line waiting to have their selections spooned out by the three men in white aprons and white caps who were so busy serving they didn't have time to stop and dry their perspiring faces. At our table my mother took solace in resuming her motherly mealtime role—"Darling, try not to lower your chin to the plate when you take a bite"—and our having Mr. Taylor seated beside us as if he were a relative or family friend, though not so novel an adventure as being thrown out of the Douglas Hotel, provided the opportunity to watch someone eat who'd grown up in Indiana. My father was the only one of us paying attention to the other diners, all of them laughing and smoking and diligently digging into the Frenchified evening special —roast beef au jus and pecan pie à la mode—while he sat there fingering his water glass, seemingly trying to figure out how the problems in their lives could be so unlike his own.

When he got around to expressing his thoughts—which continued to take precedence over his eating—it wasn't to one of us but to Mr. Taylor, who was just starting in on the piece of pie topped with American cheese that he'd chosen for dessert. "We are a Jewish family, Mr. Taylor. You know that by now, if you didn't already, because that's the reason we were evicted yesterday. That was a big shock," he said. "That's hard to get over just like that. It's a shock because though it's something that could have happened without this man being president, he is the president and he is no friend of the Jews. He is the friend of Adolf Hitler."

"Herman," my mother whispered, "you'll frighten the little one."

"The little one knows everything already," he said, and resumed addressing Mr. Taylor. "You ever listen to Winchell? Let me quote you Walter Winchell: 'Was there any more to their diplomatic understanding, other things they talked about, other things they agreed on? Did they reach an understanding about America's Jews—and if so, what was it?' That's the kind of guts Winchell has. Those are the words he has the guts to speak to the entire country."

Surprisingly, someone had stepped up so close to our table that he was hanging half over it—a heavyset, mustached elderly man with a white paper napkin jammed into his belt who seemed inflamed with whatever he had in mind to say. He had been eating at a nearby table and his companions there were all leaning our way, eager to hear what was coming next.

"Hey, what's doin', bud?" my father said. "Back up, will ya?"

"Winchell is a Jew," the man announced, "in the pay of the British government."

What happened next was that my father's hands rose violently from the table, as though to drive his knife and his fork upward into the stranger's holiday-goose of a belly. He hadn't to elaborate further to communicate his abhorrence, and yet the man with the mustache did not budge. The mustache wasn't a dark close-clipped little square patch like Hitler's but one conceived of in a less officious, more whimsical spirit, a conspicuously substantial white walrus mustache of the type displayed by President Taft on the light red 1938 fifty-cent stamp.

"If ever there was a case of a loudmouth Jew with too much power—" the stranger said.

"That is enough!" Mr. Taylor cried and, jumping to his feet, placed himself—undersized as he was—between the large figure looming over us and my outraged father, pinned in below by all that ludicrous bulk.

Loudmouth Jew. And for the second time in less than forty-eight hours.

Two of the aproned men from behind the serving counter had rushed out onto the floor of the cafeteria and taken hold of our assailant from either side. "This is not your corner saloon," one of them told him, "and don't you forget it, mister." At his table, they pushed him down into his chair, and then the one who'd chastised him came over to us and said, "I want you folks to fill your coffee cups as much as you like. Let me bring the boys some more ice cream. You folks just stay and finish up your supper. I am the owner, my name is Wilbur, and all the desserts you want is on the house. Let's bring you fresh ice water while we're at it."

"Thank you," my father said, speaking with the eerie impersonality of a machine. "Thank you," he repeated. "Thank you."

"Herman, please," my mother whispered, "let's just go."

"Absolutely not. No. We're finishing our food." He cleared his throat to continue. "We're touring Washington by night. We are not going home till we tour Washington by night."

The evening, in other words, was to be seen through to the end without our being frightened away. For Sandy and me that meant consuming big new dishes of ice cream, delivered to our table by one of the countermen.

It took a few minutes for the cafeteria to come alive again with the squeaking of chairs and the rattle of cutlery and the light tinkle of plates, if not yet the full dinnertime clamor.

"Would you like more coffee?" my father said to my mother. "You heard the owner—he wants you to fill your cup."

"No," she murmured, "no more."

"And you, Mr. Taylor—coffee?"

"Nope, I'm fine."

"So," my father said to Mr. Taylor—stiffly, lamely, but beginning again to push back at everything awful that was surging in. "What kind of job did you do before this one? Or have you always been a guide in Washington?"

And it was here that we heard once again from the man who'd stepped up to inform us that, like Benedict Arnold before him, Walter Winchell had sold out to the British. "Oh, don't you worry," he was assuring his friends, "the Jews will find out soon enough."

In all that quiet there was no mistaking what he'd said, especially as he hadn't bothered to modulate the taunt in any way. Half the diners didn't even look up, pretending to have heard nothing, but more than a few twisted round to look right at the offending objects.

I'd seen tarring and feathering only once, in a Western movie, but I thought, "We are going to be tarred and feathered," envisioning all our humiliation sticking to the skin like a coat of thick filth that you could never get off.

My father was stalled for a moment, having to decide once again whether to attempt to control the event or give in to it. "I was asking Mr. Taylor," he suddenly said to my mother while taking her hands in both of his, "about what he did before being a guide." And he looked at her like someone casting a spell, someone whose art is to prevent your will from being free of his and keep you from acting on your own.

"Yes," she said, "I heard." And then, her anguish once again filling her with tears, she nonetheless drew herself up erect in her seat and said to Mr. Taylor, "Yes, please tell us."

"Keep eating your ice cream, boys," my father said, reaching out and patting our forearms until we looked him right in the eye. "Is it good?"

"Yes," we said.

"Well, you just keep eating and take your time." He smiled to make us smile, and then said to Mr. Taylor, "The job before this one, your old job—what was it you did again, sir?"

"I was a college teacher, Mr. Roth."

"Is that right?" my father said. "Hear that, boys? You're eating your dinner with a college teacher."

"A college history teacher," added Mr. Taylor for the sake of accuracy.

"Should have known," my father admitted.

"Little college in northwest Indiana," Mr. Taylor told the four of us. "When they shut half the place down in '32, that was it for me."

"And so what'd you do then?" my father asked.

"Well, you can imagine. What with unemployment and all the strikes, I did a little of everything. Harvested mint up in the Indiana mucklands. Packed meat for the slaughterhouse in Hammond. Packed soap for Cudahy in East Chicago. Worked a year for Real Silk Hosiery Mills in Indianapolis. Even worked a stint at Logansport, at the mental hospital there, worked as an orderly for people suffering mental diseases. Hard times finally washed me up here."

"And what was the name of that college where you taught?" my father asked.

"Wabash."

"Wabash? Well," said my father, soothed by the very sound of the word, "everybody has heard of that."

"Four hundred and twenty-six students? I'm not so sure they have. What everybody has heard of is something that one of our distinguished graduates once said, though they don't necessarily know him for being a Wabash man. They know him for being U.S. vice president, 1912 to 1920. That is our two-term vice president Thomas Riley Marshall."

"Sure," my father said. "Vice President Marshall, the Democratic governor of Indiana. Vice president under another great Democrat, Woodrow Wilson. Man of dignity, President Wilson. It was President Wilson," he said, after two days of tutelage under Mr. Taylor, himself in the mood now to elucidate, "who had the courage to appoint Louis D. Brandeis to the Supreme Court. First Jewish member ever of the Supreme Court. You know that, boys?"

We did—it was hardly the first time he'd told us. It was only the first time he'd told us in a booming voice in a cafeteria like this one in Washington, D.C.

Sailing on, Mr. Taylor said, "And what the vice president said has been famous nationwide ever since. One day, in the United States Senate—while he was presiding over a Senate debate—he said to the senators there, 'What this country needs,' he said, 'is a really good five-cent cigar.'"

My father laughed—that was indeed a folksy observation that had won the heart of his whole generation and that even Sandy and I knew through his repeating it to us. So he laughed genially, and then, to further astonish not only his family but probably everyone in the cafeteria, to whom he'd already extolled Woodrow Wilson for appointing a Jew to the Supreme Court, he proclaimed, "What this country needs now is a new president."

No riot ensued. Nothing. Indeed, by not quitting he appeared almost to have won the day.

"And isn't there a Wabash River?" my father next asked Mr. Taylor.

"Longest tributary of the Ohio. Runs four hundred and seventy-five miles clear across the state east to west."

"And there is a song, too," my father remembered almost dreamily.

"Right you are," replied Mr. Taylor. "A very famous song. Maybe as famous as 'Yankee Doodle' itself. Written by Paul Dresser in 1897. 'On the Banks of the Wabash, Far Away.'"

"Of course!" cried my father.

"The favorite song," said Mr. Taylor, "of our Spanish-American War soldiers in 1898 and adopted as the state song of Indiana in 1913. March 4, to be exact."

"Sure, sure, I know that one," my father told him.

"I expect every American does," Mr. Taylor said.

And all at once, in a brisk cadence, my father began to sing it, and strongly enough for everyone in the cafeteria to hear. "'Through the sycamores the candlelights are gleaming . . .'"

"Good," said our guide with admiration, "very good," and outright bewitched by my father's baritone bravura, the solemn little encyclopedia smiled at last.

"My husband," said my dry-eyed mother, "has a lovely singing voice."

"That he does," said Mr. Taylor, and though there was no applause—other than from Wilbur, back of the serving counter—here we abruptly got up to go before we outstayed our tiny triumph and the man with the presidential mustache went berserk.

3

Following Christians

O N JUNE 22, 1941, the Hitler-Stalin Non-Aggression Pact —signed two years earlier by the two dictators only days before invading and dividing up Poland—was broken without warning when Hitler, having already overrun continental Europe, dared to undertake the conquest of the enormous landmass that stretched from Poland across Asia to the Pacific by staging a massive assault to the east against Stalin's troops. That evening, President Lindbergh addressed the nation from the White House about Hitler's colossal expansion of the war and astonished even my father by his candid praise for the German Führer. "With this act," the president declared, "Adolf Hitler has established himself as the world's greatest safeguard against the spread of Communism and its evils. This is not to minimize the effort of imperial Japan. Dedicated as the Japanese are to modernizing Chiang Kai-shek's corrupt and feudal China, they are equally dedicated to rooting out the fanatical Chinese Communist minority, whose aim is to seize control of that vast country and, like the Bolsheviks in Russia, to turn China into a Communist prison camp. But it is Hitler to whom the entire world must be grateful tonight for striking at the Soviet Union. If the German army is successful in its struggle against Soviet Bolshevism—and there is every reason to believe that it will be—America will never have to face the threat of a voracious Communist state imposing its pernicious system on the rest of the world. I can only hope that the internationalists still serving in the United States Congress recognize that if we had allowed our nation to be dragged into this world war on the side of Great Britain and France, we would now find our great democracy allied with the evil regime of the USSR. Tonight the German army may well be waging the war that would otherwise have had to be fought by American troops."

Our troops were at the ready, however, and would be, the president reminded his countrymen, for a long time to come because of the peacetime draft established by Congress at his request, twenty-four months of compulsory military training for eighteen-year-olds, followed by eight years on call in the reserves, which would contribute enormously to fulfilling his dual goal of "keeping America out of all foreign wars and of keeping all foreign wars out of America." "An independent destiny for America"—that was the phrase Lindbergh repeated some fifteen times in his State of the Union speech and again at the close of his address on the night of June 22. When I asked my father to explain what the words meant—absorbed by the headlines and weighed down by all my anxious thoughts, I was more and more asking what everything meant—he frowned and said, "It means turning our back on our friends. It means making friends with their enemies. You know what it means, son? It means destroying everything that America stands for."

Under the auspices of Just Folks—described by Lindbergh's newly created Office of American Absorption as "a volunteer work program introducing city youth to the traditional ways of heartland life"—my brother left on the last day of June 1941 for a summer "apprenticeship" with a Kentucky tobacco farmer. Because he'd never been away from home before, and because the family had never lived with such uncertainty before, and because my father objected strenuously to what the OAA's existence implied about our status as citizens—and also because Alvin, already off serving with the Canadian army, had become a perpetual source of concern—Sandy's was an emotional leave-taking. What had given Sandy strength to resist our parents' arguments against his participating in Just Folks—and planted the idea to apply in the first place—was the support he'd received from my mother's vivid younger sister, Evelyn, now executive assistant to Rabbi Lionel Bengelsdorf, who'd been appointed by the new administration to serve as the first director of the OAA office for the state of New Jersey. The announced purpose of the OAA was to implement programs "encouraging America's religious and national minorities to become further incorporated into the larger society," though by the spring of 1941 the only minority the OAA appeared to take a serious interest in encouraging was ours. It was the intention of Just Folks to remove hundreds of Jewish boys between the ages of twelve and eighteen from the cities where they lived and attended school and put them to work for eight weeks as field hands and day laborers with farm families hundreds of miles from their homes. Notices extolling the new summer program had been posted on bulletin boards at Chancellor and at Weequahic, the high school just next door, where the student population, like ours, was nearly one hundred percent Jewish. One day in April, a representative from the New Jersey OAA had come to talk to the boys twelve and over about the program's mission, and that evening Sandy showed up at the dinner table with an application blank that required a parent's signature.

"Do you understand what this program is actually trying to do?" my father asked Sandy. "Do you understand why Lindbergh wants to separate boys like you from their families and ship them out to the sticks? Do you have any idea what's behind all this?"

"But this doesn't have anything to do with anti-Semitism, if that's what you think. You have one thing on your mind and one thing only. This is just a great opportunity, that's all."

"Opportunity for what?"

"To live on a farm. To go to Kentucky. To draw all the things there. Tractors. Barns. Animals. All kinds of animals."

"But they're not sending you all that way to draw animals," my father told him. "They're sending you there to fetch the slops for the animals. They're sending you there to spread manure. You'll be so bushed by the end of the day that you won't be able to stand on your feet, let alone draw a picture of an animal."

"And your hands," my mother said. "There's barbed wire on farms. There are machines with sharp blades. You could injure your hands, and then where would you be? You'd never draw again. I thought you were going to take classes at Arts High this summer. You were going to take drawing with Mr. Leonard."

"I can always do that—this is seeing America!"

The next night Aunt Evelyn came to dinner, invited by my mother for the hours Sandy was planning to be at a friend's house doing his homework; that way he wouldn't be around to witness the argument that was certain to flare up between Aunt Evelyn and my father on the subject of Just Folks, and that did indeed erupt upon her entering the house to announce that she would be taking care of Sandy's application the moment it reached the office. "Don't do us any favors," said my unsmiling father.

"You mean to tell me you're not letting him go?"

"Why should I? Why would I?" he asked her.

"Why on earth wouldn't you," Aunt Evelyn replied, "unless you're another Jew afraid of his shadow."

Their disagreement only grew more passionate during dinner, my father maintaining that Just Folks was the first step in a Lindbergh plan to separate Jewish children from their parents, to erode the solidarity of the Jewish family, and Aunt Evelyn intimating none too gently that the greatest fear of a Jew like her brother-in-law was that his children might escape winding up as narrow-minded and frightened as he was.

Alvin was the renegade on my father's side, Evelyn was the maverick on my mother's, a substitute elementary school teacher in the Newark system who'd been active several years earlier in founding the left-wing, largely Jewish Newark Teachers Union, whose few hundred members were competing with a more staid, apolitical teachers' association to negotiate contracts with the city. Evelyn was just thirty in 1941, and until two years before, when my maternal grandmother died of heart failure after a decade as a coronary invalid, it was Evelyn who'd cared for her in the tiny top-floor apartment of a two-and-a-half-family house that mother and daughter shared on Dewey Street, not far from Hawthorne Avenue School, where Evelyn usually subbed. On the days when a neighbor wasn't free to stop by to keep an eye on our grandmother, my mother would take the bus over to Dewey Street and look after her until Evelyn got home from work, and when Evelyn went to New York to see a play with her intellectual friends on a Saturday night, either our grandmother would be driven to our house by my father to spend the evening with us or my mother would return to Dewey Street to tend to her there. Many nights Aunt Evelyn never made it home from New York—even when she'd planned to return before midnight—and so my mother would be forced to spend the night away from her husband and children. And then there were the afternoons Evelyn didn't get back until hours after school was over, because of a long-standing off-and-on love affair with a substitute teacher from North Newark, like Evelyn a forceful union advocate, and unlike Evelyn married, Italian, and the parent of three children.

My mother would always contend that if Evelyn hadn't got waylaid at home for all those years nursing their invalid mother, she would have settled down to marry after getting her teaching certificate and never have ended up falling in and out of "unsavory" relationships with married men who were her fellow teachers. Her large nose didn't prevent people from calling Aunt Evelyn "striking," and it was true, as my mother observed, that when tiny Evelyn walked into a room—a vivacious brunette with a perfect, if miniaturized, womanly silhouette, enormous dark eyes slanted like a cat's, and crimson lipstick guaranteed to dazzle—everyone turned to look, the women as well as the men. Her hair was lacquered to a metallic luster and pulled back in a chignon, her eyebrows were dramatically plucked, and when she went off to sub, she donned a brightly colored skirt with matching high-heeled shoes and a broad white belt and a semisheer, pastel-colored blouse. My father considered her apparel in poor taste for a schoolteacher, and so did the principal at Hawthorne, but my mother, who, wrongly or not, reproached herself for Evelyn's having had to "sacrifice her youth" caring for their mother, was incapable of judging her sister's boldness harshly, even when Evelyn resigned from teaching, quit the union, and, seemingly without a qualm, abandoned her political loyalties to work for Rabbi Bengelsdorf in Lindbergh's OAA.

It would be several months before it occurred to my parents that Aunt Evelyn was the rabbi's mistress and had been ever since he'd met her at a reception following his speech to the Newark Teachers Union on "The Classroom Development of American Ideals"—and they realized it only then because, on leaving the New Jersey OAA to assume the job of federal director at the national headquarters in Washington, Bengelsdorf announced to the Newark papers news of his engagement, at age sixty-three, to his thirty-one-year-old firebrand of an assistant.

When he first ran off to fight Hitler, Alvin imagined that the quickest way to see action would be aboard one of the Canadian destroyers that were protecting the merchant marine ships carrying supplies to Great Britain. Stories in the newspaper regularly reported the sinking by German submarines of one or more of the Canadian ships in the North Atlantic, sometimes as close to the mainland as the coastal fishing waters of Newfoundland—an especially ominous development for the British because Canada had become virtually their only source of arms, food, medicine, and machinery once the Lindbergh administration overturned the aid legislation enacted by the Roosevelt Congress. In Montreal Alvin met a young American defector who told him to forget about the navy—it was the Canadian commandos who were in the thick of things, carrying out nighttime raids on the Nazi-occupied continent, sabotaging utilities vital to the Germans, blowing up ammunition arsenals, and, alongside British commandos and in concert with underground European resistance movements, destroying dock and shipyard facilities up and down the coastline of western Europe. When he recounted for Alvin all the many ways the commandos taught you to kill a man, Alvin dropped his original plans and went to join up. Like the rest of the Canadian armed forces, the commandos were eager to accept qualified American citizens into their ranks, and so, after sixteen weeks of training, Alvin was assigned to an active commando unit and shipped to a secret staging area in the British Isles. And that was when we heard from him finally, receiving a six-word letter that read, "Off to fight. See you soon."

It was just days after Sandy, all on his own, took the overnight train to Kentucky that my parents received a second letter, this one not from Alvin but from the War Department in Ottawa, advising Alvin's designated next of kin that their nephew had been wounded in action and was in a convalescent hospital in Dorset, England. After the dinner dishes were cleared that night, my mother sat back down at the kitchen table with a fountain pen and the box of monogrammed stationery reserved for important correspondence. My father seated himself across from her, and I stood looking over her shoulder to observe how her cursive script uniformly unfurled because of the handwriting mechanics she'd employed as a secretary and taught early on to Sandy and me—the third and fourth fingers positioned to support the hand, and the forefinger nearer the pen point than the thumb. She spoke each sentence aloud before writing it down in case my father wanted to change or add anything.

Dearest Alvin,

This morning we received a letter from the Canadian government telling us that you were wounded in action and that you're in a hospital in England. The letter contained nothing more specific other than a mailing address for you.

Right now we are at the kitchen table, Uncle Herman, Philip, and Aunt Bess. We all want to know everything about your condition. Sandy is away for the summer, but we'll write him about you immediately.

Is there any chance you will be sent back to Canada? If so, we would drive there to see you. In the meantime, we send you our love and hope you will write us from England. Please write or ask someone to write for you. Whatever you want us to do, we will do.

Again, we love you and we miss you.

To this message we appended our three signatures. It was nearly a month before we got a response.

Dear Mr. and Mrs. Roth:

Corporal Alvin Roth received your letter of July 5. I am the senior nurse on his unit and I read the letter to him several times to be sure he understood who it was from and what it said.

Right now Cpl. Roth is not communicative. He lost his left leg below the knee and was seriously wounded in his right foot. The right foot is healing and that wound should not leave him impaired. When his left leg is ready, he will be fitted with a prosthesis and taught to walk with it.

This is a dark moment for Cpl. Roth, but I wish to assure you that in time he should be able to resume his life as a civilian with no significant physical problems. This hospital is limited to amputees and burn cases. I have seen many men undergo the same psychological difficulties as Cpl. Roth, but most of them come through, and I strongly believe that Cpl. Roth will too.

Sincerely,
Lt. A. F. Cooper

Once a week, Sandy wrote saying he was fine and reporting how hot it was in Kentucky and concluding with a sentence about life on the farm—something like "There's a bumper crop of blackberries" or "The steer are being driven crazy by flies" or "Today they're cutting alfalfa" or "Topping began," whatever that might mean. Then, below his signature—and perhaps to prove to his father that he had stamina enough to do his artwork even after working all day on the farm—he'd sketch a picture of a pig ("This pig," he noted, "weighs over three hundred pounds!") or a dog ("Suzie, Orin's dog—her specialty is scaring snakes") or a lamb ("Mr. Mawhinney took 30 lambs to the stockyards yesterday") or of a barn ("They just painted this place with creosote. P-U!"). Usually far more space was taken up by the drawing than by the message, and, to my mother's chagrin, the questions she would raise in her own weekly letter, asking if he needed clothes or medicine or money, rarely got answered. Of course I knew my mother cared for each of her children with equal devotion, but not till Sandy was gone to Kentucky did I learn how much he meant to her as someone distinct from his little brother. Though she wasn't about to grow despondent over being separated for eight weeks from a son already thirteen, all summer long there was an undercurrent of the forlorn noticeable in certain gestures and facial expressions, particularly at the kitchen table when the fourth chair drawn up for dinner remained empty night after night.

Aunt Evelyn was with us when we went to Penn Station to pick Sandy up on the late-August Saturday that he arrived back in Newark. She was the last one my father wanted coming along, but just as when, against his own inclinations, he'd eventually allowed Sandy to apply for Just Folks and accept the summer job in Kentucky, he had yielded to his sister-in-law's influence over his son to avoid making more difficult a predicament whose ultimate danger still wasn't entirely clear.

At the station, Aunt Evelyn was the first of us to recognize Sandy when he stepped from the train onto the platform, some ten pounds heavier than when he'd left and his brown hair blondish from his working in the fields under the summer sun. He'd grown a couple of inches as well, so that his pants were now nowhere near his shoe tops, and altogether my impression was of my brother in disguise.

"Hey, farmer," Aunt Evelyn called, "over here!" and Sandy came loping in our direction, swinging his bags at his sides and sporting an outdoorsy new walk to go with the new physique.

"Welcome home, stranger," my mother said, and, with the air of a young girl, happily threw her arms around his neck, and the words she murmured into his ear ("Was there ever a boy so handsome?") caused him to complain, "Ma! Cut it out!" which, of course, handed the rest of the family a big laugh. We all hugged him, and, standing beside the train he'd boarded seven hundred fifty miles away, he flexed his biceps so I could feel them. In the car, when he began answering our questions, we heard how husky his voice had become, and we heard for the first time the drawl and the twang.

Aunt Evelyn was triumphant. Sandy talked about the last job he'd had out in the fields— going around with Orin, one of the Mawhinneys' sons, picking up the tobacco leaves broken off during harvesting. They were usually the lowest on the plant, Sandy said, they were called "flyings," and it so happened they were top-grade tobacco and fetched the highest price at the market. But the men doing the cutting on a tobacco patch of twenty-five acres can't bother about the leaves on the ground, he told us, as they have to cut some three thousand sticks of tobacco a day in order to get everything housed in the curing barn in two weeks. "Whoa, whoa—what's a 'stick,' dear?" Aunt Evelyn asked, and gladly he obliged her with the lengthiest possible explanation. And so what's a curing barn, she asked, what's topping, what's suckering, what's worming— and the more questions Aunt Evelyn came up with, the more authoritative Sandy became, so that even when we got to Summit Avenue and my father pulled the car into the alleyway, he was still going on about raising tobacco as though expecting us all to head right for the backyard and start preparing the weedy patch of dirt next to the garbage cans for Newark's first crop ever of white burley. "It's the sweetened burley in Luckys," he informed us, "that gives 'em the taste," and meanwhile I was itching to feel his biceps again, which to me were no less extraordinary than the regional accent, if that's what it was— he said "cain't" for "can't" and "rimember" for "remember" and "fahr" for "fire" and "agin" for "again" and "awalkin'" and "atalkin'" for "walking" and "talking," and whatever you wanted to call that concoction of English, it wasn't what we natives of New Jersey spoke.

Aunt Evelyn was triumphant but my father was stymied, said almost nothing, and at the dinner table that evening looked especially glum when Sandy got around to reporting on what a paragon Mr. Mawhinney was. First off, Mr. Mawhinney had graduated from the College of Agriculture at the University of Kentucky, while my father, like most other Newark slum children before the World War, hadn't been educated beyond the eighth grade. Mr. Mawhinney owned not just one farm but three—the lesser two rented to tenants—land that had been in his family going back nearly to the days of Daniel Boone, and my father owned nothing more impressive than a six-year-old car. Mr. Mawhinney could saddle a horse, drive a tractor, operate a thresher, ride a fertilizer drill, work a field as easily with a team of mules as with a team of oxen; he could rotate crops and manage hired men, both white and Negro; he could repair tools, sharpen plow points and mowers, put up fences, string barbed wire, raise chickens, dip sheep, de-horn cattle, slaughter pigs, smoke bacon, sugar-cure ham—and he raised watermelons that were the sweetest and juiciest Sandy had ever eaten. By cultivating tobacco, corn, and potatoes, Mr. Mawhinney was able to make a living right out of the earth and then, at Sunday dinner (where the six-foot-three-inch, two-hundred-and-thirty-pound farmer consumed more fried chicken with cream gravy than everyone else at the table combined), eat only food that he himself had raised, and all my father could do was sell insurance. It went without saying that Mr. Mawhinney was a Christian, a long-standing member of the great overpowering majority that fought the Revolution and founded the nation and conquered the wilderness and subjugated the Indian and enslaved the Negro and emancipated the Negro and segregated the Negro, one of the good, clean, hardworking Christian millions who settled the frontier, tilled the farms, built the cities, governed the states, sat in Congress, occupied the White House, amassed the wealth, possessed the land, owned the steel mills and the ball clubs and the railroads and the banks, even owned and oversaw the language, one of those unassailable Nordic and Anglo-Saxon Protestants who ran America and would always run it—generals, dignitaries, magnates, tycoons, the men who laid down the law and called the shots and read the riot act when they chose to—while my father, of course, was only a Jew.

Sandy got the news about Alvin once Aunt Evelyn had gone home. My father was at the kitchen table working on his account books preparatory to going out to make his evening collections and my mother was in the cellar with Sandy sorting through the clothes he'd brought back from Kentucky, deciding what to repair and what to throw out before putting everything else in the washtub. My mother always did immediately whatever had to be done, and she was set on disposing of his dirty clothes before she went to bed. I was down there with them, unable to let my brother out of my sight. He'd always known everything I didn't know, and he'd come back from Kentucky knowing still more.

"I have to tell you about Alvin," my mother said to him. "I didn't want to write because . . . well, I didn't want to shock you, dear." Here, having gathered herself together to make certain she wouldn't cry, she said in a low voice, "Alvin was wounded. He's in a hospital in England. He's there recovering from his wounds."

Astonished, Sandy asked, "Who wounded him?" as though she were reporting an occurrence in our neighborhood rather than in Nazi-occupied Europe, where people were being maimed, wounded, and killed all the time.

"We don't know any details," my mother said. "But it wasn't a superficial wound. I have to tell you something very sad, Sanford." And despite her attempt to keep everyone's courage up, her voice began to waver when she said, "Alvin's lost a leg."

"A leg?" There aren't many words less abstruse than "leg," but it took some doing for him to comprehend it.

"Yes. According to a letter we got from one of his nurses, his left leg below the knee." As if it might somehow soothe him, she added, "If you'd like to read it, the letter's upstairs."

"But—how will he walk?"

"They're going to fit him with an artificial leg."

"But I don't understand who wounded him. How did he get wounded?"

"Well, they were there to fight the Germans," she said, "so it must have been one of them."

Still half staving off what was half sinking in, Sandy asked, "Which leg?"

As tenderly as she could, she repeated, "The left."

"The whole leg? The whole thing?"

"No, no, no," she rushed to reassure him. "I told you, dear—below the knee."

Suddenly Sandy began to cry, and because he was so much bigger across the shoulders and through the chest and around the wrists than he'd been just last spring, because his arms were now brawny like a man's rather than stringy like a child's, I was so startled to see tears running down his deeply tanned face that I started crying too.

"Dear, it's awful," my mother said. "But Alvin is not dead. He is still alive, and now at least he's out of the war."

"*What?*" Sandy erupted. "Did you hear what you just said to me?"

"What do you mean?" she asked.

"Didn't you hear yourself? You said, 'He's out of the war.'"

"And he is. Absolutely. And because he is, he'll now come home before anything more can possibly happen."

"But why was he even *in* the war, Ma?"

"Because—"

"Because of Dad!" Sandy shouted.

"Dear, no, this isn't true," and her hand flew up to cover her mouth as though it were she who had spoken those unpardonable words. "That is not *so*," she objected. "Alvin went off to Canada without telling us. He ran away on that Friday night. You remember how terrible it was. Nobody wanted Alvin to go to war—he just went, on his own."

"But Dad wants the whole country to go to war. Well, doesn't he? Isn't that why he voted for Roosevelt?"

"Lower your voice, please."

"First you say thank God that Alvin is out of the war—"

"Lower your *voice!*" and the tension of the day now so overwhelmed her that she lost her temper, and to the boy she had so painfully missed all summer long, she snapped, "You don't know what you're talking about!"

"But you won't *listen*," he shouted. "If it wasn't for President Lindbergh—"

That name again! I would rather have heard a bomb go off than to have to hear one more time the name that was tormenting us all.

Just then my father appeared in the dim light of the landing at the top of the cellar stairs. It was probably a good thing that from where we were standing by the deep laundry sink, all we could see of him were trousers and shoes.

"He's upset about Alvin," my mother said, looking up to explain what the shouting was about. "I made a mistake." To Sandy she said, "I should never have told you tonight. It's not easy for a boy to come home from a big experience like that . . . it's never easy to go from one place to another . . . and anyway you're so tired . . . ," and then, helpless, giving herself up to her own exhaustion, she said, "The two of you, both of you, go upstairs now so I can do the wash."

And so we turned to mount the stairs and found, fortunately, that my father had already disappeared from the landing and was off in the car to make his evening collections.

In bed, one hour later. The lights are out all over the house. We whisper.

Did you really have a good time?

I had a great time.

What made it so great?

Being on a farm is great. You get to get up early in the morning, and you're outside all day, and there are all these animals. I drew a lot of animals, I'll show you my drawings. And we had ice cream every night. Mrs. Mawhinney makes it herself. There's fresh milk there.

All milk is fresh.

No, we got it right from the cow. It was still warm. We put it on the stove and we'd boil it and just take the cream off the top, and then we'd drink it.

You couldn't get sick from it?

That's why you boil it.

But you don't just drink it right out of the cow.

I tried that once but it doesn't taste so good. It's so creamy.

Did you milk a cow?

Orin showed me how to do it. It's hard to do. Orin would squirt it, and the cats would come around, and they'd try to catch the milk.

Did you have any friends?

Well, Orin's my best friend.

Orin Mawhinney?

Yeah. He's my age. He goes to school there. He works on the farm. He gets up at four o'clock in the morning. He does chores. It's not like us. He goes to school on the bus. It's about forty-five minutes on the bus, and then he comes back in the evening, and he does some more chores, and he does his homework, and he goes to bed. He gets up at four o'clock the next morning. It's hard work to be a farmer's son.

But they're rich, aren't they?

They're pretty rich.

How come you talk like that now?

Why shouldn't I? That's the way they talk in Kentucky. You should hear Mrs. Mawhinney. She's from Georgia. She makes pancakes for breakfast every morning. With bacon. Mr. Mawhinney smokes his own bacon. In a smokehouse. He knows how to.

You ate bacon every morning?

Every morning. It's delicious. And on Sundays when we got up we had pancakes and bacon and eggs. From their own chickens. The eggs—they're almost red in the middle, they're so fresh. You go and take 'em from the chickens and bring 'em in and you eat 'em right there.

Did you eat ham?

We had ham for dinner about two times a week. Mr. Mawhinney makes his own ham. He has a special family recipe. He says if a ham isn't hung up to be aged for a year he doesn't want to eat it.

Did you eat sausage?

Yeah. He makes the sausage, too. They grind it in a sausage grinder. We had sausage sometimes instead of bacon. It's good. Pork chops. They're good too. They're great. I don't really know why we don't eat it.

Because it's stuff from a pig.

So what? Why do you think farmers raise pigs? For people to look at 'em? It's like anything else you eat. You just eat it, and it's really good.

You going to keep eating it now?

Sure.

It was really hot there, though, huh?

During the day. But we'd come in at lunchtime, and we'd have tomato and mayonnaise sandwiches. With lemonade— with lots of lemonade. We'd rest inside and then we'd go back out into the fields and do whatever we had to. Weeding. Weed all afternoon. Weed the corn. Weed the tobacco. We had a vegetable garden, me and Orin, and we'd weed that. We'd work with the hired hands, and there were some Negroes, day laborers. And there's one Negro, Randolph, who is a tenant, and he rose from hired hand. He's a grade-A farmer, Mr. Mawhinney says.

Can you understand when the Negroes talk?

Sure.

Can you imitate one?

They say " 'bacca" for tobacco. They say "I 'clare." I 'clare this and I 'clare that. But they don't talk much. Mostly they work. At hog-killing time, Mr. Mawhinney has Clete and Old Henry who gut the hogs. They're Negroes, they're brothers, and they take the intestines home and eat 'em fried. Chitterlings.

Would you eat that?

Do I look like a Negro? Mr. Mawhinney says Negroes are starting to move away from the farm because they think they can earn more money in the city. Sometimes Old Henry got arrested on Saturday nights. For drinking. Mr. Mawhinney pays the fine to get him out because he needs him on Monday.

Do they have shoes?

Some. The kids are barefoot. The Mawhinneys give them their clothes when they're done with them. But they were happy.

Anybody say anything about anti-Semitism?

They don't even think about it, Philip. I was the first Jew they ever met. They told me that. But they never said anything mean. It's Kentucky. People there are really friendly.

So, are you glad to be home?

Sort of. I don't know.

You going to go back next year?

Sure.

What if Mom and Dad won't let you?

I'll go anyway.

Seemingly as a direct consequence of Sandy's having eaten bacon, ham, pork chops, and sausage, there was no containing the transformation of our lives. Rabbi Bengelsdorf was coming to dinner. Aunt Evelyn was bringing him.

"Why us?" my father said to my mother. Dinner was over, Sandy was on his bed writing to Orin Mawhinney, and I was alone with them in the living room, intent on seeing how my father was going to take the news now that everything around us was moving at once.

"She is my sister," said my mother, a touch belligerently, "he is her boss—I can't tell her no."

"I can," he said.

"You will do nothing of the sort."

"Then explain again why we deserve this great honor? The big shot has nothing more pressing than to come here?"

"Evelyn wants him to meet your son."

"That's ridiculous. Your sister has always been ridiculous. My son is in the eighth grade at Chancellor Avenue School. He spent the summer pulling weeds. This is *all* ridiculous."

"Herman, they're coming on Thursday night, and we're going to make them welcome. You may hate him, but he's not nobody."

"I know that," he said impatiently. "That's *why* I hate him."

When he walked about the house now a copy of *PM* was constantly in his hands, either rolled up like a weapon—as though he were preparing, if called upon, to go to war himself—or turned back to a page where there was something he wanted to read aloud to my mother. He was perplexed on this particular evening as to why the Germans continued to advance so easily into Russia, and so, rattling the paper in exasperation, he all at once exclaimed, "Why don't those Russians *fight*? They have planes—why don't they use them? Why doesn't anybody over there put up a fight? Hitler walks into a country, crosses the border and walks right in, and bingo, it's his. England," he announced, "is the only country in Europe to stand up to that dog. He pounds away at those English cities every single night, and they just come back and keep on fighting him with the RAF. Thank God for the men of the RAF."

"When is Hitler going to invade England?" I asked him. "Why doesn't he invade England now?"

"That was part of the deal he made with Mr. Lindbergh up in Iceland. Lindbergh wants to be the savior of mankind," my father explained to me, "and negotiate the peace that ends the war, and so after Hitler takes Russia, and after he takes the Middle East, and after he takes everything else he could possibly want, Lindbergh will call a phony peace conference—the kind that's right up the Germans' alley. The Germans will be there, and the price for world peace and no German invasion of Great Britain will be installing in England an English fascist government. Putting a fascist prime minister in Downing Street. And when the English say no, *then* Hitler will invade, and all with the consent of our president the peacemaker."

"Is that what Walter Winchell says?" I asked, thinking that all he had explained to me was just too smart for him.

"That's what *I* say," he told me, and probably that was true. The pressure of what was happening was accelerating everyone's education, my own included. "But thank God for Walter Winchell. Without him we'd be lost. He's the last person left on the radio to speak out against these dirty dogs. It's disgusting. It's worse than disgusting. Slowly but surely, there's nobody in America willing to speak out against Lindbergh's kissing Hitler's behind."

"What about the Democrats?" I asked.

"Son, don't ask me about the Democrats. I'm angry enough as it is."

My mother had me help her set the table in the dining room on Thursday evening, and then sent me to my bedroom to change into my good clothes. Aunt Evelyn and Rabbi Bengelsdorf were to arrive at seven, forty-five minutes later than we would ordinarily have finished eating in the kitchen, but seven was the earliest the rabbi could manage to get to our house because of all his official duties. This was the very traitor whom my father, usually so respectful of the Jewish clergy, had accused aloud of making "a stupid, lying speech" in behalf of Lindbergh at Madison Square Garden, the "Jewish fake," according to Alvin, who'd guaranteed Roosevelt's defeat by "koshering Lindbergh for the goyim," and so it was puzzling to witness the lengths to which we were going to feed him. I was myself instructed beforehand not to use the fresh towels in the bathroom or to go anywhere near my father's armchair, which was for the rabbi to occupy before we ate dinner.

First we all sat stiffly in the living room while my father offered the rabbi a highball or, if he preferred, a shot of schnapps, both of which Bengelsdorf declined in favor of a glass of tap water. "Newark has the best drinking water in the world," the rabbi said, and said it as he would say everything, with deep consideration. Graciously he received the glass, on a coaster, from my mother, whom I could still recall back in October running from the radio in order not to have to hear him praise Lindbergh. "You have a most agreeable house," he said to her. "Everything in its place and everything placed perfectly. It bespeaks the love of order which I myself share. I see you have a penchant for the color green."

"Forest green," said my mother, trying to smile and trying to please but speaking with difficulty and unable as yet to look his way.

"You should take great pride in your lovely home. I am honored to be a guest here."

The rabbi was quite tall, built on the order of Lindbergh, a thin, bald-headed man in a dark three-piece suit and gleaming black shoes; his erect posture alone seemed to me to express an allegiance to mankind's highest ideals. From the mellifluous southern accent I'd heard on the radio I had envisioned somebody looking far less severe, but just his eyeglasses were intimidating, in part because they were the owlish oval spectacles that pinched the nose to stay on the face, like the ones that Roosevelt wore, and in part because the very fact that he wore them—and examined you through them microscopically—made it clear that he was not a man with whom to disagree. Yet when he spoke his tone was warm, friendly, even confiding. I kept waiting for him to treat us with contempt or order us around, but all he did was to talk in that accent (which wasn't at all like Sandy's), and so softly that at times you had to hold your breath to hear how learned he was.

"And you must be the boy," he said to Sandy, "who's made us all so proud."

"I'm Sandy, sir," Sandy replied, flushing furiously. It was, to my mind, a brilliant retort to a question that another successful boy, trying to meet the sanctioned standard of modesty, might not have been able to handle with such dispatch. No, nothing could now undo Sandy, not with those muscles and that sun-bleached hair and the abundance of pig he'd stashed away without asking permission of anyone.

"And what was it like," the rabbi asked, "to work there in the Kentucky fields under the burning sun?" He said "wuhk" for "work" and "buhning" for "burning" and "theyuh" for "there," and pronounced "Kentucky" as it was spelled and not, as Sandy now did, as though the first three letters were K-i-n.

"I learned a lot, sir. I learned a lot about my country."

Aunt Evelyn visibly approved, as well she might have, since on the phone the evening before she'd fitted him out with the answer to just such a question. Since she had always to be superior to my father, there could be no greater delight than to shape the existence of his older son right in front of his nose.

"You were on a tobacco farm, your aunt Evelyn tells me."

"Yes, sir. White burley tobacco."

"Did you know, Sandy, that tobacco was the economic foundation of the first permanent English settlement in America, at Jamestown in Virginia?"

"I didn't," he admitted, but added, "Though I'm not surprised to hear it," and, in a flash, the worst was over.

"Many mishaps beset the Jamestown pioneers," the rabbi told him. "But what saved them from starvation and saved the settlement from extinction was the cultivation of tobacco. Think of it. Without tobacco, the first representative government in the New World would never have met at Jamestown, as it did in 1619. Without tobacco, the Jamestown colony would have collapsed, the colonization of Virginia would have failed, and the First Families of Virginia, whose wealth derived from their tobacco plantations, would themselves have never come to prominence. And when you remember that the First Families of Virginia were the forebears of the Virginia statesmen who were our country's Founding Fathers, you appreciate tobacco's vital importance to the history of our republic."

"You do," Sandy answered.

"I myself," said the rabbi, "was born in the American South. I was born fourteen years after the tragedy of the Civil War. My father as a young man fought for the Confederacy. His father came from Germany to settle in Louisiana in 1850. He was a peddler. He had a horse with a wagon and he wore a long beard and he sold to the Negroes and to the white people both. Did you ever hear of Judah Benjamin?" the rabbi asked Sandy.

"No, sir." But again he quickly righted himself, this time by replying, "May I ask who he was?"

"Well, he was a Jew and second only to Jefferson Davis in

the government of the Confederacy. He was a Jewish lawyer who served Davis as attorney general, as secretary of war, and as secretary of state. Prior to the secession of the South he had served in the U.S. Senate as one of Louisiana's two senators. The cause for which the South went to war was neither legal nor moral in my judgment, yet I have always held Judah Benjamin in the highest regard. A Jew was a rarity in America in those days, in the North no less than the South, but don't think there wasn't anti-Semitism to contend with back then. Nonetheless Judah Benjamin came close to the very pinnacle of political success in the Confederate government. After the war was lost, he moved abroad to become a distinguished lawyer in England."

Here my mother removed herself to the kitchen—purportedly to check on the dinner—and Aunt Evelyn said to Sandy, "Maybe this is a good time for the rabbi to see the drawings you made on the farm."

Sandy got up and carried over to the rabbi's chair the several sketchbooks that he'd filled with drawings during the summer and that he'd been holding in his lap since we'd all gathered in the living room.

The rabbi took one of the books and began slowly turning the pages.

"Tell the rabbi a little something about each picture," Aunt Evelyn suggested.

"That's the barn," Sandy said. "That's where they hang the tobacco to cure after they harvest it."

"Well, that is a barn, all right, and a beautifully drawn barn. I very much like the pattern of light and dark. You're very talented, Sanford."

"And that's a tobacco plant growing. That's what they look like. See, it's shaped like a triangle. They're big. That one's still got the blossom on top. It's before they top it."

"And this tobacco plant," the rabbi said, turning to a new page, "with the bag on the top—that is something I've never seen before."

"That's how they get the seed. That's a seed plant. They cover the blossom with a paper bag and tie it tight. It keeps the blossom the way they want it."

"Very, very good," the rabbi said. "It isn't easy to draw a

plant accurately and still make it into a work of art. Look how you've shadowed the undersides of the leaves. Very good indeed."

"And that's a plow, of course," Sandy said, "and that's a hoe. That's a hand hoe. To do your weeding with. Though you can also use just your hands."

"And did you weed much?" the rabbi asked teasingly.

"Oh, boy," Sandy said, and Rabbi Bengelsdorf smiled, looking not at all now like a frightening figure. "And that's just the dog," Sandy went on, "Orin's dog. She's sleeping. And that's one of the Negroes, Old Henry, and those are his hands. I thought they had character."

"And who is this?"

"That's Old Henry's brother. That's Clete."

"I like the way you've rendered him. How weary the man looks, slouching like that. I know those Negroes—I grew up with them, and I respect them. And this? Just what would this be?" the rabbi asked. "Here, with the bellows."

"Well, a person's inside. That's how he sprays against tobacco worms. He has to dress like that from head to foot with big gloves and heavy clothes all buttoned up so he doesn't get burned. When he squirts the insecticide out through the bellows he can burn himself with it. It's green, the dust, and when he's finished his clothes are covered with it. I tried to get the look of the dust, I tried to make it lighter where the dust is, but I don't think it came out right."

"Well, I'm sure," said the rabbi, "that it's hard to draw dust," and began to progress a little more rapidly through the remaining pages until he came to the end and closed the book. "Kentucky was an experience that wasn't wasted on you, was it, young man?"

"I loved it," Sandy replied, and my father, who had been silent and unmoving on the sofa since yielding the rabbi his favorite chair, got up and said, "I have to help Bess," the way he might have said, "I'm now going to jump out the window and kill myself."

"The Jews of America," the rabbi told us at dinner, "are unlike any other community of Jews in the history of the world. They have the greatest opportunity accorded to our people in modern times. The Jews of America can participate fully in the national life of their country. They need no longer dwell apart, a pariah community separated from the rest. All that is required is the courage that your son Sandy displayed by going on his own into the unknown of Kentucky to work for the summer as a farm hand there. I believe that Sandy and the other Jewish boys like him in the Just Folks program should serve as models not only for every Jewish child growing up in this country but for every Jewish adult. And this is not merely a dream of mine; it is the dream of President Lindbergh."

Our ordeal had suddenly taken the worst possible turn. I'd not forgotten how in Washington my father had stood up to the hotel manager and the bullying policeman, and so now that Lindbergh's name had been spoken with deference in his house I thought the moment had come when he would stand up to Bengelsdorf.

But a rabbi was a rabbi, and he didn't.

My mother and Aunt Evelyn served the meal, three courses followed by a marble cake freshly baked in our oven that afternoon. We ate off the "good" dishes with the "good" silverware, and in the dining room no less, where we had our best rug and our best furniture and our best linens and where we ourselves ate only on special occasions. From my side of the table you could see the photographic portraits of the family dead arranged atop the breakfront that was our memorial shrine. Framed there were two grandfathers, our maternal grandmother, a maternal aunt, and two uncles, one of them Uncle Jack, Alvin's father and my father's beloved older brother. In the aftermath of Rabbi Bengelsdorf's invoking Lindbergh's name, I was more confused than ever. A rabbi was a rabbi, but Alvin meanwhile was in a Canadian army hospital in Montreal learning to walk on an artificial left leg after having lost his own left leg battling Hitler, and in my own house—where I was supposed to wear anything *except* my good clothes—I had to put on my one tie and my one jacket to impress the very rabbi who helped to elect the president whose friend was Hitler. How could I not be confused, when our disgrace and our glory were one and the same? Something essential had been destroyed and lost, we were being coerced to be other than the Americans we were, and yet, by the light of the cut-glass chandelier, amid the weighty, dark-stained suite of dining room furniture, we were eating my mother's pot roast in the company of the first famous visitor we had ever entertained.

To further confound me and make me pay the full price for my thoughts, Bengelsdorf began, all at once, to speak about Alvin, whom he'd learned about from Aunt Evelyn. "I am saddened by the casualty in your family. My heart goes out to all of you. Evelyn tells me that when your nephew is released from the hospital he will come to convalesce with you all. I'm sure you know the mental anguish that such a wound can provoke in someone still in the flower of his youth. It will require all the love and patience you can muster to bring him to where he can again resume a useful life. His story is particularly tragic because there was no necessity whatsoever for his having crossed over to Canada to join their armed forces. Alvin Roth was born a citizen of the United States, and the United States is not at war with anyone, has no intention of going to war with anyone, and doesn't require the sacrifice of life or limb in warfare from a single one of its young men. Some of us have gone to great lengths to make this so. I have encountered considerable hostility from members of the Jewish community for allying myself in the 1940 election with the Lindbergh campaign. But I have been sustained by my abhorrence of war. It is terrible enough that young Alvin should have lost his leg in a battle on the European continent having nothing to do with the security of America or the well-being of Americans . . ."

On he went, more or less repeating what he'd said at Madison Square Garden in support of America's remaining neutral, but my focus now was only on Alvin. He was coming to stay with us? I looked at my mother. She'd told us nothing about it. When would he arrive? Where would he sleep? It was bad enough, as my mother had said in Washington, that we weren't living in a normal country; now we would never again be living in a normal house. A life of even more suffering was taking shape around me, and I wanted to scream "No! Alvin can't stay here—he has only one leg!"

I was so upset that it was a while before I realized that the dining room reign of decorum had ended and my father was no longer allowing himself to be shoved aside. Somehow he had managed at last to overturn the obstacles posed by Bengelsdorf's credentials and by his own insufficiencies; he had ceased being intimidated by the rabbinical grandeur, and, urged on by his irrepressible sense of an impending disaster— and violently irritated by the condescension—he was letting Bengelsdorf have it, pince-nez and all.

"Hitler," I heard him saying, "Hitler is not business as usual, Rabbi! This madman is not making a war from a thousand years ago. He is making a war such as no one has ever seen on this planet. He has conquered Europe. He is at war with Russia. Every night he bombs London into rubble and kills hundreds of innocent British civilians. He is the worst anti-Semite in history. And yet his great friend our president takes him at his word when Hitler tells him that they have an 'understanding.' Hitler had an understanding with the Russians. Did he keep it? He had an understanding with Chamberlain. Did he keep it? Hitler's goal is to conquer the world, and that includes the United States of America. And since everywhere he goes he shoots the Jews, when the time is right he will come and shoot the Jews here. And what will our president do then? Protect us? Defend us? Our president will not lift a finger. *That* is the understanding that they reached at Iceland, and any adult who thinks otherwise is crazy."

Rabbi Bengelsdorf showed no impatience with my father but listened respectfully, as if in sympathy with at least some of what he was hearing. Only Sandy seemed to be having trouble keeping his feelings to himself, and when our father referred scornfully to Lindbergh as "our president," he turned to me and made a face that revealed how far he'd spun out of the family orbit merely by making the ordinary American's adjustment to the new administration. My mother was seated to my father's right and, when he had finished, gripped his hand in hers, though to communicate how proud she was of him or to signal him to be still wasn't clear. As for Aunt Evelyn, she took all her cues from the rabbi, concealing her thoughts behind a mask of benign sufferance while her shallow brother-in-law dared to oppose with his piddling vocabulary a scholar who could talk in ten languages.

Bengelsdorf did not immediately respond but instead created a portentous interval in which quietly to insert his rejoinder: "I was at the White House talking to the president just yesterday morning." Here he sipped from his glass of water, allowing time for us to regain self-possession. "I was congratulating him," he continued, "on the significant inroad he had made into allaying the Jewish suspiciousness that dated back to his trips to Germany in the late thirties, when he was secretly taking the measure of the German air force for the U.S. government. I informed him that any number of my own congregants who had voted for Roosevelt were now his strong supporters, grateful that he had established our neutrality and spared our country the agonies of yet another great war. I told him that Just Folks and programs like it were beginning to convince the Jews of America that he is anything but their enemy. Admittedly, before his becoming president he at times made public statements grounded in anti-Semitic clichés. But he spoke from ignorance then, and admits as much today. I am pleased to tell you that it took no more than two or three sessions alone with the president to get him to relinquish his misconceptions and to appreciate the manifold nature of Jewish life in America. This is not an evil man, not in any way. This is a man of enormous native intelligence and great probity who is rightly celebrated for his personal courage and who wants now to enlist my aid to help him raze those barriers of ignorance that continue to separate Christian from Jew and Jew from Christian. Because there is ignorance as well among Jews, unfortunately, many of whom persist in thinking of President Lindbergh as an American Hitler when they know full well that he is not a dictator who attained power in a putsch but a democratic leader who came to office through a landslide victory in a fair and free election and who has exhibited not a single inclination toward authoritarian rule. He does not glorify the state at the expense of the individual but, to the contrary, encourages entrepreneurial individualism and a free enterprise system unencumbered by interference from the federal government. Where is the fascist statism? Where is the fascist thuggery? Where are the Nazi Brown Shirts and the secret police? When have you observed a single manifestation of fascist anti-Semitism emanating from our government? What Hitler perpetrated on Germany's Jews with the passage in 1935 of the Nuremberg Laws is the absolute antithesis of what President Lindbergh has undertaken to do for America's Jews through the establishment of the Office of American Absorption. The Nuremberg Laws deprived Jews of their civil rights and did everything to exclude them from membership in their nation. What I have encouraged President Lindbergh to do is to initiate programs inviting Jews to enter as far into the national life as they like—a national life that I'm sure you would agree is no less ours to enjoy than anyone else's."

A pouring forth of sentences as informed as these had never before occurred at our dining table or probably anywhere on our block, and it was startling then—when the rabbi concluded by inquiring rather gently, even intimately, "Tell me, Herman, does what I've explained begin to address your fears?"—to hear my father respond flatly, "No. No. Not for a moment." And then, heedless of rendering an affront that would not only arouse the rabbi's displeasure but insult his dignity and provoke his vindictive contempt, my father added, "Hearing a person like you talk like that—frankly, it alarms me even more."

The following evening Aunt Evelyn phoned and bubblingly informed us that out of the one hundred New Jersey boys who'd gone west that summer under the sponsorship of Just Folks, Sandy had been selected as the statewide "recruiting officer" to speak as a veteran to eligible Jewish youngsters and their families about the OAA program's many benefits and to encourage them to apply. Thus did the rabbi extract his revenge. Our father's older son was now an honorary member of the new administration.

It was shortly after Sandy began spending his afternoons downtown at Aunt Evelyn's OAA office that my mother put on her best suit—the tailored gray jacket and skirt with the pale pinstripe that she wore to preside over PTA meetings and as a poll watcher in the school basement at election time—and went off to look for a job. At dinner she announced that she had found work selling ladies' dresses at Hahne's, a big downtown department store. She had been hired early as holiday help to work six days a week and Wednesday evenings, but as she was an experienced office secretary she harbored the hope that over the coming weeks a job might open up on the store's administrative floor and she would be retained after Christmas as a permanent employee. She explained to Sandy and me that her paycheck would contribute toward meeting the larger household bills occasioned by Alvin's return while her real intention (known to no one other than her husband) was to deposit her paychecks by mail into a Montreal bank account in case we had to flee and start from scratch in Canada.

My mother was gone, my brother was gone, and Alvin would soon be on his way home. My father had driven to Montreal to visit him in the army hospital there. One Friday morning, hours before Sandy and I got up for school, my mother made his breakfast, filled his thermos, packed food— three paper bags marked with Sandy's shading crayon, *L* for lunch, *S* for snack, *D* for dinner—and away he headed for the international border three hundred and fifty miles to the north. Since his boss could give him only the Friday off, he'd have to drive all that day to see Alvin on Saturday and then drive all day Sunday to be back for the morning staff meeting on Monday. He had a flat tire going and two more coming home and to make it to his meeting had to bypass us and drive from the highway directly downtown. By the time we saw him at dinner he'd been sleepless for over a day and without a proper wash for longer than that. Alvin, he told us, looked like a corpse, his weight down to something around a hundred pounds. Hearing this, I wondered how much the leg weighed that he'd lost, and that evening, without success, tried to weigh mine on the bathroom scale. "He's got no appetite," my father said. "They put food in front of him and he pushes it away. That boy, tough as he is, doesn't want to live, doesn't want anything except to lie there emaciated with that terrible grim face. I said, 'Alvin, I've known you since you were born. You're a fighter. You don't give up. You've got your father's strength. Your father could take the hardest blow and still keep going. So could your mother.' I told him, 'When your father died, the woman had to bounce back—she had no choice, she had you.' But I don't know what sunk in. I hope something," he said, his voice growing husky, "because while I was there, with all those sick boys in those beds all around me, while I was sitting beside his bed in that hospital—" and that was as far as he got. It was the first time I saw my father cry. A childhood milestone, when another's tears are more unbearable than one's own.

"It's because you're so tired," my mother said to him. She

got up from her chair and, trying to calm him, came around and began to stroke his head. "When you finish eating," she said, "you'll take a shower and go right to bed."

Pressing his skull firmly back into the grip of her hand, he started to sob uncontrollably. "They blew his leg off," he told her, and here my mother motioned for Sandy and me to leave her to comfort him alone.

A new life began for me. I'd watched my father fall apart, and I would never return to the same childhood. The mother at home was now away all day working for Hahne's, the brother on call was now off after school working for Lindbergh, and the father who'd defiantly serenaded all those callow cafeteria anti-Semites in Washington was crying aloud with his mouth wide open—crying like both a baby abandoned and a man being tortured—because he was powerless to stop the unforeseen. And as Lindbergh's election couldn't have made clearer to me, the unfolding of the unforeseen was everything. Turned wrong way round, the relentless unforeseen was what we schoolchildren studied as "History," harmless history, where everything unexpected in its own time is chronicled on the page as inevitable. The terror of the unforeseen is what the science of history hides, turning a disaster into an epic.

As I was on my own, I began to spend all my after-school hours with Earl Axman, my stamp mentor, and not just to pore over his collection with my magnifying glass or to look through his mother's bureau at her puzzling array of undergarments. Since my homework took no time and my only other chore was setting the table for dinner, I was now wholly available for mischief. And since, in the afternoons, Earl's mother seemed always to be off at the beauty parlor or over in New York shopping, Earl was free to provide it. He was nearly two years older than I, and because his glamorous parents were divorced—and because they were glamorous—he seemed never to have bothered being a model child. Of late, increasingly irritated by being one myself, I'd taken to mumbling in my bed, "Now let's do something awful," the suggestion with which Earl alternately thrilled and unnerved me whenever he got tired of what we were up to. Adventurousness was bound to assert its appeal sooner or later, but disillusioned by a sense that my family was slipping away from me right along with my country, I was ready to learn of the liberties a boy from an exemplary household could take when he stopped working to please everyone with his juvenile purity and discovered the guilty enjoyment of secretly acting on his own.

What I fell into with Earl was following people. He'd been doing it a couple of times a week for months now—traveling downtown alone after school and hanging around bus stops looking for men on their way home from work. When the one he settled on boarded his bus, Earl climbed aboard too, unobtrusively rode with him until he got off, got off right after him, and then from a safe distance followed him home. "Why?" I asked. "To see where they live." "But that's all? That's it?" "That's a lot. I go all over. I even leave Newark. I go anyplace I want. People live everywhere," Earl explained. "How do you get home before your mother?" "That's the trick—to go as far as I can and get back before she does." The money for the bus fares he readily confessed to stealing from his mother's handbags and then, as gleefully as if he were springing the lock on the vault at Fort Knox, opened wide a bedroom drawer where all kinds of handbags were piled haphazardly atop one another. On the weekends when he went to stay with his father in New York, he stole from the pockets of the suits hanging in his father's closet, and when four or five musicians from the Casa Loma Orchestra came over to his father's apartment to play poker on Sundays, he helpfully piled their overcoats on the bed, then went through *their* pockets and hid the change in a dirty sock at the bottom of his suitcase. Then he'd nonchalantly saunter into the living room to watch the card game all afternoon and listen to the funny stories they told about playing at the Paramount and the Essex House and the Glen Island Casino. In 1941 the band had just come back from Hollywood, where they'd been in a movie, and so between hands they talked about the stars and what they were like, inside information that Earl passed on to me and that I then repeated to Sandy, who invariably said, "That's bullshit," and warned me not to hang around with Earl Axman. "Your friend," he told me, "knows too much for a little kid." "He's got a great stamp collection." "Yeah, and he's got a mother," Sandy said, "who'll go out with anybody. She goes out with men who aren't even her age." "How do you know?" "Everybody on Summit Avenue knows." "I don't," I said. "Well," he told me, "that's not all you don't know," and, greatly pleased with myself, I thought, "Maybe there's something that you don't know either," but I nervously had to wonder if my best friend's mother wasn't what the older boys called "a whore."

It turned out to be far easier than I could have believed getting used to stealing from my mother and father, and easier than I would have thought following people, even though the first few times there wasn't a moment that didn't stun me, beginning with being downtown unwatched at three-thirty in the afternoon. Sometimes we'd go all the way to Penn Station to find someone, sometimes to Broad and Market, sometimes up Market to the courthouse to wait at the bus stop and catch our prey there. We never followed women. They didn't interest us, Earl said. We never followed anybody we thought was Jewish. They didn't interest us. Our curiosity was directed at men, the adult Christian men who worked all day in downtown Newark. Where did they go when they went home?

My apprehension was at its worst when we stepped up into the bus and paid. The fare money was stolen, we were where we shouldn't be, and where we were headed we had no idea—and by the time we got to wherever that was, I was too dizzy with emotion to understand what Earl told me when he whispered the name of the neighborhood into my ear. I was lost, a lost boy—that's what I pretended. What will I eat? Where will I sleep? Will dogs attack me? Will I be arrested and thrown in jail? Will some Christian take me in and adopt me? Or will I wind up being kidnapped like the Lindbergh child? I pretended either that I was lost in some far-off region unknown to me or that, with Lindbergh's connivance, Hitler had invaded America and Earl and I were fleeing the Nazis.

And all the while I assailed myself with my fears, we were surreptitiously turning corners and crossing streets and crouching behind trees to stay out of sight until the climactic moment when the man we were following reached his home and we watched him open the door and go in. Then we would stand off at a distance and look at the house—its door once again shut—and Earl would say something like, "That lawn's really big," or "Summer's over—why are there screens up?" or "See in the garage? That's the new Pontiac." And then, because trying to sneak up to the windows to peer in unobserved exceeded even Earl Axman's Peeping Jewism, he'd lead us back to the bus that would return us to Penn Station. Often at that hour, with everyone busy leaving work, the bus headed back downtown would be empty of passengers other than us, and so it was as though the driver were a chauffeur and the Public Service bus our private limousine and the two of us the most daring two boys alive. Earl was an extremely well-fed, white-skinned ten-year-old, already a bit of a vat, with full babyish cheeks and long dark lashes and tight black ringlets perfumed with his father's hair oil, and if the bus was empty, he would stretch himself out on the long rear seat in a pashalike posture perfectly embodying his swaggering mood, while sitting up beside him, lean and bony, I sported the half-ashamed little sidekick's smile of sublimity.

From Penn Station we'd catch the 14 home, taking our fourth bold bus ride of the afternoon. At dinner I'd think, "I followed a Christian, and nobody knows. I could have been kidnapped, and nobody knows. Using the money we've got between us, we could've, if we'd wanted . . ." and would sometimes all but give myself away to my sharp-eyed mother because beneath the kitchen table (and exactly like Earl when he was cooking up something) I couldn't stop jiggling my knee. And night after night I went to sleep under the exciting spell of the great new aim I'd unearthed for my eight-year-old life: to escape it. When at school I heard a bus through the open window climbing the Chancellor Avenue hill, all I could think about was being on board; the whole of the outside world had become a bus the way for a boy in South Dakota it was a pony—the pony that carries him to the limits of permissible flight.

I joined Earl as apprentice liar and thief in late October and, with no dwindling of the sense of momentousness, our secret jaunts continued as the weather grew colder in November and then on into December, when the Christmas decorations went up downtown and there was an excess of men to choose from at just about every bus stop. Christmas trees were for sale right on the downtown sidewalks, something I'd never seen before, and selling the trees for a buck apiece were kids who looked to be either hardship cases or toughs recently released from reform school. Money changing hands like that out in the open struck me at first as against the law and yet nobody appeared concerned with concealing the transaction. There were cops in profusion, cops with nightsticks walking the beat in their large blue overcoats, but they looked happy enough and seemed to be in on it—in on Christmas, that is. Big wind-driven blizzards had been whipping in twice a week since just after Thanksgiving, and so to either side of the freshly cleared streets grimy hillocks of snow were already banked as high as a car.

Unimpeded by the late-afternoon throngs, the vendors wrested one tree free from the others, carried it a ways onto the busy sidewalk, and propped it on its sawed-off trunk to be sized up by the customer. It was strange to see trees grown by some tree farmer miles from the city massed along the wrought-iron railings out front of the city's oldest churches and leaning in piles against the façades of the imposing banks and insurance buildings, and strange too, on a downtown street, to breathe in their rustic tang. There were no trees for sale in our neighborhood—because there was no one to buy them—and so the month of December, if it smelled at all, smelled of something a hissing alley cat had tugged from an overturned garbage can in somebody's yard, and of supper heating on the stove of a flat whose steamy kitchen window was open a crack to let in air from the alleyway, and of the bursts of noxious coal gas spewed from the furnace chimneys, and of the pail of ashes dragged up from the cellar to be emptied outdoors over slippery patches of sidewalk. Compared with the fragrances of North Jersey's damp spring and swampy summer and unsettled, moody fall, the smells of a bitter-cold winter were almost unnoticeable—or so I was convinced until I traveled downtown with Earl and saw the trees and took a whiff and discovered that, as with many things, for Christians December was otherwise. What with all of downtown strung with thousands of bulbs and the carolers singing and the Salvation Army band reveling and on every street corner another Santa Claus laughing, it was the month of the year when the heart of my birthplace was sublimely theirs and theirs alone. In Military Park there was a decorated Christmas tree forty feet tall, and from the face of the Public Service building hung a giant metal Christmas tree, illuminated by floodlights, that the *Newark News* said was eighty feet tall, while I was barely four and a half feet tall.

My final trip with Earl occurred one afternoon a few days before our Christmas vacation when we boarded the Linden bus behind a man who was carrying in either hand a department store shopping bag stuffed with gifts and decorated for the season in red and green; just ten days later Mrs. Axman would suffer a nervous breakdown and be taken away in an ambulance in the middle of the night, and soon after that, on New Year's Day 1942, Earl would be whisked off by his father, stamp collection and all. A mover's truck showed up later in January and, while I watched, took all the household furnishings away, including the bureau with Earl's mother's underwear, and no one on Summit Avenue saw the Axmans again.

Because the cold winter twilight now descended so quickly, following people home from the bus made us feel all the more satisfied with ourselves, as though we were about our business long after midnight, when other kids had been asleep for hours. The man with the shopping bags stayed on the bus past the Hillside line and over into Elizabeth and got off just past the big cemetery, not far from the corner where my mother had grown up, above her father's grocery store. We got off after him quietly enough, the two of us looking indistinguishable from a thousand other local schoolkids in the standard-issue winter camouflage of hooded mackinaw and thick woolen mittens and shapeless corduroy trousers tucked into ill-fitting rubber galoshes with half of their maddening toggles undone. But because we imagined ourselves more concealed than we were by the deepening shadows, or because our adroitness was losing its power to time, we must have tailed him less skillfully than we were practiced at doing, and thus compromised "the invincible duo," as Earl had vaingloriously dubbed the pair of Christian-trackers we'd become.

There were two long blocks to traverse, both of them lined with stately brick houses bright with Christmas lights that Earl identified in a whisper as "millionaires' mansions"; then there were two shorter blocks of much smaller, modest frame houses of the kind that by then we'd seen by the hundreds on the streets that we'd traveled, each with a Christmas wreath on the door. On the second of the two blocks the man turned onto a narrow brick pathway that curved up to a low shoebox of a shingled house that poked up prettily out of the banked snow like the edible adornment on a big frosted cake. Lamps were burning dimly upstairs and down, and the Christmas tree could be seen twinkling through one of the windows to the side of the front door. While the man set down his shopping bags to get his key out, we drew closer and closer to the undulating white lawn until, through the window, we were able to discern the ornaments decorating the tree.

"Look," Earl whispered. "See the top? At the very top of the tree—see that? It's Jesus!"

"No, it's an angel."

"What do you think Jesus is?"

I whispered back, "I thought he was their God."

"And chief of the angels—and there he is!"

This then was the culmination of our quest—Jesus Christ, who by their reasoning was everything and who by my reasoning had fucked everything up: because if it weren't for Christ there wouldn't be Christians, and if it weren't for Christians there wouldn't be anti-Semitism, and if it weren't for anti-Semitism there wouldn't be Hitler, and if it weren't for Hitler Lindbergh would never be president, and if Lindbergh weren't president . . .

Suddenly the man we'd followed, standing now in the open doorway with his shopping bags, twirled around and softly, as though exhaling a smoke ring, called, "Boys."

So flabbergasted were we by being caught that I, for one, felt summoned to step forward onto the path leading up to the house and, like the model child I'd been two months before, clear my conscience by telling him my name. Only Earl's arm held me back.

"Boys, don't hide. You don't have to," the man said.

"What now?" I whispered to Earl.

"Shhhhhh," he whispered back.

"Boys, I know you're there. Boys, it's getting awfully dark," he warned in a friendly voice. "Aren't you freezing out there? Wouldn't you like a nice cup of cocoa? Inside now, children, quickly inside now before it snows. There's hot cocoa, and I have spice cake and I have seed cake and gingerbread men, I have animal crackers frosted in all different colors, and there are marshmallows—there are marshmallows, boys, marshmallows in the cupboard that we can toast over a fire."

When I again looked at Earl to find out what to do, he was already on his way back to Newark. "Run for it," he shouted at me over his shoulder, "beat it, Phil—it's a fairy!"

4

The Stump

ALVIN WAS discharged in January 1942, after forsaking first the wheelchair and then the crutches and, over the course of a long hospital rehabilitation, having been trained by the Canadian army nurses to walk unassisted on his artificial limb. He would be receiving a monthly disability pension from the Canadian government of a hundred and twenty-five dollars, a little more than half of what my father earned each month from the Metropolitan, and an additional three hundred dollars in separation pay. As a handicapped veteran he was eligible for further benefits should he choose to remain in Canada, where foreign volunteers into the Canadian armed forces, if they wished, were granted citizenship immediately upon discharge. And why didn't he become a Canuck? asked Uncle Monty. Since he couldn't stand America anyway, why didn't he just stay up there and cash in?

Monty was the most overbearing of my uncles, which probably accounted for why he was also the richest. He'd made his fortune wholesaling fruit and vegetables down near the railroad tracks at the Miller Street market. Alvin's father, Uncle Jack, had begun the business and taken in Monty, and after Uncle Jack died Monty had taken in his youngest brother, my uncle Herbie; when he invited my father in as well—back when my parents were penniless newlyweds—my father said no, having already been sufficiently bullied by Monty while they were growing up. My father could keep pace with Monty's prodigious expenditure of energy, and his capacity to endure all manner of hardship was no less remarkable than Monty's, but he knew from the clashes of boyhood that he was no match for the innovator who'd first gambled on bringing ripe tomatoes to Newark in the wintertime by buying up carloads of green tomatoes from Cuba and ripening them in specially heated rooms on the creaky second floor of his Miller Street ware-house. When they were ready, Monty packed them four to a box, got top dollar, and was known thereafter as the Tomato King.

While we remained rent-paying tenants in a five-room second-story flat in Newark the uncles in the wholesale produce busi-ness lived in the Jewish section of suburban Maplewood, where each owned a large, white, shuttered Colonial with a green lawn out front and a polished Cadillac in the garage. For good or bad, the exalted egoism of an Abe Steinheim or an Uncle Monty or a Rabbi Bengelsdorf—conspicuously dynamic Jews all seemingly propelled by their embattled status as the off-spring of greenhorns to play the biggest role that they could commandeer as American men—was not in the makeup of my father, nor was there the slightest longing for supremacy, and so though personal pride was a driving force and his blend of fortitude and combativeness was heavily fueled, like theirs, by the grievances attending his origins as an impoverished kid other kids called a kike, it was enough for him to make some-thing (rather than everything) of himself and to do so without wrecking the lives around him. My father was born to contend but also to protect, and to inflict damage on an enemy didn't make his spirits soar as it did his older brother's (not to men-tion all the rest of the brutal entrepreneurial *machers*). There were the bosses and there were the bossed, and the bosses usually were bosses for a reason—and in business for them-selves for a reason, whether the business was construction or produce or the rabbinate or the rackets. It was the best they could come up with to remain unobstructed—and, in their own eyes, unhumiliated—not least by the discrimination of the Protestant hierarchy that kept ninety-nine percent of the Jews employed by the dominant corporations uncomplainingly in their place.

"If Jack was alive," Monty said, "the kid wouldn't have got out the front door. You should never have let him go, Herm. He runs away to Canada to become a war hero and this is where it lands him, a goddamn gimp for the rest of his life." It was the Sunday before the Saturday of Alvin's return, and Uncle Monty, wearing clean clothes instead of the badly stained windbreaker and splattered old pants and filthy cloth cap that

were his usual market attire, was leaning against our kitchen
sink, a cigarette dangling out of his mouth. My mother was
not present. She had excused herself, as she generally did when
Monty was around, but I was a small boy and mesmerized by
him, as though he were indeed the gorilla that she privately
called him when her exasperation with his coarseness got the
upper hand.

"Alvin can't bear your president," my father replied, "that's
why he went to Canada. Not so long ago you couldn't bear the
man either. But now this anti-Semite is your friend. The Depression is over, all you rich Jews tell me, and thanks not to
Roosevelt but to Mr. Lindbergh. The stock market is up, profits
are up, business is booming—and why? Because we have Lindbergh's peace instead of Roosevelt's war. And what else matters, what besides money counts with you people?" "You
sound like Alvin, Herman. You sound like a kid. What counts
besides money? Your two boys count. You want Sandy to come
home one day like Alvin? You want Phil," he said, looking over
to where I sat listening at the kitchen table, "to come home
one day like Alvin? We're out of the war, and we're staying out
of the war. Lindbergh's done me no harm that I can see." I
expected my father to respond "Just you wait," but probably
because I was there and frightened enough already, he didn't.

As soon as Monty left, my father told me, "Your uncle
doesn't use his head. Coming home like Alvin—that's not
something that's going to happen." "But what if Roosevelt is
president again? Then there would be a war," I said. "Maybe
and maybe not," my father replied, "nobody can predict that
in advance." "But if there was a war," I said, "and if Sandy was
old enough, then he would be drafted to fight in the war. And
if he fought in the war, then what happened to Alvin *could*
happen to him." "Son, anything can happen to anyone," my
father told me, "but it usually doesn't." "Except when it does,"
I thought, but I didn't dare to say as much because he was already upset by my questions and might not even know how to
answer if I kept on going. Since what Uncle Monty said to him
about Lindbergh was exactly what Rabbi Bengelsdorf had told
him—and also what Sandy was secretly saying to me—I began
to wonder if my father knew what he was talking about.

*

It was close to a year after Lindbergh took office that Alvin returned to Newark on an overnight train from Montreal, accompanied by a Canadian Red Cross nurse and missing half of one of the legs that he'd left with. We drove downtown to Penn Station to meet him as we did to meet Sandy the summer before, only this time Sandy was with us. A few weeks earlier, in the interest of family harmony, I had been allowed to go off with Aunt Evelyn and him to sit in the audience and listen as he impressed the congregation of a synagogue some forty miles south of Newark, in New Brunswick, encouraging them to enroll their children in Just Folks with stories of his Kentucky adventure and an exhibition of his drawings. My parents had made it clear to me that Sandy's job with Just Folks was something I needn't mention to Alvin; they'd themselves explain everything, but only after Alvin had a chance to get used to being home and could better understand how America had changed since he'd gone to Canada. It was a matter not of hiding anything from Alvin or of lying to him but of protecting him from whatever could interfere with his recovery.

The Montreal train was late that morning, and to pass the time—and because the political situation was with him now every moment of the day—my father had bought a copy of the *Daily News*. Seated on a bench at Penn Station, he scanned the paper, a right-wing New York tabloid that he unfailingly referred to as a "rag," while the rest of us paced the platform, anxiously waiting for the next phase of our new life to begin. When the PA system announced that the Montreal train would be arriving even later than expected, my mother, linking arms with Sandy and me, walked us back to the bench to wait there together. My father had meanwhile finished as much of the *Daily News* as he could bear and thrown it into a trash basket. Since ours was a household where nickels and dimes mattered, I was as perplexed to see him discard the paper only minutes after buying it as I'd been to see him reading it in the first place. "Can you believe these people?" he said. "This fascist dog is *still* their hero." What he didn't say was that by making good on his campaign promise to keep America out of the worldwide war, the fascist dog had by now become the hero of virtually every paper in the country with the exception of *PM*.

"Well," said my mother as the train finally entered the station and began to pull to a stop, "here comes your cousin."

"What should we do?" I asked her, as she prompted us onto our feet and the four of us stepped toward the platform's edge.

"Say hello. It's Alvin. Welcome him home."

"What about his leg?" I whispered.

"What about it, dear?"

I shrugged.

Here my father took me by the shoulders. "Don't be afraid," he said to me. "Don't be afraid of Alvin and don't be afraid of his leg. Let him see how you've grown up."

It was Sandy who broke away from us and went racing toward the car that had come to a halt a couple of hundred feet down the track. Alvin was being pushed from the train in a wheelchair by a woman in a Red Cross uniform while the person who was barreling down on him shouting his name was the only one of us who'd been won over to the other side. I didn't know any longer what to make of my brother, but then I didn't know what to make of myself, so busy was I trying to remember to conceal everyone's secrets while doing my best to suppress my fears and trying not to stop believing in my father as well as in the Democrats and FDR and whoever else could keep me from teaming up with the rest of the country in adoring President Lindbergh.

"You're back!" Sandy cried. "You're home!" And then I watched as my brother, who'd only just turned fourteen but was as strong now as a young man of twenty, dropped to his knees on the platform's concrete floor, the better to be able to throw his arms around Alvin's neck. My mother began crying then, and my father quickly took me by the hand, either to try to prevent me from going to pieces or to protect himself from his own chaos of feelings.

I thought it must be my job to run to Alvin next, and so I pulled away from my parents and broke for the wheelchair and, once there, imitating Sandy, threw *my* arms around him, only to discover how rotten he smelled. I thought at first that the smell must be coming from his leg, but it was coming from his mouth. I held my breath and shut my eyes and only released my hold on Alvin when I felt him lean forward in the chair to shake my father's hand. I noticed then the wooden crutches strapped to one side of the wheelchair, and for the first time dared to look straight at him. I'd never before seen anyone so skeletal or so dejected. His eyes showed no fear, however, or any trace of weeping, and they surveyed my father with ferocity, as though it were the guardian who had committed the unpardonable act that had rendered the ward a cripple.

"Herman," he said, but that was all.

"You're here," my father said, "you're home. We're taking you home."

Then my mother bent forward to kiss him.

"Aunt Bess," Alvin said.

The left trouser leg dropped straight down from the knee, a sight generally familiar to adults but one that startled me, even though I already knew of a man with no legs at all, a man who began at the hips and was himself no more than a stump. I had seen him before, begging on the sidewalk outside my father's downtown office, but overwhelmed as I was by the colossal freakishness, I'd never had to think much about it since there was never any danger of his coming to live in our house. He did best with his begging in baseball season when, as the men working there left the building at the end of the day, he would run through the afternoon's final scores in his incongruously deep, declamatory voice, and each of them would drop a couple of coins into the battered laundry pail that was his alms box. He moved about on—appeared, in fact, to live on—a small platform of plywood fitted beneath with roller skates. Aside from my remembering the heavy, weatherbeaten work gloves he wore all year round—to protect the hands that were his means of ambulation—I'm unable to describe the rest of his outfit because the fear of gaping merged with the terror of seeing to prevent me from ever looking long enough to register what he wore. That he dressed at all seemed as miraculous as that he was somehow able to urinate and defecate, let alone remember the ball scores. Whenever I came along to the empty insurance office on a Saturday morning with my father—largely for the delight of twirling in his desk chair while he attended to the week's mail—he and the stump of a man would always greet each other with a friendly nod. I discovered then that the grotesque injustice of a man's being halved had not merely happened, which was incomprehensible enough, but happened to someone called Robert, as commonplace as a male name could be and six letters long, like my own. "How you doin', Little Robert?" my father said as we two passed together into the building. "How you, Herman?" Little Robert would reply. Eventually I asked my father, "Does he have a last name?" "Do you?" my father asked me. "Yes." "Well, so does he." "What is it? Little Robert what?" I asked. My father thought a moment, then laughed and said, "To tell you the truth, son, I don't know."

From the moment I found out that Alvin was returning to Newark to convalesce in our house, I would involuntarily envision Robert on his platform and wearing his work gloves whenever I lay stiffly in the dark trying to force myself asleep: first my stamps covered with swastikas, then Little Robert, the living stump.

"I thought you'd be up on the leg they gave you. I thought they couldn't discharge you otherwise," I heard my father saying to Alvin. "What's happened?"

Without bothering to look at him, Alvin snapped, "Stump broke down."

"What's that mean?" my father asked.

"It's nothing. Don't worry about it."

"Does he have luggage?" my father asked the nurse.

But before she could answer, Alvin said, "Sure I got luggage. Where do you think my leg is?"

Sandy and I were headed for the baggage counter on the main concourse with Alvin and his nurse while my father hurried off to get the car from the Raymond Boulevard lot, accompanied by my mother, who went along with him at the last minute, more than likely to talk over all they hadn't anticipated about Alvin's mental state. Out on the platform, the nurse had summoned a redcap, and together they helped Alvin to a standing position and then the redcap took charge of the wheelchair while the nurse walked at Alvin's side as he hopped to the head of the escalator. There she took up her place as a human shield, and he hopped after her, clutching the moving banister as the escalator descended. Sandy and I stood at Alvin's back, out of range at last of his unfragrant breath—and where Sandy instinctively braced himself to catch him should Alvin lose his balance. The redcap, carrying upside down and over his head the wheelchair with the crutches still strapped to one side, took the stairs parallel to the escalator and was already on the main concourse to greet us when Alvin hopped from the escalator and we stepped off behind him. The redcap placed the wheelchair right side up on the concourse floor and firmly positioned it for Alvin to sit back down, but Alvin turned on his one foot and began to hop vigorously away, leaving his nurse—to whom he'd said neither thank you nor goodbye—to watch him speed off along the crowded marble floor in the direction of the baggage room.

"Can't he fall?" Sandy asked the nurse. "He's going so fast. What if he slips and falls?"

"Him?" the nurse replied. "That boy can hop anywhere. That boy can hop a very long way. He won't fall. He's the world-champion hopper. He'd have been happier to hop from Montreal than to have me helping him down here by train." She then confided to us, two protected children entirely ignorant of the bitterness of loss, "I've seen 'em angry before," she said, "I've seen the ones without *any* limbs angry, but nobody before ever angry like him."

"Angry at what?" Sandy asked anxiously.

She was a strapping woman with stern gray eyes and hair short as a soldier's under her gray Red Cross cap, but it was in the softest maternal tones, with a gentleness that came as yet another of the day's surprises, as though Sandy were one of her very own charges, that she explained, "At what people get angry at—at how things turn out."

My mother and I had to take the bus home because there wasn't enough room in the little family Studebaker. Alvin's wheelchair went into the trunk, though as it was the old unwieldy uncollapsible type, the lid of the trunk had to be tied shut with heavy twine to accommodate it. His canvas overseas bag (with the artificial leg somewhere inside) was stuffed so full that Sandy was unable to lift it even with my help, and we had to drag it across the concourse floor and through the door to the street; there my father took charge and he and Sandy laid it flat out across the back seat. Practically doubled over at the waist, Sandy was perched atop the bag for the ride home, Alvin's crutches straddling his lap. The crutches' rubber-capped tips protruded from one of the rear side-windows, and my father tied his pocket handkerchief around the ends to warn off other drivers. My father and Alvin rode up front, and I was unhappily preparing to squeeze between them just to the right of the floor shift when my mother said she wanted my company on the ride home. What she wanted, it turned out, was to prevent me from having to witness any more of the misery.

"It's okay," she said as we headed around the corner for the underpass where the line formed for the 14 bus. "It's perfectly natural to be upset. We all are."

I denied being in any way upset but found myself looking around the bus stop for somebody to follow. Easily a dozen different routes started out from this one Penn Station stop, and it happened that a Vailsburg bus bound for distant North Newark was taking on passengers at the very moment that my mother and I stood at the curbside of the underpass waiting for a 14 to show up. I spotted just the man to follow, a businessman with a briefcase who seemed to me—with my admittedly imperfect grasp of the telling characteristics that Earl was so masterfully attuned to   not to be Jewish. Yet I could only look with longing as the bus door closed behind him and he rode off without my spying on him from a nearby seat.

Once we were alone together on the bus, my mother said, "Tell me what's bothering you."

When I didn't reply she began to explain Alvin's behavior at the train station. "Alvin is ashamed. He feels ashamed for us to be seeing him in a wheelchair. When he left he was strong and independent. Now he wants to hide and he wants to scream and he wants to lash out, and it's terrible for him. And it's terrible too for a boy like you to have to see your big cousin like this. But that's all going to change. Just as soon as he understands that there's nothing about the way he looks or about what happened for him to be ashamed of, he's going to gain back the weight he lost, and he'll start to walk everywhere on his artificial leg, and he's going to look just as you remember him before he left for Canada . . . Does that help any? Does what I'm telling you reassure you at all?"

"I don't need to be reassured," I said, but what I wanted to ask was: "His stump—what does it mean that it's broken down? Do I have to look at it? Will I ever have to touch it? Are they going to fix it?"

On a Saturday a couple of weeks earlier I'd gone into the cellar with my mother and helped her empty the cartons full of Alvin's belongings, rescued by my father from the Wright Street room after Alvin had run off to join the Canadian army. Everything washable my mother scrubbed on the washboard in the divided cellar tub, soaping in one sink, rinsing in the other, and then feeding a piece at a time into the wringer while I cranked the handle to force out the rinse water. I hated that wringer; each piece of wash emerged flattened out from between its two rollers, looking as if it had been run over by a truck, and whenever I was down in the cellar for whatever reason, I was always afraid to turn my back on the thing. But now I steeled myself to drop each wet, deformed item of mangled laundry into the laundry basket and carry the basket upstairs so that my mother could dry everything on the backyard clothesline. I fed her the clothespins as she leaned from the window to hang out the wash, and while she stood in the kitchen after dinner that evening ironing the shirts and pajamas that I had just helped her to reel in, I sat at the kitchen table folding Alvin's underwear and rolling each pair of socks into a ball, determined to make everything turn out right by being the best little boy imaginable, much, much better than Sandy and better even than myself.

After school the next day, it required two trips for me to carry Alvin's good clothes around the corner to the tailor shop where they did our dry cleaning. Later in the week I picked them up and at home placed everything—topcoat, suit, sport jacket, and two pairs of his pants—on wooden hangers in the half I'd apportioned him of my bedroom closet and stacked the rest of the clean apparel in the top two drawers that had formerly been Sandy's. Since Alvin was going to be sleeping in our bedroom—to provide him with the easiest possible access to the bathroom—Sandy had already gotten himself ready to move to the sun parlor at the front of the flat by arranging his own belongings in the breakfront in the dining room, beside the linen tablecloth and napkins. One evening a few days before Alvin's scheduled return I shined his pair of brown shoes and his pair of black shoes, ignoring as best I could any uncertainty I had as to whether shining all four of them was still necessary. To make those shoes gleam, to get his good clothes clean, to neatly pile the dresser drawers with his freshly washed things—and all of it simply a prayer, an improvised prayer imploring the household gods to protect our humble five rooms and all they contained from the vengeful fury of the missing leg.

I tried to gauge from what I saw beyond the bus window how much time remained before we got to Summit Avenue and it was too late to unseal my fate. We were on Clinton Avenue just passing the Riviera Hotel, where, as I never failed to remember, my mother and father had spent their wedding night. We were clear of downtown, about halfway home, and directly ahead was Temple B'nai Abraham, the great oval fortress built to serve the city's Jewish rich and no less foreign to me than if it had been the Vatican.

"I could move into your bed," my mother said, "if that's what's bothering you. For now, until everybody gets used to everybody else again, I could sleep in your bed next to Alvin's bed and you could go in and sleep with Daddy in our bed. Would that be better?"

I said that I'd rather sleep alone in my own bed.

"What if Sandy moved back from the sun parlor to his bed," my mother suggested, "and Alvin slept in yours and you slept where Sandy was going to sleep, on the daybed in the sun parlor? Would you be lonely up at the front of the house, or is that what you would really prefer?"

Would I prefer it? I'd have loved it. But how possibly could Sandy, who was now working for Lindbergh, share a room with someone who had lost his leg going to war against Lindbergh's Nazi friends?

We were turning onto Clinton Place from the Clinton Avenue stop, the familiar residential corner where—back before Sandy deserted me for Aunt Evelyn on Saturday afternoons—he and I used to disembark for the double feature at the Roosevelt Theater, whose black-lettered marquee was a block away. Soon the bus would be sailing past the narrow alleyways and the two-and-a-half-family houses lining the level length of

Clinton Place—streets that looked much like our own but whose red-brick bank of gabled front stoops aroused not a one of the basic boyhood emotions that ours did—before arriving at the big final turn onto Chancellor Avenue. There the grinding pull up the hill would begin, past the elegant fluted piers of the spiffy new high school, on to the sturdy flagpole out front of my grade school, and through to the crest of the hill, where a band of Lenni Lenapes were said by our third-grade teacher to have lived in a tiny village, cooking their food over hot stones and drawing designs on their pots. This was our destination, the Summit Avenue stop, diagonally across from the platters of freshly dipped chocolates profligately displayed in the lace-trimmed windows of Anna Mae's, the sweetshop that had succeeded the Indians' tepees and whose tantalizing scent honeyed the air less than a two-minute walk from our house.

In other words, the time left to say yes to the sun parlor was precisely measurable and running out, movie theater by movie theater, candy store by candy store, stoop by stoop, and yet all I could say was no, no, I'll be fine where I am, until my mother had nothing soothing left to suggest and, despite herself, went gloomily silent in a very ominous, undisguised way, as though the eventfulness of the morning was at last working her over the way it had me. Meanwhile, since I didn't know how long I could go on concealing that I couldn't bear Alvin because of his missing limb and his empty trouser leg and his awful smell and his wheelchair and his crutches and the way he wouldn't look up at any of us when he talked, I began to pretend that I was following somebody on our bus who didn't look Jewish. It was then that I realized—employing all the criteria imparted to me by Earl—that my mother looked Jewish. Her hair, her nose, her eyes—my mother looked *unmistakably* Jewish. But then so must I, who so strongly resembled her. I hadn't known.

What made Alvin smell bad was all the decay in his mouth. "You lose your teeth when you've got problems," Dr. Lieberfarb explained after looking around with his little mirror and saying "Uh-oh" nineteen times, and that very afternoon he started drilling. He was going to do all that work for nothing because Alvin had volunteered to fight the fascists and because, unlike "the rich Jews" who astonished my father by imagining themselves secure in Lindbergh's America, Lieberfarb remained undeluded about what "the many Hitlers of this world" might yet have in store for us. Nineteen gold inlays was a big deal, but that's how he showed solidarity with my father, my mother, me, and the Democrats, as opposed to Uncle Monty, Aunt Evelyn, Sandy, and all the Republicans currently enjoying their countrymen's love. Nineteen inlays also took a long time, particularly for a dentist who'd trained in night school while working days packing cargo crates at Port Newark, and whose touch was never that light. Lieberfarb was drilling away for months, but within the first few weeks enough of the rot had been removed so that it was no longer such a trial to be sleeping more or less next to Alvin's mouth. The stump was something else. "Broken down" means that the end of the stump goes bad: it opens up, it cracks, it gets infected. There are boils, sores, edema, and you can't walk on it with the prosthesis and so have to be without it and resort to crutches until it heals and can take the pressure without breaking down again. At fault was the fit of the artificial leg. The doctors would tell him, "You've lost your fit," but he hadn't lost his fit, he never *had* a fit, Alvin said, because the legmaker hadn't got the measurements right to begin with.

"How long does it take to heal?" I asked him the night he finally told me what "broken down" meant. Sandy up at the front of the house and my parents in their bedroom had already been asleep for hours, and so too were Alvin and I when he began to shout "Dance! Dance!" and, with a frightening gasp, shot upright in his bed, wide awake. When I flipped on the night lamp and saw him covered with sweat, I got up and opened the bedroom door, and though suddenly covered in sweat myself, I tiptoed across the little back foyer, not to my parents' room, however, to report what had happened, but into the bathroom to get Alvin a towel. He used it to mop his face and his neck, then pulled off his pajama shirt to wipe his chest and his underarms, and now at last I saw what had become of the upper man since the lower man had been blown apart. No wounds, stitches, or disfiguring scars, but no strength either, just the pale skin of a sickly boy adhering to the knobs and ridges of bone.

This was our fourth night together. On the first three nights

Alvin had been careful to change into his pajamas in the bathroom and then to hop back to hang his clothes in the closet, and since he used the bathroom again to dress in the mornings, I hadn't as yet had to look at the stump and could pretend I didn't know it was there. At night I turned to the wall and, fatigued by all my worries, fell right off to sleep and remained asleep until sometime in the early hours when Alvin got up and hopped to the bathroom and back to bed. He did all this without turning on the light and I lay there afraid he was going to bang into something and crash to the floor. At night, his every move made me want to run away, and not merely from the stump. It was on this fourth night, when Alvin had finished drying himself off with the towel and was lying there in just his pajama bottoms, that he pulled up the pajamas' left leg to take a look at the stump. I supposed this was a hopeful sign—that he was starting to be less crazily agitated, at least with me—but I still didn't want to look his way . . . and so I did, trying to be a soldier in my bed. What I saw extending down from his knee joint was something five or six inches long that resembled the elongated head of a featureless animal, something on which Sandy, with just a few well-placed strokes, could have crayoned eyes, a nose, a mouth, teeth, and ears, and turned it into the likeness of a rat. What I saw was what the word "stump" describes: the blunt remnant of something whole that belonged there and once had been there. If you didn't know what a leg looked like, this one might have seemed normal to you, given how the hairless skin was rounded off softly at the abbreviated end as though it were nature's handiwork and not the result of a trying sequence of medical amputations.

"Is it healed?" I asked him.

"Not yet."

"How long will it take?"

"Forever," he replied.

I was stunned. Then this is endless! I thought.

"Extremely frustrating," Alvin said. "You get on the leg they make for you and the stump breaks down. You get on crutches and it starts to swell up. The stump goes bad whatever you do. Get my bandages from the dresser."

I did as he told me. I was going to have to handle the beige elasticized wrappings he used to prevent his stump from swelling when the artificial leg was off. They were coiled up in a corner of the drawer beside his socks. Each was about three inches wide and had a large safety pin stuck through the end to keep it from unrolling. I no more wanted to plunge my hand into that drawer than to go down to the cellar and stick it into the wringer, but I did, and when I delivered the bandages to the bed, one in each fist, he said, "Good boy," and was able to make me laugh by petting my head like a dog's.

Afraid to see what came next, I sat on my bed and watched.

"You put this bandage on," he explained, "to keep it from blowing up." He held the stump in one hand and with the other undid the safety pin and began to unroll one of the bandages in a crisscrossing pattern over the stump and on up to the knee joint and then several inches beyond that. "You put this bandage on to keep it from blowing up"—he repeated the words wearily, with exaggerated patience—"but you don't want bandages over the breakdown because that won't let the breakdown heal. So you're just going back and forth until you're nuts." When he finished unrolling the bandage and inserted the safety pin to fasten the end, he showed me the results. "You have to pull it tight, you see?" He began a similar routine with the second bandage. The stump—when he was through with it—again reminded me of a small animal, this time one whose head had to be muzzled extra carefully to prevent it from sinking its razor-sharp teeth into the hand of its captor.

"How do you learn that?" I asked him.

"You don't have to learn. You just put it on. Except," he suddenly announced, "it's too goddamn tight. Maybe you *do* have to learn. Goddamn son of a bitch! It's either too fucking loose or too fucking tight. It makes you nuts—the whole goddamn thing." He removed the safety pin that fastened the second bandage and then undid both bandages in order to start again. "You can see," he told me, struggling now to suppress disgust with the futility of *everything*, "how good at doing this you get," and resumed the rewrapping, which, like the healing, appeared destined to go on in our bedroom forever.

The next day when school was over, I ran straight home to a

house that I knew would be empty—Alvin was at the dentist, Sandy was off somewhere with Aunt Evelyn, the two of them inexplicably helping Lindbergh achieve his ends, and my parents wouldn't be back from work until suppertime. As Alvin had settled on using the daytime hours to allow the breakdown to heal unbandaged and the nights to wrap the stump to prevent the swelling, I readily found the two bandages in the corner of the top dresser drawer where he'd returned them rolled up that morning. I sat on the edge of my bed, turned up my left trouser leg, and, shocked to realize that what remained of Alvin's leg was not much bigger around than my own, set out to bandage myself. I'd spent the day at school mentally running through what I'd watched him do the night before, but at three-twenty, when I got home, I'd only just started to wrap the first bandage around an imaginary stump of my own when, against the flesh below my knee, I felt what turned out to be a ragged scab from the ulcerated underside of Alvin's stump. The scab must have come loose during the night—Alvin had either ignored it or failed to notice it—and now it was stuck to me and I was out way beyond what I could deal with. Though the heaves began in the bedroom, by racing for the back door and then down the back stairway to the cellar, I managed to position my head over the double sink seconds before the real puking began.

To find myself alone in the dank cavern of the cellar was an ordeal under any circumstances, and not only because of the wringer. With its smudged frieze of mold and mildew running along the cracking whitewashed walls—stains in every hue of the excremental rainbow and seepage blotches that looked as if they'd leaked from a corpse—the cellar was a ghoulish realm apart, extending beneath the whole of the house and deriving no light at all from the half-dozen slits of grime-clouded glass that looked onto the cement of the alleyways and the weedy front yard. There were several saucer-sized drains sunk into the bottom of a sloping concavity at the middle of the concrete floor. Secured in the mouth of each was a heavy black disc pierced by the concentric dime-sized perforations from which, with no difficulty, I imagined vaporous creatures spiraling malevolently up from the earth's innards into my life. The cellar was a place bereft not just of a sunny window but of every human assurance, and when I came to study Greek and Roman mythology in a freshman high school class and read in the textbook about Hades, Cerberus, and the River Styx, it was always our cellar that I was reminded of. One 30-watt bulb hung over the washtub into which I'd vomited, a second hung in the vicinity of the coal furnaces—ablaze and bulkily aligned together like the three-personed Pluto of our underworld—and another, almost always burned out, was suspended from an electrical cord inside each of the storage bins.

I could never accept that the wintertime responsibility would fall to me for shoveling coal into our family's furnace first thing each morning, then banking the fire before going to bed, and once a day carrying a pailful of cold ashes out to the ashcan in the backyard. Sandy had by now grown strong enough to take over from my father, and in a few more years, when he went off like every other eighteen-year-old American boy to receive his twenty-four months of military training in President Lindbergh's new citizen Army, I would inherit the job and relinquish it only when I too was conscripted. Imagining a future when I'd be in the cellar manning the furnace all alone was, at nine, as upsetting as thinking about the inevitability of dying, which had also begun tormenting me in bed every night.

But I mainly feared the cellar because of those who were already dead—my two grandfathers, my mother's mother, and the aunt and uncle who once constituted Alvin's family. Their bodies may have been interred just off Route 1 on the Newark-Elizabeth line, but in order to patrol our affairs and scrutinize our conduct their ghosts resided two stories beneath our flat. I had little or no recollection of any of them other than of the grandmother who'd died when I was six, and yet whenever I was headed for the cellar by myself, I took care to warn each in turn that I was on my way and to beg them to keep their distance and not to besiege me once I was in their midst. When Sandy was my age he used to arm himself against his brand of fear by barreling down the cellar stairs shouting, "Bad guys, I know you're down there—I've got a gun," while I would descend whispering, "I'm sorry for whatever I did that was wrong."

There was the wringer, the drains, the dead—the ghosts of the dead watching and judging and condemning as I vomited into the double sink where my mother and I had washed Alvin's clothes—and there were the alley cats who would disappear into the cellar when the outside back door was left ajar and then yowl from wherever in the dark they were crouched, and there was the agonized cough of our downstairs neighbor Mr. Wishnow, a cough that sounded from the cellar as though he were being ripped apart by the teeth of a two-man saw. Like my father, Mr. Wishnow was an insurance agent with the Metropolitan, but for over a year he had been on disability pay, too ill with cancer of the mouth and the throat to do anything but stay at home and listen to the daytime radio serials when he wasn't asleep or uncontrollably coughing. With the blessing of the home office, his wife had taken over for him—the first female insurance agent in the history of the Newark district—and now kept the same long hours as my father, who generally had to go back out after dinner to make his collections and canvassed for prospective customers most every Saturday or Sunday, weekends being the only time when he could hope to find a breadwinner at home to listen to his spiel. Before my mother had herself begun to work as a saleslady at Hahne's, she would stop downstairs a couple of times a day to see how Mr. Wishnow was doing; and now, when Mrs. Wishnow called to say she couldn't be home in time to cook a proper dinner, my mother would prepare a little more of whatever we were eating and Sandy and I, before we were allowed to sit down to our own meal, each carried a warm plateful of food to the first floor on a tray, one for Mr. Wishnow and one for Seldon, the Wishnows' only child. Seldon would open the door for us and we would maneuver our trays through the foyer and into the kitchen, absorbed in trying not to spill anything as we set them on the table where Mr. Wishnow was already waiting, a paper napkin tucked into the top of his pajamas but looking in no way able to feed himself, however desperately in need of nutrition. "You boys all right?" he would ask us in the shredded rag of a voice that was left to him. "How about a joke for me, Phillie? I could use a good joke," he allowed, but without bitterness, without sadness, merely demonstrating the soft, defensive joviality of someone still hanging on for no seeming reason. Seldon must have told his father that I could make the kids laugh at school, and so I would teasingly be asked to tell him a joke when just by his proximity he'd have obliterated my capacity to speak. The best I could do was to try to look at somebody whom I knew to be dying—and, worse, *resigned* to dying—without allowing my eyes to see in his the gruesome evidence of the bodily misery he was being made to pass through on the way to a spectral life in our cellar with all the other dead. Sometimes, when Mr. Wishnow's supply of medicine had to be refilled at the drugstore, Seldon would hurry up the stairs to ask if I wanted to go with him, and because I had learned from my parents that Seldon's father was doomed—and because Seldon himself acted as if he knew nothing about it—there was no way I could think of to refuse him, even though I'd never liked being with anyone so nakedly eager to be befriended. Seldon was a child transparently under the sway of his loneliness, undeservedly rich with sorrow and working much too hard to achieve the permanent smile, one of those skinny, pallid, gentle-faced boys who embarrass everyone by throwing a ball like a girl but also the smartest kid in our class and the schoolwide whiz at arithmetic. Oddly, there was nobody in gym class better than Seldon at scrambling up and down the ropes that dangled from the gymnasium's high ceiling, his aerial nimbleness integrally related—according to one of our teachers—to his unchallengeable adroitness with numbers. He was already a little champ at chess, which his father had taught him, and so whenever I accompanied him to the drugstore I knew there was no way to prevent my winding up later at the chessboard in his family's darkened living room—dark to save electricity and dark because the drapes were now drawn all the time to keep the neighborhood's morbidly curious from peering in at Seldon's step-by-step descent into fatherlessness. Undeterred by my stern resistance, Solitary Seldon (as he'd been nicknamed by Earl Axman, whose mother's overnight mental collapse had been a startling parental catastrophe of another order) would try to teach me for the millionth time how to move the pieces and play the game while, behind the back bedroom door, his father coughed so frequently and with so much force that there seemed to be not one father but four, five, six fathers in there coughing themselves to death.

*

In less than a week it was I and not Alvin who was bandaging his stump, and by then I'd practiced enough on myself—and without again throwing up—that he hadn't once to complain of the bandages being too loose or too tight. I did this nightly —even after the stump had healed and he was walking regularly on the artificial leg—to stave off a resurgence of the swelling. All the while the stump was healing, the artificial leg had been at the back of the clothes closet, largely hidden from sight by the shoes on the floor and by the trousers hanging down from the crossrod. It still took some doing not to notice it, but I was determined and didn't know what it was made of till the day Alvin took it out to put on. Except for its eerily replicating the shape of the lower half of a real lower limb, everything about it was horrible, but horrible and a wonder both, beginning with what Alvin called his harness: the dark leather thigh-corset that laced up the front and extended from just below the buttock to the top of the kneecap and that was attached to the prosthesis by hinged steel joints on either side of the knee. The stump, with a long white woolen sock pulled over it, fit snugly into a cushioned socket carved into the top of the prosthesis, which was fashioned of hollowed-out wood with air holes punched into it and not, as I'd been imagining, of a length of black rubber resembling a comic-book bludgeon. At the end of the leg was an artificial foot that flexed only a few degrees and was cushioned with a sponge sole. It screwed neatly into the leg without any of the hardware showing, and though it looked more like a wooden shoe-tree than a living foot with five separate toes, when Alvin slipped into his socks and shoes—the socks washed by my mother, the shoes shined by me—you'd have thought that the feet were both his own.

The first day back on his artificial leg Alvin exercised in the alleyway by walking back and forth from the garage at the far end to the scrawny hedge enclosing the tiny front yard, but never a step farther, to where he could be seen by someone out on the street. The second day he again exercised alone in the morning, but when I got home from school he took me outdoors with him for another session, this time not just concentrating on his walking but pretending that the soundness of his stump and the fit of his prosthesis—and the long future ahead as a one-legged man—weren't weighing on his mind. The following week Alvin was wearing the leg around the house all day, and the week after that, he said to me, "Go get the football." Only we didn't own a football—owning a football was as big a deal as owning cleats or shoulder pads, and no kid had one who wasn't "rich." And I couldn't just go and sign one out from the playground back of the school unless we were going to use it right there, so what I did—I who'd not stolen anything so far other than some change from my parents' pockets—what I did without a moment's hesitation was to stroll down Keer Avenue to where there were one-family houses with front and back lawns and case every driveway until I saw what I was after—a football to steal, a real leather Wilson football, scuffed from the pavement, with worn leather lacing and a bladder you inflated, that some kid with money had left unattended. I tucked it under my arm and took off, tearing all the way up the hill to Summit Avenue as if I were returning a kickoff for old Notre Dame.

That afternoon we practiced pass plays in the alleyway for close to an hour, and at night, when we examined the stump together behind our bedroom's closed door, we saw not one sign of its breaking down, even though while tossing me his perfect left-handed spirals Alvin had been taking practically the whole of his weight on the artificial limb. "I didn't have a choice" is the defense I would have formulated had I been caught in the act on Keer Avenue that day. My cousin Alvin wanted a football, Your Honor. He lost his leg fighting Hitler and now he's home and he wanted a football. What else could I possibly do?

By then a month had passed since the awful homecoming at Penn Station and, though it wasn't necessarily pleasant, I'd feel no revulsion to speak of when, while going for my shoes in the morning, I reached to the back of the closet for Alvin's prosthesis and handed it across to where he was seated on the bed in his undershorts, waiting his turn in the bathroom. The grimness was fading and he'd begun gaining weight, gorging himself between meals on fistfuls of whatever was in the refrigerator, and his eyes didn't look so enormous, and his hair had grown thick again, wavy hair so black it had a waxen sheen, and as he sat there semihelpless with his stump exposed, there was more each morning for a boy who worshiped him to worship, and what there was to pity was a little less impossible to bear.

Soon Alvin was no longer confining himself to the alleyway, and without having to rely on the crutches or the cane that it humiliated him to use in public, he was all over the place on his artificial leg, shopping for my mother at the butcher's, the bakery, and the vegetable store, buying a hotdog for himself down at the corner, taking the bus not only to the dentist on Clinton Avenue but all the way on to Market Street to buy a new shirt at Larkey's—and also, as I didn't yet know, dropping by the playing fields back of the high school with his separation pay in his pocket to see who might be hanging around wanting to play poker or shoot craps. After school one day, the two of us made room in the storage bin for the wheelchair, and that night after dinner I reported to my mother something that had dawned on me at school. Wherever I was and no matter what I was supposed to be doing, I found myself thinking about Alvin and how I could get him to forget about his prosthesis—and so I said to my mother, "If Alvin had a zipper on the side of his pant leg, it would be easier for him, wouldn't it, to get in and out of his pants when he's got his leg on?" The next morning, on her way to work, my mother dropped off a pair of Alvin's army trousers with a neighborhood seamstress who worked out of her house, and the seamstress was able to open the side seam and sew in a zipper that extended some six inches up the uncuffed left pant leg. That night when Alvin pulled on the trousers after having undone the zipper, the pant leg passed easily up over the prosthesis without his having to curse everyone on earth just because he was getting dressed. And when he closed the zipper, you couldn't see it. "You don't even know it's there!" I cried. In the morning, we put all his other trousers in a paper bag for my mother to take to the seamstress to fix. "I couldn't live without you," Alvin said to me when we went to bed that night. "I couldn't put my pants on without you," and he gave me to keep forever the Canadian medal that he'd been awarded "for performance under exceptional circumstances." It was a circular silver medal, on one side King George VI in profile and on the other a triumphant lion standing on the body of a dragon. I of course cherished it and began to wear it regularly, but with the narrow green ribbon from which it hung pinned to my undershirt so no one would see it and question my loyalty to the United States. I left it in my drawer at home only on days I had gym and we had to strip off our outer shirts to exercise.

And where did this leave Sandy? Because he was himself so busy, he seemed at first not to notice my breakneck transformation into personal valet to a decorated Canadian war hero who'd now gone ahead and decorated me; and when he did—and was made miserable at first not so much because of Alvin's involvement with me, which was bound to follow from our new sleeping arrangement, but because of the hostile indifference Alvin evinced toward him—it was too late to oust me from the great supporting role (with its nauseating duties) that I'd virtually been forced to undertake and that, to Sandy's surprise, had elicited such sublime recognition in the waning years of my long career as his little brother.

And all of this had been achieved without my once alluding to Sandy's affiliation, by way of Aunt Evelyn and Rabbi Bengelsdorf, with our present hateful administration. Everyone, including my brother, had avoided speaking of the OAA and Just Folks anywhere near Alvin, convinced that until he came to understand how the enormous popularity of Lindbergh's isolationist policies had begun to win even the support of many Jews—and how it was far less traitorous than it might appear for a Jewish boy Sandy's age to have been drawn to the adventure that Just Folks offered—there'd be nothing to mitigate the outrage of the most self-sacrificing and staunchest Lindbergh-hater of us all. But Alvin seemed already to have sensed that Sandy had let him down and, being Alvin, didn't bother disguising his feelings. I'd said nothing, my parents had said nothing, certainly Sandy hadn't said anything to incriminate himself in Alvin's eyes, and yet Alvin had come to know (or to behave as though he knew) that the first one to welcome him home at the train station had also been first to sign on with the fascists.

Nobody was sure what Alvin was going to do next. There would be problems finding a job because not everyone was going to hire somebody who was considered a cripple, a traitor, or both. However, it was essential, my parents said, to thwart any inclination Alvin might have to do nothing and just sulk and feel sorry for himself for the rest of his life while squeaking by on his pension. My mother wanted him to use his monthly disability check to put himself through college. She had asked around and been told that if he spent a year at Newark Academy, earning B's for the courses he'd got D's and F's in at Weequahic, more than likely he'd be able to get into the University of Newark the following year. But my father couldn't imagine Alvin voluntarily going back to the twelfth grade, even at a downtown private school; at twenty-two and after all he'd been through, he needed as quickly as possible to get a job with a future, and for this my father proposed Alvin's contacting Billy Steinheim. Billy was the son who'd befriended Alvin back when he was Abe's driver, and if Billy was willing to make the case to his father for giving Alvin a second chance, maybe they would agree to find a place for him in the firm, a lowly job for now but one in which he could redeem himself in Abe Steinheim's eyes. If need be, and only if need be, Alvin could get a start with Uncle Monty, who'd already come around to offer his nephew work at the produce market; that had been in those bad early days when Alvin's stump was seriously broken down and he was still in bed most of the time and wouldn't allow the shades to be raised in our room out of his dread of catching so much as a glimpse of the little world in which he'd once been whole. Driving home from Penn Station in the car with my father and Sandy, he'd shut his eyes once the high school came into view rather than be reminded of the innumerable times he'd come bounding out of that building at the end of the day unimpeded by bodily torment and equipped to pursue whatever he wanted.

It was on the very afternoon before Uncle Monty's visit that I was a little late returning from school—it had been my turn to stay to clean the blackboards—and got home to discover that Alvin was gone. I couldn't find him in his bed or in the bathroom or anywhere else in the flat, and so I ran outside to look for him in the backyard and then, bewildered, raced back into the house where, from the foot of the stairwell, I heard faint moaning sounds rising from below—ghosts, the suffering ghosts of Alvin's mother and father! When I edged down the cellar stairs to see if they could be seen there as well as heard, what I saw instead, up by the front wall of the cellar, was Alvin himself peering out of the horizontal little glass slit that looked at street level onto Summit Avenue. He was in his bathrobe, a hand to help him maintain his balance clutching the narrow sill. The other hand I couldn't see. He was using it for something that I was too young to know anything about. Through a little circle of window that had been cleared of grime, he was watching the high school girls who lived on Keer Avenue walk home from Weequahic along our street. Their legs scooting by the front hedge was about all that he could have possibly seen, but seeing that much was enough and caused him to moan with what I took to be anguish at his no longer himself having two legs to walk on. I retreated silently up the stairs and out the back door and squatted in the farthest corner of our garage, plotting to run away to New York to live with Earl Axman. Only because it was getting dark and I had homework to do, did I return to the house, stopping first to peek into the cellar to see if Alvin was still there. He wasn't, and so I dared to descend the stairs, dashing quickly past the wringer and around the drains, and once at the window and up on my toes— intending only to look out at the street the way he did—I discovered the whitewashed wall beneath the window slick and syrupy with an abundance of goo. Since I didn't know what masturbation was, I of course didn't know what ejaculate was. I thought it was pus. I thought it was phlegm. I didn't know what to think, except that it was something terrible. In the presence of a species of discharge as yet mysterious to me, I imagined it was something that festered in a man's body and then came spurting from his mouth when he was completely consumed by grief.

The afternoon Uncle Monty stopped by to see Alvin, he was on his way downtown to Miller Street, where, since he was fourteen years old, he'd been working all night long at the market, arriving at around five and getting home only at nine the next morning to eat his big meal and go to sleep for the day. That was the life lived by the richest member of our family. His two children fared better. Linda and Annette, who were a little older than Sandy and exhibited the painful shyness of girls who tiptoe around a tyrannical father, had lots of clothes and attended suburban Columbia High School in Maplewood, where there were more Jewish kids who had lots of clothes and whose fathers, like Monty, each owned a Caddy for themselves and had a second car in the garage for the convenience of the wife and the grown children. Living with them all in the big Maplewood house was my grandmother, who also had a lot of clothes, all bought for her by her most successful son and none of which she wore other than on the High Holidays and when Monty made her get dressed up to go out to eat with the family on Sundays. The restaurants weren't sufficiently kosher to meet her standards, so all she ever ordered was the à la carte prisoner's meal of bread and water, and then she never knew how to act in a restaurant anyway. Once when she saw a busboy carrying a staggering load of dishes back to the kitchen, she'd gotten up to go over and help him. Uncle Monty cried, "Ma! No! *Loz im tsu ru!* Let the boy be!" and when she slapped his hand away had to be pulled back to the table by the sleeve of her ridiculously sequined dress. There was a black woman, known as "the girl," who came by bus from Newark to clean two days a week, but that didn't stop Grandma from going down on her knees when no one was around to scrub the kitchen and bathroom floors or from doing her own wash on a washboard despite the presence in Monty's finished basement of a brand-new $99 Bendix Home Laundry. My aunt Tillie, Monty's wife, was endlessly complaining because her husband slept all day and was never home at night, though everyone else in the family considered that—far more than her own new Oldsmobile—to be her good luck.

Alvin was lying in bed and still in pajamas at four in the afternoon on that January day when Monty first dropped by to see him and to dare ask the question whose answer none of us exactly knew—"How the hell did you manage to lose a leg?" Since Alvin had been so uncompanionable when I got home from school, responding with a grunt of disgust to whatever I offered to cheer him up, I hardly expected our least lovable relative to elicit any response at all.

But the intimidating presence of Uncle Monty, with the ever-present cigarette dangling from the corner of his mouth, was such that not even Alvin, in those early days, could tell him to shut up and go away. On that particular afternoon Alvin couldn't begin to mimic the brash defiance that had enabled him to hop like a marvel across the Penn Station concourse upon arriving back home as an amputee.

"France," Alvin hollowly replied to the big question.

"Worst country in the world," Monty told him, and with no lack of certainty. As a twenty-one-year-old in the summer of 1918, Monty had himself fought in France against the Germans in the second bloody Battle of the Marne, and then in the Argonne Forest when the Allies broke through on the Germans' western front, and so, of course, he knew everything about France.

"I'm not asking you where," Monty said, "I'm asking you how."

"How," repeated Alvin.

"Spit it out, kid. It'll do you good."

He knew that too—what would do Alvin good.

"Where were you," he asked, "when you got hit? And don't tell me 'the wrong place.' All your life you been in the wrong place."

"We were waiting for the boat to get us out."

Here he closed his eyes as though hoping never to open them again. But instead of stopping right there, as I was praying for him to do—"Shot a German," he suddenly said.

"And?" said Monty.

"He was out there screaming for the rest of the night."

"So? So? Go on. So he was screaming. So what?"

"So near dawn, before the boat's due in, I crawled over to where he was. Maybe fifty yards away. By then he was already dead. But I crawled around to the top of him and I shot him twice in the head. Then I spit on the son of a bitch. And in that second they threw the grenade. I got it in both legs. On one of my legs the foot was twisted around. Broken and twisted. That one they could fix. They operated and fixed it. They put a cast on it. They straightened it out. But the other was gone. I looked down and I saw one foot backwards and one leg dangling. The left leg just about amputated already."

There it was, and nothing like the heroic reality that I had so shallowly imagined.

"Out in no man's land all alone," Monty told him, "could be you were hit by one of your own. It's not yet light, it's half-light, a guy hears gunfire, he panics—bingo, he yanks the pin."

As for that surmise, Alvin had nothing to say.

Anyone else might have understood and relented, if only because of the perspiration beading Alvin's forehead and the droplets pooled in the hollow of his throat and the fact that he still wouldn't open his eyes. But not my uncle—he understands and *doesn't* relent. "And how come you didn't get left there? After pulling that stunt, how come they didn't just leave you to die?"

"There was mud everywhere" was Alvin's vacant reply. "The ground was mud. All I remember is that there was mud."

"Who saved you, misfit?"

"They took me. I must have been out of it. Came and took me."

"I'm trying to picture your brain, Alvin, and I can't. Spits. He spits. And that's the story of how he loses a leg."

"Some things you don't know why you do them." It was I who was speaking. What did I know? But I was telling my uncle, "You just do them, Uncle Monty. You can't not."

"You can't not, Phillie, when you're a professional misfit." To Alvin he said, "So now what? You going to lay there living off disability checks? You going to live like a sharpie off your luck? Or would you maybe consider supporting yourself like the rest of us dumb mortals do? There's a job at the market for you when you're up out of bed. You start at the bottom, hosing down the floor and grading tomatoes, you start at the bottom with the buggy-luggers and the schleppers, but there's a job there working for me, and a paycheck every week. You pocket half the take at the Esso station, but I'll go with you anyway because you're still Jack's kid, and for my brother Jack I do anything. I wouldn't be where I am without Jack. Jack taught me the produce business and then he died. Just like Steinheim wanted to teach you the building business. But nobody can teach you, misfit. Throws the keys in Steinheim's face. Too big for Abe Steinheim. Only Hitler is big enough for Alvin Roth."

In the kitchen, in a drawer with the potholders and the oven thermometer, my mother kept a long stiff needle and heavy thread to truss up the Thanksgiving turkey after it was stuffed. It was the only instrument of torture, aside from the wringer, that I could think of that we owned, and I wanted to go in and get it and use it to shut my uncle's mouth.

At the bedroom door, before leaving for the market, Monty turned back to summarize. Bullies love to summarize. The redundant upbraiding summary—nothing to equal it outside the old-fashioned flogging. "Your buddies risked everything to save you. Went in and dragged you out under fire. Didn't they? And for what? So you could spend the rest of your life shooting craps with Margulis? So you can play seven-card stud up at the schoolyard? So you can go back and pump gas and steal Simkowitz blind? You make every mistake in the book. Everything you do you do wrong. Even shooting Germans you do wrong. Why is that? Why do you throw keys at people? Why do you spit? Someone who is already dead—and you spit? Why? Because life wasn't handed to you on a silver platter like it was handed to the rest of the Roths? If it wasn't for Jack, Alvin, I wouldn't be standing here wasting my breath. There is nothing you have earned. Let's be clear about that. Nothing. For twenty-two years you have remained a disaster. I'm doing this for your father, sonny, not for you. I'm doing it for your grandmother. 'Help the boy,' she tells me, so I'm helping you. Once you figure out how you want to make your fortune, come around on your pegleg and we'll talk."

Alvin didn't cry, didn't curse, didn't holler, even after Monty was out the back door and into his car and he could have unleashed his every evil thought. He was too far gone to roar that day. Or even to crack. Only I did, after he refused to open his eyes and look at me when I begged him to; only I cracked, alone later in the one place in our house where I knew I could go to be apart from the living and all that they cannot not do.

5

Never Before

H ERE'S HOW Alvin came to have it in for Sandy.
Before leaving him alone on the morning of his first
Monday back, my mother had made Alvin promise to use his
crutches to get around on until one of us was home to fetch
for him. But Alvin so despised being on crutches that he refused even by himself to submit to the stability they provided.
At night, when we were in our beds and the lights were out,
Alvin would get me laughing by explaining why crutching
wasn't so simple as my mother thought. "You go to the bathroom," Alvin said, "and they're always falling. They're always
clattering. They're always making a fucking noise. You go to
the bathroom, you've got these crutches, you try to get your
cock, and you can't get your cock because your crutches are in
the way. You gotta get rid of the crutches. Then you're standing on one leg. That's not so good. You lean one way or another, you splatter all over the place. Your father tells me to sit
down to piss. Know what I say? 'I'll sit when you do, Herman.'
Fucking crutches. Standing on one leg. Taking your dick out.
Jesus. Pissing is hard enough to do as it is." I'm laughing uncontrollably now not only because the story is especially funny
as he half whispers it in the darkened room, but because never
before has a man revealed himself to me this way, using the
prohibited words so freely and openly cracking toilet jokes.
"Come on," Alvin says, "own up to it, kiddo—pissing's not
something that's as easy as it looks."

So it happened that on that first Monday morning alone,
when the amputation was still a limitless loss that he assumed
would impede and torment him forever, he took the fall that
no one in the family knew about other than me. He was standing braced against the kitchen sink, where, without the aid of
his crutches, he'd gone for a glass of water. When he turned to

start back to the bedroom he forgot (for all possible reasons) that he had just the one leg and, instead of hopping, did what everyone else did in our house—began to walk and of course toppled over. The pain shooting up from the butt end of his stump was worse than the pain in the missing segment of his leg—pain, Alvin explained to me after I first watched him succumb to a siege in the bed beside me, "that grabs you and won't let you go," though no limb is left to cause it. "There's pain where you are," Alvin said when the time had come to reassure me with some kind of comical remark, "and there's pain where you ain't. I wonder who thought that up."

The English hospital gave the amputees morphine to control the pain. "You're always calling for it," Alvin told me. "And whenever you do they give it to you. You push a button for the nurse and when she gets to you, you tell her, 'Morphine, morphine,' and then you're pretty much out of it." "How much did it hurt in the hospital?" I asked him. "It was no fun, kiddo." "Was that the worst pain you ever had?" "Worst pain I ever had," he replied, "was when my father closed the door of the car on my finger when I was six years old." He laughed, and so I laughed. "My father said—when he saw me crying like hell, this little stinker about that high—my father said, 'Stop crying, that doesn't do any good.'" Quietly laughing again, Alvin said, "And that was probably worse than the pain. My last memory of him, too. Later that day he keeled over and died."

Writhing on the kitchen linoleum, Alvin had no one to call for help, let alone for a shot of morphine; everybody was off either at school or at work, and so, in time, it was necessary to grope his way across the kitchen and the foyer to his bed. But just as he was positioning himself to push up from the floor, he spotted Sandy's art portfolio. Sandy still used the portfolio to preserve his large pencil and charcoal drawings between tracing paper and to carry them with him when he had to take the drawings somewhere to show. It was too large to store in the sun parlor, and so he'd left it behind in our room. Mere curiosity impelled Alvin to fish the portfolio out a ways from beneath the bed, but because he was unable right off to determine its purpose—and because all he really wanted was to be back under the covers—he was ready to forget about it when he noticed the ribbon that held the two halves together. Existence was worthless, living was unendurable, he still throbbed with pain from the mindless accident at the kitchen sink, and so for no reason other than that he felt himself powerless to carry off a physical task any more formidable, he fiddled with the ribbons until he undid the bow.

What he found inside were the three portraits of Charles A. Lindbergh as an aviator that Sandy had told my parents he'd destroyed two years back as well as those that he'd drawn at the behest of Aunt Evelyn once Lindbergh became president. I'd only seen the new ones myself when Aunt Evelyn took me along to New Brunswick to hear Sandy give his Just Folks recruitment speech in the synagogue basement. "This shows President Lindbergh signing into law the Universal Conscription Act, designed to keep America at peace by teaching our youth the skills necessary to protect and defend the nation. This one shows the president at a draftsman's drawing board, adding his aeronautical suggestions to the design for the nation's newest fighter-bomber. Here I show President Lindbergh relaxing at the White House with the family dog."

Each of the new Lindbergh portraits exhibited as a prelude to Sandy's New Brunswick talk Alvin examined on the bedroom floor. Then, despite the destructive urge aroused by his registering the skill so meticulously expended on these beautiful likenesses, he placed them between the leaves of tracing paper and shoved the portfolio back under the bed.

Once Alvin was out and around in the neighborhood, he hadn't to rely only on Sandy's Lindbergh drawings to realize that, while he'd been making raids on ammo depots in France, Roosevelt's Republican successor had come to be, if not entirely trusted by the Jews, accepted as tolerable for the time being even among those of our neighbors who had started out hating him as passionately as my father did. Walter Winchell persisted in attacking the president on his Sunday-night radio show, and everybody on the block devotedly tuned him in to give credence, while they listened, to his alarming interpretations of the president's policies, but as nothing that they feared had come to pass since the inauguration, our neighbors slowly began putting more faith in Rabbi Bengelsdorf's optimistic assurances than in Winchell's dire prophecies. And not just the neighbors but Jewish leaders all over the country began openly to acknowledge that Newark's Lionel Bengelsdorf, far from having betrayed them by endorsing Lindy in the 1940 election, had been prescient enough to see where the nation was headed and that his elevation to the directorship of the Office of American Absorption—and the administration's foremost adviser on Jewish affairs—was the direct result of his having cleverly gained Lindbergh's confidence as an early supporter. If the president's anti-Semitism had somehow been neutralized (or, more remarkably, eradicated), Jews were willing to attribute the miracle to the influence of the venerable rabbi who was soon to become—another miracle—an uncle by marriage to Sandy and me.

One day early in March I wandered over, uninvited, to the dead-end street backing onto the school playground where Alvin had begun shooting craps and playing stud poker if the afternoon was warm enough and it wasn't raining. He was rarely in the house anymore when I got home after school, and though generally he made it back by five-thirty for dinner, after dessert he'd head out to the hotdog hangout a block from our house to meet up with his old high school friends, a few of whom used to pump gas at the Esso station owned by Simkowitz and had been fired along with him for stealing from the boss. I'd be asleep by the time he got in for the night, and only when he removed his leg and began hopping to and from the bathroom did I open my eyes and mumble his name before falling back to sleep. Some seven weeks after he'd moved into the bed beside mine, I ceased to be indispensable and abruptly found myself bereft of the mesmeric surrogate he'd been for Sandy, vanished now from my side into the stardom masterminded for him by Aunt Evelyn. The maimed and suffering American pariah who had come to loom larger for me than any man I'd ever known, including my father, whose passionate struggles had become my own, whose future I fretted over when I should have been listening to the teacher in class, had begun to buddy up with the same good-for-nothings who'd helped turn him into a petty thief at sixteen. What he appeared to have lost in combat, along with his leg, was every decent habit inculcated in him when he was living as my parents' ward. Nor did he display any interest in the fight against fascism, which, two years earlier, no one could restrain him from joining. In fact, why he went scooting out of the house on his artificial leg every night was, at the beginning anyway, largely to avoid having to sit in the living room while my father read the war news aloud from the paper.

There was no campaign against the Axis powers that my father didn't agonize about, particularly when things went badly for the Soviet Union and Great Britain and it was clear how urgently they needed the U.S. arms embargoed by Lindbergh and the Republican Congress. By this time my father could deploy the terminology of a war strategist quite proficiently when he expatiated on the need for the British, Australians, and Dutch to prevent the Japanese—who, in sweeping across Southeast Asia, exhibited all the righteous cruelty of the racially superior—from proceeding westward into India and southward into New Zealand and on to Australia. In the early months of 1942 the Pacific war news that he read to us was uniformly bad: there was the successful Japanese drive into Burma, the Japanese capture of Malaya, the Japanese bombing of New Guinea, and, after devastating attacks from the sea and air and the capturing of tens of thousands of British and Dutch troops on the ground, the fall of Singapore, Borneo, Sumatra, and Java. But it was the progress of the Russian campaign that upset my father most. The year before, when the Germans appeared to be on the verge of overrunning every major city in the western half of the Soviet Union (including Kiev, from whose environs my maternal grandparents had emigrated to America in the 1890s), the names of even lesser Russian cities, like Petrozavodsk, Novgorod, Dnepropetrovsk, and Taganrog, had become as familiar to me as the capitals of the forty-eight states. In the winter of 1941–42 the Russians had staged the impossible counterattacks that broke the sieges of Leningrad, Moscow, and Stalingrad, but by March the Germans had regrouped from their winter catastrophe and, as demonstrated by the troop movements mapped out in the *Newark News*, were reinforcing for a spring offensive to conquer the Caucasus. My father explained that what made the prospect of a Russian collapse so awful was that it would represent to the world the invincibility of the German war machine. The vast natural resources of the Soviet Union would fall into German hands and the Russian people would be forced to serve the Third Reich. Worst of all "for us" was that with Germany's eastward advance millions and millions of Russian Jews would come under the control of an occupying army equipped in every way to implement Hitler's messianic program to deliver humanity from the clutches of the Jews.

According to my father, the brutal triumph of antidemocratic militarism was imminent just about everywhere, the massacre of Russian Jewry, including members of my mother's extended family, was all but at hand, and Alvin didn't care one bit. No longer was he burdened by concern for anyone's suffering other than his own.

I found Alvin down on the good knee of the real leg, dice in hand and the pile of bills beside him secured by a jagged chunk of cement. With the prosthetic leg jutting straight out in front of him, he looked like a squatting Russian dancing one of those crazy Slavic jigs. There were six other gamblers tightly encircling him, three still in the game, clutching what was left of their dough, two who were broke and just standing around—whom I vaguely recognized as ex-Weequahic washouts now in their twenties—and the long-legged guy hovering over him, Alvin's "partner," as it turned out, Shushy Margulis, a skinny zoot-suiter with a sinewy build and a gliding gait, the hanger-on from Alvin's gas station days whom my father most despised. Shushy was known to us kids as the Pinball King because a racketeer uncle whom he boasted about *was* the pinball king—and king as well of all illegal slots down in Philadelphia, where he reigned—and also because of the hours he spent racking up scores by banging away at the pinball machines in the neighborhood candy stores, shoving the machine, cursing it, violently shaking it from side to side until play was terminated either by the colored lights flashing "Tilt" or by the store owner chasing him out. Shushy was the famous comedian who entertained his admirers by gleefully tossing lit matches into the mouth of the big green mailbox across from the high school, and who had once eaten a live praying mantis on a bet, and who, during his short-lived academic career, liked to hand the crowd a laugh outside the hotdog hangout by limping across Chancellor Avenue with one hand raised to stop the oncoming traffic—limping badly, tragically, though nothing was wrong with him. By this time he was already into his thirties and still living with his seamstress mother in one of the little flats at the top of a two-and-a-half-family house next door to the synagogue on Wainwright Street. It was to Shushy's mother, known sympathetically to one and all as "poor Mrs. Margulis," that my mother had taken Alvin's pants to have the zippers sewn in—poor Mrs. Margulis not merely because she survived as a widow by doing piecework at slave wages for a Down Neck dress manufacturer but because her sharpie son seemed never to have held a job other than as a runner for the bookie who worked out of the poolroom around the corner from their house and just down the street from the Catholic orphanage on Lyons Avenue.

The orphanage stood within the fenced-off grounds of St. Peter's, the parish church that oddly monopolized some three square blocks at the very heart of our unredeemable neighborhood. The church itself was topped by a tall bell tower and an even taller steeple that was capped by a cross that rose divinely above the telephone wires. Locally there was no building that high to be seen until you proceeded nearly a mile down the Lyons Avenue hill to my birthplace, the Beth Israel Hospital, where every boy I knew had been born as well and, at the age of eight days, ritually circumcised in the hospital's sanctuary. Flanking the bell tower of the church were two smaller steeples that I never cared to examine because the faces of Christian saints were said to be carved into the stone, and the church's high, narrow stained-glass windows told a story that I didn't want to know. Near the church was a small rectory; like most everything else situated within the black iron palings of this alien world it had been built during the latter part of the previous century, several decades before the first of our houses went up and the western edge of the Weequahic neighborhood took shape as Newark's Jewish frontier. Behind the church was the grammar school serving the orphans—there were about a hundred of them—and a smaller number of local Catholic kids. The school and the orphanage were run by an order of nuns, German nuns, I remember being told. Jewish children raised even in tolerant households like mine would generally cross the street on the rare occasions we saw them swishing our way in their witchy attire, and family lore had it that when my brother, as a small child sitting alone on our front stoop one afternoon, spotted a pair of them approaching from Chancellor Avenue, he had called excitedly to my mother, "Look, Ma—the nuts."

A convent stood next to the orphans' residence. Both were simple red-brick buildings, and at the end of a summer's day you'd sometimes catch a glimpse of the orphans—white children, girls and boys, aged from about six to fourteen—sitting outdoors on the fire escape. I have no memory of seeing the orphans in a group anywhere else, certainly not running freely about the streets the way we did. A swarm of them would have discomfited me no less than did the unsettling appearance of the nuns, primarily because they were orphaned but also because they were said to be both "neglected" and "indigent."

Back of the residence hall, and unlike anything to be seen in our neighborhood—or anywhere else in an industrial city of close to half a million   was a truck farm of the kind that made New Jersey "the Garden State," back when compact family vegetable farms able to turn a small profit dotted the undeveloped rural reaches of the state. The food grown and harvested at St. Peter's went to feed the orphans, the dozen or so nuns, the old monsignor in charge, and the younger priest who was his assistant. With the help of the orphans, the land was worked by a resident German farmer called Thimmes—unless I'm remembering incorrectly and that was the name of St. Peter's monsignor, who'd been running the place for years.

At our public elementary school less than a mile away it was rumored that the nuns who instructed the orphans in class routinely smacked the stupidest of them across the hands with wooden rulers and that when a boy's offense was so gross as to be intolerable the monsignor's assistant was called in to beat him across the buttocks with the same whip the farmer used on the swaybacked pair of lumbering workhorses that pulled the plow for the spring planting. These horses we all knew and recognized because from time to time they'd wander together across the farm to the little wooded meadow at the southern boundary of St. Peter's domain and stick their heads inquisitively out above

the gate that backed onto Goldsmith Avenue, where the crap
game I'd come upon was taking place.

There was a chain-link fence about seven feet high at the edge
of the playground on the near side of Goldsmith Avenue and a
wire fence set in posts at the wooded edge of the truck farm on
the far side, and since no houses had as yet gone up anywhere
nearby and there was never much foot or automobile traffic to
speak of, an almost sylvan seclusion was conveniently provided
there for the neighborhood's tiny handful of losers to pursue
their pleasures out of harm's way. The closest I'd ever come to
one of these sinister conclaves before was when, during some
playground game, I'd had to chase a ball that had rolled to
where they all huddled together just beyond the fence, uttering imprecations at one another and saving their sweet talk for
the dice.

Now, I was no righteous little foe of crapshooting, and I had
begged Alvin to teach me how to play one afternoon when he
was still on crutches and my mother had instructed me to accompany him to his dentist appointment and do things like
drop his fare into the fare box and hold his crutches for him
while he hopped onto the street from the bus's back door. That
night, when everyone else had gone to sleep and we'd switched
off the table lamp on the stand between our beds, he watched
with a smile as, by the beam of my flashlight, I whispered,
"Dice be nice," and soundlessly rolled three consecutive sevens
across my sheets. Yet as I watched him now in the clutches of
his inferiors, and remembered all that my family had sacrificed
to prevent him from turning himself into a replica of Shushy,
every obscenity I'd learned as his roommate flooded foully
into my mind. I cursed him in behalf of my father, my mother,
and especially my ostracized brother—was it for this that all of
us had agreed to endure Alvin's objectionable behavior toward
Sandy? Was it for this that he'd run off to fight in the war? I
thought, "Take your fucking medal, gimp, and shove it!" If
only he would learn his lesson by losing every last penny of his
disability pension, but in fact he couldn't stop himself from
winning, any more than he could stop himself from abandoning the desire to ever again be anyone's hero, and, having already raked in a big wad of bills, he held the dice to my lips

and, in a gravelly voice with which he intended to be funny for his friends, he instructed me, "Blow on 'em—baby." I blew, he rolled and won yet again. "Six and one—making what?" he asked. "Seven," I obediently answered, "the hard way."

Shushy reached down to muss my hair and began calling me Alvin's mascot, as though "mascot" could encompass what I'd resolved to be for Alvin since he'd come home, as though a word so hollow and childish could account for why Alvin's King George medal was pinned to my undershirt. Shushy was dressed in a chocolate-colored double-breasted gabardine suit, with pegged trousers and wide, padded shoulders and flamboyant lapels, his favored getup whenever he went bopping around the neighborhood snapping his fingers—and, in my mother's words, "wasting his life"—while back in their tiny attic flat his mother hemmed a hundred dresses a day to meet the family's bills.

When he missed his point, Alvin drew all his winnings together and ostentatiously stuffed the bundle into his pocket—the man who broke the bank behind the high school. Then, by grasping the chain-link fence, he pulled himself to his feet. I knew (and not just from observing the tortured way he began limping about to get himself going) that a big boil had erupted on his stump the night before and that he wasn't in the best of shape that day. But he refused any longer to be seen on crutches by anyone outside the family, and before going off to team up with sleazy Shushy—and spend another day blatantly repudiating all the ideals that had made him a cripple—he harnessed the stump into the prosthesis however much it hurt.

"Goddamn legmaker" was all he said by way of complaint as he came up to put his hand on my shoulder.

"Can I go home now?" I whispered.

"Sure, why not?" and then he took two ten-dollar bills out of his pocket—nearly half my father's weekly paycheck—and flattened them against the palm of my hand. Never before had money seemed like something alive.

Instead of heading back across the playground, I took a slightly longer route home, proceeding down the Goldsmith Avenue hill to Hobson Street so that I could look up close at the orphanage horses. I had never dared to reach over and touch them, and before that day I'd never spoken to them the way other kids did, satirically calling these mud-spattered beasts drooling gooey saliva "Omaha" and "Whirlaway," which were the names of two of the greatest Kentucky Derby winners of our day.

I stopped a safe distance back from where the darkly gleaming high-relief eyes peered out above the orphanage fence, impassively monitoring through their long lashes the no man's land separating the stronghold of St. Peter's from the neighborhood of Jews beyond the pale. The chain was unlooped and hanging down off the gate. I had only to yank up on the latch and swing the gate open and the horses would be free to gallop away. The temptation was enormous—as was the spite.

"Fucking Lindbergh," I said to the horses, "Nazi fucking bastard Lindbergh!" and then, for fear that if I did fling open the gate, instead of the horses running free they'd use their big teeth to drag me into the orphanage, I darted down the street and, turning on Hobson, raced past the block-long row of four-family houses and out to the corner of Chancellor Avenue, where housewives I recognized were in and out of the grocery and the bakery and the butcher shop, and older boys whose names I knew were riding their bikes, and the tailor's son was carrying over either shoulder a load of newly pressed clothes for delivery, and where Italian singing issued onto the street through the shoemaker's doorway, his radio tuned as always to WEVD—the EVD to honor the persecuted socialist hero Eugene V. Debs—and where I was safe from Alvin, Shushy, the horses, the orphans, the priests, the nuns, and the parochial-school whip.

When I turned back up the hill toward home a man neatly dressed in a business suit fell in step beside me. It was still too early for the local workingmen to be getting home for dinner, and so I knew right off to be suspicious.

"Master Philip?" he inquired with a broad smile. "Do you ever listen to *Gangbusters* on the radio, Master Philip? About J. Edgar Hoover and the FBI?"

"Yes."

"Well, I work for Mr. Hoover. He's my boss. I'm an agent from the FBI. Here," he said, and he removed a billfold from an inside coat pocket and flipped it open to show me his badge. "If you wouldn't mind, I'd like to ask a few little questions."

"I don't mind, but I'm on my way home. I have to get home."

Immediately I thought about the two ten-dollar bills. If he searched me, if he had a warrant to search me, wasn't he going to find all that money and assume it was stolen? Wouldn't anybody? And until ten minutes earlier, for an entire lifetime, I'd been walking around with my pockets empty, out on the street without a penny to my name! My allowance of five cents a week I saved in a jelly jar with a slit Sandy chiseled into the lid with the can opener blade of his Boy Scout knife. Now I was walking around like a bank robber.

"Don't be frightened. Calm down, Master Philip. You've heard *Gangbusters*. We're on your side. We protect you. I just want to ask a few questions about your cousin Alvin. How's he doing?"

"He's fine."

"How's his leg coming along?"

"Good."

"He's able to walk okay?"

"Yes."

"Wasn't that him I saw over where you just came from? Wasn't that Alvin behind the playground? Out on the sidewalk, wasn't that Alvin with Shushy Margulis?"

I didn't reply, and so he said, "It's okay if they're shooting craps. That's no crime. That's just part of being a big man. Alvin must have shot craps a lot in the army hospital up in Montreal."

When I still wouldn't speak, he asked, "What were the fellas talking about?"

"Nothing."

"All afternoon they're out there, and they're talking about nothing?"

"They were just saying how much they were losing."

"Nothing else? Nothing about the president? You know who the president is, don't you?"

"Charles A. Lindbergh."

"Nothing about President Lindbergh, Master Philip?"

"Not that I heard," I answered truthfully.

But might he not have overheard *me* saying what I'd said to the horses? Impossible—and yet by now I was sure that he knew every move I'd made since Alvin came home from the war and gave me his medal. It was indisputable that he knew that I was wearing the medal. Why else was he looking me over from head to toe?

"Did they talk about Canada?" he asked. "About going to Canada?"

"No, sir."

"Call me Don, why don't you? And I'll call you Phil. You know what a fascist is, don't you, Phil?"

"I think so."

"Did they call anybody a fascist that you remember?"

"No."

"Don't rush yourself. Don't rush to answer. Take all the time you need. Try hard to remember. It's important. Did they call anybody a fascist? Did they say anything about Hitler? You know who Hitler is."

"Everybody does."

"He's a bad man, isn't he?"

"Yes," I said.

"He's against the Jews, isn't he?"

"Yes."

"Who else is against the Jews?"

"The Bund."

"Anyone else?" he asked.

I knew enough not to mention Henry Ford, America First, the southern Democrats, or the isolationist Republicans, let alone Lindbergh. Over the past few years, the list I heard at home of prominent Americans who hated Jews was far longer than that, and then there were the ordinary Americans, tens of thousands of them, maybe millions of them, like the beer drinkers we didn't want to live beside in Union and the owner of the hotel in Washington and the mustached diner who'd insulted us in the cafeteria near Union Station. "Don't talk," I told myself, as though a protected boy of nine were mixed up with criminals and had something to hide. But I must already have begun to think of myself as a little criminal because I was a Jew.

"And who else?" he repeated. "Mr. Hoover wants to know who else. Come clean, Phil."

"I *am*," I insisted.

"How's your aunt Evelyn doing?"

"She's fine."

"She's getting married. Isn't that right, that she's getting married? You can at least answer that."

"Yes."

"And do you know who she's marrying?"

"Yes."

"You're a smart boy. I think you know more—a lot more. But you're too smart to tell me, aren't you?"

"She's marrying Rabbi Bengelsdorf," I said. "He's head of the OAA."

My saying that made him laugh. "Okay," he told me, "you go on home. Go home and eat your matzohs. Isn't that what makes you so smart? Eating the matzohs?"

We were now at the corner of Chancellor and Summit, and I could see the stoop of our house down at the end of the block. "Bye!" I cried, and didn't wait for the light to change but ran for home before I fell into his trap, if I hadn't fallen into it already.

There were three police cars parked on the street in front of our house, our alleyway was blocked off by an ambulance, and a couple of cops stood on the stoop talking together while another was posted beside the back door. The women on the block, most of them still in their aprons, were on their front stoops trying to figure out what was going on, and all the kids were huddled on the sidewalk across the street from our house, peering out at the cops and the ambulance from between the row of parked cars. Never before could I remember them silently gathered together like that, looking so apprehensive.

Our downstairs neighbor was dead. Mr. Wishnow had committed suicide. That was why everything I could never have expected to see was now right outside the door of our house. Weighing barely eighty pounds, he had been able to strangulate himself by stringing the living room curtain cords over the wooden rod in the back-foyer coat closet, then looping them around his neck and falling forward off the edge of the kitchen chair where he'd seated himself inside the closet. When Seldon, home from school, went to put his coat away, he found his father, in his pajamas, hanging face-down on the closet floor amid the family's rubbers and galoshes. My first thought on learning the news was that I no longer had to be fearful of hearing a coughing fit emanating from the dying man in the first-floor flat whenever I was alone in the cellar, or of hearing him in my bed on the floor above when I was trying to fall asleep. But then I realized that the ghost of Mr. Wishnow would now join the circle of ghosts already inhabiting the cellar and that, just because I was relieved he was dead, he would go out of his way to haunt me for the rest of my life.

Since I didn't know what else to do, I at first kneeled at the side of the parked cars, hiding there with the other kids. None of them had a conception any larger than my own of the cataclysm that had befallen the Wishnows, but it was from their whisperings that I pieced together how Mr. Wishnow had died and how he'd been found and learned that Seldon and his mother were inside with one of the policemen and the medics. And with the corpse. The corpse was what the kids were all waiting to see. I waited with them rather than wind up entering the back hallway just as they were carrying Mr. Wishnow down the stairs. Nor did I want to get home and have to sit there alone until my mother, my father, or Sandy appeared. As for Alvin, I wanted never to see him again or to be questioned about him by anyone.

The woman who emerged from the house accompanying the medics wasn't Mrs. Wishnow but my mother. I couldn't understand why she was home from work until it dawned on me that the dead father they were carrying away was my own. Yes, of course—*my* father had committed suicide. He couldn't take any more of Lindbergh and what Lindbergh was letting the Nazis do to the Jews of Russia and what Lindbergh had done to our family right here and so it was he who had hanged himself—in *our* closet.

I didn't have hundreds of memories of him then, I had just one, and it did not seem to me at all important enough to be the memory I ought to be having. Alvin's last memory of his father was of him closing the car door on his little boy's finger —mine of my father was of him greeting the stump of a man who begged every day outside his office building. "How you doin', Little Robert?" my father said, and the stump of a man replied, "How you, Herman?"

It was here that I edged myself between the closely parked cars and darted out across the street.

When I saw that the sheet covering my father's body and face couldn't possibly allow him to breathe, I began to wail.

"Don't, don't, darling," my mother said. "There's nothing to be frightened of." She put her arms around my head, held me to her, and repeated, "There's nothing to be frightened of. He was sick and he was suffering and he died. Now he's not suffering anymore."

"He was in the closet," I said.

"No, he wasn't. He was in his bed. He died in his bed. He was very, very sick. You knew that. That was why he coughed all the time."

By now the ambulance doors were swung open to receive the stretcher. The medics carefully maneuvered it inside and pulled the doors shut behind them. My mother stood next to me on the street, holding my hand in hers and to my amazement looking perfectly composed. Only when I made a move to break away from her and run after the ambulance, only when I cried, "He can't breathe!" did she finally realize what was torturing me.

"It's Mr. Wishnow—it's Mr. *Wishnow* who is dead." She shook me, gently shook me back and forth to bring me to my senses. "It's *Seldon's* father, dear—he died from his illness this afternoon."

I couldn't tell if she was lying to keep me from becoming more hysterical or if she was telling the wonderful truth.

"Seldon found him in the closet?"

"No. I told you—no. Seldon found his father in his bed. Seldon's mother wasn't home so he called the police. I came because Mrs. Wishnow called me at the store and asked me to help her. Do you understand? Daddy's at work. Daddy's working. Oh, what on earth have you been thinking? Daddy will be home for dinner very soon. So will Sandy. There's nothing to be afraid of. Everybody will be home, everybody is coming home, we'll have our dinner," she said reassuringly, "and everything is going to be fine."

*

But nothing was "fine." The FBI agent who'd grilled me about Alvin on Chancellor Avenue had earlier stopped by Hahne's dress department to question my mother, then by the Metropolitan's Newark office to question my father, and, just after Sandy left Aunt Evelyn's office for home, he had boarded my brother's bus and, from the seat alongside him, conducted yet another interrogation. Alvin wasn't at dinner to hear about any of this—just as we were sitting down to eat, he'd phoned and told my mother not to save anything for him. It seemed that every time he'd made a killing at poker or craps, Alvin took Shushy downtown with him to the Hickory Grill for a charcoal-broiled steak dinner. "Alvin's partner in crime," my father called Shushy. What he called Alvin that evening was ungrateful, stupid, reckless, ignorant, and incorrigible.

"And bitter," said my mother, sadly, "so bitter because of his leg."

"Well, I'm sick and tired of his leg," said my father. "He went to war. Who sent him? I didn't. You didn't. Abe Steinheim didn't. Abe Steinheim wanted to send him to college. He went to war on his own, and he's lucky he wasn't killed. He's lucky it was just his leg. This is it, Bess. I've had it with that boy. The FBI questions my children? Bad enough they harass you and me—and in my office, mind you, in front of the Boss! No," he told her. "This has to stop and stop now. This is a home. We are a family. He has dinner downtown with Shushy? Let him go live with Shushy."

"If only he would go to school," my mother said. "If only he would take a job."

"He has a job," my father replied. "Bum."

After we'd finished eating, my mother put a meal together for Seldon and Mrs. Wishnow, and my father helped her carry the plates downstairs while Sandy and I were left with the dinner dishes. We set to work at the sink as we did most nights, except that I couldn't shut up. I told him about the crap game. I told him about the FBI agent. I told him about Mr. Wishnow. "He didn't die in his bed," I said. "Mother's not telling us the truth. He committed suicide, only she doesn't want to say it. Seldon found him in the closet when he got home from school. He hung himself. That's why the police came."

"Did he turn colors?" my brother asked me.

"I only saw him under the sheet. Maybe it was colors—I don't know. I don't *want* to know. It was bad enough when they jiggled the stretcher that you could see him move." That I had thought at first it was my father under the sheet I didn't say aloud for fear that if I did it would turn out to be true. The fact that my father was alive, vividly alive—angry at Alvin and threatening to throw him out of the house—had no impact on my thinking.

"How do you know he was in the closet?" Sandy asked.

"That's what all the kids said."

"And you believe them?" Because of his fame, he was becoming a very hard boy whose tremendous confidence now sounded more and more like lordly arrogance whenever he spoke about me or my friends.

"Well, why were all the police here? Just because he died? People die all the time," I said, trying, however, not to believe it. "He killed himself. He had to."

"And is that against the law, killing yourself?" my brother asked me. "What were they going to do, put him in jail for killing himself?"

I didn't know. I didn't know any longer what the law was and so I didn't know what might or might not be against it. I didn't seem to know whether my own father—who'd just headed downstairs with my mother—was really alive or pretending to be alive or being driven around dead in the back of that ambulance. I didn't know anything. I didn't know why Alvin was bad now instead of good. I didn't know if I had dreamed that an FBI agent had questioned me on Chancellor Avenue. It had to be a dream and yet couldn't be if everybody else said they'd been questioned too. Unless that was the dream. I felt woozy and thought I was going to faint. I'd never before seen anyone faint, other than in a movie, and I'd never before fainted myself. I'd never before looked at my house from a hiding place across the street and wished that it was somebody else's. I'd never before had twenty dollars in my pocket. I'd never before known anyone who'd seen his father hanging in a closet. I'd never before had to grow up at a pace like this.

Never before—the great refrain of 1942.

"You better call Mom," I told my brother. "Call her—tell

her to come home right away!" But before Sandy could reach the back door to rush down to the Wishnows, I was vomiting into the dishtowel still in my hand, and when I collapsed it was because my leg had been blown off and my blood was everywhere.

I remained in bed with a high fever for six days, so weak and lifeless that the family doctor stopped by every evening to check on the progress of my disease, that not uncommon childhood ailment called why-can't-it-be-the-way-it-was.

The next day for me was Sunday. It was late afternoon, and Uncle Monty was visiting. Alvin was there too, and from what I could overhear from my bed of what was being said in the kitchen, he hadn't been seen anywhere around since Mr. Wishnow had committed suicide on Friday and he'd walked away from that crap game with his bundle of fives, tens, and twenties. But since dinnertime Friday I'd been away myself, off with the horses and their hooves, enveloped by kaleidoscopic hallucinations of the orphanage workhorses pursuing me to the edge of the earth.

And now Uncle Monty again, again Uncle Monty attacking Alvin, and with words I could not believe were being spoken in our house in the presence of my mother. But then, Uncle Monty knew how to subdue Alvin in ways that my father just couldn't employ.

By nightfall, after all the shouting had subsided into lamentations for my late uncle Jack and Monty's booming voice had gone hoarse, Alvin accepted the job at the produce market that he'd refused to consider when Monty had offered it first. As unmanned as he'd been by his mutilation on the morning he arrived at Penn Station in the care of that hulking Canadian nurse, as overridden by defeat as when, from his wheelchair, he wouldn't dare to look a one of us in the eye, Alvin consented to dissolve his partnership with Shushy and to give up gambling on the neighborhood streets. A hater no less of subservience than of weeping, he astonished everyone by breaking into guilty tears and begging forgiveness and agreeing to stop being a brute to my brother, an ingrate to my mother and father, and a bad influence on me, and to treat us with the appreciation we were due. Uncle Monty warned Alvin that if he didn't abide by his promises and continued instead to sabotage Herman's household, the Roths would be finished with him for good.

Though Alvin appeared to be trying hard to make a go of the menial donkeywork that was his first job, he didn't last long enough at the market to rise even a notch above sweeping and fetching. One day, when he'd been there little more than a week, the FBI came around to inquire about him, the same agent using the same menacingly innocuous questions he'd asked my family and me, only insinuating now to the other produce workers that Alvin was a self-declared traitor plotting with anti-American malcontents like himself to assassinate President Lindbergh. The charges were ludicrous, and yet tame as Alvin had been all that week—tame as he'd sworn and dedicated himself to remaining—he was fired on the spot and, on the way out, instructed by one of the goons in charge never to come anywhere near the market again. When my father got on the phone to his brother demanding to know what had happened, Monty replied that he'd had no choice—he'd been ordered to get rid of his nephew by Longy's boys. Newark's Longy Zwillman, who'd grown up like my father and his brothers a son of immigrants in the old Jewish slums, ran the Jersey rackets back then, the ruthless potentate of everything from bookmaking and strikebreaking to the trucking and hauling services foisted on merchants like Belmont Roth. Because the feds were the last people Longy needed snooping around, Alvin lost the job, cleared out of our house, and left the city in under twenty-four hours, this time not across the international border for Montreal and the Canadian commandos but just over the Delaware for Philadelphia and a job with Shushy's uncle the gambling-machine king, a racketeer seemingly more tolerant of traitors than his peerless counterpart up in North Jersey.

In the spring of 1942, to celebrate the success of the Iceland Understanding, a state dinner was given at the White House by President and Mrs. Lindbergh to honor Foreign Minister Joachim von Ribbentrop, who was known to have touted Lindbergh to his Nazi colleagues as Germany's ideal American presidential candidate long before the Republican Party drafted Lindbergh at its 1940 convention. Von Ribbentrop was the

258 THE PLOT AGAINST AMERICA

negotiator seated at Hitler's side throughout the Iceland meetings and the first Nazi leader to be invited to America by *any* government official or agency since the fascists had come to power nearly ten years before. No sooner was the announcement of the von Ribbentrop dinner made public than strong criticism was voiced by the liberal press, and rallies and demonstrations were staged all across the country protesting the White House decision. For the first time since he left office, former president Roosevelt emerged from seclusion to make a brief nationwide address from Hyde Park urging President Lindbergh to rescind the invitation "for the sake of all freedom-loving Americans, and particularly the tens of millions of Americans of European stock whose ancestral countries must live beneath the Nazis' crushing yoke."

Roosevelt was immediately attacked by Vice President Wheeler for "playing politics" with a sitting president's conduct of foreign affairs. It wasn't merely cynical, said the vice president, but utterly irresponsible of him to argue for the same dangerous policies that had all but dragged America into a bloody European war while the New Deal Democrats were running the country. Wheeler was himself a Democrat, a former three-term senator from Montana and the first and only member of the opposition party to be chosen to share a ticket with a presidential candidate since Lincoln picked Andrew Johnson as his second-term running mate in 1864. Early in his political career, Wheeler was so far to the left that he'd been the voice of Butte's radical labor leaders, the enemy of Anaconda Copper—the mining company that ran Montana pretty much like a company store—and, as an early supporter of FDR's, had been suggested as his vice presidential candidate in 1932. He'd first departed the Democratic Party in 1924 to team up with Wisconsin's reformist senator Robert La Follette on the union-supported Progressive Party presidential ticket, and then, after abandoning La Follette and his supporters in the non-Communist American left, he joined Lindbergh and the right-wing isolationists in helping to found America First, attacking Roosevelt with antiwar statements so extreme that they prompted the president to label his criticism "the most untruthful, dastardly, unpatriotic thing that has been said in public life in my generation." Wheeler had been chosen by the

Republicans to be Lindbergh's running mate in part because his own political machine in Montana had helped to elect Republicans to Congress throughout the late thirties but mainly to persuade the American people of the strength of the bipartisan support for isolationism and to have on the ticket a combative, un-Lindbergh-like candidate whose job would be to attack and revile his own political party at every opportunity, as he did in the press conference from the vice president's office when he predicted that if the reckless "war-minded" rhetoric in Roosevelt's message from Hyde Park was any indication of the campaign the Democrats intended to wage in the forthcoming elections, they would suffer even greater congressional losses than they had in the 1940 Republican landslide.

The very next weekend, the German-American Bund filled Madison Square Garden with a near-capacity crowd, some twenty-five thousand people who had turned out to support President Lindbergh's invitation to the German foreign minister and to denounce the Democrats for their renewed "warmongering." During Roosevelt's second term, the FBI and congressional committees investigating the Bund's activities had immobilized the organization, designating it a Nazi front and bringing criminal charges against leaders in its high command. But under Lindbergh, government efforts at harassing or intimidating Bund members ceased and they were able to regain their strength by identifying themselves not only as American patriots of German extraction opposed to America's intervention in foreign wars but as staunch enemies of the Soviet Union. The deep fascist fellowship uniting the Bund was now masked by vociferous patriotic declamations on the peril of a worldwide Communist revolution.

As an anti-Communist rather than a pro-Nazi organization, the Bund was as anti-Semitic as before, openly equating Bolshevism with Judaism in propaganda handouts and harping on the number of "prowar" Jews—like Treasury Secretary Morgenthau and financier Bernard Baruch, who'd been Roosevelt confidants—and, of course, holding fast to the purposes enunciated in their official declaration on first organizing in 1936: "to combat the Moscow-directed madness of the Red world menace and its Jewish bacillus-carriers" and to promote "a free Gentile-ruled United States." Gone, however, from the 1942

Madison Square Garden rally were the Nazi flags, the swastika armbands, the straight-armed Hitler salute, the storm trooper uniforms, and the giant picture of the Führer that had been on display for the first rally, on February 20, 1939, an event promoted by the Bund as "George Washington Day Birthday Exercises." Gone were the wall banners proclaiming "Wake up America—Smash Jewish Communists!" and the references by speechmakers to Franklin D. Roosevelt as "Franklin D. Rosenfeld" and the big white buttons with the black lettering that had been distributed to Bund members to stick into their lapels, the buttons that read:

KEEP AMERICA
OUT OF
THE JEWISH WAR

Meanwhile, Walter Winchell continued to refer to the Bundists as "Bundits," and Dorothy Thompson, the prominent journalist and wife of novelist Sinclair Lewis, who'd been expelled from the 1939 Bund rally for exercising what she called her "constitutional right to laugh at ridiculous statements in a public hall," went on denouncing their propaganda in the same spirit she'd demonstrated three years earlier when she'd exited the rally shouting, "Bunk, bunk, bunk! *Mein Kampf*, word for word!" And on his Sunday-night program following the Bund rally, Winchell contended, with his usual cocksureness, that growing hostility to the von Ribbentrop state dinner marked the end of America's honeymoon with Charles A. Lindbergh. "The presidential blunder of the century," Winchell called it, "the blunder of blunders for which the reactionary Republican henchmen of our fascist-loving president will pay with their political lives in the November elections."

The White House, accustomed to nearly universal deification of Lindbergh, seemed stymied by the strong disapproval that the opposition was so rapidly able to muster against him, and though the administration sought to distance itself from the Bund's New York rally, the Democrats—determined to associate Lindbergh with the organization's ignominious reputation —held a Madison Square Garden rally of their own. Speaker after speaker scathingly denounced "the Lindbergh Bundists," until to everyone's astonished delight, FDR himself appeared on the platform. The ten-minute ovation his presence elicited would have gone on even longer had not the former president called out forcefully, above the roar, "My fellow Americans, my fellow Americans—I have a message for both Mr. Lindbergh and Mr. Hitler. The moment compels my stating with a candor they cannot misunderstand that it is we, and not they, who are the masters of America's destiny," words so stirring and dramatic that every human being in that crowd (and in our living room and in the living rooms up and down our street) was swept away by the joyous illusion that the nation's redemption was at hand.

"The only thing we have to fear," FDR told his audience—recalling the opening seven words of a sentence as renowned as any ever spoken at a first inaugural—"is the obsequious yielding to his Nazi friends by Charles A. Lindbergh, the shameless courting by the president of the world's greatest democracy of a despot responsible for innumerable criminal deeds and acts of savagery, a cruel and barbaric tyrant unparalleled in the chronicle of man's misdeeds. But we Americans will not accept a Hitler-dominated America. We Americans will not accept a Hitler-dominated world. Today the entire globe is divided between human slavery and human freedom. We—choose—freedom! We accept only an America consecrated to freedom! If there is a plot being hatched by antidemocratic forces here at home harboring a Quisling blueprint for a fascist America, or by foreign nations greedy for power and supremacy—a plot to suppress the great upsurge of human liberty of which the American Bill of Rights is the fundamental document, a plot to replace American democracy with the absolute authority of a despotic rule such as enslaves the conquered people of Europe—let those who would dare in secret to conspire against our freedom understand that Americans will not, under any threat or in the face of any danger, surrender the guarantees of liberty framed for us by our forefathers in the Constitution of the United States."

Lindbergh's response came a few days afterward—he donned his Lone Eagle flying gear and early one morning took off from Washington in his two-engine Lockheed Interceptor to meet with the American people face to face and reassure them that every decision he made was designed solely to increase their security and guarantee their well-being. That's what he did when the smallest crisis loomed, flew to cities in every region of the country, this time to as many as four and five in a single day owing to the Interceptor's phenomenal speed, and everywhere his plane set down the cluster of radio microphones was waiting for him as were the local bigwigs, the wire-service stringers, the city's reporters, and the thousands of citizens who had gathered to catch sight of their young president in his famous aviator's windbreaker and leather cap. And each time he landed, he made it clear that he was flying the country unescorted, without either Secret Service or Air Corps protection. This was how safe he considered the American skies to be; this was how secure the *country* was now that his administration, in little more than a year, had dispelled all threat of war. He reminded his audiences that the life of not a single American boy had been put at risk since he'd come to office and would not be put at risk so long as he remained in office. Americans had invested their faith in his leadership, and every promise he had made to them he had kept.

That was all he said or had to say. He never mentioned von Ribbentrop's name or FDR's or made reference to the German-American Bund or the Iceland Understanding. He said nothing in support of the Nazis, nothing to reveal an affinity with their leader and his aims, not even to note with approval that the German army had recovered from its winter losses and that all along the Russian front, the Soviet Communists were being pushed farther eastward toward their ultimate defeat. But then everyone in America knew that it was an unshakable conviction of the president's, as it was of his party's dominant right wing, that the best protection against the spread of Communism across Europe, into Asia and the Middle East, and as far as to our own hemisphere was the total destruction of Stalin's Soviet Union by the military might of the Third Reich.

In his low-key, taciturn, winning way, Lindbergh told the airfield crowds and the radio listeners who he was and what he'd done, and by the time he climbed back aboard his plane to take off for his next stop, he could have announced that, following the von Ribbentrop White House dinner, the First Lady would be inviting Adolf Hitler and his girlfriend to spend the Fourth of July weekend as vacation guests in the Lincoln

bedroom of the White House and still have been cheered by
his countrymen as democracy's savior.

My father's boyhood friend Shepsie Tirschwell had been one of
several projectionist-editors at the Newsreel Theater on Broad
Street since its opening in 1935 as the city's only all-news movie
house. The Newsreel's one-hour show comprised news clips,
shorts, and "The March of Time," and it ran daily from early
morning until midnight. Every Thursday, out of thousands of
feet of news film supplied by companies like Pathé and Paramount, Mr. Tirschwell and the three other editors selected
stories and spliced together an up-to-the-minute show so that
regular customers like my father—whose office on Clinton
Street was only a few blocks away—could keep pace with national news, important happenings worldwide, and exciting
moments from championship sports matches that, back in the
radio era, could be seen on film nowhere but at a movie theater.
My father would try to find an hour each week to catch a complete show, and when he did, he'd recount over dinner what
he'd seen and whom. Tojo. Pétain. Batista. De Valera. Arias.
Quezon. Camacho. Litvinov. Zhukov. Hull. Welles. Harriman.
Dies. Heydrich. Blum. Quisling. Gandhi. Rommel. Mountbatten. King George. La Guardia. Franco. Pope Pius. And that
was but an abbreviated list of the tremendous cast of newsreel
characters prominent in events that my father told us we would
one day remember as history worthy of passing on to our own
children.

"Because what's history?" he asked rhetorically when he was
in his expansive dinnertime instructional mode. "History is
everything that happens everywhere. Even here in Newark.
Even here on Summit Avenue. Even what happens in his house
to an ordinary man—that'll be history too someday."

On the weekends when Mr. Tirschwell was working, my father would take Sandy and me to be further educated at the
Newsreel Theater. Mr. Tirschwell would leave free passes at
the box office for us, and each time my father brought us up to
the projection booth after the show would give the same civics
lecture. He'd tell us that in a democracy, keeping abreast of
current events was a citizen's most important duty and that
you could never start too early to be informed about the news

of the day. We'd gather close to the film projector, each of whose parts he'd name for us, and then we'd look at the framed photographs on the walls that had been taken at the theater's black-tie opening night, when Newark's first and only Jewish mayor, Meyer Ellenstein, had cut the ribbon strung across the lobby and welcomed the famous guests, among whom, as Mr. Tirschwell told us, pointing to their pictures, was the former U.S. ambassador to Spain and the founder of Bamberger's department store.

What I liked best about the Newsreel Theater was that the seats were constructed so that even an adult didn't have to get up to let others by, that the projection booth was said to be soundproof, and that on the carpet in the lobby was a design of motion picture reels that you could step on when you went in and out. Not until I think back to those consecutive Saturdays in 1942, when Sandy was fourteen and I was nine and we were taken by my father specifically to see the Bund rally one week and FDR addressing the anti-Ribbentrop Garden rally the next, am I able to remember anything much other than the narrating voice of Lowell Thomas, who introduced most of the political news, and of Bill Stern, who enthusiastically reported on sports. But the Bund rally I've not forgotten because of the hatred instilled in me by the Bundists up on their feet chanting von Ribbentrop's name as though it were he who was now president of the United States, and FDR's speech I've not forgotten because when he proclaimed to the anti-Ribbentrop rally, "The only thing we have to fear is the obsequious yielding to his Nazi friends by Charles A. Lindbergh," a good half of the movie audience booed and hissed while the rest, including my father, clapped as loudly as they could, and I wondered if a war might not break out right there on Broad Street in the middle of the day and if, when we left the darkened theater, we'd find downtown Newark a rubble heap of smoking ruins and fires burning everywhere.

It wasn't easy for Sandy to sit through those two Saturday-afternoon shows at the Newsreel Theater, and since he'd already understood beforehand that it wasn't going to be, he at first refused my father's invitation and agreed to come along with us only when he was ordered to do so. By the spring of 1942, Sandy was a few months from beginning high school, a lean, tall, good-looking boy whose attire was neat, whose hair was combed, and whose posture, standing or sitting, was as perfect as a West Point cadet's. His experience as a leading young spokesman for Just Folks had endowed him, in addition, with an air of authority seldom seen in one so young. That Sandy should prove himself so adept at influencing adults and that he should have developed a reverential following among the younger neighborhood kids who were eager to emulate him and qualify for the Office of American Absorption's summer farm program had surprised my parents and made their older child more intimidating to have around the house than he was back when everyone thought of him as an affable, fairly ordinary boy with a gift for drawing people's likenesses. To me he'd always been the mighty one because of his seniority; now he seemed mightier than ever and easily aroused my admiration despite my having turned away from him because of what Alvin had described as his opportunism—though even the opportunism (if Alvin was correct and that was the word for it) seemed another remarkable attainment, the emblem of a calm, self-aware maturity knowingly wedded to the ways of the world.

Of course, the concept of opportunism was barely familiar to me at the age of nine, yet its ethical status Alvin communicated clearly enough by the disgust with which he'd pronounced his indictment and what he added by way of amplification. He was still fresh from the hospital then and far too miserable to show much restraint.

"Your brother's nothing," he informed me from his bed one night. "He's less than nothing." And that was when he labeled Sandy opportunistic.

"Is he? Why?"

"Because people are, because they look for the advantage for themselves and the hell with everything else. Sandy's a fucking opportunist. So's your bitch aunt with the big pointy tits. So's the great rabbi. Aunt Bess and Uncle Herman are honest people. But Sandy—selling out to these bastards right off the bat? At his age? With his talent? A real fucking doozy, this brother of yours."

Selling out. Language also new to me, but now no more difficult to understand than "opportunist."

"He just drew some pictures," I explained.

But Alvin was in no mood to have me try to downplay the existence of those pictures, especially as he'd somehow come to know about Sandy's affiliation with Lindbergh's Just Folks. I didn't have the courage to ask how he'd found out what I'd determined never to tell him, though what I figured was that, after accidentally uncovering the artwork beneath the bed, he must have gone ahead to scavenge the drawers of the dining room breakfront, where Sandy stored his school notebooks and his writing paper, and found there all the evidence necessary to hate Sandy forever.

"It doesn't mean what you think," I said, but immediately I had to think what else it *could* mean. "He's doing it to protect us," I announced. "So we don't get in trouble."

"Because of me," Alvin said.

"No!" I protested.

"But that's what he told you. So the family won't get in trouble because of Alvin. That's how he justifies this shit he's up to."

"But why else *would* he be doing it?" I asked this as guilelessly as a child could and with all of a child's cunning—and with no idea of how to begin to extricate myself from a conflict I had only intensified by lying idiotically in my brother's defense. "What's wrong with what he's doing if he's trying to help?"

He merely replied, "I don't believe you, ace," and, because I was no match for Alvin, I gave up trying to believe myself. Though if only Sandy *had* told me he was leading a double existence! If only he *was* making the best of a terrible situation and masquerading as a Lindbergh loyalist to protect us! But having seen him lecturing an audience of Jewish adults in that New Brunswick synagogue basement, I knew how convinced he was of what he was saying and how he gorged on the attention it brought him. My brother had discovered in himself the uncommon gift to be somebody, and so while making speeches praising President Lindbergh and while exhibiting his drawings of him and while publicly extolling (in words written by Aunt Evelyn) the enriching benefits of his eight weeks as a Jewish farm hand in the Gentile heartland—while doing, if the truth be known, what I wouldn't have minded doing myself, by doing what was normal and patriotic all over America and aberrant and freakish only in his home—Sandy was having the time of his life.

Then came history's next outsized intrusion: an engraved invitation from President and Mrs. Charles A. Lindbergh for Rabbi Lionel Bengelsdorf and Miss Evelyn Finkel to attend a state dinner in honor of the German foreign minister on the evening of Saturday, April 4, 1942. The cross-country solo flying tour of thirty cities had raised Lindbergh's reputation as a nononsense realist and plain-talking man of the people higher even than it had been before Winchell had labeled the von Ribbentrop dinner "the political blunder of the century." Soon the editorial pages of the country's largely Republican press were crowing that it was FDR and the Democrats whose blunder it had been to deliberately misrepresent as a sinister conspiracy what was no more than a cordial White House dinner for a foreign dignitary.

Stunned as my parents were to learn of the invitation, there was nothing much for them to do about it. Months earlier they had registered with Evelyn their disappointment in her for having become another of the small band of misguided Jews to serve as underlings to those now in power. It made no sense to challenge yet again her remote administrative connection to the president of the United States, especially since they knew that it wasn't ideological conviction that animated her, as it appeared to have back in her union days, or just craven political ambition, but the exhilaration of having been rescued by Rabbi Bengelsdorf from her life as a substitute teacher living in an attic flat on Dewey Street and removed to a life at court as miraculously as Cinderella. However, when she phoned unexpectedly one evening to tell my mother that she and the rabbi had arranged for my brother to accompany them to the von Ribbentrop dinner . . . well, at first no one was willing to believe her. It was still barely possible to accept that Evelyn could herself have stepped overnight from our local little society into "March of Time" celebrity, but now Sandy as well? His preaching for Lindbergh in synagogue basements wasn't improbable enough? This simply could not be so, my father insisted—meaning that it mustn't be so, that, credibility aside, it was too repellent to be so. "It only proves," he told my brother, "that your aunt is nuts."

And maybe she was—driven temporarily nuts by an exaggerated sense of her newfound importance. How else could she have mustered the audacity to seek an invitation to such a great event for her fourteen-year-old nephew? How else could she have prevailed on Rabbi Bengelsdorf to make so outlandish a request of the White House other than by insisting with the uncompromising tenacity of a self-absorbed screwball on the way up? Over the phone my father spoke to her as calmly as he could. "Enough of this foolishness, Evelyn. We're not important people. Leave us alone, please. There's too much for an ordinary person to put up with as it is." But my aunt's commitment to liberating an exceptional nephew from the confines of an ignorant brother-in-law's insignificance (so that he could play a leading role in the world like her) was by now unassailable. Sandy was to attend the dinner as a testament to the success of Just Folks, he was to attend as nothing less than the nationwide representative of Just Folks, and no ghetto father was going to stop him—or her. She got in her car, and fifteen minutes later the reckoning came.

After he hung up, my father did nothing to conceal his outrage, and his voice rose and rose as if he were Uncle Monty. "In Germany Hitler has the decency at least to bar the Jews from the Nazi Party. That and the armbands, that and the concentration camps, and at least it's clear that dirty Jews aren't welcome. But here the Nazis pretend to invite the Jews *in*. And why? To lull them to sleep. To lull them to sleep with the ridiculous dream that everything in America is hunky-dory. But *this*?" he cried. "*This*? Inviting them to shake the blood-stained hand of a Nazi criminal? Unbelievable! Their lying and their scheming do not stop for a minute! They find the best boy, the most talented boy, the hardest-working, most grown-up boy . . . No! They have mocked us enough with what they are doing to Sandy! He is not going anywhere! They have already stolen my country—they are not stealing my son!"

"But nobody," Sandy shouted, "is mocking *anybody*. This is a great *opportunity*." "For an opportunist," I thought, but kept my mouth shut.

"Be still," my father told him, just that, and the quiet sternness was more effective than the anger in causing Sandy to understand that he was on the brink of the worst hour of his life.

Aunt Evelyn was knocking and my mother got up to open the back door. "What is this woman doing *now*?" my father called after her. "I tell her to leave us alone—and so here she comes, crazy as a coot!"

My mother was by no means at odds with my father's resolve, but she did manage to look imploringly at him as she left the kitchen, hoping she might dispose him to be somewhat merciful however little mercy Evelyn deserved for the reckless stupidity with which she had exploited Sandy's zeal.

Aunt Evelyn was astonished (or pretended to be) by my parents' inability to grasp what it meant for a boy Sandy's age to be invited to the White House, what it would mean for his future to have been a dinner guest at the White House . . . "I am not impressed by *the White House!*" my father cried, hammering on the table to shut her up after she'd said "the White House" for the fifteenth time. "I am only impressed by who lives there. And the person who lives there is a Nazi." "He is not!" Evelyn insisted. "And do you want to tell me that Herr von Ribbentrop isn't a Nazi either?" In response, she called my father a frightened, provincial, uncultivated, narrow-minded . . . and he called her an unthinking, gullible, social-climbing . . . and the quarrel raged across the table, each hotly spitting out indictments to increase the fury of the other, until something Aunt Evelyn said—something relatively mild, as it turned out, about all the strings Rabbi Bengelsdorf had pulled for Sandy— was one absurdity too many for him, and he got up from the table and told her to leave. He walked out of the kitchen and into the rear foyer, where he opened the door to the stairwell, and from there he called to her, "Get out. Go. And don't come back. I never want to see you in this house again."

She couldn't believe it any more than the rest of us. It seemed to me to be a joke, a line tossed off in an Abbott and Costello movie. Get out, Costello. If you're going to carry on like that, leave this house and never come back.

My mother got up from where the three adults had been sitting with their tea and followed him out into the foyer.

"The woman is an idiot, Bess," my father said to her, "a childish idiot who understands nothing. A *dangerous* idiot."

"Close the door, please," my mother said to him.

"Evelyn," he called. "Now. Immediately. Leave."

"Don't do this," my mother whispered.

"I am waiting for your sister to get out of my house," he replied.

"Our house," my mother said, and she came back into the kitchen. "Ev, go home," she said softly, "so everything can quiet down." Aunt Evelyn's face was on the table, hidden in her hands. My mother took her by the arm and lifted her to her feet and walked her to the back door and out of the house, our assertive, effervescent aunt looking as though she had been hit by a bullet and was being carried off to die. Then we heard my father slam the door.

"The woman thinks it's a *party*," he said to Sandy and me when we stepped out into the foyer to view the aftermath of the battle. "She thinks it's a *game*. You've been to the Newsreel Theater. I took you boys. You know what you saw there."

"Yes," I said. I felt I had to say something since my brother was now refusing to speak. He had stoically endured Alvin's remorseless ostracism and he had stoically endured the Newsreel Theater and now he was stoically enduring the banishment of his favorite aunt—at fourteen already at one with the family's obstinate men, determined to stand up to anything.

"Well," my father said, "it's *not* a game. It's a fight. Remember that: a fight!"

Again I said yes.

"Outside in the world . . ." But here he stopped. My mother hadn't returned. I was nine and thought that she would never return. And it may have been that my father, at forty-one, thought so too: my father, who had been freed by hardship of many fears, was not free of the fear of losing his precious wife. Catastrophe was no longer far from anyone's mind, and he was looking at his children as though we were suddenly as bereft of a mother as Earl Axman was on the night of Mrs. Axman's nervous breakdown. When my father went to the living room to look out the front windows, Sandy and I trailed closely behind. Aunt Evelyn's car was no longer at the curb. And my mother wasn't standing on the sidewalk or on the stoop or out in the alleyway or even across the street—nor was she in the cellar when my father ran down the cellar stairs calling her name. Nor was she with Seldon and his mother. They were eating in their kitchen when my father knocked and the three of us were let in.

My father said to Mrs. Wishnow, "Did you see Bess?"

Mrs. Wishnow was a beefy woman, tall and ungainly, who walked around with her fists clenched and who, amazingly to me, was said to have been a laughing, lighthearted girl when my father knew her and her family down in the Third Ward before the Great War. Now that she was both mother and family breadwinner, my parents were constantly extolling her unstinting exertions in behalf of Seldon. That *her* life was a fight was indisputable: you had only to look at her fists.

"What's wrong?" she asked him.

"Isn't Bess here?"

Seldon left the kitchen table to come out and say hello to us. Since his father's suicide, my aversion to him had grown stronger, and at the end of the day I hid back of the school when I knew he was out front waiting to walk me home. And though we lived just one short block from the school, in the morning I'd tiptoe down the stairs and leave the house fifteen minutes before I had to in order to beat him out the door. But then late in the afternoon I would invariably run into him, even if I was at the other end of the Chancellor Avenue hill. I'd be on a household errand and there would be Seldon at my heels, acting as if he'd turned up by accident. And whenever he came by to try to teach me to play chess, I would pretend I wasn't home and not answer the door. If my mother was around she would try to persuade me to play with him by reminding me of the very thing that I wanted to forget. "His father was a wonderful chess player. Years ago he was champion at the Y. He taught Seldon, and now Seldon has no one to play with, and he wants to play with you." I'd tell her that I didn't like or understand the game or know how to play it, but finally there'd be no choice and Seldon would show up with the chess board and his chessmen and I'd sit down across from him at the kitchen table where he'd immediately begin to remind me how his father had made the board and found the chess pieces. "He went into New York, and he knew just the places to go to, and he found just the right pieces—aren't they beautiful? They're made of special wood. And he made this board. He found the wood, and he cut it—you see how the different colors are?" and the only way I found to stop him from perpetually going on about his terrifyingly dead father was to bombard him with the latest toilet jokes I'd heard at school.

When we were headed upstairs again I realized that my father was now going to marry Mrs. Wishnow, and that one evening soon the three of us would carry our belongings down the back stairway and move in with her and Seldon, and that on the way to school as on the way home there would be no way ever again of avoiding Seldon and his unceasing need to draw sustenance from me. And once back in the house, I would have to put my coat away in the closet where Seldon's father had hanged himself. Sandy would sleep in the Wishnow sun parlor, as he had in ours when Alvin lived with us, I'd sleep in the back bedroom beside Seldon, while in the other bedroom my father would sleep where Seldon's father used to sleep, alongside Seldon's mother and her clenched fists.

I wanted to go to the corner and get on a bus and disappear. I still had Alvin's twenty dollars hidden in the tip of a shoe at the bottom of my closet. I'd take the money and get on a bus and down at Penn Station buy a one-way ticket for the train to Philadelphia. There I would find Alvin, and never live with my family again. Instead I would stay with Alvin and look after his stump.

My mother called home after she had put Aunt Evelyn to bed. Rabbi Bengelsdorf was in Washington, but he had talked with Evelyn on the phone and afterward spoke to my mother, assuring her that he knew better than her dunce of a husband what was and was not in the interest of the Jews. How Herman had treated Evelyn would not be forgotten, he said, especially after all he himself had gone out of his way to do for her nephew at Evelyn's request. The rabbi concluded by telling my mother that appropriate action would be taken when the time came.

Around ten, my father went to pick my mother up and drive her home. Sandy and I were already in pajamas when she came into the room and sat down on my bed and took my hand. I'd never seen her so exhausted—not completely depleted like Mrs. Wishnow but hardly the untiring mother full of contentment who used to live so energetically inside her skin back when her worries were merely the ones of making do for her family on a husband's take-home pay of less than fifty dollars a week. A downtown job, a house to run, a tempestuous sister, a determined husband, a headstrong fourteen-year-old, an apprehensive nine-year-old—not even the simultaneous inundation of all these concerns with all their exacting demands need have been overly burdensome for a woman so resourceful, if only there weren't Lindbergh, too.

"Sandy," she said, "what shall we do? Should I explain to you why Daddy doesn't think you should go? Can we do that together quietly? At some point we have to talk everything through. Just you and me off by ourselves. Sometimes Daddy can fly off the handle, but I don't—you know that. You can trust me to listen to you. But we have to get some perspective on what is going on. Because maybe it really isn't a good thing for you to be drawn any further into something like this. Maybe Aunt Evelyn made a mistake. She's overexcited, darling. She's been like that all her life. Something out of the ordinary happens and she loses all perspective. Daddy thinks . . . Shall I continue, dear, or do you want to go to sleep?"

"Do what you want," Sandy said flatly.

"Continue," I said.

My mother smiled at me. "Why? What do you want to know?"

"What everyone's yelling for."

"Because everybody sees things differently." Kissing me goodnight, she said, "Because there's a lot on everyone's mind," but when she leaned toward Sandy's bed to kiss him, he turned his face into the pillow.

Usually my father was off to work before Sandy and I were awake, and my mother would be up early to eat breakfast with him and to make our lunch sandwiches and wrap them in wax paper and put them in the refrigerator and then would herself leave for work after seeing that we two were ready for school. The following day, however, my father didn't leave for his office until he'd had a chance to clarify for Sandy why he was not going to the White House and why he was no longer to participate in any of the programs sponsored by the OAA.

"These friends of von Ribbentrop," he explained to Sandy,

"are no friends of ours. Every dirty scheme that Hitler has foisted on Europe, every filthy lie he has told other countries, has come through the mouth of Mr. von Ribbentrop. Someday you'll study what happened at Munich. You'll study the role that Mr. von Ribbentrop played in tricking Mr. Chamberlain into signing a treaty that wasn't worth the paper it was written on. Read *PM* about this man. Listen to Winchell about this man. Foreign Minister von Ribbensnob, Winchell calls him. You know what he did for a living before the war? Sold champagne. A liquor salesman, Sandy. A fake—a plutocrat and a thief and a fake. Even the 'von' in his name is a fake. But you know none of this. You know nothing about von Ribbentrop, you know nothing about Göring, you know nothing about Goebbels and Himmler and Hess—but I *do* know. Did you ever hear about the castle in Austria where Herr von Ribbentrop wines and dines the rest of the Nazi criminals? Know how he got it? He stole it. The nobleman who owned it Himmler threw into a concentration camp, and now it is the property of the liquor salesman! Do you know where Danzig is, Sandy, and what happened to it? Do you know what the Treaty of Versailles is? Did you hear of *Mein Kampf*? Ask Mr. von Ribbentrop— he'll tell you. And I will tell you too, though not from the Nazi point of view. I follow things, and I read things, and I know who these criminals are, son. And I am not allowing you anywhere near them."

"I'll never forgive you for this," Sandy replied.

"But you will," my mother said to him. "One day you'll understand that what Daddy wants for you is only what's in your best interest. He's right, dear, believe me—you have no business with such people. They are only making you their tool."

"Aunt Evelyn?" Sandy asked. "Aunt Evelyn is making me into a 'tool'? Getting me invited to the White House—that's making me into a 'tool'?"

"Yes," my mother said sadly.

"No! That isn't true!" he said. "I'm sorry but I can't let Aunt Evelyn down."

"Your aunt Evelyn," my father told him, "is the one who let *us* down. Just Folks," he said contemptuously. "The only purpose of this so-called Just Folks is to make Jewish children into a fifth column and turn them against their parents."

"Bullshit!" Sandy said.

"Stop that!" my mother said. "Stop that right now. Do you realize that we're the only family on the block going through anything like this? The only family in this entire neighborhood. Everybody else knows by now just to continue living as they were living before the election and to forget who the president is. And that's what we're doing too. Bad things have happened, but now they're over. Alvin is gone and now Aunt Evelyn is gone, and everything is going to get back to normal."

"And when are we moving to Canada," Sandy asked her, "because of your persecution complex?"

Pointing his finger, my father said, "Don't mimic your stupid aunt. Don't talk back like that ever again."

"You're a dictator," Sandy said to him, "you're a dictator *worse* than Hitler."

Because my parents had each been raised in a household where an old-country father had not hesitated to discipline his children in accordance with traditional methods of coercion, they were themselves incapable of ever hitting Sandy or me and disapproved of corporal punishment for anyone. Consequently, all my father did in response to being told by a child of his that he was worse than Hitler was to turn away in disgust and leave for work. But he was hardly out the back door when my mother raised her hand and, to my astonishment, smacked Sandy across the face. "Do you know what your father has just done for you?" she shouted at him. "Don't you understand yet what you were about to do to yourself? Finish your breakfast and go to school. And you be home when school is over. Your father laid down the law—you better obey it."

He didn't flinch when she hit him, and now, all resistance, he undertook to enlarge his heroism by brazenly telling her, "I'm going to the White House with Aunt Evelyn. I don't care whether you ghetto Jews like it or not."

To add to the morning's ugliness, to add to the nerve-shattering implausibility of all our disorder, she made him pay in full for his filial defiance by dealing him a second blow, and this time he burst into tears. And had he not, this prudent mother of ours would have raised her gentle, kindly mothering hand and hit him a third, a fourth, and a fifth time. "She doesn't know what she's doing." I thought, "she's somebody else—*everybody* is," and I grabbed my schoolbooks and ran down the back stairs to the alleyway and out to the street, and, as if the day weren't already gruesome enough, there was Seldon waiting on the front stoop to walk me to school.

On the way home from work a couple of weeks later my father stopped off at the Newsreel Theater to catch the filmed coverage of the von Ribbentrop dinner. It was then that he learned from Shepsie Tirschwell, whom he visited up in his booth after the show, that on the first of June his old boyhood friend was leaving for Winnipeg with his wife, his three children, his mother, and his wife's elderly parents. Representatives of Winnipeg's small Jewish community had helped Mr. Tirschwell to find work as a projectionist at a neighborhood movie house there and had located apartments for the entire family in a modest Jewish neighborhood much like our own. The Canadians had also arranged a low-interest loan to pay for the Tirschwells' move from America and to assist with the support of the in-laws until Mrs. Tirschwell found a job in Winnipeg that would enable her to cover her parents' living expenses. Mr. Tirschwell told my father that he hated parting from his native city and his dear old friends and that of course he regretted leaving his one-of-a-kind job at Newark's most important theater. There was much to leave and much to lose, but he was convinced by all the raw unedited film he'd been watching for the past several years from newsreel crews working around the world that the secret side of the pact reached in Iceland between Lindbergh and Hitler in 1941 provided for Hitler first to defeat the Soviet Union, then to invade and conquer England, and only after that (and after the Japanese had overrun China, India, and Australia, thus completing the creation of their "New Order in Greater East Asia") for America's president to establish the "American Fascist New Order," a totalitarian dictatorship modeled on Hitler's that would set the stage for the last great continental struggle—the German invasion, conquest, and Nazification of South America. Two years down the line, with Hitler's swastika flying from London's houses of Parliament, the Rising Sun flying over Sydney, New Delhi, and Peking, and Lindbergh having been elected to the presidency for another four years, the U.S. border with Canada would be closed, diplomatic relations between the two countries would be severed, and, so as to focus Americans on the grave internal danger that necessitated the curtailment of their constitutional rights, the onslaught would begin en masse against America's four and a half million Jews.

In the wake of von Ribbentrop's Washington visit—and the triumph it represented for the most dangerous of Lindbergh's American supporters—this was Mr. Tirschwell's forecast, and it was so much more pessimistic than anything my father was predicting that he decided not to repeat it to us or, when he got home from the Newsreel Theater for dinner early that evening, to say anything about the Tirschwells' imminent departure, certain that the news would terrify me, rile Sandy, and set my mother clamoring to emigrate at once. Since Lindbergh's inauguration a year and a half earlier, there were estimated to be only two to three hundred Jewish families who had taken up permanent residence in the haven of Canada; the Tirschwells were the first such fugitives that my father knew personally, and learning of their decision had left him shaken.

And then there was the shock of seeing on film the Nazi von Ribbentrop and his wife warmly greeted on the White House portico by the president and Mrs. Lindbergh. And the shock of seeing all the prominent guests stepping from their limousines and smiling with anticipation at the prospect of dining and dancing in von Ribbentrop's presence—and among the guests, seemingly no less thrilled than the others by the disgusting occasion, Rabbi Lionel Bengelsdorf and Miss Evelyn Finkel. "I could not believe it," my father said. "The smile on her face is a mile wide. And the husband-to-be? He looks like he thinks the dinner is for him. You should see this man—nodding at everyone as if he actually mattered!" "But why did you go," my mother asked him, "when it was bound to upset you like this?" "I went," he told her, "because every day I ask myself the same question: How can this be happening in America? How can people like these be in charge of our country? If I didn't see it with my own eyes, I'd think I was having a hallucination."

Though we had only just begun dinner, Sandy set down his silverware, mumbled "But nothing is happening in America, *nothing*," and left the table—and not for the first time since the morning my mother had smacked him across the face. At meals now, should the smallest reference be made to the news, Sandy would get up and without explanation or apology disappear into our room, pulling the door shut behind him. The first few times my mother got up after him and went in to talk with him and to invite him back to the table, but Sandy would sit at his desk sharpening a charcoal pencil or doodling with it on his drawing pad until she let him be. My brother wouldn't even speak to me when, merely out of loneliness, I dared to ask how much longer he was going to act like this. I began to wonder if he might not pick up and leave home, and not for Aunt Evelyn's but to live with the Mawhinneys on their Kentucky farm. He'd change his name to Sandy Mawhinney and we'd never see him again, just as we were never going to see Alvin. And nobody need bother to kidnap him—he'd do it himself, hand himself over to the Christians so as never again to have anything to do with Jews. Nobody needed to kidnap him because Lindbergh had kidnapped him already, along with everyone else!

Sandy's behavior so unsettled me that, in the evenings, I took to doing my homework out of sight of him at the kitchen table. That was how I came to overhear my father—who was in the living room with my mother, reading the evening paper there while Sandy remained in contemptuous seclusion at the back of the flat—reminding her that our private turmoil was exactly the sort of dissension that the Lindbergh anti-Semites had hoped to stir up between Jewish parents and their children with programs like Just Folks. Understanding this, however, had only hardened his resolve not to follow Shepsie Tirschwell's lead and leave.

"What are you talking about?" said my mother. "Are you telling me that the Tirschwells are going to Canada?" "In June, yes," he replied. "Why? Why June? What's happening in June? When did you find out? Why didn't you say something?" "Because I knew it would upset you." "And it has—why shouldn't it? Why," she demanded to know, "why, Herman, are they leaving in June?" "Because in Shepsie's judgment the time has come. Let's not discuss it," my father said softly. "The little one is in the kitchen, and he's frightened enough. If Shepsie feels it's time, that is his decision for himself and his family, and good luck to him. Shepsie sits and watches the latest news hour after hour. The news is Shepsie's life, and the news is terrible, and so it affects how he thinks, and this is the decision he came up with." "The man came up with the decision," my mother said, "because he is *informed*." "I am also informed," he said sharply. "I am no less informed—I have just reached a different conclusion. Don't you understand that these anti-Semitic bastards *want* us to run away? They want to get the Jews so fed up with everything," he told her, "that they leave for good, and then the goyim will have this wonderful country all to themselves. Well, I have a better idea. Why don't *they* leave? The whole bunch of them—why don't they all go live under their Führer in Nazi Germany? Then *we* will have a wonderful country! Look, Shepsie can do whatever he thinks is right, but we aren't going anywhere. There is still a Supreme Court in this country. Thanks to Franklin Roosevelt, it is a liberal Supreme Court, and it is there to look after our rights. There is Justice Douglas. There is Justice Frankfurter. There is Justice Murphy and Justice Black. They are there to uphold the law. There are still good men in this country. There is Roosevelt, there is Ickes, there is Mayor La Guardia. In November there is a congressional election. There is still the ballot box and people can still vote without anybody telling them what to do." "And what will they vote for?" my mother asked, and immediately answered herself. "The American people will vote," she said, "and the Republicans will be even *stronger*." "Quiet. Try to keep your voice down, will you? When November comes," he told her, "we'll find out the results, and there'll be time then to decide what to do." "And if there isn't time?" "There will be. Please, Bess," he said, "this cannot go on every night." And his was the last word, though it was probably only because of me doing my homework in the kitchen that my mother forced herself to say no more.

The next day, right after school, I walked down Chancellor Avenue and around to Clinton Place and then beyond the high school to where I figured chances were slight that anybody would recognize me and waited there for a bus downtown to the Newsreel Theater. I'd checked the newspaper timetable the night before. There was an hour-long show beginning at five minutes to four, which meant that I could catch a five o'clock 14 at the Broad Street stop across from the theater and be safely back in time for dinner, or even earlier, depending on when von Ribbentrop was slotted into the program. One way or another, I had to see Aunt Evelyn at the White House, and not because, like my parents, I was appalled and outraged by what she was doing but because her having gone there at all seemed to me more remarkable than anything that could possibly befall a member of our family—except for what had befallen Alvin.

NAZI BIGWIG WHITE HOUSE GUEST—that was the black-lettered headline spelled out across either side of the theater's triangular marquee, and along with my being downtown without my brother or Earl Axman or one of my parents, it made me feel powerfully delinquent when I stepped up to the box-office window and asked for a ticket.

"Unaccompanied by an adult? No, sir," the woman selling tickets told me. "I'm an orphan," I told her. "I live at the orphanage on Lyons Avenue. The sister sent me to do a report on President Lindbergh." "Where's her note?" I'd carefully written one out on the bus, using a blank page from my notebook, and handed it through the money slot. It was modeled after the notes of permission my mother wrote for school trips, only it was signed "Sister Mary Catherine, St. Peter's Orphanage." The woman looked at it without reading it, then beckoned for me to push my money over. I gave her one of Alvin's tens—a huge bill for a kid my size, let alone an orphan from St. Peter's—but she was busy and gave back nine-fifty in change and slipped me a ticket without any fuss. She failed, however, to return the note. "I need that," I said. "Let's go, sonny," she said impatiently, and motioned for me to make room for the people still lining up for the next show.

I got inside just as the lights went out and the martial music came on and the film began to roll. Because seemingly every man in Newark (the theater drew only a very few women) wanted to get a look at the unlikely White House guest, the place was filled to capacity for this late-Friday-afternoon show and the only empty seat I could find was in the far reaches of the balcony—anyone entering now would have to stand at the back of the orchestra's last row. A great excitement came over me, not only because of my having pulled off something that was not expected of me, but because enveloped by the fumes of the hundreds of cigarettes and the extravagant odor of the five-cent cigars, I felt deep in the virile magic of a boy masquerading as a man among men.

British land on Madagascar to take over French naval base.

Pierre Laval, chief of Vichy French government, denounces British move as "act of aggression."

RAF bombs Stuttgart third consecutive night.

British fighter planes in savage air battle over Malta.

German army resumes assault on USSR in the Kerch Peninsula.

Mandalay falls to Japanese army in Burma.

Japanese army launches new drive in jungles of New Guinea.

Japanese army marches into Yunnan province of China from Burma.

Chinese guerrillas raid city of Canton, killing five hundred Japanese troops.

A multitude of helmets, uniforms, weapons, buildings, harbors, beaches, flora, fauna—human faces of every race—but otherwise the same inferno again and again, the unsurpassable evil from whose horrors the United States, of all the great nations, was alone in being spared. Picture after picture of misery without end: the mortars bursting, the infantrymen doubled over and running, marines with raised rifles wading ashore, airplanes dropping bombs, airplanes blown apart and spiraling to earth, the mass graves, the kneeling chaplains, the improvised crosses, the sinking ships, the drowning sailors, the sea in flames, the shattered bridges, the tank bombardment, the targeted hospitals sheared in two, pillars of fire coiling upward from bombed-out oil tanks, prisoners corralled in a sea of mud, stretchers bearing living torsos, bayoneted civilians, dead babies, beheaded bodies bubbling blood . . .

And then the White House. A twilit spring evening. Shadows falling across the sprawl of lawn. Blooming bushes. Flowering trees. Limousines driven by liveried chauffeurs and everyone exiting them in formal attire. From the marble hallway beyond the open portico doors, a string ensemble playing last year's number one hit song, "Intermezzo," popularized from a theme in Wagner's *Tristan and Isolde*. Gracious smiles. Quiet laughter. The lean, beloved, handsome president. Beside him the talented poetess, daring aviatrix, and decorous socialite who is the mother of their murdered child. The loquacious, silver-haired honored guest. The elegant Nazi spouse in her long satin gown. Welcoming words, witticisms, and the Old World gallant, steeped in the theatrics of the royal court and looking in his evening clothes like a million bucks, charmingly kissing the First Lady's hand.

Had it not been for the Iron Cross, awarded to the foreign minister by his Führer and embellishing the pocket just inches below the impeccably arranged silk handkerchief, as persuasively civilized a sham as human cunning could devise.

And there! Aunt Evelyn, Rabbi Bengelsdorf—past the marine guards, through the doorway, and gone!

They couldn't have been on the screen for as long as three seconds, and yet the rest of the national news and the closing sports clips were incomprehensible to me and I kept hoping for the film to spin back to the moment where my aunt materialized asparkle with the gems previously the property of the rabbi's late wife. Among the many improbabilities that the cameras established as irrefutably real, Aunt Evelyn's disgraceful triumph was for me the least real of all.

When the show was over and the lights went up, a uniformed usher was standing in the aisle motioning with his flashlight. "You," he said. "You come with me."

He led me into the crowd that was emptying out of the lobby and through a door he unlocked with a key and then up a narrow stairway that I recognized from when Sandy and I had been brought here to see the Madison Square Garden von Ribbentrop rallies. "How old are you?" the usher asked me.

"Sixteen."

"That's a good one. Keep it up, kid. Get yourself in more hot water."

"I have to go home now," I told him. "I'm going to miss my bus."

"You're going to miss a lot more than that."

He rapped sharply on the famous soundproof door to the Newsreel's projection booth and Mr. Tirschwell let us in.

He was holding the note from Sister Mary Catherine.

"I don't see how I cannot show this to your parents," he told me.

"It was just a joke," I said.

"Your father's coming to pick you up. I telephoned his office to tell him you were here."

"Thank you," I said as politely as I had been taught to say it. "Please sit down."

"But it was a joke," I repeated.

Mr. Tirschwell was preparing the reels for the new show. I saw when I got to looking around that many of the signed photos of the theater's renowned patrons had been removed from the walls, and realized that Mr. Tirschwell had begun to gather together the mementos he was taking to Winnipeg. And I realized too that the gravity of such a move might alone have been enough to account for the sternness with which he was treating me. Yet he also struck me as the exacting sort of adult whose sense of responsibility often extends to what is none of his business. It would have been hard to tell from either his looks or his speech that he'd grown up in a Newark tenement with my father. He was an understated, distinctly more polished and prideful version than my father of the scantily educated slum child who'd lifted himself out of his parents' immigrant poverty almost entirely by virtue of a vigilant, programmatic industriousness. Ardor, for these men, was all they had to go on. What their Gentile betters called pushiness was generally just this—the ardor that was everything.

"If I go outside," I said, "I can still get the bus and be home in time for dinner."

"Stay where you are, please."

"But what did I do wrong? I wanted to see my aunt. This isn't fair," I said, dangerously close to crying. "I wanted to see my aunt at the White House, that's all."

"Your aunt," he said, and he gritted his teeth so as to say no more.

Of all things, his disdain for Aunt Evelyn triggered my tears. Here Mr. Tirschwell lost his patience. "Are you suffering?" he asked sardonically. "What, what are you suffering? Do you have any idea what people are going through all over the world? Did you understand nothing of what you just saw? I only hope that in the future you're spared any real reason to cry. I hope and pray that in the days ahead your family—" He stopped abruptly, clearly unaccustomed to an undignified eruption of irrational emotion, particularly in the handling of an insignificant child.

Even I could understand that his argument was with something other than me, but that didn't lessen the shock of my having to bear the brunt of it.

"What's going to happen in June?" I asked him. It was the unanswered question that I'd overheard my mother ask my father the night before.

Mr. Tirschwell continued scanning my face as though trying to determine how lacking in intelligence I was. "Pull yourself together," he finally said. "Here," and handed me his handkerchief. "Dry your eyes."

I did as he told me, but when I repeated, "What's going to happen? Why are you going to Canada?" the exasperation all at once disappeared from his voice and something emerged both stronger and milder—*his* intelligence.

"I have a new job there," he replied.

That he was sparing me terrified me, and I was again in tears.

My father arrived some twenty minutes later. Mr. Tirschwell handed him the note I'd written to get myself into the theater, but my father didn't take the time to read it until he had steered me by the elbow out of the theater and into the street. That's when he hit me. First my mother hits my brother, now my father reads the words of Sister Mary Catherine and, for the first time ever, wallops me, without restraint, across the face. As I am already overwrought—and nothing like as stoical as Sandy—I break down uncontrollably alongside the ticket booth, in plain view of all the Gentiles hurrying home from their downtown offices for a carefree spring weekend in Lindbergh's peacetime America, the autonomous fortress oceans away from the world's war zones where no one is in jeopardy except us.

6

Their Country

May 22, 1942

Dear Mr. Roth:

In compliance with a request from Homestead 42, Office of American Absorption, U.S. Department of the Interior, our company is offering relocation opportunities to senior employees like yourself, deemed qualified for inclusion in the OAA's bold new nationwide initiative.

It was exactly eighty years ago that the U.S. Congress passed the Homestead Act of 1862, the famous legislation, unique to America, which granted 160 acres of unoccupied public land virtually free to farmers willing to pull up stakes and settle the new American West. Nothing comparable has been undertaken since then to provide adventurous Americans with exciting new opportunities to expand their horizons and to strengthen their country.

Metropolitan Life is proud to be among the very first group of major American corporations and financial institutions selected to be participants in the new Homestead program, which is designed to give emerging American families a once-in-a-lifetime opportunity to move their households, at government expense, in order to strike roots in an inspiring region of America previously inaccessible to them. Homestead 42 will provide a challenging environment steeped in our country's oldest traditions where parents and children can enrich their Americanness over the generations.

Upon receipt of this announcement you should immediately contact Mr. Wilfred Kurth, the Homestead 42 representative in our Madison Avenue office. He will personally answer all your questions and his staff will courteously assist you in every way they can.

Congratulations to you and your family for having been chosen from among numerous deserving candidates at Metropolitan Life to be among the company's first pioneering "homesteaders" of 1942.

Sincerely yours,
Homer L. Kasson
Vice President for Employee Affairs

Several days had to pass before my father could summon the composure to show the company's letter to my mother and to break the news that as of September 1, 1942, he was being transferred from the Metropolitan's Newark district to a district office opening in Danville, Kentucky. On a map of Kentucky that had been included in the Homestead 42 packet presented to him by Mr. Kurth, he located Danville for us. Then he read aloud from a page in a Chamber of Commerce pamphlet entitled *The Blue Grass State*. " 'Danville is the county seat of rural Boyle County. It sits in beautiful Kentucky countryside about sixty miles south of Lexington, the state's second-biggest city after Louisville.' " He began flipping through the pamphlet to find still more interesting facts to read aloud that would somehow mitigate the senselessness of this turn of events. " 'Daniel Boone helped to blaze "the Wilderness Road," which opened the way to the settlement of Kentucky . . . In 1792, Kentucky became the first state west of the Appalachians to join the Union . . . The population of Kentucky in 1940 was 2,845,627.' The population of Danville—let me get it here— Danville's population was 6,700."

"And how many Jews in Danville," my mother asked, "of the six thousand and seven hundred? How many in the whole state?"

"You already know, Bess. There are very few. All I can tell you is that it could be worse. It could be Montana, where the Gellers are going. It could be Kansas, where the Schwartzes are going. It could be Oklahoma, where the Brodys are going. Seven men are leaving from our office, and I am the luckiest, believe me. Kentucky is a beautiful place with a beautiful climate. It is not the end of the world. We will wind up living out there just about the way we live here. Maybe better, given that everything is cheaper and the climate's so nice. There's going to be school for the boys, there's going to be the job for me, there's going to be the house for you. Chances are we'll be able to afford to buy a place of our own where the boys can each have a separate room and a yard out back to play in."

"And just where do they get the gall to do this to people?" my mother asked. "I am dumbfounded, Herman. Our families are here. Our lifelong friends are here. The children's friends are here. We have lived in peace and harmony here all of our lives. We are only a block from the best elementary school in Newark. We are a block from the best high school in New Jersey. Our boys have been raised among Jews. They go to school with other Jewish children. There is no friction with the other children. There is no name-calling. There are no fights. They have never had to feel left out and lonely the way I did as a child. I cannot believe the company is doing this to you. The way you have worked for those people, the hours that you put in, the effort—and this," she said angrily, "is the reward."

"Boys," my father said, "ask me what you want to know. Mother is right. This is a big surprise for all of us. We are all a little dumbfounded. So ask whatever is on your mind. I don't want anybody to be confused about anything."

But Sandy wasn't confused, nor did he look dumbfounded in any way. Sandy was thrilled and barely able to hide his glee, and all because he knew exactly where to find Danville, Kentucky, on the map—fourteen miles from the Mawhinneys' tobacco farm. It could have been that he'd also known we would be moving there long before any of the rest of us did. My father and mother may not have said as much, but then, precisely because of what no one was saying, even I could understand that my father's being selected as one of his district's seven Jewish "homesteaders" was no more fortuitous than his assignment to the company's new Danville office. Once he'd opened the back door to our flat and told Aunt Evelyn to leave the house and never come back, our fate could have played out no other way.

It was after dinner and we were in the living room. Serenely unperturbed, Sandy was drawing something and had no questions to ask, and I—looking outside with my face pressed to the screen of the open window—I had no questions to ask either, and so my father, grimly absorbed in his thoughts, and knowing he'd been defeated, began to pace the floor, and my mother, on the sofa, murmured something under her breath, refusing to resign herself to what awaited us. In the drama of confrontation, in the struggle against we knew not what, each had taken on the role that the other had played in the lobby of the Washington hotel. I realized how far things had gone and how terribly confusing everything now was and how calamity, when it comes, comes in a rush.

Since about three it had been squalling steadily, but abruptly the wind-driven downpour stopped and the sun came blazing out as though the clocks had been turned ahead and, over in the west, tomorrow morning was now set to begin at six P.M. today. How could a street as modest as ours induce such rapture just because it glittered with rain? How could the sidewalk's impassable leaf-strewn lagoons and the grassy little yards oozing from the flood of the downspouts exude a smell that roused my delight as if I'd been born in a tropical rain forest? Tinged with the bright after-storm light, Summit Avenue was as agleam with life as a pet, my own silky, pulsating pet, washed clean by sheets of falling water and now stretched its full length to bask in the bliss.

Nothing would ever get me to leave here.

"And who will the boys play with?" my mother asked.

"There are plenty of children in Kentucky to play with," he assured her.

"And who will I talk to?" she asked. "Who will I have there like the friends I've had my whole life?"

"There are women there, too."

"Gentile women," she said. Ordinarily my mother drew no strength from scorn, but she spoke scornfully now—that's how perplexed she was and how endangered she felt. "Good Christian women," she said, "who will fall all over themselves to make me feel at home. They have no right to do this!" she proclaimed.

"Bess, please—this is what it is like to work for a big company. Big companies transfer people all the time. And when they do, you have to pick up and go."

"I'm talking about the government. The *government* cannot do this. They cannot force people to pick up and go—that is not in any constitution that I ever heard of."

"They aren't forcing us."

"Then why are we going?" she asked. "Of course they are forcing us. This is *illegal*. You cannot just take Jews because they're Jews and force them to live where you want them to. You cannot take a city and just do what you want with it. To get rid of Newark as it is, with Jews living here like everyone else? What business is it of theirs? This is against the law. Everyone *knows* it is against the law."

"Yeah," said Sandy without bothering to look up from what he was sketching, "why don't we sue the United States of America?"

"You *can* sue," I told him. "In the Supreme Court."

"Ignore him," my mother told me. "Until your brother learns to be civil, we just continue to ignore him."

Here Sandy got up and took his drawing materials into our bedroom. Unable any longer to witness the spectacle of my father's defenselessness and my mother's anguish, I unlocked the front door and raced down the front stairs and out into the street where the kids who'd finished their dinner were already dropping Popsicle sticks into the gutters and watching them cascade over the iron grate into the gurgling sewer along with the natural detritus shaken by the storm from the locust trees and the swirl of candy wrappers, beetles, bottle caps, earthworms, cigarette butts, and, mysteriously, inexplicably, predictably, the single mucilaginous rubber. Everybody was out having one last good time before they had to turn in for bed —and all of them still capable of having a good time because none had a parent working for any of the corporations collaborating with Homestead 42. Their fathers were men who worked for themselves or with a partner who was a brother or an in-law and so they weren't going to have to go anywhere. But I wasn't going anywhere either. I would not be driven by the United States government from a street whose very gutters gushed with the elixir of life.

Alvin was in the rackets in Philadelphia, Sandy lived in exile in our house, and my father's authority as a protector had been drastically compromised if not destroyed. Two years earlier, to preserve our chosen way of life, he had mustered his strength to drive over to the home office and, face to face with the big boss, to decline the promotion that would have advanced his career and increased his earnings but at the price of taking us to live in heavily Bundist New Jersey. Now he no longer had it in him to challenge an uprooting potentially no less hazardous, having concluded that confrontation was futile and our fate out of his hands. Shockingly enough, my father had been rendered impotent by his company's having obediently joined hands with the state. There was nobody left to protect us except me.

After school the next day, I covertly headed off again for the downtown bus, this time for the number 7 line, whose route ran some three-quarters of a mile from Summit Avenue, on the far side of the farmed acreage of the orphan asylum, out where St. Peter's Church fronted the thoroughfare of Lyons Avenue and where, in the shadow of its cross-capped steeple, I was even less likely to be spotted by a neighbor or a schoolmate or a family friend than when I made it my business to walk past the high school and down to Clinton Place to take the 14.

I waited at the bus stop outside the church beside two nuns identically buried within the coarse heavy cloth of those voluminous black habits that I'd never had a chance to study as I did that day. Back then, a nun's habit reached to her shoes, and that, along with the brilliant white, starched arc of cloth that starkly framed her facial features and obliterated all lateral vision—the stiffened wimple that hid scalp, ears, chin, and neck and was itself enfolded in an extensive white headcloth—made of the traditionally dressed Catholic nuns the most archaic-looking creatures I had ever seen, far more startling to behold in our neighborhood than even the creepily morticianlike priests. No buttons or pockets were visible, and thus there was no way to figure out how that sheath of thickly gathered curtaining got hooked up or how it was taken off or whether it ever was taken off, given that overlaying everything was a large metal cross suspended from a long cord necklace, and strung beads, big and shiny as "killer" marbles, that dangled several feet down from the front of a black leather belt, and, secured to the headcloth, a black veil that broadened at the back and fell straight to the waist. Other than within the naked little region that was the wimpled, plain, unornamented face, no nap, no softness, no fuzziness anywhere.

I assumed these were two of the nuns who supervised the

lives of the orphans and taught in the parochial school. Neither
looked my way and, on my own, without a wisecracking sidekick like Earl Axman, I didn't dare to look at them other than
in stolen glances, though even while I stared at my own two
feet, the clever child's capacity for self-censorship deserted me
and I confronted the mysteries again and again, all the questions concerning their female bodies and its lowliest functions,
and all tending toward depravity. Despite the seriousness of
the afternoon's secret mission and everything that rode on its
outcome, I couldn't manage to be anywhere near a nun, let
alone a pair of them, without a mind awash in my none-too-
pure Jewish thoughts.

The nuns took the two seats behind the driver and, though
most of the seats farther to the rear were empty, I sat down
across the narrow aisle from the two of them, in the seat just
back from the turnstile and the fare box. I'd had no intention
of sitting there, didn't understand why I was doing so, but instead of moving off to where I could be out from under the
sway of unfettered curiosity, I opened my notebook to pretend
to do my schoolwork, simultaneously hoping and dreading
that I'd overhear them say something in Catholic. Alas, they
were silent, praying I supposed, and no less spellbinding for doing it on a bus.

Some five minutes from downtown, there was a musical
clacking of rosary beads as together they rose to disembark at
the wide intersection of High Street and Clinton Avenue. On
one side of the junction there was an auto dealer's lot and on
the other the Hotel Riviera. As they passed, the taller of the
nuns smiled down at me from the aisle and, with a vague sadness in her quiet voice—perhaps because the Messiah had
come and gone without my knowing it—commented to her
companion, "What a well-scrubbed, cute little boy."

She should have known what I'd been thinking. Then again,
maybe she did.

A few minutes later, before the bus took the big final turn
off Broad Street and started down Raymond Boulevard for its
last stop outside Penn Station, I too got off and began running
toward the Federal Office Building on Washington Street, where
Aunt Evelyn had her office. Inside the lobby I was told by an
elevator operator that the OAA was on the top floor, and when

I got there I asked for Evelyn Finkel. "You're Sandy's brother," the receptionist announced. "You could be his little twin," she added appreciatively. "Sandy's five years older," I told her. "Sandy's a wonderful, wonderful boy," she said, "everybody loved having him around," and then she buzzed Aunt Evelyn's office. "Nephew Philip's here, Miss F.," she announced, and within seconds, Aunt Evelyn had swept me past the desks of some half-dozen men and women working at their typewriters and into her office overlooking the public library and the Newark Museum. She was kissing me and hugging me and telling me how much she had missed me, and, despite all my apprehensions—beginning, of course, with the fear that my meeting with our estranged aunt would be discovered by my parents—I proceeded as I had planned by confiding in Aunt Evelyn how I had secretly gone alone to the Newsreel Theater to see her at the White House. I sat in the chair at the side of her desk—a desk easily twice the size of my father's just over on Clinton Street—and asked her to tell me what it had been like to eat dinner with the president and Mrs. Lindbergh. When she began to answer in elaborate detail—and with an eagerness to impress that didn't quite make sense to a mere child already overwhelmed by the magnitude of her betrayal— I couldn't believe I was so easily tricking her into thinking that this was why I was here.

There were two big maps pierced with clumps of colored pins and fixed to an enormous cork bulletin board on the wall back of her desk. The larger map was of the forty-eight states and the smaller of just New Jersey, whose long inland river boundary with neighboring Pennsylvania we had been taught in school to identify as the uncanny outline of an Indian chief's profile, the brow up by Phillipsburg, the nostrils down by Stockton, and the chin narrowing into the neck in the vicinity of Trenton. The state's densely populated easternmost corner, encompassing Jersey City, Newark, Passaic, and Paterson, and extending northward to the ruler-straight border with the southernmost counties of the state of New York, denoted the upper back end of the Indian's feathered headdress. That was how I saw it then, and how I continue to see it; along with the five senses, a child of my background had a sixth sense in those days, the geographic sense, the sharp sense of where he lived and who and what surrounded him.

On Aunt Evelyn's spacious desktop, beside separately framed pictures of my dead grandmother and of Rabbi Bengelsdorf, there was a large autographed photo of President and Mrs. Lindbergh standing together in the Oval Office and a smaller photo of Aunt Evelyn in her evening gown shaking the president's hand. "That's the reception line," she explained. "On the way into the state dining room, the guests each file past the president and the First Lady and the evening's honored guest. You're introduced by name and they take a photograph and the White House sends it to you."

"Did the president say anything?"

"He said, 'Nice to have you here.'"

"Are you allowed to say anything back?" I asked.

"I said, 'I'm honored, Mr. President.'" She made no effort to disguise how important that exchange had been to her and perhaps to the president of the United States. As always with Aunt Evelyn, there was something very winning about her enthusiasm, though in the context of my household's confusion, I couldn't miss what was diabolical about it as well. Never in my life had I so harshly judged any adult—not my parents, not even Alvin or Uncle Monty—nor had I understood till then how the shameless vanity of utter fools can so strongly determine the fate of others.

"Did you meet Mr. von Ribbentrop?"

Now almost girlishly bashful, she replied, "I danced with Mr. von Ribbentrop."

"Where?"

"There was dancing after dinner in a big tent on the White House lawn. It was a beautiful night. An orchestra and dancing, and Lionel and I were introduced to the foreign minister and his wife, and we got to talking, and then he just bowed and asked me to dance. He's known to be an excellent dancer, and he is, it's true—a perfectly magical ballroom dancer. And his English is faultless. He studied at the University of London and then lived for four years as a young man in Canada. His great youthful adventure, he calls it. I found him a very charming gentleman and *highly* intelligent."

"What'd he say?" I asked.

"Oh, we talked about the president, about the OAA, about our lives—we talked about everything. He plays the violin, you know. He's like Lionel, a man of the world who can talk knowledgeably about anything. Here, look, darling—look at what I was wearing. Do you see the bag I was carrying? It's gold mesh. See this? See the scarabs? Gold, enamel, and turquoise scarabs."

"What's a scarab?"

"It's a beetle. It's a gem that's cut to resemble a beetle. And it was made right here in Newark by the family of the first Mrs. Bengelsdorf. Their workshop was world famous. They made jewelry for the kings and queens of Europe and all of the wealthiest people in America. Look at my engagement ring," she said, placing her perfumed little hand so close to my face I felt like a dog suddenly and wanted to lick it. "See the stone? That is an emerald, my dearest dear child."

"A real one?"

She kissed me. "A real one! And in the photo, here—that's a link bracelet. It's gold with sapphires and pearls. *Real* ones!" she said, kissing me again. "The foreign minister said he'd never seen a bracelet more beautiful anywhere. And what do you think that is around my neck?"

"A necklace?"

"A festoon necklace."

"What's 'festoon'?"

"A chain of flowers, a garland of flowers. You know the word 'festival.' You know 'festivities.' And you know 'feast,' too, don't you? Well, they're all related. And look, the two brooches, see them? They're sapphires, darling—Montana sapphires set in gold. And do you see who is wearing them? Who? Who is that? It's Aunt Evelyn! It's Evelyn Finkel of Dewey Street! At the White House! Isn't it unbelievable?"

"I guess so," I said.

"Oh, sweetheart," she said, drawing me to her and kissing me now all over my face, "I guess so too. I'm so glad you came to see me. I've missed you so," and she stroked me then as if to find out if my pockets were stuffed with stolen goods. Only years later did I come to understand that her skillful way with her groping hands may well have been what accounted for the

rapid renovation of Aunt Evelyn's life by a figure of the stature
of Lionel Bengelsdorf. Brilliant and erudite though the rabbi
was, superior to everyone even in his egoism, Aunt Evelyn
must never have been at a loss with him.

The paradise of envelopment that followed was, of course,
unidentifiable at the time. Wherever I put my own two hands,
there was the soft surface of her body. Wherever I moved my
face, there was the thickness of her scent. Wherever I looked,
there was her clothing, new spring wrappings so light and
gauzy that they didn't even veil the sheen of her slip. And there
were the eyes of another human being as I'd never quite seen
them before. I had not reached the age of desire, was blinded,
of course, by the word "aunt," still found the random little
stiffening of my acorn of a penis the puzzling nuisance it had
always been, and so the delight that I took nestling into the
curvaceousness of my mother's thirty-one-year-old sister, a
tiny, lively Thumbelina seemingly timid in no way and formed
after the model of hills and apples, was a lifeless feeling of
frenzy and nothing more, as though a rare, imperfectly printed
treasure of a stamp that I knew to be priceless had accidentally
turned up on an ordinary letter dropped by the postman into
our Summit Avenue mailbox.

"Aunt Evelyn?"

"My darling."

"Do you know that we're moving to Kentucky?"

"Uh-huh."

"I don't want to go, Aunt Evelyn. I want to stay at my school."

She stepped sharply back from me, and with the air now of
anything but a paramour, asked, "Who sent you here, Philip?"

"Sent me? Nobody."

"Who sent you to see me? Tell the truth."

"It is the truth. Nobody."

She returned to the chair behind the desk, and the look in
her eyes made it necessary for me to do everything I could not
to get up and run. But I wanted what I wanted too much to run.

"There's nothing to be afraid of in Kentucky," she said.

"I'm not afraid. I just don't want to have to move."

Even her silence was all-embracing and, if I had indeed been
lying, would have forced from me the confession she wanted.
Her life, poor woman, was a perpetual state of intensity.

"Can't Seldon and his mother go instead of us?" I asked.

"Who is Seldon?"

"The boy downstairs whose father died. His mother works for the Metropolitan now. How come we have to go and they don't?"

"Wasn't it your father who put you up to this, dear?"

"No. No. Nobody even knows I'm here."

But I saw she still didn't believe me—her aversion to my father was too precious to be dislodged by the obvious truth.

"Does Seldon want to go with you to Kentucky?" she asked me.

"I didn't ask him. I don't know. I just thought I'd ask you if they could go instead."

"My dear little boy, do you see the New Jersey map? Do you see these pins in the map? Each one represents a family chosen for relocation. Now look at the map of the whole country. See all the pins there? Those represent the location to which each New Jersey family has been assigned. Making these assignments involves the cooperation of many, many people, in this office, in the Washington headquarters, and in the state to which each family is moving. The biggest and most important corporations in New Jersey are relocating employees in a partnership with Homestead 42, and so much more planning, much, much more than you can begin to imagine, has gone into all of this. And, of course, no decision is made by any one person. But even if it was, and I were that person, and I could do something to keep you near your friends and your school, I would continue to think that you for one are going to benefit enormously by becoming something more than another Jewish child whose parents have made him too frightened ever to leave the ghetto. Look what your family has done to Sandy. You saw your brother in New Brunswick that night. You saw him talking to all those people about his adventure on the tobacco farm. Do you remember that night?" she asked me. "Weren't you proud of him?"

"Yes."

"And did it sound as though living in Kentucky was frightening and that Sandy was ever, for a moment, afraid?"

"No."

Here, having reached into her desk for something, she got up and came around again to where I was sitting. Her pretty face, with its large features and thickly applied makeup, suddenly looked to me preposterous—the carnal face of the ravenous mania to which, in my mother's judgment, her emotional younger sister had helplessly fallen prey. To be sure, for a child in the court of Louis XIV the ambitions and satisfactions of such a relative would never have attained the same intimidating aura of significance that Aunt Evelyn's did for me, nor would the worldly advancement of a cleric like Rabbi Bengelsdorf have seemed the least bit scandalous to my parents were they themselves raised at court as a marquis and a marchioness. Probably I couldn't have done any worse—I might well have done a lot better—seeking solace from the two nuns on the Lyons Avenue bus than from someone reveling in the pleasures of the standard, petty corruptions that proliferate wherever people compete for even the tiniest advantages of rank.

"Be brave, darling. Be a brave boy. Do you want to sit on the front stoop of Summit Avenue for the rest of your life, or do you want to go out into the world like Sandy did and prove that you are as good as anyone? Suppose I'd been afraid to go to the White House and meet the president because people like your father say things about him and call him names. Suppose I'd been afraid to meet the foreign minister because they call *him* names. You cannot go around being afraid of everything that isn't familiar to you. You cannot grow up to be frightened like your parents. Promise me you won't."

"I promise."

"Here," she said, "I have a treat for you." And she handed me one of two little cardboard packets that she had been holding in her hand. "I got this for you at the White House. I love you, sweetheart, and I want you to have it."

"What is it?"

"An after-dinner chocolate. It's a chocolate wrapped in gold paper. And you know what's embossed right on the chocolate? The presidential seal. Here's one for you, and if I give you Sandy's, will you bring it to him for me?"

"Okay."

"This is what's on your table at the White House at the end of the meal. Chocolates in a silver dish. And the moment I saw them there I thought of the two boys in the world I most want to make happy."

I got up, clutching the chocolates in my hand, and Aunt Evelyn put her arm tightly around my shoulder and walked me out past all the people working for her and into the corridor, where she pressed the button for the elevator.

"What is Seldon's last name?" she asked me.

"Wishnow."

"And he's your best friend."

How could I explain that I couldn't bear him? And so at last I lied and said, "Yes, he is," and, since my aunt did indeed love me and was not herself lying when she said she wanted to make me happy, only a few days later, after I'd finally disposed of the White House chocolates by waiting until no one was around and throwing them over the orphanage fence, Mrs. Wishnow received a letter from the Metropolitan informing her that she and her family were fortunate enough to have been chosen to move to Kentucky as well.

On a Sunday afternoon at the end of May, a confidential meeting was convened in our living room for the Jewish insurance agents who, along with my father, were being relocated from the Metropolitan's Newark office under the auspices of Homestead 42. They all came with just their wives, having agreed that it would be best to leave the children at home. Earlier in the afternoon Sandy and I, joined by Seldon Wishnow, had arranged the chairs for the meeting, including a set of bridge chairs we'd carried upstairs from the Wishnows'. Afterward Mrs. Wishnow drove the three of us to the Mayfair Theater in Hillside, where we would catch a double feature and then be picked up by my father when the meeting was over.

The other guests were Shepsie and Estelle Tirschwell, who were only days from moving their family to Winnipeg, and Monroe Silverman, a distant cousin who'd recently opened a law office in Irvington, just above the haberdashery store owned by my father's second-older brother, Lenny, the uncle who supplied Sandy and me with new school clothes "at cost." When my mother suggested—out of her enduring respect for everything that one is taught to respect—that Hyman Resnick, our local rabbi, should be invited to attend the meeting, nobody else among the organizers who'd assembled in our kitchen the week before showed much enthusiasm for the idea and, after a deferential few minutes of discussion (during which my father said diplomatically what he always said diplomatically about Rabbi Resnick, "I like the man, like his wife, no doubt in my mind he does an excellent job, but he's really not very brilliant, you know"), my mother's proposal was tabled. Even though, to the delight of a small child, these intimate friends of our family spoke in as wide and entertaining a range of voices as the characters on *The Fred Allen Show* and were each as distinctively different-looking as the comic-strip figures in the evening paper—this was back when evolution's sly wit was still rampantly apparent, long before the youthful renovation of face and figure became a serious adult aspiration—they were very similar people at the core: they raised their families, budgeted their money, attended to their elderly parents, and cared for their modest homes alike, on most every public issue thought alike, in political elections voted alike. Rabbi Resnick presided over an unimposing yellow-brick synagogue at the edge of the neighborhood where everyone showed up in their High Holiday best for the three days each year of Rosh Hashanah and Yom Kippur observances but otherwise returned there for little else, except, when necessary, to dutifully recite the daily prayer for the dead during the period prescribed. A rabbi was to officiate at weddings and funerals, to bar mitzvah their sons, to visit the ill in the hospital, and to console the bereft at the shiva; beyond that he did not play a role of any importance in their day-to-day lives, nor did any of them—including my respectful mother—expect him to, and not just because Resnick wasn't that brilliant. Their being Jews didn't issue from the rabbinate or the synagogue or from their few formal religious practices, though over the years, largely for the sake of living parents who came once a week to visit and eat, several of the households, ours among them, were kosher. Their being Jews didn't even issue from on high. To be sure, each Friday at sundown, when my mother ritually (and touchingly, with the devotional delicacy she'd absorbed as a child from watching her own mother) lit the Sabbath candles, she invoked the Almighty by his Hebrew title but otherwise no one ever made mention of "Adonoy." These were Jews who needed no large terms of reference, no profession of faith or doctrinal creed, in order to be Jews, and they certainly needed no other language—they had one, their native tongue, whose vernacular expressiveness they wielded effortlessly and, whether at the card table or while making a sales pitch, with the easygoing command of the indigenous population. Neither was their being Jews a mishap or a misfortune or an achievement to be "proud" of. What they were was what they couldn't get rid of—what they couldn't even begin to want to get rid of. Their being Jews issued from their being themselves, as did their being American. It was as it was, in the nature of things, as fundamental as having arteries and veins, and they never manifested the slightest desire to change it or deny it, regardless of the consequences.

I'd known these people all my life. The women were close and reliable friends who exchanged confidences and swapped recipes, who commiserated with one another on the phone and looked after one another's children and regularly celebrated one another's birthdays by traveling the twelve miles to Manhattan to see a Broadway show. The men had not only worked for years in the same district office but met to play pinochle on the two evenings a month the women had their mahjong game, and from time to time, on a Sunday morning, a group of them went off to the old sweatbaths on Mercer Street with their young sons in tow—the offspring of this set happened all to be boys somewhere between Sandy's age and mine. On Decoration Day, the Fourth of July, and Labor Day the families would usually organize a picnic some ten miles west of our neighborhood at the bucolic South Mountain Reservation, where the fathers and the sons tossed horseshoes and chose up sides for softball and listened to a ball game on somebody's static-ridden portable radio, the most magical technology known to our world. The boys weren't necessarily the best of friends but we felt connected through our fathers' affiliation. Of us all, Seldon was the least robust, least confident, and, most painfully for him, least lucky, and yet it was to Seldon that I had managed to contract myself for the remainder of boyhood and probably beyond. He'd begun to shadow me more doggedly since he and his mother had learned of their relocation, and I could only think that because we two were going to be the sole Jewish pupils in the Danville elementary school system, I'd be expected—by the Danville Gentiles no less than by our parents—to be his natural ally and closest companion. Seldon's omnipresence might not be the worst that was awaiting me in Kentucky, but to the imagination of a nine-year-old it registered as an unendurable ordeal and accelerated the urge to rebel.

How? I didn't know yet. All I'd felt so far was the pre-mutinous roiling, and all I'd done about it was to find a small, water-stained cardboard suitcase forgotten beneath the usable luggage in our cellar storage bin and, after cleaning it of mildew inside and out, hidden the clothing there that I surreptitiously took, piece by piece, from Seldon's room whenever my mother dragooned me into enduring my hour downstairs as a peevish student of chess. I would have taken my own clothes to stow away in the suitcase except that I knew my mother would discover what was missing and one day soon I'd have to come up with an explanation. She still did the wash on the weekends and put the laundered clothes back—as well as the dry cleaning that it was my job to collect from the tailor shop on Saturdays—and so mapped out in her head was an inventory of everyone's wardrobe that was complete down to the location of the last pair of socks. On the other hand, stealing clothes from Seldon was a snap, and—what with his having latched on to me as his other self—vengefully irresistible. Underclothes and socks were easy enough to get out of the Wishnow apartment—and down the cellar stairs to the suitcase—tucked beneath my undershirt. Stealing and hiding a pair of his trousers, a sport shirt, and a pair of his shoes posed a more difficult problem, but suffice it to say that Seldon was distractible enough for the theft to be accomplished and, for a time, to go unnoticed.

Once having gathered together everything of his I needed, I couldn't have said what I planned to do next. He and I were about the same size, and on the afternoon when I dared to secrete myself in the bin and change out of my clothes and into Seldon's, all I did was to stand there and whisper, "Hello. My name is Seldon Wishnow," and feel like a freak, and not just because Seldon had become such a freak to me and I was being him but because it was clear from all my transgressive sneaking around Newark—and culminating in this costume party in the dark cellar—that I had become a far bigger freak myself. A freak with a trousseau.

The $19.50 left from Alvin's $20 also went into the suitcase, under the clothes. I then hurriedly got back into my own clothes, shoved the cardboard suitcase beneath the other luggage, and, before the angry ghost of Seldon's father could strangle me to death with a hangman's rope, ran for the alleyway and the outdoors. Over the next few days I was able to forget what I'd hidden and the unspecified purpose it was meant to serve. I could even count this latest little escapade as nothing seriously aberrant and as harmless as following Christians with Earl, until the evening when my mother had to rush downstairs to sit and hold Mrs. Wishnow's hand and make her a cup of tea and put her to bed, so wretched and distraught was Seldon's overworked mother because of her son's inexplicably "losing his clothes."

Seldon meanwhile was up in our flat, where he'd been sent to do his homework with me. He was plenty distraught himself. "I didn't lose them," he said through his tears. "How could I lose a pair of shoes? How could I lose a pair of pants?"

"She'll get over it," I said.

"No, not her—she doesn't get over anything. 'You're going to send us to the poorhouse,' she told me. Everything to my mother is 'the last straw.'"

"Maybe you left them at gym class," I suggested.

"How could I? How could I get out of gym class without any clothes on?"

"Seldon, you had to leave them somewhere. Think."

The next morning, before I headed for school and my mother left for work, she suggested my making a gift to Seldon of a set of my own clothes to replace his that had disappeared. "There's the shirt that you never wear—the one from Uncle Lenny's that you say is too green. And the pair of Sandy's corduroy trousers, the brown ones that never fit you right—I'm sure they would fit Seldon just fine. Mrs. Wishnow is beside herself, and it would be such a thoughtful gesture on your part," she said.

"And underwear? Do you want to give him my underwear too? Should I take it off now, Ma?"

"That's not necessary," she said, smiling to soothe my irritation. "But the green shirt and the brown corduroys and maybe one of your old belts that you don't use. It's entirely up to you, but it would mean a lot to Mrs. Wishnow, and to Seldon it would mean the world. Seldon worships you. You know that."

I immediately thought, "She knows. She knows what I did. She knows everything."

"But I don't want him walking around in my clothes," I said. "I don't want him telling everyone in Kentucky, 'Look at me, I'm wearing Roth's clothes.'"

"Why don't you worry about Kentucky when and if we go to Kentucky."

"He'll wear them to school *here*, Ma."

"What is the *matter* with you?" she replied. "What is going on with you? You're turning into—"

"So are you!" and I ran off with my books to school, and when I got home for lunch at noon I pulled from the bedroom closet the green shirt I hated and the brown corduroy pants that never fit and brought them downstairs to Seldon, who was in his kitchen eating the sandwich his mother had left for him and playing chess with himself.

"Here," I said, throwing the clothes on the table. "I'm giving you these," and then I told him, for all the good it did in rerouting the direction of either of our lives, "Only stop following me around!"

There were leftover delicatessen sandwiches for our supper when Sandy, Seldon, and I got back from the movies. The adults, who'd eaten in the living room when their meeting was through, had by now all left for home, except for Mrs. Wishnow, who sat at the kitchen table with her fists clenched, still embattled, still grappling day in and day out with everything determined to crush her and her fatherless son. She listened, along with the three of us, to the Sunday-night comedy shows and, while we ate, watched Seldon the way an animal watches over her newborn when she's caught a whiff of something stealthily creeping their way. Mrs. Wishnow had washed and dried the dishes and put them away in the pantry cupboard, my mother was in the living room pushing the carpet sweeper over the rug, and my father had collected and put out the garbage and carried the Wishnows' set of bridge chairs downstairs to return them to the back of the closet where Mr. Wishnow had killed himself. The reek of tobacco smoke pervaded the house despite every window having been thrown open and the ashes and butts flushed down the toilet and the glass ashtrays rinsed clean and stacked away in the breakfront's liquor cabinet (from which not a bottle had been removed that afternoon nor—in keeping with the matter-of-fact temperance practiced in the bulk of the homes of that first industrious American-born generation—a drop requested by a single guest).

For the moment, our lives were intact, our households were in place, and the comfort of habitual rituals was almost powerful enough to preserve a child's peacetime illusion of an eternal, unhounded now. We had the radio going with our favorite programs, we had dripping corned beef sandwiches for supper and rich coffee cake for dessert, we had the resumption of the routines of the school week before us and a double feature under our belts. But because we had no idea what our parents had decided about the future—had as yet no way of telling whether Shepsie Tirschwell had persuaded them to immigrate to Canada, whether cousin Monroe had come through with an affordable legal maneuver to challenge the relocation plan without getting everyone fired, or whether, after poring over the ins and outs of their government-ordained displacement as unemotionally as it was in them to do, they'd found no alternative but to accept that the guarantees of citizenship no longer fully extended to them—the embrace of the totally familiar wasn't the Sunday-night debauch it would ordinarily have been.

Seldon had got mustard all over his face when he hungrily attacked his sandwich, and it surprised me to see his mother reach over to wipe it off with a paper napkin. His letting her do it surprised me even more. I thought, "It is because he has no father," and though by now I believed that about everything that concerned him, probably this time I was right. I thought, "This is the way it's going to be in Kentucky." The Roth family against the world, and Seldon and his mother for dinner forever.

Our voice of belligerent protest, Walter Winchell, came on at nine. Everyone had been waiting on successive Sunday evenings for Winchell to lay into Homestead 42, and when he failed to, my father attempted to rid himself of his agitation by sitting down to compose a letter to the one man aside from Roosevelt whom he considered America's last best hope. "This is an experiment, Mr. Winchell. This is the way Hitler did it. The Nazi criminals start with something small, and if they get away with it," he wrote, "if no one like you raises a cry of alarm . . ." but he never proceeded to list the horrors that could ensue, because my mother was sure that the letter would wind up in the office of the FBI. It is mailed to Walter Winchell, she reasoned, but it never reaches Walter Winchell—at the post office it's diverted to the FBI and placed in a folder labeled "Roth, Herman," to be filed beside the existing folder labeled "Roth, Alvin."

My father argued, "Never. Not the U.S. Mail," but my mother's commonsensical reply stripped him on the spot of what little remained of his certainty. "You're sitting there writing Winchell," she said, "you're predicting to him how these people will stop at nothing once they know what they can get away with. And now you're trying to tell me that they can't do what they want to the postal system? Let someone else write to Walter Winchell. Our children have been questioned by the FBI already. The FBI is already watching like a hawk because of what Alvin did." "But that," he told her, "is *why* I'm writing him. What else should I do? What more *can* I do? If you know, advise me. Should I just sit here waiting for the worst to happen?"

In his helpless bewilderment she saw her opportunity, and, not because she was callous but because she was desperate, she seized it and thereby humbled him further. "You don't see Shepsie sitting around writing letters and waiting for the worst to happen," she said. "No," he replied, "not Canada again!" as though Canada were the name of the disease insidiously debilitating us all. "I don't want to hear it. Canada," he told her firmly, "is not a solution." "It's the *only* solution," she pleaded. "I am not running away!" he shouted, startling everyone. "This is our country!" "No," my mother said sadly, "not anymore. It's Lindbergh's. It's the goyim's. It's their country," she said, and her breaking voice and the shocking words and the nightmare immediacy of what was mercilessly real forced my father, in the prime of his manhood, fit, focused, and undiscourageable as any forty-one-year-old could possibly be, to see himself with mortifying clarity: a devoted father of titanic energy no more capable of protecting his family from harm than was Mr. Wishnow hanging dead in the closet.

To Sandy—still silently enraged by the injustice of having been stripped of his precocious importance—neither of them sounded anything but stupid, and alone with me he didn't hesitate to speak of them in the language he'd picked up from Aunt Evelyn. "Ghetto Jews," Sandy told me, "frightened, paranoid ghetto Jews." At home he sneered at just about everything they said, on any subject, and then sneered at me when I appeared to be skeptical of his bitterness. He might anyway have begun by now to seriously enjoy sneering, and perhaps even in ordinary times our mother and father might have found themselves having to tolerate as best they could a restless adolescent's contemptuous derision, but back in 1942 what made it more than merely exasperating was the ambiguously menacing predicament throughout whose duration he would continue disparaging them right to their faces.

"What's 'paranoid'?" I asked him.

"Somebody afraid of his shadow. Somebody who thinks the whole world's against him. Somebody who thinks Kentucky is in Germany and that the president of the United States is a storm trooper. These people," he said, mimicking our captious aunt whenever she would superciliously distinguish herself from the Jewish rabble. "You offer to pay their moving expenses, you offer to throw open the gates for their children . . . Know what paranoid is?" Sandy said. "Paranoid is nuts. The two of them are bats—they're crazy. And you know what's made them crazy?"

The answer was Lindbergh, but I didn't dare say it to him. "What?" I asked.

"Living like a bunch of greenhorns in a goddamn ghetto. You know what Aunt Evelyn says Rabbi Bengelsdorf calls it?"

"Calls what?"

"The way these people live. He calls it 'Keeping faith with the certainty of Jewish travail.' "

"And what's that supposed to mean? I don't understand. Translate, please. What's 'travail'?"

"Travail? Travail is what you Jews call *tsuris.*"

*

The Wishnows had gone back downstairs and Sandy had settled into the kitchen to finish his homework when my parents, at the front of the house, tuned the living room radio to Walter Winchell. I was in bed with the lights out: I didn't want to hear another panic-stricken word from anyone about Lindbergh, von Ribbentrop, or Danville, Kentucky, and I didn't want to think about my future with Seldon. I wanted only to disappear into forgetful sleep and to wake up in the morning somewhere else. But because it was a warm night and the windows were wide open, I couldn't help, at the stroke of nine, but be beset from virtually every quarter by the renowned Winchell radio trademark—the clatter of dots and dashes sounding over the telegraph ticker and signaling in Morse code (which Sandy had taught me) absolutely nothing. And then, above the ticker's dimming clatter, the red-hot blast of Winchell himself issuing from all the houses on the block. "Good evening, Mr. and Mrs. America . . ." followed by the staccato barrage of the long-hoped-for words—at last the purgative Winchell scourge that would change everything. In normal times, when it was generally within the power of my mother and father to set things right and explain away enough of the unknown to make existence appear to be rational, it wasn't at all like this, but because of the maddening here and now, Winchell, even to me, had become an out-and-out god and more important by far than Adonoy.

"Good evening, Mr. and Mrs. America and all the ships at sea. Let's go to press! Flash! To the glee of rat-faced Joe Goebbels and his boss, the Berlin butcher, the targeting of America's Jews by the Lindbergh fascists is officially under way. The phony moniker for phase one of organized Jewish persecution in the land of the free is 'Homestead 42.' Homestead 42 is being aided and abetted by the most respectable of America's robber barons—but don't worry, they'll be rewarded in giveaway tax breaks by Lindbergh's Republican henchmen in the next pro-greed Congress.

"Item: Whether the Homestead 42 Jews end up in concentration camps à la Hitler's Buchenwald has yet to be decided by Lindbergh's two top swastinkers, Vice President Wheeler and Secretary of the Interior Henry Ford. Did I say 'whether'? Pardon my German. I meant when.

"Item: Two hundred and twenty-five Jewish families have already been told to vacate the cities of America's northeast in order to be shipped thousands of miles from family and friends. This first shipment has been kept strategically small in order to escape national attention. Why? Because it marks the beginning of the end for the four and a half million American citizens of Jewish descent. The Jews will be scattered far and wide to wherever Hitlerite America Firsters flourish. There the right-wing saboteurs of democracy—the so-called patriots and the so-called Christians—can be turned against these isolated Jewish families overnight.

"And who's next, Mr. and Mrs. America, now that the Bill of Rights is no longer the law of the land and the racial haters are running the show? Who's next under the Wheeler-Ford pogrom-plan for government-funded persecution? The long-suffering Negroes? The hard-working Italians? The last of the Mohicans? Who else among us is no longer welcome in Adolf Lindbergh's Aryan America?

"Scoop! This reporter has learned that Homestead 42 was in the works on January 20, 1941, the day the American Fascist New Order moved its mob into the White House, and was signed into the Iceland sellout between the American Führer and his Nazi partner in crime.

"Scoop! This reporter has learned that only in return for the gradual relocation—and eventual mass imprisonment—of America's Jews by the Lindbergh Aryans would Hitler agree to spare the British Isles from a massive armed invasion across the English Channel. The two beloved Führers agreed in Iceland that massacring blue-eyed, blond-haired bona fide Aryans didn't make sense unless you definitely had to. And it comes as no surprise that Hitler will most definitely have to if Oswald Mosley's British fascist party fails to take dictatorial control of 10 Downing Street before 1944. That's when the master race plans to wrap up the Nazi enslavement of three hundred million Russians and to raise the swastika over the Moscow Kremlin.

"And how long will the American people stand for this treachery perpetrated by their elected president? How long will Americans remain asleep while their cherished Constitution is torn to shreds by the fascist fifth column of the Republican right marching under the sign of the cross and the flag?

Stay with me, your New York correspondent Walter Winchell, for my next big bombshell about Lindbergh's treasonous lies.

"I'll be back in a flash with a flash!"

Three things then happened at once: the calming voice of announcer Ben Grauer started hawking hand lotion for the program's sponsor; the phone began to ring in the hallway outside my bedroom as it never did after nine in the evening; and Sandy exploded. Addressing only the radio (but so passionately that my father was instantly roused from his living room chair), he began to shout, "You filthy liar! You lying prick!"

"Whoa," said my father, rushing into the kitchen. "Not in this house. Not that language. That is enough."

"But how can you *listen* to this crap? *What* concentration camps? There are no concentration camps! Every word is a lie —bullshit and more bullshit to get you people to tune in! The whole country knows Winchell's full of hot air—it's only you people who don't."

"And which people exactly is that?" I heard my father say.

"I lived in Kentucky! Kentucky is one of the forty-eight states! Human beings live there like they do everywhere else! It is not a concentration camp! This guy makes millions selling his shitty hand lotion—and *you* people believe him!"

"I told you already about the dirty words, and now I'm telling you about this 'you people' business. 'You people' one more time, son, and I am going to ask you to leave the house. If you want to go live in Kentucky instead of here, I'll drive you down to Penn Station and you can catch the next train out. Because I know very well what 'you people' means. And so do you. So does everyone. Don't you use those two words in this house ever again."

"Well, in my opinion Walter Winchell is full of it."

"Fine," he said. "That is your opinion and you are entitled to it. But other Americans hold a different opinion. It so happens that millions and millions of Americans listen to Walter Winchell every single Sunday night—and they are not just what you and your brilliant aunt call 'you people.' His program is still the highest-rated news show on the air. Franklin Roosevelt confided to Walter Winchell things he would never tell another newspaperman. And listen to me, will you—these are *facts*."

"But I *can't* listen to you. How can I listen to you when you tell me about 'millions' of people? Millions of people are nothing but idiots!"

Meanwhile my mother had answered the phone in the hall, and from my bed I could now hear her speaking as well. Yes, she said, of course they had Winchell on. Yes, it was terrible, it was worse than they thought, but at least now it was out in the open. Yes, Herman would call as soon as the Winchell show was over.

Four consecutive times she had this conversation, but when the phone rang a fifth time, she didn't jump to answer, even though the caller had to have been another of their friends shaken by Winchell's rapid-fire disclosures—she didn't answer because the commercial was finished and she and my father were back beside the radio in the living room. And Sandy was now in the bedroom, where I pretended to be asleep while he got himself ready for bed by the night light, the small lamp with the pump-handle switch that he had made from scratch in shop class back when he was merely an artistic boy engrossed by what he could fashion with his own skillful hands and blessedly uncontaminated by ideological battling.

Our phone hadn't been used so incessantly so late at night since the death of my grandmother a couple of years back. It was close to eleven before my father had returned everyone's call, and another hour before my parents left the kitchen, where they'd been quietly conversing together, and themselves went to bed. And it was another two hours after that before I could assure myself that they were sound asleep and that, in the bed beside mine, my brother was no longer glaring at the ceiling but was also asleep, and that I could safely get up without being discovered and make my way to the back door and undo the lock and slip out of the flat and pad down the stairs into the cellar and, in the dark, steer myself barefoot across the dank floor to our storage bin.

There was nothing impulsive or hysterical driving me, nothing melodramatic about my decision, nothing reckless that I could see. People said afterward that they'd had no idea that beneath the fourth-grade patina of obedience and good manners I could be such a surprisingly irresponsible, daydreaming child. But this was no shallow daydream. I wasn't playing at make-believe, and I wasn't making mischief for mischief's sake. As it turned out, the mischief-making with Earl Axman had been valuable training but undertaken for a purpose entirely different. I surely didn't feel as though I were rushing head-long into insanity, not even when I stood in the dark bin removing my pajamas and stepping into Seldon's pants while at the same time mentally warding off the ghost of his father and trying not to be terrified by Alvin's empty wheelchair. I wasn't being swallowed up by anything other than the determination to resist a disaster our family and our friends could no longer elude and might not survive. Later my parents said, "He didn't know what he was doing," and "sleepwalking" became the official explanation. But I was fully awake and my motivation never obscure to me. All that was obscure was whether I would succeed. One of my teachers suggested that I had been suffering from "delusions of grandeur" inspired by what I was learning in school about the Underground Railroad, organized before the Civil War to assist the slaves in making their way north to freedom. Not so. I wasn't at all like Sandy, in whom opportunity had quickened the desire to be a boy on the grand scale, riding the crest of history. I wanted nothing to do with history. I wanted to be a boy on the smallest scale possible. I wanted to be an orphan.

There was only one thing I couldn't leave behind—my stamp album. Perhaps if I could have been sure that it would be preserved undisturbed after I was gone, I wouldn't, at the last moment, on the way out of my bedroom, have stopped to open my dresser drawer and, as quietly as I could, lifted it from where it was stored beneath my socks and my underclothes. But it was intolerable to think of my album ever being broken up or thrown out or, worst of all, given away wholly intact to another boy, and so I took it under my arm, and along with it the musket-shaped letter opener I'd bought at Mount Vernon whose beak of a bayonet I used to neatly slice open the only mail ever addressed to me, other than birthday cards—the packets of "approvals" sent regularly from Boston 17, Massachusetts, by "the world's largest stamp firm," H. E. Harris & Co.

I remember nothing between my stealing out of the house and starting down the empty street toward the orphanage grounds and my waking up the next day to see my grim-faced parents at the foot of my bed and to be told by a doctor busily extracting some kind of tube from my nose that I was a patient in Beth Israel Hospital and that though I probably had a terrible headache, I was going to be all right. My head did hurt, excruciatingly, but it wasn't from a blood clot's putting pressure on the brain—a possibility they feared when I was found bleeding and unconscious—and not because there was brain damage. X-rays ruled out a skull fracture and the neurological examination showed no damage to the nerves. Other than a three-inch-long laceration requiring eighteen stitches that were removed the following week, and the fact that I had no memory of the blow itself, nothing serious was wrong with me. A routine concussion, the doctor said—that's all that was causing the pain as well as the amnesia. I'd probably never remember being kicked by the horse—or the series of events leading to that collision—but the doctor said that was routine, too. Otherwise my memory was intact. Luckily. He used that word several times and it sounded like ridicule in my aching head.

They kept me for observation all that day and overnight—rousing me just about every hour to be sure I didn't slip into unconsciousness again—and the next morning I was discharged and instructed only to go easy with physical activities for a week or two. My mother had taken off from work to be with me at the hospital and she was there to take me home on the bus. Because my head didn't stop hurting for some ten days, and because there was nothing to be done about it, I was kept home from school, but otherwise I was said to be fine, and fine thanks primarily to Seldon, who, from a distance, had witnessed almost everything that I was unable to remember. If Seldon hadn't sneaked out of bed when he heard me coming down the back stairs, hadn't followed me in the dark along Summit Avenue and across the high school playing field to the Goldsmith Avenue side of the orphanage and through the unlatched gate and into the orphanage woods, I probably would have lain there unconscious in his clothes until I bled to death. Seldon ran all the way back to our house, woke my parents, who immediately dialed the operator for help, and got in our car with them and directed them to the very spot where I was. It was by then close to three in the morning and pitch black;

kneeling beside me on the damp ground, my mother pressed a
towel she'd brought with her against my head to stanch the
bleeding while my father covered me with an old picnic blanket that was in the trunk of the car and kept me warm until the
ambulance arrived. My parents organized my rescue, but Seldon Wishnow saved my life.

I had apparently startled the two horses when, disoriented, I
began stumbling about in the dark where the woods opened
out into the farming field, and when I turned to try to escape
the horses and make it back to the street through the woods
one of them reared up, I tripped and fell, and the other horse,
in fleeing, nicked me with a hoof high on the back of my skull.
For weeks Seldon recounted excitedly to me (and, of course,
to the entire school) every detail of my nocturnal attempt to run
away from home and be taken in by the nuns as a familyless
child—in his telling, savoring particularly the mishap with the
workhorses as well as the fact that, outdoors in the middle of
the night, barefoot and in just his pajamas, he had twice traversed the mile of abrasive terrain between the orphanage
woods and our house.

Unlike his mother and my parents, Seldon couldn't get over
the thrill of discovering that it wasn't he who had inexplicably
"lost" his clothes but I who had stolen them to use for my
getaway. This utter improbability established, as never before,
a value to his own existence that had previously escaped his
attention. Telling the story with all the prestige of savior and
co-conspirator both—and showing everyone who'd look at
them his scraped feet—seemed to make Seldon significant at
last even in his own eyes, a daredevil of a boy able to compel a
hero's attention for the first time in his life, while I was devastated, not only by the shame of it all, which was more unbearable and longer lasting than the headache, but because my
stamp album, my greatest treasure, that which I could not live
without, was gone. I didn't remember having taken it with me
until the day after I got home from the hospital and got up in
the morning to get dressed and saw that it was missing from
beneath my socks and my underwear. The reason I stored it
there in the first place was so as to see it first thing every morning when I dressed for school. And now the first thing I saw
on my first morning home was that the biggest thing I had

ever owned was gone. Gone and irreplaceable. Like—and utterly unlike—losing a leg.

"Ma!" I shouted. "Ma! Something terrible happened!"

"What is it?" she cried, and came running from the kitchen into my room. "What's wrong?"

She thought, of course, that I'd begun to bleed from my stitches or that I was about to faint or that the headache was more than I could stand.

"My stamps!" That was all I could say, and she was able to figure out the rest.

What she did then was to go looking for them. All alone she went into the orphanage woods and searched the ground where I'd been discovered, but she was unable to find the album anywhere—found not so much as a single stamp.

"Are you sure you had them?" she asked when she got home.

"Yes! Yes! They're there! They have to be there! I can't lose my stamps!"

"But I looked and looked. I looked everywhere."

"But who could have taken them? Where could they be? They're mine! We've got to find them! They're my stamps!"

I was inconsolable. I envisioned a horde of orphans spotting the album in the woods and tearing it apart with their filthy hands. I saw them pulling out the stamps and eating them and stomping on them and flushing them by the handful down the toilet in their terrible bathroom. They hated the album because it wasn't theirs—they hated the album because nothing was theirs.

Because I asked her to, my mother told neither my father nor my brother what had become of my stamps or about the money in Seldon's pants. "In the pocket, when we found you, there were nineteen dollars and fifty cents. I don't know where it came from and I don't want to know. That episode is over and done with. I opened a savings account for you at the Howard Savings Bank. I deposited it for you there for your future." Here she handed me a little bankbook with my name written inside it and "$19.50" the first and only item stamped in black on the deposit page. "Thank you," I said. And then she made the judgment of her second son that I believed she carried with her to her grave. "You are the strangest child," she told me. "I had no idea," she said. "I didn't begin to know." And then she handed me my letter opener, the miniaturized pewter musket from Mount Vernon. The stock was scratched and dirty and the bayonet bent slightly out of shape. She had found it that afternoon when, unknown to me, she had raced back from work at lunch hour and returned for a second time to comb through the soil of the orphanage woods in search of the tiniest remnant of the stamp collection that had dissolved into thin air.

7

The Winchell Riots

THE DAY before I discovered that my stamps were gone, I'd learned of my father's decision to quit his job. Only minutes after I got home from the hospital on Tuesday morning, he drove up to our house and into the alley in Uncle Monty's truck with the slatted-wood sides and parked it there behind Mrs. Wishnow's car, having just finished his first night of work at the Miller Street market. From then on, Sunday night through Friday morning, he'd come home at nine, ten A.M., wash up, eat his big meal, go to bed and be asleep by eleven, and when I returned from school I had to be careful not to slam the back door and wake him. A little before five in the afternoon he'd be up and gone, because by about six or seven the farmers began arriving at the market with their produce, and then anywhere from ten P.M. to four in the morning the retail grocers would be coming in to buy, along with the restaurant owners and the hotelkeepers and the last of the city's horse-and-wagon peddlers. He'd survive through the long night on the thermos of coffee and the couple of sandwiches my mother had prepared for him to take to work. On Sunday mornings he'd visit his mother at Uncle Monty's or Monty would bring her to the house to see us, and he'd spend the rest of Sunday sleeping, and again we'd have to be quiet so as not to disturb him. It was a hard life, especially since on occasion he had to drive out well before dawn to farmers in Passaic and Union counties and bring their produce in all by himself if Uncle Monty could get a better deal that way.

I knew it was a hard life because when he got home in the morning he'd have a drink. Ordinarily in our house a bottle of Four Roses lasted for years. My mother, a caricature of a teetotaler, couldn't stand the look of a foaming glass of beer, let alone the smell of straight whiskey, and when did my father ever take a drink, other than on their anniversary or when his boss came for dinner and he served him Four Roses on the rocks? But now he would get home from the market and, before he changed out of his dirty clothes and took his shower, he'd pour the whiskey into a shot glass, tilt back his head, and take it down in one gulp, making the face of a man who'd just bit into a light bulb. "Good!" he'd say aloud. "Good!" Only then could he ease up enough to eat a full meal without getting indigestion.

I was dumbfounded, and not only by the abrupt decline in my father's vocational status—not only by the truck in the alleyway and the thick-soled boots on the feet of a man who had previously gone off to work in a suit and a tie and polished black shoes, not only by the preposterousness of his slugging down his shot and having his dinner alone at ten in the morning—but by my brother as well, by *his* unforeseen transformation.

Sandy wasn't angry any longer. He wasn't contemptuous. He wasn't superior-acting in any way. It was as though he too had taken a blow to the head, but one that, instead of bringing on amnesia, had rejuvenated the quiet, conscientious boy whose satisfactions emanated not from his being a precocious big shot full of contrary opinions but from that strong, even current of an interior life that carried him steadily along from morning to night and that, in my eyes, had always made him genuinely superior to the other kids his age. Or perhaps it was that the passion for stardom—along with the capacity for conflict—had been spent; perhaps he had never possessed the necessary egoism, and was secretly relieved no longer having to be publicly stupendous. Or perhaps he'd just never believed in what he was supposed to be promulgating. Or perhaps, while I lay unconscious in the hospital with a possibly life-threatening hematoma, my father had given him the talking-to that had done the trick. Or perhaps, in the wake of the crisis I'd precipitated, he was merely concealing the stupendous self *behind* the old Sandy, masquerading, calculating, cleverly waiting in hiding until . . . until who knew what befell us next. At any rate, for now the shock of circumstances had steered my brother back into the family fold.

And my mother was no longer a working woman. There

wasn't nearly what she'd hoped to accumulate in the Montreal savings account, but enough to get us across the border and started in Canada if we should have to flee at a moment's notice. She'd left her job at Hahne's no less expeditiously than my father had jettisoned the security of his twelve-year affiliation with the Metropolitan to foil the government's plans for our transfer to Kentucky and safeguard us against the anti-Semitic subterfuge that he, along with Winchell, understood Homestead 42 to be. She was back running the household full-time and would once again be there when we came home for lunch and got home from school, and during the summer vacation she'd be there to monitor Sandy and me so that we didn't again spin out of control owing to lack of supervision.

A father remodeled, a brother restored, a mother recovered, eighteen black silk sutures stitched in my head and my greatest treasure irretrievably lost, and all with a wondrous fairy-tale swiftness. A family both declassed and rerooted overnight, facing neither exile nor expulsion but entrenched still on Summit Avenue, whereas in three short months, Seldon—to whom I was helplessly yoked now that he was going around the neighborhood reveling in having prevented me from bleeding to death while disguised in his clothes—Seldon was shipping out. As of September 1, Seldon would be off living with his mother, the only Jewish kid in Danville, Kentucky.

My "sleepwalking" would likely have caused an even more humiliating scandal than it did in our immediate locale had not Walter Winchell been fired by Jergens Lotion only hours after coming off the air on the Sunday night that I'd run away. There was the truly shocking news that nobody could believe and that Winchell wasn't about to let the country forget. After ten years as America's leading radio reporter, he was replaced at nine P.M. the following Sunday by yet another dance band broadcasting from yet another sophisticated supper club on the terrace of a midtown Manhattan hotel. Jergens's first charge against him was that a broadcaster with a weekly nationwide audience of more than twenty-five million had essentially "cried fire in a crowded theater"; the second was that he had slandered a president of the United States with malicious accusations "that only the most outrageous demagogue would contrive to arouse the passions of the mob."

Even the moderate *New York Times*, a paper founded and owned by Jews—and highly esteemed for that reason by my father—and by no means uncritical of Lindbergh's policy toward Hitler's Germany, announced its unqualified support of the action taken by Jergens Lotion in an editorial entitled "A Professional Disgrace." "A competition has been in progress for some time," wrote the *Times*,

> among anti-Lindbergh entrepreneurs to determine who can produce the most outrageous accounts of the motives of the Lindbergh administration. With one bombastic stride, Walter Winchell has moved to the head of the pack. The borderline scruples and questionable taste of Mr. Winchell have tumbled over into an outburst of vitriol that is as unpardonable as it is unethical. With accusations so far-fetched that even a lifelong Democrat may find himself feeling unexpected sympathy for the president, Winchell has disgraced himself irredeemably. Jergens Lotion is to be commended for the speed with which it has removed him from the airwaves. Journalism as it is practiced by the Walter Winchells of this country is an insult as much to our enlightened citizenry as to the journalistic standards of accuracy, fairness, and responsibility, toward which Mr. Winchell, his cynical tabloid cohorts, and their money-hungry publishers have always displayed the utmost contempt.

In a subsequent attack delivered in behalf of the Lindbergh administration and published by the *Times* as the first and lengthiest of the letters elicited by its editorial, one eminent correspondent, after alluding gratefully to the editorial and reinforcing its argument by further examples of Winchell's ostentatious abuse of the First Amendment, concluded: "The attempt to inflame and frighten his fellow Jews is no less detestable than the disregard for the norms of decency that your paper so forcefully condemns. Certainly nothing is so heinous as preying upon the historical fears of a persecuted people, particularly when full participation in an open society free of oppression is precisely what the present administration is working to achieve for this same group through the efforts of the Office of American Absorption. For Walter Winchell to

characterize Homestead 42, a program designed to broaden
and enrich the involvement of America's proud Jewish citizens
in the national life, as a fascistic strategy to isolate Jews and
exclude them from the national life is the height of journalistic
recklessness and an illustration of the Big Lie technique that is
today the greatest threat to democratic freedom everywhere."

The letter was signed "Rabbi Lionel Bengelsdorf, Director,
Office of American Absorption, Department of the Interior,
Washington, D.C."

Winchell's response came in the column he wrote for the
Daily Mirror, the New York paper belonging to America's
wealthiest publisher, William Randolph Hearst, who owned a
chain of some thirty right-wing papers and half a dozen popular magazines as well as King Features, where Winchell was
syndicated and read by many millions more. Hearst despised
Winchell's political allegiances, particularly his glorification of
FDR, and would have fired him years earlier had it not been
that the very New Yorkers for whose nickels the *Mirror* competed against the *Daily News* found irresistible the gutter
charm of the columnist's singular concoction of muckraking
contentiousness and cloying patriotism. According to Winchell,
why Hearst finally did fire him had less to do with the long-
standing animosity between the columnist and his publisher
than with pressure from the White House that even a ruthless
old tycoon as powerful as Hearst could not dare to resist for
fear of the consequences.

"The Lindbergh fascists"—so began the characteristically
brazen, unregenerate Winchell column published just days after
he'd lost his radio contract—"have openly begun their Nazi
assault on freedom of expression. Today Winchell's the enemy
to be silenced . . . Winchell 'the warmonger,' 'the liar,' 'the
alarmist,' 'the Commie,' 'the kike.' Today yours truly, tomorrow every newscaster and reporter who dares to tell the truth
about the fascist plot to destroy American democracy. Honorary Aryans like the rabid rabbi Lyin' Lionel B. and the snooty
Park Avenue proprietors of the gutless *New York Times* aren't
the first ultracivilized Jewish Quislings to grovel before an
anti-Semitic master because they're just too, too refined to
fight like Winchell . . . and they won't be the last. The jerks
at Jergens aren't the first corporate cowards to play ball with

the dictatorial lying machine that is now ruining this country . . . and they won't be the last, either."

And that column—which proceeded to list some fifteen more of his personal enemies who qualified as America's leading fascist collaborators—was, in fact, to be *his* last.

Three days later, after visiting Hyde Park to make certain that FDR was still determined not to come out of political retirement to run for a third term, Winchell announced his candidacy for president of the United States in the next general election. Until then, those considered in the running were Roosevelt's secretary of state, Cordell Hull; the former secretary of agriculture and the vice presidential candidate on the 1940 ticket, Henry Wallace; Roosevelt's postmaster general and the chairman of the Democratic Party, James Farley; Supreme Court Justice William O. Douglas; and two middle-of-the-road Democrats, neither of them New Dealers, former Indiana governor Paul V. McNutt and Senator Scott W. Lucas of Illinois. There was also an unconfirmed report (circulated and perhaps originated by Winchell back when he was still making $800,000 a year circulating unconfirmed reports) that should the convention wind up deadlocked, as could easily happen with so unexciting a slate of candidates, Eleanor Roosevelt, a forceful political and diplomatic presence during her husband's two terms—and still a popular figure whose blend of outspokenness and aristocratic reserve had gained her an enormous following among the party's liberal constituency as well as numerous mocking enemies in the right-wing press— would appear on the convention floor the way Lindbergh did at the 1940 Republican Convention and sweep the nomination by acclamation. But once Walter Winchell became the first Democratic candidate to enter the race, and to do so almost thirty months in advance of the '44 election, in advance even of the midterm congressional elections—and to do so immediately after the noisy fracas that resulted from his having been "purged" from his profession by "the strong-arm putsch tactics of the fascist gang in the White House" (as Winchell described his enemies and their methods in announcing his candidacy)—the one-time gossip columnist became the man to beat, the only Democrat with a name known to everyone and audacious enough to assault with ferocity an incumbent as beloved as Lindy.

Republican leaders didn't deign to take Winchell seriously, assuming either that the irrepressible performer was putting on a self-glorifying sideshow to sucker funds out of a handful of rich diehard Democrats or that he was a flamboyant stalking horse for FDR (or perhaps for Roosevelt's ambitious wife), at once stirring up and measuring whatever underground anti-Lindbergh sentiment might possibly exist in a nation where polls showed that Lindbergh continued to be supported by a record eighty to ninety percent of every classification and category of voter, except the Jews. Winchell, in short, was the candidate of the Jews, and himself a Jew of the coarsest type, in no way resembling the inner circle of well-bred, dignified Jewish Democrats like Roosevelt's wealthy friend Bernard Baruch or the banker and New York governor Herbert Lehman or the recently retired Supreme Court justice Louis Brandeis. And as if being a Jew of no background who embodied just about every vulgar trait that made Jews less than welcome in the better strata of American social and business society weren't enough to render him an irrelevant impertinence on the political scene anywhere other than the heavily Jewish precincts of New York City, there was his reputation as an adulterous philanderer with a penchant for seducing long-legged showgirls and his profligate nightlife among the loose-living Hollywood and Broadway celebrities who drank to all hours at New York's Stork Club to make him anathema to the straitlaced multitude. His candidacy was a joke and the Republicans treated it as nothing more.

But on our street that week, in the immediate aftermath of the firing of Winchell and his instantaneous resurrection as a presidential candidate, the significance of the two events was almost all that neighbors could talk about among themselves. After nearly two years of never knowing whether to believe the worst, of trying to focus on the demands of their day-to-day lives and then helplessly absorbing every rumor about what the government had in store for them, of never being able to justify either their alarm or their composure with hard fact—after so much perplexity, they were so ripe for delusion that, when the parents gathered on their beach chairs to chat together in the alleyways at night, the guessing game that invariably started up could go on without letup for hours: Who would be vice president on the Winchell ticket? Whom would he appoint to his cabinet? Whom would he appoint to the Supreme Court? Who would turn out to be the greater leader, FDR or Walter Winchell? They plunged headlong into a thousand fantasies, and the very small children also caught the spirit and went skipping and dancing about, chanting, "Wind-shield for pres-i-dent . . . Wind-shield for pres-i-dent." Of course, that no Jew could ever be elected to the presidency—least of all a Jew with a mouth as unstoppable as Winchell's—even a kid as young as I was already accepted, as if the proscription were laid out in so many words in the U.S. Constitution. Yet not even that iron-clad certainty could stop the adults from abandoning common sense and, for a night or two, imagining themselves and their children as native-born citizens of Paradise.

The wedding of Rabbi Bengelsdorf and Aunt Evelyn took place on a Sunday in the middle of June. My parents were not invited, nor did they expect or want to be, and yet nothing could be done to ease my mother's distress. I'd overheard her crying from behind her bedroom door before, and though it wasn't a usual occurrence or one I liked, in all the months during which my parents struggled to assess the menace posed by the Lindbergh administration and to determine the response sensible for a Jewish family to take, I'd never known her to be so inconsolable. "Why does this have to happen too?" she asked my father. "They're only getting married," he told her. "It isn't the end of the world." "But I can't stop thinking about my father," she said. "Your father died," he said, "my father died. They weren't young men, they got sick and they died." It would have been hard to imagine a tone any more sympathetic than his, but her misery was such that the gentler his voice, the worse she suffered. "And I think," she said, "about my mother, how Momma wouldn't know what to make of anything anymore." "Honey, it could all be a lot more terrible—you know that." "And it will be," my mother said. "Maybe not, maybe not. Maybe everything is starting to change. Winchell—" "Oh, please, Walter Winchell won't—" "Shhh, shhh," he said to her, "the little one."

And so I understood that Walter Winchell wasn't, in fact, the candidate of the Jews—he was the candidate of the children of the Jews, something we were being given to clutch at, the way not too many years before we'd been given the breast not merely for nutrients but for the alleviation of babyhood's fears.

The wedding ceremony was held at the rabbi's temple and the reception afterward in the ballroom of the Essex House, Newark's most luxurious hotel. The notables who attended, each accompanied by a wife or a husband, were listed inside a box separate from the wedding story itself and directly beside photographs of the bride and groom that appeared in the *Newark Sunday Call.* The list was surprisingly long and impressive, and I present it here to explain why I, for one, had to wonder if my parents and their Metropolitan friends weren't completely out of touch with reality to imagine that any harm could befall them because of a government program being administered by a luminary of the stature of Rabbi Bengelsdorf.

To begin with, there were Jews in abundance at the wedding ceremony, among them family and friends, congregants from Rabbi Bengelsdorf's temple, admirers and colleagues from around New Jersey, and others who had traveled from all over the country to be present. And many Christians were there as well. And, according to the article in the *Sunday Call*—which took up one and a half of the two society pages that day—among the several invited guests who were unable to attend but who sent their best wishes through Western Union, was the wife of the president, the First Lady, Anne Morrow Lindbergh, identified as a close friend of the rabbi's, "a fellow New Jerseyite and a fellow poet" with whom he shared "cultural and intellectual interests" and met frequently "over afternoon tea for a White House tête-à-tête to discuss philosophy, literature, religion, and ethics."

Representing the city were the two highest-ranking Jews ever in Newark's government, the two-term ex-mayor, Meyer Ellenstein, and the city clerk, Harry S. Reichenstein, and five of the slew of Irishmen currently most prominent in the city, the director of Public Safety, the director of the Department of

Revenue and Finance, the director of Parks and Public Property, the city's chief engineer, and the corporation counsel. Newark's federal postmaster was there, and the head librarian of the Newark Public Library as well as the president of the library's board of trustees. Among the distinguished educators attending the wedding were the president of the University of Newark, the president of Newark College of Engineering, the superintendent of schools, and the headmaster of St. Benedict's Prep. And an array of distinguished clergymen—Protestant, Catholic, and Jewish—were also among those present. From the First Baptist Peddie Memorial Church, the city's largest Negro congregation, there was Reverend George E. Dawkins; from Trinity Cathedral, Reverend Arthur Dumper; from Grace Episcopal Church, Reverend Charles L. Gomph; from St. Nicholas Greek Orthodox Church, on High Street, Reverend George E. Spyridakis; and from St. Patrick's Cathedral, the Very Reverend John Delaney.

Absent—and glaringly so to my parents, though nowhere alluded to in the newspaper story—was Rabbi Bengelsdorf's antagonist and the foremost of Newark's rabbis, Joachim Prinz of Congregation B'nai Abraham. Before Rabbi Bengelsdorf's rise to national prominence, Rabbi Prinz's authority among Jews throughout the city, in the wider Jewish community, and among scholars and theologians of every religion had far exceeded his elder colleague's, and it was he alone of the Conservative rabbis leading the city's three wealthiest congregations who had never flinched in his opposition to Lindbergh. The other two, Charles I. Hoffman of Oheb Shalom and Solomon Foster of B'nai Jeshurun, were in attendance, however, and Rabbi Foster presided over the wedding ceremony.

Present as well were the presidents of Newark's four major banks, the presidents of two of its largest insurance companies, the president of its biggest architecture firm, the two founding partners of its most prestigious law firm, the president of the Newark Athletic Club, the owner of three of the big downtown movie houses, the president of the Chamber of Commerce, the president of New Jersey Bell Telephone, the editors in chief of the two daily papers, and the president of P. Ballantine, Newark's most famous brewery. From the Essex County government there was the supervisor of the Board of

Freeholders and three members of the board, and from the New Jersey judiciary were the vice chancellor of the Court of Chancery and an associate justice from the state's Supreme Court. From the State Assembly there was the majority speaker and three of the four assemblymen from Essex County, and from the State Senate a representative from Essex County. The ranking state official was a Jew, Attorney General David T. Wilentz, who had successfully led the prosecution of Bruno Hauptmann, but the state official whose presence most impressed me was Abe J. Greene, another Jew but more importantly New Jersey's boxing commissioner. One of Jersey's two U.S. senators was there, the Republican W. Warren Barbour, as was our congressman Robert W. Kean. From the District Court of the United States for the District of New Jersey there was a circuit judge, two district judges, and the district attorney (whose name I recognized from listening to *Gangbusters*), John J. Quinn.

A number of close associates of the rabbi at the national headquarters of the OAA and several officials representing the Department of the Interior had come up from Washington, and though there was nobody at the wedding from the very highest echelons of the federal government, there was an eloquent proxy representing no less a personage than the president himself: the telegram from the First Lady that was read aloud by Rabbi Foster at the reception, after which reading the wedding guests rose spontaneously to applaud the First Lady's sentiments and were then asked by the groom to remain standing and to join with him and his bride in singing the National Anthem.

The lengthy text of the telegram was carried in full by the *Sunday Call*. It went as follows:

My dear Rabbi Bengelsdorf and Evelyn:
    My husband and I send you our heartfelt best wishes, and we join in wishing you the most blissful happiness.
    We were delighted to have an opportunity to meet Evelyn at the White House State Dinner for the German Foreign Minister. She is an enchanting, energetic young woman, clearly a most worthy and upright person, and it took no more than the few moments I spent chatting with her for me to recognize the

gifts of personality and intellect that won her the devotion of a man as extraordinary as Lionel Bengelsdorf.

I recall today the splendidly succinct lines of poetry my meeting with Evelyn brought to mind that evening. The poet is Elizabeth Barrett Browning, and the words with which she begins the fourteenth of her *Sonnets from the Portuguese* embody just such womanly wisdom as I saw emanating from Evelyn's astonishingly dark and beautiful eyes. "If thou must love me," wrote Mrs. Browning, "let it be for naught / Except for love's sake only . . ."

Rabbi Bengelsdorf, you have been more than a friend since we met here in the White House after the ceremony establishing the Office of American Absorption; since your moving to Washington to become the OAA director, you have been an invaluable mentor. Our engrossing conversations, along with the enlightening books you have generously given me to read, have taught me much, not just about the Jewish faith but about the tribulations of the Jewish people and the sources of the great spiritual strength which has been the mainspring of their survival for three thousand years. I am all the richer for having discovered through you how profoundly rooted my own religious heritage is in yours.

Our greatest mission as Americans is to live in harmony and brotherhood as a united people. I know from the excellent work you are both doing for the OAA how dedicated the two of you are to helping us achieve this precious goal. Of the many blessings bestowed upon our nation by God, none is more valuable than our having among us citizens like yourselves, proud, vital champions of an indomitable race whose ancient concepts of justice and freedom have sustained our American democracy since 1776.

> With every best wish,
> Anne Morrow Lindbergh

The second time the FBI entered our lives, it was my father who was under surveillance. The same agent who'd stopped to question me about Alvin, on the day that Mr. Wishnow hanged himself (and who'd questioned Sandy on the bus, my mother at the store, and my father at the office), showed up at the produce market and hung around the diner where the men would go to eat and get coffee in the middle of the night and, behaving as he'd done when Alvin began working for Uncle Monty, started asking around now about Alvin's uncle Herman and what he was saying to people about America and our president. Word got back to Uncle Monty through one of Longy Zwillman's henchmen, who passed on to Uncle Monty what Agent McCorkle had reported to him—namely, that after having housed and fed a traitor who'd fought for a foreign country, my father had now quit a good job with Metropolitan Life rather than participate in a government program designed to unify and strengthen the American people. Uncle Monty told Longy's guy that his brother was a poor schnook with no education who had two kids and a wife to support and couldn't do much harm to America by schlepping produce crates six nights a week. And Longy's guy listened sympathetically, according to Uncle Monty, who, with none of the decorum ordinarily practiced in our house, told us the whole story in our kitchen one Saturday afternoon—"and still the guy says to me, 'Your brother's gotta go.' So I told him, 'This is all bullshit. Tell Longy this is all part of the bullshit against Jews.' And the guy is himself a Jew, Niggy Apfelbaum, but what I say does not make a dent. Niggy goes back to Longy, and he tells him Roth don't do as he's told. What happens next? The Long One himself shows up, right there in my stinky little office and wearing a silk handmade suit. Tall, soft-spoken, dressed to kill—you see how he gets the movie stars. I said to him, 'I remember you from grade school, Longy. I could see even then you were going places.' So Longy says to me, 'I remember you, too. I could see even then you were going nowhere.' We started to laugh, and I told him, 'My brother needs a job, Longy. Can I not give my own brother a job?' 'And can I not have the FBI snooping around?' he asks me. 'I know all this,' I say, 'and didn't I get rid of my nephew Alvin because of the FBI? But with my own brother, it's not the same, is it? Look,' I tell him, 'twenty-four hours and I'll fix everything. If I don't, if I can't, Herman goes.' So I wait till after we close up the next morning, and I walk over to Sammy Eagle's, and sitting at the bar is the mick shmegeggy from the FBI. 'Let me buy your breakfast,' I tell him, and I order him a boilermaker, and I sit down next to him and I say, 'What do you got against Jews, McCorkle?' 'Nothing,' he says. 'Then why are you after my brother like this? What did he do to anybody?' 'Look, if I had something against Jews, would I be sitting here in Eagle's, would Sammy Eagle be my friend if I did?' He calls down the bar for Eagle to come over. 'Tell him,' McCorkle says, 'do I have anything against Jews?' 'Not that I know,' Eagle says. 'When your boy had the bar mitzvah, didn't I come and give him a tie clasp?' 'He still wears it,' Eagle tells me. 'See?' McCorkle says. 'I'm just doing my job, the way Sammy does his and you do yours.' 'And that's all my brother is doing,' I tell him. 'Fine. Good. So don't say I'm against the Jews.' 'My error,' I tell him, 'I apologize.' And meantime I slip him the envelope, the little brown envelope, and that's that."

Here my uncle turned to me and said, "I understand you're a horse thief. I understand you stole a horse from the church. Smart boy. Let me see." I leaned over and showed him where the horse's hoof had opened up my head. He laughed when he ran his finger lightly over the length of the scar and around the shaved patch where the hair was just growing in. "May you have many more," he told me—and then, as he'd been doing for as long as I could remember, he lifted me roughly onto one of his knees so that I could straddle it like, of all things, a horse. "You been to a bris, ain't you?" he asked, and began to give me the up-and-down ride by raising and lowering his thigh. "You know when they circumcise the baby at the bris, you know what they do, don't you?" "They cut off the foreskin," I said. "And what do they do with the little foreskin? After it's off—do you know what they do?" "No," I told him. "Well," said Uncle Monty, "they save them up, and when they got enough they give them to the FBI to make agents out of." I couldn't help myself, and even though I knew I wasn't sup-posed to—and even though last time he'd told me the joke, he'd said, "They send them to Ireland to make priests out of"—I began to laugh. "What was in the envelope?" I asked him. "Take a guess," he said. "I don't know. Money?" "Money is right. You're a bright little horse thief. The money that makes all trouble go away."

Only later did I learn from my brother, who'd overheard my parents talking in their bedrooom, that the full amount of the bribe given to McCorkle was to be repaid to Uncle Monty, out of my father's already paltry paycheck, at the rate of ten dollars per week over the next six months. And my father could do nothing about it. About the laboriousness of the work, about the mortifications attendant upon serving his brother, all he ever said was "He's been this way since he's ten years old, he'll be this way till he dies."

Aside from Saturdays and Sunday mornings, my father was hardly to be seen that summer. My mother, on the other hand, was now around all the time, and since Sandy and I had to be home at noon for lunch and again in the midafternoon to check in with her and be accounted for, neither of us could stray very far, and in the evenings we were forbidden to go anywhere beyond the school playing field a block from the house. Either my mother was keeping a very strict vigil over herself or she'd managed temporarily to make peace with all her chagrin, because though my father had taken a steep pay cut and the household budget required some difficult trimming, she showed no disabling signs of the improbabilities she'd confronted over the past year. Her resilience had a lot to do with her being back at a job whose compensations mattered more to her than those derived from selling dresses, work she hadn't shrunk from doing but that seemed to her meaningless measured against her normal pursuits. Just how troubling her worries continued to be would only be clear to me when a letter arrived from Estelle Tirschwell, reporting on the family's progress in Winnipeg. Every lunchtime I brought the mail upstairs with me from our mailbox in the front entryway, and if there was an envelope bearing Canadian postage, she immediately sat down at the kitchen table and, while Sandy and I ate our sandwiches, read the letter to herself twice over, then folded it up to carry around in her apron pocket to look at another ten times before passing it on to my father to read when he got up to go to the market—the letter for my father, the canceled Canadian stamps for me, to help get me started on a new collection.

Sandy's friends were suddenly the girls his age, the teenage girls whom he knew from school but had never examined so covetously before. He went to find them at the playground where the organized summer activities took place all day and into the early evening. I was there too, accompanied regularly

now by Seldon. I'd watch Sandy with fluctuating feelings of
trepidation and delight, as though my own brother had become a pickpocket or a professional shill. He'd park himself on
a bench near the ping-pong table, where the girls tended to
congregate, and he'd start making pencil drawings in his sketchpad of the cutest around; invariably they'd want to see the
drawings, and so before the day was over, chances were good
he'd be walking dreamily out of the playground hand in hand
with one of them. Sandy's strong proclivity for infatuation was
no longer galvanized by propagandizing for Just Folks or topping tobacco for the Mawhinneys but fomented by these girls.
Either the fresh excitement of desire had transformed his existence with the same incredible swiftness that Kentucky had
and, at fourteen and a half, he'd been recast anew in a single
hormonal blast or, as I believed—with my own proclivity to
grant him omnipotence—getting girls to go off with him was
simply an amusing ruse, how he was biding his time until . . .
Always with Sandy I thought there must be a great deal more
going on than I could begin to understand, when in fact, despite the handsome boy's air of self-assurance, he had no more
idea than anyone else why he took the bait. Lindbergh's Jewish
tobacco farmer discovers breasts, and suddenly he turns up as
just another teenager.

My parents ascribed the girl-craziness to defiance, to "rebel-
liousness," to a compensatory display of independence following his forced retirement from the Lindbergh cause, and seemed
willing to consider it relatively harmless. One of the girls'
mothers felt otherwise evidently, and called to say so. When
my father got home from work, there was a long conversation
between my mother and father behind their bedroom door,
and then another between my brother and my father behind the
bedroom door, and for the rest of the week Sandy was not allowed to leave the vicinity of the house. But they couldn't, of
course, keep him cooped up on Summit Avenue for the whole
of the summer, and soon he was back at the playground confidently drawing pictures of the pretty ones, and whatever
these girls allowed him to do with his hands when they went
off by themselves—which couldn't have been much for eighth-
graders as ignorant of sex as kids that young were back in those
years—they didn't rush home to report, and so there were no

more excited phone calls for my parents to contend with in the midst of all their other troubles.

Seldon. Seldon was *my* summer. Seldon's muzzle in my face like a dog's, and kids I'd known all my life laughing and calling me Sleepy, kids with their arms raised stiffly out in front of them and walking with slow, clumpy, zombie steps, supposedly in imitation of me lurching toward the orphanage in my sleep, and the team in the field all chanting "Hi ho Silver!" whenever I came to bat in a choose-up game.

There would be no big end-of-summer picnic up at the South Mountain Reservation on Labor Day that year because all of my parents' Metropolitan friends had left Newark with their boys by September to settle in around the country before the start of the school year. One by one, throughout that summer, each of the families drove up on a Saturday to visit and say goodbye. It was awful for my parents, who alone of the group from the local Metropolitan district designated for relocation by Homestead 42 had chosen to stay where we were. These were their dearest friends, and the hot Saturday afternoons with the tearful adults embracing out on the street while all the children forlornly looked on—afternoons that ended with the four of us who were remaining behind waving goodbye from the curb as my mother called after the departing car, "Don't forget to write!"—were the most harrowing moments so far, when our defenselessness became real to me and I sensed the beginning of the destruction of our world. And when I realized that my father, of all these men, was the most obstinate, helplessly bonded to his better instincts and their excessive demands. I only then understood that he had quit his job not merely because he was fearful of what awaited us down the line should we agree like the others to be relocated but because, for better or worse, when he was bullied by superior forces that he deemed corrupt it was his nature not to yield—in this instance, to resist either running away to Canada, as my mother urged our doing, or bowing to a government directive that was patently unjust. There were two types of strong men: those like Uncle Monty and Abe Steinheim, remorseless about their making money, and those like my father, ruthlessly obedient to their idea of fair play.

"Come," my father said, trying to perk us up on the Saturday when the last of the six homesteading families had seemingly vanished forever. "Come on, boys. We're going out for ice cream." The four of us walked down Chancellor to the drugstore, where the pharmacist was one of his oldest insurance customers and where in summertime it was generally more pleasant than it was out on the street, what with the awnings unfurled to prevent the sun's rays from piercing the plate glass window and the paddle blades of the three ceiling fans creaking softly as they revolved overhead. We slipped into a booth and ordered sundaes, and though my mother could not bring herself to eat despite my father's prompting, she was able eventually to stop the tears from running down her face. We, after all, were no less enjoined to an unknowable future than were our exiled friends, and so we sat spooning our sundaes in the awninged semidarkness of the cool pharmacy, everyone speechless and completely spent, until my mother at last looked up from the paper napkin she was neatly shredding and, with that wry, stripped-down smile that comes when one is entirely cried out, said to my father, "Well, like it or not, Lindbergh is teaching us what it is to be Jews." Then she added, "We only think we're Americans." "Nonsense. No!" my father replied. "*They* think we only think we're Americans. It is not up for discussion, Bess. It is not up for negotiation. These people are not understanding that I take this for *granted*, goddamnit! Others? He dares to call us *others*? *He's* the other. The one who looks most American—and he's the one who is least American! The man is unfit. He shouldn't be there. He shouldn't be there, and it's as simple as that!"

For me the hardest departure to stomach was Seldon's. Of course I was delighted to see him go. All summer long I'd been counting the days. Yet that early morning in the last week of August when the Wishnows drove off with two mattresses strapped to the car roof (lifted there and tied down beneath a tarp the night before by my father and Sandy) and clothing jammed to the top of the old Plymouth's back seat (stacks of clothing, including several items of my own, that my mother and I had helped them to carry from the house), I was the one, grotesquely enough, who couldn't stop crying. I was remembering an afternoon when Seldon and I were just six years old, and Mr. Wishnow was alive and seemingly well and still working every day for the Metropolitan, and Mrs. Wishnow was still a housewife like my mother, absorbed by her family's everyday needs and even, on occasion, looking after me if my mother had to be off doing her PTA work and Sandy wasn't around and I was home by myself after school. I was remembering the generic maternalism that she shared with my mother —the succoring warmth I wallowed in as a matter of course— and that I experienced so strikingly on the afternoon that I got stuck in their bathroom and couldn't get out. I was remembering how kind she'd been to me while I repeatedly tried and failed to open the door, spontaneously caring for me as though, regardless of differences in appearance and temperament and immediate circumstance, the four of us—Seldon and Selma, Philip and Bess—were all one and the same. I was remembering Mrs. Wishnow when what was uppermost in her mind was what was uppermost in my mother's mind—back when she was just another watchful member of the local matriarchy whose overriding task was to establish a domestic way of life for the next generation. I was remembering Mrs. Wishnow unperturbed, when her fists weren't clenched and her face full of pain.

It was a small bathroom, exactly like ours, quite confining, the door next to a toilet and the toilet abutting a sink and a bathtub squeezed in beside that. I pulled on the door but it didn't open. At home I would just have closed it behind me, but at the Wishnows' I locked it—something I'd never done before in my life. I locked it and I peed and I flushed and I washed my hands and, because I didn't want to touch their towel, wiped them dry on the back of the legs of my corduroys —everything was fine, and then I went to exit the bathroom, and I couldn't undo the lock above the doorknob. I could turn it a little ways but then it would catch and stop. I didn't bang on the door or rattle the doorknob, I just kept trying to turn the lock as quietly as I could. But it wouldn't go, and so I sat back down on the toilet and I thought that maybe it would somehow work itself out. I sat there for a while but then I got lonesome and stood up and tried the lock again. It still wouldn't uncatch, and I started to knock lightly on the door, and Mrs. Wishnow came and said, "Oh, the lock on the door does that sometimes. You have to turn it like this." She explained how to do it, but I still couldn't get it open, and so very calmly she said, "No, Philip, while you're turning it you have to pull it *back*," and though I tried to do as she told me it still didn't work. "Dear," she said, "turn and back simultaneously —turn and back at the same time." "Which way is back?" I said. "Back. Back towards the wall." "Oh, the wall. Okay," I said, but I couldn't get it right no matter what I did. "It won't work," I said, and I began to sweat, and then I heard Seldon. "Philip? It's Seldon. Why did you lock it? We weren't going to come in." "I didn't say you were," I said. "Then why did you lock it?" "I don't know," I said. "Do you think we should call the fire department, Mom? They can get him out with a ladder." "No, no, no," Mrs. Wishnow said. "Come on, Philip," Seldon said, "it's not that hard." "But it is. It's stuck." "How's he gonna get out, Ma?" "Seldon, be still. Philip?" "Yes." "Are you all right?" "Well, it's hot in here. It's getting hot." "Take a glass of cold water, dear. There's a glass in the medicine cabinet. Take a glass of water and slowly drink it and you'll be fine." "Okay." But the glass had something slimy at the bottom, and though I took it out, I only pretended to drink from it and drank instead from my cupped hands. "Ma," Seldon said, "what's he doing wrong? Philip, what are you doing wrong?" "How do I know?" I said. "Mrs. Wishnow? Mrs. Wishnow?" "Yes, dear." "It's getting too hot in here. I'm really starting to sweat." "Then open the window. Open the little window in the shower. Are you tall enough to do that?" "I think so." I took off my shoes and stepped into the shower in just my socks, and standing on my tiptoes I was able to reach the window—a smallish window of pebbled glass that looked onto the alleyway—but when I tried to open it, it was stuck too. "It won't go," I said. "Bang it a little, dear. Bang the frame at the bottom, but not too hard, and I'm sure it will open." I did as she told me but couldn't get it to budge. By now my shirt was saturated with sweat, and so I angled myself to be able to give the window a good strong shove upwards, but in turning I must have struck the shower handle with my elbow because suddenly the water was on. "Oh, no!" I said, and ice-cold water was pouring over my head and down the back of my shirt, and I jumped out of the shower and onto the tile floor.

"What happened, dear?" "The shower started." "How?" Seldon said. "How could the shower start?" "I don't know!" "Are you very wet?" she asked me. "Sort of." "Get a towel," she told me. "Get a towel out of the closet. The towels are in the closet." We had the same narrow little bathroom closet directly upstairs over the Wishnows' bathroom closet, and we used it for towels too, but when I went to open theirs, I couldn't—the door was stuck. I yanked but it wouldn't open. "What is it now, Philip?" "Nothing." I couldn't tell her. "Did you take a towel?" "Yes." "Then dry yourself off. And you must stay calm. There's nothing to worry about." "I am calm." "Sit down. Sit down and dry yourself off." I was soaking wet, and now the floor was getting wet, and I sat on the toilet seat, and that's when I saw a bathroom for what it is—the upper end of a sewer—and that's when I felt the tears begin to well up. "Don't worry," Seldon called in to me, "your mother and father will be home soon." "But how will I get *out*?" And all at once the door was open—and there was Seldon and behind him his mother. "How'd you do that?" I said. "I opened the door," he said. "But how?" He shrugged. "I pushed. I just pushed. It was open all the time." And that was when I began to bawl and Mrs. Wishnow took me in her arms and said, "That's okay. Things like this happen. They can happen to anyone." "It was open, Ma," Seldon said to her. "Shhh," she told him. "Shhh. It doesn't matter," and then she came into the bathroom and turned off the cold water—which was still streaming into the tub—and, without any problem she opened the closet door and took out a fresh towel and began to dry my hair and my face and my neck, all the while gently telling me that it didn't matter and that these things happened to people all the time.

But that was long before everything else went wrong.

The congressional campaign began at eight A.M. the Tuesday after Labor Day, with Walter Winchell up on a soapbox at Broadway and 42nd Street—the celebrated crossroads where he'd announced his presidential candidacy from atop the very same genuine wooden soapbox—and looking in broad daylight exactly as press photos pictured him broadcasting from the NBC studio Sunday nights at nine: jacketless, in his shirtsleeves, with the cuffs rolled up and his tie yanked down and, pushed back from his forehead, the hardboiled newsman's fedora. Within only minutes some half-dozen mounted New York City policemen were already needed to divert traffic away from the eager stream of working people charging onto the street to hear and see him in the flesh. And once word spread that the orator with the bullhorn wasn't just another Bible bore prophesying doom for sinful America but the Stork Club habitué only recently the country's most influential radio broadcaster and the city's most nefarious tabloid journalist, the number of onlookers grew from the hundreds to the thousands—nearly ten thousand people all told, said the papers, up from the subways and emptying out of the buses, drawn by the maverick and his immoderation.

"The broadcasting cowards," he told them, "and the billionaire publishing hooligans controlled from the White House by the Lindbergh gang say Winchell was canned for crying 'Fire!' in a crowded theater. Mr. and Mrs. New York City, the word wasn't 'fire.' It was 'fascism' Winchell cried—and it still is. Fascism! Fascism! And I will continue crying 'fascism' to every crowd of Americans I can find until Herr Lindbergh's pro-Hitler party of treason is driven from the Congress on Election Day. The Hitlerites can take away my radio microphone, and they've done just that, as you know. They can take away my newspaper column, and they have done that, as you know. And when, God forbid, America goes fascist, Lindbergh's storm troopers can lock me away in a concentration camp to shut me up—and they will do that too, as you know. They can even lock *you* away in a concentration camp to shut *you* up. And I hope by now that you damn well know that. But what our homegrown Hitlerites cannot take away is my love for America and yours. My love for democracy and yours. My love for freedom and yours. What they cannot take away—unless the gullible and the sheepish and the terrified are patsies enough to return them to Washington one more time—is the power of the ballot box. The Hitlerite plot against America must be stopped—and stopped by you! By you, Mr. and Mrs. New York! By the voting power of the freedom-loving people of this great city on Tuesday, November 3, nineteen hundred and forty-two!"

All that day—September 8, 1942—and into the evening, Winchell climbed atop his soapbox in every neighborhood in Manhattan, from Wall Street, where he was largely ignored, to Little Italy, where he was shouted down, to Greenwich Village, where he was ridiculed, to the Garment District, where he was intermittently cheered, to the Upper West Side, where he was welcomed as their savior by the Roosevelt Jews, and eventually north to Harlem, where, in the crowd of several hundred Negroes who gathered at dusk to hear him speak at the corner of Lenox Avenue and 125th Street, a few laughed and a handful applauded but most remained respectfully dissatisfied, as though to work his way into their antipathies would require his delivering a very different spiel.

It was difficult to ascertain the impact Winchell made on the voting public that day. To Winchell's former paper, Hearst's *Daily Mirror*, the ostensible effort to gather local grass-roots support for routing the Republican Party from Congress nationwide looked more like a publicity stunt than anything else—a predictably egomaniacal publicity stunt by an unemployed gossip columnist who could not bear being out of the spotlight—and especially so since not a single Democratic congressional candidate running for election in Manhattan chose to appear anywhere within hearing distance of the Winchell bullhorn. If any candidates were out campaigning, they stayed far from wherever Winchell repeatedly committed the political blunder of associating the name of Adolf Hitler with that of an American president whose heroics the world still idolized, whose achievement even the Führer respected, and whom an overwhelming majority of his countrymen continued to adore as their nation's godlike catalyst of peace and prosperity. In a brief, sardonic editorial, "At It Again," the *New York Times* was able to reach but one conclusion about the latest of Winchell's "self-serving shenanigans": "There is nothing Walter Winchell has more talent for," wrote the *Times*, "than himself."

Winchell spent a full day in each of the other four boroughs of the city, and the following week headed north to Connecticut. Though still in want of a Democratic candidate willing to wed a fledgling congressional campaign to his inflammatory rhetoric, Winchell went ahead to set up his soapbox outside the gates to the factories of Bridgeport and at the entrance to

the shipyards in New London, where he pushed back his fedora, pulled down his tie, and cried "Fascism! Fascism!" into
the face of the crowd. From Connecticut's industrial coast he
traveled north again to the working-class enclaves of Provi-
dence and then crossed from Rhode Island into the factory
towns of southeastern Massachusetts, addressing tiny street-
corner gatherings in Fall River, Brockton, and Quincy with no
less fervor than he'd expended in his maiden speech in Times
Square. From Quincy he went on to Boston, where he planned
to spend three days moving through Irish Dorchester and
South Boston into the Italian North End. However, on his
first afternoon at South Boston's busy Perkins Square the few
jeering hecklers who'd been baiting him as a Jew ever since his
departing his native New York—and his leaving behind there
the police protection guaranteed him by Fiorello La Guardia,
the city's anti-Lindbergh Republican mayor—burgeoned into
a mob waving handmade placards reminiscent of the banners
and signs beautifying the Bund rallies in Madison Square Garden. And the moment Winchell opened his mouth to speak,
somebody brandishing a burning cross rushed toward the
soapbox to set him aflame and a gun was fired twice into the
air, either as a signal from the organizers to the rioters or as a
warning to the marked man from "Jew York," or as both.
There in the old brick cityscape of little family-run shops and
streetcars and shade trees and small houses, each topped back
then, before TV, only by the appendage of a towering chimney,
in the Boston where the Depression had never ended, amid
the storefronts sacred to the American main street—the ice
cream parlor, the barber shop, the pharmacy—and just up the
way from the dark, spiky outline of St. Augustine's Church,
thugs with clubs surged forward screaming "Kill him!" and,
two weeks from its inception in New York's five boroughs, the
Winchell campaign, as Winchell had imagined it, was under
way. He had at last brought the Lindbergh grotesquery to the
surface, the underside of Lindbergh's affable blandness, raw
and undisguised.

Though the Boston police did nothing to restrain the rioters
—the gunshots had sounded a full hour before a squad car
drove up to survey the scene—the plainclothes team of armed
professional bodyguards who'd been stationed at Winchell's

side throughout the trip managed to douse the flames consuming one of his trouser legs and, having freed him from the
first wave of the crowd after only a few blows had fallen, to lift
him into a car parked just yards from the soapbox and drive
him to Carney Hospital on Telegraph Hill, where he was
treated for facial wounds and minor burns.

His first visitor at the hospital wasn't the mayor, Maurice
Tobin, or Tobin's defeated mayoral rival, ex-governor James M.
Curley (another FDR Democrat who, like the Democrat Tobin,
wanted no part of Walter Winchell). Nor was it the local congressman, John W. McCormack, whose roughneck brother, a
bartender known as Knocko, presided over the neighborhood
with as much authority as the popular Democratic representative. To everyone's surprise, beginning with Winchell himself,
his first visitor was a patrician Republican of distinguished New
England lineage, the two-term Massachusetts governor, Leverett Saltonstall. On hearing of Winchell's hospitalization, Governor Saltonstall had left his State House office to communicate
his concern directly to Winchell (whom privately he could only
have despised), and to promise a thorough investigation into
the well-plotted, obviously premeditated pandemonium that,
by a mere fluke, had produced no fatalities. He also assured
Winchell of protection by the state police—and, if need be, by
the National Guard—for as long as Winchell campaigned in
Massachusetts. And before the governor left the hospital, he
saw to it that two armed troopers were stationed at the door
only feet from Winchell's bed.

The *Boston Herald* interpreted Saltonstall's intervention as a
political maneuver to gain him recognition as a courageous,
honorable, fair-minded conservative who could serve his party
as a dignified replacement in 1944 for the Democratic vice
president, Burton K. Wheeler, who'd done the job required in
the 1940 campaign but whose imprudence as an orator many
Republicans now believed might compromise their president
the second time around. In a hospital press conference where
Winchell appeared before the photographers in his robe, with
surgical dressings half covering his face and a heavily bandaged
left foot, he welcomed Governor Saltonstall's offer but declined
assistance in a message (cast, now that he was under assault, in
language more statesmanlike than his standard feverish patter)

that was distributed to the two dozen reporters from the radio
and the press who had converged on his room. The statement
began, "On the day when a candidate for the presidency of the
United States requires a phalanx of armed police officers and
National Guardsmen to protect his right to free speech, this
great country will have passed over into fascist barbarism. I
cannot accept that the religious intolerance emanating from
the White House has already so corrupted the ordinary citizen
that he has lost all respect for fellow Americans of a creed or
faith different from his own. I cannot accept that the abhorrence for my religion shared by Adolf Hitler and Charles A.
Lindbergh can already have corroded . . ."

From then on, anti-Semitic agitators hunted Winchell down
at every crossing, though without success in Boston, where
Saltonstall had ignored Winchell's grandstanding and directed
his troops to impose order, employing force if need be, and to
carry the violent off to jail, a command that they undertook to
execute, however reluctantly. Meanwhile—using a cane to support himself because of his burned foot and with his jaw and
forehead still bandaged—Winchell proceeded to draw an angry
mob chanting "Kike go home!" in every single parish where
he displayed his stigmata to the faithful, from Gate of Heaven
Church in South Boston to St. Gabriel's Monastery in Brigh-
ton. Beyond Massachusetts, in communities in upper New
York State, in Pennsylvania, and throughout the Midwest that
were already notorious for their bigotry—and to which
Winchell's explosive strategy inevitably pointed him—most of
the local authorities did not share Saltonstall's unwillingness to
tolerate civil unrest, and so, despite the doubling of his entourage of plainclothes bodyguards, the candidate came close to
getting himself mauled each time he stepped onto the soapbox
to denounce "the fascist in the White House" and to assign
responsibility directly to the president's "religious hatred" for
"fostering unheard-of Nazi barbarism in the American streets."

The worst and most widespread violence occurred in Detroit, the midwestern headquarters of the "Radio Priest" Father Coughlin and his Jew-hating Christian Front and of the
crowd-pleasing minister known as "the dean of anti-Semites,"
Reverend Gerald L. K. Smith, who preached that "Christian
character is the true basis of real Americanism." Detroit, of

course, was also home to the American automobile industry and to Lindbergh's elderly secretary of the interior, Henry Ford, whose avowedly anti-Semitic newspaper, the *Dearborn Independent*, published in the 1920s, addressed itself to "an investigation of the Jewish Question" that Ford ultimately reprinted in four volumes, totaling nearly one thousand pages, entitled *The International Jew*, in which he directed that in the cleansing of America "the International Jew and his satellites, as the conscious enemies of all that Anglo-Saxons mean by civilization, are not spared."

It was to be expected that organizations like the American Civil Liberties Union and eminent liberal journalists like John Gunther and Dorothy Thompson would be outraged by the Detroit riots and immediately make public their disgust, but so too were many conventional middle-class Americans, who, even if they found Walter Winchell and his rhetoric repugnant and understood him to be "asking for trouble," were also appalled by the eyewitness reports of how the rioting that had begun at Winchell's first stop in Hamtramck (the residential section inhabited chiefly by auto workers and their families and said to contain the world's largest Polish population outside Warsaw) had suspiciously spread within minutes to 12th Street, to Linwood and then to Dexter Boulevard. There, in the city's biggest Jewish neighborhoods, shops were looted and windows broken, Jews trapped outdoors were set upon and beaten, and kerosene-soaked crosses were ignited on the lawns of the fancy houses along Chicago Boulevard and out front of the modest two-family dwellings of the housepainters, plumbers, butchers, bakers, junk dealers, and grocers who lived on Webb and Tuxedo and in the little dirt yards of the poorest Jews on Pingry and Euclid. In midafternoon, only moments before the school day ended, a firebomb was thrown into the front foyer of Winterhalter Elementary School, where half the students were Jewish, another into the foyer of Central High, whose student body was ninety-five percent Jewish, another through a window at the Sholem Aleichem Institute—a cultural organization Coughlin had ridiculously identified as Communist— and a fourth outside another of Coughlin's "Communist" targets, the Jewish Workers' Alliance. Next came the attack on houses of worship. Not only were windows broken and walls

defaced on some half of the city's thirty-odd Orthodox synagogues, but as evening services were scheduled to begin an
explosion went off on the steps of the prestigious Chicago
Boulevard temple Shaarey Zedek. The explosion there caused
extensive damage to the exotic centerpiece of architect Albert
Kahn's Moorish design—the three massive arched doorways
that conspicuously exhibited to a working-class populace a
distinctively un-American style. Five passersby, none of whom
happened to be Jews, were injured by flying debris from the
façade, but no casualties were otherwise reported.

By nightfall, several hundred of the city's thirty thousand
Jews had fled and taken refuge across the Detroit River in
Windsor, Ontario, and American history had recorded its first
large-scale pogrom, one clearly modeled on the "spontaneous
demonstrations" against Germany's Jews known as *Kristallnacht*, "the Night of Broken Glass," whose atrocities had been
planned and perpetrated by the Nazis four years earlier and
which Father Coughlin in his weekly tabloid, *Social Justice*,
had defended at the time as a reaction by the Germans against
"Jewish-inspired Communism." Detroit's *Kristallnacht* was
similarly justified on the editorial page of the *Detroit Times* as
the unfortunate but inevitable and altogether understandable
backlash to the activities of the troublemaking interloper the
paper identified as "the Jewish demagogue whose aim from
the outset had been to incite the rage of patriotic Americans
with his treasonous rabble-rousing."

The week after the September assault on Detroit's Jews—
which was addressed with dispatch by neither Michigan's
governor nor the city's mayor—new violence was directed at
homes, shops, and synagogues in Jewish neighborhoods in
Cleveland, Cincinnati, Indianapolis, and St. Louis, violence
that Winchell's enemies attributed to his deliberately challenging appearances in those cities after the cataclysm that he'd
instigated in Detroit, and that Winchell himself—who, in Indianapolis, barely escaped being crushed by a paving stone
hurled from a rooftop that had broken the neck of the body-
guard stationed beside him—explained by the "climate of
hate" emanating from the White House.

Our own street in Newark was many hundreds of miles from
Dexter Boulevard in Detroit, nobody around had ever been to

Detroit, and before September 1942 all that the boys on the block knew about Detroit was that organized baseball's only Jewish player was the Tigers' star first baseman, Hank Greenberg. But then came the Winchell riots, and suddenly even the children could recite the names of the Detroit neighborhoods that had been shaken by violence. Parroting what they heard from their parents, they would argue back and forth as to whether Walter Winchell was courageous or foolish, self-sacrificing or self-serving, and whether or not he was playing right into Lindbergh's hands by allowing the Gentiles to tell themselves that the Jews had brought their misery on themselves. They argued over whether it would be better if—before Winchell set off a nationwide pogrom—he desisted and allowed "normal" relations to be restored between the Jews and their fellow Americans or whether in the long run it would be better for him to continue to raise the alarm among the country's more complacent Jews—and to arouse the conscience of Christians —by exposing the menace of anti-Semitism from one end of America to the other. On the way to school, on the playground after school, between classes in the school corridors, you would see the smartest kids standing toe to toe, kids Sandy's age as well as a few no older than me, heatedly debating whether Walter Winchell's crisscrossing the country with his soapbox to flush into the open the German-American Bundists and the Coughlinites and the Ku Klux Klanners and the Silver Shirts and the America Firsters and the Black Legion and the American Nazi Party, whether getting these organized anti-Semites and their thousands of unseen sympathizers to reveal themselves for what they were—and to reveal the president for what *he* was, a chief executive and commander in chief who hadn't yet bothered to acknowledge that anything like a state of emergency existed, let alone called in federal troops to prevent further rioting—was good for the Jews or bad for the Jews.

After Detroit, the Jews of Newark—numbering some fifty thousand in a city of well over half a million—began to ready themselves for serious violence erupting on their own streets, either because of a Winchell visit to New Jersey when he swung back east or because of the riots inevitably spilling over into cities where, as in Newark, there was a heavily Jewish neighborhood abutting large communities of working-class Irish,

Italians, Germans, and Slavs that were already home to a goodly number of bigots. The assumption was that these people wouldn't require much encouragement to be molded into a mindless, destructive mob by the pro-Nazi conspiracy that had successfully plotted the riot in Detroit.

Almost overnight, Rabbi Joachim Prinz, along with five other eminent Newark Jews—including Meyer Ellenstein—established the Newark Committee of Concerned Jewish Citizens. Quickly the group became a model for similar ad hoc Jewish citizens' groups in other big cities that were determined to ensure their communities' safety by enlisting the authorities to draw up contingency plans to prepare for the worst possibility. The Newark committee arranged first for a City Hall meeting—presided over by Mayor Murphy, whose election had ended Ellenstein's eight-year tenure—with Newark's police chief, fire chief, and director of the Department of Public Safety. The next day the committee met at the State House in Trenton with Democratic governor Charles Edison, the superintendent of the New Jersey State Police, and the commanding officer of the New Jersey National Guard. Attorney General Wilentz, an acquaintance of all six committee members, also attended, and, in the bulletin the Newark committee issued to the Jersey papers, he was reported to have assured Rabbi Prinz that anyone attempting an assault on the Jews of Newark would be prosecuted to the full extent of the law. The committee next telegrammed Rabbi Bengelsdorf, requesting a meeting with him in Washington, but was informed that theirs was a local and not a federal issue and advised to address their concern, as they were doing, to state and city officials.

Partisans of Rabbi Bengelsdorf lauded him for keeping himself aloof from the sordid Walter Winchell affair while quietly, in private White House conversations with Mrs. Lindbergh, urging assistance to those innocent Jews throughout the country who were tragically paying for the iniquitous conduct of the renegade candidate, a provocateur cynically encouraging American citizens who needed in no way to feel besieged to cling to their oldest, most crippling anxieties. The Bengelsdorf supporters constituted an influential clique drawn from the highly assimilated upper echelon of German Jewish society. A good many of them had been born to wealth and were among the first Jewish generation to attend elite secondary schools and Ivy League colleges, where, because their numbers were minute, they had mingled with the non-Jews, whom they subsequently associated with in communal, political, and business endeavors and who sometimes appeared to accept them as equals. To these privileged Jews there was nothing suspicious about the programs designed by Rabbi Bengelsdorf's agency to assist poorer, less cultivated Jews in learning to live in closer harmony with the nation's Christians. What was unfortunate, in their opinion, was that Jews like us continued to huddle together in cities like Newark out of a xenophobia fostered by historical pressures that no longer existed. The status conferred by economic and vocational advantage inclined them to believe that those who lacked their prestige were rebuffed by the larger society more because of insular clannishness than because of any pronounced taste for exclusiveness on the part of the Christian majority, and that neighborhoods like ours were less the result of discrimination than its breeding grounds. They recognized, of course, that there were pockets of backward people in America among whom virulent anti-Semitism was still their strongest, most obsessive passion, but that seemed only another reason for the director of the OAA to encourage Jews handicapped by the limitations of a segregated existence to at least permit their children to enter the American mainstream and show themselves there to be nothing like the caricature of the Jew disseminated by our enemies. Why these wealthy, urbane, self-assured Jews particularly abhorred the self-caricaturing Winchell was because he so deliberately reinforced the very hostility that they imagined themselves to have propitiated by their exemplary behavior toward their Christian colleagues and friends.

Aside from Rabbi Prinz and ex-mayor Ellenstein, the four remaining members of the Newark committee were the elderly civic leader responsible for the success of the Americanization programs for immigrant children in the Newark school system —and the wife of Beth Israel Hospital's leading surgeon— Jenny Danzis; the department store executive and son of the founder of S. Plaut & Co., as well as ten-time president of the Broad Street Association, Moses Plaut; the prominent city property owner and past president of the Newark Conference of Jewish Charities, community leader Michael Stavitsky; and the chief of Beth Israel's medical staff, Dr. Eugene Parsonette. That Newark's leading mobster, Longy Zwillman, hadn't been enlisted to join a group of local Jews as distinguished as this was no surprise to anyone, even though Longy was a wealthy man of enormous influence and hardly less distressed than Rabbi Prinz by the menace posed by the anti-Semites who, under the pretext of being provoked by Walter Winchell, had ushered in what looked to many like stage one of the resolution of Henry Ford's "Jewish Question."

Longy set out separately, apart from the many civil authorities who had promised Rabbi Prinz their fullest cooperation, to ensure that if and when the Newark cops and the New Jersey state troopers failed to respond any more vigorously than the police had to the disorder in Boston and Detroit, the city's Jews would not be left unprotected. Bullet Apfelbaum, the close associate known throughout the city as Longy's chief enforcer —and the older brother of Niggy Apfelbaum—was assigned by Longy to supplement the good work of the Newark Committee of Concerned Jewish Citizens by recruiting that scattering of incorrigible Jewish kids who had failed to graduate from high school and training them as cadre for a hastily assembled volunteer corps to be called the Provisional Jewish Police. These were the local boys without any of the ideals that were embedded in the rest of us, who'd already begun to emanate an aura of lawlessness as far back as the fifth grade, inflating condoms in the school toilet and breaking into fistfights on the 14 bus and wrestling till they bled onto the concrete sidewalk outside the movies, the ones who, during their years in school, parents directed their children to have nothing to do with and who were now in their twenties and occupied running numbers and shooting pool and washing dishes in the kitchens of one or another of the neighborhood's delicatessen restaurants. To most of us they were known, if at all, only by the hoodlum magic of their supercharged nicknames—Leo "the Lion" Nusbaum, Knuckles Kimmelman, Big Gerry Schwartz, Dummy Breitbart, Duke "Duke-it-out" Glick—and by their double-digit IQ scores.

And now they were stationed on every second street corner, our neighborhood's handful of flops, spitting expertly into the

gutter from between their teeth and signaling back and forth
by whistling with their fingers angled deep in their mouths.
Here they were, the callous and the obtuse and the mentally
deficient, the Jews' very own deviants strolling the streets like
sailors on shore leave looking for a fight. Here they were, the
brainless few we had been raised to pity and fear, the Stone
Age oafs and the seething runts and the ominous, swaggering
weightlifters, buttonholing kids like me out on Chancellor
Avenue and telling us to keep our baseball bats at the ready in
case we were called in the night to take to the streets and going
around to the Y in the evenings and to the ball fields on Sundays and to the local stores during the week, shanghaiing the
able-bodied from among the neighborhood's grown men so as
to bring to a total of three on each block a squad they could
count on in an emergency. They embodied everything crude
and despicable that our parents had hoped to leave behind,
along with their childhood pennilessness, in the Third Ward
slums, and yet here were our demons got up as our guardians,
each with a loaded revolver strapped to his calf, a gun on loan
from the collection of Bullet Apfelbaum, who was known by
everyone to have devoted his existence to loyally intimidating
folks on Longy's behalf, threatening them, beating them, torturing them, and—despite the fact that, in imitation of a boss
easily thirty pounds leaner and a foot taller, Bullet was never to
be seen other than in a three-piece suit adorned with a neatly
folded silk pocket handkerchief the color of his tie and wearing
an expensive Borsalino debonairly angled only inches above what
was admittedly the ungenerous glower of an extremely severe
judge of human nature—ending their lives for them, should
that be the boss's pleasure.

What made the death of Walter Winchell worthy of instantaneous nationwide coverage wasn't only that his unorthodox
campaign had touched off the century's worst anti-Semitic rioting outside Nazi Germany, but that the murder of a mere
candidate for the presidency was unprecedented in America.
Though Presidents Lincoln and Garfield had been shot and
killed in the second half of the nineteenth century and McKin-
ley at the start of the twentieth, and though in 1933 FDR had
survived an assassination attempt that had instead taken the

life of his Democratic supporter Chicago's Mayor Cermak, it wasn't until twenty-six years after Winchell's assassination that a second presidential candidate would be gunned down—that was New York's Democratic senator Robert Kennedy, fatally shot in the head after winning his party's California primary on Tuesday, June 4, 1968.

On Monday, October 5, 1942, I was home alone after school listening on our living room radio to the final innings of the fifth game of the World Series between the Cardinals and the Yankees, when, in the top of the ninth, with the Cardinals coming to bat in a 2–2 tie—and leading the Series three games to one—the play-by-play broadcast was halted by a voice with that finely articulated, faintly Anglicized diction prized in a network news announcer back in radio's earlier days: "We interrupt this program to bring you an important bulletin. Presidential candidate Walter Winchell has been shot and killed. We repeat: Walter Winchell is dead. He has been assassinated in Louisville, Kentucky, while addressing an open-air political rally. That is all that is known at this time of the Louisville assassination of Democratic presidential candidate Walter Winchell. We return to our regularly scheduled program."

It wasn't quite five P.M. My father had just left for the market in Uncle Monty's truck, my mother had gone out to Chancellor Avenue a few minutes earlier to buy something for dinner, and my single-minded brother was off in search of a trysting place to resume importuning one of his after-school girls to grant him access to her chest. I heard shouting in the street, then a scream from a nearby house, but the game had come back on and the suspense was tremendous: Red Ruffing pitching to the Cardinals' rookie third baseman Whitey Kurowski, Cardinals catcher Walker Cooper on first base with his sixth hit in five games, and the Cardinals needing only this victory to take the Series. Rizzuto had homered for the Yankees, the portentously surnamed Enos Slaughter had homered for the Cardinals, and, as histrionic little fans like to tell one another, I "knew" before Ruffing had even fired his first pitch that Kurowski was about to hit a second Cardinal home run and give the Cards their fourth straight victory after an opening-day loss. I couldn't wait to run outside crying, "I knew it! I called it! Kurowski was due!" But when Kurowski homered and the game was over and I was out the door and headed at top speed down our alleyway, I saw two members of the Jewish police—Big Gerry and Duke Glick—running from one side of the street to the other to bang on doors and shout into hallways, "They shot Winchell! Winchell is dead!"

Meanwhile more kids were rushing out of their houses, delirious with World Series excitement. But no sooner did they hit the street howling Kurowski's name than Big Gerry began barking at them, "Go get your bats! The war is on!" And he didn't mean the war against Germany.

By evening there wasn't a Jewish family on our street that wasn't barricaded behind double-locked doors, their radios playing nonstop to catch the latest bulletin and everyone phoning to tell everyone else that Winchell had said nothing remotely inflammatory to the Louisville crowd, that he had, in fact, begun his speech in what could only have been intended as an open appeal to civic self-esteem—"Mr. and Mrs. Louisville, Kentucky, proud citizens of the unique American city that is home to the greatest horse race in the world and birthplace of the very first Jewish justice of the United States Supreme Court—" and yet before he could speak aloud the name of Louis D. Brandeis, he'd been brought down by three bullets to the back of the head. A second report, aired just moments later, identified the spot where the murder occurred as only a few yards from one of the most elegant municipal buildings constructed in the Greek Revival style in the whole of Kentucky, the Jefferson County Courthouse, with its commanding statue of Thomas Jefferson facing the street and a long, wide staircase leading up to the grandly columned portico. The shots that killed Winchell appeared to have been fired from one of the courthouse's large, austere, beautifully proportioned front windows.

My mother began making her first calls immediately upon coming in from shopping. I had stationed myself just inside the door to tell her about Walter Winchell the instant she got home, but by then she already knew the little there was to be known, first because the butcher's wife had phoned the store to repeat the news bulletin to her husband just as he was wrapping my mother's order, and then because of the bewilderment apparent among the people out on the street, who were already

scurrying for the safety of their homes. Failing to reach my father, whose truck hadn't yet pulled up at the market, she of
course began to worry about my brother, who was cutting it
close once again and probably wouldn't come rushing up the
back stairs until seconds before he was due at the kitchen table
with his hands washed of the day's dirt and his face scrubbed
clean of lipstick. It was the worst moment imaginable for either
of them to be away and their precise whereabouts unknown,
but without taking time to unbag the groceries or to register
her alarm, my mother said to me, "Get me the map. Get your
map of America."

There was a large folding map of the North American continent squared away in a pocket inside volume one of the encyclopedia set sold to us by a door-to-door salesman the year I
started school. I rushed into the sun parlor, where, shelved
between the brass George Washington bookends bought at
Mount Vernon by my father, was the whole of our library: the
six-volume encyclopedia, a leather-bound copy of the United
States Constitution awarded by Metropolitan Life, and the
unabridged Webster's dictionary that Aunt Evelyn had given
Sandy for his tenth birthday. I opened the map and spread it
across the kitchen table's oilcloth covering, whereupon my
mother —using the magnifying glass that I'd received from my
parents for a seventh-birthday gift along with my irreplaceable,
unforgotten stamp album—searched for the speck in north-
central Kentucky that was the city of Danville.

In only seconds the two of us were back at the telephone
table in the foyer, above which hung yet another of my father's
awards for selling insurance, a framed copper engraving replicating the Declaration of Independence. Local dial service
within Essex County was barely ten years old and probably a
good third of the people in Newark didn't as yet have any
phone service at all—and most who did were, like us, on a party
line—and so the long-distance call was still a wondrous phenomenon, not only because making one was far from an ordinary household experience for a family of our means but
because no technological explanation, however basic, could
remove it entirely from the realm of magic.

My mother spoke to the operator very precisely to be sure
that nothing went wrong and we weren't charged by mistake

for anything extra. "I want to make a long-distance person-to-person call, operator. To Danville, Kentucky. Person-to-person to Mrs. Selma Wishnow. And please, operator, when my three minutes are up, don't forget to tell me."

There was a long pause while the operator got the number from the directory operator. When my mother finally heard the call being placed, she signaled for me to put my ear beside hers but not to speak.

"Hello!" Answering enthusiastically is Seldon.

Operator: "This is long distance. I have a person-to-person call for Mrs. Selma Wistful."

"Uh-uh," Seldon mumbles.

"Is this Mrs. Wistful?"

"Hello? My mother's not home right now."

Operator: "I'm calling for Mrs. Selma Wistful—"

"Wishnow," my mother shouts. "*Wish-now.*"

"Who's that?" Seldon says. "Who's calling?"

Operator: "Young lady, is your mother home?"

"I'm a boy," Seldon says. Taken aback. Another blow. They won't stop coming. Yet he does sound girlish, his voice higher-pitched even than when he'd been living downstairs. "My mother's not home from work yet," Seldon says.

Operator: "Mrs. Wishnow is not at home, madam."

My mother looks at me and says, "What could have happened? The boy is alone. Where could she be? He's all by himself. Operator, I'll talk to anyone."

Operator: "Go ahead, sir."

"Who's this?" Seldon asks.

"Seldon, it's Mrs. Roth. From Newark."

"Mrs. Roth?"

"Yes. I'm calling long distance to speak to your mother."

"From Newark?"

"You know who I am."

"But it sounds like you're just down the street."

"Well, I'm not. This is a long-distance call. Seldon, where's your mother?"

"I'm just having a snack. I'm waiting for her to come home from work. I'm having some Fig Newtons. And some milk."

"Seldon—"

"I'm waiting for her to come home from work—she works

late. She always works late. I just sit here. Sometimes I have a snack—"

"Seldon, stop right there. Be still a moment."

"And then she comes home and she makes dinner. But she's late every night."

Here my mother turns to me and makes to hand me the phone. "Talk to him. He won't listen when I speak."

"Talk to him about what?" I say, waving the phone away.

"Is Philip there?" Seldon asks.

"Just a moment, Seldon," my mother says.

"Is Philip there?" Seldon repeats.

To me, my mother says, "Take the phone, please."

"But what am I supposed to say?" I ask.

"Just get on the phone," and she places the receiver in my one hand and lifts the speaker for me to hold in the other.

"Hello, Seldon?" I say.

Softly tentative, unbelieving, he replies, "Philip?"

"Yes. Hi, Seldon."

"Hey, you know, I don't have any friends in school."

I tell him, "We want to speak to your mother."

"My mother's at work. She works late every night. I'm having a snack. I'm having some Fig Newtons and a glass of milk. It's going to be my birthday in about a week and my mother said I could have a party—"

"Seldon, wait a minute."

"But I don't have any friends."

"Seldon, I have to ask my mother a question. Just wait." I muzzle the speaker and whisper to her, "What am I supposed to say to him?"

My mother whispers, "Ask him if he knows what happened today in Louisville."

"Seldon, my mother wants to know if you know what happened today in Louisville."

"I live in Danville. I live in Danville, Kentucky. I'm just waiting for my mom to come home. I'm having a snack. Did something happen in Louisville?"

"Just a minute, Seldon," I say. "Now what?" I whisper to my mother.

"Just talk to him, please. Keep talking to him. And if the operator says the three minutes are up, you tell me."

"Why are you calling?" Seldon asks. "Are you going to come visit?"

"No."

"Remember when I saved your life?" he says.

"Yes, I do. I remember."

"Hey, what time is it there? Are you in Newark? Are you on Summit Avenue?"

"We told you we were. Yes."

"It's really clear, isn't it? It sounds like you're just down the block. I wish you could come over and have a snack with me, and then you could be here for my birthday party next week. I don't have any friends to invite to my birthday party. I don't have anybody to play chess with. I'm sitting here now practicing my opening move. Remember my opening move? I move out the pawn that's just in front of the king. Remember when I tried to teach you? I move out the king's pawn, remember? Then I put out the bishop, then I move the knight, and then the other knight—and remember the move when there's no pieces between the king and one of the rooks? When I move my king over two spaces to protect him?"

"Seldon—"

My mother whispers, "Tell him you miss him."

"Ma!" I say to her.

"Tell him, Philip."

"I miss you, Seldon."

"Do you want to come over for a snack then? I mean it sounds like—are you really just down the street?"

"No, this is a long-distance phone call."

"What time is it there?"

"It's, uh—about ten to six."

"Oh, it's ten to six here. My mom should already be home around five. Five-thirty the latest. One night she came home at *nine*."

"Seldon," I say, "do you know that Walter Winchell was killed?"

"Who's that?" he asks.

"Let me finish. Walter Winchell was killed in Louisville, Kentucky. In your state. Today."

"I'm sorry to hear that. Who is that?"

Operator: "Your three minutes are up, sir."

"Is that your uncle?" Seldon asks. "Is that your uncle who came to see you? Is he dead?"

"No, no," I say, and I'm thinking that, alone now out in Kentucky, he sounds as though *he* were the one who was kicked in the head. He sounds stunned. Stunted. He sounds *stopped*. And yet he was the smartest kid in our class.

My mother takes the phone. "Seldon, this is Mrs. Roth. I want you to write something down."

"Okay. I have to go find a piece of paper. And a pencil."

Waiting. Waiting. "Seldon?" my mother says.

More waiting.

"Okay," he says.

"Seldon, write this down. This is now costing a lot of money."

"I'm sorry, Mrs. Roth. I just couldn't find a pencil in the house. I was at the kitchen table. I was having a snack."

"Seldon, write down that Mrs. Roth—"

"Okay."

"—called from Newark."

"From Newark. Gosh. I wish I was still in Newark, living downstairs. You know, I saved Philip's life."

"Mrs. Roth called from Newark to be sure—"

"Just a minute. I'm writing."

"—to be sure everything is okay."

"Is something supposed to not be okay? I mean Philip's all right. And you're okay. Is Mr. Roth okay?"

"Yes, thank you for asking, Seldon. Tell your mother that's why I called. There's nothing to worry about here."

"Should I be worried about something?"

"No. Just eat your snack—"

"I think I've had enough Fig Newtons now, but thanks anyway."

"Goodbye, Seldon."

"I like Fig Newtons, though."

"Goodbye, Seldon."

"Mrs. Roth?"

"Yes?"

"Is Philip going to come visit me? It's my birthday next week and I don't have anybody to invite for my birthday party. I don't have any friends in Danville. The kids here call me Saltine. I have to play chess with a kid who's six years old. He lives next door. He's the only one I can play with. One kid. I taught him chess. Sometimes he makes moves you can't do. Or he moves his queen and I have to tell him not to. I win all the time but it's really no fun. But I have nobody else to play with."

"Seldon, it's hard for everyone. It's hard for everyone now. Goodbye, Seldon." And she placed the receiver onto the hook and began to sob.

Only days before, on October first, the two Summit Avenue flats vacated in September by the "homesteaders of 1942"—the one beneath ours and another across the street, three doors down—were occupied by Italian families up from the First Ward. Essentially their new living quarters had been assigned to them by outright government edict, though with the sweetening incentive of a rent discount of fifteen percent (or $6.37 on their monthly $42.50) over a five-year period, that money to be paid directly to the landlord by the Department of the Interior over the life of the initial three-year lease and for the first two years of a lease's three-year renewal. Such arrangements derived from a previously unpublicized section of the homesteading plan called the Good Neighbor Project, designed to introduce a steadily increasing number of non-Jewish residents into predominantly Jewish neighborhoods and in this way "enrich" the "Americanness" of everyone involved. What one heard at home, however—and sometimes even at school from our teachers—was that the underlying goal of the Good Neighbor Project, like that of Just Folks, was to weaken the solidarity of the Jewish social structure as well as to diminish whatever electoral strength a Jewish community might have in local and congressional elections. If the displacing of Jewish families and their replacement by the conscripting of Gentile families followed the timetable of the agency's master plan, a Christian majority might well be dominant in at least half of America's twenty most heavily populated Jewish neighborhoods as early as the start of Lindbergh's second term and a resolution of America's Jewish Question close at hand, by one means or another.

The family conscripted to move in downstairs from us—a mother, a father, a son, and a grandmother—were the Cucuzzas. Because of my father's years of canvassing the First Ward, where the customers whose tiny premiums he collected each month were by and large Italians, he was already familiar with the new tenants, and consequently, when he got home from work on the morning after Mr. Cucuzza, a night watchman, had trucked the family's possessions up from their cold-water flat in a tenement building on a side street not far from Holy Sepulchre Cemetery, my father stopped off first at the downstairs door to see if, despite his appearing there without a coat and a tie and with dirty hands, the elderly grandmother would recognize him as the insurance man who'd sold her husband the policy that had provided the family with the means to bury him.

The "other" Cucuzzas (relatives of "our" Cucuzzas, who'd moved from their own First Ward cold-water flat to the house three doors away) were a much larger family—three sons, a daughter, the two parents, and a grandfather—and potentially noisier, more disruptive neighbors. They were associated through the grandfather and the father with Ritchie "the Boot" Boiardo, the mobster who ruled Newark's Italian precincts and constituted the city's only serious competitor to Longy's underworld monopoly. To be sure, the father, Tommy, was but one of a bevy of underlings and, like his own retired father, doubled as a waiter at Boiardo's popular restaurant, the Vittorio Castle, when he wasn't making the rounds of the taverns, barber shops, brothels, schoolyards, and candy stores of the Third Ward slums to extract their pocket change from the Negroes who faithfully played the daily numbers game. Regardless of religion, the other Cucuzzas were hardly the sort of neighbors my parents wanted anywhere near their impressionable young sons, and to comfort us at breakfast on Sunday morning my father explained how much worse off we would have been if we'd gotten the numbers runner and his three boys instead of the night watchman and his son, Joey, an eleven-year-old recently enrolled at St. Peter's and, by my father's report, a good-natured kid with a hearing problem who had little in common with his roughneck cousins. Whereas down in the First Ward all four of Tommy Cucuzza's kids had gone to the local public school, here they'd been enrolled along with Joey at St. Peter's rather than at a public school like ours, brimming with brainy little Jews.

*

Since my father had left work only a few hours after the Winchell assassination and, over Uncle Monty's angry objections, driven back home to spend the remainder of that tense evening beside his wife and his children, the four of us were seated together at the kitchen table waiting for the radio to bring fresh news when Mr. Cucuzza and Joey came up the back stairway to pay a visit. They knocked on the door and then had to wait on the landing until my father was sure who was there.

Mr. Cucuzza was a bald, hulking man, six and a half feet tall, weighing over two hundred and fifty pounds, and he was dressed for work in his night watchman's uniform, a dark blue shirt, freshly pressed dark blue trousers, and a wide black belt that along with holding up his trousers supported several pounds of the most extraordinary collection of equipment I'd ever been close enough to reach out and touch. There were keys in bunches each the size of a hand grenade hanging to the side of either pants pocket, there was a set of real handcuffs, and a night watchman's clock in its black case dangled by a strap from the polished belt buckle. At first glance, I took the clock for a bomb, but there was no mistaking for other than what it was the pistol in a holster at his waist. A longish flashlight that had to have doubled as a blackjack was stuck lamp upward into his back pocket, and high on one sleeve of his starched workshirt was a triangular white patch whose blue lettering read "Special Guard."

Joey was also big—only two years my senior and already twice my weight—and to me the equipment he sported was nearly as intriguing as his father's. Looking like a wad of molded bubble gum plugging the hole of his right ear was a hearing aid attached by a thin wire to a round black case with a dial on the front that he wore clipped to his shirt pocket; another wire attached to a battery about the size of a large cigarette lighter that he carried around in his pants pocket. And in his hands he carried a cake, a gift from his mother to mine.

Joey's gift was the cake, Mr. Cucuzza's was a pistol. He owned two, one that he wore for work and the other that he kept hidden away at home. He'd come to offer my father the spare.

"Nice of you," my father said to him, "but I really don't know how to shoot."

"You pulla the trig'." Mr. Cucuzza had a surprisingly soft voice for someone so enormous, though with a raspy edge to it, as if it had been exposed too long to the weather during his hours of walking the watchman's beat. And his accent was so enjoyable to hear that when I was alone I sometimes pretended that the way he talked was the way I talked too. How many times did I entertain myself by saying aloud "You pulla the trig'"? With the exception of Joey's American-born mother, our Cucuzzas all had oddish voices, the bewhiskered grandmother's being oddest of all, odder even than Joey's, which sounded less like a voice than like the uninflected echo of a voice. And odd not just because she went around speaking only Italian, whether to others (including me) or to herself while she swept the back stairway or kneeled in the dirt planting her vegetables in our minute backyard or just stood muttering in the dark doorway. Hers was oddest because it sounded like a man's—she looked like a tiny old man in a long black dress and she sounded like one too, particularly when barking the commands and decrees and injunctions that Joey never dared disobey. The playful half of him, the soul that the nuns and the priests never saw enough of to save, was virtually all that I ever encountered when we two were alone. Why it was hard to feel too sorry about his hearing was because Joey was himself a very jolly, prankish boy with his own brand of hooting laughter, a talkative, curious, monumentally gullible boy whose mind moved quickly if unpredictably. It was hard to feel sorry for him, yet when he was around his family Joey's obedience was so painstakingly thorough that I found it almost as astonishing to contemplate as the painstakingly thorough lawlessness of a Shushy Margulis. There couldn't have been a better son in all of Italian Newark, which was why my own mother soon found him irresistible—his faultless filial devotion and his long dark eyelashes, the way he imploringly looked at adults, waiting to be told what to do, allowed her to set aside the uneasy aloofness that was her inbuilt defense against Gentiles. The old-country grandmother, however, gave her— and me—the willies.

"You aim," Mr. Cucuzza explained to my father, using a finger and a thumb to demonstrate, "and uhyou shoot. You aim and uhyou shoot and that's it."

"I don't need it," my father said.

"But ifuh they come roun'," Mr. Cucuzza said, "how you gonna protect?"

"Cucuzza, I was born in the city of Newark in the year nineteen hundred and one," my father told him. "All my life I have paid my rent on time, I have paid my taxes on time, and I have paid my bills on time. I've never cheated on an employer for as much as a dime. I have never tried to cheat the United States government. I believe in this country. I love this country."

"Me too," said our massive new downstairs neighbor, whose wide black belt might have been hung with shrunken heads, given the enchantment that it continued to cast over me. "I come-uh here I was uhten. Best country anyplace. No Mussolini here."

"I'm glad you feel that way, Cucuzza. It's a tragedy for Italy, it's a human tragedy for people like you."

"Mussolini, Hitler—make-uh me sick."

"You know what I love, Cucuzza? Election Day," my father told him. "I love to vote. Since I was old enough, I have not missed an election. In 1924 I voted against Mr. Coolidge and for Mr. Davis, and Mr. Coolidge won. And we all know what Mr. Coolidge did for the poor people of this country. In 1928 I voted against Mr. Hoover and for Mr. Smith, and Mr. Hoover won. And we know what *he* did for the poor people of this country. In 1932 I voted against Mr. Hoover for the second time and for Mr. Roosevelt for the first time, and, thank God, Mr. Roosevelt won, and he put America back on its feet. He took this country out of the Depression and he gave the people what he promised—a new deal. In 1936 I voted against Mr. Landon and for Mr. Roosevelt, and again Mr. Roosevelt won —two states, Maine and Vermont, that is all Mr. Landon is able to carry. Can't even carry Kansas. Mr. Roosevelt sweeps the country by the biggest presidential vote there has ever been, and once again he keeps every promise to the working people that he made in that campaign. And so what do the voters up and do in nineteen hundred and forty? They elect a fascist instead. Not just an idiot like Coolidge, not just a fool like Hoover, but an out-and-out fascist with a medal to prove it. They put in a fascist and a fascist rabble-rouser, Mr. Wheeler,

as his sidekick, and they put Mr. Ford into the cabinet, not
only an anti-Semite right up there with Hitler but a slave driver
who has turned the workingman into a human machine. And
so tonight you come to me, sir, in my own home, and you
offer me a pistol. In America in the year nineteen hundred and
forty-two, a brand-new neighbor, a man I do not even know
yet, has to come here and offer me a pistol in order for me to
protect my family from Mr. Lindbergh's anti-Semitic mob.
Well, don't you think I'm not grateful, Cucuzza. I will never
forget your concern. But I am a citizen of the United States of
America, and so is my wife, and so are my children, and so," he
said, his voice catching, "and so was Mr. Walter Winchell—"

But now, suddenly, there is a radio bulletin *about* Walter
Winchell. "Shhh!" my father says. "Shhh!" as though in the
kitchen someone other than himself had been the orator holding forth. We all listen—even Joey appears to listen—the way
birds flock to migrate and fish swim in a school.

The body of Walter Winchell, slain that day at a political rally
in Louisville, Kentucky, by a suspected American Nazi Party
assassin working in collaboration with the Ku Klux Klan, will
be carried overnight by train from Louisville to Pennsylvania
Station in New York City. There, by order of Mayor Fiorello
La Guardia and under the protection of the New York City
police, the body will lie in state in the great hall of the train
station throughout the morning. According to Jewish custom,
a funeral service will be held that same day, at two P.M. in
Temple Emanu-El, New York's largest synagogue. A public-
address system will broadcast the proceedings beyond the
temple to a gathering of mourners on Fifth Avenue expected
to number in the tens of thousands. Along with Mayor La
Guardia, speakers will include Democratic senator James
Mead, New York's Jewish governor, Herbert Lehman, and the
former president of the United States, Franklin D. Roosevelt.

"It's happening!" my father cries. "He's back! FDR is back!"

"We need him bad," Mr. Cucuzza says.

"Boys," he asks, "do you understand what is happening?"
and here he throws his arms around Sandy and me. "It's the
beginning of the end of fascism in America! No Mussolini
here, Cucuzza—no more Mussolini here!"

8

Bad Days

A LVIN APPEARED at our house the next night, driving a brand-new green Buick and with a fiancée named Minna Schapp. "Fiancée" always got me when I heard the word spoken as a kid. It made whoever she was sound like somebody special—then she showed up and she was just some girl who, when she met the family, was afraid to say the wrong thing. The special one here wasn't the intended wife anyway but the intended father-in-law, a masterful deal-maker prepared to deliver Alvin from the game-machine business—where, assisted by two strong-arm thugs who lifted the freight and fended off evildoers, my cousin was employed trucking and setting up the illegal machines—and into a hand-tailored Hong Kong silk suit and a white-on-white monogrammed shirt as an Atlantic City restaurateur. Though Mr. Schapp had himself started out in the twenties as Pinball Billy Schapiro, a two-bit hustler associated with the worst hoods from the most rundown row houses on the most violent streets of the South Philly badlands —among them the uncle of Shushy Margulis—by 1942 the return on the pinballs and the slots amounted to upward of fifteen thousand unreported dollars each week, and Pinball Billy had been regenerated as William F. Schapp II, highly esteemed member of the Green Valley Country Club, of the Jewish fraternal organization Brith Achim (where on Saturday nights he took his dynamic wife in her gigantic jewels to dance to the music of Jackie Jacobs and his Jolly Jazzers), and of Har Zion Synagogue (through whose burial society he purchased a family plot in a beautifully landscaped corner of the synagogue's cemetery), as well as the maharajah of an eighteen-room mansion in suburban Merion and wintertime occupant of a poor boy's dream of a penthouse suite annually reserved for him at the Miami Beach Eden Roc.

At thirty-one, Minna was eight years Alvin's senior, a butterycomplexioned woman with a browbeaten look who, when she even dared to speak in her babyish voice, enunciated each word as though she had only just learned to tell time. She was every inch the child of overbearing parents, but because the father owned, in addition to the Intercity Carting Company—the public face of the gaming-machine operation—half an acre of lobster house across from the Steel Pier where people lined up twice around the block to get in on weekends, and because back in the early thirties, when Prohibition ended and Pinball Billy's lucrative side interest in Waxey Gordon's interstate boot-legging syndicate suddenly dried up, he'd established Philadelphia's "Original Schapp's"—the steak house popular with what in Philly they called the Jew Mob—Pinball Billy figured strongly with Alvin as Minna's advocate. "The contract goes like this," Schapp told him when he handed Alvin the cash to buy his daughter's engagement ring. "Minna takes care of your leg, you take care of Minna, and I take care of you."

That's how my cousin came to don the hand-tailored suits and to arrogate to himself the glamorous responsibility for ushering to their tables big-name customers such as Jersey City's crooked mayor, Frank Hague; New Jersey's light-heavyweight champion, Gus Lesnevich; and racket tycoons like Cleveland's Moe Dalitz, Boston's King Solomon, L.A.'s Mickey Cohen, and even "the Brain" himself, Meyer Lansky, when they were in town for a gangland convention. And regularly, every September, to welcome fresh from her pageant triumph, the newly crowned Miss America with all her befuddled relatives in tow. Once everyone was lavishly complimented and into their silly lobster bibs, it was Alvin's pleasure to signal to the waiter, by a snap of his fingers, that the house would pick up the tab.

Pinball Billy's one-legged future son-in-law soon gained a nickname of his own, Showy, bestowed on him, as Alvin told everyone, by Allie Stolz, the contender for the world light-weight title. Alvin was up from Philly to visit with Stolz—like Gus Lesnevich, a Newark boy—the day he and Minna wound up at our house for dinner. Stolz had fought and lost a fifteen-round decision against the lightweight champion in Madison Square Garden the previous May and was training that fall at Marsillo's Market Street gym for a November fight against Beau Jack that would gain him a shot at Tippy Larkin if he won.

"Once Allie gets past Beau Jack," Alvin said, "there's just Larkin between him and the title, and Larkin's got a glass jaw."

Glass jaw. Phony-baloney. A going-over. A hard guy. What's his beef? I'll take the grunt. The oldest dodge in the world. Alvin had a new vocabulary and a whole new ostentatious way of talking that it clearly pained my parents to hear. Yet when he said adoringly of Stolz's generosity, "Allie's a guy who is rapid with the dollar," I couldn't wait to sound like a hard guy myself by repeating the amazing expression at school along with the extensive medley of slang that Alvin now used just for the word "money."

Minna was silent during the meal—though my mother tried mightily to draw her out—I was overcome by shyness, and my father could think of nothing but the synagogue bombing that had taken place in Cincinnati the previous night and the looting of Jewish-owned stores in American cities scattered across two time zones. This was the second night in a row that he'd walked out on Uncle Monty rather than leave the family alone on Summit Avenue, but he couldn't worry about his brother's wrath at a time like this, and instead all through dinner kept getting up to go into the living room to turn on the radio and hear what news there was in the aftermath of the Winchell funeral. Alvin, meanwhile, was able to talk only about "Allie" and his quest for the world boxing crown as though the lightweight contender native to Newark embodied Alvin's profoundest conception of the human race. Could the abandonment have been any more complete of the moral code that had cost him his leg? He had disposed of whatever once stood between him and the aspirations of a Shushy Margulis—he had disposed of us.

I wondered, when I met her, if Alvin had even told Minna that he was an amputee. It didn't occur to me that her subjugated personality was precisely what made her the first and only woman Alvin *could* tell, nor did I understand that Minna was the evidence of his incapacity with women. His stump, in fact, constituted Alvin's greatest *success* with Minna, particularly after Schapp died in 1960 and Minna's worthless brother took over the slots, while Alvin was content just to acquire the restaurants and to begin running with the best-looking hookers in two states. Whenever the stump cracked and got sore and bloody and infected—which it did as a result of his

many follies—Minna immediately stepped in and wouldn't
allow him to wear his prosthesis. Alvin would say to her, "For
Christ's sake, don't worry about it, it'll be all right," but here
alone Minna prevailed. "You can't put a load on that leg,"
she'd tell him, "till you get it fixed"—meaning the artificial leg,
which was always, in the legmaker's phrase that Alvin had
taught me back when I, not yet nine, was the mothering
Minna, "losing its fit." When Alvin got older and his stump
broke down all the time from bearing all the weight he'd
gained, when he had to be without the prosthesis for weeks on
end until it healed, Minna would drive him to the public beach
in the summertime and watch fully clothed from under a big
umbrella while he played for hours in the all-healing surf, bob-
bing in the waves and floating on his back and spouting saltwa-
ter geysers into the air and then, to throw a scare into the
tourists crowding the beach, emerging from the water screaming "Shark! Shark!" while pointing in horror at his stump.

Alvin showed up with Minna for dinner after phoning that
morning to tell my mother that he was going to be in North
Jersey and wanted to stop by to thank his aunt and uncle for all
they had done for him when he'd come home from the commandos and given everyone a hard time. He had a lot to be
grateful for, he said, and he wanted to make peace with the
two of them and to see the two boys, and to introduce his fiancée. That's what he said and that may even have been what
he had in mind before he came face to face with my father and
the memory of my father's reforming instincts—and the fact of
their innate antipathy, the antipathy as human types that was
really there from the start—and it was why, when I got home
from school and heard the news, I dug down into my drawer
and found his medal and, for the first time since he'd left for
Philly, pinned it back on my undershirt.

Of course it was hardly an ideal day for a conciliatory visit
from the family's black sheep. There'd been no anti-Semitic
violence reported in Newark or in the other major New Jersey
cities during the night, but the firebombing of the synagogue
that subsequently burned to the ground some hundred miles
up the Ohio River from Louisville, in Cincinnati, and the random window-smashing and looting of Jewish-owned stores in
eight other cities (St. Louis, Buffalo, and Pittsburgh the three

largest) did nothing to diminish fear that the spectacle of Walter Winchell's Jewish funeral just across the Hudson in New York—and the demonstrations and counter-demonstrations coinciding with all the solemn observances—could easily provoke an outbreak of violence a lot closer to home. At school, first thing in the morning, a special half-hour assembly program had been called for grades four through eight. Along with a representative from the Board of Education, a deputy from Mayor Murphy's office, and the current president of the PTA, the principal spelled out the measures being taken to ensure our safety during the day and offered ten rules that would protect us from harm on our way to and from school. While no mention was made of Bullet Apfelbaum's Jewish police—who'd been on the streets all night long and were still there in the morning, drinking hot coffee out of thermoses and eating powdered doughnuts donated by Lehrhoff's bakery when Sandy and I started off for school—we were assured by the mayor's deputy that "until normal conditions are restored," extra details of city police would be patrolling the neighborhood and we were instructed not to be alarmed if we found a uniformed policeman stationed at each of the school doors and a policeman in the corridors. Two mimeographed sheets were then distributed to every pupil, one listing the rules to obey on the street, which our teachers would go over with us when we returned to our homerooms, and the other to take to our parents to advise them of the new safety procedures. If there were questions, our parents should direct them to Mrs. Sisselman, the PTA president who'd succeeded my mother.

We ate in the dining room, where we last had a meal when Aunt Evelyn had brought Rabbi Bengelsdorf to meet us. After Alvin's call, my mother (whose inability to hold a personal grudge Alvin would have known he could count on the moment he heard her answer the phone) went off to buy food for a dinner that would especially please him, and this despite the anxiety aroused in her each time she had to unlock the door and go back out on the street. That armed Newark cops were now walking the beat and cruising the local streets in squad cars gave her only slightly more assurance than did the glimpses of Bullet Apfelbaum's Jewish police, and so, like anyone else shopping in a city under siege, she wound up all but running back and forth to Chancellor Avenue to pick up everything she needed. In the kitchen she proceeded to bake the chocolate layer cake with chocolate icing and chopped walnuts that had been Alvin's favorite and to peel the potatoes and chop the onions for the latkes that Alvin could devour by the batch, and the house still smelled of the baking and frying and broiling that had been touched off by the unexpected homecoming when Alvin drove his new Buick into the alleyway. There (where we'd run pass plays together with the football I stole) Alvin pulled up behind the little Ford pickup that Mr. Cucuzza used to move people's furniture as a second job and that happened to be parked in the garage because it was the night watchman's day off, and on his day off he slept round the clock.

Alvin arrived wearing a pearl-gray sharkskin suit padded heavily at the shoulders, perforated two-tone wingtip shoes with taps on the toes, and bearing gifts for all: Aunt Bess's was a white apron decorated with red roses, Sandy's a sketchpad, mine a Phillies cap, and Uncle Herman's a certificate entitling a family of four to a free lobster dinner at the Atlantic City restaurant. His giving us all presents reassured me that just because he'd run off to Philadelphia, he hadn't forgotten all the good stuff he'd found in our house in the years preceding his losing his leg. It certainly did not look then and there as though we were a divided family or that when dinner was over—and Minna already in the kitchen taking a lesson in latke-making from my mother—a battle royal could possibly break out between my father and Alvin. Perhaps if Alvin hadn't shown up in his flashy clothes and his snazzy car all but seething with the raw carnality of Marsillo's gym and exuberant with the imminent acquisition of undreamed-of wealth . . . perhaps if Winchell hadn't been assassinated twenty-four hours earlier and the worst that had been feared when Lindbergh first took office hadn't seemed closer to befalling us than ever before . . . perhaps then the two grown men who mattered most to me throughout my childhood might never have come so close to murdering each other.

Before that night, I'd had no idea my father was so well suited for wreaking havoc or equipped to make that lightning-quick transformation from sanity to lunacy that is indispensable in enacting the unbridled urge to destroy. Unlike Uncle Monty he preferred never to speak of the ordeal of a Jewish tenement kid on Runyon Street before World War One, when the Irish, armed with sticks and rocks and iron pipes, regularly came streaming up through the viaduct underpasses of the Iron-bound section seeking vengeance against the Christ-killers of the Jewish Third Ward, and much as he enjoyed taking Sandy and me to Laurel Garden on Springfield Avenue when tickets to a good match came his way, men fighting each other outside a boxing ring appalled him. That he'd always had a muscular physique I knew from a snapshot taken when he was eighteen and pasted by my mother into the family photo album along-side the only other photograph surviving from his youth, a picture of him at the age of six standing next to Uncle Monty, three years older and close to a foot and a half taller—two ragtag kids stiffly posing in their ancient overalls and their dirty shirts and with their caps pushed back just far enough to reveal the cruelty of their haircuts. In that sepia photo of him at eighteen he's already a million miles from childhood, a full-fledged force of nature standing cross-armed in his bathing suit on the sunny beach at Spring Lake, New Jersey, the im-movable keystone at the base of a human pyramid of six raffish hotel waiters enjoying their afternoon off. As evidenced in that 1919 photo, he'd been powerful through the chest right from the start, and the yoke-bearing shoulders and brawny arms he had somehow retained even through his years knocking on doors for Metropolitan Life, so that now, at forty-one, after having worked hauling heavy crates and lifting hundred-pound sacks six nights a week all through September, there was prob-ably more explosive strength stored up in that body than ever before in his life.

Prior to that night, it would have been as impossible for me to envision him beating somebody up—let alone battering bloody his beloved older brother's fatherless son—as to imag-ine him atop my mother, especially as there was no taboo stronger among Jews with our impoverished European origins and our tenaciously held American ambitions than the perva-sive, unwritten prohibition against settling disputes by force. In that era, the common Jewish propensity was by and large nonviolent as well as nonalcoholic, a virtue whose shortcoming was the failure to educate the bulk of the young of my generation in the combative aggression that was the first law of other ethnic educations and indisputably of great practical value when you couldn't negotiate your way out of violence or manage to run away. Among, say, the several hundred boys in my elementary school between the ages of five and fourteen who were not chromosomally preordained to be top-flight lightweights like Allie Stolz or successful racketeers like Longy Zwillman, surely far fewer fistfights broke out than in any of the other neighborhood schools in industrial Newark, where the ethical obligations of a child were differently defined and schoolmates demonstrated their belligerence by means not readily available to us.

So then, for every reason imaginable it was a devastating night. I didn't have the capacity in 1942 to begin to decipher all the awful implications, but just the sight of my father's and Alvin's blood was stunning enough. Blood spattered the length and breadth of our imitation Oriental rug, blood dripping from the splintered remains of our coffee table, blood smeared like a sign across my father's forehead, blood spurting from my cousin's nose—and the two of them not so much fistfighting, not so much wrestling as caroming, with a terrible bony thwack colliding, rearing back and charging in like men with antlers branching from their brows, fantastical, cross-species creatures sprung from mythology into our living room and pulping each other's flesh with their massive, snaggletoothed horns. Inside a house you usually scale down your movements, you scale down your speed, but here the scale of things was reversed and terrifying to behold. The South Boston riots, the Detroit riots, the Louisville assassination, the Cincinnati firebombing, the mayhem in St. Louis, Pittsburgh, Buffalo, Akron, Youngstown, Peoria, Scranton, and Syracuse . . . and now this: in an ordinary family living room—traditionally the staging area for the collective effort to hold the line *against* the intrusions of a hostile world—the anti-Semites were about to be abetted in their exhilarating solution to America's worst problem by our taking up the cudgels and hysterically destroying ourselves.

The horror ended with Mr. Cucuzza, in his nightshirt and his nightcap (attire I'd never before seen on anyone, man or boy, other than in a funny movie), crashing into our flat with his pistol drawn. A frantic wail rose from Joey's Old World grandmother, appropriately swathed like the Calabrian Queen of the Shades at the foot of our landing—and from within our own flat came a noise equally hair-raising the instant the splintered back door flew open and my mother saw that the nightshirted intruder was armed. Minna began bringing up into her hands everything she'd just swallowed at dinner, I couldn't help myself and promptly urinated, while Sandy, who alone among us was able to find the right words and the vocal strength to utter them, cried, "Don't shoot! It's Alvin!" But Mr. Cucuzza was a professional guardian of private property trained to act now and draw distinctions later and—without pausing to ask "Who's Alvin?"—immobilized my father's assailant in a strangulating half nelson with one arm while holding the pistol to his head with the hand of the other.

Alvin's prosthesis had cracked in two, his stump was torn to shreds, and one of his wrists was broken. Three of my father's front teeth were shattered, two ribs were fractured, a gash was opened along his right cheekbone that had to be sutured with almost twice as many stitches as were needed to close the wound inflicted on me by the orphanage horse, and his neck was so badly wrenched that he had to go around in a high steel collar for months afterward. The glass-topped coffee table with the dark mahogany frame that my mother had saved over the years to buy at Bam's (and where, at the conclusion of a pleasant hour of evening reading, she would set down, with its ribboned bookmark in place, the new novel by Pearl Buck or Fannie Hurst or Edna Ferber borrowed from the local pharmacy's tiny rental library) lay in fragments all across the room, and microscopic crumbs of glass were embedded in my father's hands. The rug, the walls, and the furniture were speckled with chocolate icing (from the slices of layer cake they had been eating when they sat down over dessert to talk together in the living room) as well as with their blood, and then there was the smell of it—the airless, gag-inducing slaughterhouse smell.

It's so heartbreaking, violence, when it's in a house—like seeing the clothes in a tree after an explosion. You may be prepared to see death but not the clothes in the tree.

And all of it the result of my father's failing to understand that Alvin's nature was never really reformable, despite the lecturing and the hectoring love—all of it the result of having taken him in to save him from what it was simply in his nature to become. All of it the result of my father's looking Alvin over and remembering the tragically evanescent life of Alvin's late father, and, in his despair, sadly shaking his head and saying, "A Buick automobile, a sharpie's suits, the scum of the earth for your friends—but do you know, do you care, does it bother you at all, Alvin, what's happening in this country tonight? It did years ago, damn it. I can remember clear as day when it did. But now no. Now it's big cigars and motor cars. But do you have any idea at all what is happening to the Jews even while we sit here?"

And Alvin, whose lot had finally come to something, whose prospects never before had been so hopeful, could not bear and would not endure being informed by the custodian whose tutelage had once meant everything—by the relative who, when no one else would have him, had twice taken him to live in a homey little Weequahic flat amid a kindly family and their benign concerns—that he had come to nothing. His voice husky with the grievance of the injured party, his delivery staccato and without a single caesura to let anything in that wasn't retaliatory, all calumny, all castigation, all coercion and fatuous bluff, Alvin shouted at my father, "The *Jews*? I wrecked my *life* for the Jews! I lost my fuckin' *leg* for the Jews! I lost my fuckin' leg for *you*! What did I give a shit either way about Lindbergh? But you send me to go fuckin' fight him, and the stupid fuckin' kid I am, I *go*. And look, *look*, Uncle Fucking Disaster—*I have no fucking leg*!"

Here he hiked up a handful of the pearl-gray fabric in which he was so lustrously clad to reveal where there was indeed no longer a lower limb of flesh and blood and muscle and bone. And then, insulted, negated, inwardly once again the unmanned man (and the bum kid), he added his final heroic touch by spitting into my father's face. A family, my father liked to say, is both peace and war, but this was family war as I could never have imagined it. Spitting into my father's face the way he'd spit into the face of that dead German soldier!

If only he had been allowed to go along unrehabilitated, on

his own stinking trajectory, but that hadn't happened, and so this was how the great menace undid us and the abomination of violence entered our house, and I saw how bitterness blinds a man and the defilement it spawns.

And why, why did he go to fight in the first place? Why did he fight and why did he fall? Because there is a war going on, he chooses that way—the raging, rebellious instinct historically trapped! If only the times were different, if only he had been smarter . . . But he wants to fight. He's like the very fathers he wants to be rid of. That's the tyranny of the problem. Trying to be faithful to what he's trying to be rid of. Trying to be faithful and to get rid of what he's faithful to at the same time. And that's why he went to fight in the first place, as best I can figure it out.

Later that night, after a pair of Alvin's buddies had pulled up in a Caddy with Pennsylvania plates (one of them to get Alvin and Minna over to Allie Stolz's doctor's office on Elizabeth Avenue, the other to drive their Buick back to Philly); after my father was home from the Beth Israel emergency room (where they'd plucked the glass out of his hands and stitched up his face and x-rayed his neck and taped his ribcage and, on his way out, handed him codeine tablets to take for the pain); after Mr. Cucuzza, who'd rushed my father to the hospital in his pickup, had returned him safely to the befouled and littered battlefield that was now our flat, the gunshots erupted on Chancellor Avenue. Shots, screaming, shouting, sirens—the pogrom had begun, and it was only seconds before Mr. Cucuzza charged back up the stairs he'd only just descended and banged once on our broken back door before rushing in.

Desperate for sleep, I was dragged from bed by my brother, but when my legs wouldn't work and kept collapsing from uncontrollable fear, I had to be carried off in his arms by my father. My mother—who instead of going to bed and trying to sleep had donned her apron and a pair of rubber gloves and set about to purge the house of its filth with a bucket and a broom and a mop—my meticulous mother, weeping amid the wreckage of her living room, was guided to the door by Mr. Cucuzza, and the four of us were herded down the stairs and into the Wishnows' old flat to take cover there.

This time when Mr. Cucuzza offered a pistol, my father accepted it. His poor human body was black-and-blue and bandaged just about everywhere, his mouth was full of broken teeth, and still he sat with us on the floor in the Cucuzzas' windowless back foyer, regarding the weapon in his hands with all his concentration, as though it were no longer just a weapon but the most serious thing entrusted to him since he'd first been given his infant babies to hold. My mother sat straight up between Sandy's self-conscious stoicism and my stupefied inertness, gripping us each by the arm closest to her and doing all she could to keep a thin layer of courage from revealing her terror to the children. Meanwhile the biggest man I'd ever seen moved with a pistol through the darkened flat, stealthily advancing from window to window to ascertain with the eagle-eyed thoroughness of the veteran night watchman whether anyone lurked anywhere nearby with an ax, a gun, a rope, or a can of kerosene.

Joey, his mother, and his grandmother had been directed by Mr. Cucuzza to remain in their beds, though the old lady could not resist the magnetism of all that turbulence and the picture we four presented of sheer plight. Snarling in tiny bursts of raw Italian that could not have been complimentary to her guests, she peered out from the doorway of the dark kitchen—where she customarily slept in her clothes on a cot next to the stove—fixing us in the crosshairs of her madness (because mad she was) as if she were the patron saint of anti-Semitism whose silver crucifix had engendered it all.

The firing went on for less than an hour but we didn't head back upstairs until dawn, and didn't learn, until after Mr. Cucuzza bravely ventured forth as a scout to where Chancellor Avenue was cordoned off, that the gun battle had been not between the city police and the anti-Semites but between the city police and the Jewish police. There'd been no pogrom in Newark that night, just a shootout, extraordinary for having occurred within earshot of our house but otherwise not much different from the disorder that could erupt in any large city after dark. And though three Jews had been killed—Duke Glick, Big Gerry, and Bullet himself—it wasn't necessarily because they were Jews ("though it didn't hurt," my uncle Monty said) but because they were exactly the sort of thugs that the new mayor wanted off the streets, primarily to signal to Longy that he was no longer an honorary member of the city's Board of Commissioners (a position he was rumored—by Meyer Ellenstein's enemies—to have held under Murphy's Jewish predecessor). Nobody bothered taking the police commissioner too seriously when he explained to the *Newark News* that it was the "trigger-happy vigilantes" who, without provocation, had opened fire a little before midnight on two foot patrolmen walking their beat, nor, among our neighbors, was there any noticeable expression of grief because of how the three—dangerous people in their own right whose protection nobody decent would have dreamed of requesting—had been unceremoniously mowed down. Of course, it was awful that the blood of violent men should stain the pavement where the neighborhood children wended their way to school every day, but at least it wasn't blood shed in a clash with the Klan or the Silver Shirts or the Bund.

No pogrom, and yet at seven that morning my father was on the phone long-distance to Winnipeg to admit to Shepsie Tirschwell that the Jews were so frightened and the anti-Semites so emboldened that it was no longer possible in Newark—where fortunately the prestige of Rabbi Prinz had continued to exert an influence over the powers that be and nothing worse than relocation had as yet been forced on a single Jewish family—to live as normal people. Whether outright government-sanctioned persecution was inevitable, nobody could say for sure, but the fear of persecution was such that not even a practical man grounded in his everyday tasks, a person who tried his best to contain the uncertainty and the anxiety and the anger and operate according to the dictates of reason, could hope to preserve his equilibrium any longer.

Yes, my father admitted, he had been wrong all along and Bess and the Tirschwells had been right—and then, as best he could, he shook off his abashment over everything he'd mismanaged and badly misjudged, including the improbable violence that had smashed to bits, along with our coffee table, that lifelong barrier of rigid rectitude that had stood between his harsh upbringing and his mature ideals. "That's it," he told Shepsie Tirschwell, "I can't live any longer not knowing what will happen tomorrow," and their phone conversation moved on to emigration and the steps to be taken and the arrangements to be made, so that by the time Sandy and I left the house, there was no misunderstanding that, quite incredibly, we'd been overpowered by the forces arrayed against us and were about to flee and become foreigners. I wept all the way to school. Our incomparable American childhood was ended. Soon my homeland would be nothing more than my birthplace. Even Seldon in Kentucky was better off now.

But then it was over. The nightmare was over. Lindbergh was gone and we were safe, though never would I be able to revive that unfazed sense of security first fostered in a little child by a big, protective republic and his ferociously responsible parents.

Drawn from the Archives of Newark's Newsreel Theater

Tuesday, October 6, 1942

Thirty thousand mourners stream through the great hall of Pennsylvania Station to view Walter Winchell's flag-draped coffin. The turnout exceeds even the expectations of New York mayor Fiorello La Guardia, whose decision it was to transform the assassination into the occasion for a citywide day of mourning for "American victims of Nazi violence," culminating in a funeral oration to be delivered by FDR. Outside the station (as at numerous other locations throughout the city), silent men and women dressed in somber clothing distribute half-dollar-sized black buttons whose white lettering poses the question "Where is Lindbergh?" Just before noon, Mayor La Guardia arrives at the studio of the city radio station, where he removes his wide-brimmed black Stetson (a memento of his boyhood roots in the Arizona Territory as the son of a U.S. Army bandmaster) to recite the Lord's Prayer; then he puts the hat back on to read aloud, in Hebrew, the Jewish prayer for the dead. At the stroke of noon, by decree of the City Council, a minute of silence is observed in the five boroughs. The New York police are in evidence everywhere, chiefly to oversee the protest demonstrations organized by the array of right-wing groups located in preponderantly German Yorkville—the Manhattan neighborhood north of the Upper East Side and south of Harlem that is the main headquarters for the American Nazi movement—and that militantly endorse the president and his policies. At one P.M. an honor guard of motorcycles manned by policemen wearing black armbands aligns itself with the funeral cortege forming outside Penn Station and, with the mayor leading the way from a motorcycle sidecar, escorts the cortege slowly northward up Eighth Avenue, eastward along 57th Street, northward again on Fifth Avenue to 65th Street and Temple Emanu-El. There, among the dignitaries summoned by La Guardia to fill the temple's every last seat, are the ten members of Roosevelt's 1940 cabinet, Roosevelt's four Supreme Court appointees, President Philip Murray of the CIO, President William Green of the AFL, President John L. Lewis of the United Mine Workers, Roger Baldwin of the American Civil Liberties Union, as well as past and current Democratic governors, senators, and congressmen from New York, New Jersey, Pennsylvania, and Connecticut, among them the Democrats' defeated 1928 presidential aspirant, former New York governor Al Smith. Loudspeakers installed overnight by municipal laborers and wired to telephone poles and barber poles and door lintels throughout the city carry the memorial service to the New Yorkers who've assembled on the streets of every Manhattan neighborhood (except Yorkville) and to the thousands of out-of-towners who have congregated alongside them—all those Mr. and Mrs. Americas who'd been listening to Walter Winchell weekly since he first came on the air and who have journeyed to his hometown to pay their respects. And virtually every man, woman, and child among them wears that now ubiquitous badge of defiant solidarity, the black-and-white "Where is Lindbergh?" button.

Fiorello H. La Guardia—the down-to-earth idol of the city's working people; the flamboyant ex-congressman who'd belligerently represented a congested East Harlem district of poor Italians and Jews for five terms, who as early as 1933 described Hitler as a "perverted maniac" and called for a boycott of German goods; the tenacious spokesman for the unions, the needy, and the unemployed who'd battled almost single-handedly against Hoover's do-nothing congressional Republicans during the first dark year of the Depression and, to the dismay of his own party, called for taxation to "soak the rich"; the liberal anti-Tammany reform Republican who has been the three-term Fusion mayor of the country's most populous city, the metropolis that is home to the largest concentration of Jews in the hemisphere—La Guardia is alone among the members of his party in displaying his contempt for Lindbergh and for the Nazi dogma of Aryan superiority that he (himself the son of an unobservant Jewish mother from Austrian Trieste and a free-thinker Italian father who came to America as a ship's musician) has identified as the precept at the heart of Lindbergh's credo and of the huge American cult that worships the president.

La Guardia stands beside the coffin and addresses the dignitaries with that same excitable, high-pitched voice in which he famously narrated the Sunday comic strips over the city's radio station to the city's children every Sunday morning during a New York newspaper strike, like the best of uncles proceeding patiently, panel by panel, balloon by balloon, from Dick Tracy to Little Orphan Annie and on through the rest of the serialized funnies.

"We can dispense with the cant at the start," says the mayor. "Everybody knows that Walter was not a lovely human being. Walter was not the strong, silent type who hides everything but the muckraker who hates everything hidden. As anybody who ever turned up in his column can tell you, Walter was not always as accurate as he might have been. He was not shy, he was not modest, he was not decorous, discreet, kindly, et cetera. My friends, if I were to list for you everything lovely that W.W. was not, we'd be here till next Yom Kippur. I'm afraid that the late Walter Winchell was just one more doozy of a specimen of the imperfect man. In declaring himself a candidate for the presidency of the United States were his motives pure as Ivory soap? Walter Winchell's motives? Was his preposterous candidacy uncontaminated by a raving ego? My friends, only a Charles A. Lindbergh has motives pure as Ivory soap when he runs for the American presidency. Only a Charles A. Lindbergh is decorous, discreet, et cetera—oh, and accurate too, wholly accurate always when every few months he summons up the gregariousness to address his ten favorite platitudes to the nation. Only a Charles A. Lindbergh is a selfless ruler and a strong, silent saint. Walter, on the other hand, was Mr. Gossip Columnist. Walter, on the other hand, was Mr. Broadway:

liked the ponies, liked the late hours, liked Sherman Billingsley
—somebody once told me that he even liked the girls. And the
repeal of that 'noble experiment,' as Mr. Herbert Hoover
called it, the repeal of the hypocritical, expensive, stupid, un-
enforceable Eighteenth Amendment, was no more ignoble to
Walter Winchell than it was to the rest of us here in New York.
In short, Walter lacked every gleaming virtue demonstrated daily
by the incorruptible test pilot ensconced in the White House.

"Oh yes, several more differences that are perhaps worth
noting between fallible Walter and infallible Lindy. Our president is a fascist sympathizer, more than likely an outright
fascist—and Walter Winchell was the enemy of the fascist. Our
president is no lover of Jews and more than likely a dyed-in-
the-wool anti-Semite while Walter Winchell was a Jew and the
unwavering, vociferous enemy of the anti-Semite. Our president is an admirer of Adolf Hitler and more than likely a Nazi
himself—and Walter Winchell was Hitler's first American
enemy and his worst American enemy. There's where our imperfect Walter was incorruptible—where it mattered. Walter is
too loud, Walter talks too fast, Walter says too much, and yet,
by comparison, Walter's vulgarity is something great, and Lindbergh's decorum is hideous. Walter Winchell, my friends, was
the enemy of Nazis *everywhere*, not excluding the Dieses and
the Bilbos and the Parnell Thomases who serve their Führer
in the United States Congress, not excluding the Hitlerites who
write for the *New York Journal-American* and the *New York
Daily News*, not excluding those who royally fete Nazi murder-
ers in our American White House at the taxpayer's expense.
And it was *because* he was Hitler's enemy and it was *because* he
was the Nazis' enemy that Walter Winchell was gunned down
yesterday in the shadow of the statue of Thomas Jefferson in
gracious old Louisville's most historic and beautiful public
square. For speaking his mind in the state of Kentucky, W.W.
was assassinated by the Nazis of America, who, thanks to the
silence of our strong, silent, selfless president, today run ram-
pant throughout this great land. It can't happen here? My
friends, it *is* happening here—and where is Lindbergh? *Where
is Lindbergh?*"

Out in the streets, those listening together around the loudspeakers take up the mayor's cry, and soon their chant is cas-

cading eerily across the entire city—"Where is *Lind*-bergh? Where is *Lind*-bergh?"—while inside the synagogue the mayor repeats and repeats his four irate syllables, angrily banging the pulpit not like an orator theatrically emphasizing a point but like an outraged citizen demanding the truth. "Where is Lindbergh?" This is the snarling peroration with which the red-faced La Guardia readies the assembled mourners for the climactic appearance of Franklin D. Roosevelt, who stuns even his closest political cronies (Hopkins, Morgenthau, Farley, Berle, Baruch, all sitting behatted only feet from the coffin of the martyred candidate, whose brand of megalomania was never to the taste of the White House inner circle, however useful a mouthpiece he may have been to their boss) by ordaining as Winchell's successor the cunning, contemptuous, short-tempered, bullheaded, roly-poly politico standing five feet two inches tall and known affectionately to his devoted constituents as the Little Flower. From the pulpit of Temple Emanu-El, the nominal head of the Democratic Party pledges his support to New York's Republican mayor as a "national unity" candidate to oppose Lindbergh's quest for a second term in 1944.

Wednesday, October 7, 1942
Piloted by President Lindbergh, the *Spirit of St. Louis* departs from Long Island in the morning, lifting off from the runway that served as the point of embarkation for the transatlantic solo flight of May 20, 1927. With no protective escort, the plane speeds through a cloudless autumn sky across New Jersey, Pennsylvania, Ohio, and down to Kentucky. Only an hour before he is to set down in the midday sunshine at the Louisville commercial airport is the White House notified by the president of his destination. His timing allows just enough notice for Louisville mayor Wilson Wyatt and the city and its citizens to prepare for the president's arrival. A mechanic is at the ready on the ground to check over the plane and tune and equip it for the return flight.

Of Louisville's 320,000 residents, the police estimate that at least a third have made the five-mile trek out from the city and are already packing the fields and the roads adjacent to Bowman Field when the president lands and smoothly taxies his plane to a platform where a microphone has been hooked up for him to address the vast crowd. When finally the great din of their greeting begins to diminish and his voice can be heard, the president makes no mention of Walter Winchell, does not allude to the assassination two days earlier or to the funeral the day before or to the speech made by Mayor La Guardia on the occasion of his anointment as Winchell's successor by Franklin Roosevelt in a New York synagogue. He does not have to. That La Guardia is, like Winchell before him, no more than a stalking horse for FDR in his dictatorial quest for an unprecedented third presidential term, and that those behind the "vicious La Guardia libel of our president" are the very same people who would have forced America to go to war in 1940, has already been colorfully explained to the nation by Vice President Wheeler in an impromptu Washington speech before the American Legion convention the previous evening.

All that the president says to the crowd is "Our country is at peace. Our people are at work. Our children are at school. I flew down here to remind you of that. Now I'm going back to Washington so as to keep things that way." An innocuous enough string of sentences, but to these tens of thousands of Kentuckians who've been the subject of national interest for two full days it is as though he has announced the end of all hardship on earth. Pandemonium once again, while the president, as laconic as ever and bidding farewell with just a single wave, squeezes his lanky frame back into the plane's cockpit, and from the airstrip a smiling mechanic signals with his wrench that everything's checked out and ready to go. The engine turns, the Lone Eagle waves a final goodbye, and with a rush and a roar the *Spirit of St. Louis* lifts free of Daniel Boone's gorgeous wilderness state, inch by inch, foot by foot, until at last (like the barnstorming, skydiving, wing-walking stunt pilot he'd been as a kid, flying low over the farming towns of the West—and to the delight of the delirious crowd) Lindy clears by no more than a hairsbreadth the telephone wires strung from the poles along Route 58. Rising steadily into the stream of a warm, gentle tailwind, the most famous small plane in aviation history—the modern-day counterpart of Columbus's *Santa María* and the Pilgrims' *Mayflower*— disappears eastward, never to be seen again.

*

Thursday, October 8, 1942

Ground searches of the regular flight path between Louisville and Washington yield no evidence of wreckage despite the perfect fall weather that makes it possible for local search parties to penetrate deep into the rugged mountains of West Virginia and to range over the harvested farmlands of Maryland and for state authorities to dispatch police launches up and down the Maryland and Delaware coastlines throughout the daylight hours. In the afternoon the Army, Coast Guard, and Navy join the search, along with hundreds of men and boys in every county from every state east of the Mississippi who have volunteered to assist the National Guard units called out by the state governors. Yet by dinnertime in Washington there is still no reported sighting of the plane or its wreckage, and so at eight P.M. the cabinet is summoned to an emergency meeting at the vice president's home. There Burton K. Wheeler announces that, after consulting with the First Lady and the majority leaders of the House and the Senate and the chief justice of the Supreme Court, he has deemed it in the country's best interest to assume the duties of acting president in accordance with Article II, Section 1 of the U.S. Constitution.

In dozens of newspapers, the evening headline, printed in the boldest, blackest type seen on America's front pages since the stock market crash of 1929 (and intended to shame Fiorello La Guardia), somberly reads: WHERE IS LINDBERGH?

Friday, October 9, 1942

By the time Americans awaken to begin their day, martial law has been imposed throughout the continental United States and in the territories and possessions. At noon Acting President Wheeler travels under military guard to the Capitol, where he announces to an emergency closed-door session of Congress that the FBI has received information establishing that the president has been kidnapped and is being held by parties unknown at a location somewhere in North America. The acting president assures the Congress that all steps are being taken to secure the president's release and to bring the perpetrators of the crime to justice. In the meantime the country's borders with Canada and Mexico have been sealed, airports and seaports have been shut down, and law and order, says the acting president, is to be maintained in the District of Columbia by the U.S. armed forces and elsewhere by the National Guard in cooperation with the FBI and local police authorities.

AGAIN!

So reads the one-word headline carried on every Hearst paper in the country and printed above pictures of the little Lindbergh baby, last photographed alive in 1932, only days before his kidnapping at the age of twenty months.

Saturday, October 10, 1942
    German state radio announces that the kidnapping of Charles A. Lindbergh, thirty-third president of the United States and signatory to America's historic Iceland Understanding with the Third Reich, has been discovered to have been perpetrated by a conspiracy of "Jewish interests." Top-secret Wehrmacht intelligence data are cited to corroborate initial reports from the Ministry of State that the plot was masterminded by the warmonger Roosevelt—in collusion with his Jewish Treasury secretary, Morgenthau, his Jewish Supreme Court justice, Frankfurter, and the Jewish investment banker Baruch—and that it is being financed by the international Jewish usurers Warburg and Rothschild and carried out under the command of Roosevelt's mongrel henchman, the half-Jew gangster La Guardia, mayor of Jewish New York City, along with the powerful Jewish governor of New York State, the financier Lehman, in order to return Roosevelt to the White House and launch an all-out Jewish war against the non-Jewish world. The intelligence data, which have been turned over to the FBI by the German embassy in Washington, allege that the assassination of Walter Winchell was planned and executed by the same cabal of Roosevelt Jews—and responsibility for the crime predictably attributed by them to Americans of German descent—so as to foster the vicious "Where is Lindbergh?" campaign, which in turn moved the president to take to the air and fly to the scene of the assassination to reassure the citizens of Louisville, Kentucky, who were justifiably fearful of organized Jewish retaliation. But there—according to the Wehrmacht reports—as the president addressed the crowd, an airport mechanic

bribed by the Jewish conspiracy (who has himself vanished and is believed to have been murdered by order of La Guardia) rendered the aircraft's radio inoperative. No sooner had the president taken off for Washington than he was unable to make contact with the ground or with other aircraft and had no choice but to capitulate when the *Spirit of St. Louis* was corralled by high-flying British fighter planes, which forced him to deviate from his course and to land, some hours later, at an airstrip secretly maintained by international Jewish interests across the Canadian border from Lehman's state of New York.

In America, the German announcement prompts Mayor La Guardia to tell City Hall reporters, "Any American who can believe that lollapalooza of a Nazi lie has sunk to the lowest possible level." Nonetheless, both the mayor and the governor are said by informed sources to have been interviewed at length by agents of the FBI, and Secretary of the Interior Ford is demanding that Mackenzie King, prime minister of Canada, conduct an intensive search on Canadian soil for President Lindbergh and his captors. Acting President Wheeler is reported to be examining the German documentation with White House aides but will make no comment about the allegations until the search for the president's plane has been completed. Navy destroyers along with Coast Guard PT boats are now looking for signs of an air crash as far north as Cape May, New Jersey, and as far south as Cape Hatteras, North Carolina, while ground units of the Army, Marine Corps, and National Guard continue to search in twenty states for clues to the missing plane's whereabouts.

The National Guard units enforcing the nationwide curfew report no incidents of violence prompted by the president's disappearance. Under martial law, America remains calm, though the Grand Wizard of the Ku Klux Klan and the leader of the American Nazi Party have jointly called upon the acting president "to implement extreme measures to protect America from a Jewish coup d'état."

Meanwhile a committee of American Jewish clergymen led by Rabbi Stephen Wise of New York telegrams the First Lady expressing their deepest sympathy in her family's hour of need. Rabbi Lionel Bengelsdorf is seen entering the White House in the early evening, reportedly there at Mrs. Lindbergh's request to offer spiritual guidance to the family during what is now the third day of their vigil. The White House invitation to Rabbi Bengelsdorf is widely interpreted to indicate the First Lady's refusal to accept that "Jewish interests" have had anything to do with her husband's disappearance.

Sunday, October 11, 1942

At church services around the country, prayers are offered in behalf of the Lindbergh family. The three major radio networks cancel regularly scheduled programs to broadcast the services conducted at Washington's National Cathedral, where the First Lady and her children are in attendance, and for the remainder of the day and into the evening, programming is devoted exclusively to inspirational music. At eight P.M. Acting President Wheeler addresses the nation, assuring his fellow Americans that he has no plans to abandon the search. He reports that at the invitation of the Canadian prime minister representatives from American law enforcement agencies will assist the Royal Canadian Mounted Police in scouring the eastern half of the U.S.-Canada border and the southernmost counties of the easterly Canadian provinces.

Having emerged as official spokesman for the First Lady, Rabbi Lionel Bengelsdorf tells a large group of reporters waiting on the White House portico that Mrs. Lindbergh urges the American people to ignore speculation emanating from any foreign government concerning the circumstances of her husband's disappearance. She would remind the public, the rabbi says, that in 1926, as an airmail pilot on the St. Louis–Chicago run, the president twice survived, without injury, crashes that demolished his aircraft, and that as of the moment it is the First Lady's belief that the president will once again be found to have survived should there have been another crash. The First Lady remains unconvinced, says the rabbi, by the evidence of a kidnapping that has been presented to her by the acting president. When Rabbi Bengelsdorf is asked why Mrs. Lindbergh cannot speak for herself and why the press is being prevented from questioning her directly, he replies, "Bear in mind that this is not the first time in her thirty-six years that Mrs. Lindbergh has been required to deal with inquiries from the press while enduring the gravest of family crises. I would think that Americans are altogether willing to accept whatever arrangement the First Lady decides will best protect her and her children's privacy for however long the search continues." When he is asked if there is any truth to rumors that Mrs. Lindbergh is too distraught to make her own decisions and that it is Lionel Bengelsdorf who is reaching her decisions for her, the rabbi replies, "Anyone who observed the demeanor of the First Lady at the cathedral this morning is able to see for himself that she is wholly competent intellectually, in complete possession of all her faculties, and that, despite the magnitude of the situation, neither her reason nor her judgment has been in any way impaired."

Despite the rabbi's assurances, stories go out over the wire services reporting on suspicions voiced by a "highly placed government official"—believed to be Secretary Ford—that the First Lady has become the captive of "Rabbi Rasputin," the Jewish spokesman considered comparable in his influence over the president's wife to the lunatic Siberian peasant monk who insidiously controlled the minds of the czar and czarina of Russia and all but ruled the imperial palace in the days leading up to the Russian Revolution and whose mad reign ended only when he was murdered by a conspiracy of patriotic Russian aristocrats.

Monday, October 12, 1942

The London morning papers report that British intelligence has forwarded to the FBI German coded communications proving beyond a doubt that President Lindbergh is alive and in Berlin. British intelligence ascertains that on October 7, in keeping with a long-standing plan conceived by Air Marshal Hermann Göring, the president of the United States succeeded in ditching the *Spirit of St. Louis* at predetermined coordinates in the Atlantic approximately three hundred miles east of Washington. There he rendezvoused with a waiting German U-boat whose crew transferred him to a German naval vessel waiting off the coast of Portugal to take him to Italian-occupied Cotor in Montenegro, on the Adriatic Sea. The wreckage of the president's plane was commandeered and taken on board by a German military freighter, dismantled, crated, and transported to a Gestapo warehouse in Bremen. The president himself was flown from a Cotor airstrip to Germany in a camouflaged Luftwaffe plane, accompanied by Air Marshal Göring, and upon his arrival at a Luftwaffe airbase was driven to Hitler's Berchtesgaden hideaway to confer with the Führer.

Serbian resistance groups in Yugoslavia confirm the British intelligence reports on the basis of information supplied by sources within the German-instituted Belgrade government of General Milan Nedich, whose interior ministry directed the naval operation at the port of Cotor.

In New York, Mayor La Guardia tells reporters, "If it is true that our president has voluntarily fled to Nazi Germany, if it is true that, since his taking the oath of office, he has been working from the White House as a Nazi agent, if it is true that our domestic and foreign policies have been dictated to the president by the Nazi regime that today tyrannizes the entire European continent, then I lack the words to describe a treason whose wickedness is without equal in human history."

Despite the imposition of martial law and a nationwide curfew, and despite the presence of heavily armed National Guard troops patrolling the streets of every major American city, anti-Semitic riots begin just after sundown in Alabama, Illinois, Indiana, Iowa, Kentucky, Missouri, Ohio, South Carolina, Tennessee, North Carolina, and Virginia, and continue throughout the night and into the early morning. Not until approximately eight A.M. are federal troops—dispatched by Acting President Wheeler to support the National Guard units—able to quell these disturbances and to bring under control the worst of the fires the rioters have set. By then 122 American citizens have lost their lives.

Tuesday, October 13, 1942

In a noontime radio address, Acting President Wheeler places responsibility for the riots on "the British government and their warmongering American supporters."

"Having falsely disseminated the vilest charges that could possibly be leveled against a patriot of the stature of Charles A. Lindbergh, just what did these people expect from a nation already grieving over the disappearance of a beloved leader? To advance their own economic and racial interests," says the acting president, "these people choose to try to the limit the conscience of a heartsick nation, and just what do they then expect will occur? I can report that order has been restored to our ravaged cities throughout the South and the Midwest, but at what cost to the equanimity of our nation?"

A statement from the president's wife is subsequently delivered by Rabbi Lionel Bengelsdorf. Once again the First Lady counsels her countrymen to ignore all unverifiable hypotheses about her husband's disappearance emanating from foreign capitals, and she requests of the U.S. government the immediate termination of the weeklong search for her husband's plane. The First Lady wishes the country to recall the tragic plight of Amelia Earhart, the greatest of woman aviators, who, following the lead of President Lindbergh, made her heralded solo flight across the Atlantic in 1932, only to disappear without a trace in 1937 while attempting a solo flight across the Pacific. "As an experienced aviator in her own right," Rabbi Bengelsdorf tells the press, "the First Lady has concluded that something very like what happened to Amelia Earhart appears now to have overtaken the president. Life is not without risk, and aviation, of course, is not without risk, particularly for those like Amelia Earhart and Charles A. Lindbergh, whose daring and courage as solo aviators launched the aeronautical age in which we now live."

Requests by reporters to meet with the First Lady are once again politely declined by her official spokesman, prompting Secretary Ford to demand the arrest of Rabbi Rasputin.

Wednesday, October 14, 1942

In the early evening Mayor La Guardia calls a press conference to point in particular to three manifestations of the "sheer derangement that is threatening the nation's sanity."

First, a front-page *Chicago Tribune* article, datelined Berlin, reports that the twelve-year-old son of President and Mrs. Lindbergh—the child believed to have been kidnapped and murdered in New Jersey in 1932—has been reunited with his father at Berchtesgaden after having been rescued by the Nazis from a dungeon in Kraków, Poland, where he had been held prisoner in the city's Jewish ghetto ever since his disappearance and where, each year, blood was drawn from the captive boy to be used in the ritual preparation of the community's Passover matzohs.

Second, House Republicans introduce a bill calling for a declaration of war against the Dominion of Canada should Prime Minister King fail to reveal the whereabouts of America's missing president within forty-eight hours.

Third, law enforcement agencies in the South and the Midwest report that the "so-called anti-Semitic riots" of October 12 were instigated by "local Jewish elements" working as part of "a far-reaching Jewish conspiracy intent on undermining the country's morale." Of the 122 killed in the rioting, 97 have already been identified as "Jewish provocateurs" seeking to deflect suspicion from the very group responsible for the disorder and plotting to take control of the federal government.

Mayor La Guardia says, "There's a plot afoot all right, and I'll gladly name the forces propelling it—hysteria, ignorance, malice, stupidity, hatred, and fear. What a repugnant spectacle our country has become! Falsehood, cruelty, and madness everywhere, and brute force in the wings waiting to finish us off. Now we read in the *Chicago Tribune* that all these years clever Jewish bakers have been using the blood of the kidnapped Lindbergh child for making Passover matzohs in Poland—a story just as nutty today as when it was first concocted by anti-Semitic maniacs five hundred years ago. How it must please the Führer to be poisoning our country with this sinister nonsense. Jewish interests. Jewish elements. Jewish usurers. Jewish retaliation. Jewish conspiracies. A Jewish war against the world. To have enslaved America with this hocus-pocus! To have captured the mind of the world's greatest nation without uttering a single word of truth! Oh, the pleasure we must be affording the most malevolent man on earth!"

Thursday, October 15, 1942
Just before dawn Rabbi Lionel Bengelsdorf is taken into custody by the FBI under suspicion of being "among the ringleaders of the Jewish conspiratorial plot against America." At the same time the First Lady, said to be suffering from "extreme nervous exhaustion," is transferred by ambulance from the White House to Walter Reed Army Hospital. Others arrested in the early-morning roundup include Governor Lehman, Bernard Baruch, Justice Frankfurter, Frankfurter protégé and Roosevelt administrator David Lilienthal, New Deal

advisers Adolf Berle and Sam Rosenman, labor leaders David Dubinsky and Sidney Hillman, economist Isador Lubin, leftist journalists I. F. Stone and James Wechsler, and socialist Louis Waldman. More arrests are said to be imminent, but the FBI has not disclosed whether the charge of conspiring to kidnap the president will be brought against any or all of the suspects.

Tank and infantry units of the U.S. Army enter New York to assist the National Guard in putting down sporadic antigovernment street violence. In Chicago, Philadelphia, and Boston attempts to mount protest demonstrations against the FBI— demonstrations in violation of martial law—result only in minor injuries, though arrests numbering in the hundreds are reported by police.

In Congress, leading Republicans praise the FBI for thwarting the conspirators' plot. In New York, Mayor La Guardia is joined at a press conference by Eleanor Roosevelt and Roger Baldwin of the ACLU. They demand the immediate release of Governor Lehman along with his alleged co-conspirators. La Guardia is subsequently arrested at the mayor's mansion.

To address an emergency protest rally convened by a New York citizens' committee, former president Roosevelt travels from his home at Hyde Park to New York; "for his own protection" he is promptly taken into custody by the police. The U.S. Army shuts down all newspaper offices and radio stations in New York, where the after-dark martial-law curfew will be enforced round the clock until further notice. Tanks close off all bridges and tunnels into the city.

In Buffalo the mayor announces his intention to distribute gas masks to the city's citizens, and the mayor of nearby Rochester initiates a bomb shelter program "to protect our residents in the event of a surprise Canadian attack." An exchange of small-arms fire is reported by the Canadian Broadcasting Corporation on the border between Maine and the province of New Brunswick, not far from Roosevelt's summer home on Campobello Island in the Bay of Fundy. From London, Prime Minister Churchill warns of an imminent German invasion of Mexico, purportedly to protect American's southern flank while the United States sets about to wrest control of Canada from the British. "It is no longer a matter," says Churchill, "of the great American democracy taking military action to save us. The time has come for American citizens to take civil action to save themselves. There are not two isolated historical dramas, the American and the British, and there never were. There is only one ordeal, and now as in the past we face it in common."

Friday, October 16, 1942

Beginning at nine A.M., a radio transmitter secreted somewhere in the nation's capital broadcasts the voice of the First Lady, who, with the assistance of Lindbergh loyalists inside the Secret Service, has managed to escape from Walter Reed, where—alleged by authorities to be a mental patient in the care of Army psychiatrists—she has been straitjacketed and held prisoner for nearly twenty-four hours. The tone is appealingly gentle, the words uttered without a trace of harshness or righteous contempt—altogether the evenly paced voice of someone entirely respectable who is educated to face down sorrow and disappointment without ever losing her self-restraint. She is no cyclone, yet the undertaking is extraordinary and she shows no fear.

"My fellow Americans, unlawfulness on the part of America's law enforcement agencies cannot and will not be allowed to prevail. In my husband's name, I ask all National Guard units to disarm and disband and for our guardsmen to return to civilian life. I ask all members of the United States armed forces to leave our cities and to regroup at their home bases under the command of their authorized senior officers. I ask the FBI to release all of those arrested on charges of conspiring to harm my husband and to restore immediately their full rights as citizens. I ask law enforcement authorities throughout the nation to do the same with those who have been detained in local and state jails. There is not a shred of evidence that a single detainee is in any way responsible for whatever befell my husband and his plane on or after Wednesday, October 7, 1942. I ask the New York City police to vacate the illegally occupied premises of government-sequestered newspapers, magazines, and radio stations and that these facilities resume their normal activities as guaranteed under the First Amendment to the Constitution. I ask the Congress of the United States to initiate proceedings to remove from office the current acting president of the United States and to appoint a new president in accordance with the Presidential Succession Act of 1886, which designates the secretary of state as next in line for the presidency should the vice presidency be vacant. The Succession Act of 1886 also states that, under the circumstances described, Congress shall decide whether to call a special presidential election, and so I ask the Congress to do just that and to authorize a presidential election that will coincide with the congressional election scheduled for the first Tuesday after the first Monday of November."

Her morning broadcast is repeated by the First Lady every half hour until, at noon, she announces that, in defiance of the acting president—whom she charges by name with having ordered her illegal abduction and confinement—she is returning to take up residence with her children at the White House. Deliberately appropriating for her peroration echoes of American democracy's most revered text, she concludes, "I will not yield to or be intimidated by the illegal representatives of a seditious administration, and I ask no more of the American people than that they follow my example and refuse to accept or support government conduct that is indefensible. The history of the present administration is a history of repeated injuries and usurpations, all having in direct object the establishment of an absolute tyranny over these states. This government has been deaf to the voice of justice and has extended over us an unwarrantable jurisdiction. Consequently, in defense of those same inalienable rights claimed in July of 1776 by Jefferson of Virginia and Franklin of Pennsylvania and Adams of Massachusetts Bay, and by the authority of the same good people of these United States, and appealing to the same supreme judge of the world for the rectitude of our intentions, I, Anne Morrow Lindbergh, a native of the state of New Jersey, a resident of the District of Columbia, and the spouse of the thirty-third president of the United States, declare that injurious history of usurpation to be ended. Our enemies' plot has failed, liberty and justice are restored, and those who have violated the Constitution of the United States shall now be addressed by the judicial branch of government, in strict keeping with the law of the land."

"Our Lady of the White House"—as Harold Ickes grudgingly

christens Mrs. Lindbergh—returns to the presidential living quarters early that evening, and from there, marshaling the power of her mystique as sorrowing mother of the martyred infant and resolute widow of the vanished god, engineers the speedy dismantling by Congress and the courts of the unconstitutional Wheeler administration, whose criminality, in a mere eight days in office, has far exceeded that of Warren Harding's Republican administration twenty years earlier.

The restoration of orderly democratic procedures initiated by Mrs. Lindbergh culminates two and a half weeks later, on Tuesday, November 3, 1942, in a sweep by the Democrats of the House and the Senate and the landslide victory of Franklin Delano Roosevelt for a third presidential term.

The next month—following the devastating surprise attack on Pearl Harbor by the Japanese and, four days later, the declaration of war on the United States by Germany and Italy—America enters the global conflict that had begun in Europe some three years earlier with the German invasion of Poland and had since expanded to encompass two-thirds of the world's population. Disgraced by their collusion with the acting president and demoralized by their colossal electoral defeat, the few Republicans remaining in Congress pledge their support to the Democratic president and his fight to the finish against the Axis powers. The House and the Senate approve America's going to war without a dissenting vote in either chamber, and the day following his inauguration, President Roosevelt issues Proclamation No. 2568, "Granting a Pardon to Burton Wheeler." In part it reads:

> As a result of certain acts occurring before his removal from the Office of Acting President, Burton K. Wheeler has become liable to possible indictment and trial for offenses against the United States. To spare the country the ordeal of such a criminal prosecution against a former Acting President of the United States and to protect against the disruptive distraction of such a spectacle during a time of war, I, Franklin Delano Roosevelt, President of the United States, pursuant to the pardon power conferred upon me by Article II, Section 2 of the Constitution, have granted and by these presents do grant a full, free, and absolute pardon unto Burton Wheeler for all offenses against the United States which he, Burton Wheeler, has committed or

may have committed or taken part in during the period from October 8, 1942, through October 16, 1942.

As everyone knows, President Lindbergh was not found or heard from again, though stories circulated throughout the war and for a decade afterward, along with the rumors about other prominent missing persons of that turbulent era, like Martin Bormann, Hitler's private secretary, who was thought to have eluded the Allied armies by escaping to Juan Perón's Argentina —but who more likely perished during the last days of Nazi Berlin—and Raoul Wallenberg, the Swedish diplomat whose distribution of Swedish passports saved some twenty thousand Hungarian Jews from extermination by the Nazis, although he himself disappeared, probably into a Soviet jail, when the Russians occupied Budapest in 1945. Among the dwindling number of Lindbergh conspiracy scholars, reports on clues and sightings have continued to appear in intermittently published newsletters devoted to speculation on the unexplained fate of America's thirty-third president.

The most elaborate story, the most unbelievable story— though not necessarily the least convincing—was first made known to our family by Aunt Evelyn after Rabbi Bengelsdorf's arrest, her source none other than Anne Morrow Lindbergh, who allegedly confided the details to the rabbi just days before she was removed from the White House against her will and held prisoner in the psychiatric wing of Walter Reed.

Mrs. Lindbergh, reported Rabbi Bengelsdorf, traced everything to the 1932 kidnapping of her infant son Charles, secretly plotted and financed, she maintained, by the Nazi Party shortly before Hitler came to power. According to the rabbi's recapitulation of the First Lady's story, the baby had been passed on for safekeeping by Bruno Hauptmann to a friend living near him in the Bronx—a fellow German immigrant who in actuality was a Nazi espionage agent—and only hours after having been lifted from the Hopewell, New Jersey, crib and carried down the makeshift ladder in Hauptmann's arms, Charles Jr. had already been smuggled out of the country and was en route to Germany. The corpse found and identified as the Lindbergh baby ten weeks later was another child, selected by the Nazis to be murdered because of its resemblance to the

Lindbergh baby and then, when the body was already decomposing, planted in the woods near the Lindbergh home to ensure Hauptmann's conviction and execution and to keep secret the true circumstances of the kidnapping from everyone but the Lindberghs themselves. Through a Nazi spy stationed as a foreign newspaper correspondent in New York, the couple had been informed early on of Charles's arrival, healthy and unharmed, on German soil and assured that the best of care would be given him by a specially selected team of Nazi doctors, nurses, teachers, and military personnel—care merited by his status as firstborn son of the world's greatest aviator—provided that the Lindberghs cooperated fully with Berlin.

As a result of this threat, for the next ten years the lot of the Lindberghs and their kidnapped child—and, gradually, the destiny of the United States of America—was determined by Adolf Hitler. Through the skill and efficiency of his agents in New York and Washington—and in London and Paris after the celebrated couple, complying with orders, "fled" to live as expatriates in Europe, where Lindbergh began regularly to visit Nazi Germany and extol the achievements of its military machine—the Nazis set about to exploit Lindbergh's fame in behalf of the Third Reich and at the expense of America, dictating where the couple would reside, whom they would befriend, and, above all, what opinions they would espouse in their public utterances and published writings. In 1938, as a reward for Lindbergh's graciously accepting a prestigious medal from Hermann Göring at a Berlin dinner in the aviator's honor, and after numerous pleading letters that were secretly channeled from Anne Morrow Lindbergh to the Führer himself, the Lindberghs were at last allowed to visit their child, by then a handsome fair-haired boy of almost eight who, from the day he'd arrived in Germany, had been raised as a model Hitler youth. The German-speaking cadet did not understand, nor was he told, that the famous Americans to whom he and his classmates were introduced following parade exercises at their elite military academy were his mother and father, nor were the Lindberghs permitted to speak to him or to be photographed with him. The visit came at just the moment when Anne Morrow Lindbergh had concluded that the Nazis' kidnapping story was an unspeakably cruel hoax and that the time was long overdue for the Lindberghs to free themselves from their bondage to Adolf Hitler. Instead, after seeing Charles alive for the first time since his disappearance in 1932, the Lindberghs left Germany irreversibly in thrall to their country's worst enemy.

They were ordered to end their expatriation and return to America, where Colonel Lindbergh was to take up the cause of America First. Speeches were provided, written in English, denouncing the British, Roosevelt, and the Jews and supporting America's neutrality in the European war; detailed instructions specified where and when speeches were to be delivered, even the type of apparel to be donned for each public appearance. Every political stratagem originating in Berlin Lindbergh enacted with the same meticulous perfectionism that distinguished his aeronautical pursuits, right down to the night that he arrived in aviator attire at the Republican Convention and accepted the nomination for the presidency with words written for the occasion by Nazi propaganda minister Joseph Goebbels. The Nazis plotted every maneuver of the election campaign that followed, and once Lindbergh had defeated FDR, it was Hitler himself who took charge, proceeding to prepare —in weekly meetings with Göring, his designated successor and director of the German economy, and Heinrich Himmler, overlord of Germany's internal affairs and chief of the Gestapo, the police agency charged with Charles Lindbergh Jr.'s custody —a foreign policy for the United States that would best serve Germany's wartime objectives and his grand imperial design.

Soon Himmler began to interfere directly in U.S. domestic affairs by bringing pressure on President Lindbergh—humorously belittled in the Gestapo chief's memos as "our American Gauleiter"—to institute repressive measures against the four and a half million American Jews, and it was here, according to Mrs. Lindbergh, that the president undertook, if only passively at the start, to assert his resistance. To begin with, he ordered the establishment of the Office of American Absorption, in his judgment an agency inconsequential enough to leave the Jews essentially unharmed while seemingly meeting—with token programs like Just Folks and Homestead 42—Himmler's directive "to inaugurate in America a systematic process of marginalization that will lead in the foreseeable future to the confiscation of all Jewish wealth and the total disappearance of the Jewish population, their appurtenances, and their property."

Heinrich Himmler was hardly one to be misled by such a transparent deception or to bother to disguise his disappointment when Lindbergh dared to justify himself—through von Ribbentrop, whom Himmler dispatched to Washington, supposedly on a ceremonial state visit, to assist the president in formulating more stringent anti-Jewish measures—by explaining to the supreme commandant of Hitler's concentration camps that guarantees embedded in the U.S. Constitution, combined with long-standing American democratic traditions, made it impossible for a final solution to the Jewish problem to be executed in America as rapidly or efficiently as on a continent where there was a thousand-year history of anti-Semitism deeply rooted in the common people and where Nazi rule was absolute. During the state dinner given in von Ribbentrop's honor, the president was taken aside by his esteemed guest and handed a cablegram, decoded moments earlier at the German embassy, that constituted in its entirety Himmler's reply. "Think of the child," the cablegram read, "before you again respond with such poppycock. Think of brave young Charles, an outstanding German military cadet who already at the age of twelve knows better than his celebrated father the value assigned by our Führer to constitutional guarantees and democratic traditions, especially where the rights of parasites are concerned."

The dressing-down by Himmler of "the Lone Eagle with the chicken heart" (as Lindbergh was described in Himmler's internal memo) marked the beginning of Lindbergh's repudiation as a minion useful to the Third Reich. By defeating Roosevelt and the anti-Nazi interventionists in Roosevelt's party he had provided the German army with additional time to quell the continuing and unexpected resistance from the Soviet Union without Germany's running the risk of having simultaneously to confront the industrial and military might of the United States. Even more imporant, Lindbergh's presidency furnished German industry and the German scientific establishment— already secretly developing a bomb of unparalleled explosive force powered by atomic fission, as well as a rocket engine capable of conveying this weapon across the Atlantic—with a further two years in which to complete preparation for the apocalyptic struggle with the United States whose outcome, as envisioned by Hitler, would determine the course of Western civilization and the progress of mankind for the next millennium. Had Himmler found in Lindbergh the visionary Jew-hater the German high command had been led to expect from intelligence reports, rather than what Himmler contemptuously dubbed "a dinner-party anti-Semite," perhaps the president would have been permitted to complete his term in office and to serve a second four years before retiring and ceding the government to Henry Ford, whom Hitler had already settled on as Lindbergh's successor, despite Ford's advanced age. Had Himmler been able to rely on an American president of unimpeachable American credentials to implement the final solution to America's Jewish problem, it would, of course, have been preferable to the employment at a later date of German resources and personnel to fulfill that mission in North America, and Lindbergh's plane would not have had to disappear from the skies, as was deemed necessary by Berlin, on Wednesday, October 7, 1942—nor would Acting President Wheeler have assumed power the following evening and, to the astonished delight of those who'd considered him till then nothing more than a buffoon, proved himself a genuine leader in a matter of days by spontaneously implementing the very measures that von Ribbentrop had proposed to Lindbergh and that, as Himmler believed, the American hero had failed to carry out because of the puerile moral objections of his wife.

Within an hour of Lindbergh's disappearance, Mrs. Lindbergh had been informed by the German embassy that responsibility for her child's well-being was now hers alone and that, should she do anything other than vacate the White House and withdraw in silence from public life, Charles Jr. would be removed from his military academy and dispatched to the Russian front for the November offensive on Stalingrad and remain on duty there as the Third Reich's youngest combat infantryman until he valiantly expired on the field of battle for the greater glory of the German people.

This is the story whose gist Aunt Evelyn conveyed to my mother when she appeared at our house in the hours after Rabbi Bengelsdorf was taken in handcuffs from their Washington hotel by agents of the FBI. More fully elaborated, it is the story told in *My Life Under Lindbergh*, the 550-page apologia published as an insider's diary just after the war by Rabbi Bengelsdorf and dismissed then in a press statement by a spokesman for the Lindbergh family as "a reprehensible calumny with no basis in fact, motivated by vengeance and greed, sustained by egomaniacal delusion, invented for the sake of crass commercial exploitation, and one that Mrs. Lindbergh will not dignify with a further response." When my mother first heard the story it seemed to her conclusive evidence that the shock of witnessing Rabbi Bengelsdorf's arrest had temporarily caused her sister to lose her mind.

The day after Aunt Evelyn's surprise visit was Friday, October 16, 1942, when Mrs. Lindbergh, before returning to the White House, went on the air from a secret Washington location and, based solely on her authority as "spouse of the thirty-third president of the United States," pronounced the "injurious history of usurpation" implemented by the administration of the acting president "to be ended." Whether any harm befell her kidnapped child as a consequence of the First Lady's bravery, whether Charles Jr. had ever even survived his infancy to suffer the dreadful fate that Himmler had promised, let alone to endure the childhood of a privileged ward and treasured hostage of the German state, whether Himmler, Göring, and Hitler had anything of importance to do with fostering Lindbergh's rise to political eminence as an America Firster or shaping U.S. policy during the twenty-two-month Lindbergh presidency or implementing Lindbergh's mysterious disappearance—have been matters of controversy for over half a century, though by now a far less impassioned and widespread controversy than when, for some thirty-odd weeks in 1946 (and despite its oft-quoted characterization by Westbrook Pegler, the dean of America's Roosevelt-hating right-wing journalists, as "the crackpot diary of a certifiable mythomaniac"), *My Life Under Lindbergh* remained at the top of the American bestseller lists along with two personal biographies of FDR, who had died in office the previous year, only weeks before the unconditional surrender of Nazi Germany to the Allies marked the end of World War Two in Europe.

9

Perpetual Fear

THE CALL from Seldon came when my mother, Sandy, and I were already in bed. This was Monday, the twelfth of October, and at dinnertime we had heard the reports on the radio of the rioting that had broken out in the Midwest and the South following the announcement by British intelligence that President Lindbergh had deliberately ditched his plane three hundred miles out to sea and from there had been whisked by the navy and air corps of Nazi Germany to a secret rendezvous with Hitler. Not until the next day were the morning papers able to furnish details of the riots sparked by this dispatch, though barely minutes after the news had reached us at our kitchen table, my mother had guessed correctly whom the rioters had targeted and why. It was by then three days since the border to Canada had been closed, and even to me, who found leaving America an unbearable prospect, it was clear that my father's refusal to listen to my mother and get us out of the country months before was the gravest mistake he'd ever made. He was now back working nights at the market, my mother went into the streets every day to shop for groceries—quixotically, she had attended a meeting at school one afternoon for the prospective poll watchers in the November election—Sandy and I went off to school each morning with our friends, but nonetheless, by the beginning of the second week of Acting President Wheeler's administration, the fear was everywhere, and this despite Mrs. Lindbergh's advising Americans to dismiss the reports emanating from foreign countries about the president's whereabouts, despite the ascendancy as a newsworthy figure of Rabbi Bengelsdorf, a member now of our family, an uncle by marriage who'd even eaten dinner once in our house but who couldn't do a thing to help us and wouldn't if he could because of the contempt he and my father harbored each for the other. The fear was everywhere, the *look* was everywhere, in the eyes of our protectors especially, the look that comes in the split second after you have locked the door and realize you don't have the key. We had never before observed the adults all helplessly thinking the same thoughts. The strongest among them did their best to be calm and brave and to sound realistic when they told us that our worries would soon be over and the regular round of life restored, but when they turned on the news they were devastated by the speed with which everything dreadful was happening.

Then, on the evening of the twelfth—while each of us lay in bed unable to sleep—the phone rang: Seldon calling collect from Kentucky. It was ten at night and his mother still wasn't home, and since he knew our number by heart (and didn't know whom else to call), he cranked the phone, got the operator, and, in a rush, trying to articulate all the necessary words before the power of speech deserted him, said to her, "Collect, please. Newark, New Jersey. 81 Summit Avenue. Waverley 3–4827. My name is Sheldon Wishnow. I want to speak person-to-person to Mr. or Mrs. Roth. Or Philip. Or Sandy. Anyone, operator. My mother's not home. I'm ten. I haven't eaten and she's not here. Operator, please—Waverley 3–4827! I'll talk to anybody!"

That morning Mrs. Wishnow had driven to Louisville, to the Metropolitan regional office, to report at the company's request to her district supervisor. Louisville was more than a hundred miles from Danville, and the roads were so bad most of the way that it was going to take practically all day just to get there and back. Why the district supervisor couldn't have written a letter or picked up the phone to tell her what he had to say nobody ever understood, nor was the man himself ever asked to explain. My father's guess was that the company intended to fire her that day—to have her turn in her ledger with its handwritten record of collections and then to send her on her way, unemployed after a mere six weeks on the job and seven hundred miles from home. She'd done no business to speak of in those first weeks out in the rural reaches of Boyle County, though not for lack of hard work—primarily it was because there wasn't the business there to do. In fact, every last one of the transfers made by the Metropolitan under the auspices of Homestead 42 were turning into catastrophes for the agents formerly from the Newark district. In the barely inhabited corners of those distant states to which they and their families had been relocated, none of them were ever going to be able to earn a quarter of the amount of commissions they were accustomed to making in metropolitan North Jersey—and so, if only for that reason, my father had been wonderfully prescient in quitting his job and going to work instead for Uncle Monty. He hadn't been quite so prescient about getting us over the Canadian border before it closed down and martial law was declared.

"If she was alive . . ." Seldon told my mother, after she'd accepted the charges and taken his call, "if she was alive . . ." In the beginning, because of his crying, that was all he was able to say, and even those four words were barely comprehensible.

"Seldon, that's enough of that. You're doing this to yourself. You're making yourself hysterical. Of course your mother's alive. She's just late getting home—that's all that has happened."

"But if she was alive she would *call*!"

"Seldon, what if she's only caught in traffic? What if something happened to the car and she's had to pull over to get it fixed? Didn't that happen before, when you were here in Newark? Remember that night when it was raining and she had a flat and you came upstairs to stay with us? It's probably nothing more than a flat tire, so please, dear, calm down. You must stop crying. Your mother is fine. It only upsets you to say what you're saying, and it is not true, so please, please, right now, just make an effort and try to calm down."

"But she's dead, Mrs. Roth! Just like my father! Now *both* my parents are dead!" And, of course, he was right. Seldon knew nothing about the riots way off in Louisville and little about what was going on in the rest of America. Since there was no room left in Mrs. Wishnow's life for anything other than the child and the job, there was never a newspaper to read in the Danville house, and when the two of them sat down to dinner in Danville they didn't have the news on the way we did in Newark. More than likely she was too exhausted in Danville to listen to it, by now too benumbed to register any misfortune other than her own.

But Seldon had it perfectly right: Mrs. Wishnow was dead, though no one would know until the following day, when the burnt-out car containing his mother's remains was found smoldering in a drainage ditch alongside a potato field in the flat country just south of Louisville. Apparently she had been beaten and robbed and the car set ablaze within the first minutes of the evening's violence, which had not been restricted to the downtown Louisville streets where there were Jewish-owned shops or to the residential streets where the handful of Louisville's Jewish citizens lived. The Klansmen knew that once the torches were lit and the crosses burning, the vermin were going to try to get out, and so they were ready for them, not only on the main road leading north to Ohio but along the narrow country roads heading south, which was where Mrs. Wishnow paid with her life for the slander of Lindbergh's good name, first by the late Walter Winchell and now by the Jewish-controlled propaganda machine of Prime Minister Churchill and King George VI.

My mother said, "Seldon, you must take something to eat. That will help calm you down. Go to the refrigerator and get something to eat."

"I ate the Fig Newtons. There's none left."

"Seldon, I'm talking about your eating a meal. Your mother will be home very soon, but meanwhile you can't sit there waiting for her to feed you—you have to feed yourself, and not on cookies. Put the phone down and go look in the refrigerator and then come back and tell me what's in there that you could eat."

"But it's long distance."

"Seldon, do as I say."

To Sandy and me, gathered closely around her in the back foyer, my mother said, "She's very late, and he hasn't eaten, and he's all alone, and she hasn't phoned, and the poor child is frantic and starving to death."

"Mrs. Roth?"

"Yes, Seldon."

"There's pot cheese. It's old, though. It doesn't look too good."

"What else is in there?"

"Beets. In a bowl. Leftovers. They're cold."

"And anything else?"

"I'll look again—just a minute."

This time when Seldon put down the phone, my mother said to Sandy, "How far from Danville are the Mawhinneys?"

"With the truck about twenty minutes."

"In my dresser," my mother said to my brother, "in the top, in my change purse—their number is there. It's on a piece of paper in my little brown change purse. Get it for me, please."

"Mrs. Roth?" Seldon said.

"Yes. I'm here."

"There's butter."

"That's all? Isn't there any milk? Isn't there juice?"

"But that's breakfast. That's not dinner."

"Are there Rice Krispies, Seldon? Are there Corn Flakes?"

"Sure," he said.

"Then get whichever cereal you like best."

"Rice Krispies."

"Get the Rice Krispies, take out the milk and the juice, and I want you to make yourself breakfast."

"Now?"

"Do as I say, please," she told him. "I want you to eat breakfast."

"Is Philip there?"

"He's here, but you cannot talk to him. You have to eat first. I'm going to call you back in half an hour, after you've eaten. It's ten after ten, Seldon."

"In Newark it's ten after ten?"

"In Newark and Danville both. It's exactly the same time in both places. I'm going to call you back at quarter to eleven," she told him.

"Can I talk to Philip then?"

"Yes, but I want you to sit down first with everything you need at the kitchen table. I want you to use a spoon and a fork and a napkin and a knife. Eat slowly. Use dishes. Use a bowl. Is there any bread?"

"It's stale. It's just a couple of slices."

"Do you have a toaster?"

"Sure. We brought it here in the car. Remember the morning when we all packed the car?"

"Listen to me, Seldon. Concentrate. Make yourself some toast, with the cereal. And use the butter. Butter it. And pour yourself a big glass of milk. I want you to eat a good breakfast, and when your mother comes in, I want you to tell her to call us immediately. She can call here collect. Tell her not to worry about the charges. It's important for us to know when she's home. But either way, in half an hour I'm calling you back, so don't you go anywhere."

"It's dark out. Where would I go?"

"Seldon, eat your breakfast."

"Okay."

"Goodbye," she said. "Goodbye, for now. I'll call you back at quarter to eleven. You stay where you are."

Next she phoned the Mawhinneys. My brother handed her the piece of paper with the number and she asked the operator to put through the call and when somebody answered at the other end, she said, "Is this Mrs. Mawhinney? This is Mrs. Roth. I'm Sandy Roth's mother. I'm calling you from Newark, New Jersey, Mrs. Mawhinney. I'm sorry if I woke you up, but we need you to help us with a little boy who's alone in Danville. What? Yes, of course, yes."

To us she said, "She's getting her husband."

"Oh, no," my brother moaned.

"Sanford, this is not the time for that. I don't like what I'm doing either. I realize I don't know these people. I realize they're not like us. I know farmers go to bed early and get up early and that they work very hard. But you tell me what else I should do. That little boy is going to go crazy if he's left alone any longer. He doesn't know where his mother is. Somebody has to be there. He's had too many shocks for someone his age already. He lost his father. Now his mother is missing. Can't you understand what this means?"

"Sure I can," said my brother indignantly. "Sure I understand."

"Good. Then you understand that somebody has to go to him. Somebody—" but then Mr. Mawhinney got on the phone, and my mother explained to him why she was calling, and he immediately agreed to do all she asked. When she hung up she said, "At least there's some decency left in this country. At least there's some decency *somewhere*."

"I told you," my brother whispered.

Never would she seem more remarkable to me than she did

that night, and not merely for the abandon with which she was accepting and making phone calls to and from Kentucky. There was more, much more. There was, to begin with, Alvin's assault on my father the week before. There was my father's explosive response. There was the wreckage of our living room. There was my father's broken teeth and broken ribs, the stitches in his face and the brace on his neck. There was the shootout on Chancellor Avenue. There was our certainty that it was a pogrom. There were the sirens all night long. There was the screaming and the shouting in the streets all night long. There was our hiding in the Cucuzzas' foyer, the loaded pistol in my father's lap, the loaded pistol in Mr. Cucuzza's fist—and that was just the week before. There was also the month before, the year before, and the year before that—all those blows, insults, and surprises intent on weakening and frightening the Jews that still hadn't managed to shatter my mother's strength. Before I heard her telling Seldon, from more than seven hundred miles away, to make himself something to eat and to sit down and eat it, before I heard her calling the Mawhinneys—churchgoing Gentiles whom she'd never laid eyes on—to enlist them in saving Seldon from going mad, before I heard her asking to speak to Mr. Mawhinney and then telling him that if something serious had happened to Mrs. Wishnow the Mawhinneys needn't worry they'd be stuck with Seldon, that my father was prepared to get in the car and drive to Kentucky to bring Seldon back to Newark (and promising Mr. Mawhinney this even while no one knew just how far the Wheelers and the Fords intended to allow the American mob to go), I hadn't understood anything of the story that was her life in those years. Till Seldon's frantic phone call from Kentucky, I'd never totted up the cost to my mother and father of the Lindbergh presidency—till that moment, I'd been unable to add that high.

When my mother phoned Seldon at quarter to eleven she explained the plan worked out with the Mawhinneys. He was to put his toothbrush, pajamas, underwear, and a pair of clean socks into a paper bag, and he was to get on a heavy sweater and his warm coat and his flannel cap, and he was to wait in the house for Mr. Mawhinney to come for him in his truck. Mr. Mawhinney was a very kind man, my mother told Seldon, a kind, generous man with a nice wife and four children whom Sandy knew from the summer he lived at the Mawhinney farm.

"Then she *is* dead!" Seldon screamed.

No, no, no, absolutely not—his mother would be coming to pick him up at the Mawhinneys' the next morning and to drive him from there to school. Mr. and Mrs. Mawhinney would arrange all that for him and he wasn't to worry about a thing. But meanwhile there was work to do: in his best hand-writing Seldon was to write a note for his mother and leave it on the kitchen table, a note telling her that he was going to be at the Mawhinneys' for the night and leaving the Mawhinneys' phone number for her. He was also to tell her in the note to call Mrs. Roth collect in Newark the moment that she got in. Then Seldon was to sit in the living room and wait there until he heard Mr. Mawhinney outside blowing the horn, then he was to turn off all the lights in the house . . .

She took him through each stage of his departure and then, at what financial expense I couldn't begin to calculate, she continued to stay on the line until he'd done what she'd directed him to do and had come back to the phone to tell her that he'd done it, and still she didn't hang up or stop reassuring him about everything until at last Seldon shouted, "It's him, Mrs. Roth! He's blowing the horn!" and my mother said, "Okay, good, but calmly now, Seldon, calmly—take your bag, turn out the lights, don't forget to lock the door on the way out, and tomorrow morning, bright and early, you're going to see your mother. Now, good luck, dear, and don't run, and— Seldon? Seldon, hang up the phone!" But this he neglected to do. In his hurry to flee as fast as he could that frightening, lonely, parentless house, he left the phone dangling, though it hardly mattered. The house could have burned to the ground and it wouldn't have mattered because Seldon was never to set foot inside it again.

On Sunday, October 18, he arrived back on Summit Avenue. My father, accompanied by Sandy, drove out to Kentucky to get him. The casket containing Mrs. Wishnow's remains followed after them by train. I knew that in her car she had been burned beyond recognition, yet I kept envisioning her inside the casket with her fists still clenched. And alternately envisioning myself locked in their bathroom with Mrs. Wishnow just outside telling me how to open the door. How patient she'd been! How like my own mother! And now she was inside a casket, and I was the one who had put her there.

That was all I could think on the night that my mother, like a combat officer, led Seldon to organize his dinner and to organize his departure and to get himself safely into the Mawhinneys' hands. I did it. That was all I could think then and all I can think now. I did this to Seldon and I did this to her. Rabbi Bengelsdorf had done what he had done, Aunt Evelyn had done what she had done, but I was the one who had started it off—this devastation had been done by me.

On Thursday, October 15—the day the Wheeler putsch reached the heights of illegality—our phone rang at quarter to six in the morning. My mother thought it was my father and Sandy calling with bad news from Kentucky, or worse, someone calling about the two of them, but for now the bad news was from my aunt. Only minutes earlier FBI agents had knocked at the door of the Washington hotel room where Rabbi Bengelsdorf was living. Aunt Evelyn had traveled down just the day before from Newark and so happened to be there for the night—otherwise she might not have known the circumstances of his disappearance. The agents didn't bother to wait for anyone inside to open the door; the hotel manager's master key obligingly opened it for them, and after presenting a warrant for Rabbi Bengelsdorf's arrest and waiting silently while he dressed, they escorted him in handcuffs from the room without a word of explanation to Aunt Evelyn, who immediately after watching them drive off with him in an unmarked car called my mother to ask for help. But this was hardly the time when my mother was going to leave me in somebody else's care to travel for five hours by train so as to assist a sister from whom she'd been estranged now for months. A hundred and twenty-two Jews had been murdered three days earlier—among them, as we had only just learned, Mrs. Wishnow—my father and Sandy were still off on their perilous journey to rescue Seldon, and nobody knew what was in store even for those of us at home on Summit Avenue. The shootout with the city police that had resulted in the deaths of three local thugs was the worst that had happened in Newark so far; nonetheless, its having happened around the corner on Chancellor

Avenue had left everyone on the street feeling as though a wall had been pulled down that previously protected their families—not the wall of the ghetto (which had protected no one, certainly not from fear and the pathologies of exclusion), not a wall intended to shut them out or to seal them in, but a sheltering wall of legal assurances standing between them and the derangements of a ghetto.

At five that afternoon, Aunt Evelyn showed up at our door, more crazed than she'd been on the phone in the wake of Rabbi Bengelsdorf's arrest. No one in Washington was either willing or able to tell her where her husband was being held, or if he was even alive any longer, and then when she heard of the arrests of seemingly impregnable figures like Mayor La Guardia, Governor Lehman, and Justice Frankfurter, she had succumbed to her panic and taken the train up from Washington. Fearful of returning alone to the rabbi's Elizabeth Avenue mansion—fearful too that if she called first she'd be told by my mother that she was to stay away—she'd taken a taxi from Penn Station directly to Summit Avenue to beg to be let in. Only a couple of hours earlier a shocking bulletin had come over the air—the news that President Roosevelt, upon entering New York to attend an evening protest rally at Madison Square Garden, had been "detained" by the New York police —and it was this that had prompted my mother to leave the house and, for the first time since I'd started kindergarten in 1938, to come pick me up at the end of the school day. Till then she had been as willing as everyone else on the street to abide by Rabbi Prinz's instructions for the community to carry on as usual and to leave security matters to his committee, but that afternoon she decided that events had now overtaken the rabbi's wisdom, and alongside a hundred other mothers who had reached a similar conclusion, she had turned up looking to retrieve her child when the last bell sounded and kids began pouring out of the exit doors for home.

"They're after me, Bess! I have to hide—you have to hide me!"

As if enough of our world hadn't been turned upside down in little over a week, there was my vibrant, haughty aunt, the wife (or perhaps by now the widow) of the most significant personage any of us had ever laid eyes on—there was tiny Aunt

Evelyn, without her makeup, her hair in disarray, an ogress suddenly, made as ugly and vulnerable-looking by disaster as by her own theatricality. And there was my mother blocking our doorway and looking angrier than I could ever have imagined her. Never had I seen her in such a fury, nor had I heard her utter a curse word. I didn't even know she knew how to.

"Why don't you go to the von Ribbentrops' to hide?" my mother said. "Why don't you go to your friend Herr von Ribbentrop for protection? Stupid girl! What about *my* family? Don't you think that we're afraid too? Don't you think that we're in danger too? Selfish little bitch—we're *all* afraid!"

"But they're going to arrest me! They'll torture me, Bessie, because I know the truth!"

"You cannot stay here! That's out of the question!" my mother said. "You have a house, money, servants—you have everything to protect you. We have nothing like that, nothing at all like that. Leave, Evelyn! Go! Get out of this house!"

Astonishingly, my aunt turned to me to plead for sanctuary. "Darling boy, sweetheart—"

"How dare you!" my mother shouted, and slammed the door shut, barely missing the hand that Aunt Evelyn had helplessly extended toward mine.

The next moment she threw her arms so tightly around me that against my forehead I could feel her heart thump.

"How will she get home?" I asked.

"The bus. It's not our concern. She'll take the bus like everyone else."

"But what did she mean about the truth, Ma?"

"Nothing. Forget what she meant. Your aunt is not our concern anymore."

Back in the kitchen, she buried her face in her hands and was all at once convulsed with weeping. The responsible parental scruples gave way, and with it the strength she rigorously employed to hide her weaknesses and hold things together.

"How can Selma Wishnow be dead?" she asked. "How can they arrest President Roosevelt? How can any of this be happening?"

"Because Lindbergh disappeared?" I asked.

"Because he *appeared*," she replied. "Because he appeared in the first place, a goyisch idiot flying a stupid plane! Oh, I should never have let them go to get Seldon! Where is your brother? Where is your father?" Where too, she seemed to be asking, is that orderly existence once so full of purpose, where is the great, great enterprise of our being the four of us? "We don't even know where they are," she said, but sounding as though it were she who was lost. "To send them off like that . . . What was I thinking? To let them go when the entire country . . . when . . ."

Deliberately she stopped herself there, but the trend of her thought was clear enough: when the goyim are killing Jews in the street.

There was nothing for me to do except watch until the weeping had drained her to the dregs, whereupon my whole idea of her underwent a startling change: my mother was a fellow creature. I was shocked by the revelation, and too young to comprehend that there was the strongest attachment of all.

"How could I turn her away?" she said. "Oh, darling, what, oh what, would Grandma say now?"

Remorse, predictably, was the form taken by her distress, the merciless whipping that is self-condemnation, as if in times as bizarre as these there were a right way and a wrong way that would have been clear to somebody else, as if in confronting such predicaments the hand of stupidity is ever far from guiding anyone. Yet she reproached herself for errors of judgment that were not only natural when there was no longer a logical explanation for anything but generated by emotions she had no reason to doubt. The worst of it was how convinced she was of her catastrophic blunder, though, had she gone against her instincts, she would have had no less reason to deplore what she'd done. What it came down to for the child who was watching her being battered about by the most anguishing confusion (and who was himself quaking with fear) was the discovery that one could do nothing right without also doing something wrong, so wrong, in fact, that especially where chaos reigned and everything was at stake, one might be better off to wait and do nothing—except that to do nothing was also to do something . . . in such circumstances to do nothing was to do quite a lot—and that even for the mother who performed each day in methodical opposition to life's unruly flux, there was no system for managing so sinister a mess.

*

In light of the day's drastic developments (which not even passage of the Alien and Sedition Acts of 1798, not even what Jefferson called the Federalist "reign of witches," remotely equaled for tyrannical intolerance or treachery) there were emergency meetings called for that evening at the four local schools that together enrolled nearly all the Jewish pupils in Newark's elementary education system. Each meeting was to be presided over by a member of the Committee of Concerned Jewish Citizens. A sound truck had come by late in the afternoon asking everyone to spread word of the meeting among their neighbors. People were invited to bring their children if they did not wish to leave them home alone, and they were assured that a full-scale police mobilization throughout the South Ward—police protection extending as far east as Freling-huysen Avenue and as far north as Springfield Avenue—had been promised to Rabbi Prinz by Mayor Murphy. The department's entire complement of mounted police—two platoons of twelve divided up and stabled in four different precincts—was to be called out specifically to patrol the streets to the west of the Weequahic section bordering Irvington (where, the previous night, a Jewish-owned liquor store on the main shopping street had been burned to the ground after being broken into and looted) and the streets to the south bordering Union County and the towns of Hillside (in my eyes renowned for the sizable Bristol-Myers plant along Route 22 that manufactured the Ipana tooth powder we used, where, the day before, a synagogue's windows had been smashed) and Elizabeth (where my mother's immigrant parents had settled at the turn of the century—where, most intriguingly to a nine-year-old, the New Jersey Pretzel Factory on Livingston Street was said to hire deaf-mutes from the state to do the pretzel bending—and where graves had been desecrated in the Temple B'nai Jeshurun cemetery, just a few blocks from the Weequahic Park golf course).

Shortly before six-thirty, my mother headed quickly down the street for the emergency meeting at Chancellor Avenue School. I remained at home, delegated by her to answer the phone and to accept the charges should my father call from the road. The Cucuzzas had promised her that they would look after me until she returned home, and, indeed, even as she was descending the stairs, Joey was climbing them, three at a time, dispatched by Mrs. Cucuzza to keep me company while I waited —in vain, as it turned out—for the long-distance call informing us that my father and my brother were both all right and would soon be arriving home with Seldon. Because under martial law the Army had commandeered the facilities of Bell Telephone for military use, the long-distance services still open to civilians were jammed, and forty-eight hours had passed since we'd last heard anything from my father.

As the Newark–Hillside line ran only a couple of hundred yards south of our house, it was possible that night, even with the windows closed, to find reassurance of sorts in the loud clattering of the police horses as they paraded up and down the Keer Avenue hill just around the corner. And when I threw open my bedroom window and leaned out over the darkening alleyway to listen, I could manage to hear them, if only faintly, when they sauntered on a ways to where Summit Avenue petered out and became Hillside's Liberty Avenue. Liberty ran through Hillside to Route 22, which proceeded westward into Union and from there swept southward into the vast Christian unknown of those authentically Anglo-Saxon-sounding towns of Kenilworth, Middlesex, and Scotch Plains.

These weren't the suburbs of Louisville, but they were farther west than I'd ever been, and though you had to traverse another three New Jersey counties just to reach the eastern border of Pennsylvania, on the night of October 15 I was able to alarm myself with a nightmarish vision of America's anti-Semitic fury roaring eastward through the pipeline of 22 and surging from 22 into Liberty Avenue and pouring from Liberty Avenue straight into our Summit Avenue alleyway and on up our back stairs like the waters of a flood had it not been for the sturdy barrier presented by the gleaming bay haunches of the horses of the Newark police force, whose strength and speed and beauty Newark's preeminent rabbi, the nobly named Prinz, had caused to materialize at the end of our street.

As was to be expected, Joey could hear next to nothing of what was going on outdoors, and so took to running from room to room, peering out of windows at either end of the house to try to get a glimpse of the anatomy of at least one of the horses—horses of a bloodline with limbs much longer, muscled torsos much slimmer, skulls elongated and much more exquisite than those of the inelegant orphanage plowhorse that had kicked my head in—and also to catch sight of the uniformed cops, each with two rows of brass buttons shining down the length of his double-breasted, snug-fitting tunic and a holstered pistol riding one hip.

Several years earlier my father had taken Sandy and me to Weequahic Park one Sunday morning to toss horseshoes at the public pitch, and a mounted policeman went racing across the park in pursuit of somebody who'd snatched a woman's purse —a moment in Newark out of the court of King Arthur. It was days before the thrill wore off and I could stop being stirred up by the gallantry of it all. They recruited the most supple and athletic of the cops to train as mounted policemen, and a small kid could be mesmerized just watching one who'd been lazing majestically down the street stop to write a parking ticket and then lean way over in the saddle so as to place the ticket under the car's windshield wiper, a physical gesture, if ever there was one, of magnificent condescension to the machine age. At the city's famous Four Corners there were mounted patrol posts each facing a different point of the compass, and on a Saturday lots of kids were taken downtown to see the horses on duty there and to pet their noseless noses and to feed them sugar cubes and to learn that each policeman up on a horse was worth four men on foot and, of course, to ask the usual questions of the mounted cops, such as "What's his name?" and "Is the horse real?" and "What's his foot made out of?" Sometimes you might see a police horse tied up at the side of a busy downtown street, undisturbed and calm as could be beneath the blue and white saddlecloth marked with the insignia *NP*, a gelding well over six feet high and weighing a thousand pounds, with a menacingly long nightstick belted to his flank and looking as blasé as the most gorgeous movie star while the policeman who had just dismounted stood nearby in his deep blue jodhpurs and high black boots, his pornographic leather holster molded perfectly in the engorged shape of the male genitalia, indifferent to injury amid the pandemonium of honking cars and trucks and buses and smartly signaling with his arms so as to restore a smooth flow of traffic to the city.

These were the cops with a talent for everything—even, to my father's chagrin, for galloping into a strike crowd and sending picketers flying—and that they were so very close by looking so glamorously heroic helped to shore up my nerves for the calamity to come.

In the living room Joey took off his hearing aid and presented it to me, gave it to me, incomprehensibly *shoved* it at me —the earpiece along with the black microphone case, the battery, and all its wires. I didn't know why he thought I should want it, particularly on a night like this, but there the whole contraption was, cradled in the palms of my two hands and, if possible, looking more gruesome than it did when he wore it. I didn't know whether he expected me now to interrogate him about it or to admire it or to try to disassemble and fix it. It turned out that he wanted me to wear it.

"Put it on," he told me in his hollow, honking voice.

"Why?" I shouted. "It's not going to fit me."

"It don't fit nobody," he said. "Put it on."

"I don't know how," I complained in my loudest voice, and so Joey clipped the microphone case to my shirt and dropped the battery into my pants pocket and, after he checked all the wiring, left it to me to insert the molded earpiece. I did so by closing my eyes and pretending it was a seashell and that we were down the shore and he wanted me to listen to the roar of the ocean . . . but I had to suppress the heaves when I managed to jiggle it into place, still stickily warm from the interior of his ear.

"Okay, now what?"

Whereupon he reached over and, as though it were the switch to the electric chair he was throwing and I were Public Enemy Number One, he gleefully turned the dial at the center of the microphone case.

"I don't hear anything," I told him.

"Wait'll I louden it."

"Is wearing this thing going to make me deaf?" and I saw myself made both deaf *and* dumb, and trapped in Elizabeth for the rest of my life bending pretzels in the New Jersey Pretzel Factory.

He laughed heartily at my saying that, though I hadn't meant it as a joke.

"Look," I said, "I don't want to do this. Not now. There's a lot going on outside that's not so great, you know."

But he was oblivious of what was not so great, either because he was Catholic and had nothing to worry about or simply because he was irrepressible Joey.

"You know what the crook said who sold it? He ain't even a doctor," Joey told me, "but he gives me the bullshit test anyway. He takes his pocket watch out and he holds it right up to my ear and he says to me, 'Can you hear the watch tick, Joey?' and I can hear a little, and so he starts backing away, and he says, 'Can you hear it now, Joey?' and I can't, I can't hear nothing, and so he writes some numbers down on a piece of paper. Then he takes two half-dollars out of his pocket and it's the same thing. He clicks them by my ear, clicks them together, and he says, 'Can you hear the coins click, Joey?' and then he starts walking away again, and I see him clicking them, but I can't hear nothing no more. 'The same,' I tell him—and so he writes that down. Then he looks at what he wrote down, looks real real hard, then he takes this tin piece of shit out of a drawer. He puts it on me, all the pieces, and he tells my father, 'Your boy is going to hear the grass growing, that's how good this model is,'" and with that Joey began to turn the dial again until what I heard was water running into a bathtub—and I was the bathtub. Then he spun it vigorously—and there was thunder.

"Cut it out!" I cried. "That's enough!" but Joey was joyfully leaping about, and so I reached up and yanked the earpiece out of my ear and was derailed for the moment thinking that, on top of Mayor La Guardia's being under arrest and President Roosevelt's being under arrest and even Rabbi Bengelsdorf's being under arrest, the new boy downstairs wasn't going to be any more of a picnic than the one before him had been, and this was when I determined to run away again. I was still too much of a fledgling with people to understand that, in the long run, nobody is a picnic and that I was no picnic myself. First I couldn't stand Seldon downstairs and now I couldn't stand Joey downstairs, and I determined then and there to run away from both of them. I would run away before Seldon got here, I would run away before the anti-Semites got here, I would run away before Mrs. Wishnow's body got here and there was a funeral that I had to go to. Under the protection of the mounted police, I would run away that very night from everything that was after me and everything that hated me and wanted to kill me. I would run away from everything I'd done and everything I hadn't done, and start out fresh as a boy nobody knew. And I realized, all at once, where to run away to—to Elizabeth, to the pretzel factory. I'd tell them in writing that I was a deaf-mute. They'd give me a job making pretzels, and I'd never speak and I'd pretend not to hear, and nobody would find out who I was.

Joey said, "You know about the kid who drank the horse's blood?"

"What horse's blood?"

"St. Peter's horse. This kid, he got in at night, into the farm, and drank the horse's blood. They're looking for him."

"Who is?"

"The guys. Nick. Those guys. The older guys."

"Who's Nick?"

"One of the orphans. He's eighteen. The kid that did it's a Jew like you. They know for sure he's a Jew, and they're going to find him."

"How come he drank the horse's blood?"

"Jews drink blood."

"You don't know what you're talking about. I don't drink blood. Sandy doesn't drink blood. My parents don't drink blood. Nobody I *know* drinks blood."

"This kid does."

"Yeah? And what's his name?"

"Nick don't know yet. But they're looking for him. Don't worry, they'll get him."

"And what will they do then, Joey? Drink *his* blood? *Jews don't drink blood.* Saying that is *crazy.*" I handed his hearing aid back to him—thinking that I could now add Nick to everything else I was having to flee—and soon Joey began racing from window to window again, trying to get a look at the horses, until, when he could no longer bear being out of range of a spectacle comparable in his mind to Buffalo Bill's Wild West Show coming to town and raising the big top in front of our house, he upped and flew out the door and that was the last I saw of him that night. There was rumored to be a police horse in Newark who munched on chewing tobacco, like the cop who rode him, and who was able to add numbers by tapping his right front hoof, and Joey later claimed that he'd seen him there on our block, a horse from the Eighth Precinct called Ned, who let kids swing from his tail without kicking out at them with his hind legs. And maybe he did meet the fabled Ned, and maybe that had made it all worth it. Nonetheless, for deserting me that night, for never returning, for succumbing to his love of excitement rather than obeying his mother's orders, Joey was soundly punished when his father got home from work the following morning, *his* horselike haunches thrashed mercilessly with the black strap off the night watchman's time clock.

Once Joey had disappeared, I double-locked the door behind him and would have turned on the radio to distract me from my worries if I hadn't been afraid of yet another bulletin interrupting a regularly scheduled program and relaying to me, all by myself, even more horrible news than had been coming at us throughout the day. It wasn't long before I started thinking again about running away to the pretzel factory. I remembered the article about the factory that had appeared in the *Sunday Call* about a year before and that I'd cut out to bring to school for a report I had to make on a New Jersey industry. In the article the owner, a Mr. Kuenze, had been quoted as debunking the idea, prevalent apparently throughout the world, that it took years to teach somebody to become a pretzel maker. "I can teach them overnight," he said, "if they can be taught." A lot of the article had been about a controversy over the need for salt on a pretzel. Mr. Kuenze claimed that salt on the outside was unnecessary and that he put it on only "to satisfy the trade." The important thing, he said, was to put salt in the dough, which he alone did, of all the pretzel makers in the state. The article said that Mr. Kuenze had one hundred employees, a good many deaf-mutes among them but also "boys and girls who work after school."

I knew which bus went by the pretzel factory—it was the same one that Earl and I had taken on the afternoon we'd followed home to Elizabeth the Christian whom Earl had spotted as a fairy just in the nick of time. I'd have to pray that the fairy wouldn't be on the same bus—if by chance he was, I'd get off and take the next one. What I'd have to have with me was a note, a note this time not from Sister Mary Catherine but from a deaf-mute. "Dear Mr. Kuenze. I read about you in the *Sunday Call*. I want to learn to make pretzels. I'm sure I can be taught overnight. I am deaf and dumb. I am an orphan. Will you give me a job?" And I signed it "Seldon Wishnow." I couldn't for the life of me think of another name.

I needed a note, and I needed clothes. I had to look to Mr. Kuenze like a kid he could trust, and I couldn't turn up without clothes. And this time I needed a plan, what my father called "a long-range plan." It came to me immediately: my long-range plan would be to save enough of the money I earned at the pretzel factory to buy a one-way train ticket to Omaha, Nebraska, where Father Flanagan ran Boys Town. I knew about Boys Town and Father Flanagan—as did every boy in America —from the movie with Spencer Tracy, who won an Academy Award for playing the famous priest and then donated his Oscar to the real Boys Town. I was five when I saw it at the Roosevelt with Sandy on a Saturday afternoon. Father Flanagan took in boys from the street, some of them already thieves and little gangsters, and brought them out to his farm, where they were fed and clothed and received an education and where they played baseball and sang in a choir and learned to become good citizens. Father Flanagan was father to all of them, regardless of race or creed. Most of the boys were Catholic, some Protestant, but a few needy Jewish boys lived on the farm as well—this I knew from my parents, who, like thousands of other American families who'd seen the movie and wept, made an annual ecumenical contribution to Boys Town. Not that I'd identify myself as Jewish once I reached Omaha. I'd say—speaking aloud at long last—that I didn't know what I was or who. That I was nothing and nobody—just a boy and nothing more, and hardly the person responsible for the death of Mrs. Wishnow and the orphaning of her son. Let my family raise her son as their son from here on out. He could have my bed. He could have my brother. He could have my future. I'd make my life with Father Flanagan in Nebraska, which was even farther from Newark than Kentucky.

Suddenly I thought of another name and rewrote the note, signing it "Philip Flanagan." Then I started for the cellar to get the cardboard suitcase in which I'd hidden Seldon's stolen clothes before running away the first time. This time I'd pack the suitcase with my own clothes and in my pocket carry the miniature pewter musket that I had bought at Mount Vernon and used to slice open the envelopes from the stamp company back when I owned a serious collection and was getting mail. Its bayonet measured barely an inch in length, but leaving home for good I would need something for protection, and a letter opener was all I had.

Minutes later, descending the stairs with a flashlight, I was able to derive the strength to keep my legs from collapsing by realizing that this was the last occasion I'd ever have to go down into that cellar and confront the wringer or the alley cats or the drains or the dead. Or that dank, befouled wall facing the street on which one-legged Alvin had once spattered his grief.

It wasn't cold enough yet for us to start burning coal, and when, from the foot of the cellar stairs, I turned my flashlight on the ash-colored hulk of the fireless furnaces they looked to me like those ostentatious burial vaults where, for all the good it does them, the rich and mighty inter themselves. I stood there hoping that the ghost of Seldon's father would have gone off to Kentucky (perhaps unseen in the trunk of my father's car) to fetch his dead wife but understanding full well that he hadn't, that his business as a ghost was here with me—that his spectral heart seethed with curses, and all of them for me. "I didn't mean for them to move," I whispered. "That was a mistake. I'm not who's really responsible. I didn't mean to make Seldon the target."

I was prepared, of course, for the silence that inevitably surrounded my pleading utterances to the merciless dead, and instead heard my name pronounced in response—and by a woman! From beyond the furnaces, a woman moaning my name! Dead only hours and already back to begin haunting me for the rest of my life!

"I know the truth," she said, and there, emerging like an oracular priestess out of the Delphi of our storage bin, came my aunt. "They're after me, Philip," Aunt Evelyn said. "I know the truth, and they're going to kill me!"

*

Because she had to use the toilet and to eat something—because I didn't know what I could do other than to give my aunt whatever she needed—I had no choice but to bring her back upstairs with me. I sliced a piece of bread from the half a loaf that was left from dinner, buttered it, poured her a glass of milk, and, after she'd gone to the bathroom—and I'd pulled the kitchen shades so that nobody could see in from across the way—she came into the kitchen and feverishly gobbled everything down. Her coat and her purse were in her lap and she was still wearing her hat, and I hoped that as soon as she'd had enough to eat, she'd get up and go home so that I could go down and get the suitcase, pack it, and run away before my mother returned from the meeting. But once she'd eaten she began to babble, repeating again and again that she knew the truth and because of that they were going to kill her. They'd called out the mounted police, she informed me, to find where she was hiding.

In the silence that followed that startling remark—which, in those circumstances, when suddenly there were no longer any predictable happenings, I was enough of a child to almost believe—we followed the audible progress of a single horse prancing up the block toward Chancellor Avenue. "They know I'm here," she said.

"They don't, Aunt Evelyn," but the words had no hold on me as I spoke them. "*I* didn't know you were here."

"Then why did you come looking for me?"

"I didn't. I was looking for something else. The police are outside," I told her, convinced that I was deliberately lying even while speaking as earnestly as I could, "the police are outside because of the anti-Semitism. They're patrolling the streets to protect us."

She smiled the smile reserved for trusting souls. "Tell me another one, Philip."

Now *nothing* that I knew coincided with anything either of us was saying. The shadow of her madness had crept over me without my as yet understanding that while hiding in our storage bin—or perhaps earlier than that, while watching the FBI take the rabbi away in handcuffs—she had indeed lost her mind. Unless, of course, she'd already begun hopelessly slipping into insanity the night at the White House when she danced with von Ribbentrop. That was to be my father's theory—that long before the rabbi's arrest, when Bengelsdorf was astonishing all of Jewish Newark with the unseemliness of how high he had climbed in the president's esteem, she'd abandoned herself to the same credulity that had transformed the entire country into a madhouse: the worship of Lindbergh and his conception of the world.

"Do you want to lie down?" I asked, dreading that she would say yes. "Do you need to rest? Do you want me to call the doctor?"

Here she took my hand so firmly that her fingernails bit into my flesh. "Philip dearest, I know *everything*."

"Do you know what happened to President Lindbergh? Is that what you mean?"

"Where is your mother?"

"At school. At a meeting."

"You'll bring me food and water, darling boy."

"I will? Sure. Where?"

"To the cellar. I can't drink from the laundry sink. Someone will find me."

"You don't want that," I said, thinking immediately of Joey's grandmother and the fiery breath of madness that wafted from *her*. "I'll bring everything." But having promised her that, I couldn't possibly run away.

"Would you happen to have an apple?" asked Aunt Evelyn.

I opened the refrigerator. "No, no apple. We're out of apples. My mother hasn't been able to do much shopping. But there's a pear, Aunt Evelyn. You want that?"

"Yes. And another piece of bread. Make another piece of bread."

Her voice kept changing. Now she sounded as though we were doing nothing more than getting ready for a picnic, making the best of what we had on hand to take to Weequahic Park to eat by the lake under a tree, as though the events of the day were as unimportant to us as probably they were to everybody else in America: a minor nuisance to the Christians, if that. As there were more than thirty million Christian families in America and only about a million Jewish families, why, really, should it bother them?

I cut a second slice from the loaf for her to take down to the cellar and smeared it extra heavily with butter. If asked later about the bread missing from the loaf, I'd say that Joey ate it, that and the pear, before he ran off to see the horses.

When she got home to learn that my father hadn't called, my mother was unable to hide her response. Forlornly she looked at the kitchen clock, remembering perhaps the time that it used to be at this hour: bedtime, when all that was required was for the children to wash their faces and brush their teeth for the day dense with fulfillable duties to be rounded off to the satisfaction of all. Now *that* was nine o'clock—or so we'd been led to believe by that wholly convincing, immutable life-likeness that now turned out to have been a sham.

And the day in, day out routine of school—was that a sham too, a cunning deception perpetrated to soften us up with rational expectations and foster nonsensical feelings of trust? "Why no school?" I asked when she told me that tomorrow we'd have the day off. "Because," my mother replied, making recourse to the colorless formulation suggested to the parents in order for them to be truthful without frightening the children unduly, "the situation has further deteriorated." "What situation?" I asked. "Our situation." "Why? What happened now?" "Nothing happened. It's just better that you children stay home tomorrow. Where is Joey? Where is your friend?" "He ate some bread, and he took the pear, and he left. He took the pear out of the refrigerator and ran outside. He went to see the horses." "And you're sure that no one phoned?" she asked, simply too exhausted to be angry with Joey for letting her down at a moment like this. "I want to know why there's no school, Ma." "Must you know tonight?" "Yes. Why can't I go to school?" "Well . . . it's because there may be a war with Canada." "With *Canada*? When?" "No one knows. But it's best if you all stay home until we see what's going on." "But why are we going to war with Canada?" "Please, Philip, I can't take much more tonight. I've told you everything I know. You insisted and I told you. Now we just have to wait. We have to wait and see like everyone else." And then, as if the unknown whereabouts of my father and brother hadn't given rein to her worst imaginings—which was that we two were now, like the Wishnows, just a widow and her son—she said (trying doggedly to follow the protocol of the old nine o'clock), "I want you to wash up and go to bed."

Bed—as though as a place of warmth and comfort, rather than an incubator for dread, bed still existed.

War with Canada was far less of an enigma to me than what Aunt Evelyn was going to use for a toilet during the night. As best I could understand, the United States was at last entering into the worldwide war, not on the side of England and the British Commonwealth, whom everyone had expected we would support while FDR was president, but on the side of Hitler and Hitler's allies, Italy and Japan. Moreover, two full days had passed since we had heard from my father and Sandy, and for all we knew they had been killed as horribly as Seldon's mother by the rioting anti-Semites; there was, in addition, to be no school tomorrow, suggesting to me that there might never be school again if President Wheeler was now to inflict on us the laws we knew to have been imposed by the Nazis on the Jewish children of Germany. A political catastrophe of unimaginable proportions was transforming a free society into a police state, but a child is a child, and all I could think about in my bed was that when the time came to move her bowels, Aunt Evelyn would have to do it on our storage bin floor. This was the uncontrollable event that weighed on me in lieu of everything else, that loomed over me like the embodiment of everything else, and that blotted out everything else. The most negligible danger of all, and it came to assume such momentous significance that around midnight I tiptoed into the bathroom and at the back of the bottom shelf of the towel closet I found the bedpan we had bought for Alvin to use in an emergency when he first got home from Canada. I was already at the back door and ready to carry the bedpan down to Aunt Evelyn when my mother confronted me in her nightgown, aghast at the picture I presented of a small boy so overwhelmed he was going out of his mind.

Minutes later Aunt Evelyn was being led by my mother up the stairwell and into our apartment. There's no need to describe the disturbance this caused in the Cucuzza household or the antagonistic response to the frightful figure of my aunt by that frightful figure who was Joey's grandmother—the farcical edge of suffering is familiar to everyone. I was sent to sleep in my parents' bed, and my mother and Aunt Evelyn took over my room, where my mother's next great task was to prevent her sister from getting up out of Sandy's bed and stealing into the kitchen to turn on the gas and kill us all.

The round trip of fifteen hundred miles was the adventure of Sandy's lifetime. It was something more fateful for my father. His Guadalcanal, I suppose, his Battle of the Bulge. At forty-one he was too old to be drafted when, that December, with Lindbergh's policies discredited and Wheeler disgraced and Roosevelt back in the White House, America finally went to war against the Axis powers, so this was as close as he would ever come to the fear, fatigue, and physical suffering of the frontline soldier. Wearing his high steel neck brace and nursing two broken ribs and a sutured facial wound and exhibiting a mouthful of broken teeth—and carrying Mr. Cucuzza's extra pistol in the glove compartment for protection against the people who'd already murdered 122 Jews in those very regions of the country toward which the car was headed—he drove the seven hundred and fifty miles to Kentucky stopping only to get gas and go to the toilet. And after sleeping at the Mawhinneys' for five hours and eating something, turned around and started back, though now with a painful infection simmering along the length of his suture and with Seldon, sick to his stomach and feverish in the back seat, hallucinating about his mother and all but performing feats of magic to do what he could to bring her back.

The trip out had taken just over twenty-four hours, but the one back took three times as long because of the many times they had to stop for Seldon to vomit by the side of the road or to pull down his pants and squat in a ditch, and because, in just a twenty-mile radius of Charleston, West Virginia (where they went round in circles, hopelessly lost, instead of proceeding east and north toward Maryland), the car broke down on six separate occasions in little over a day: once in the midst of the railroad tracks, power lines, and massive conveyors of Alloy, a town of two hundred where enormous mounds of ore and silica surrounded the factory buildings of the Electro-Metallurgical Company plant; once in the nearby little town of Boomer, where flames from the coke ovens reached so high my father, standing after sundown in the middle of the unlighted street, could read (or misread) the road map by the incandescence; once in Belle, yet another of those tiny, hellish industrial hamlets, where the fumes from the Du Pont ammonia plant almost knocked them flat when they got out of the car to lift the hood and try to figure out what was wrong; again in South Charleston, the city that looked to Seldon like "a monster" because of the steam and the smoke wreathing the freight yards and the warehouses and the long dark roofs of the soot-blackened factories; and twice on the very outskirts of the state capital, Charleston. There, around midnight, in order to call a tow truck, my father had to cross a railroad embankment on foot and then descend a hill of junk to a bridge that spanned a river lined with coal barges and dredging barges and tugboats to go looking for a riverfront dive with a pay phone, meanwhile leaving the two boys alone together in the car just across the river road from an endless jumble of a plant—sheds and shanties, sheet-iron buildings and open coal cars, cranes and loading booms and steel-frame towers, electric ovens and roaring forges, squat storage tanks and high cyclone fences—a plant that was, if you believed the sign the size of a billboard, "The World's Biggest Manufacturer of Axes, Hatchets, and Scythes."

That factory brimming with sharpened blades dealt the final blow to the little that was left of Seldon's equilibrium—by morning he was screaming that he was going to be scalped by the Indians. And oddly he was on to something: an analogy could be made, even if one weren't delirious, to the uninvited white settlers who first poured through the Appalachian barrier into the favorite hunting grounds of the Delaware and Algonquin tribes, except that instead of alien, strange-looking whites affronting the local inhabitants with their rapaciousness, these were alien, strange-looking Jews provocative merely by their presence. This time around, though, those violently defending their lands from usurpation and their way of life from destruction weren't Indians led by the great Tecumseh but upright American Christians unleashed by the acting president of the United States.

It was by then October 15—the very Thursday when Mayor La Guardia was arrested in New York, when the First Lady was incarcerated at Walter Reed, when FDR was "detained" along with the "Roosevelt Jews" alleged to have masterminded the kidnapping of Lindbergh *père*, when Rabbi Bengelsdorf was arrested in Washington and Aunt Evelyn went to pieces in our storage bin. On that same day my father and Sandy were searching the West Virginia mountains for the county's one licensed physician (as opposed to the licensed barber, who'd already offered his services), to try to get him to give Seldon something to quiet him down. The man they found on a rural dirt road was over seventy and reeking of whiskey, a good, kind, spry old "Doc" who ran a country clinic out of a little frame house where the patients who lined up waiting their turn on the front porch were, as Sandy later described them to me, the raggediest-looking bunch of white people he had ever seen. The doc figured Seldon's delirium stemmed mainly from dehydration and directed Seldon to spend an hour taking down ladle after ladle of water from the well out near the creekbed behind the house. He also drained the pus from my father's infected face to prevent blood poisoning, which in those days, when antibiotics were just discovered and not widely available, would probably have spread through his system and killed him before he made it home. The old guy displayed less talent stitching the wound back up than he had in diagnosing the incipient septicemia, with the result that for the rest of his life my father looked as though he'd sustained a dueling scar while a student at Heidelberg. Afterward it seemed not simply a sign of the contingencies of that trip but, to me, the imprint of his insane stoicism. When finally he reached Newark he was so depleted by fever and chills—and a racking cough no less alarming than Mr. Wishnow's—that Mr. Cucuzza took him straight from our kitchen, where he'd fainted at the dinner table, and once again to the Beth Israel Hospital, where he very nearly died from pneumonia. But there was no way of stopping him until Seldon was saved. My father was a rescuer and orphans were his specialty. A displacement even greater than having to move to Union or to leave for Kentucky was to lose one's parents and be orphaned. Witness, he would tell you, what had happened to Alvin. Witness what had happened to his sister-in-law after Grandma had died. No one should be motherless and fatherless. Motherless and fatherless you are vulnerable to manipulation, to influences—you are rootless and you are vulnerable to everything.

Sandy in the meantime perched on the railing of the clinic's front porch sketching the patients, one of them a thirteen-year-old girl named Cecile. These were the years when my precocious brother was three different boys in the course of twenty-four months, the years when, for all his unflappability, he could seem to do nothing satisfactory even by excelling: my parents didn't like it when he went to work for Lindbergh and became Aunt Evelyn's oratorical boy wonder and New Jersey's leading authority on tobacco farming, they didn't like it when he left Lindbergh for the girls and overnight became the neighborhood's youngest Don Juan, and now, having volunteered to guide my father a quarter of the way across the continent to the Mawhinney farm—and hoping by an exhibition of genuine bravery to recapture his prestige as the older son and reenter the family from which he'd been torn away—he virtually subverted his cause by an amusement that must have seemed to him wholly harmless for being "artistic": drawing nubile Cecile. When my father—with a new bandage covering his cheek —came out of the doctor's office and saw what Sandy was up to, he took him by the belt of his trousers and dragged him, sketchpad and all, clear off the side of the porch and out to the road and into the car. "Are you crazy," my father whispered, peering furiously down at him over his neck brace, "are you nuts, drawing her?" "It's only her face," Sandy tried to explain, holding the sketchpad to his chest—and lying. "I don't care what it is! You never heard of Leo Frank? You never heard of the Jew they lynched in Georgia because of that little factory girl? Stop *drawing* her, damn it! Stop drawing *any* of them! These people don't *like* being drawn—can't you see that? We came out to Kentucky to get this boy because they have burned his mother to death in her car! For Christ's sake, put those drawing things away, and don't draw any more girls!"

Finally back on the road again, they had no idea that Philadelphia (which my father was hoping to reach by dawn of the seventeenth) had been occupied by tanks and troops of the U.S. Army, nor did my father know that Uncle Monty, indifferent to my mother's pleading and impervious to any hardship not his own, had fired him for not showing up at work a second week in a row. My father chooses resistance, Rabbi Bengelsdorf chooses collaboration, and Uncle Monty chooses himself.

To get to Boyle County and the Mawhinneys' they had traveled diagonally south across New Jersey to Camden, across the Delaware to Philadelphia, south from there to Baltimore, west and south across the length of West Virginia, and then into Kentucky until, a hundred or so miles on, they reached Lexington and, near a place called Versailles, turned south again for Boyle County's rolling hills. My mother tracked their trip on my encyclopedia's foldout map of the forty-eight states and the ten Canadian provinces, which she spread across the dining room table to look at whenever her anxiety overtook her, while out on the road Sandy, armed with a flashlight for the dark hours, charted their course on an Esso road map and kept an eye out for suspicious-looking characters, especially when they were passing through some grim one-street town whose name he couldn't even find on the map. Excluding the six times that the car broke down on the way back, Sandy counted at least another six in West Virginia when my father—who didn't like the look of a battered truck that was following behind them or of the pickups parked haphazardly by some roadside saloon or of the overalled kid in the gas station who'd pumped their gas and checked the car's front end and then spat on the ground when he took their money—had asked Sandy to open the glove compartment and pass him Mr. Cucuzza's spare pistol to hold in his lap while he drove, and each time sounding as though he, who'd never fired a shot in his life, wouldn't hesitate, if he had to, to pulla the trig'.

Sandy, who once he got home drew from memory his boyhood masterpiece—the illustrated history of their great descent into the hard American world—admitted to having been frightened just about all the time: frightened when they passed through cities where Ku Klux Klansmen had to be lying in wait for any Jew foolhardy enough to be driving through, but no less frightened when they were out beyond the ominous cities, beyond the faded billboards and the tiny filling stations and the last of the shacks where the poorest of people in their threadbare clothes lived—dilapidated timber shacks that Sandy rendered meticulously, underpinned at the four corners by rickety stone piles, with cutout holes for windows and a crudely built chimney crumbling at one end and, on the weather-worn roof, a few scattered rocks holding down the loose shingles—and into what my father called "the wilds." Frightened, said Sandy, speeding past the cows and the horses and the barns and the silos without another car in sight, frightened making hairpin turns up in the mountains without either a shoulder or a guardrail at the side of the road, and frightened when the paved road turned to gravel and the forest closed around them as though they were Lewis and Clark. And especially frightened because our car had no radio, and they didn't know whether the killing of Jews had stopped or whether they might be driving right into the thick of the country's murderous rage against people like us.

Seemingly the sole interlude that *hadn't* frightened my brother was what had so scared my father out front of the doctor's house: Sandy's drawing a picture of the West Virginia mountain girl whose looks had clearly gotten him all worked up. As it turned out, she'd been exactly the age of "the little factory girl" (as the whole country came to know her) murdered in Atlanta some thirty years earlier by her Jewish supervisor, a married businessman of twenty-nine named Leo Frank. The famous 1913 case of poor Mary Phagan—found dead with a noose around her neck on the floor of the pencil factory basement after going to Frank's office on the day of the murder to collect her pay envelope—had been all over the front pages, North *and* South, at about the time my father, an impressionable boy of twelve who'd only recently left school to help support the family, was at work in an East Orange hat factory, obtaining a first-class education there in the commonplace libel that linked him inextricably to the crucifiers of Christ. After Frank's conviction (on not entirely reliable circumstantial evidence that is all but discredited today), a fellow prison inmate became a statewide hero by slashing his throat and nearly killing him. One month later, a lynch mob of respectable citizens finished the job by abducting Frank from his jail cell and—much to the satisfaction of my father's co-workers on the factory floor—hanging "the sodomite" from a tree in Marietta, Georgia (Mary Phagan's hometown), as public warning to other

"Jewish libertines" to stay the hell out of the South and away from their women.

To be sure, the Frank case was only a part of the history that fed my father's sense of danger in rural West Virginia on the afternoon of October 15, 1942. It all goes further back than that.

This was how Seldon came to live with us. After their safe return to Newark from Kentucky, Sandy moved into the sun parlor and Seldon took over where Alvin and Aunt Evelyn had left off—as the person in the twin bed next to mine shattered by the malicious indignities of Lindbergh's America. There was no stump for me to care for this time. The boy himself was the stump, and until he was taken to live with his mother's married sister in Brooklyn ten months later, I was the prosthesis.

POSTSCRIPT

Note to the Reader
A True Chronology of the Major Figures
Other Historical Figures in the Work
Some Documentation

Note to the Reader

The Plot Against America is a work of fiction. This postscript is intended as a reference for readers interested in tracking where historical fact ends and historical imagining begins. The facts presented below are drawn from the following sources: John Thomas Anderson, *Senator Burton K. Wheeler and United States Foreign Relations* (dissertation presented to the graduate faculty, University of Virginia), 1982; Neil Baldwin, *Henry Ford and the Jews: The Mass Production of Hate*, 2001; A. Scott Berg, *Lindbergh*, 1998; Biography Resource Center, *Newark Evening News* and *Newark Star-Ledger*; Allen Bodner, *When Boxing Was a Jewish Sport*, 1997; William Bridgwater and Seymour Kurtz, eds., *The Columbia Encyclopedia*, 1963; James Mac-Gregor Burns, *Roosevelt: The Soldier of Freedom*, 1970, and *Roosevelt: The Lion and the Fox*, 1984; Wayne S. Cole, *America First: The Battle Against Intervention, 1940–41*, 1953; Sander A. Diamond, *The Nazi Movement in the United States, 1924–1941*, 1974; John Drexel, ed., *The Facts on File Encyclopedia of the Twentieth Century*, 1991; Henry Ford, *The International Jew: The World's Foremost Problem*, vol. 3, *Jewish Influences in American Life*, 1920–1922; Neal Gabler, *Winchell: Gossip, Power, and the Culture of Celebrity*, 1994; Gale Group Publishing, *Contemporary Authors*, vol. 182, 2000; John A. Garraty and Mark C. Carnes, eds., *American National Biography*, 1999; Susan Hertog, *Anne Morrow Lindbergh: Her Life*, 1999; Richard Hofstadter and Beatrice K. Hofstadter, eds., *Great Issues in American History: From Reconstruction to the Present Day, 1864–1981*, vol. 3, 1982; Joseph G. E. Hopkins, ed., *Dictionary of American Biography*, supplements 3–9, 1974–1994; Joseph K. Howard, "The Decline and Fall of Burton K. Wheeler," *Harper's Magazine*, March 1947; Harold L. Ickes, *The Secret Diary of Harold L. Ickes*, vol. 3, 1954; Thomas Kessner, *Fiorello H. La Guardia and the Making of Modern New York*, 1989; Herman Klurfeld, *Winchell: His Life and Times*, 1976; Anne Morrow Lindbergh, *The Wave of the Future: A Confession of Faith*, 1940; Albert S. Lindemann, *The Jew Accused: Three Anti-Semitic Affairs (Dreyfus, Beilis, Frank), 1894–1915*, 1991; Arthur Mann, *La Guardia: A Fighter Against His Times, 1882–1933*, 1959; Samuel Eliot Morison and Henry Steele Commager, *The Growth of the American Republic*, vol. 2, 1962; Charles Moritz, ed., *Current Biography Yearbook, 1988*, 1988; John

Morrison and Catherine Wright Morrison, *Mavericks: The Lives and Battles of Montana's Political Legends*, 1997; *Random House Dictionary of the English Language*, 1983; Arthur M. Schlesinger, Jr., *The Coming of the New Deal, 1933–1935*, 1958, and *The Politics of Upheaval, 1935–1936*, 1960 (vols. 2 and 3 of *The Age of Roosevelt*); Peter Teed, *A Dictionary of Twentieth-Century History, 1914–1990*, 1992; Walter Yust, ed., *Britannica Book of the Year Omnibus, 1937–1942*, and *Britannica Book of the Year, 1943*; Ben D. Zevin, ed., *Nothing to Fear: The Selected Addresses of Franklin D. Roosevelt, 1932–1945*, 1961.

A True Chronology of the Major Figures

FRANKLIN DELANO ROOSEVELT
1882–1945

NOVEMBER 1920. After serving as assistant secretary of the navy under Wilson, Roosevelt runs as vice president on Democratic ticket with Governor James M. Cox of Ohio; Democrats defeated in Harding landslide.

AUGUST 1921. Stricken with polio, which leaves him badly crippled for life.

NOVEMBER 1928. Elected to first of two two-year terms as Democratic governor of New York, while national ticket, headed by ex-governor Alfred E. Smith, loses to Herbert Hoover. As governor, Roosevelt strongly establishes himself as a progressive liberal, an advocate of government relief for Depression victims, including unemployment insurance, and a foe of Prohibition. After landslide 1930 gubernatorial victory, becomes Democratic presidential front-runner.

JULY–NOVEMBER 1932. Selected as presidential candidate by Democrats at July convention; in November, defeats President Hoover with 57.4 percent of vote, and Democrats sweep both houses of Congress.

MARCH 1933. Inaugurated as president March 4; with nation paralyzed by Depression, proclaims in inaugural address that "the only thing we have to fear is fear itself." Quickly proposes New Deal recovery legislation for agriculture, industry, labor, and business, and relief programs for mortgage holders and the unemployed. Cabinet includes Harold L. Ickes, secretary of the interior; Henry A. Wallace, secretary of agriculture; Frances Perkins—first ever woman cabinet appointee —secretary of labor; and Henry Morgenthau, Jr.—the country's second Jew ever to be a cabinet member—secretary of the Treasury (to replace the ill secretary, William Woodin, on November 17, 1933). Begins brief national radio broadcasts from White House, known as fireside chats, and engages reporters in informative press conferences.

NOVEMBER 1933–DECEMBER 1934. Recognizes Soviet Union and soon starts rebuilding the U.S. fleet, in part owing to Japanese activities in Far East. By '34 black voters have shifted political loyalty from Lincoln's Republican Party to Roosevelt's Democratic Party in response to president's programs for the underprivileged.

1935. Burst of reform initiatives, referred to as "second New Deal," results in the Social Security Act, the National Labor Relations Act, as well as the WPA (Works Progress Administration), which employs two million workers a month. Signs first of several neutrality measures in response to unsettled European situation.

NOVEMBER 1936. Defeats Kansas Republican governor Alfred M. Landon, winning every state except Maine and Vermont; Democrats enlarge congressional lead. In inaugural address asserts, "Here is a challenge to our democracy . . . I see one-third of a nation ill-housed, ill-clad, ill-nourished." By 1937, economic recovery well under way, but economic crisis follows and, along with labor unrest, leads to Republican congressional victories in 1938.

SEPTEMBER–NOVEMBER 1938. Apprehensive over Hitler's intentions in Europe, appeals to Nazi leader to accept negotiated settlement in dispute with Czechoslovakia. At September 30 Munich conference, Britain and France capitulate to German demand for Czech Sudetenland and the dismemberment of Czechoslovakia; German troops, led by Hitler, enter in October (and, five months later, conquer the entire country, granting Slovakia independence as a German-backed fascist republic). In November Roosevelt orders enormous increase in production of combat airplanes.

APRIL 1939. Asks Hitler and Mussolini to agree for a period of ten years to refrain from attacking weaker European nations; Hitler replies in a Reichstag speech by heaping scorn on Roosevelt and boasting of German military might.

AUGUST–SEPTEMBER 1939. Telegrams Hitler asking him to negotiate settlement with Poland over territorial dispute; Hitler responds by invading Poland on September 1. England and France declare war on Hitler, and World War Two begins.

SEPTEMBER 1939. European war prompts Roosevelt to seek changes in Neutrality Act to allow Britain and France to obtain arms from U.S. When Hitler invades Denmark, Norway, Belgium, the Netherlands, Luxembourg, and France in first half of 1940, Roosevelt significantly increases U.S. arms production.

MAY 1940. Establishes Council of National Defense and, later, Office of Production Management, to prepare industry and armed forces for possible war.

SEPTEMBER 1940. Japan, at war with China and having invaded French Indochina (and having already annexed Korea in 1910 and occupied Manchuria in 1931), signs triple alliance with Italy and Germany in Berlin. At Roosevelt's urging, Congress passes first peacetime conscription bill in U.S. history, requiring all men between twenty-one and thirty-five to register for the draft and arranging for the induction into armed services of 800,000 draftees.

NOVEMBER 1940. Denounced by right-wing Republicans as a "war-monger," and campaigning as an avowed enemy of Hitler and fascism pledged to do everything possible to keep America out of the European war, Roosevelt wins unprecedented third term, by 449 to 82 electoral votes, defeating the Republican Wendell L. Willkie in an election in which national defense and U.S. relationship to the war are major issues; Willkie carries only Maine, Vermont, and the isolationist Midwest.

JANUARY–MARCH 1941. Inaugurated January 20. In March Congress passes his Lend-Lease Act, authorizing president to "sell, transfer, lend, lease" armaments, foodstuffs, and services to countries whose defense he deems vital to the defense of the U.S.

APRIL–JUNE 1941. After German army invades Yugoslavia and then Greece, Hitler breaks joint non-aggression pact and invades Russia. In April U.S. takes Greenland under protection; in June Roosevelt authorizes landing of U.S. forces in Iceland and extends Lend-Lease to Russia.

AUGUST 1941. Meeting at sea, Roosevelt and Churchill draw up Atlantic Charter of "common principles," containing eight-point declaration of peace aims.

SEPTEMBER 1941. Announces that Navy has been ordered to destroy any German or Italian submarines entering U.S. waters and threatening U.S. defense; asks Japan to begin military evacuation of China and Indochina, but minister, General Tojo, refuses.

OCTOBER 1941. Asks Congress to amend Neutrality Act to allow arming of U.S. merchant ships and to permit them to enter combat zones.

NOVEMBER 1941. Massive Japanese striking force secretly assembles in Pacific while negotiations with U.S. on military and economic issues appear to continue with arrival in U.S. of Japanese envoys for "peace talks."

DECEMBER 1941. Japan launches surprise attack on U.S. possessions in the Pacific and Far Eastern possessions of Great Britain; after emergency address by president, Congress unanimously declares war on Japan the next day. On December 11 Germany and Italy declare war on the U.S.; Congress, in response, declares war on Germany and Italy. (Casualty figures for Japanese attack on Pearl Harbor: 2,403 American sailors, soldiers, marines, and civilians killed; 1,178 wounded.)

1942. Directing the war effort occupies president almost entirely. In his annual message to Congress he stresses increased war production, declares that "our objectives are clear—smashing the militarism imposed by the warlords on their enslaved peoples." Proposes record $58,927,000,000 budget to accommodate war expenses. With Churchill, announces creation of unified military command in Southeast Asia. Strategy conference with Churchill in June results in November invasion of French North Africa by Allied troops under command of General Dwight D. Eisenhower (German army driven from Africa seven months later); president assures France, Portugal, and Spain that Allies have no designs on their territories. In June asks Congress to recognize existence of state of war against fascist regimes of Romania, Bulgaria, and Hungary, allied with Axis powers. In July appoints commission to try eight Nazi saboteurs arrested by federal agents after landing on U.S. shores from enemy submarine; following secret trial, two are imprisoned and six are executed in Washington. In September, president's emissary Wendell Willkie received by Stalin in Moscow, where he urges second military front in Western Europe. In October president makes secret two-week tour of war production facilities and announces objectives are being met. Asks Congress to expand draft to eighteen- and nineteen-year-olds.

JANUARY 1943–AUGUST 1945. European war (and Hitler's concurrent massacre of Europe's Jews and the expropriation of their property) lasts until 1945. In April Mussolini executed by Italian partisans, and Italy surrenders. Germany surrenders unconditionally on May 7, a week after the suicide of Adolf Hitler in his Berlin bunker and less than a month after the sudden death, from a cerebral hemorrhage, of President Roosevelt—then in the first year of a fourth presidential term—and the swearing-in of his successor, Vice President Harry S. Truman. War ends in Far East when Japan surrenders unconditionally on August 14. World War Two is over.

CHARLES A. LINDBERGH
1902–1974

MAY 1927. Charles A. Lindbergh, a twenty-five-year-old Minnesota-born stunt flier and airmail pilot, flies the monoplane *Spirit of St. Louis* from New York to Paris in thirty-three hours and thirty minutes; his completing first nonstop transatlantic solo flight makes him a celebrity around the globe. President Coolidge awards Lindbergh Distinguished Flying Cross and commissions him colonel in U.S. Army Air Corps Reserve.

MAY 1929. Lindbergh marries Anne Morrow, the twenty-three-year-old daughter of U.S. ambassador to Mexico.

JUNE 1930. Charles A. Lindbergh, Jr., born to Charles and Anne Lindbergh in New Jersey.

MARCH–MAY 1932. Charles Jr. kidnapped from family's secluded new house on 435 acres in rural Hopewell, New Jersey; some ten weeks later, decomposing corpse of baby discovered by chance in nearby woods.

SEPTEMBER 1934–MARCH 1935. A poor German immigrant carpenter and ex-convict, Bruno R. Hauptmann, arrested in Bronx, New York, for kidnap and murder of Lindbergh baby. Six-week trial in Flemington, New Jersey, characterized by press as "trial of the century." Hauptmann found guilty and executed in electric chair April 1936.

APRIL 1935. Anne Morrow Lindbergh publishes first book, *North to the Orient*, an account of her 1931 air adventures with Lindbergh; becomes a top bestseller and receives the National Booksellers Award as the most distinguished nonfiction book of the year.

DECEMBER 1935–DECEMBER 1936. Seeking privacy, Lindberghs leave America with their two small children and, until their return in spring 1939, reside mainly in small village in Kent, England. At the invitation of U.S. military, Lindbergh travels to Germany to report on Nazi aircraft development; makes repeated visits for this purpose over the next three years. Attends 1936 Berlin Olympics, where Hitler is in attendance, and later writes of Hitler to a friend, "He is undoubtedly a great man, and I believe has done much for the German people." Anne Morrow Lindbergh accompanies her husband to Germany and afterward writes critically of the "strictly puritanical view at home that dictatorships are of necessity wrong, evil, unstable and no good can come of them—combined with our funny-paper view of Hitler as a clown—combined with the very strong (naturally) Jewish propaganda in the Jewish-owned papers."

OCTOBER 1938. Service Cross of the German Eagle—a gold medallion with four small swastikas, conferred on foreigners for service to the Reich—presented to Lindbergh, "by order of the Führer," by Air Marshal Hermann Göring at American embassy dinner in Berlin. Anne Morrow Lindbergh publishes second account of her flying adventures, *Listen! the Wind*, a nonfiction bestseller despite her husband's growing unpopularity among American antifascists and the refusal by some Jewish booksellers to stock the book.

APRIL 1939. After Hitler invades Czechoslovakia, Lindbergh writes in his journal, "Much as I disapprove of many things Germany has done, I believe she has pursued the only consistent policy in Europe in recent years." At request of Air Corps chief, General "Hap" Arnold, and with approval of President Roosevelt—who dislikes and distrusts him—goes on active duty as colonel in U.S. Army Air Corps.

SEPTEMBER 1939. In journal entries after Germany invades Poland on September 1, Lindbergh notes the need to "guard ourselves against attack by foreign armies and dilution by foreign races . . . and the infiltration of inferior blood." Aviation, he writes, is "one of those priceless possessions which permit the White race to live at all in a pressing sea of Yellow, Black, and Brown." Earlier in year he notes, of a private conversation with a high-ranking member of the Republican National Committee and the conservative newsman Fulton Lewis, Jr., "We are disturbed about the effect of the Jewish influence in our press, radio, and motion pictures . . . It is too bad because a few Jews of the right type are, I believe, an asset to any country." In an April 1939 diary entry (omitted in 1970 from his published *Wartime Journals*) he writes, "There are too many Jews in places like New York already. A few Jews add strength and character to a country, but too many create chaos. And we are getting too many." In April 1940, speaking over the Columbia Broadcasting System, he says, "The only reason that we are in danger of becoming involved in this war is because there are powerful elements in America who desire us to take part. They represent a small minority of the American people, but they control much of the machinery of influence and propaganda. They seize every opportunity to push us closer to the edge." When Idaho Republican senator William E. Borah encourages Lindbergh to run for president, Lindbergh says he prefers to take political positions as a private citizen.

OCTOBER 1940. In spring America First Committee founded at Yale University Law School to oppose FDR's interventionist policies and promote American isolationism; in October Lindbergh addresses meeting of three thousand at Yale, advocating that America recognize "the new powers in Europe." Anne Morrow Lindbergh publishes third book, *The Wave of the Future*, a brief anti-interventionist tract subtitled "A Confession of Faith," which arouses enormous controversy and immediately becomes top nonfiction bestseller despite denunciation by Secretary of the Interior Harold Ickes as "the Bible of every American Nazi."

APRIL–AUGUST 1941. Addresses ten thousand at America First Committee rally in Chicago, another ten thousand at New York rally, prompting his bitter enemy Secretary Ickes to call him "the No. 1 United States Nazi fellow traveler." When Lindbergh writes to President Roosevelt complaining about Ickes's attacks on him, particularly for accepting the German medal, Ickes writes, "If Mr. Lindbergh feels like cringing when he is correctly referred to as a knight of the German Eagle, why doesn't he send back the disgraceful decoration and be done with it?" (Earlier, Lindbergh had declined returning the medal on grounds that it would constitute "an unnecessary insult" to the Nazi leadership.) President openly questions Lindbergh's loyalty, prompting Lindbergh to tender his resignation as Army colonel to Roosevelt's secretary of war. Ickes notes that while Lindbergh is swift in renouncing his Army commission, he remains adamant in refusing to return the medal received from Nazi Germany. In May, along with Senator Burton K. Wheeler of Montana, who is seated on the platform beside Anne Morrow Lindbergh, Lindbergh addresses twenty-five thousand at America First rally at Madison Square Garden; his appearance greeted with cries from the audience of "Our next president!" and his speech followed by a four-minute ovation. Speaks against American intervention in European war to large audiences across the country throughout spring and summer.

SEPTEMBER–DECEMBER 1941. Delivers his "Who Are the War Agitators?" radio speech to an America First rally in Des Moines on September 11; audience of eight thousand cheers when he names "the Jewish race" as among those most powerful and effective in pushing the U.S.—"for reasons which are not American"—toward involvement in the war. Adds that "we cannot blame them for looking out for what they believe to be their own interests, but we also must look out for ours. We cannot allow the natural passions and prejudices of other peoples to lead our country to destruction." Des Moines speech is attacked the next day by both Democrats and Republicans, but Senator Gerald P. Nye, Republican from North Dakota and staunch America Firster, defends Lindbergh from critics and reiterates charge against the Jews, as do other supporters. December 10 address, scheduled for Boston America First rally, canceled by Lindbergh after Japanese attack on Pearl Harbor and U.S. declaration of war on Japan, Germany, and Italy. Activities of America First Committee terminated by leadership, and organization disbands.

JANUARY–DECEMBER 1942. Travels to Washington to seek reinstatement in Air Corps, but key Roosevelt cabinet members strongly oppose, as does much of the press, and Roosevelt says no. Repeated attempts to find position in aviation industry also fail, despite a lucrative association during the late twenties and early thirties with Transcontinental Air Transport ("the Lindbergh Line") and as highly paid consultant with Pan American Airways. In spring finally finds work, with government approval, as consultant to Ford's bomber development program, outside Detroit at Willow Run, and family moves to Detroit suburb. (The September afternoon President Roosevelt visits Willow Run to inspect war production projects, Lindbergh makes it his business to be away.) Participates in experiments at Mayo Clinic aeromedical laboratory to decrease physical dangers of high-altitude flying; later participates as test pilot in experiments with oxygen equipment at high altitudes.

DECEMBER 1942–JULY 1943. Takes active role in training pilots for

Navy/Marine Corps Corsair, fighter plane that he helps develop for United Aircraft in Connecticut.

AUGUST 1943. Anne Morrow Lindbergh, now mother of four children, publishes *The Steep Ascent*, a novella about a dangerous flying adventure; her first publishing failure, largely owing to hostility of reviewers and readers toward the prewar politics of the Lindbergh family.

JANUARY–SEPTEMBER 1944. After stint in Florida testing a variety of warplanes, including Boeing's new B-29 bomber, receives government permission to go to South Pacific to study Corsairs in action; once there, begins to fly combat and bombing runs against Japanese targets from New Guinea base, at first as observer but soon, with great success, as enthusiastic participant. Teaches pilots how to increase combat range by conserving fuel in flight. Having flown fifty missions—and downed a Japanese fighter plane—returns to America in September to resume work with United Aircraft's fighter program, and family moves from Michigan to Westport, Connecticut.

FIORELLO H. LA GUARDIA
1882–1947

NOVEMBER 1922. Having served congressional terms representing Lower East Side of Manhattan just before and after World War One, La Guardia is returned to Congress and serves five consecutive terms as Republican representative for the Italian and Jewish constituency of East Harlem. Leads House in opposing President Harding's sales tax and denouncing his failure to address economic hard times; also opposes Prohibition.

NOVEMBER 1924. In presidential election, outspokenly supports Progressive Party candidate Robert M. La Follette rather than the Republican, President Coolidge.

JANUARY 1931. New York governor Franklin D. Roosevelt calls governors' conference to deal with Depression problems of unemployment; La Guardia praises him for promoting inquiry leading to labor and unemployment legislation that he himself had urged unsuccessfully on President Hoover.

1932. As a maverick Republican—and defeated lame-duck congressman—is chosen by president-elect Roosevelt to introduce New Deal legislation in lame-duck Seventy-second Congress after Democrats' 1932 landslide victory.

NOVEMBER 1933. Running as anti-Tammany candidate, elected Republican-Fusion (and later, in addition, American Labor Party) mayor of New York for first of three consecutive terms; sets out as activist mayor to bring economic recovery to Depression New York by fostering public works projects and establishing and increasing public services. Denounces fascism and American Nazis; in response to Nazis labeling him "Jew Mayor of New York," quips, "I never thought I had enough Jewish blood in my veins to justify boasting of it."

SEPTEMBER 1938. After Hitler dismembers Czechoslovakia, La Guardia attacks Republican isolationists and takes side of FDR in growing interventionist controversy.

SEPTEMBER 1940. Though Wendell Willkie is said to be considering him for vice presidential running mate, La Guardia again deserts Republicans, as he did in 1924; with Senator George Norris forms Independents for Roosevelt and openly campaigns for Roosevelt third term.

AUGUST–NOVEMBER 1940. With war looming, Roosevelt favors La Guardia for secretary of war but chooses Republican Henry Stimson instead, appointing La Guardia chairman of the American side of the U.S.-Canadian Defense Board.

APRIL 1941. Accepts unpaid position as FDR's director of civilian defense while continuing to hold office as mayor of New York.

FEBRUARY–APRIL 1943. Presses Roosevelt to return him to active Army duty as brigadier general, but Roosevelt, having failed to grant him a cabinet position or consider him for a running mate, declines, on advice of intimates who consider La Guardia too provocative; the disappointed mayor returns to his "street-cleaner's uniform."

AUGUST 1943. Wartime racial strife that previously struck Beaumont, Mobile, Los Angeles, and Detroit—where there are thirty-four deaths in June 21 riots—erupts in New York's Harlem. After nearly three days of vandalism, looting, and bloodshed, La Guardia praised by black leaders for strong, compassionate leadership during riots that leave 6 dead, 185 injured, and $5 million in property damage.

MAY 1945. A month after FDR's death, announces he will not run for a fourth term; famously, before his retirement, he reads the funnies over the radio to New York youngsters during a newspaper strike. After leaving office, accepts directorship of UNRRA (United Nations Relief and Rehabilitation Administration).

WALTER WINCHELL

1897–1972

1924. Ex-vaudevillian Walter Winchell hired by *New York Evening Graphic* and soon gains popularity as Broadway reporter and columnist.

JUNE 1929. Goes to work as columnist for William Randolph Hearst's *New York Daily Mirror*, a job he will keep for over thirty years. Hearst's King Features syndicates Winchell column nationwide; it eventually appears in more than two thousand papers. Inventor of modern gossip column naturally becomes regular at New York celebrity night spot the Stork Club.

MAY 1930. Makes radio debut as Broadway gossip newscaster; moves on to great popularity with *Lucky Strike Dance Hour* program and, in December 1932, on Sundays at nine P.M., the program for Jergens Lotion on the NBC Blue Network. Weekly Winchell quarter hour of insider gossip and general news soon claims radio's largest audience, and his opening gambit—"Good evening, Mr. and Mrs. America and all the ships at sea, let's go to press!"—becomes part of American parlance.

MARCH 1932. Begins covering Lindbergh kidnapping case, aided in his coverage by tips from FBI chief J. Edgar Hoover; continues to cover the case through the arrest of Bruno Hauptmann in 1934 and the trial in 1935.

FEBRUARY 1933. Almost alone among public commentators and among well-known Jews, begins public attack on Hitler and American Nazis, including Bund leader Fritz Kuhn; continues attack on radio and in column until outbreak of World War Two; coins neologisms "razis" and "swastinkers" to ridicule the Nazi movement.

JANUARY–MARCH 1935. Lauded for his work covering Hauptmann trial by J. Edgar Hoover. Hoover and Winchell subsequently trade information about American Nazis that winds up in Winchell's column.

1937. Support in column for Roosevelt and New Deal leads to May White House invitation and regular communication between the president and Winchell. Feud grows between Hearst and Winchell over Winchell's public support of FDR. Friendship develops between Winchell and New York neighbor, mobster Frank Costello.

1940. Winchell's combined audience for column and newscast estimated at fifty million, more than a third of America's population; his annual salary of $800,000 places him among highest-paid Americans. Winchell steps up attack on pro-Nazi activities with features in his column such as "The Winchell Column vs. The Fifth Column." Strongly endorses FDR for unprecedented third term; writes pseudonymous columns for *PM* attacking Republican candidate Willkie after Hearst censors Winchell's criticism of Willkie in *Daily Mirror*.

APRIL–MAY 1941. Attacks Lindbergh for isolationist and pro-German statements; warns Nazi foreign minister von Ribbentrop that America has the will to fight, and is then attacked by Senator Burton K. Wheeler for "blitzkrieging the American people into this war."

SEPTEMBER 1941. After Lindbergh's Des Moines speech charging Jews with pushing America toward war, writes that Lindbergh's "halo has become his noose" and repeatedly attacks Lindbergh as well as Senators Wheeler, Nye, Rankin, and others he identifies as pro-Nazi.

DECEMBER 1941–FEBRUARY 1972. After America's entrance into World War Two, Winchell's newscasts and columns deal predominantly with war news; as lieutenant commander in naval reserve, presses FDR for assignment and is called to active duty in November 1942. With end of war, turns to far right; becomes fierce foe of Soviet Union and anti-Communist supporter of Senator Joseph McCarthy. Fades into near obscurity in mid-1950s; at his death in 1972, funeral attended only by his daughter.

BURTON K. WHEELER
1882–1975

NOVEMBER 1920–NOVEMBER 1922. After defying Montana's powerful giant, Anaconda Copper Mining Company, as Montana state legislator and after opposing human rights violations committed during postwar Red Scare, Wheeler is badly defeated in 1920 run for governor, but in 1922 elected as Democrat to U.S. Senate for the first of four terms with the strong backing of farmers and labor. Over the years, converts Montana state government into bipartisan Wheeler machine.

FEBRUARY–NOVEMBER 1924. Chosen to head Senate inquiry into Teapot Dome graft scandal, which leads to resignation of President Coolidge's attorney general, Harry M. Dougherty, and humiliation of Coolidge's Justice Department. Abandons Democrats—and Democratic ticket headed by John W. Davis—to run for vice president on Progressive Party ticket with Wisconsin senator Robert M. La Follette. Coolidge overwhelmingly defeats both Democrats and Progressives, though latter party polls six million votes nationwide and nearly forty percent of vote in Montana.

1932–1937. Prior to Democratic Convention in 1932, visits sixteen states to promote Roosevelt nomination. Despite being the first national figure to endorse Democratic candidate and by and large sympathetic to New Deal social reform, in 1937 Wheeler bitterly opposes the president over his legislative proposal to enlarge Supreme Court and "pack" it with New Deal supporters; Wheeler's leadership leads to controversial bill's defeat, and aggravates personal enmity between him and the president.

1938. Wheeler's Montana machine works to undermine his Democratic rival, Congressman Jerry O'Connell, aiding election to the House of Jacob Thorkelson, a right-wing Republican labeled by Walter Winchell the "mouthpiece of the Nazi movement in Congress."

Thorkelson calls Winchell a "Jewish vilifier" and files suit against him after Winchell includes Thorkelson in *Liberty* magazine series of articles called "Americans We Can Do Without." Congressman O'Connell, commenting on electoral activities of Wheeler Democrats, describes Wheeler as a "Benedict Arnold to his party and a traitor to his president."

1940–1941. Wheeler for President club formed in Montana by influential Democrats; in his home state and elsewhere, considered a formidable contender for Democratic nomination until Roosevelt announces his candidacy for a third term. In Senate, Wheeler increasingly aligned with Republicans and southern Democrats against liberal Roosevelt wing of Democratic Party. Vociferously opposes American intervention in European war. In June 1940 threatens to bolt Democratic Party "if it is going to be a war party." Meets that month to make plans "for countering war agitation and propaganda" with Charles A. Lindbergh and a group of isolationist senators; on Senate floor, defends Lindbergh against accusations of being pro-Nazi, and some months later, after Roosevelt publicly compares Lindbergh to a Civil War "Copperhead" (a northerner who sympathized with the South), calls the remark "shocking and appalling to every right-thinking American." Speaking over NBC radio network, proposes an eight-point peace proposal for negotiating with Hitler and receives congratulatory telegram from Lindbergh. Meets with Yale students planning to organize America First Committee and assumes role of unofficial adviser; along with Lindbergh, becomes most popular speaker at AFC rallies. Speaks out against draft, calling Roosevelt's peacetime conscription proposal "a step toward totalitarianism." On Senate floor, arguing against Lend-Lease bill, says, "If the American people want a dictatorship—if they want a totalitarian form of government and if they want war—this bill should be steamrollered through Congress, as is the wont of President Roosevelt." Claims Lend-Lease, if passed, "will plow under every fourth American boy," prompting Roosevelt to label Wheeler's remark "the most untruthful . . . most dastardly, unpatriotic thing . . . that has been said in public life in my generation." Publicly—and prematurely—reveals that U.S. is sending troops to Iceland; White House, along with Prime Minister Churchill, accuses Wheeler of endangering American and British lives. Again charged with compromising military secrecy when, in November 1941, he leaks to isolationist *Chicago Tribune* a classified War Department document disclosing U.S. strategy in the event of war.

DECEMBER 1941–DECEMBER 1946. Following Pearl Harbor, supports war effort, arguing, however, that America's alliance with Soviet

Union aids survival of Communist government. In 1944, claiming "Communists are behind MVA," sides against liberals and with Montana Power Company and Anaconda Copper Company in helping defeat Missouri Valley counterpart to Tennessee Valley Authority (TVA). Subsequently loses last of Montana Democratic support and is defeated in 1946 Senate primary campaign by young Montana liberal Leif Erickson.

1950s. Practices law in Washington, D.C. Allies himself ideologically and politically with Senator Joseph McCarthy.

HENRY FORD
1863–1947

1903–1905. First Ford automobile, the two-cylinder, eight-horsepower Model A, designed by Henry Ford and manufactured by his newly incorporated Ford Motor Company, appears in 1903, selling for $850. Higher-priced models appear over next few years.

1908. Designed for rural America, Model T Ford is introduced and, until 1927, is the only model built by the company. Makes Ford the country's premier auto manufacturer, fulfilling his plan to "build a motorcar for the great multitude."

1910–1916. With his automotive associates, establishes a manufacturing process of sequential production and division of labor that evolves into the continuously moving assembly line—considered the greatest industrial advance since the advent of the Industrial Revolution—which leads to mass production of Model T. In 1914 Ford announces a basic wage of $5 for an eight-hour day; offer extends, in fact, to only a portion of Ford work force. Nonetheless his advocating the "Five Dollar Day" brings Ford much praise and fame as an enlightened businessman, if not as an enlightened thinker. "I don't like to read books," he explains. "They muss up my mind." "History," he declares, "is more or less bunk."

1916–1919. Name put into nomination for presidency at Republican National Convention and gains thirty-two first-ballot votes. Moves successfully to wield absolute power over all Ford enterprises. By 1916, company producing two thousand cars a day, with a production total to date of one million Model T's. At outbreak of World War One becomes active as pacifist opponent of war and attacks war profiteering. Announces to meeting of Ford officials, "I know who caused the war. The German-Jewish bankers. I have the evidence here. Facts. The German-Jewish bankers caused the war." With American entry into war, pledges to "operate without one cent of profit" in fulfilling government contracts, but neglects to do so. At urging of President

Wilson, runs for Senate as a Democrat—though formerly identified as a Republican—and is defeated in close election. Attributes his losing to Wall Street "interests" and "the Jews."

1920. In May, *Dearborn Independent*—local weekly bought by Ford in 1918—prints first of ninety-one detailed articles devoted to exposing "The International Jew: The World's Problem"; in ensuing issues, serializes the text of the fraudulent *Protocols of the Learned Elders of Zion* while claiming the document—and its revelation of a Jewish plan for world domination—to be authentic. Circulation rises to close to 300,000 by second year of publication; subscriptions to paper are forced upon Ford dealers as a company product, and the strongly anti-Semitic articles are collected in a four-volume edition, *The International Jew: The World's Foremost Problem*.

1920s. Five millionth Ford car produced in 1921; more than half of cars sold in America are Model T's. Develops huge River Rouge plant and industrial city in Dearborn. Acquires forests, iron mines, and coal mines to supply auto company with raw materials. Diversifies Ford line of cars. His 1922 autobiography, *My Life and Work*, is a nonfiction bestseller, and the Ford name and legend are known throughout the world. Polls show him running ahead of President Harding in popularity, and is spoken of as potential Republican presidential candidate; in the fall of 1922 considers presidential run. Adolf Hitler, in 1923 interview, says, "We look to Heinrich Ford as the leader of the growing fascist movement in America." In mid-twenties, a suit for defamation filed against him by a Chicago Jewish lawyer is settled out of court, and in 1927, he retracts his attacks on Jews, agrees to discontinue anti-Semitic publications, and shuts down *Dearborn Independent*, a deficit enterprise that had cost him close to $5 million. When Lindbergh flies the *Spirit of St. Louis* to Detroit in August 1927, he meets Ford at Ford Airport and takes him in the famous plane for his first flight. Lindbergh interests Ford in aviation manufacturing. The two meet afterward numerous times, and in a 1940 Detroit interview Ford explains, "When Charles comes out here, we only talk about the Jews."

1931–1937. Competition from Chevrolet and Plymouth and impact of Depression produce large company losses despite innovation of Ford V-8 engine. Poor labor relations at River Rouge plant caused by speedup, job insecurity, and labor espionage. Efforts by United Auto Workers to organize Ford, along with General Motors and Chrysler, meet with violence and intimidation by Ford; Detroit vigilante group beats up labor organizers at River Rouge. Ford Company's labor policies condemned by National Labor Relations Board and considered worst in auto industry.

1938. In July, on his seventy-fifth birthday, accepts Service Cross of

the German Eagle from Hitler's Nazi government at a birthday dinner in Detroit for fifteen hundred prominent citizens. (Same medal
awarded to Lindbergh in October ceremony in Germany, causing
Interior Secretary Ickes to tell a December meeting of the Cleveland
Zionist Society, "Henry Ford and Charles A. Lindbergh are the only
two free citizens of a free country who obsequiously have accepted
tokens of contemptuous distinction at a time when the bestower of
them counts that day lost when he can commit no new crimes against
humanity.") Suffers first of two strokes.

1939–1940. With outbreak of World War Two joins his friend
Lindbergh in supporting isolationism and America First Committee.
Shortly after Ford is appointed to America First executive committee,
Lessing J. Rosenwald, Jewish director of Sears, Roebuck and Company, resigns because of Ford's anti-Semitic reputation. For a while
meets regularly with anti-Semitic radio priest Father Coughlin, whose
activities Roosevelt and Ickes believe Ford is financing. Lends financial support to the anti-Semitic demagogue Gerald L. K. Smith for his
weekly radio broadcast and his living expenses. (Some years later,
Smith reprints Ford's *International Jew* in a new edition and maintains into the 1960s that Ford "never changed his opinion of Jews.")

1941–1947. Suffers second stroke. Company converts to defense
production as war approaches; during war, produces B-24 bomber at
huge Willow Run facility, where Lindbergh is hired as consulting adviser. Because of illness, Ford no longer able to run company and resigns in 1945. Dies April 1947, and 100,000 mourners view the body.
Vast fortune in company stock goes mainly to Ford Foundation, soon
the world's wealthiest private foundation.

Other Historical Figures in the Work

BERNARD BARUCH (1870–1965) Financier and government adviser. As
director of War Industries Board under Woodrow Wilson, mobilized
nation's industrial resources for World War One. Member of the
White House circle during Roosevelt administrations. Appointed by
Truman as U.S. representative to U.N. Atomic Energy Commission
in 1946.

RUGGIERO "RITCHIE THE BOOT" BOIARDO (1890–1984) Newark
crime figure and local rival to racketeer Longy Zwillman; his influence
strongest in the city's Italian First Ward, where he owned a popular
restaurant.

LOUIS D. BRANDEIS (1856–1941) Born in Louisville, Kentucky, to cultivated immigrant Jewish family from Prague. Public interest and

labor attorney in Boston. Early organizer of Zionist movement in America. Appointed by President Wilson as associate justice of Supreme Court, but only after intense four-month controversy in Senate Judiciary Committee and around the country, which Brandeis attributed to his being first Jew nominated to the court. Served twenty-three years, until 1939.

CHARLES E. COUGHLIN (1891–1979) Roman Catholic priest and pastor of the Shrine of the Little Flower in Royal Oak, Michigan. Regarded Roosevelt as a Communist and fervently admired Lindbergh. In the 1930s, disseminated strongly anti-Semitic ideas in a weekly nationwide radio broadcast and his periodical *Social Justice*, which was barred from the U.S. Mail during the war for violating the Espionage Act and ceased publication in 1942.

AMELIA EARHART (1897–1937) In 1932, set transatlantic record of fourteen hours and fifty-six minutes for flight from Newfoundland to Ireland; first woman to make unaccompanied flights across Atlantic and across Pacific from Honolulu to California. Her plane lost somewhere over the Pacific in 1937 attempt to fly around the world with navigator Frederick J. Noonan.

MEYER ELLENSTEIN (1885–1963) After careers as a dentist and a lawyer, chosen by fellow Newark city commissioners in 1933 to be mayor of Newark. The city's first and only Jewish mayor, served two terms, 1933–1941.

EDWARD FLANAGAN (1886–1948) In 1904, emigrated from Ireland to the U.S., where he began studies for priesthood; ordained 1912. In 1917, to provide for the welfare of homeless boys of all races and religions, founded Father Flanagan's Home for Boys in Omaha. Became national figure in 1938 because of popular film about Boys Town, starring Spencer Tracy as Father Flanagan.

LEO FRANK (1884–1915) Manager of Atlanta pencil factory, found guilty of murdering Mary Phagan, a thirteen-year-old employee, on April 26, 1913; assaulted with a knife while prisoner and later forcibly removed from jail by local citizens and lynched, August 1915. Anti-Semitism believed to have played important part in dubious conviction.

FELIX FRANKFURTER (1882–1965) Roosevelt-appointed associate justice of U.S. Supreme Court, 1939–1962.

JOSEPH GOEBBELS (1897–1945) An early member of the Nazi Party, in 1933 became Hitler's propaganda minister and culture czar, responsible for overseeing the press, radio, movies, and theater, and mounting public spectacles such as parades and mass rallies. Among the most devoted and brutal of Hitler's associates. In April 1945, with Germany destroyed and the Russians entering Berlin, he and his wife killed their six young children and together committed suicide.

HERMANN GÖRING (1893–1946) Founder and first head of the Gestapo, or secret police, and responsible for creation of the German air force. In 1940 Hitler named him as his successor, but dismissed him near war's end. Convicted at Nuremberg for war crimes and sentenced to death, he committed suicide two hours before execution.

HENRY (HANK) GREENBERG (1911–1986) Slugging first baseman for Detroit Tigers in 1930s and 1940s; fell two home runs short of Babe Ruth's record in 1938. Hero to Jewish baseball fans, he was first of two Jewish players elected to baseball's Hall of Fame.

WILLIAM RANDOLPH HEARST (1863–1951) American publisher, considered the foremost proponent of the sensational, jingoistic "yellow journalism" addressed to a mass audience; his newspaper empire flourished into the 1930s. Originally aligned with Democratic populists, became increasingly right wing and a bitter enemy of FDR's.

HEINRICH HIMMLER (1900–1945) Nazi leader, commander of the SS, which controlled concentration camps, and chief of the Gestapo; in charge of racial "purification" programs, and second in power only to Hitler. Poisoned himself and died after being captured by British troops in May 1945.

J(OHN) EDGAR HOOVER (1895–1972) Director of the Federal Bureau of Investigation (originally the Bureau of Investigation, a subsidiary of the Department of Justice), 1924–1972.

HAROLD L. ICKES (1874–1952) A progressive Republican turned Democrat, served nearly thirteen years as Roosevelt's secretary of the interior, making his the second-longest tenure of any Roosevelt cabinet member. A dedicated conservationist and an active foe of fascism.

FRITZ KUHN (1886–1951) German-born veteran of World War One, emigrated to America in 1927, and by 1938, as Bundesleiter who considered himself the American Führer, had established the German-American Bund as most powerful, most active, and richest Nazi group in U.S., with membership of twenty-five thousand. Convicted of larceny in 1939, denaturalized in 1943, deported to Germany in 1945. In 1948, convicted by German denazification court of attempting to transplant Nazism to U.S. and of having close ties to Hitler; sentenced to ten years at hard labor.

HERBERT H. LEHMAN (1878–1963) A partner in Lehman Brothers, banking house founded by his family. Lieutenant governor of New York under Governor Roosevelt; succeeded Roosevelt as governor, 1932–1942. New Deal supporter and strong interventionist. As Democratic senator from New York (1949–1957), early opponent of Senator Joseph McCarthy.

JOHN L. LEWIS (1880–1969) American labor leader. In 1935, as president of the United Mine Workers, broke with the American Federation of Labor (AFL) to form the new Committee for Industrial Organization, which became the Congress of Industrial Organizations in 1938. Initially a supporter of Roosevelt's, backed Republican Willkie in 1940 election and resigned CIO presidency after Willkie's defeat. Strikes by UMW during the war led to further enmity between Lewis and the administration.

ANNE SPENCER MORROW LINDBERGH (1906–2001) American author and aviator. Born to wealth and privilege in Englewood, New Jersey; her father, Dwight Morrow, a partner in the investment firm of J. P. Morgan and Co., the U.S. ambassador to Mexico during the Hoover administration, and a Republican senator from New Jersey; and her mother, Elizabeth Reeve Cutter Morrow, a writer, an educator, and, briefly, the acting president of Smith College, where Morrow received an A.B. in literature in 1928. Introduced to Charles Lindbergh the year before, while visiting her family at the ambassador's residence in Mexico City. For details of Morrow's life after that meeting, see True Chronology, Charles A. Lindbergh.

HENRY MORGENTHAU, JR. (1891–1967) Roosevelt-appointed secretary of the Treasury, 1934–1945.

VINCENT MURPHY (1888–1976) Meyer Ellenstein's successor as mayor of Newark, 1941–1949. Democratic nominee for governor of New Jersey in 1943 and dominant figure in New Jersey labor for thirty-five years after his 1933 election as secretary-treasurer of state Federation of Labor.

GERALD P. NYE (1892–1971) Ardently isolationist Republican senator from North Dakota, 1925–1945.

WESTBROOK PEGLER (1894–1969) Right-wing journalist whose column "As Pegler Sees It" appeared in Hearst newspapers from 1944 to 1962. In 1941 won Pulitzer Prize for exposé of labor racketeering. Fierce critic of the Roosevelts and the New Deal, which he characterized as Communist-inspired, and openly hostile toward the Jews. Close supporter and friend of Senator Joseph McCarthy, and adviser to McCarthy's investigating committee.

JOACHIM PRINZ (1902–1988) Rabbi, author, and civil rights activist, served as rabbi of Temple B'nai Abraham, Newark, 1939–1977.

JOACHIM VON RIBBENTROP (1893–1946) Hitler's chief foreign policy adviser in 1933 and minister for foreign affairs, 1938–1945. With Soviet foreign minister Molotov signed 1939 non-aggression pact that included secret agreement to partition Poland. Pact opened way for World War Two. Found guilty of war crimes at Nuremberg and, on October 16, 1946, became first of condemned Nazis to be hanged.

ELEANOR ROOSEVELT (1884–1962) Niece of Theodore Roosevelt, wife of her distant cousin FDR, and mother of their daughter and five sons. As First Lady, made speeches for liberal social causes, lectured on the status of minorities, the underprivileged, and women, spoke out against fascism, wrote daily syndicated column for sixty newspapers, and during World War Two was cochair of the Office of Civilian Defense. As U.N. delegate appointed by President Truman, supported establishment of a Jewish state, and in 1952 and 1956 campaigned for Adlai Stevenson for president. Appointed again as delegate to U.N. by President Kennedy, whose Bay of Pigs invasion she opposed.

LEVERETT SALTONSTALL (1892–1979) Descendant of Sir Richard Saltonstall, an original member of the Massachusetts Bay Company who arrived in America in 1630. Republican governor of Massachusetts, 1939–1944; Republican senator, 1944–1967.

GERALD L. K. SMITH (1898–1976) Minister and famous orator, allied first with Huey Long and later with Father Coughlin and Henry Ford, both of whom supported him in his unrelenting hatred of Jews. His anti-Semitic magazine, *The Cross and the Flag*, blamed the Jews for causing the Depression and World War Two. In 1942, polled 100,000 votes in Michigan as Republican nominee for Senate. Maintained that Roosevelt was a Jew, that *The Protocols of the Learned Elders of Zion* was an authentic document, and, after the war, that the Holocaust had never taken place.

ALLIE STOLZ (1918–2000) Lightweight boxer from Jewish Newark. Won 73 of 85 fights, losing two title fights in the 1940s; the first, a controversial fifteen-round decision, to champion Sammy Angott; the second—leading to his retirement in 1946—a thirteenth-round knockout, to champion Bob Montgomery.

DOROTHY THOMPSON (1893–1961) Journalist, political activist, and columnist syndicated in 170 newspapers during the 1930s. Early foe of Nazism and Hitler and bitter critic of Lindbergh's politics. Married to novelist Sinclair Lewis in 1928 and divorced in 1942. Opposed Zionism and supported Palestinian Arabs in 1940s and 1950s.

DAVID T. WILENTZ (1894–1988) New Jersey attorney general (1934–1944) whose prosecution of the Lindbergh baby kidnapping case led to the conviction and execution of Bruno Hauptmann. Later, influential in New Jersey Democratic organization and adviser to three Democratic governors of the state.

ABNER "LONGY" ZWILLMAN (1904–1959) Newark-born Prohibition era bootlegger who was leading New Jersey mobster from 1920s to 1940s. Member of East Coast racketeering's "Big Six," among them Lucky Luciano, Meyer Lansky, and Frank Costello. Extensive criminal activities exposed by Senate Crime Committee's televised hearings in 1951. Committed suicide eight years later.

Some Documentation

Speech by Charles Lindbergh, "Who Are the War Agitators?," delivered at the America First Committee's rally in Des Moines on September 11, 1941. The text that follows appears at www.pbs.org/wgbh/amex/lindbergh/filmmore/reference/primary/desmoinesspeech.html.

It is now two years since this latest European war began. From that day in September, 1939, until the present moment, there has been an ever-increasing effort to force the United States into the conflict.

That effort has been carried on by foreign interests, and by a small minority of our own people; but it has been so successful that, today, our country stands on the verge of war.

At this time, as the war is about to enter its third winter, it seems appropriate to review the circumstances that have led us to our present position. Why are we on the verge of war? Was it necessary for us to become so deeply involved? Who is responsible for changing our national policy from one of neutrality and independence to one of entanglement in European affairs?

Personally, I believe there is no better argument against our intervention than a study of the causes and developments of the present war. I have often said that if the true facts and issues were placed before the American people, there would be no danger of our involvement.

Here, I would like to point out to you a fundamental difference between the groups who advocate foreign war, and those who believe in an independent destiny for America.

If you will look back over the record, you will find that those of us who oppose intervention have constantly tried to clarify facts and issues; while the interventionists have tried to hide facts and confuse issues.

We ask you to read what we said last month, last year, and even before the war began. Our record is open and clear, and we are proud of it.

We have not led you on by subterfuge and propaganda. We have not resorted to steps short of anything, in order to take the American people where they did not want to go.

What we said before the elections, we say again and again, and again today. And we will not tell you tomorrow that it was just campaign oratory. Have you ever heard an interventionist, or a British agent, or a member of the administration in Washington ask you to go back and study a record of what they have said since the war started? Are their self-styled defenders of democracy willing to put the issue of war to a vote of our people? Do you find these crusaders for foreign freedom of speech, or the removal of censorship here in our own country?

The subterfuge and propaganda that exists in our country is obvious on every side. Tonight, I shall try to pierce through a portion of it, to the naked facts which lie beneath.

When this war started in Europe, it was clear that the American people were solidly opposed to entering it. Why shouldn't we be? We had the best defensive position in the world; we had a tradition of independence from Europe; and the one time we did take part in a European war left European problems unsolved, and debts to America unpaid.

National polls showed that when England and France declared war on Germany, in 1939, less than 10 percent of our population favored a similar course for America.

But there were various groups of people, here and abroad, whose interests and beliefs necessitated the involvement of the United States in the war. I shall point out some of these groups tonight, and outline their methods of procedure. In doing this, I must speak with the utmost frankness, for in order to counteract their efforts, we must know exactly who they are.

The three most important groups who have been pressing this country toward war are the British, the Jewish and the Roosevelt administration.

Behind these groups, but of lesser importance, are a number of capitalists, Anglophiles, and intellectuals who believe that the future of mankind depends upon the domination of the British empire. Add to these the Communistic groups who were opposed to intervention until a few weeks ago, and I believe I have named the major war agitators in this country.

I am speaking here only of war agitators, not of those sincere but misguided men and women who, confused by misinformation and frightened by propaganda, follow the lead of the war agitators.

As I have said, these war agitators comprise only a small minority of our people; but they control a tremendous influence. Against the determination of the American people to stay out of war, they have marshaled the power of their propaganda, their money, their patronage.

Let us consider these groups, one at a time.

First, the British: It is obvious and perfectly understandable that Great Britain wants the United States in the war on her side. England is now in a desperate position. Her population is not large enough and her armies are not strong enough to invade the continent of Europe and win the war she declared against Germany.

Her geographical position is such that she cannot win the war by the use of aviation alone, regardless of how many planes we send her. Even if America entered the war, it is improbable that the Allied armies could invade Europe and overwhelm the Axis powers. But one thing is certain. If England can draw this country into the war, she can shift to our shoulders a large portion of the responsibility for waging it and for paying its cost.

As you all know, we were left with the debts of the last European war; and unless we are more cautious in the future than we have been in the past, we will be left with the debts of the present case. If it were not for her hope that she can make us responsible for the war financially, as well as militarily, I believe England would have negotiated a peace in Europe many months ago, and be better off for doing so.

England has devoted, and will continue to devote every effort to get us into the war. We know that she spent huge sums of money in this country during the last war in order to involve us. Englishmen have written books about the cleverness of its use.

We know that England is spending great sums of money for propaganda in America during the present war. If we were Englishmen, we would do the same. But our interest is first in America; and as Americans, it is essential for us to realize the effort that British interests are making to draw us into their war.

The second major group I mentioned is the Jewish.

It is not difficult to understand why Jewish people desire the overthrow of Nazi Germany. The persecution they suffered in Germany would be sufficient to make bitter enemies of any race.

No person with a sense of the dignity of mankind can condone the persecution of the Jewish race in Germany. But no person of honesty and vision can look on their pro-war policy here today without seeing the dangers involved in such a policy, both for us and for them. Instead of agitating for war, the Jewish groups in this country should be opposing it in every possible way for they will be among the first to feel its consequences.

Tolerance is a virtue that depends upon peace and strength. History shows that it cannot survive war and devastation. A few far-sighted Jewish people realize this and stand opposed to intervention. But the majority still do not.

Their greatest danger to this country lies in their large ownership and influence in our motion pictures, our press, our radio and our government.

I am not attacking either the Jewish or the British people. Both races, I admire. But I am saying that the leaders of both the British and the Jewish races, for reasons which are as understandable from their viewpoint as they are inadvisable from ours, for reasons which are not American, wish to involve us in the war.

We cannot blame them for looking out for what they believe to be their own interests, but we also must look out for ours. We cannot allow the natural passions and prejudices of other peoples to lead our country to destruction.

The Roosevelt administration is the third powerful group which has been carrying this country toward war. Its members have used the war emergency to obtain a third presidential term for the first time in American history. They have used the war to add unlimited billions to a debt which was already the highest we have ever known. And they have just used the war to justify the restriction of congressional power, and the assumption of dictatorial procedures on the part of the president and his appointees.

The power of the Roosevelt administration depends upon the maintenance of a wartime emergency. The prestige of the Roosevelt administration depends upon the success of Great Britain to whom the president attached his political future at a time when most people thought that England and France would easily win the war. The danger of the Roosevelt administration lies in its subterfuge. While its members have promised us peace, they have led us to war heedless of the platform upon which they were elected.

In selecting these three groups as the major agitators for war, I have included only those whose support is essential to the war party. If any one of these groups—the British, the Jewish, or the administration—stops agitating for war, I believe there will be little danger of our involvement.

I do not believe that any two of them are powerful enough to carry this country to war without the support of the third. And to these three, as I have said, all other war groups are of secondary importance.

When hostilities commenced in Europe, in 1939, it was realized by these groups that the American people had no intention of entering the war. They knew it would be worse than useless to ask us for a declaration of war at that time. But they believed that this country could be entered into the war in very much the same way we were entered into the last one.

They planned: first, to prepare the United States for foreign war under the guise of American defense; second, to involve us in the war, step by step, without our realization; third, to create a series of incidents which would force us into the actual conflict. These plans were, of course, to be covered and assisted by the full power of their propaganda.

Our theaters soon became filled with plays portraying the glory of war. Newsreels lost all semblance of objectivity. Newspapers and magazines began to lose advertising if they carried anti-war articles. A smear campaign was instituted against individuals who opposed intervention. The terms "fifth columnist," "traitor," "Nazi," "anti-Semitic" were thrown ceaselessly at any one who dared to suggest that it was not to the best interests of the United States to enter the war. Men lost their jobs if they were frankly anti-war. Many others dared no longer speak.

Before long, lecture halls that were open to the advocates of war were closed to speakers who opposed it. A fear campaign was inaugurated. We were told that aviation, which has held the British fleet off the continent of Europe, made America more vulnerable than ever before to invasion. Propaganda was in full swing.

There was no difficulty in obtaining billions of dollars for arms under the guise of defending America. Our people stood united on a program of defense. Congress passed appropriation after appropriation for guns and planes and battleships, with the approval of the overwhelming majority of our citizens. That a large portion of these appropriations was to be used to build arms for Europe, we did not learn until later. That was another step.

To use a specific example; in 1939, we were told that we should increase our air corps to a total of 5,000 planes. Congress passed the necessary legislation. A few months later, the administration told us that the United States should have at least 50,000 planes for our national safety. But almost as fast as fighting planes were turned out from our factories, they were sent abroad, although our own air corps was in the utmost need of new equipment; so that today, two years after the start of war, the American army has a few hundred thoroughly modern bombers and fighters—less in fact, than Germany is able to produce in a single month.

Ever since its inception, our arms program has been laid out for the purpose of carrying on the war in Europe, far more than for the purpose of building an adequate defense for America.

Now at the same time we were being prepared for a foreign war, it was necessary, as I have said, to involve us in the war. This was accomplished under that now famous phrase "steps short of war."

England and France would win if the United States would only repeal its arms embargo and sell munitions for cash, we were told. And then a familiar refrain began, a refrain that marked every step we took toward war for many months—"the best way to defend America and keep out of war," we were told, was "by aiding the Allies."

First, we agreed to sell arms to Europe; next, we agreed to loan arms to Europe; then we agreed to patrol the ocean for Europe; then we occupied a European island in the war zone. Now, we have reached the verge of war.

The war groups have succeeded in the first two of their three major steps into war. The greatest armament program in our history is under way.

We have become involved in the war from practically every standpoint except actual shooting. Only the creation of sufficient "incidents" yet remains; and you see the first of these already taking place, according to plan—a plan that was never laid before the American people for their approval.

Men and women of Iowa: only one thing holds this country from war today. That is the rising opposition of the American people. Our system of democracy and representative government is on test today as it has never been before. We are on the verge of a war in which the only victor would be chaos and prostration.

We are on the verge of a war for which we are still unprepared, and for which no one has offered a feasible plan for victory—a war which cannot be won without sending our soldiers across the ocean to force a landing on a hostile coast against armies stronger than our own.

We are on the verge of war, but it is not yet too late to stay out. It is not too late to show that no amount of money, or propaganda, or patronage can force a free and independent people into war against its will. It is not yet too late to retrieve and to maintain the independent American destiny that our forefathers established in this new world.

The entire future rests upon our shoulders. It depends upon our action, our courage, and our intelligence. If you oppose our intervention in the war, now is the time to make your voice heard.

Help us to organize these meetings; and write to your representatives in Washington. I tell you that the last stronghold of democracy and representative government in this country is in our house of representatives and our senate.

There, we can still make our will known. And if we, the American people, do that, independence and freedom will continue to live among us, and there will be no foreign war.

From Lindbergh *by A. Scott Berg*, 1998

Peace, Lindbergh felt, could exist only so long as "we band together to preserve that most priceless possession, our inheritance of European blood, only so long as we guard ourselves against attack by foreign armies and dilution by foreign races." He viewed aviation as "a gift from heaven to those Western nations who were already the leaders of their era . . . a tool specially shaped for Western hands, a scientific art which others only copy in a mediocre fashion, another barrier between the teeming millions of Asia and the Grecian inheritance of Europe—one of those priceless possessions which permit the White race to live at all in a pressing sea of Yellow, Black, and Brown."

Lindbergh believed the Soviet Union had become the most evil empire on earth and that Western civilization depended on repelling it and the Asiatic powers that lay beyond its borders—the "Mongol and Persian and Moor." He wrote that it also depended on "a united strength among ourselves; on a strength too great for foreign armies to challenge; on a Western Wall of race and arms which can hold back either a Genghis Khan or an infiltration of inferior blood . . ." (page 394)

EXIT GHOST

For B. T.

Before death takes you, O take back this.
—Dylan Thomas, "Find Meat on Bones"

1

The Present Moment

I HADN'T been in New York in eleven years. Other than for surgery in Boston to remove a cancerous prostate, I'd hardly been off my rural mountain road in the Berkshires in those eleven years and, what's more, had rarely looked at a newspaper or listened to the news since 9/11, three years back; with no sense of loss—merely, at the outset, a kind of drought within me—I had ceased to inhabit not just the great world but the present moment. The impulse to be in it and of it I had long since killed.

But now I'd driven the hundred and thirty miles south to Manhattan to see a urologist at Mount Sinai Hospital who specialized in performing a procedure to help the thousands of men like me left incontinent by prostate surgery. By going in through a catheter inserted in the urethra to inject a gelatinous form of collagen where the neck of the bladder meets the urethra, he was getting significant improvement in about fifty percent of his patients. These weren't great odds, especially as "significant improvement" meant only a partial alleviation of the symptoms—reducing "severe incontinence" to "moderate incontinence" or "moderate" to "light." Still, because his results were better than those that other urologists had achieved using roughly the same technique (there was nothing to be done about the other hazard of radical prostatectomy that I, like tens of thousands of others, had not been lucky enough to escape—nerve damage resulting in impotence), I went to New York for a consultation, long after I imagined myself as having adapted to the practical inconveniences of the condition.

In the years since the surgery, I even thought I'd surmounted the shaming side of wetting oneself, overcome the disorienting shock that had been particularly trying in the first year and a half, during the months when the surgeon had given me reason to think that the incontinence would gradually disappear over time, as it does in a small number of fortunate patients. But despite the dailiness of the routine necessary to keep myself clean and odor-free, I must never truly have become accustomed to wearing the special undergarments and changing the pads and dealing with the "accidents," any more than I had mastered the underlying humiliation, because there I was, at the age of seventy-one, back on the Upper East Side of Manhattan, not many blocks from where I'd once lived as a vigorous, healthy younger man—there I was in the reception area of the urology department of Mount Sinai Hospital, about to be assured that with the permanent adherence of the collagen to the neck of the bladder I had a chance of exerting somewhat more control over my urine flow than an infant. Waiting there envisioning the procedure, sitting and flipping through the piled-up copies of *People* and *New York* magazine, I thought, Entirely beside the point. Turn around and go home.

I'd been alone these past eleven years in a small house on a dirt road in the deep country, having decided to live apart like that some two years before the cancer was diagnosed. I see few people. Since the death, a year earlier, of my neighbor and friend Larry Hollis, two, three days can go by when I speak to no one but the housekeeper who comes to clean each week and her husband, who is my caretaker. I don't go to dinner parties, I don't go to movies, I don't watch television, I don't own a cell phone or a VCR or a DVD player or a computer. I continue to live in the Age of the Typewriter and have no idea what the World Wide Web is. I no longer bother to vote. I write for most of the day and often into the night. I read, mainly the books that I first discovered as a student, the masterpieces of fiction whose power over me is no less, and in some cases greater, than it was in my initial exciting encounters with them. Lately I've been rereading Joseph Conrad for the first time in fifty years, most recently *The Shadow-Line*, which I'd brought with me to New York to look through yet again, having read it all in one go only the other night. I listen to music, I hike in the woods, when it's warm I swim in my pond, whose temperature, even in summer, never gets much above seventy degrees. I swim there without a suit, out of sight of everyone, so that if in my wake I leave a thin, billowing cloud of urine that visibly discolors the surrounding pond waters, I'm largely unperturbed and feel nothing like the chagrin that would be sure to crush me should my bladder involuntarily begin emptying itself while I was swimming in a public pool. There are plastic underpants with strongly elasticized edges designed for incontinent swimmers that are advertised as watertight, but when, after much equivocation, I went ahead and ordered a pair from a pool-supply catalogue and tried them out in the pond, I found that though wearing these biggish white bloomers beneath a bathing suit diminished the problem, it was not sufficiently eradicated to subdue my self-consciousness. Rather than take the chance of embarrassing myself and offending others, I gave up on the idea of swimming regularly down at the college pool for the bulk of the year (with bloomers under my suit) and continued to confine myself to sporadically yellowing the waters of my own pond during the Berkshires' few months of warm weather, when, rain or shine, I do my laps for half an hour every day.

A couple of times a week I go down the mountain into Athena, eight miles away, to shop for groceries, to get my clothes cleaned, occasionally to eat a meal or buy a pair of socks or pick up a bottle of wine or use the Athena College library. Tanglewood isn't far away, and I drive over to a concert there some ten times during the summer. I don't give readings or lectures or teach at a college or appear on TV. When my books are published, I keep to myself. I write every day of the week—otherwise I'm silent. I am tempted by the thought of not publishing at all—isn't the work all I need, the work and the working? What does it matter any longer if I'm incontinent and impotent?

Larry and Marylynne Hollis had moved up from West Hartford to the Berkshires after he'd retired from a lifelong position as an attorney with a Hartford insurance company. Larry was two years my junior, a meticulous, finicky man who seemed to believe that life was safe only if everything in it was punctiliously planned and whom, during the months when he first tried to draw me into his life, I did my best to avoid. I submitted eventually, not only because he was so dogged in his desire to alleviate my solitude but because I had never known anyone like him, an adult whose sad childhood biography had, by his own estimate, determined every choice he had made since his mother had died of cancer when he was ten, a mere four years after his father, who owned a Hartford linoleum store, had been bested no less miserably by the same disease. An only child, Larry was sent to live with relatives on the Naugatuck River southwest of Hartford, just outside bleak, industrial Waterbury, Connecticut, and there, in a boy's diary of "Things to Do," he laid out a future for himself that he followed to the letter for the rest of his life; from then on, everything undertaken was deliberately causal. He was content with no grade other than an A and even as an adolescent vigorously challenged any teacher who'd failed to accurately estimate his achievement. He attended summer sessions to accelerate his graduation from high school and get to college before he turned seventeen; he did the same during his summers at the University of Connecticut, where he had a full-tuition scholarship and worked in the library boiler room all year round to pay for his room and board so he could get out of college and change his name from Irwin Golub to Larry Hollis (as he'd planned to do when he was only ten) and join the air force, to become a fighter pilot known to the world as Lieutenant Hollis and qualify for the GI Bill; on leaving the service, he enrolled at Fordham and, in return for his three years in the air force, the government paid for his three years of law school. As an air force pilot stationed in Seattle he vigorously courted a pretty girl just out of high school who was named Collins and who met exactly his specifications for a wife, one of which was that she be of Irish extraction, with curly dark hair and with ice-blue eyes like his own. "I did not want to marry a Jewish girl. I did not want my children to be raised in the Jewish religion or have anything to do with being Jews." "Why?" I asked him. "Because that's not what I wanted for them" was his answer. That he wanted what he wanted and didn't want what he didn't want was the answer he gave to virtually every question I asked him about the utterly conventional structure he'd made of his life after all those early years of rushing and planning to build it. When he first knocked on my door to introduce himself—only a few days after he and Marylynne had moved into the house nearest to mine, some half mile down our dirt road—he immediately decided that he didn't want me to eat alone every night and that I had to take dinner at his house with him and his wife at least once a week. He didn't want me to be alone on Sundays—he couldn't bear the thought of anyone's being as alone as he'd been as an orphaned child, fishing in the Naugatuck on Sundays with his uncle, a dairy inspector for the state—and so he insisted that every Sunday morning we had a hiking date or, if the weather was bad, Ping-Pong matches, Ping-Pong being a pastime that I could barely tolerate but that I obliged him by playing rather than have a conversation with him about the writing of books. He asked me deadly questions about writing and was not content until I had answered them to his satisfaction. "Where do you get your ideas?" "How do you know if an idea is a good idea or a bad idea?" "How do you know when to use dialogue and when to use straight storytelling without dialogue?" "How do you know when a book is finished?" "How do you select a first sentence? How do you select a title? How do you select a last sentence?" "Which is your best book?" "Which is your worst book?" "Do you like your characters?" "Have you ever killed a character?" "I heard a writer on television say that the characters take over the book and write it themselves. Is that true?" He had wanted to be the father of one boy and one girl, and only after the fourth girl was born did Marylynne defy him and refuse to continue trying to produce the male heir that had been in his plans from the age of ten. He was a big, square-faced, sandy-haired man, and his eyes were crazy, ice-blue and crazy, unlike Marylynne's ice-blue eyes, which were beautiful, and the ice-blue eyes of the four pretty daughters, all of whom had gone to Wellesley because his closest friend in the air force had a sister at Wellesley and when Larry met her she exhibited just the sort of polish and decorum that he wanted to see in a daughter of his. When we would go to a restaurant (which we did every other Saturday night—that too he would have no other way) he could be counted on to be demanding with the waiter. Invariably there was a complaint about the bread. It wasn't fresh. It wasn't the kind he liked. There wasn't enough for everyone.

One evening after dinner he came by unexpectedly and gave me two orange kittens, one long-haired and one short-haired, just over eight weeks old. I had not asked for two kittens, nor had he apprised me of the gift beforehand. He said he'd been to his ophthalmologist for a checkup in the morning, seen a

sign by the receptionist's desk saying she had kittens to give
away. That afternoon he went to her house and picked out the
two most beautiful of the six for me. His first thought on seeing the sign was of me.

He put the kittens down on the floor. "This isn't the life you
should have," he said. "Whose is?" "Well, mine is, for one. I
have everything I ever wanted. I won't have you experiencing
the life of a person alone any longer. You do it to the goddamn
utmost. It's too extreme, Nathan." "As are you." "The hell I
am! I'm not the one who lives like this. All I'm pushing on you
is a little normality. This is too separate an existence for any
human being. At least you can have a couple of cats for company. I have all the stuff for them in the car."

He went back outside, and when he returned he emptied
onto the floor a couple of large supermarket bags containing
half a dozen little toys for them to bat around, a dozen cans of
cat food, a large bag of cat litter and a plastic litter box, two
plastic dishes for their food, and two plastic bowls for their
water.

"There's all you'll need," he said. "They're beauties. Look at
them. They'll give you a lot of pleasure."

He was exceedingly stern about all this, and there was nothing I could say except, "It's very thoughtful of you, Larry."

"What will you call them?"

"A and B."

"No. They need names. You live all day with the alphabet.
You can call the short-haired one Shorty and the long-haired
one Longy."

"That's what I'll do then."

In my one strong relationship I had fallen into the role that
Larry prescribed. I was basically obedient to Larry's discipline,
as was everyone in his life. Imagine, four daughters and not a
single one of them saying, "But I'd rather go to Barnard, I'd
rather go to Oberlin." Though I never had a sense of his being
a frightening paternal tyrant when I was with him and the family, how strange it was, I thought, that as far as I knew not one
of them had ever objected to her father's saying it's Wellesley
for you and that's it. But their willingness to be will-less as
Larry's obedient children was not quite as remarkable for me

to contemplate as was my own. Larry's path to power was to have complete acquiescence from the beloved in his life—mine was to have no one in my life.

He'd brought the cats on a Thursday. I kept them through Sunday. During that time I did virtually no work on my book. Instead I spent my time throwing the cats their toys or stroking them, together or in turn in my lap, or just sitting and looking at them eating, or playing, or grooming themselves, or sleeping. I kept their litter box in a corner of the kitchen and at night put them in the living room and shut my bedroom door behind me. When I awoke in the morning the first thing I did was rush to the door to see them. There they would be, just beside the door, waiting for me to open it.

On Monday morning I phoned Larry and said, "Please come and take the cats."

"You hate them."

"To the contrary. If they stay, I'll never write another word. I can't have these cats in the house with me."

"Why not? What the hell is wrong with you?"

"They're too delightful."

"Good. Great. That's the idea."

"Come and take them, Larry. If you like, I'll return them to the ophthalmologist's receptionist myself. But I can't have them here any longer."

"What is this? An act of defiance? A display of bravado? I'm a disciplined man myself, but you put me to shame. I didn't bring two people to live with you, God forbid. I brought two cats. Tiny *kittens*."

"I accepted them graciously, did I not? I've given them a try, have I not? Please take them away."

"I won't."

"I never asked for them, you know."

"That doesn't prove anything to me. You ask for nothing."

"Give me the phone number of the ophthalmologist's receptionist."

"No."

"All right. I'll take care of it myself."

"You're crazy," he said.

"Larry, I can't be made into a new being by two kittens."

"But that's exactly what is happening. Exactly what you won't *allow* to happen. I cannot understand it—a man of your intelligence turning himself into this kind of person. It's beyond me."

"There are many inexplicable things in life. You shouldn't trouble yourself over my tiny opacity."

"All right. You win. I'll come, I'll get the cats. But I'm not finished with you, Zuckerman."

"I have no reason to believe that you are finished or that you can be finished. You're a little crazy too, you know."

"The hell I am!"

"Hollis, please, I'm too old to work myself over anymore. Come get the cats."

Just before the fourth daughter was to be married in New York City—to a young Irish-American attorney who, like Larry, had attended Fordham Law School—he was diagnosed with cancer. The same day the family went down to New York to assemble for the wedding, Larry's oncologist put him into the university hospital in Farmington, Connecticut. His first night in the hospital, after the nurse had taken his vital signs and given him a sleeping pill, he removed another hundred or so sleeping pills secreted in his shaving kit and, using the water in the glass by his bedside, swallowed them in the privacy of his darkened room. Early the next morning, Marylynne received the phone call from the hospital informing her that her husband had committed suicide. A few hours later, at her insistence —she hadn't been his wife all those years for nothing—the family went ahead with the wedding, and the wedding luncheon, and only then returned to the Berkshires to plan his funeral.

Later I learned that Larry had arranged with the doctor beforehand to be hospitalized that day rather than the Monday of the following week, which he could easily have done. In that way the family would be together in one place when they got the news that he was dead; moreover, by killing himself in the hospital, where there were professionals on hand to attend to his corpse, he had spared Marylynne and the children all that he could of the grotesqueries attendant upon suicide.

He was sixty-eight years old when he died and, with the exception of the plan recorded in his "Things to Do" diary to one day have a son named Larry Hollis Jr., he had, amazingly, achieved every last goal that he had imagined for himself when he was orphaned at ten. He had managed to wait long enough to see his youngest daughter married and into a new life and still wind up able to avoid what he most dreaded—his children witnessing the excruciating agonies of a dying parent that he had witnessed when his father and his mother each slowly succumbed to cancer. He had even left a message for me. He had even thought to look after me. In the mail the Monday after the Sunday when we all learned of his death, I received this letter: "Nathan, my boy, I don't like leaving you like this. In this whole wide world, you cannot be alone. You cannot be without contact with anything. You must promise me that you will not go on living as you were when I found you. Your loyal friend, Larry."

So was that why I remained in the urologist's waiting room— because one year earlier, almost to the day, Larry had sent me that note and then killed himself? I don't know, and it wouldn't have mattered if I did. I sat there because I sat there, flipping through magazines of the kind I hadn't seen for years —looking at photos of famous actors, famous models, famous dress designers, famous chefs and business tycoons, learning about where I could go to buy the most expensive, the cheapest, the hippest, the tightest, the softest, the funniest, the tastiest, the tackiest of just about anything produced for America's consumption, and waiting for my doctor's appointment.

I'd arrived the afternoon before. I'd reserved a room at the Hilton, and after unpacking my bag, I went out to Sixth Avenue to take in the city. But where was I to begin? Revisiting the streets where I'd once lived? The neighborhood places where I used to eat my lunch? The newsstand where I bought my paper and the bookstores where I used to browse? Should I retrace the long walks I used to take at the end of my workday? Or since I no longer see that many of them, should I seek out other members of my species? During the years I'd been gone there'd been phone calls and letters, but my house in the Berkshires is small and I hadn't encouraged visitors, and so, in time, personal contact became infrequent. Editors I'd worked with over the years had left their publishing houses or retired.

Many of the writers I'd known had, like me, left town. Women I'd known had changed jobs or married or moved away. The first two people I thought to drop in on had died. I knew that they had died, that their distinctive faces and familiar voices were no more—and yet, out in front of the hotel, deciding how and where to reenter for an hour or two the life left behind, contemplating the simplest ways of putting a foot back in, I had a moment not unlike Rip Van Winkle's when, after having slept for twenty years, he came out of the mountains and walked back to his village believing he'd merely been gone overnight. Only when he unexpectedly felt the long grizzled beard that grew from his chin did he grasp how much time had passed and in turn learned that he was no longer a colonial subject of the British Crown but a citizen of the newly established United States. I couldn't have felt any more out of it myself had I turned up on the corner of Sixth Avenue and West 54th with Rip's rusty gun in my hand and his ancient clothes on my back and an army of the curious crowding around to look me over, this eviscerated stranger walking in their midst, a relic of bygone days amid the noises and buildings and workers and traffic.

I started toward the subway to take a train downtown to Ground Zero. Begin there, where the biggest thing of all occurred; but because I've withdrawn as witness and participant both, I never made it to the subway. That would have been wholly out of character for the character I'd become. Instead, after crossing the park, I found myself in the familiar rooms of the Metropolitan Museum, wiling away the afternoon like someone who had no catching up to do.

The next day when I left the doctor's office, I had an appointment to return the following morning for the collagen injection. There'd been a cancellation, and he could fit me in. The doctor would prefer it, his nurse told me, if, after the hospital procedure, I stayed overnight in my hotel rather than return immediately to the Berkshires—complications rarely occurred in the aftermath of the procedure, but remaining nearby till the next morning was a worthwhile precaution. Barring any mishap, by then I could leave for home and resume my usual activities. The doctor himself expected a considerable improvement, not excluding the possibility of the injection's restoring close to complete bladder control. On occasion the collagen "traveled," he explained, and he'd have to go in a second or third time before getting it to adhere permanently to the neck of the bladder; then again, one injection could suffice.

Fine, I said, and instead of reaching a decision only after I'd had a chance to think everything over back home, I surprised myself by seizing at the opening in his schedule, and not even when I was out of the encouraging environment of his office and in the elevator to the main floor was I able to summon up an ounce of wariness to restrain my sense of rejuvenation. I closed my eyes in the elevator and saw myself swimming in the college pool at the end of the day, carefree and without fear of embarrassment.

It was ludicrous to feel so triumphant, and perhaps a measure less of the transformation promised than of the toll taken by the discipline of seclusion and by the decision to excise from life everything that stood between me and my task—the toll of which till then I'd remained oblivious (willed obliviousness being a primary component of the discipline). In the country there was nothing tempting my hope. I had made peace with my hope. But when I came to New York, in only hours New York did what it does to people—awakened the possibilities. Hope breaks out.

One floor below the urology department, the elevator stopped and a frail, elderly woman got on. The cane she carried, along with a faded red rainhat pulled low over her skull, gave her an eccentric, yokelish look, but when I heard her speaking quietly with the doctor who'd boarded the elevator with her—a man in his mid-forties who was lightly guiding her by the arm—when I heard the foreign tinge to her English, I took a second look, wondering whether she was someone I'd once known. The voice was as distinctive as the accent, especially as it wasn't a voice one would associate with her wraith-like looks but a young person's voice, incongruously girlish and innocent of hardship. I know that voice, I thought. I know the accent. I know the woman. On the main floor, I was crossing the hospital lobby just behind them, heading for the street, when I happened to overhear the elderly woman's name spoken by the doctor. That was why I followed her out the hospital door and to a luncheonette a few blocks south on Madison. I did indeed know her.

It was ten-thirty, and only four or five customers were still eating breakfast. She took a seat in a booth. I found an empty table for myself. She didn't seem to be aware of my having followed her or even of my presence a few feet away. Her name was Amy Bellette. I'd met her only once. I'd never forgotten her.

Amy Bellette was wearing no coat, just the red rainhat and a pale cardigan sweater and what registered as a thin cotton summer dress until I realized that it was in fact a pale blue hospital gown whose clips had been replaced at the back with buttons and around whose waist she wore a ropelike belt. Either she's impoverished or she's crazy, I thought.

A waiter took her order, and after he walked away she opened her purse and took out a book and while reading it casually reached up and removed the hat and set it down beside her. The side of her head facing me was shaved bald, or had been not too long ago—fuzz was growing there—and a sinuous surgical scar cut a serpentine line across her skull, a raw, well-defined scar that curved from behind her ear up to the edge of her brow. All her hair of any length was on the other side of her head, graying hair knotted loosely in a braid and along which the fingers of her right hand were absent-mindedly moving—freely playing with the hair as the hand of any child reading a book might do. Her age? Seventy-five. She was twenty-seven when we met in 1956.

I ordered coffee, sipped it, lingered over it, finished it, and without looking her way, got up and left the luncheonette and the astonishing reappearance and pathetic reconstitution of Amy Bellette, one whose existence—so rich with promise and expectation when I first encountered her—had obviously gone very wrong.

The procedure the next morning took fifteen minutes. So simple! A wonder! Medical magic! I saw myself once again swimming laps in the college pool, clad in only an ordinary bathing suit and leaving no stream of urine in my wake. I saw myself going blithely about without carrying along a supply of the absorbent cotton pads that for nine years now I had worn day and night cradled in the crotch of my plastic briefs. A painless fifteen-minute procedure and life seemed limitless again. I was a man no longer powerless over something so elementary as managing to piss in a pot. To possess control over one's bladder—who among the whole and healthy ever considers the freedom that bestows or the anxious vulnerability its loss can impose on even the most confident among us? I who'd never thought along these lines before, who from the age of twelve was bent on singularity and welcomed whatever was unusual in me—I could now be like everyone else.

As though the ever-hovering shadow of humiliation isn't, in fact, what *binds* one to everyone else.

Well before noon I was back in my hotel. I had plenty to keep me busy while I waited out the day before returning home. The previous afternoon—after deciding to leave Amy Bellette undisturbed—I'd gone down to the Strand, the venerable used-book store south of Union Square, and for under a hundred dollars I'd been able to purchase original editions of the six volumes of E. I. Lonoff's short stories. The books happened also to be in my library at home, but I'd bought them anyway and carried them back to the hotel in order to skip chronologically through the various volumes during the hours I would have to remain in New York.

When you undertake an experiment like this after spending twenty or thirty years away from a writer's work, you can't be sure what you're going to turn up, about either the datedness of the once admired writer or the naiveté of the enthusiast you once were. But by midnight I was no less convinced than I was in the 1950s that the narrow range of Lonoff's prose and the restricted scope of his interests and the unyielding restraint he employed, rather than collapsing inward a story's implications and diminishing its impact, produced instead the enigmatic reverberations of a gong, reverberations that left one marveling at how so much gravity and so much levity could be joined, in so small a space, to a skepticism so far-reaching. It was precisely the limitation of means that made of each little story not something stultifying but a feat of magic, as if a folk tale or a fairy tale or a Mother Goose rhyme were inwardly illuminated by the mind of Pascal.

He was as good as I had thought. He was better. It was as though there were some color previously missing or withheld from our literary spectrum and Lonoff alone had it. Lonoff *was* that color, a twentieth-century American writer unlike any other, and he had been out of print for decades. I wondered if his achievement would have been so completely forgotten if he had finished his novel and lived to see it published. I wondered if he *had* been working on a novel at the end of his life. If not, how was one to understand the silence preceding his death, those five years that coincided with the breakup of his marriage to Hope and the new life undertaken alongside Amy Bellette? I could still remember the mordant, uncomplaining way he had described to me, a worshipful young acolyte eager to emulate him, the monotony of an existence that was composed of pains-takingly writing his stories throughout the day, reading studi-ously, with a notebook at his side, in the evening, and, nearly mute from mental fatigue, sharing meals and a bed with a loyal, wretchedly lonely wife of thirty-five years. (For discipline is imposed not just on oneself but on those in one's orbit.) One might have imagined a regeneration of intensity—and, with it, of productivity—in an original writer of such imposing forti-tude, still not quite into his sixties, who had arranged finally to escape this imprisoning regimen (or whose wife had forced him, by her angry, precipitate departure) and to take as his mate a charming, intelligent, adoring young woman half his age. One might have imagined that after tearing himself away from the rural landscape and the married life that together held him in check—that made the artistic enterprise for him so ruthlessly rock-bottom a sacrifice—E. I. Lonoff wouldn't have had to be quite so severely punished for his waywardness, needn't have had to be reduced to so annihilating a silence just for daring to believe that he might be permitted to rewrite fifty times over his paragraph a day while living in something other than a cage.

What *was* the story of those five years? Once something did happen to that sedate, reclusive writer who—assisted by the forlorn irony that pervaded his view of the world—had bravely resigned himself to nothing's ever happening to him, what then ensued? Amy Bellette would know—*she* was what had hap-pened to him. If somewhere there was the manuscript of a Lonoff novel, finished or unfinished, she'd know about that, too. Unless the entire estate had passed on to Hope and the three children, the manuscript would be in her hands. And should the novel legally belong to the immediate family that had survived the author and not to her, Amy, who'd have been at his side while the book was being written, would have read every page of every draft and would know how well or how poorly the new venture had gone. Even if his death had cut short its completion, why hadn't finished sections of it been published in the literary quarterlies that used to regularly run his stories? Was it because the novel was no good that no one had seen to its publication? And if so, was that failure the consequence of his having left behind everything that he had counted on to chain him to his talent, of his having at long last gained the freedom and found the pleasure against which captivity had been designed to protect him? Or could he never subdue the shame of subverting his suffering at Hope's expense? But wasn't it Hope who had done the subverting *for* him—by doing the leaving? In so resolute and experienced a writer— one for whom realizing his distinctly laconic brand of vernacular fluency had been a perpetual ordeal to be surmounted only by the most diligent application of patience and will—why a five-year block? Why should so ordinary a renovation—the middle-age life change, commonly thought to be replenishing, of taking a new mate and setting up house in a new locale— cripple a man with the forbearance of a Lonoff?

If that's what had crippled him.

By the time I was ready for sleep, I knew how off the mark these questions might be in helping to understand what it was that stifled Lonoff in his final years. If, between the ages of fifty-six and sixty-one, he had failed at writing a novel, it was probably because (as he may always have suspected) the novelist's passion for amplification was just another form of excess that ran counter to his own special gift for condensation and reduction. A novelist's passion for amplification probably explained my having spent my day raising such questions in the first place.

What it didn't explain was my failing to introduce myself to Amy Bellette in that coffee shop and to find out from her, if not everything there was to know, whatever she was willing to tell.

*

The three children were grown and gone by the time I met Lonoff and Hope in 1956, and though the grinding discipline of his daily writing life was in no way altered by their dispersal —no more than by the disappearance of passion that dogs connubial life—Hope's response to her isolation in the remote Berkshire farmhouse was vividly on display in just the few hours I was there. Having valiantly tried to remain calm and sociable during dinner on the evening I arrived, she'd eventually broken down and, after hurling a wine glass at the wall, had run from the table in tears, leaving Lonoff to explain to me—or, as it happened, to feel unobliged to explain—what was going on. At breakfast the following morning, where Amy and I both were present and where the incendiary houseguest with her enchantingly serene, self-possessed demeanor—with the clarity of her mind, with her play-acting, with her mystery, with the sparklingness of her comedy—was being especially delightful, Hope's stoic façade had given way again, but this time when she left the table it was to pack a bag and to put on her coat and, despite the freezing weather and the snowy roads, to walk out the front door, announcing that she was leaving the post of great writer's neglected wife to none other than Lonoff's former student and (from all indications) his paramour. "This is officially your house!" she'd notified the young victor, and left for Boston. "You will now be the person he is not living with!"

I left only an hour later and never saw any of them again. It was by a fluke that I'd been there for the blowup at all. From a nearby writers' colony where I'd been staying, I had sent Lonoff a packet of my first published short stories, along with an earnest introductory letter, and in this way managed to wangle the dinner invitation that had turned into an overnight stay only because bad weather had prevented me from departing till the next day. In the late forties, into the fifties, and until his death from leukemia in 1961, Lonoff was probably America's most esteemed short story writer—if not that to the country at large, then among many in the intellectual and academic elites —the author of six collections whose mingling of comedy and darkness had desentimentalized totally the standard hard-luck saga of the immigrant Jew; his fiction read like an unfolding of disjointed dreams, yet without sacrificing the factuality of time and place to surreal fakery or magic-realist gimmickry. The annual output of stories had never been great, and in his last five years, when he was supposedly working on a novel, his first, and the book that admirers claimed would win him international recognition and the Nobel Prize that should already have been his, he published no stories at all. Those were the years when he made his home with Amy in Cambridge and was affiliated loosely with Harvard. He had never married Amy; apparently, during those five years, he had never legally been free to marry anyone. And then he was dead.

The evening before I was to leave for home, I went to eat at a small Italian restaurant not far from the hotel. The ownership hadn't changed since I'd last eaten there back in the early nineties, and to my surprise I was greeted by name by the youngest of the family, Tony, who seated me at the corner table I'd always liked best because it was the quietest in the place.

You depart while others, unamazingly enough, stay behind to continue doing what they've always done—and, upon returning, you are surprised and momentarily thrilled to see that they are still there, and, too, reassured by there being somebody who is spending his whole life in the same little place and who has no desire to go.

"You moved away, Mr. Zuckerman," Tony said. "We don't ever see you."

"I moved up north. I live in the mountains now."

"It must be beautiful there. Nice and quiet to write."

"It is," I said. "How's the family?"

"Everybody's good. Celia, though, she passed. Remember my aunt? Who was at the register?"

"Sure I do. I'm sorry to hear Celia's gone. Celia wasn't that old."

"No, not at all. But last year she got sick, and she went like that. But you look good," he said. "You want something to drink? Chianti, right?"

Though Tony's hair had gone the same steel gray as his grandfather Pierluigi's—as revealed in the oil painting of the restaurant's immigrant founder, handsome as an actor in his chef's apron, that still hung just beside the coat-check room—and though Tony's frame had grown big and soft since I'd last seen him, in his early thirties, back when he was the only lean and bony member remaining in his well-fed restaurant clan, back some hundred thousand bowls of pasta ago, the menu itself hadn't changed, the specialties hadn't changed, the bread in the bread basket hadn't changed, and when the dessert cart was navigated past my table by the head waiter, I saw that the head waiter hadn't changed nor had the desserts. You would think that my relationship to all of this could not have shifted one iota, that once I had my drink in my hand and was chewing on a chunk of Italian bread of the kind that I'd eaten here dozens of times before I'd feel pleasantly at home, and yet I didn't. I felt like an impostor, pretending to be the man Tony had once known and suddenly craving to be him. But by living mostly in solitude for eleven years, I had got rid of him. I had gone off to flee a genuine menace; in the end, I stayed away to be rid of what no longer remained of interest and, as who doesn't dream of being, to be rid of the lingering consequences of a life's mistakes (for me, repeated marital failure, furtive adultery, the emotional boomerang of erotic attachment). Presumably by taking action rather than just dreaming of it, I had got rid of myself in the process.

I'd brought something to read, just as I used to do when I ate at Pierluigi's by myself. Living alone, I'd become habituated to reading with my meals, but on this night I set the paper down on the table and instead looked around at those eating their dinner in New York City on the evening of October 28, 2004. One of city life's notable satisfactions: strangers fostering the chimera of human accord by eating together in a good little restaurant. And I was one among them. Late in the day to find so commonplace an experience momentous, but I did.

Only with my coffee did I open the paper, the current issue of *The New York Review of Books*. I hadn't seen a copy since leaving New York. I hadn't wanted to see one, though I'd been a subscriber since the paper's inauguration in the early sixties and, in its first years, an occasional contributor. In passing a newsstand on the way to Pierluigi's I had caught a glimpse of the top of the front page, where above a set of David Levine caricatures of the presidential candidates there was printed an unfurled banner on which yellow lettering announced "Special Election Issue"—and beneath that, above a list of some dozen

contributors, the words "The Election and America's Future"
—and I had paid the newsdealer four dollars and fifty cents
and carried the paper off with me to the restaurant. But now I
was sorry I'd bought it, and even when curiosity got the best
of me, instead of starting with the table of contents and the
opening pages of the election symposium, I began my reimmersion by tiptoeing in at the back, reading the classified adver-
tisements. "BEAUTIFUL photographer/art educator, loving
mother . . ." "COMPLEX, THOUGHTFUL, DESIROUS and desirable woman, legally married . . ." "ENERGETIC, FUN-LOVING,
FIT, established man of many interests . . ." "GREEN-EYED,
funny, kooky, curvaceous . . ." I skipped to "Real Estate," and
in the brief "Rentals" column—above the much longer "International Rentals" column, where the residences available were
mainly in Paris and London—I came upon an ad so pointedly
addressed to me that I felt myself being urged on, as though
with a whip, by chance, sheer chance that seemed brimming
with intention.

> RELIABLE writing couple in early thirties wishes to swap homey,
> book-lined 3-room Upper West Side apartment for quiet rural
> retreat one hundred miles from New York. New England pre-
> ferred. Immediate exchange, ideally for one year . . .

Without waiting—as precipitously as I had gone ahead with
the collagen injection I'd intended to think about back home
before committing myself to having it, as precipitously as I'd
bought *The New York Review*—I went down the stairway alongside the kitchen to where I remembered a pay phone hung on
the wall across from the men's room. I'd copied the phone
number onto a piece of scrap paper on which I'd written the
name "Amy Bellette." Quickly I dialed and told the man who
answered that I was responding to his ad to exchange residences for a year. I owned a small house in rural western Massachusetts, located on a dirt road atop a mountain and across
from a large marshy swamp that was a bird and wildlife refuge.
New York was a hundred and twenty-eight miles away, my
nearest neighbors were half a mile away, and it was eight miles
down the mountain to a college town where you could find a
supermarket, a bookstore, a wine shop, a good campus library,
and a convivial bar with edible food. If that sounded like what

he had in mind, I'd be interested in stopping by, I said, and seeing the apartment and discussing a swap. I was only blocks away from the Upper West Side; if it wasn't an inconvenience I could be there in minutes.

The man laughed. "You sound like you want to move in tonight."

"If you'll move out tonight," I told him, and I meant it.

Before returning to my table, I stopped off in the men's room and ducked into the single stall, where I lowered my trousers to learn whether the procedure had begun to work. To blot out what I saw I shut my eyes, and to blot out what I felt I cursed aloud. "A fucking dream!" by which I meant the dream of being suddenly like everyone else.

I set about removing the absorbent cotton pad from my plastic briefs and replacing it with a fresh one from a small packet I carried in my inside jacket pocket. I wrapped the dirty pad in toilet paper, threw it into a covered wastebasket beside the sink, washed and dried my hands, and, fighting off the gloom, went upstairs to pay my bill.

I walked to West 71st Street, startled, at Columbus Circle, to see that the bulky fortress of the Coliseum had metamorphosed into a pair of glass skyscrapers joined at the hip and lined at street level with swanky shops. I wandered into the arcade and out, and when I continued north on Broadway I felt not so much that I was in a foreign country as that some optical trick were being played on me, that things appeared as in the reflection of a fun-house mirror, everything simultaneously familiar and unrecognizable. Not without some hardship, as I've said, I'd conquered the solitary's way of life; I knew its tests and satisfactions and over time had shaped the scope of my needs to its limitations, long ago abandoning excitement, intimacy, adventure, and antagonisms in favor of quiet, steady, predictable contact with nature and reading and my work. Why invite the unanticipated, why court any more shocks or surprises than those that aging would be sure to deliver without my prompting? Yet I continued up Broadway—past the crowds at Lincoln Center that I did not wish to join, the theater complexes whose movies I had no inclination to see, the leather goods shops and the gourmet food shops whose merchandise I didn't care to buy—unwilling to oppose the power of the crazed hope of rejuvenation that was affecting all my actions, the crazed hope of the procedure's reversing the strongest side of my decline, and aware of the mistake I was making, a revenant, a man who'd cut himself off from sustained human contact and its possibilities yielding to the illusion of starting again. And not through my own distinctive mental capacities but through the body refashioned, life seeming limitless again. Of course this is the wrong thing to do, the insane thing to do, but if so, I thought, what is the right thing to do, the sane thing, and who am I to claim that I ever knew enough to do it? I did what I did—that's all one knows looking backward. I made the ordeal that was mine out of the inspiration and the ineptitude that were mine—the inspiration *was* the ineptitude—and more than likely I am now doing the same. And at this batty speed, no less, as though fearful that my insanity is going to evaporate at any minute and I'm going to stop being able to go on with all that I'm doing that I know very well I shouldn't be doing.

The elevator of the small six-story white-brick apartment building took me to the top floor, where I was greeted at the doorway of apartment 6B by a chubby young man with a soft, agreeable manner who immediately said, "You're the writer." "I am. And you?" "*A* writer," he said with a smile. He led me inside and introduced me to his wife. "Yet a third writer," he said. She was a tall, slender young woman who, unlike her husband, no longer had a playful, childlike aspect in evidence anywhere, at least not tonight. Her long, narrow face was curtained by straight, fine black hair that fell to her shoulders and a little below, the cut seemingly designed to conceal some disfiguring blemish, though by no means one that was physical—she had an impeccable, creamily soft surface, whatever else she might be hiding. That she was boundlessly loved by her husband and the source of his sustenance was apparent in the undisguised tenderness with which his every gaze and gesture enveloped her, even when what she said was not necessarily to his liking. It was clear that she was considered by them the more brilliant of the two and that his personality was swaddled in hers. Her

name was Jamie Logan, his Billy Davidoff, and as they walked
me through the apartment, he seemed to take pleasure in def-
erentially calling me Mr. Zuckerman.

It was an attractive apartment of three spacious rooms, furnished with pricey European-designed modern furniture and
Oriental throw rugs and a beautiful Persian rug in the living
room. There was a large workspace in the bedroom overlooking a tall plane tree in the rear yard and another workspace in
the living room, which looked across to a church. Books were
piled everywhere, and hanging on the walls where there
weren't book-laden shelves were framed photographs of statu-
ary in Italian cities taken by Billy. Who was funding the modest
opulence of these two thirty-year-olds? My guess was that the
money was his, that they had met at Amherst or Williams or
Brown, a tame, wealthy, kindhearted Jewish boy and an intense
poor girl, Irish, maybe half Italian, who from grade school on
had never stopped excelling, self-propelled, perhaps even
something of a climber . . .

I had it wrong. The money was hers and it came from Texas.
Her father was a Houston oilman with origins as American as
American origins could be. Billy's Jewish family owned a luggage and umbrella shop in Philadelphia. The two had met in
the graduate writing program at Columbia. Neither had as yet
published a book, though five years earlier she'd had a short
story in *The New Yorker* that had prompted inquiries about a
novel from agents and publishers. I wouldn't have guessed
right off that hers was the more developed creative disposition.

After I was shown around, we sat in the quiet living room,
where the windows were double-glazed. The small Lutheran
church across the street, a charming little building with narrow
windows and pointed arches and a rough stone façade, though
probably built in the early 1900s, seemed designed to transport
its Upper West Side congregants back five or six centuries to a
rural village in northern Europe. Immediately outside the window the fanlike leaves of a thriving ginkgo tree were just beginning to lose their summertime green. A recording of Strauss's
Four Last Songs had been playing softly in the background when
I'd come into the apartment, and when Billy went to turn off
the CD player, I wondered if the *Four Last Songs* were what he
or Jamie happened to have been listening to before I came or if

my arrival had prompted one or the other of them to play such dramatically elegiac, ravishingly emotional music written by a very old man at the close of his life.

"His favorite instrument is the female voice," I said.

"Or two," said Billy. "His favorite combination was two women singing together. The end of *Rosenkavalier.* The end of *Arabella.* In *The Egyptian Helen.*"

"You know Strauss," I said to him.

"Well, my favorite instrument is the female voice too."

His intention in saying that was to flatter his wife, but I pretended otherwise. "Do you write music as well?" I asked him.

"No, no," said Billy. "I have a hard enough time with fiction."

"Well, my house in the woods," I told them, "is no more peaceful than this."

"We're leaving for only a year," Billy said.

"May I ask why?"

"Jamie's idea," he answered, sounding not as tamed as I'd imagined him.

Reluctant to appear to interrogate her, I merely looked her way. Her sensual presence was strong—perhaps she kept herself on the thin side so it wouldn't be stronger. Or maybe so it would, since her breasts weren't those of an undernourished woman. She wore jeans and a low-cut, lacy silk blouse that resembled a little lingerie top—that *was* a little lingerie top, I realized upon looking again—and wrapping her torso was a longish cardigan with a thick edge of wide ribbing and a tie of the same ribbing pulled loosely around her narrow waist. It was a garment at the other end of the spectrum of female apparel from the hospital gown Amy Bellette had converted into a dress, its color paler and softer than tan and woven of a thick, soft cashmere. The sweater could easily have cost a thousand bucks, and she looked languid wearing it, languid and in enticing repose, as though she were wearing a kimono. She spoke rapidly and quietly, however, as highly complicated people will do, under pressure particularly.

"Why are you coming to New York?" was Jamie's response to my gaze.

"I have a friend who's ill here," I said.

I still had no clear idea what I was doing in their apartment, what it was I wanted. To make things different for myself? Exactly how? To see a Victorian replica of a medieval church out the window while I worked rather than my mammoth maples and uneven stone walls? To see cars moving when I looked down to the street below rather than the deer and the crows and the wild turkeys that populated my woods?

"She has a brain tumor," I explained, merely out of a need to talk. To talk to her.

"Well, we're leaving," Jamie told me, "because I don't wish to be snuffed out in the name of Allah."

"Isn't that unlikely," I asked, "on West Seventy-first?"

"This city is at the heart of their pathology. Bin Laden dreams only of evil, and he calls that evil 'New York.'"

"I wouldn't know," I said. "I don't see any papers. I haven't for years. I picked up a *New York Review* for the ads. I have no idea what's going on."

"You do know about the election," Billy said.

"Practically nothing," I said. "People don't talk openly about politics in the hick town where I live, certainly never to an outsider like me. I don't turn on the TV much. No, I don't know a thing."

"You haven't followed the war?"

"No."

"You haven't followed Bush's lies?"

"No."

"That's hard to believe," Billy said, "when I think of your books."

"I've served my tour as exasperated liberal and indignant citizen," I said, seemingly talking to him while once again talking for her, and out of a motive hidden even from myself when I began, out of a yearning whose might I would have hoped had all but withered away. Whatever the force prying me back open at seventy-one—whatever the force that had sent me down to New York to the urologist in the first place—was quickly regathering its strength in the presence of Jamie Logan wearing her widenecked thousand-buck cardigan sweater hanging loose over a low-cut camisole. "I don't wish to register an opinion, I don't want to express myself on 'the issues'—I don't even want to know what they are. It no longer suits me to know, and what doesn't suit me, I expunge. That's why I live where I do. That's why you want to live where I do."

"Why Jamie wants to," Billy said.

"It's so. I'm scared all the time," she said. "A new vantage point might help." Here she broke off, but not because she had thought better of admitting her fears to someone interested in swapping his safely remote rural residence for a potentially imperiled New York apartment, but because Billy was looking at her as though she were deliberately attempting to provoke him in front of me. If his relationship to her was worshipful, it wasn't exclusively worshipful. This was a marriage, after all, and he could be tried by his lovely wife as well.

"Are others leaving," I asked her, "because they're frightened of a terrorist attack?"

"Others have certainly been talking about it," Billy allowed.

"Some have left," Jamie put in.

"People you know?" I asked.

"No," Billy said decisively. "We'll be the first."

With a smile not overly generous, with what I, transfixed by her (subjugated as quickly as I imagined Billy to have been, though for reasons having to do with finding myself at the other edge of experience from him, at the rim that borders oblivion), took to be the air of a temptress—a tauntingly aloof temptress—Jamie added, "I like to be first."

"Well, if you want my place," I said, "it's yours. Here, I'll draw a diagram of the house."

When I got back to the hotel, I phoned Rob Massey, the local carpenter who's worked for ten years as my caretaker, and his wife, Belinda, who during that time has been cleaning my place once a week and who does the grocery shopping when I don't want to drive the eight miles into Athena. I read out a list to them of what I wanted packed and brought to New York and told them about the young married couple who would be moving up to my place the following week and living there for the next year.

"I hope this doesn't have to do with your health," Rob said. It was Rob who'd driven me to Boston and then home from the hospital when I'd had my prostate surgery nine years earlier, and Belinda who'd cooked for me and, with great sickroom sensitivity and gentleness, assisted me during the uncomfortable weeks of recovery. I hadn't been hospitalized since or ill with anything other than a cold, but they were a kindly, childless middle-aged couple—a wiry, shrewd, agreeable husband and a buxom, gregarious, hyperefficient wife—and since the operation they had treated my slightest needs as if they were of uppermost importance. I couldn't have done better if I'd had children of my own to watch me grow old, and might have done a lot worse. Neither had read a word I'd written, though whenever they spotted my name or my photo in a paper or a magazine, Belinda never failed to clip the article and bring it to me. I'd thank her, admit I hadn't seen it, and, later, to ensure that I didn't inadvertently offend this warm, bighearted woman who believed I kept the clippings in what she referred to as my "scrapbook," I'd tear it into the tiniest, unrecognizable pieces before throwing it into the garbage, unread. That stuff too I'd expunged long ago.

For my seventieth birthday Belinda had cooked a dinner of venison steaks and red cabbage for the three of us to eat at my place. The meat—hunted down by Rob in the woods back of my house—was wonderful, and so was the cheery generosity and warm affection of my two friends. They toasted me with champagne and gave me a maroon lamb's wool sweater they'd bought for me down in Athena; then they asked me to make a speech about what it was like to be seventy. After donning their sweater, I rose from my chair at the head of the table and said to them, "It'll be a short speech. Think of the year 4000." They smiled, as though I were about to crack a joke, and so I added, "No, no. Think seriously about 4000. Imagine it. In all its dimensions, in all its aspects. The year 4000. Take your time." After a minute of sober silence, I quietly said to them, "That's what it's like to be seventy," and sat back down.

Rob Massey was the fantasy caretaker, the caretaker everybody wants, Belinda the fantasy cleaning woman, the cleaning woman everyone wants, and though I no longer had Larry Hollis watching over me, I still had the two of them, and all the time I devoted to my writing, even the writing itself, was in part the result of their looking so well after everything else. And now I was letting them go.

"My health's fine. I've just got some work to do down here,

and so I exchanged houses with them. I'll stay in touch with you, and if there's anything I should know, call me collect."

Good-naturedly, Rob said to me, "Nathan, nobody's called anybody collect for twenty years."

"Is that so? Well, you know what I mean. I'm going to tell them to keep Belinda on once a week and to turn to you two if anything goes wrong. I'll pay you directly, unless Jamie Logan or Billy Davidoff asks you to do something especially for them, and that you can work out together." It gave me a surprising pang to say Jamie's name and to think that I was not only losing her along with Rob and Belinda but arranging for the loss of her to befall me. It was as if I were losing the thing I loved best in the world.

I told them that after I'd moved into the West 71st Street apartment we'd make arrangements for them to drive my stuff down to the city and for one of them then to drive my car back and, while I was away, for them to keep the car in their garage and be sure to run it from time to time. I had finished a book two months earlier and hadn't yet begun another one, so there were no manuscripts or notebooks to transport. Had there been a new book under way I probably wouldn't have contemplated the move at all; if I had, I certainly wouldn't have left the manuscript to anyone's care other than my own. What's more, had I to return for any reason to my house in the woods, I knew I would never head back to New York again, though not for Jamie's reasons, not because of the fear of terrorist danger, but because everything essential I had where I was, the unbroken stretches of tranquil time that my writing now required, the books I needed to satisfy my interests, and an environment in which I could best maintain my equilibrium and keep myself fit to work for as long as I could. All the city would add was everything I'd determined I no longer had use for: Here and Now.

Here and Now.

Then and Now.

The Beginning and the End of Now.

These were the lines that I jotted onto the scrap of paper where I'd previously written Amy's name and the phone number of my new New York apartment. Titles for something. Perhaps this. Or should I just come right out with it—call it *A Man in Diapers*. A book about knowing where to go for your agony and then going there for it.

The next morning I received a phone call from the urologist's office asking if everything was all right and if I'd noticed any change in my condition—a fever, pain, anything out of the ordinary. I said I felt fine but reported that, as best I could tell, the incontinence hadn't lessened. The doctor's calm, comforting nurse advised me to continue to be patient and to wait to see if there was an improvement, which was not an unlikely possibility, even in some cases weeks after the procedure, and she reminded me that it required a second and sometimes a third procedure to achieve the desired effect and that one could safely undergo the procedure once a month for three months. "By giving you a narrower opening, the chances are good that we will have reduced or controlled the dripping. Please don't fail to contact us and let the doctor know exactly what's going on. Whatever happens, we'd like you to call us here within a week. Do that for us, Mr. Zuckerman, please."

The urge was overwhelming now to cut loose from the shallow, soft-headed fantasy of regeneration, get my car from the garage around the corner, and speed north for home, where I could quickly put my thoughts back where they belonged, under the transforming exigencies of prose fiction, which allow for no sweet dreams. What you do not have, you live without —you're seventy-one, and that's the deal. The vainglorious days of self-assertion are over. Thinking otherwise is ridiculous. There was no need to learn anything more about Amy Bellette or Jamie Logan, nor was there any need to learn anything about myself. That too was ridiculous. The drama of self-discovery was long over. I had not lived as a child all these years, and I knew more than was useful on the subject as it was. Until well into my sixties, I'd not looked away, drifted off, turned my back, I'd tried my best to show no fear, but whatever work might remain could be completed without knowing or hearing more about Al Qaeda, terrorism, the war in Iraq, or the possible reelection of Bush. It was not advisable to collide with all this indignant, highly emotional crisis-brooding—I'd been more than susceptible to my own obsessive brand during the Vietnam years—and if I moved back to the city it wouldn't be long before I was blanketed by it and by the not necessarily enlightening loquaciousness that accompanied such brooding and that, at the end of a nightlong spell submerged in its emptiness, could leave you seething like a lunatic, shattered and stupid, and that surely had contributed to Jamie Logan's decision to take flight.

Or was the history of the past few years sufficient in itself to lead her to expect a second gruesome Al Qaeda attack that would carry her off along with Billy and thousands more? I had no way of judging if she'd concluded correctly or was half demented by the situation (as perhaps the rational, patient young husband believed), or if her foresight was to be substantiated by bin Laden, or if by staying I'd be inflicting on myself a blow more devastating than the disorientation visited on Rip Van Winkle. As a onetime creature of intense responsiveness who'd over the preceding decade tautened himself into a low-keyed solitary, I'd got out of the habit of giving in to every impulse that crossed my nerve endings, and yet, in just my few days back, I had arrived at what might turn out to be the most thoughtless snap decision I'd ever made.

The hotel phone rang. A man who introduced himself as a friend of Jamie Logan's and Billy Davidoff's. Knew Jamie from Harvard, where she was two years ahead of him. A freelance journalist. Richard Kliman. Wrote on literary and cultural subjects. Articles in the *Times* Sunday magazine, *Vanity Fair*, *New York*, and *Esquire*. Was I free today? Could he take me to lunch?

"What do you want?" I asked.

"I'm writing about an old acquaintance of yours."

I was no longer skilled in indulging journalists, if I ever had been, nor was I heartened at being so easily located, touching as it did on the immediate circumstances that had first exiled me from New York.

Without explanation, I hung up. Kliman called back within seconds. "We were cut off," he said.

"I cut us off."

"Mr. Zuckerman, I'm writing a biography of E. I. Lonoff. I asked Jamie for your number because I know you met Lonoff and corresponded with him back in the 1950s. I know that as a young writer you were his great admirer. I'm now just a few years older than you were then. I'm not the prodigy you were —this is my first book, and it's not fiction. But I'm trying to do no more or less than you did. I know what I'm not, but I also know what I am. I'm trying to give it everything I have. If you'd like to call and ask Jamie to confirm my credentials—"

No, I'd like to call and ask Jamie why she had informed Mr. Kliman of my whereabouts.

"The last thing Lonoff wanted was a biographer," I said. "He had no ambition to be talked about. Or read about. He wanted anonymity, a harmless enough preference achieved automatically by most and surely a desire easy enough to respect. Look, he's been dead for over forty years. Nobody reads him. Nobody remembers him. Next to nothing is known about him. Any biographical treatment would be largely imaginary— in other words, a travesty."

"But *you* read him," Kliman responded. "You even mentioned his work to us when you came to have lunch at the Signet Society with a bunch of students back in my sophomore year. You told us which stories of his to read. I was there. Jamie was a member and she invited me to come along. Do you remember the Signet Society, the arts club where you had lunch at a big communal table, and afterward we went into the living room—remember that? The evening before, you'd read from your work in Memorial Hall, and one of the students invited you, and you agreed to come for lunch before you left the next day."

"No, I don't remember," I said, though I did—the reading because it was the last I'd given before my prostatectomy and the last ever, and I even remembered the lunch, when Kliman spoke of it, because of the dark-haired girl who'd sat looking at me from across the table. That must have been Jamie Logan at twenty. She'd pretended on West 71st Street that we'd never met, but we had, and I'd noticed her then. What struck me as unusual? Was it merely that she was the prettiest of them all? That could have done it, of course—that and the self-assured reserve suggested by a serene silence that might as easily have indicated that she was just too shy at the time to speak up, though not so shy that she couldn't stare and invite being stared back at in turn.

"You're still interested in him," Kliman was saying. "I know because only the other day you bought the clothbound Scribner's edition of the stories. At the Strand. A friend of mine works at the Strand. She told me. She was thrilled to see you there."

"A tactically stupid remark to make to a recluse, Kliman."

"I'm not a tactician. I'm an enthusiast."

"How old are you?"

"Twenty-eight," he said.

"What's your game?" I asked.

"What motivates me? I'd say the spirit of inquiry. I'm driven by my curiosity, Mr. Zuckerman. That's not necessarily something that makes me popular. It already hasn't made me popular with you. But to answer the question, that's the drive that's strongest."

Was he naively obnoxious or obnoxiously naive or just young or just cunning? "Stronger than the drive to kick off a career?" I asked. "To make a splash?"

"Yes, sir. Lonoff is an enigma to me. I'm trying to puzzle him out. I want to do him justice. I thought you could help. It's important to speak to people who knew him. Some still live, fortunately. I need people who knew him to corroborate my idea of him or, if they see fit, to challenge it. Lonoff was in hiding, not just as a man but as a writer. The hiding was the catalyst for his genius. The wound and the bow. Lonoff kept a great secret from his early years. It's only coincidental that he lived in Hawthorne country, but it's been argued that Nathaniel Hawthorne lived with a great secret too, and one not that dissimilar. You know what I'm talking about."

"I have no idea."

"Hawthorne's son wrote that Melville had been convinced in his later years that all his life Hawthorne had 'concealed some great secret.' Well, I'm more than convinced that was true of E. I. Lonoff. It helps to explain many things. His work among them."

"Why does his work need explaining?"

"As you said, nobody reads him."

"Nobody reads anyone when you think about it. On the other hand, as I needn't bother to tell you, there's a huge popular appetite for secrets. As for the biographical 'explanation,' generally it makes matters worse by adding components that aren't there and would make no aesthetic difference if they were."

"I know what you're telling me," he said, clearly prepared to shake off what I was telling him, "but I can't be that cynical and do the job decently. The disappearance of Lonoff's fiction is a cultural scandal. One of many, but one I can try to address."

"So," I said, "you've taken it upon yourself to undo the scandal by revealing the great secret from his early years that explains everything. I assume the great secret is sexual."

Dryly he said, "That's very astute of you, sir."

I would have hung up again, but I was the curious one now, curious to see how dogged and smug he intended to be. Without its ever turning outright belligerent, the unfaltering forward march of the voice made clear he was prepared to do battle. It was, unexpectedly, a passing rendition of me at about that stage, as though Kliman were mimicking (or, as now seemed more to the point, deliberately mocking) my mode of forging ahead when *I* started out. There it was: the tactless severity of vital male youth, not a single doubt about his coherence, blind with self-confidence and the virtue of knowing what matters most. The ruthless sense of necessity. The annihilating impulse in the face of an obstacle. Those grand grandstand days when you shrink from nothing and you're only right. Everything is a target; you're on the attack; and you, and you alone, are right.

The invulnerable boy who thinks he's a man and is seething to play a big role. Well, let him play it. He'll find out.

"I wish you weren't entirely antagonistic," he said, though it didn't sound now as if he cared. "I wish you'd give me the chance to explain to you the significance of his story as I see it and how it explains what happened to his writing when he left Hope and went off with Amy Bellette."

His saying "when he left Hope" galled me. I understood him—the uncompromising tenacity, the bluntness, the indomitable virus of superiority (he was going to be kind enough to explain things to me)—but that didn't mean I had to trust him. Other than hearsay and gossip, what could he know about "when he left Hope"?

"That needs no explaining either," I said.

"A thoroughly documented critical biography could go a long way toward resurrecting Lonoff and restoring his rightful place in twentieth-century literature. But his children won't talk to me, his wife is the oldest person in America with Alzheimer's and *can't* talk to me, and Amy Bellette no longer bothers to answer my letters. I've also sent you letters you haven't answered."

"I don't remember any."

"They were sent in care of your publisher, the proper method, I thought, of contacting someone known to be as private as you. The envelopes came back with a sticker attached: 'Return to sender. Unsolicited mail no longer accepted.' "

"That's a service any publisher will provide. I learned about it first from Lonoff. When I was your age."

"On that sticker that you use, that's Lonoff's language—his formulation?"

It *was* Lonoff's language—I couldn't have improved on it—but I didn't answer.

"I've found out a lot about Miss Bellette. I want to verify it. I need a credible source. You're certainly that. Are you in touch with her?"

"No."

"She lives in Manhattan. She works as a translator. She has brain cancer. If the cancer gets worse before I get to speak with her again, everything she knows will be lost. She could tell me more than anyone."

"To what end tell you more?"

"Look, old men hate young men. That goes without saying."

So offhand, the cryptic flash of wisdom he suddenly displays. Is this generational dispute something he read about or something someone told him about or something that he knows from his own prior experience, or did the awareness of it arrive out of the blue? "I'm just trying to be responsible," Kliman added, and now it was the word "responsible" that galled me.

"Isn't Amy Bellette why you're in New York?" he asked. "That's what you told Billy and Jamie, that you were here to attend to a friend with cancer."

"This time when you're cut off," I said, "don't call back."

Billy phoned fifteen minutes later to apologize for any

indiscretion he or Jamie had committed. He hadn't known that our meeting was to be treated as confidential, and he was sorry for the discomfort they may have caused. Kliman, who had just phoned them to report how badly things had gone with me, was a college boyfriend of Jamie's she was friendly with still, and she had meant no harm in telling him who it was that had answered their ad. Billy said that—wrongly, as he now understood it—neither he nor Jamie had foreseen my objections to talking to the biographer of E. I. Lonoff, a writer I was known by all of them to admire. He assured me that they wouldn't again make the mistake of speaking about the arrangement we'd reached, though I had to realize that once I moved into their place, it wouldn't be long before their network of friends and acquaintances knew who was there, and, likewise, once they'd moved into my place . . .

He was polite and thorough, he made sense, and so I said, "No harm done." Of course Kliman had been a boyfriend of Jamie's. Another reason I couldn't bear him. *The* reason.

"Richard can be insistent," Billy said. "But," he repeated, "we do want to apologize for telling him where you're staying. That was thoughtless."

"No harm done," I repeated, and once again told myself to get in the car and drive home. New York was full of people motivated by "the spirit of inquiry," and not all of them ethically up to the job. If I were to take over the 71st Street apartment—and the telephone there—I would unavoidably find myself in the sort of circumstances that were superfluous to me and that, as I had just demonstrated, I no longer had the wherewithal to finesse. Not that my curiosity hadn't been aroused by what Kliman was insinuating about Lonoff. Not that I wasn't surprised by the unlikeliness of my coming upon Lonoff's Amy for the first time in close to fifty years, and by my following her from the hospital to that luncheonette, and by Kliman's then calling to tell me about Amy's brain cancer and to try to tantalize me with his insider's knowledge of Lonoff's Hawthorne-like "secret." For one who had cultivated seclusion and bound himself to repetitiveness and thrown in his lot with monotony, who had banished everything deemed by him nonessential (purportedly in the service of his work, more likely at the mercy of a failing), it was like being overwhelmed by some rare astronomical event, as though an eclipse of the sun had taken place in the way eclipses had occurred throughout the prescientific eons: without resident earthlings anticipating their imminence.

Precipitously stepping into a new future, I had retreated unwittingly into the past—a retrograde trajectory not that uncommon, but uncanny anyhow.

"We want to invite you to spend election night with us," Billy said. "It'll just be Jamie and me. We're going to be at home to watch the results. We can have dinner here. Stay afterward for as long as you like. Why don't you come?"

"Tuesday night?"

He laughed. "Still the first Tuesday after the first Monday in November."

"I will be there," I said, "I accept," thinking not of the election but of Billy's wife and Kliman's former girlfriend and of the pleasure I could no longer provide a woman, even should the opportunity present itself. Old men hate young men? Young men fill them with envy and hatred? Why shouldn't they? The preposterous was seeping in fast from every quarter, and my heart pounded away with lunatic eagerness, as if the medical procedure to remedy incontinence had something to do with reversing impotence, which of course it did not—as though, however sexually disabled, however sexually unpracticed I was after eleven years away, the drive excited by meeting Jamie had madly reasserted itself as the animating force. As though in the presence of this young woman there was hope.

Through a single, brief meeting with Billy and Jamie I was not merely dropping back into a world of ambitious literary youth that was of no interest to me but opening myself to the irritants, stimulants, temptations, and dangers of the present moment. In my case, the specific danger threatening me back when I decided to leave the city for good—the danger of fatal attack —didn't emanate from the menace of Islamic terrorism but from death threats that I'd begun to receive and that the FBI determined to be issuing from a single source. Each was written on a picture postcard bearing a postmark from somewhere in northern New Jersey, the region where I'd been raised. The same location never appeared on a postmark twice, though the figure pictured on the front of the card was invariably the current pope, John Paul II, either blessing the crowd at St. Peter's or kneeling at prayer or sitting resplendent in brocaded white robes. The first postcard read:

> Dear Jew Bastard, We are part of a new international organization to counter the growth of the racist, filth-laden philosophy ZIONISM. As yet another Jew parasitizing "goy" countries and their inhabitants, you have been marked down to be targeted. Because of the location of your Jew York apartment, it has fallen to this "department" to do the "targeting." This notice marks the beginning.

The second card bearing John Paul's picture carried the same salutation and message, the text's only alteration in the conclusion: "NOTICE NUMBER TWO, JEW!"

Now, I had received communications as vile and ominous in the past, but never more than a couple a year, and most years none at all. Also, on the streets of New York, strangers would intermittently gravitate toward me and initiate a difficult encounter because of something in my fiction that enticed them or that infuriated them or that enticed them because it infuriated them or that infuriated them because it enticed them. I'd been through more than one such unsettling intrusion because of the conception of their author that the books had inspired in minds easily swayed into fantasy by fiction. But this was being *targeted*: not only did these postcards arrive weekly for months on end, but during this same period a reviewer living in the Midwest who'd once written a laudatory review of a book of mine in *The New York Times Book Review* also received a threatening postcard picturing the pope, his addressed to him at the college where he taught, in care of the "Department of Sycophancy and English." No salutation. Just this, written in a tiny hand:

> Only a cheap little asskissing two-bit fucking "English professor" would have stooped to calling this Jew bastard's latest pile of dogshit "his richest and most rewarding." What a tragedy that scum like you get away with wrenching young minds out of shape. AK-47 fire. That remedy would restore American higher education to what it once was. Or help to.

It was my New York lawyer who put me in touch with the FBI. As a result, I was visited at my apartment on East 91st Street by an agent named M. J. Sweeney, a small, sprightly southerner in her early forties, who took all of the cards (which she sent on to Washington, along with the one received by the reviewer, for examination and analysis) and who advised me of the precautions I should observe, as though she were instructing me in the basic rules of a sport or game I was unfamiliar with. I wasn't to leave a building without first scrutinizing the street in both directions and across the way for anyone suspicious-looking. On the street, if approached by people I didn't know, I was to keep my eyes on their hands instead of their faces to be sure they didn't reach for a weapon. There were more suggestions like these, and I immediately set out to follow them, but not with much conviction that they would furnish serious protection against someone dedicated to gunning me down. The words "AK-47 fire," which had appeared first in the reviewer's postcard, now began to turn up in the messages addressed to me. Some weeks, "AK-47 fire," written with a black felt-tip marker in characters two inches high, constituted the entire message.

M.J. and I spoke each time a new postcard arrived, and I would photocopy both sides before putting the original in an envelope and mailing it off to her. When I called one day to tell her that my latest book had been nominated for a prize and I was expected to attend the award ceremony in a midtown Manhattan hotel, she asked, "What kind of security do they have?" "I would think very little." "It's open to the public?" "It's not *not* open to the public," I said; "I can't imagine anybody determined to get in having trouble. I'd guess there'll be around a thousand people." "Well, watch yourself," she said. "You sound as if you don't think I ought to show up." "I can't speak for the FBI," M.J. said. "The FBI cannot advise you on this." "Should I happen to win, if I have to go up on the stage to accept the prize, I'd make an easy target, would I not?" "If I were speaking as a friend," she replied, "I'd say you would." "If you were speaking as a friend, what would you suggest I do?" "Does it mean a lot to you to be there?" "It means nothing." "Well, if it were me to whom it meant nothing," M.J.

said, "and I'd just got twenty-some death threats in the mail, I wouldn't go anywhere near the place."

The next morning I rented a car and drove to western Massachusetts, and within forty-eight hours I'd bought my cabin, two large rooms with a big stone fireplace in one and a wood stove in the other and between them a small kitchen with a window looking out back onto a grove of twisted old apple trees to a good-sized oval swimming pond and a big storm-damaged willow tree. The twelve acres were situated across from a picturesque swamp where waterfowl were plentiful and a couple hundred feet back from a dirt road that you followed for close to three miles before you reached the blacktop that wound five more miles down the mountain to Athena. Athena was where E. I. Lonoff was teaching when I met him in 1956, along with his wife and Amy Bellette. The Lonoff house, built in 1790 and passed down over the years through his wife's family, was a ten-minute drive from the house I'd just bought. It was because this locale had been Lonoff's place of refuge that I had instinctively chosen it as my own—because of that and because I was twenty-three years old when I'd met him, and never forgotten it.

I'd learned to use a rifle in the army, and so I bought a .22 at a local gun shop and spent a few afternoons firing alone in the woods until I got the hang of it again. I kept the rifle in a closet next to my bed and a box of ammunition beside it on the closet floor. I arranged to have a security system installed that connected to the local state troopers' barracks, and to have outdoor spotlights fixed at the corners of my roof so that the grounds wouldn't be pitch-black if I got home after dark. Then I called M.J. and told her what I'd done. "Maybe I'm worse off out here in the woods, but so far I'm feeling less exposed and anxious than I felt in the city. I'm keeping my apartment for the time being, but I'm going to live up here for now, till there are no more death threats coming my way." "Does anybody know where you are?" "So far only you. I've arranged for my mail to be forwarded elsewhere." "Well," M.J. said, "it wouldn't have been my first recommendation, but you must do whatever makes you feel safe." "I'll be in and out of the city, but I'll be living here." "Good luck," she said, then went on to tell me she'd now have to transfer my file to the Boston office. After she said goodbye and hung up, I agonized all night long over what I had done, convinced that all the while I'd been receiving the death threats, it had been M. J. Sweeney who had been the barrier between me and my correspondent's AK-47.

When the death threats eventually stopped coming by mail I didn't forsake the cabin. By then it had turned into a home, and there I lived those eleven years writing books, staying fit, getting cancer, taking the radical cure, and, off by myself, without my quite knowing it or my keeping track, advancing in age by the day. The habit of solitude, of solitude without anguish, had taken hold of me, and with it the pleasures of being unanswerable and being free—paradoxically, free above all of oneself. For days on end of only work, I would feel sweetened by luxurious contentment. Loneliness, raving loneliness, was sporadic and amenable to strategy: should it sweep over me during the day, I'd leave my desk and go for a five-mile walk in the woods or along the river, and when it insinuated itself at night, I'd temporarily put aside the book I was reading and listen to something requiring the whole of my attention—something, say, like a Bartók quartet. Thus did I restore stability and make the loneliness bearable. All in all, being without any need to play a role was preferable to the friction and agitation and conflict and pointlessness and disgust that, as a person ages, can render less than desirable the manifold relations that make for a rich, full life. I stayed away because over the years I conquered a way of life that I (and not just I) would have thought impossible, and there's pride taken in that. I may have left New York because I was fearful, but by paring and paring and paring away, I found in my solitude a species of freedom that was to my liking much of the time.

I shed the tyranny of my intensity—or, perhaps, by living apart for over a decade, merely reveled in its sternest mode.

It was on the last day of June 2004 that the name "AK-47" returned to alarm me. I know it was on June 30 because that's the day that the female snapping turtles in my part of New England make their annual trek out from their watery habitat to find an open sandy spot to dig a nest for their eggs. These are strong, slow-moving creatures, large turtles with sawtooth armored shells a foot or more in diameter and long, heavily scaled tails. They appear in abundance at the south end of Athena, troops of them crossing the two-lane macadam road that leads into town. Drivers will patiently wait for minutes on end so as not to hit them as they emerge from the deep woods whose marshes and ponds they inhabit, and it is the annual custom of many local residents like me not merely to stop but to pull over and step out onto the shoulder of the road to watch the parade of these rarely seen amphibians, lumbering forward inch by inch on the powerful, foreshortened, scaly legs that end in prehistoric-looking reptilian claws.

Every year you hear pretty much the same joking and laughter and wonderment from the onlookers, and from the pedagogical parents who've brought their children around to see the show you learn yet again how much the turtles weigh, and how long their necks are, and how strong their bite is, and how many eggs they lay, and how long they live. Then you get back in the car and drive into town to do your errands, as I did on that sunny day just four months before I traveled down to New York to inquire about the collagen treatment.

After having parked diagonally alongside the town green, I ran into several of the local merchants I know who'd come out of their shops to momentarily bask in the sunshine. I stood and talked for a while—about very little, all of us assuming the amiable attitude of men who think only the best of everything, a haberdasher, a liquor store owner, and a writer all exuding the contentment of Americans living safely beyond the reach of the nerve-racking world.

It was after I'd crossed the street and was on my way to the hardware store that I suddenly heard "AK-47" muttered into my ear by the person who had just passed me, heading in the other direction. I swung around and from the mass of his back and the pigeon-toed gait recognized him right off. He was the painter whom I'd hired the summer before to paint the outside of my house, and whom, because he failed to turn up for work just about every other day—and when he put in an appearance did so for no more than two or three hours—I'd had to fire less than halfway into the job. He then sent me a bill so exorbitant that rather than argue with him—and because, on the phone or in person, we'd had noisy arguments nearly every day about either his hours or his absences—I turned the bill over to my local lawyer to deal with. The housepainter's name was Buddy Barnes and rather too late I learned that he was one of Athena's leading alcoholics. I'd never much liked the bumper sticker on his car that read CHARLTON HESTON IS MY PRESIDENT, but I paid little attention to it because, though the legendary movie star had been renowned as the celebrity president of the recklessly irresponsible National Rifle Association, he was well on his way to dementia by the time I got around to hiring Buddy, and the bumper sticker struck me as foolish and innocuous more than anything else.

I was stunned, of course, by what I'd heard on the street, so stunned that rather than give myself a moment to contemplate how best to respond or to determine whether I should respond at all, I raced across to the green, where he had just climbed into his pickup truck. I called his name and banged a fist on his fender until he rolled his window down. "What did you just say to me?" I asked him. Buddy had an almost angelic pink-complexioned look for a gruff-mannered man in his forties, angelic despite the blond hairs growing thinly under his nose and on his chin. "I got nothing to say to you," he replied in his customary high-pitched howl. "What did you say to me, Barnes?" "Je-*sus*," he replied, rolling his eyes. "Answer me. Answer me, Barnes. Why did you say that to me?" "You're hearing things, nutcase," he said. Then, throwing the truck into reverse, he backed out, and with a teenage tire-screech, he was gone.

In the end, I decided that the incident had nothing like the dramatic meaning I had first lighted on. Yes, "AK-47" was what he said, and yes, I was so sure that as soon as I got home, I placed a call to the New York office of the FBI to speak to M. J. Sweeney, only to be told that she had left the agency two years earlier. I reminded myself that those postcards had been sent to me months before I had moved up here and before anybody like Buddy Barnes knew of my existence. It was impossible for Barnes to have sent them, especially as they were postmarked from cities and towns in north Jersey, over a hundred miles south of Athena, Massachusetts. His intending to harass me with the very word that I'd been harassed with through the mails some eleven years earlier was nothing but the weirdest of coincidences.

Nonetheless, for the first time since I'd bought the .22 and practiced firing it in the woods, I opened the box of ammunition and instead of keeping the weapon as I had all these years, standing unloaded at the back of my bedroom closet, I slept with it loaded, on the floor by the side of my bed. And I did this until I left for New York, even after I wondered whether Buddy had said nothing at all to me, even after I concluded that on that beautiful early summer morning, when I'd enjoyed the sight of the female snapping turtles laboriously crossing the road to fulfill their reproductive function, I'd had the most lifelike of auditory hallucinations, one whose cause was inexplicable, at least to me.

The incontinence was wholly unaffected by the collagen treatment, and when I reported this on the morning of the election, the doctor's office recommended that I schedule an appointment for a second procedure the following month. If there was an improvement in the interim, I could always cancel it; if not, the procedure would be repeated. "And if it's not effective?" "Then we repeat it. The third time, we don't go in through the urethra," the nurse explained, "but through the scars from the prostate operation. Just a puncture. Local anesthetic. No pain." "And if a third procedure doesn't work?" I asked. "Oh, that's a long way off, Mr. Zuckerman. Let's just take one step at a time. Don't lose heart. This is not going to come to nothing."

As if incontinence weren't indignity enough, one had then to be addressed like a churlish eight-year-old balking at taking his cod liver oil. But that's how it goes when an elderly patient refuses to resign himself to the inevitable travails and totter politely toward the grave: doctors and nurses have a child on their hands who must be soothed into soldiering on in behalf of his own lost cause. That, at any rate, was my thinking when I hung up the phone, drained of pride and feeling all the limitations of my strength, the man at the point where he fails whether he resists or acquiesces.

What surprised me most my first few days walking around the city? The most obvious thing—the cell phones. We had no reception as yet up on my mountain, and down in Athena, where they do have it, I'd rarely see people striding the streets talking uninhibitedly into their phones. I remembered a New York when the only people walking up Broadway seemingly talking to themselves were crazy. What had happened in these ten years for there suddenly to be so much to say—so much so pressing that it couldn't wait to be said? Everywhere I walked, somebody was approaching me talking on a phone and someone was behind me talking on a phone. Inside the cars, the drivers were on the phone. When I took a taxi, the cabbie was on the phone. For one who frequently went without talking to anyone for days at a time, I had to wonder what that had previously held them up had collapsed in people to make incessant talking into a telephone preferable to walking about under no one's surveillance, momentarily solitary, assimilating the streets through one's animal senses and thinking the myriad thoughts that the activities of a city inspire. For me it made the streets appear comic and the people ridiculous. And yet it seemed like a real tragedy, too. To eradicate the experience of separation must inevitably have a dramatic effect. What will the consequence be? You know you can reach the other person anytime, and if you can't, you get impatient—impatient and angry like a little stupid god. I understood that background silence had long been abolished from restaurants, elevators, and ballparks, but that the immense loneliness of human beings should produce this boundless longing to be heard, and the accompanying disregard for being overheard—well, having lived largely in the era of the telephone booth, whose substantial folding doors could be tightly pulled shut, I was impressed by the conspicuousness of it all and found myself entertaining the idea for a story in which Manhattan has turned into a sinister collectivity where everyone is spying on everyone else, everyone being tracked by the person at the other end of his or her phone, even though, incessantly dialing one another from wherever they like in the great out of doors, the telephoners believe themselves to be experiencing the maximum freedom. I knew that merely by thinking up such a scenario I was at one with all the cranks who imagined, from the beginnings of industrialization, that the machine was the enemy of life. Still, I could not help it: I did not see how anyone could believe he was continuing to live a human existence by walking about talking into a phone for half his waking life. No, those gadgets did not promise to be a boon to promoting reflection among the general public.

And I noticed the young women. I couldn't fail to. The days were still warm in New York and women were clad in ways I couldn't ignore, however much I wanted not to be aroused by the very desires actively quelled through living in seclusion across the road from a nature preserve. I knew from my trips down to Athena how much of themselves college girls now exposed with neither shame nor fear, but the phenomenon didn't stun me until I got to the city, where the numbers were vastly multiplied and the age range expanded and I enviously understood that women dressing as they did meant that they weren't there only to be looked at and that the provocative parade was merely the initial unveiling. Or perhaps it meant that to someone like me. Maybe I had got it all wrong and this was just how they dressed now, how T-shirts were cut now, how clothes were designed now for women, and though walking around in tight shirts and low-cut shorts and enticing bras and with their bellies bare looks like it means that they're all available, they're not—and not only not to me.

But it was noticing Jamie Logan that bewildered me most. I hadn't sat so close to such an irresistible young woman in years, perhaps not since I last sat opposite Jamie herself in the dining room of a Harvard arts club. Nor had I understood how disconcerted I had been by her until we'd all agreed on the exchange of residences and I left to go back to the hotel and found myself thinking how pleasant it would be if no swap took place—if Billy Davidoff stayed where he wanted to stay, which was right there, across from the little Lutheran church on West 71st Street, while Jamie escaped her dread of terrorism by coming back to the tranquil Berkshires with me. She had a huge pull on me, a huge gravitational pull on the ghost of my desire. This woman was in me before she even appeared.

The urologist who had diagnosed the cancer when I was sixty-two had commiserated with me afterward by saying, "I know it's no comfort, but you're not alone—this disease has reached epidemic proportions in America. Your struggle is shared by many others. In your case, it's just too bad that I couldn't have made the diagnosis ten years from now," suggesting that the impotence brought on by the removal of the prostate might by then seem a less painful loss. And so I set out to minimize the loss by struggling to pretend that desire had naturally abated, until I came in contact for barely an hour with a beautiful, privileged, intelligent, self-possessed, languid-looking thirty-year-old made enticingly vulnerable by her fears and I experienced the bitter helplessness of a taunted old man dying to be whole again.

2

Under the Spell

O N T H E walk from my hotel up to West 71st Street I
stopped at a liquor store to buy a couple of bottles of
wine for my hosts and then proceeded quickly on my way to
watch the election results of a campaign that, for the first time
since I was made aware of electoral politics—when Roosevelt
defeated Willkie in 1940—I knew barely anything about.

I had been an avid voter all my life, one who'd never pulled
a Republican lever for any office on any ballot. I had campaigned for Stevenson as a college student and had my juvenile
expectations dismantled when Eisenhower trounced him, first
in '52 and then again in '56; and I could not believe what I saw
when a creature so rooted in his ruthless pathology, so transparently fraudulent and malicious as Nixon, defeated Humphrey
in '68, and when, in the eighties, a self-assured knucklehead
whose unsurpassable hollowness and hackneyed sentiments
and absolute blindness to every historical complexity became
the object of national worship and, esteemed as a "great communicator" no less, won each of his two terms in a landslide.
And was there ever an election like Gore versus Bush, resolved
in the treacherous ways that it was, so perfectly calculated to
quash the last shameful vestige of a law-abiding citizen's naiveté? I'd hardly held myself aloof from the antagonisms of
partisan politics, but now, having lived enthralled by America
for nearly three-quarters of a century, I had decided no longer
to be overtaken every four years by the emotions of a child—
the emotions of a child and the pain of an adult. At least not so
long as I holed up in my cabin, where I could manage to remain in America without America's ever again being absorbed
in me. Aside from writing books and studying once again, for
a final go-round, the first great writers I read, all the rest that
once mattered most no longer mattered at all, and I dispelled
a good half, if not more, of a lifetime's allegiances and pursuits.
After 9/11 I pulled the plug on the contradictions. Otherwise,
I told myself, you'll become the exemplary letter-to-the-editor

madman, the village grouch, manifesting the syndrome in all its seething ridiculousness: ranting and raving while you read the paper, and at night, on the phone with friends, roaring indignantly about the pernicious profitability for which a wounded nation's authentic patriotism was about to be exploited by an imbecilic king, and in a republic, a king in a free country with all the slogans of freedom with which American children are raised. The despising without remission that constitutes being a conscientious citizen in the reign of George W. Bush was not for one who had developed a strong interest in surviving as reasonably serene—and so I began to annihilate the abiding wish *to find out.* I canceled magazine subscriptions, stopped reading the *Times,* even stopped picking up the occasional copy of the *Boston Globe* when I went down to the general store. The only paper I saw regularly was the *Berkshire Eagle,* a local weekly. I used the TV to watch baseball, the radio to listen to music, and that was it.

Surprisingly, it took only weeks to break the matter-of-fact habit that informed much of my nonprofessional thinking and to feel completely at home knowing nothing of what was going on. I had banished my country, been myself banished from erotic contact with women, and was lost through battle fatigue to the world of love. I had issued an admonition. I was out from under my life and times. Or maybe just down to the nub. My cabin could as well have been adrift on the high seas as set twelve hundred feet up on a rural road in Massachusetts that was less than a three-hour drive east to the city of Boston and about the same distance south to New York.

The television set was on when I arrived, and Billy assured me the election was in the bag—he was in touch with a friend at Democratic national headquarters, and their exit polls showed Kerry winning all the states he needed. Billy graciously accepted the wine and told me that Jamie had gone out to buy food and should be back at any minute. Once again he was expansively agreeable and exuded a jovial softness, as though he weren't yet and probably never would be expert at wielding authority. Is he a throwback, I wondered, or do they still exist like this, middle-class Jewish boys who continue to be branded with the family empathy that, despite the unmatchable satisfaction of its cradling sentiments, can leave one unprepared for the nastiness of less kindly souls? In the Manhattan literary milieu particularly, I would have expected something other than the brown eyes weighty with tenderness and the full angelic cheeks that lent him the air, if not still of a protected small boy, then of the generous young man wholly unable to inflict a wound or laugh with scorn or shirk the smallest responsibility. I speculated that Jamie might be a lot more than could be managed by the sweet selflessness of one whose every word and gesture was permeated with his decency. The trusting innocence, the mildness, the sympathetic understanding—what a setup for the rogue with an eye to stealing the wife whose infidelity would be unimaginable to him.

The phone rang just as Billy was preparing to open one of the bottles of wine, and he handed it across to me to uncork while he snatched up the phone and said, "What now?" After a moment he looked up to tell me, "New Hampshire's sewed up. D.C.?" Billy then asked the friend who was phoning. To me again he said, "In D.C. they're going eight to one for Kerry. That's the key—the blacks are turning out en masse. Okay, great," Billy said into the phone, and upon hanging up told me happily, "So we live in a liberal democracy after all," and, to toast the mounting thrill, he poured each of us a big glass of wine. "These guys would have devastated the country," he said, "had they won a second term. We've had bad presidents and we've survived, but this one's the bottom. Serious cognitive deficiencies. Dogmatic. A tremendously limited ignoramus about to wreck a very great thing. There's a description in *Macbeth* that's perfect for him. We read aloud together, Jamie and I. We're doing the tragedies. It's in the scene in act three with Hecate and the witches. 'A wayward son,' Hecate says, 'spiteful and wrathful.' George Bush in six words. It's all so awful. If you're for your kids and God, you're a Republican— meanwhile, the people who are being screwed the most are his base. It's amazing they pulled it off for even one term. It's terrifying to think what they would have done with a second term. These are terrible, evil guys. But their arrogance and their lies finally caught up with them."

My mind still full of my own thoughts, I allowed a couple of minutes more for him to continue to watch the first election results trickle in before I asked, "How did you meet Jamie?"

"Miraculously."

"You were students together."

He smiled most appealingly, when, given my thoughts, he would have done better pulling the dagger that had done in Duncan. "That makes it no less miraculous," he said.

I saw there was no need to stop myself from hurtling forward for fear of being found out. Clearly Billy couldn't begin to imagine that someone of my years might be asking about his young wife because his young wife was now all I could think about. There was my age to mislead him, and my eminence too. How could he possibly believe the worst about a writer he'd begun reading in high school? It was like meeting Henry Wadsworth Longfellow. How could the author of "The Song of Hiawatha" take a licentious interest in Jamie?

To be on the safe side, I asked first about him.

"Tell me about your family," I said.

"Oh, I'm the only reading person in the family, but that doesn't matter; they're good people. In Philly now for four generations. My great-grandfather started the family business. He was from Odessa. His name was Sam. His customers called him Uncle Sam the Umbrella Man. He made and repaired umbrellas. My grandfather expanded into luggage. In the teens and the twenties, train travel boomed and suddenly everybody needed a piece of luggage. And people were traveling by ship, transatlantic ships. It was the era of the wardrobe trunk—you know, the big, heavy trunks people took on long journeys that opened up vertically and had hangers and drawers in them."

"I know them well," I said. "And the others, the smaller black ones that opened up horizontally like a pirate's chest. I had a trunk like that to go off to college with. Nearly everyone did. It was constructed of wood and the corners were sheathed in metal and the fancy ones were girdled with bands of embossed metal and the lock was brass and made to withstand an earthquake. You used to ship your trunk by Railway Express. You'd take it down to the train station and leave it with the clerk at the Railway Express desk. The guy at Newark's Penn Station in those days still wore the green eyeshade and kept his

pencil tucked behind his ear. He'd weigh the trunk and you'd
pay per pound and off your socks and underwear would go."

"Yes, every city of any size had a luggage store, and the department stores all had luggage departments. It's airline stew-
ardesses," Billy told me, "who revolutionized how Americans
felt about luggage in the fifties—people saw that it could be
light and chic. That's about when my father went into the
business and modernized the store and changed the name to
Davidoff's Fashionable Luggage. Until then, the place was still
known by the original name, Samuel Davidoff and Sons. About
this time along came the luggage on wheels—and that, vastly
abridged, is the story of the luggage business. The full version
runs to a thousand pages."

"You're writing about the family business, are you?"

He nodded and he shrugged and he sighed. "*And* the family. I'm trying to, anyway. I more or less grew up in the store.
I've heard a thousand stories from my grandfather. Every time
I go to see him I fill another notebook. I've got stories enough
to last a lifetime. But it's all a matter of how, isn't it? I mean,
how you tell them."

"And Jamie. How did she grow up?"

And so he told me, lavishly expatiating on her accomplish-
ments: about Kinkaid, the exclusive private school in Houston
from which she'd graduated valedictorian; about her stellar
academic career at Harvard, where she graduated summa cum
laude; about River Oaks, the wealthy Houston neighborhood
where her family lived; about the Houston Country Club, where
she played tennis and swam and had come out as a debutante
against her will; about the conventional mother she tried so
hard to accommodate and the difficult father she could never
please; about the favorite haunts she took Billy to visit when
they first went together to Houston for Christmas; about the
places where she played as a child that he wanted her to show
him and the menacing beauty of the ugly Houston bayous at
dawn and Jamie's defiantly swimming in the murky water with
a wild older sister, who, he informed me, pronounced the
word "buy-ohs," like the old Houstonians.

I had simply asked him to tell me about her; what I'd gotten
was a speech appropriate to the dedication of some grand edifice. There was nothing strange about such a staunchly tender

performance—men who fall madly in love can make Xanadu of Buffalo if that's where their beloved was raised—and yet the ardor for Jamie and Jamie's Texas girlhood was so undisguised that it was as though he were telling me about somebody he had dreamed up in jail. Or about the Jamie that *I* had dreamed up in jail. It was as it should be in a masterpiece of male devotion: his veneration for his wife was his strongest tie to life.

He was elegiac when recounting to me the route they jog together when they visit her folks.

"River Oaks, where they live—it's an anomaly in Houston. Old neighborhood with old houses, though there are some nice ones that have been torn down for McMansions. Jamie's is one of the few neighborhoods in Houston where there's still some feeling for the past. Beautiful houses, big oaks, magnolias, a few pines. Huge manicured gardens. Teams of gardeners. Mexican. Thursdays and Fridays the streets are lined with the pickup trucks of gardening companies and with armies of workers out clipping and manicuring and mowing and planting for the weekend, for the parties and gatherings that are going to go on. We jog through the older part of River Oaks, where the original oil families have had their big spreads for two and three generations. We jog past the older houses and run along kind of a busy street, and then we get to the bayou that runs from River Oaks down through a park where you can jog for miles and miles until you get to downtown. Or we run along the bayou and back. Just after dawn it's cool and it's wonderful. The quiet, discreet part of River Oaks, where people aren't consuming conspicuously and parking multiple Mercedeses in front of their McMansions, is a beautiful community. There's a rose garden we especially like, a community project, kept up and cared for by the residents. I love the mornings running past that rose garden with Jamie. Some of the old estates back up onto the bayou, and to get to where we can see the bayou and run by it, we have to get out of River Oaks. And so there's the rest of Houston. River Oaks is an insular, prosperous haven of uniformity, old-money families and new-money families at the top of the Houston caste system, and a lot of the rest of the city is hot and humid and flat and ugly—tattoo parlors next to office buildings, running-shoe stores in rickety houses, everything just jumbled together. The most

beautiful thing in the city to me is the old cemetery with the
old live-oak trees where some of Jamie's family are buried,
right down by the bayous, almost downtown."

"Is Jamie's an old- or a new-money family?" I asked Billy.

"Old. The old money is oil money, and the new money is
professional money."

"How old is the old money?"

"Well, not that old, because Houston's relatively young. But
since the oil tycoons like Jamie's grandfather, whenever that
would have been."

"And how did the old Houston money feel about your being
a Jew?" I asked.

"Her parents weren't thrilled. The mother just cried. It was
the father who took the cake. When Jamie came home to tell
them we were engaged, he put his head in his hands, and that's
what he did from then on, every time my name was mentioned.
She'd e-mail him from back east and he deliberately wouldn't
answer her for three, four weeks at a time. She'd check her e-mail
hourly and he would not have answered her. An authentically
coarse tyrant, this guy. A travesty of a father. Selfish. Thoughtless. Big temper. Utterly irrational. Domineering. Venomous. No
good boorish bastard through and through. Imagine: trying,
by not answering her, to break his own daughter down, con-
sciously and deliberately exploiting a daughter's decency to
make her feel herself in the wrong. Wants to *crush* her. And, of
course, to crush me too. I had never laid eyes on him, nor he
on me, yet he wanted to harm me nonetheless. And who had
ever purposefully set out to harm me before? To my knowledge,
Mr. Zuckerman, no one. But this brute feels himself wholly
entitled to do harm to a man his daughter happens to love!
Now, Jamie is a good daughter, a very good daughter—she'd
given her all trying to love this person who was persistently on
the wrong side of the argument, tried as hard as she could
however much she'd hated his bullying of her mother and his
politics and his arrogant right-wing friends. After one three-
week silence, he finally sends her a one-sentence e-mail: 'I love
you, sweetheart, but I cannot accept that boy.' But Jamie Logan's got guts, dignity and guts, and even though the old man
held the purse strings, even though he began to hint, not very
subtly, that if she went through with marrying a Jew he would

cut her off, she wouldn't break. She stuck it out, and eventually the bigoted son of a bitch had to either swallow his animus and accept me or lose his beloved summa-cum-laude child. A lesser girl of twenty-five, one lacking Jamie's courage, lacking Jamie's independence, would have capitulated. But Jamie is a lesser nothing. Jamie is neither spoiled nor a fraud nor without a sense of honor and would never dream of submitting to what she could not stand. Jamie is the best. She said to me, 'I love you and I want you and I will not be a slave to his dough.' She as good as told him to take the money and shove it, and so in the end *she* crushed *him*. Oh, Mr. Zuckerman, it was a thing of beauty watching Jamie hold out. Though you would have thought that the father would have been used to it by the time she got around to me. 'It' being Jamie and Jews. Their country club lets in Jews now. That wouldn't have been the case in her grandparents' time, or even as recently as fifteen years ago, with her parents' generation. It's all pretty new. Like letting Jews and blacks into Kinkaid. That's relatively new. The Jewish girls were Jamie's study buddies. You can imagine how much the great hothead loved that. But they were talented and smart, and they didn't try to hide their bookishness to be popular. The brother of one of Jamie's Jewish girlfriends—Nelson Speilman, who attended St. John's, the other prestigious prep school in Houston—was her boyfriend for two years, until he went off to Princeton the year before she graduated from Kinkaid. Jamie was one of the dedicated studious ones in a very protected place where to be socially acceptable was everything. It's a school where the football team votes for the homecoming queen, and the girls can't be seen with a public school boy, only with Kinkaid or St. John's boys. The Kinkaid boys drive Broncos and hunt and watch sports, and all of them want to go to UT, and there's a lot of drinking and a lot of parental looking-the-other-way at the drinking."

"You know a lot about her school. You know a lot about her city."

"I'm fascinated," he said with a laugh. "I am. I'm a slave to Jamie's background."

"And that never happened with any girl you'd taken out before her?"

"Never."

"Well," I said, "that's probably as good a reason to marry as any."

"Oh," he said jokingly, "there are a few more."

"I can imagine," I said.

"She makes me proud of her all the time. Do you know what she did four years back when her older sister, Jessie, the wild one, was in the last stages of Lou Gehrig's disease? She picked up and got on a plane to Houston and stayed there at Jessie's bedside and nursed her till she died. Stayed there night and day for five horrible, misery-ridden months while I was here in New York. It's a nightmarish disease. It's usually not till their mid-fifties that people come down with it, but Jessie was thirty when suddenly her hands and feet began to weaken, and the diagnosis was made. Over time, all the motor neurons go, but because the brain alone is spared, the person is fully cognizant that she's a living corpse. In the end, all Jessie could move were her eyelids. That's how she communicated with Jamie—by blinking. For five months Jamie didn't leave her side. At night she slept on a cot in Jessie's room. Early on, their mother had gone to pieces and was utterly useless, and their father, from start to finish, was himself to a T—would have nothing to do with the daughter who'd inconvenienced him by coming down with a fatal disease. Wouldn't tend to her, after a while wouldn't even go into her room to say a fatherly word to soothe her, let alone touch her or give her a kiss. Went on making money as though everything at home was just fine, while his younger daughter, twenty-six, was helping his older daughter, thirty-four, to die. But the night before it happened, the night before Jessica succumbed, he was in the kitchen with Jamie, where the maid was preparing them something to eat, and all at once he broke down. In the kitchen, he finally broke down and began to sob his heart out like a child. He clung to Jamie and you know what he said to her? 'If only it were me instead of her.' And you know what Jamie said back to him? 'If only it were.' That's the girl I fell for. That's the girl I married. That's Jamie."

When Jamie came through the door carrying her bags of food, she said, "On the street somebody told me Ohio doesn't look good."

"I just spoke to Nick," Billy said. "Kerry's going to win Ohio."

She turned to me. "I don't know what I'd do if Bush gets back in. It'll be the end of the road for a whole way of political life. All their intolerance focuses on a liberal society. It'll mean that the values of liberalism will continue to be reversed. It'll be terrible. I don't think I could live with it."

As she was hurriedly speaking, Billy had taken the groceries from her and gone into the kitchen to sort things out.

"It's a flexible instrument that we've inherited," I told her. "It's amazing how much punishment we can take."

My effort to be consoling seemed to strike her as condescension, and she all but snapped at me for the imagined affront. "Have you ever lived through an election like this one? With the magnitude of this one?"

"Some. This is one I haven't followed."

"Haven't you?"

"I told you the other night—I don't follow such things."

"So you don't care who wins." She gave me a hard look of disapproval for the willed quality of my obliviousness.

"I didn't say that."

"These are terrible, evil people," she told me, echoing her husband. "I know these people. I grew up with these people. It wouldn't just be a shame if they won—it could prove to be a tragedy. The turn to the right in this country is a movement to replace political institutions with morality—*their* morality. Sex and God. Xenophobia. A culture of total intolerance . . ."

She was too agitated by the menacing world she lived in to stop herself—and, for whatever reason, to be entirely civil to me—and so I listened to her while making no further foolish attempt to embark on the knightly quest for the Holy Grail of her attention. The slender, full-breasted frame and the curtain of black hair pleased me no less than on the evening I'd come to look at the apartment. She'd returned from shopping wearing a wine-colored, closely fitted corduroy blazer, which she'd taken off after Billy had relieved her of the groceries—taken off along with her low-heeled dark brown boots. Beneath the blazer she wore a ribbed black cashmere turtleneck that was also close-fitting, as were the dark denim jeans that flared just a bit at the bottom, probably to accommodate the boots. To walk around the apartment she'd put on a pair of flat shoes that looked like ballet slippers. Though the calculation was subtle, she didn't look as if she were necessarily pursuing guileless ends by the way she dressed or as if she lacked confidence in her power to arouse the admiration of men. Did she care one way or another whether I was as wowed as the others? If not, why had she gotten herself up so appealingly just to go for the groceries and watch the election results? Though maybe any unknown guest would have prompted her to choose to wear something attractive. Regardless, the lure of the apparel was matched by the voice, the rapid speech, warm and musical even when she was upset, and with a lot of Texas in it, or her part of Texas, a relaxing of vowels, a softening, particularly in the soft "I," and then her connecting the words a little lazily, one word running into the next. It wasn't the kind of twang that's harsh on the ear—not the Wild West Texas accent that George W. Bush took on but the well-bred Texas accent belonging more to the South that his Yankee father picked up. There's a gentility to it, certainly as spoken by Jamie Logan. Maybe it's just the accent of the cream of River Oaks and the Kinkaid School.

I was as glad as Billy that she was home. It didn't matter if the clothes had nothing to do with my presence. In its deliberateness, there was something intensely exciting about her not giving me a tumble. There is no situation that infatuation is unable to feed on. Looking at her provided a visual jolt—I allowed her into my eyes the way a sword swallower swallows a sword.

As though to an ailing child, Billy said, "You're not going to be devastated. You're going to be dancing in the street."

"No," she replied, "no, this country is a haven of ignorance. I know—I come from the fountainhead. Bush talks right to the ignorant core. This is a very backward country, and the people are so easily bamboozled, and he's exactly like a snake-oil salesman . . ." She must have been angrily brooding aloud for months now, and so, for the moment, she seemed to give out, and I wondered if she was someone who didn't ever know how to say anything unseriously, or if the election overrode everything and for now I could have no idea what Jamie was like without an ordeal and whether her response to the great world was ever anything but painfully intense.

We arranged ourselves around the coffee table with the plates, the cutlery, and the linen napkins Billy had set out, taking what we wanted from the platters of food and, while we steadily emptied my two bottles of wine, watching the screen where the available results were being tabulated state by state. By a little after ten the phone calls from Nick at Democratic headquarters were becoming less optimistic, and by a quarter to eleven they were dour. "The exit polls," Billy told us after hanging up, "aren't proving to be accurate. Things don't look good in Ohio, and he's not going to win Iowa *or* New Mexico. Florida is lost."

Most of this we knew from watching television, but Jamie had no faith in the television tabulations, and so the call from Nick caused her to cry, a little drunkenly, "This is now the night before it all got even worse! I don't know what to think!" while I thought, At some point capitulation will kick in, but till then it'll be a big job to exorcise the illusions. Till then she'll be thrashing around in pain or hiding away like a wounded animal. Hiding away in my house. In these clothes. In no clothes. In my bed, beside Billy, unclothed.

"I don't know what to think!" she cried again. "There's nothing to stop them now, except Al Qaeda."

"Sweetheart," Billy said softly, "we don't yet know what will happen. Let's wait it out."

"Oh, the world is so dim," Jamie exclaimed with tears in her eyes. "Last time it seemed like a fluke. There was Florida. There was Nader. But this I don't understand! I can't believe it! It's incredible! I'm going to go out and get an abortion. I don't care if I'm pregnant or not. Get an abortion while you can!"

She was looking at me when she made this bitter joke, now without antipathy—looking at me the way somebody being helped from a burning building or freed from a car crash looks at you, as though as an observer you might have something to say that could account for the catastrophe that's altered everything. All the things I thought to tell her would likely strike her as cant. I thought to repeat, It's amazing how much punishment we can take. I thought to say, If in America you think like you do, nine times out of ten you fail. I thought to say, It's bad, but not like waking up the morning after Pearl Harbor was bombed. It's bad, but not like waking up the morning after Kennedy was shot. It's bad, but not like waking up the morning after Martin Luther King was shot. It's bad, but not like waking up the morning after the Kent State students were shot. I thought to say, We have all been through it. But I said nothing. She didn't want words anyway. She wanted murder. She wanted to wake up the morning after George Bush had been shot.

It was Billy who said, "Something will be their undoing, honey. Terror will be their undoing."

"Oh, what's the sense of living with it?" Jamie asked, and so deep was her dismay, and so close to the surface her vulnerability, that she broke into sobs.

Each of their cell phones started ringing then—the cruelly disappointed friends calling, many of them in tears as well. The first time, as Jamie said, it seemed like a fluke, but this was their idealism's second staggering electoral shock and the dawning of the hard realization that they could not will this country back into being the Roosevelt stronghold it had been some forty years before they were born. For all their sharpness and articulateness and savoir-faire, and despite Jamie's knowledge of rich Republican America and the brand of ignorance bred in Texas, they'd had no idea who the great mass of Americans were, nor had they seen so clearly before that it was not those educated like themselves who would determine the country's fate but the scores of millions unlike them and unknown to them who had given Bush a second chance, in Billy's words, "to wreck a very great thing."

I sat there, in what was soon to be the home where I would awaken every morning, and listened to the two of them, who'd soon be waking up each day in my house, a place where, if you liked, you could erase the rage about how much worse it all was than you thought and the sorrow over how far down your country had sunk and, if you were young and hopeful and engaged by your world and still enraptured by your expectations, learn instead to relinquish caring about America in 2004—to live and not be on the rack because of how stupid and corrupt it all is—by looking for fulfillment to your books, your music, your mate, and your garden. Watching these two, I got the sense easily enough of why anyone their age with their commitments would want to flee the pain-inducing lover their country had become.

"Terrorism?" Jamie cried into her phone. "But all the states that were touched by terrorism, the places where it happened and the places where people came from who were killed—all of them voted for Kerry! New York, New Jersey, D.C., Maryland, Pennsylvania—none of them wanted Bush! Look at the map east of the Mississippi. It's the Union versus the Confederacy. The same split. Bush carried the old Confederacy!"

"Do you want to know the sick next war?" Billy was telling someone. "They need a victory. They need a clean victory and without a messy occupation. Well, it's sitting ninety miles off the Florida coast. They'll connect Castro to Al Qaeda and go to war against Cuba. The provisional government is already in Miami. The property maps have already been drawn up. Wait and see. In their war against the infidel, Cuba will be next. Who is there to stop them? They don't even need Al Qaeda. They're intent on more violence, and Cuba's criminal enough on its own. The constellation that elected him will love it. Drive the last of the Communists into the sea."

I hung around long enough to be able to overhear them talk to their folks. By then they were feeling so drained that all they could do was wish they had parents with whom they could emotionally give way and be succored in return. Both were dutiful children, so when the time came they dutifully phoned, but Jamie's parents, as I knew from Billy's rendering of Jamie's Houston, were members of the same country club as the elder George Bush—and so on the phone Jamie vainly tried to remember that she was a married woman living more than a thousand miles away from where she was indoctrinated in privilege by archconservative Texans, led by the father, whom she mainly despised for his unconscionable disregard for her dying sister and whom she had flatly and obstinately defied by daring him to disinherit her by boldly marrying a Jew.

She had by now become something a good deal more than somebody beautiful I was staring at. In her voice you could hear just how battered she was, not least by the fact that her parents were the very sort of people her liberal conscience couldn't abide, and yet she still happened to be their daughter and still needed, apparently, to lay her troubles at their feet. You could hear both the great bond and the great struggle against. You could hear all it had cost her to forge a new being and all the good it had done.

Billy's parents in Philadelphia were by no means alien or adversarial or distasteful, but clearly very dear to him; yet when he hung up the phone, he shook his head and had to empty his half-full wine glass before he spoke. His gentle face could not hide the disappointment or the humiliation that he felt, and the tender heart attuned always to the feelings of others would not allow for an airing of the disgust that might have gone a ways toward easing the pain. At the moment a tender heart had no useful function, and Billy was at sea. "My father voted for Bush," he said, as surprised as if he'd discovered that his father had robbed a bank. "My mother told me. When I asked her why, she said, 'Israel.' She had him all lined up to vote for Kerry, and when he comes out of the booth he tells her, 'I did it for Israel.' 'I could have killed him,' my mother said. 'He still believes they'll find the weapons of mass destruction.'"

When I returned to the hotel, I wrote this little scene:

                              HE
You didn't tell me that we met before.

                              SHE
I didn't think it was worth mentioning. I didn't think you'd remember.

                              HE
I thought perhaps *you* didn't remember.

                              SHE
No, I remember.

                              HE
You remember where we met?

                              SHE
The Signet.

                              HE
Right. Do you remember that day at all?

SHE

I remember it quite well. I was a member of the Signet but I didn't go to lunch there much. And a friend of mine called to tell me that she had invited you to lunch the next day, and she wasn't sure if you would show up but you'd said that you would and that I ought to come. So I did. I brought Richard, and luckily I got to sit at your table instead of the table in the other room. And I sat down and you came in and sat at our table, and I watched you during lunch.

HE

You didn't speak, but you did stare.

SHE

(*Laughing apologetically*) I'm sorry if I was forward.

HE

I stared back at you. And not merely in self-defense. Do you remember that?

SHE

I thought perhaps I was imagining that. I couldn't believe I could get a response. I couldn't believe you'd take any notice of me. I had you down for inaccessible. You remember sitting opposite me, truly?

HE

It's only ten years ago.

SHE

Ten years is a long time to remember somebody you don't speak to. What impression did I make on you?

HE

I couldn't tell if you were shy or just had great serene reserve.

SHE

Both.

HE

Did you go to the reading the night before?

SHE

Yes. I remember sitting in the living room on the leather sofas after lunch. About half of us stayed. I thought what an awkward thing this must be for this man. All of us crowding around him, waiting for him to say something that we can all go home and write in our journals.

HE

Did you go home and write in your journal?

SHE

I'll have to go and check in my journal. I can do that, you know. I could if you wanted me to. I keep them all. What did you think of that day?

HE

I don't remember what I thought. It was not unusual to be asked to do such a thing. Usually it's a class you're asked to attend. You do it, and then you go home. But why didn't you mention it the other day, when we met?

SHE

Why bring up that I gawked at you once over lunch? I don't know, I wasn't keeping it a secret. We're exchanging houses. I didn't see any reason to talk about when I sat in an audience and stared at you in college. Why did *you* agree to go and have lunch with a bunch of undergraduates?

HE

I must have thought it might be interesting. The night before I'd just read for an hour and taken some questions. I hadn't met anyone other than the people who'd invited me. I don't remember anything about it except you.

SHE

(*Laughing*) Are you flirting with me?

HE

Yes.

SHE

That seems so unlikely it's almost hard to believe.

HE

It shouldn't be. It's not unlikely at all.

On rereading the scene in bed before I went to sleep, I thought: If ever there was something that didn't need doing, it's this. Now you are taken up with her totally.

It was dreadful in New York the next day, a lot of enraged people walking around looking glum and disbelieving. It was quiet, the traffic so thin you could barely hear it in Central Park, where I had gone to meet Kliman on a bench not far from the Metropolitan. There had been a message from him on my voice mail at the hotel when I got back around midnight from West 71st Street. It would have been easy enough to ignore it and I intended to, until, under the spell of this impetuous reimmersion—and stimulated by the prospect of a meeting with Amy Bellette, whose whereabouts I could probably extract from him—I phoned Kliman the next morning at the number he'd left, despite my having twice hung up on him the day before.

"Caligula wins," he said upon answering the phone. He was expecting someone else, and after a second's pause I said, "So it seems, but this is Zuckerman." "It's a dark day, Mr. Zuckerman. I've been eating crow all morning. I couldn't believe it would happen. People voted for moral values? What values are those? Lying to get us into a war? The idiocy! The idiocy! The Supreme Court. Rehnquist will be dead by tomorrow. Bush'll make Clarence Thomas chief justice. He'll have two, three, maybe even four appointments—horrendous!"

"You left a message last night about our meeting."

"Did I?" he asked. "I haven't slept. Nobody I know has slept. A friend of mine who works at the Forty-second Street library phoned to tell me that there are people crying on the library steps."

I was familiar with the theatrical emotions that the horrors of politics inspire. From the 1965 transformation into a Vietnam hawk of the peace candidate Lyndon Johnson until the 1974 resignation of all-but-impeached Richard Nixon, they were a staple in the repertoire of virtually everyone I knew. You're heartbroken and upset and a little hysterical, or you're gleeful and vindicated for the first time in ten years, and your only balm is to make theater of it. But I was merely onlooker and outsider now. I did not intrude on the public drama; the public drama did not intrude on me.

"Religion!" Kliman cried. "Why don't they put their trust in crystal gazing as a means of apprehending the truth? Suppose evolution should turn out to be a crock, suppose Darwin *was* nuts. Could he begin to be as nuts as Genesis on the origins of man? These are people who don't believe in knowledge. They don't believe in knowledge in exactly the same way I don't believe in faith. I feel like going outside," Kliman told me, "and delivering a long speech."

"Wouldn't help," I told him.

"You've been around. What does?"

"The senile solution: forget it."

"You're not senile," Kliman said.

"But I've forgotten it."

"All of it?" he asked, providing a glimpse of a possible relationship he might try to work up and exploit: the young man asking the older man for his sage advice.

"Everything," I replied truthfully enough—and as though I'd fallen for his ploy.

Kliman was jogging around the oval of the big green lawn and waved at me when I approached the Central Park bench where we were to meet. I waited for him, thinking that once I had made the original mistake—of coming to New York for the collagen procedure—thinking things through had given way to meandering erratically into a renewal I'd had no idea I had the slightest longing for. To disrupt the basic unity of one's life and change the patterns of predictability at seventy-one? What could be more fraught with the likelihood of disorientation, frustration, even of collapse?

Kliman said, "I had to get those shits out of my head. I thought a run would do it. Didn't work."

He wasn't a genial, chubby Billy but well over two hundred pounds, easily six-three, a large, agile, imposing young man with a lot of dark hair and pale gray eyes that were the wonder that pale gray eyes are in the human animal. A beautiful fullback built to pile-drive. My first (untrustworthy) impression was of someone also constrained by a generalized bafflement—at only twenty-eight bowed by the unwillingness of the world to submit without objection to his strength and beauty and the pressing personal needs they served. That's what was in his face: the angry recognition of an unexpected, wholly ridiculous resistance. He had to have been a very different sort of lover for Jamie from the young man she married. Where Billy had the soft, skillful tact of an obliging brother, Kliman had retained much of the schoolyard menace. That's what I perceived when he phoned me at the hotel, and so it was: self-control was not his watchword. Soon enough, it turned out not to be mine.

In running shorts, running shoes, and a damp sweatshirt, he sat dejectedly beside me, his elbows on his knees and his head in his hands. Dripping with sweat—this is how he comes to meet someone who is a key component of his first big professional endeavor, someone he desperately wants to win over. Well, he's genuine, I thought, whatever else he may be, and, if an opportunist, not quite the slick, self-interested opportunist I had imagined from our first conversation.

He wasn't finished expressing himself about the election. "That a right-wing administration motivated by insatiable greed and sustained by murderous lies and led by a privileged dope should answer America's infantile idea of morality—how do we live with something so grotesque? How do you manage to insulate yourself from stupidity so bottomless?"

They were some six to eight years out of college, I thought, and so Kerry's loss to Bush was taking a prominent place in the cluster of extreme historical shocks that would mentally shape their American kinship, as Vietnam had publicly defined their parents' generation and as the Depression and the Second World War had organized the expectations of my parents and their friends. There had been the barely concealed chicanery that had given Bush the presidency in 2000; there had been the terrorist attacks of 2001 and the indelible memory of the doll-like people leaping from the high windows of the burning towers; and now there was this, a second triumph by the "ignoramus" they loathed as much for his undeveloped mental faculties as for his devious nuclear fairy tales, to enlarge the common experience that would set them apart from their younger brothers and sisters as well as from people like me. To them Bush Junior's was never an administration but a regime that had seized power by judicial means. They were meant to be reclaiming their franchise in 2004, and horribly they didn't, leaving them with the feeling, along about eleven last night, not only of having lost but in some way or other of having been defrauded again.

"You wanted to tell me Lonoff's unpardonable secret," I said.

"I never said 'unpardonable.'"

"You were suggesting that much."

"Do you know about his childhood?" he asked me. "Do you know anything about his growing up? Can I trust you not to repeat what I'm about to tell you?"

I leaned back on the bench and erupted with my first laugh since returning to New York. "You want to shout from the rooftops whatever it is that constitutes this utterly private man's carefully kept and plainly humiliating 'great secret,' and you ask me to be discreet enough not to repeat it? You're about to write a book to destroy the dignity that he rigidly protected and that meant everything to him and was legitimately his, and you ask if *I* can be trusted?"

"But this is the same as the phone call. You're being awfully hard on someone you don't even know."

I thought, But I do know you. You're young and you're handsome and nothing gives you more assurance than being devious too. You have a taste for deviousness. It's another of your entitlements to do harm should you want to. And, strictly speaking, it's not harm that you do—merely the fulfilling of a right you would be a fool to relinquish. I know you: you wish to gain the approval of the adults you clandestinely set about to defile. There's a cunning pleasure in that, and safety too.

There was some foot traffic around the big oval lawn, women pushing baby carriages, elderly folks on the arms of black caretakers, and a couple of joggers in the distance whom I at first took for Billy and Jamie.

I could have been a fifteen-year-old boy on that bench, my mind given over completely to the new girl who'd been seated next to me on the first day of school.

"Lonoff declined membership in the National Institute of Arts and Letters," Kliman was telling me. "Lonoff wouldn't contribute a biography to *Contemporary Authors*. Lonoff never in his life gave an interview or made a public appearance. He did everything to remain as invisible as he could out there in the boondocks where he lived. Why?"

"Because he preferred the contemplative life to any other. Lonoff wrote. Lonoff taught. In the evenings Lonoff read. He had a wife and three children, beautiful, unspoiled rural surroundings, and a pleasant eighteenth-century farmhouse full of fireplaces. He made a modest income that sufficed. Order. Security. Stability. What more did he need?"

"To hide. Why else did he wear that bridle all his life? He stood perpetual vigil over himself—it's in his life, it pervades his work. He sustained his constraints because he lived in fear of exposure."

"And you are to do him the favor of exposing him," I said.

There was a moment of unhappiness while he searched for a reason not to punch me in the mouth for having failed to be bowled over by his eloquence. I remembered such moments easily enough, having known them myself as a literary young man just about his age and fresh to New York, where I'd been treated by writers and critics then in their forties and fifties as though I didn't and couldn't know anything about anything, except a little something perhaps about sex, knowledge they considered essentially fatuous, though of course they were themselves endlessly at the mercy of their desires. But as for society, politics, history, culture, as for "ideas"—"You don't even understand when I say you don't understand," one of them liked to tell me while waving his finger in my face. These were my notables, the intellectually exceptional American sons of immigrant Jewish housepainters and butchers and garment workers who were then in their prime, running *Partisan Review* and writing for *Commentary* and *The New Leader* and *Dissent*, irascible rivals sharply contentious with one another, bearing the emotional burden of having been raised by semiliterate Yiddish-speaking parents whose immigrant limitations and meager culture evoked ire and tenderness in equally crippling portions. If I dared to speak, these elders would scornfully shut me up, sure that I knew nothing because of my age and my "advantages"—advantages wholly imagined by them, their intellectual curiosity curiously never extending to anyone younger, unless the younger one was much younger and pretty and a woman. In their later years, marital hardships having left them badly bruised (and financially busted), the diseases of age and difficult children having taken their toll, a few of them softened toward me and became friends and didn't necessarily dismiss everything I had to say all the time.

"You see—I'm reluctant even to tell you," Kliman said at last. "You jump on me when I ask if I can tell you something in confidence, but why do you think I bother to ask?"

"Kliman, why don't you forget about whatever it is you think you've found out? Nobody knows who Lonoff is anymore. What's the point?"

"*That.* He should be in the Library of America. Singer is, with three volumes of stories. Why not E. I. Lonoff?"

"So you're going to redeem Lonoff's reputation as a writer by ruining it as a man. Replace the genius of the genius with the secret of the genius. Rehabilitation by disgrace."

When, after another angry pause, he resumed speaking, it was in the voice you use with a child who's failed to understand for the umpteenth time. "It won't be ruined," he explained to me, "if the book is written the way I intend to write it."

"Doesn't matter how you write it. The scandal will do the job by itself. You won't restore him to his place—you'll deprive him of his place. And what is it that happened anyway? Someone remember something 'inappropriate' Lonoff did fifty years ago? Defiling revelations about another contemptible white male?"

"Why do you insist on trivializing what I want to do? Why do you rush to cheapen what you know nothing about?"

"Because the dirt-seeking snooping calling itself research is just about the lowest of literary rackets."

"And the savage snooping calling itself fiction?"

"You characterizing me now?"

"I'm characterizing literature. It nurtures curiosity too. It says the public life is not the real life. It says there is something beyond the image you set out to give—call it the truth of the self. I'm not doing anything other than what you do. What any thinking person does. Curiosity is nurtured by *life.*"

We had come to our feet at the same time. There is no doubt that I should have walked quickly away from those pale gray eyes, eerily lit up now by our antipathy. For one thing, I could tell that the pad cradled in my plastic underwear to absorb and contain my urine was heavily soaked and that it was time to hurry back to the hotel to wash and change myself. There is no doubt that I should have said no more. Why else had I lived apart from people for eleven years if not to say not one word more than was in my books? Why else had I given up reading the papers and listening to the news and watching television if not to hear nothing further about all that I couldn't stand and was powerless to alter? I lived, by choice, where I could no longer be drawn down into the disappointments. Yet I couldn't stop myself. I was back, I was on a tear, and nothing could have inspired me more than the risk I was taking, because not only was Kliman forty-three years younger than me, a hulking, muscular figure wearing just his running attire, but he was enraged by the very resistance that he could not abide.

"I'm going to do everything I can to sabotage you," I told him. "I'm going to do everything I can to see that no book by you about Lonoff ever appears anywhere. No book, no article, nothing. Not a word, Kliman. I don't know the great secret that you turned up, but it's never going to see the light of day. I can prevent your being published, and, whatever the expense, whatever the effort, I will."

Back in the drama, back in the moment, back into the turmoil of events! When I heard my voice rising, I did not rein it in. There is the pain of being in the world, but there is also the robustness. When was the last time I had felt the excitement of taking someone on? Let the intensity out! Let the belligerence out! A resuscitating breath of the old contention luring me into the old role, both Kliman and Jamie having the effect of rousing the virility in me again, the virility of mind and spirit and desire and intention and wanting to be with people again and have a fight again and have a woman again and feeling the pleasure of one's power again. It's all called back—the virile man called back to life! Only there is no virility. There is only the brevity of expectations. And that being so, I thought, in taking on the young and courting all the dangers of someone of this age intermingling too closely with people of that age, I can only end up bloodied, a big fat target of a scar for unknowing youth, savage with health and armed to the teeth with time. "I'm warning you, Kliman—leave Lonoff alone."

People walking round the oval looked our way as they passed.

Some slowed to a stop, fearful that an elderly man and a young man were about to commence swinging at each other, most likely out of some dispute over the election, and that a slaughter was in store.

"You stink," he shouted at me, "you smell bad! Crawl back into your hole and die!" Shambling athletically, loose and limber, he sprinted off, calling back over the swell of his shoulder, "You're dying, old man, you'll soon be dead! You smell of decay! You smell like death!"

But what could a specimen like Kliman know about the smell of death? All I smelled of was urine.

I had come to New York only because of what the procedure had promised. I had come in search of an improvement. However, in succumbing to the wish to recover something lost—a wish I'd tried to put down long ago—I had opened myself up to believing I could somehow perform again as the man I once was. A solution was obvious: in just the time it took to return to the hotel—and to undress, shower, and put on fresh clothes —I decided to abandon the idea of exchanging residences and leave immediately for home.

Jamie answered when I phoned. I said I had to talk to her and Billy, and she replied, "But Billy's not here. He left about two hours ago to go look at your house. He should be at your caretaker's soon to pick up a key. He was going to call me when he arrived."

But I had no knowledge of having arranged for Billy to see the house or for Rob to give him the key so he could let himself in. When had these arrangements been made? Couldn't have been the night before. Had to have been the night we met. Yet I had no memory of making them.

Alone in my hotel room, without even Jamie's face before me, I felt myself flushing furiously, though, in fact, in recent years I had been having a problem remembering any number of small things. To address the difficulty, I had begun to keep, along with my daily calendar, a lined school composition book —the kind with the black-and-white marbled covers that has the multiplication tables inside the back—in which to list each day's chores and, in more abbreviated form, to note my phone calls, their content, and the letters I wrote and received. Without the chore book, I could (as I'd just proven) easily forget whom I had spoken to about what as recently as yesterday, or what someone was supposed to be doing for me the following day. I had started accumulating chore books some three years before, when I first realized that a perfectly reliable memory was beginning to fray, back when drawing a blank was no more than a minor nuisance and before I came to understand that the process of my forgetting things was ongoing and that if my memory continued to deteriorate at the pace at which it had advanced in these first few years, my ability to write could be gravely impaired. If one morning I should pick up the page I'd written the day before and find myself unable to remember having written it, what would I do? If I lost touch with my pages, if I could neither write a book nor read one, what would become of me? Without my work, what would be left of me?

I did not let on to Jamie that I didn't know what she was talking about and that I had begun to live in a world full of holes, my mind—from the minute I hit New York as an alien species, as a stranger to the world everyone else was inhabiting —swinging to and fro from obsession to forgetfulness. It's as though a switch has been pulled, I thought, as though they're starting to shut the circuits down one by one. "Any questions," I said, "have him call me. Rob knows more about the place than I do, and Billy will make out fine."

I wondered if I hadn't just repeated to her what I had said to them on the occasion of arranging for Billy's inspection of the house.

It was not the time to explain that I'd changed my mind. That would have to wait until Billy got home. Maybe by then he'd have found my little house unsuitable and everything could be resolved without difficulty.

"I would have thought you would have gone with him. Especially as you're not in great shape."

"I'm in the middle of a story," she said, but I didn't believe that writing was her reason for staying. Kliman was her reason for staying. She's the one who wants to move up to Massachusetts; isn't she the one who would check out the house? She's stayed to see Kliman.

"And how do you like your America now," she asked me, "on the first day of the second coming?"

"The pain will recede," I said.

"But Bush won't. Cheney won't. Rumsfeld won't. Wolfowitz won't. That Rice woman won't. The war won't recede. Nor will their arrogance. This useless, stupid war! And soon they'll work up another useless, stupid war. And another and another until everyone on earth will want to blow us up."

"Well, chances are slight of your being blown up at my place," I said, having phoned a moment earlier intending to rescind the agreement that would have furnished her the haven of my place. But I didn't want the phone call to end. She needn't say anything inviting or provocative. She had merely to speak into my ear to furnish a pleasure I hadn't known for years.

"I met your friend," I said.

"You thoroughly befuddled my friend."

"How would you know? I only just left him."

"He phoned from the park."

"As a child at the beach, I once watched while an ambitious swimmer drowned far out at sea," I told her. "Nobody had known he was in trouble until it was too late. With a cell phone, he could have dialed for help, just like Kliman, the instant the tide began to pull him away from shore."

"What do you have against him? Why do you belittle him? What do you even know of him?" Jamie asked. "He's in awe of you, Mr. Zuckerman."

"I honestly felt the fervor running in another direction."

"It was an important encounter for him," she said. "There's nothing in his life these days but Lonoff. He wants to resurrect a writer he considers great and whose work is lost."

"To resurrect him *how* is the question."

"Richard is a serious man."

"Why do you act as his advocate?"

"I 'act as his advocate' because I know him."

I preferred not to think too graphically about why she was arguing the cause of the serious man who had been a boyfriend at college and with whom (I could imagine all too easily) the link had remained sexual even after her marriage to devoted Billy . . . who was not there, by the way; who at this moment was a hundred miles north of New York while his wife was alone in their apartment across from the church, suffering Bush's reelection.

There could be nothing better to round out the folly of my coming back for the reasons I did—and then thinking that I should remain for an entire year—than my trying to get to see Jamie before Billy returned.

"So you know about the scandal," I said.

"What scandal?"

"The Lonoff scandal. Kliman hasn't told you?"

"Of course not."

"But of course he has—you especially, boasting of what he alone knows and of the great uses to be made of his discovery."

This time she didn't bother with the denial.

"You know the whole story," I said.

"If you didn't want the whole story from Richard, why should you want it from me?"

"May I come by?"

"When?"

"Now."

She left me dazed by quietly saying, "If you wish."

I began to pack my things to leave New York. I tried to fill my mind with all that I had to do at home in the coming weeks, to think of the relief to be found in my daily routines and in giving up on any further medical procedures. Never again would I create a circumstance where piercing regret, in its thirst for recompense, would be permitted to determine my next step. Then I set out for West 71st Street, yielded immediately to the ruthlessness of a desperate infatuation guaranteed to be anything but harmless to a man bearing between his legs a spigot of wrinkled flesh where once he'd had the fully functioning sexual organ, complete with bladder sphincter control, of a robust adult male. The once rigid instrument of procreation was now like the end of a pipe you see sticking out of a field somewhere, a meaningless piece of pipe that spurts and gushes intermittently, spitting forth water to no end, until a day arrives when somebody remembers to give the valve the extra turn that shuts the damn sluice down.

She'd been reading the *New York Times* for every bit of news about the election. The pages of the paper were strewn across the orange-gold intricacies of the softly worn Persian carpet, and her face bore traces of real misery.

"It's too bad Billy couldn't be here today," I said. "It's not good to be alone with so much disappointment."

She shrugged helplessly. "We thought there'd be jubilation."

While I was on my way, she'd prepared coffee for us and we sat across from each other in a pair of black leather Eames chairs by the window, sipping from our cups in silence. Expressing our uncertainty in silence. Accepting the unpredictability of what was to come in silence. Hiding our confusion in silence. I hadn't noticed on my previous visits that there were two orange cats in residence until one pounced weightlessly onto her lap and lay there being stroked by Jamie while I, observing, continued to say nothing. The other appeared from nowhere to straddle her bare feet, creating the pleasant illusion (in me) that it was her feet and not himself that he had set to purring. One was longhaired and one was shorthaired, and the sight of them astonished me. They were what the two kittens Larry Hollis had given me would have grown up to look like had I kept them for more than three days.

Though she was wearing a faded blue sweatshirt and loose-fitting gray workout pants, I was no less transfixed by her beauty. And we were alone, and so, far from feeling like some personage able to inspire awe, I felt myself stripped of my status by her hold over me, all the more so since she herself appeared so depleted by Kerry's defeat and the fearsome uncertainties it aroused.

In keeping with my wildly fluctuating behavior in New York, I now wondered what the writing of Lonoff's biography could possibly have to do with me. After my visit to his house in 1956, I'd never again been in his presence, and the one letter I sent him after that visit he had not answered, thus stifling any dream I may have had of his serving as master to my apprenticeship. As regards either a biography or a biographer, I had no responsibility to E. I. Lonoff or his heirs. It was seeing Amy Bellette after so many years—especially seeing her infirm and disfigured, evicted from the dwelling of her own body—and after that going out to buy his books and rereading them at the hotel, that had set in motion the response that Kliman would elicit with his allusions to a sinister Lonoff "secret." Surely if I had been at home and received a letter out of the blue from some Kliman or other, more or less inveigling me for the same reasons, I wouldn't have bothered to reply, let alone have threatened to all but destroy him should he dare to pursue this project further. Left merely to his own devices, Kliman wasn't likely to succeed in his grandiose plans; probably the greatest encouragement he'd had so far wasn't from a literary agent or a publishing house but from my strenuous opposition. And now here I was with Jamie, ending our silence by asking, "Whom am I dealing with? Will you tell me? Who is this boy?"

Suspiciously she said, "What do you want to know?"

"How does he come to imagine himself adequate to this job? Have you known him for long?"

"Since he was eighteen. Since his freshman year. I've known him ten years."

"Where is he from?"

"He's from Los Angeles. His father is a lawyer. An entertainment lawyer, a notoriously aggressive one. His mother is entirely different from his father. She's a professor of, I think, Egyptology, at UCLA. She meditates for a couple of hours every morning. She claims to be able to make a green ball of light levitate in front of her at the end of her meditations on a good day."

"How did you meet her?"

"Through him, of course. Whenever they'd come to town they'd take his friends out to dinner. Just as when my parents came to town, he was among my friends, and he would go out to dinner with us."

"So he grew up in a professional household."

"Well, he grew up with a headstrong, aggressive father and an intellectual and quiet mother. He's smart. He's very smart. He's very sharp. Yes, he's got his own aggressiveness, which clearly has put you off. But he's no dummy. There's no reason why he shouldn't be able to write a book—other than why anybody shouldn't be able to write a book."

"Why is that?"

"Because it's hard."

She was studiously saying no more than she was saying, trying to impress me with her unimpressibility and determined not to submit but merely to answer. She was strongly disinclined to appear to be a pushover because of the differences in status and age. Despite her obvious complacency about her effect on men, she hadn't seemed to realize as yet that she had already triumphed and the pushover was me.

"What was he like to you?" I asked.

"When?"

"When you were friends."

"We had a wonderful time together. We had fathers comparably bullheaded to contend with, so we had plenty of survival stories to swap. That's how we got so devoted so quickly—they provided us with delightful tales of horror and mirth. Richard's robust and energetic and always up for trying new things, and he's fearless. He holds nothing back. He's adventurous and he's fearless and he's free."

"Aren't you a little over the top?"

"I'm accurately answering your questions."

"Fearless of what, may I ask?"

"Of contempt. Of disapproval. He doesn't have the limitations that other people have about being in the group of people they feel comfortable with. There's nothing hesitant about him. He's a succession of decisive deeds."

"And he gets along with the notoriously aggressive father?"

"Oh, I think they fight. They're both fighting men, so they fight. I don't think it's taken so seriously, as if I were to fight with my mother. They'll fight like dogs on the phone and the next night they're back on the phone as though nothing had ever happened. That's the way it is with them."

"Tell me more."

"What more do you want to know?"

"Whatever you're not telling me." Of course I wanted to know only about her. "Did you ever visit him in Los Angeles?"

"Yes."

"And?"

"He lives in a big house in Beverly Hills. It's, in my book, extremely ugly. It's large, it's ostentatious. Not at all cozy. His mother collects, I guess you'd call it ancient art—sculpture, little objects. And there are display cases, niches in the wall that are too large—the way everything there is too large—for what they hold. It's a place without any warmth. Too many columns. Too much marble. A huge pool in the back yard. Extremely landscaped. Very manicured. That's not his world. He went to college in the Northeast. He's come to New York. He's chosen to live in New York and work in the literary world and not become super-rich and live in a marble palace in L.A. and hound people for a living. He's got the skills to be a professional hound—he learned them from his father—but that's not what he wants."

"The parents are still married?"

"Shockingly, yes. I don't know what they have in common. She meditates and then goes off to work all day. He's at work all the time. They share the house together, I guess. I never saw them talk about anything with each other."

"Is he in touch with them?"

"I suppose so. He doesn't talk about them."

"He wouldn't call his parents on election night."

"I suppose not. Though I'm sure his parents would be much more pleasant to talk to on election night than mine. They're good L.A. liberals."

"And his friends in New York?"

Here she sighed, the first irritated sign of impatience. Till then she'd been completely unrattled and calculatingly aloof. "He's gotten occupied with a group of men he met at the gym. They're young professionals, probably between twenty-five and forty. They all play basketball together and he hangs out with them a lot. Lawyers. Media people. Some of our mutual friends from college work at magazines and in publishing. He's got a good friend who started a video game company."

"I think he should go in with that friend. I think he should be in video games. Let him be fearless there. Because he thinks this is a game. He thinks 'Lonoff' is the *name* of a game."

"You're wrong," she said, and betrayed herself with a quick smile for having so flatly let me know that. "He comes across to you like his father, this bullying man, but he's much more his mother. He's an intellectual. He's thoughtful. Yes, he's got extraordinary energy. Dynamic and exciting and strong and obstinate and sometimes scary, too. But he's not a thoughtless opportunist out for himself."

"I would have said that's just what he was."

"What kind of opportunist goes after a literary biography of

a writer who by now is virtually unknown? If he were an opportunist, he'd follow in his father's footsteps. He wouldn't
write a biography of a writer nobody under fifty has heard of."

"You're selling him. You're idealizing him."

"Not at all. I know him a lot better than you do and I'm
trying to correct you. You need a corrective."

"He's not serious. There's no sobriety in him. It's all audacity, defiance, and highjinks. There's no gravity."

"Perhaps he doesn't have the restraint other people have or
the finesse, but he's not without sobriety."

"And integrity. Is he at all corrupted by integrity? I don't
think scheming is foreign to Kliman. Is integrity lurking anywhere?"

"You're not describing him, Mr. Zuckerman—you're bur-
lesquing him. It's true that he doesn't always get why he shouldn't
behave the way he does. But he has his principles. Look,
Richard's not alone—he lives in a careerist world, a world where
if you're not careerist you feel like a failure. A world that's all
about reputation. You're an older person coming back, and
you don't know what it is to be young now. You're from the
1950s and he's from now. You're Nathan Zuckerman. It's
probably been a long time since you had contact with people
who aren't established in their professional lives. You don't
know what it is not to be safe in a reputation in a world where
reputation is everything. But if you're not a Zen master in this
careerist world, if you're a part of it and struggling to be recognized, are you, ipso facto, the evil enemy? Admittedly,
Richard is not perhaps the most profound person I know, but
there's no reason why, in the world of his experience, he would
anticipate that his headlong pursuit of what he's pursuing
should be offensive to anyone."

"I would say, on the subject of his profundity, that he's not
half as profound as your husband. And that your husband is
not a tenth as careerist as Kliman, and doesn't feel like a failure
because of it."

"He doesn't feel like a success either. But basically that's true."

"Lucky girl."

"Very lucky. I love my husband very much."

All the faultless display of self-assurance had done in under
ten minutes was to deepen my desire and make her far and

away the biggest problem of my life. The velocity of the attraction allows for no resignation and contains no resignation—there is only room for the greed of desire.

"Surely you would agree that Kliman, at the least, is a very disagreeable person."

"I wouldn't agree," she replied.

"And the secret? The pursuit of the secret? Lonoff's great secret?"

Without altering her rhythmic stroking of the cat, she replied, "Incest."

"And how does Kliman know this?"

"He has documentation. He's been in touch with some people. Beyond that, I don't know."

"But I was with Lonoff. I met Lonoff. I've read all of Lonoff more than once. This is impossible to believe."

With just a whisper of superiority, she said, "It's always impossible to believe."

"It's nonsense," I insisted. "Incest with whom?"

"A half-sister," Jamie said.

"Like Lord Byron and Augusta."

"Not at all like them," she answered—and sharply this time—and proceeded to exhibit her (or Kliman's) erudition on the subject. "Byron and his half-sister barely knew each other as children. They were only lovers when they were adults and she was the mother of three children. The sole similarity is that Lonoff's half-sister was also older. She was from the father's first marriage. The girl's mother died when she was small, the father quickly remarried, and Lonoff was born. She was then three years old. They grew up together. They were raised as brother and sister."

"Three years old. That means she was born in 1898. She must be gone a long time now."

"She had children. The youngest son is still alive. He must be eighty or more. In Israel. She left America to live in Palestine after they were discovered. The parents took her there to escape the disgrace. Lonoff stayed behind and set off on his own. He was seventeen by then."

The story I knew of Lonoff's origins was similar only up to a point. The parents had emigrated from Russia's Jewish Pale to Boston but in time found American society repellently materialistic, and when Lonoff was seventeen, they moved on to pre-Mandate Palestine. It was true that Lonoff had remained behind, but not because he was abandoned as a deviant wrongdoer of a son; he was a fully grown American boy and preferred to become an American-speaking American man rather than a Hebrew-speaking Palestinian Jew. I'd never heard anything about a sister or any other sibling, but then, since he was devoted to preventing his fiction from being speciously misinterpreted as a gloss on his life, Lonoff had never revealed more than the most rudimentary facts of his biography to anyone, except perhaps to his wife, Hope, or to Amy.

"When did this affair begin?" I asked.

"He was fourteen."

"Who told Kliman about it—the son in Israel?"

"Richard would have told you who told him, if you'd let him," she said. "He'd have told you all of this himself. He would have known the answers to every one of your questions."

"And told how many besides me? How many besides you?"

"I don't see what crime he's committing by telling whoever he wants to tell. You wanted me to tell you. That's why you called and came here. Have I now committed a crime? I'm sorry that the thought of an incestuous Lonoff tortures you. It's hard for me to believe that the man who wrote your books would rather he be sanctified."

"It's a long way from reckless accusation to sanctification. Kliman can't possibly prove anything about intimate events that he claims happened close to one hundred years ago."

"Richard's not reckless. I told you: he is adventurous. He's drawn to daring ventures. What's wrong with that?"

Daring ventures. I had gorged on them.

I said, "Has Kliman spoken to the son in Israel, to Lonoff's nephew?"

"Several times."

"And he corroborates the story. He's given him a record of the copulations. Is there a log that young Lonoff kept?"

"The son denies everything, of course. The last time he and Richard spoke, he threatened to come to the U.S. and initiate a lawsuit should Richard make public any such characterization of his mother."

"And Kliman maintains that he's lying for the obvious reasons, or that he just doesn't know—what mother would confide such a secret to her son? Look, too little can be known for him to conclude anything about incest. There's the not-so that reveals the so—that's fiction; and then there's the not-so that just isn't so—that's Kliman."

Jamie promptly stood, sliding the one cat off her lap and dislodging the other from her feet. "I don't see that this conversation is going in a helpful direction. I shouldn't have intervened. I shouldn't have invited you here to try to do Richard's bidding for him. I have sat obediently and answered your questions. I didn't raise a single objection while you took your deposition. I answered you honestly and have been nothing but respectful, if not downright slavish. I'm sorry if anything I've said or how I've said it has rubbed you the wrong way. But without intending to, that's what I've done."

I stood too—only inches away from her—and said, "It's I who's rubbed you the wrong way. Beginning with the deposition." It was the moment to tell her that the deal was off. But I could only keep her realistically in my thoughts if the deal was on and we went ahead to exchange my house for their apartment. Then she would be living amid my things and I amid hers. Could there have been a more ridiculous motive for maintaining the impetuous arrangement I wanted so badly to break? I was hardly unaware of the flimsiness of the reasons I kept turning up to materially alter my life, and yet all that was happening seemed to be happening despite my awareness and without regard for my condition.

The phone rang. It was Billy. She listened for a long time before telling him that I happened to be right there. He must then have asked her why I was, because she replied, "He wanted to look at the apartment again. I'm showing him around."

Yes, Kliman *was* the lover. She was so used to lying to Billy —to cover her tracks with Kliman—that she'd lied to him now about me. As earlier she'd lied to me on the phone about Kliman. Either that or I was so blinded by her appeal that my mind was riveted to the one thing as it hadn't been for years. Hadn't she lied to her young husband simply because it was easier than going into the truth while I was present and they were miles apart?

There was nothing Jamie could do or say to which I did not register a disproportionate response, including her casual chit-chat with Billy on the phone. I was continuously unstable. There was no repose. I might have been gazing upon young womanhood for the very first time. Or the last. All-enveloping either way.

I left without daring to touch her. Without daring to touch her face, though it was well within my reach throughout what she had characterized as my deposing her. Without daring to touch the long hair that was within my reach. Without daring to place my hand on her waist. Without daring to say that we'd met once before. Without daring to say whatever words a man mutilated as I was says to a desirable woman forty years his junior that will not leave him covered in shame because he is overcome by temptation for a delight he cannot enjoy and a pleasure that is dead. I was in deep enough with nothing having happened between us but our abrasive little talk about Kliman, Lonoff, and the allegation of incest.

I was learning at seventy-one what it is to be deranged. Proving that self-discovery wasn't over after all. Proving that the drama that is associated usually with the young as they fully begin to enter life—with adolescents, with young men like the steadfast new captain in *The Shadow-Line*—can also startle and lay siege to the aged (including the aged resolutely armed against *all* drama), even as circumstance readies them for departure.

Maybe the most potent discoveries are reserved for last.

SITUATION: *The young husband is away, the sweet, obliging husband who adores her. It's November 2004. She's scared and distraught over the election, over Al Qaeda, over an affair with a college boyfriend who's around and still in love with her, and over "daring ventures" of a kind she married to renounce. She is wearing the soft cashmere sweater, wheat or camel in color, something paler and softer than tan. Wide cuffs hang off her wrists, and loose sleeves connect to the body of the sweater quite low. The cut is reminiscent of a kimono, or better yet, a late-nineteenth-century men's smoking jacket. A thick edge of wide ribbing runs around the neck and all the way to the sweater's bottom edge, creating a collar effect, although there is no actual collar: the sweater lies flat against her. Low on the waist, a tie made of the same broad ribbing is cinched in a careless half-bow. The sweater hangs open from the neck almost to the waist, giving a long, narrow glimpse of her mostly concealed body. Because the sweater is so loosely draped, her body is mostly hidden. But he can tell she is slim—only a thin woman can carry off such roomy clothing successfully. The sweater reminds him of an extremely short bathrobe, and so, although he can see little of her, he has the impression he is in her bedroom and will soon see more. The woman wearing this sweater must be well-off (to afford such an expensive item) and also she must place high value on her physical pleasure (since she has chosen to spend her money on clothing used almost exclusively for lolling about the house).*

To be performed with appropriate pauses, as each will sometimes stop to think before answering the other's question.

MUSIC: *Strauss's* Four Last Songs. *For the profundity that is achieved not by complexity but by clarity and simplicity. For the purity of the sentiment about death and parting and loss. For the long melodic line spinning out and the female voice soaring and soaring. For the repose and composure and gracefulness and the intense beauty of the soaring. For the ways one is drawn into the tremendous arc of heartbreak. The composer drops all masks and, at the age of eighty-two, stands before you naked. And you dissolve.*

SHE

I understand why you're coming back to New York, but why did you go away in the first place?

HE

Because I began to get a series of death threats in the mail. Postcards with death threats on one side and a picture of the pope on the other. I went to the FBI, and the FBI told me what to do.

SHE

Did they ever find the person?

HE

No, they never did. But I stayed where I was.

SHE

So—screwballs send death threats to writers. We weren't
alerted in the MFA program.

HE

Well, I'm not the first, even in recent years, who's received
death threats. The case of Salman Rushdie is most famous.

SHE

That's true. Of course.

HE

I don't compare my situation to his. But leaving Salman Rushdie aside, I can't imagine that what happened to me has happened to me alone. You have to ask yourself if the threat is
prompted by what the writer writes or if there are people who
just become inflamed by certain names and who obey urges
that are alien to the rest of us. They may only have to see a
photograph in a newspaper to become inflamed. Imagine what
can happen should they go ahead and open one of your books.
They experience your words as malevolent, as a spell cast over
them that they cannot bear. Even civilized people have been
known to throw a book they hate across the room. For those
less restrained, it's only a small step to loading the pistol. Or
they may genuinely loathe what you are, as they perceive what
you are—as we know from the motives of the Twin Towers
terrorists. Rage is plentiful out there.

SHE

Yes, the rage is out there, and it's unrivaled and insane.

HE

And it's frightened you silly.

SHE

It has. I'm in a state. Just being nervous and afraid all the time
—and the shame associated with being like that. At home I've
become silent and narcissistic and obsessed with my own
safety, and my writing is awful.

HE

Were you always frightened of the rage?

SHE

No, it's a recent thing. All the trust has gone out of me. You don't merely have your enemies now. The people who are meant to protect you, they've become your enemy. The people who are meant to take care of you, they've become your enemy. It's not Al Qaeda that scares me—it's my own government.

HE

Al Qaeda doesn't scare you? You're not afraid of the terrorists?

SHE

Yes. But the deeper fear is roused by the people who are supposed to be on my side. There will always be enemies out in the world, but . . . in your turning to the FBI, if at a certain point you had started to feel not that it was the FBI who was protecting you from the person who was sending the death threats but that it was the FBI who was endangering you, that would have given a whole new depth to the terror, and that's why I feel as I do now.

HE

And you think you won't have these fears up where I live?

SHE

I think living there will quell my more reasonable anxieties by taking away the aspect of physical danger, and I think that will calm me down somewhat. I don't think it will get rid of my own rage—my rage at my government—but I can't do anything right now, I feel so on edge. Since I can't even begin to know what to do, I *have* to go away. May I ask you something? (*Politely laughing beforehand at her presumptuousness*)

HE

Of course.

SHE

Do you think you would have gone away anyway if you hadn't gotten the death threats? Do you think at a certain point you would have left anyway?

HE

I don't honestly know. I was alone. I was free. My work is portable. I had reached an age where I was no longer looking for certain kinds of involvement.

SHE

How old were you when you left?

HE

Sixty. Seems quite old to you.

SHE

Yes. Yes, it does.

HE

How old are your parents?

SHE

My mother is sixty-five and my father is sixty-eight.

HE

I was just a bit younger than your mother when I left.

SHE

That's a different thing from what we're doing now. Billy is not too pleased about the whole thing. Or about what it's revealed about me.

HE

Well, he can write there too.

SHE

I think it will be good for both of us, and I think he'll see that in time. He's more adaptable to begin with.

HE

Is there anything that you wish you weren't leaving behind? What will you miss?

SHE

I'll miss some friends. But it's good to be without them for a while.

HE

Do you have a lover?

SHE

Why do you say that?

HE

Because of the way you say you'll miss some friends.

SHE

No. Yes.

HE

You do. How long have you been married?

SHE

Five years. We were young.

HE

Does Billy know you have a lover?

SHE

No, no he doesn't.

HE

Does he know your lover?

SHE

He does.

HE

What does your lover think about your going away? Does he even know you're going away? Is he angry about it?

SHE

He doesn't know yet.

HE

You haven't told him?

SHE

No.

HE

Are you telling the truth?

SHE

Yes.

HE

Why are you telling the truth?

SHE

Something about you seems trustworthy. I've read you. You're not easily scandalized. I imagine from what I've read of your work that you're a curious person rather than one who makes superficial judgments. I guess there's a pleasure in having a curious person's curiosity fixed on you.

HE

Are you trying to make me jealous?

SHE

(*Laughing*) No. Are you jealous?

HE

I am.

SHE

(*A bit startled*) Really. Of my lover?

HE

Yes.

SHE

How could that be?

HE

Does it seem so impossible to you?

SHE

It seems very strange to me.

HE

Truly?

SHE

Truly.

HE

You don't know how attractive you are.

SHE

Why did you come here today?

HE

To be alone with you.

SHE

I see.

HE

Yes, to be alone with you.

SHE

Why do you want to be alone with me?

HE

Shall I be truthful?

SHE

I've been truthful with you.

HE

Because it excites me to be alone with you.

SHE

Good. I suppose it excites me to be alone with you too. Perhaps for different reasons. We could probably both use a little excitement.

HE

Doesn't your lover supply the excitement?

SHE

He's been around my life a long time. Being my lover is a relatively recent development. There's nothing new.

HE

He was your lover in college.

SHE

But then he wasn't for many years. It's going backwards with him. The absorption is long over. It's retrograde now.

HE

So your lover is not exciting. And your marriage is not exciting. Did you expect marriage to be exciting?

SHE

(*Laughing*) Yes.

HE

You did really?

SHE

Yes.

HE

Didn't they teach you anything at Harvard?

SHE

(*Laughs softly again*) We were very in love when we got married, and the prospect of the future, of merely having a future, seemed glorious. To get married seemed like the greatest adventure possible. The newest thing we could possibly do. The great next step. (*Silence*) Are you glad you went away? Are you glad you did what you did?

HE

I would have answered differently several weeks ago. I would have answered differently several hours ago.

SHE

What's changed that answer?

HE

Meeting a young woman like you.

SHE

What interests you so much about me?

HE

Your youth and your beauty. The speed with which we've entered into communication. The erotic environment you create out of words.

SHE

New York is full of beautiful young women.

HE

I've been without the companionship of a woman and all that goes with it for years now. This is a startling turn of events and not necessarily in my interest. Someone wrote—I don't remember who—"Great love later in life comes at cross-purposes to everything."

SHE

Great love? Can you explain yourself, please?

HE

It's a sickness. It's a fever. It's a kind of hypnosis. I can only explain it by saying that I want to be alone in a room with you. I want to be under your spell.

SHE

Well, I'm glad. I'm glad you're getting what you want. It's a good thing.

HE

It's heartbreaking.

SHE

Why?

HE

Why do you think? You're a writer. You want to be a writer. Why would a man of seventy-one find this heartbreaking?

SHE

(*Delicately*) Because you have all this feeling again and you can't take it to its next step.

HE

That's correct.

SHE

But there's pleasure in this, isn't there?

HE

Of the heartbreaking variety.

SHE

(*She's learned something*) Hmmm. (*After a long pause, with mock theatricality*) Oh, what is to be done?

HE

Do you have any suggestions?

SHE

No. I have no idea what's to be done. I'm going away because I can't think what to do about anything.

HE

You seem close to tears all the time.

SHE

(*Laughing*) Well, it helps me not, I'll tell you that.

HE

(*Laughs too, but remains silent. The flirtation is infernal, the man within the man in flames.*)

SHE

Have you been out today? The whole city is close to tears. Yes, yes, I'm close to tears. It's momentous for me, you can imagine. Can you imagine how we felt last night when—

HE

I was here. I saw it. Did you notice that I was here?

SHE

And you obviously noticed I was here. Something seized you, though, before you met me. It wasn't me. You decided to come see our apartment. Something seized you—what was it? You know, the death threats don't explain to me the extreme thing that you've done with your life. However much you explain by saying I'm a writer who's had these threats made against my life, it is an extreme thing to have done, to go off and live the way you have. I have to keep wondering, What's the real story there? So there were these postcards. So what? The postcards are a pretext. You go away for a year, if it's the postcards, and you have friends and girlfriends, and in time the postcards stop and you come back. But a man who sequesters himself, secludes himself the way you did, does so for a much larger reason. People don't give up on life for a completely circumstantial and external reason like a death threat.

HE

What might that larger reason be?

SHE

Escaping pain.

HE

What pain?

SHE

The pain of being present.

HE

Aren't you describing yourself?

SHE

Perhaps. The pain of being present in the present moment. Yes, that could be said to describe very neatly the extreme thing I'm doing. But for you it wasn't merely the present moment. It was being present at all. It was being present in the presence of *anything*.

HE

Did you ever read a short novel called *The Shadow-Line*?

SHE

By Conrad? No. I remember a boyfriend telling me about it once, but I never read it.

HE

The opening line goes, "Only the young have such moments." These are moments Conrad describes as "rash." In the first few pages he lays everything out. "Rash moments"—the two words make up the entire sentence. He goes on, "I mean moments when the still young are inclined to commit rash actions, such as getting married suddenly or else throwing up a job for no reason." It goes like that. But these rash moments don't just happen in youth. Coming here last night was a rash moment. Daring to return is another. With age there are rash moments too. My first was leaving, my second is returning.

SHE

Billy thinks that he's indulging a rash moment on my part because if he doesn't, I'll get swamped with depression and fear. But he thinks that it's a rash moment. I never thought of myself as a desperate person. I hate to think that I'd be doing something desperate.

HE

I think you'll like it there. I'll miss you.

SHE

Well, it's your house. You can come up. You can have forgotten something and come up. We can have lunch.

HE

You can have forgotten something and come down.

> SHE

Sure.

> HE

Okay. You're less curt with me than you were last night. The fact that I haven't followed Bush's lies shouldn't make me an antagonist.

> SHE

Was I nasty?

> HE

I didn't feel that you cared for me much. Unless I intimidated you.

> SHE

Of course you did. I read all those books in college and all the ones since. You might not be aware of it, locked up alone in the Berkshires, but there are many like me, people my age, and older (*laughing*) and younger, for whom you fill an important need. We admire you.

> HE

Well, I haven't seen myself in the public mirror for many years. I don't know that.

> SHE

I just told you.

> HE

I still don't know it. But it's wonderful to learn of your admiration, because I've quickly come to admire you.

> SHE

(*Astonished*) You've come to admire me? Why?

> HE

I hate to say this to you, but "someday you'll understand." (*She laughs*)

> HE

You postmodernists laugh a lot.

> SHE

I laugh because I find things funny.

HE

Are you laughing at me?

SHE

I'm laughing at the situation. You're speaking to me like you're my father. Someday I'll understand. Is the pleasure in the doing of it or only in the having done it? Writing, I mean. I'm changing the subject.

HE

In the doing of it. The pleasure of the having done it lasts a short time. There's pleasure in holding the bundle of pages in your hand, and there's pleasure when the first copy arrives. I pick it up and set it down a hundred times. I eat with it beside me. I've taken it to bed with me.

SHE

I know that. When my story was published, I slept with the copy of *The New Yorker* under my pillow.

HE

You're a very charming young woman.

SHE

Thank you, thank you.

HE

This is why I live in the country.

SHE

I understand.

HE

It's all a little distressing for me to come back to New York, and this is a little distressing too. I think I better go.

SHE

Okay. Perhaps we'll see each other alone and talk again.

HE

That would do it to me, my friend.

SHE

I would like to be your friend.

HE

Why?

SHE

Because I have no one like you.

HE

You don't know me.

SHE

I don't. I have no interactions like this.

HE

Must you use that language? You're a writer—give up "interactions."

SHE

(*Laughing*) I have no conversations like this. I have no situations like this.

HE

I didn't mean to correct you. It's not my business. Excuse me.

SHE

I understand. If you want to get together and talk again, my number is your number. You can always call me.

HE

It's not as if I answered a rental ad. It's as if I answered the personals. "Exceedingly attractive, well-educated WMF occasionally available for intimate conversation . . ." I got more than a new apartment, didn't I?

SHE

Maybe a friend, too.

HE

But this is not a friendship I can have.

SHE

What can you have?

HE

Not much, it seems. Precious things having been taken away has created a predicament that can't be overcome by hard work, et cetera. Do you follow me?

SHE

I don't quite understand. Do you just mean getting older, or is there something else in particular?

HE

(*Laughing*) I suppose I just mean getting older.

SHE

I understand now.

HE

This is killing me, so I'm going to leave. I'm not going to follow my inclination and try to kiss you.

SHE

Okay.

HE

That wouldn't get us anywhere.

SHE

You're right. I'm glad you came by this afternoon, though. I'm very glad.

HE

Are you a seductress?

SHE

No, no, absolutely not.

HE

You have a husband, you have a lover, and now you want to have me as a friend. Do you collect men? Or do men collect you?

SHE

(*Laughing*) I suppose I've collected men and that they've collected me.

HE

You're only thirty. Have you collected many men?

SHE

I don't know what's considered many. (*She laughs again*)

HE

I mean since you left college, between commencement day
and this afternoon, which has concluded with your collecting
me with your seductive power . . . But you're acting childishly
now, as though you don't possess such power. Has nobody
ever told you about your power?

SHE

I've been told. I was laughing because if you include yourself
as a collected man, I wouldn't know how to count the men
I've collected.

HE

You have collected me.

SHE

And yet you will not call me again. And you will not kiss me.
We may not even see each other again, except with my husband, when we exchange keys, so I don't see how I've collected
you.

HE

Because a meeting like this for a man like me is devastating.

SHE

I certainly don't want to devastate you. I'm sorry if I have.

HE

I'm sorry I couldn't devastate *you*.

SHE

You've given me pleasure.

HE

As I said, this is killing, so I'm going to have to go.

SHE

Thank you for coming by.

*On the street, starting back on foot to the hotel, thinking of the
scene just enacted—and if he feels himself to be an actor, coming
from having rehearsed a scene from an unproduced play, it's because she seemed so like an actress to him, a highly intuitive, intelligent young actress who listens carefully and concentrates totally*

and responds quietly—he is reminded of the scene in A Doll's House *when the dying, lovesick sophisticate Dr. Rank is summoned to spend a moment with her by Torvald Helmer's beautiful wife, the spoiled tease, flirtatious young Nora. The light fading, the room getting smaller, a cab or two going by in the street, the city receding while everything around them becomes close and dark. These two people taking their time with each other, listening to each other. So sexual and so sad. Thick with each of their pasts, though neither knows much of the other's. The pace of it, all that silence and what might be in there. Each of them desperate for entirely different reasons. For him, however, the last desperate scene, most certainly with a cunningly gifted actress slyly passing herself off as a novice writer. A scene constituting the opening of* He and She, *a play of desire and temptation and flirtation and agony—agony all the time—an improvisation best aborted and left to die. Chekhov has a story called "He and She." Other than the title, he remembers nothing of the story (perhaps there is no such story), though from words of advice about such storytelling in a letter Chekhov wrote while still quite young, he can remember the key sentence even now. A letter by a greatly admired writer he read in his twenties is still fresh to him, while the time and place of appointments he made the day before he now forgets completely. "The center of gravity," wrote Chekhov in 1886, "should reside in two: he and she." It should. It has. It won't ever again.*

My bag was where I had left it, half packed on the hotel dresser when I had rushed off earlier for West 71st Street. A light flashing on my phone indicated that I had a message. But I still didn't know from whom because once I'd got back to the room, all I'd done was to sit at the undersized desk by the window looking down on the 53rd Street traffic, and once again, on hotel stationery, set down as quickly as I could an exchange with Jamie that had not taken place. My chore book recorded what I did do and what I was scheduled to do as an aid to a failing memory; this scene of dialogue unspoken recorded what hadn't been done and was an aid to nothing, alleviated nothing, achieved nothing, and yet, just as on election night, it had seemed terribly necessary to write the instant I came through the door, the conversations she and I don't have more affecting even than the conversations we do have, and the imaginary "She" vividly at the middle of her character as the actual "she" will never be.

But isn't one's pain quotient shocking enough without fictional amplification, without giving things an intensity that is ephemeral in life and sometimes even unseen? Not for some. For some very, very few that amplification, evolving uncertainly out of nothing, constitutes their only assurance, and the unlived, the surmise, fully drawn in print on paper, is the life whose meaning comes to matter most.

3

Amy's Brain

WHEN AT last I lifted the phone to take the message, there was the voice I'd overheard while leaving the hospital the previous Thursday, the youthful voice of the aged Amy Bellette. "Nathan Zuckerman," she said, "I learned your whereabouts from a note left in my mailbox by a colossal pest named Richard Kliman. I don't know if you want to bother to respond or whether you even remember me. We met in Massachusetts in 1956. In the winter. I'd been E. I. Lonoff's student at Athena College. I was working in Cambridge. You were a fledgling writer at the Quahsay Colony. We both stayed as the Lonoffs' guests that night. A snowy evening in the Berkshires a very long time ago. I'll understand if you don't care to call back." She left her number and hung up.

Once again, not thinking, not even about Kliman's motive, which was inscrutable to me—what could he possibly expect to get out of putting Amy and me together? But I did not linger on Kliman, nor did I consider what could have prompted this frail woman who was either recovering or dying from brain cancer to contact me once she learned through Kliman that I was nearby. Nor did I stop to wonder why it should be so easy provoking a response in me when I wanted only to undo the error of trying to ameliorate things and return home to resume living as more than my incapacities.

I dialed her number as though it were the code to restoring the fullness that once encompassed us all; I dialed as though spinning a lifetime counterclockwise were an act as natural and ordinary as resetting the timer on the kitchen stove. My heartbeat was discernible again, not because I was anxiously anticipating being within arm's reach of Jamie Logan but from envisioning Amy's black hair and dark eyes and the confident look on her face in 1956—from remembering her fluency and her charm and her quick mind, crammed back then with Lonoff and literature.

While the phone rang I recalled watching at the luncheonette as she removed the faded red rainhat to reveal her disfigured skull and the battering that bad luck had provided. "Too late," I'd thought, and got up and paid for my coffee and left without intruding. "Leave her to her fortitude."

The setting was a standard-issue Hilton hotel room, bland and drained of anything personal, but my determination to reach her had transported me nearly fifty years back, when gazing upon an exotic girl with a foreign accent seemed to an untried boy the answer to everything. I dialed the number now as a divided being no more or less integrated than anyone else, as the fledgling she'd met in 1956 *and* as the improbable onlooker (with the unforeseeable biography) that he had become by 2004. Yet never was I less free of that fledgling and his tangle of innocent idealism, precocious seriousness, excitable curiosity, and wanton desire, still comically ungratified, than while I waited for her to answer. When she did, I didn't know whom to picture at the other end of the line: Amy then or now. The voice conveyed the radiant freshness of a young girl about to break into a dance, but the head carved up by a surgeon's knife remained too grim an image to suppress.

"I saw you at a luncheonette on Madison and Ninety-sixth," Amy said. "I was too shy to speak. You're so important now."

"Am I? Not out where I live. How are you, Amy?" I asked, saying nothing about having been so stunned by the brutality of her transformation that I'd been too shy myself to approach her. "I remember very clearly that night we all met. The snowy night in 1956. I didn't realize he was still married to his wife at the time of his death until I read the obituary. I thought he had married you."

"We never married. He couldn't do it. That was all right. We were together for four years, mainly in Cambridge. We lived a year in Europe, we came home, he wrote and he wrote, he taught a little, he got sick, and he died."

"He was writing a novel," I said.

"In his late fifties writing a first novel. If the leukemia hadn't killed him, that novel would have."

"Why?"

"The subject. When Primo Levi killed himself everyone said it was because of his having been an inmate at Auschwitz. I thought it was because of his *writing* about Auschwitz, the labor of the last book, contemplating that horror with all that clarity. Getting up every morning to write that book would have killed anyone."

She was speaking of Levi's *The Drowned and the Saved*.

"Manny was that miserable." It was the first time I'd ever called him Manny. In 1956 I was Nathan, she was Amy, and he and Hope were Mr. and Mrs. Lonoff.

"Things combined to make him unhappy."

"So it was a hard time for you then," I said, "having gotten what the two of you wanted."

"It was a hard time because I was young enough to think that it was what he wanted, too. He knew it was nothing more than what he thought he wanted. Once he was rid of her and at last with me, everything changed—he was gloomy, he was remote, he was irascible. He was conscience-stricken, and it was terrible. When we were living in Oslo there were nights when I lay beside him, making no movement, rigid with anger. Sometimes I prayed he would die in his sleep. Then he became ill and it was idyllic again. It was the way it had been when I was his student. Yes," she said, underscoring the fact she wouldn't hide, "that's what happened: in adversity it was strangely rapturous, and when there was no obstacle we were miserable."

"That's imaginable," I said, and I was thinking, Rapture. Yes, I remember rapture. It comes at a very high price.

"Imaginable," she replied, "but startling."

"No. Not at all. Please go on."

"The last few weeks were hideous: he was confused and slept most of the time. He would make noises sometimes and wave his hands in the air, but there was nothing he said that you could understand. A few days before he died he had a gigantic rage. We were in the bathroom. I was kneeling in front of him changing his diaper. 'This is like college hazing,' he said. 'Get out of this bathroom!' and he hit me. He'd never hit anyone in his life. I can't tell you how elated I was. He still had strength enough to strike me like that. He's not going to die! He's not going to die! For days he'd been barely conscious. Or he'd hallucinate. 'I'm on the floor,' he'd cry from bed. 'Pick me up from the floor.' The doctor came and gave him morphine. Then one morning he spoke. He had been unconscious all of the day before. He said, 'The end is so immense, it is its own poetry. It requires little rhetoric. Just state it plainly.' I didn't know if he was quoting somebody, remembering something from all his reading, or if this was the final message. I couldn't ask. It didn't matter. All I did was to hold his head and say it back to him. I couldn't help myself any longer. I cried terribly. But I said it. 'The end is so immense, it is its own poetry. It requires little rhetoric. Just state it plainly.' And Manny nodded as best he could, and I've looked for that quotation ever since, Nathan. I can't find it. Who said that, who wrote that? 'The end is so immense . . .' "

"It sounds like him. His aesthetic in a nutshell."

"And he said more. I had to keep my ear to his mouth to hear him. Barely audibly, he said, 'I want a shave and a haircut. I want to be clean.' I found a barber. It took him more than an hour because Manny couldn't hold his head up. When it was over I showed the barber to the door and gave him twenty dollars. When I got back to the bed Manny was dead. Dead but clean." Here she broke off, though only for an instant, and I had nothing to say anyway. I'd known he died, and now I knew how, and though we'd met but that once, it still came as a shock. "I had it, and I'm glad I did, the four years of it," she told me, "every day and night of it. I'd see his bald head shining under his reading lamp, I'd see him sitting there every evening after dinner, carefully underlining what he was reading and stopping to think and jotting down a sentence in his spiral notebook, and I'd think, There is only one such man."

A woman who's lived fifty years remembering four years—an entire life defined by that. "I have to tell you," I said, "Kliman's pestering me about him too."

"I figured as much when he was the one who led me to you. He wants to write the biography that I'd hoped nobody would. A biography, Nathan. I don't want that. It's a second death. It puts another stop to a life by casting it in concrete for all time. The biography's the patent on the life—and who is this boy to hold that patent? Who is he to be Manny's judge? Who is he to fix him forever in people's minds? Doesn't he seem to you exceedingly shallow?"

"It doesn't matter what he seems or even what he is. That you don't want him is all that matters. What can you do to stop him?"

"Me?" She laughed weakly. "Why, nothing. The manuscripts of all the stories are at Harvard. He can go look at those, anyone can, though when I last checked, not a single person had asked to see them for thirty-two years. Fortunately nobody seems willing to talk to Mr. Kliman, nobody that I know of, anyway. I certainly won't see him, not again. But none of that need necessarily stop him. He can make it all up out of whole cloth, and one has no legal remedy. You can't libel the dead. And if he libels the living, if he manipulates the facts to suit himself, who has resources sufficient to sue him or the publisher he sells his trash to?"

"The Lonoff children. What about them?"

"That's a saga for another time. They never much liked the awestruck young girl who steals the renowned old man. Or the renowned old man who abandons the aging wife for the awestruck young girl. He would never have left if Hope hadn't forced the issue, but the children would have preferred that he remain with their mother till he was properly asphyxiated. His tenacity, his austerity, his achievement—it was as if he'd been selected to climb Mount Everest, then he got to the top and couldn't breathe. The daughter despised me most. A spotlessly virtuous person, dresses in burlap and reads only Thoreau—I could deal with her, but I never learned how not to be affronted by the Lady Sneerwells. They either sneered at me or ignored me. These were the good women of the tolerant, liberal community of Cambridge, Massachusetts, circa 1960, when one of the routine pleasures of faculty wives was moral disapproval. Manny would say, 'You go through too much emotion over something inconsequential.' Manny was the master of the impersonal way of considering everything, but I wasn't able to acquire that skill, even from the man who taught me to read, to write, to think, to know what was worth knowing and what wasn't. 'Stop being so intimidated. These are comical people out of *School for Scandal*.' He's the one who named the wife of our distinguished dean Lady Sneerwell. When we went out to a dinner party in Cambridge, it could be, for me, unendurable. That's why I wanted us to live abroad."

"And for him it wasn't unendurable."

"He was not bothered by such things. In public he could make light of the general prejudice. He had the substance for it. But I was just the pretty girl who'd been his student at Athena. I'd known worse as a child, far worse, of course, but back then I had a family encircling me."

"What became of Hope?" I asked.

"She's in some kind of facility in Boston. She has Alzheimer's disease," Amy said, confirming what I'd been told by Kliman. "She's over a hundred."

"Perhaps I can see you," I said. "May I take you to dinner? Could I possibly take you to dinner tonight?"

Her light, pleasant laugh belied what she was about to say. "Oh, I'm no longer the girl you were mooning over that night in 1956. The next morning, when all the hoopla took place— do you remember the high, hysterical hoopla of Hope pretending to run away from home to leave him to me? That's the morning you told me—do you recall?—that I bore 'some resemblance to Anne Frank.'"

"I recall that."

"I've had brain surgery, Nathan. You won't be dining with an ingénue."

"I'm not as I was either. Though you sound no less beguiling. I never learned where that accent originated. I never found out where you were from. It must have been Oslo. Where you knew worse was as a Jewish child under the Nazis in Oslo. That must have been why you and he went there to live."

"You sound like the biographer now."

"The biographer's enemy. The biographer's obstacle. This boy would get it all so wrong, it'd exceed even Manny's worst fears. I'll help," I said, "however I can," which undoubtedly was what she'd been hoping to hear when she was prompted to contact me in the first place.

So we made a date for that night, without a word spoken about the revelation with which Kliman hoped to launch a literary career.

Yet otherwise, we'd said so much. Two people, I thought, who met only once, and they go straight to the heart of it and are not cautious with each other at all. There was something exciting about that, though what it told me was that she was probably no less steeped in isolation than I. Or maybe there was immediate intimacy between two total strangers just because they had known each other before. Before what? Before it all happened.

I gave myself fifteen minutes to walk from the hotel to the restaurant where I was to meet Amy at seven. Tony was there to welcome me and to accompany me to my table. "After all these years," he said cheerily, pulling back a chair for me.

"You're going to see more of me, Tony. I'm coming down to the city for a while."

"Good for you," he said. "After 9/11 some of our regulars, they took their kids and they moved to Long Island, they moved upstate, they moved to Vermont—they moved all over, they went everywhere. I respect what they did, but it was panic, you know. It died down quick but I gotta be truthful—we lost some wonderful customers after that thing. You alone, Mr. Zuckerman?"

"There'll be two of us," I said.

But she never came. I'd neglected to bring her phone number with me, so I couldn't call to find out if there was anything wrong. I thought perhaps she was too ashamed to let me see up close a debilitated old woman with a head half shaved and a disfiguring scar. Or maybe she had thought better of trying to get me to intervene on her behalf with Kliman and revealing to me, as she would have to, the putative episodes of Lonoff's early life that she, as guardian of the memory of this meticulously private man, dreaded being made public.

I waited for over an hour—holding off ordering anything but a glass of wine on the chance that she might still show up—before it occurred to me that this was not the restaurant where we had agreed to meet. I'd come to Pierluigi's automatically, certain that I'd suggested our eating there, and now I couldn't remember whether I had asked Amy to suggest a restaurant that she might like. If I had, clearly I couldn't recall which restaurant it was. And the thought that she might have been sitting there alone all this time imagining that I had stood her up—because of how she'd described her appearance—made me rush downstairs to the telephone to call my hotel and learn if there were any messages. There was one: "I waited an hour and left. I understand."

Earlier in the day I had stopped at a drugstore to buy the toilet articles that I'd forgotten to bring from home. When I'd paid, I asked the salesclerk, "Could you put these in a box for me?" She looked at me blankly. "We don't have boxes," she said. "I meant a bag," I said, "in a bag, please." A tiny error, but unsettling anyway. I was misspeaking like this almost daily now, and despite the entries I dutifully made in my chore book, despite a persistent attempt to remain concentrated on what I was doing or planning to do, I was forgetting things frequently. While talking on the telephone, I'd begun to notice that well-intentioned people sometimes tried to be obliging by finishing or filling in my thoughts before I'd realized that I'd hesitated or paused in search of the next word, or that they would genially overlook the error when I produced (as I had for my cleaning woman Belinda only the other day) an unintended coinage like "heartbed" for "heartfelt," or when I addressed an acquaintance down in Athena by someone else's name, or when someone's name slipped my mind as I was addressing the person and I had to struggle silently to find it. Nor did vigilance seem much help against what felt less like the erosion of memory than like a slide into senselessness, as though something diabolical residing in my brain but with a mind of its own—the imp of amnesia, the demon of forgetfulness, against whose powers of destruction I could bring no effective counterforce—were prompting me to suffer these lapses solely for the fun of watching me degenerate, the ultimate gleeful goal to turn someone whose acuity as a writer was sustained by memory and verbal precision into a pointless man.

(That is why, uncharacteristically, I'm working here as rapidly as I can while I can, though unable to proceed anywhere near as rapidly as I should because of the very mental impediment that I'm struggling to outflank. Nothing is certain any longer except that this will likely be my last attempt to persist in groping for words to combine into the sentences and paragraphs of a book. Because permanent groping is what it is now, a groping that goes well beyond the anxious groping for fluency that writing is to begin with. During the last year of working on the novel recently sent off to my publisher, I discovered that I had to labor every day against the threat of incoherence. When I had finished—when, after four drafts, that is, I could go no further—I couldn't tell whether it was the reading of the completed manuscript that was itself marred by a disordered mind or whether my reading was accurate and the disordered mind was what was itself mirrored in the writing. As usual, I sent the manuscript to my shrewdest reader, ages ago a fellow student with me at the University of Chicago, whose intuition I trust absolutely. When he gave me his report on the phone, I knew that he had laid aside his customary candor and, out of kindness, was dissembling when he declared that he wasn't this book's best audience and apologized for having nothing useful to say, on the grounds that he found himself so out of touch with a protagonist toward whom I was altogether sympathetic that he'd been unable to sustain the interest to be helpful.

I did not press him, nor was I even puzzled. I understood the tactic that concealed his thoughts, though knowing as well as I do the critical attributes of my friend, and that his observations were never accidental, I would have had to be extremely naive to be untroubled by it. Instead of suggesting that I embark on a fifth draft—because of his having surmised from the fourth that making the substantial changes he'd had in mind was to lay an exorbitant demand on what remained intact of *my* attributes—he thought it best to blame a nonexistent limitation of his own, such as lack of imaginative sympathy, rather than what he had concluded was now missing in me. If I had interpreted his response correctly—if, as I believed, his reading painfully replicated mine—what was I to do with a book that I had worked on for close to three years and considered at once unsatisfactory yet finished? Having never before confronted this predicament—having been able in the past to summon the inventiveness and marshal the energy to battle through to a resolution—I thought of what two American writers of the highest rank had done when they sensed a decline in their powers or a weakness in a piece of work that stubbornly resisted remedying. I could do as Hemingway did—and not just near the end of his life, when the monumental strength and the active existence and the enjoyment of violent conflict were displaced by the bludgeonings of physical pain, alcoholic decay, mental fatigue, and suicidal depression, but in the grand years, when his force was bottomless, his belligerence radiant, and the preeminence of his prose established throughout the world—and put the manuscript aside, either to attempt to rewrite it later or to leave it unpublished for good. Or I could do what Faulkner did and doggedly submit the completed manuscript for publication, permitting the book that he'd labored over unstintingly, and that he could take no further, to reach the public as it was and to yield whatever satisfactions it could.

I needed a strategy by which to endure and go on—as who doesn't?—and, for better or worse, mistakenly or not, the latter was the one I chose, though only vaguely believing that it would have the less damaging effect on my ability to forge ahead, into the twilight of my talent, without an excess of disgrace. And that was before the struggle got as bad as it is now and the deterioration had advanced to the point where even the most uncertain safeguard is nowhere to be found—where it's a matter not just of my no longer being able, after a day or two, to remember the details of the previous chapter but, improbably, of being unable, after only a few minutes, to remember much of the previous page.

By the time I'd decided to seek medical help in New York, the leakage I'd been experiencing wasn't just from my penis, nor was the failure of function restricted to the bladder's sphincter—nor was the crisis waiting to alter me next one that I could continue to hope would isolate the loss in the body alone. This time it was my mind, and this time my foreboding was being given more than a moment's notice, though, for all I knew, not much more.)

I excused myself to Tony and left the restaurant without eating and returned to the hotel. But at the room I couldn't find Amy's number anywhere. I was sure I'd written it on a scrap of notepaper on the night table, but it was neither there nor on the bed itself nor on top of the bureau nor down on the carpet, which I examined with the fingertips of one hand as I slowly traversed it on my knees. I looked under the bed, but it wasn't there either. I checked the pockets of all the clothes I'd brought with me, even those I hadn't worn. Thoroughly I combed the room, searching places where it couldn't possibly be, like the mini-bar, until it occurred to me to take out my wallet, and there was the scrap of paper with the phone number—where it had been all along. I hadn't forgotten to take it with me to Pierluigi's, I'd forgotten that I'd taken it.

My phone light was blinking. Thinking this call might be a second, longer message from Amy, I picked up the phone and listened. It was Billy Davidoff calling from my own house. "Nathan Zuckerman, it's a wonderful place. Small, but suits us perfectly. I've taken photos—I hope you don't mind. Jamie will be delighted by the house, the pond, the swamp across the way—by everything, the whole setting. And Rob Massey is a jewel. Let's complete the formalities as soon as possible. We'll draw up whatever document's required. Rob says he's going to drive your things down when you're installed, but if there's anything you need right away, I can bring it with me tonight. I'll be here another hour if you want to call back. Speak to you later. And thanks. Living here is going to be a great help."

Help to Jamie, he meant. Anything for Jamie. So much devotion, and such pleasure in providing it. What does Billy want? Whatever Jamie wants. What pleases Billy? Whatever pleases Jamie. What absorbs attentive Billy? Jamie! Jamie! Delighting Jamie! Should that worshipful accord unbelievably never lose its power, lucky pair! But should she one day spurn his close attention, withhold her approbation, resist arousal by his passion, miserable, vulnerable, tenderized man! He'll never spend a day without her without thinking of her fifty times. She'll ride roughshod over her successors forever. He'll think about her till he dies. He'll think about her *while* he dies.

It was eight-thirty. If Billy was to be there for another hour, he wouldn't be arriving at West 71st Street until around twelve. I could phone her under the pretext of arranging the date for the exchange of residences that I no longer wanted. I could call and tell the truth, say to her, "I want to see you—it's unbearable not to be able to see you." Until midnight this young woman in whose proximity I'd been just three times, and fleetingly, would be sitting at home with her cats—or with the cats and Kliman.

Call off the experiment in self-torture. Get the car and go. Your great exploration is over.

The second message was from Kliman. He asked if I would talk to Amy Bellette for him: she had made promises before having surgery, and now she refused to honor them. He had a copy of the first half of the existing manuscript of Lonoff's novel, and no good was going to be served by his not being allowed to read the rest, as she had assured him he would be only two months earlier. She'd given him Lonoff family photos. She'd given him her *blessing*. "If you can, Mr. Zuckerman, please help. She's not the person she was. It's the surgery. It's all they removed, the damage that's been done. There's a huge mental deficit where there wasn't before. But maybe she'd listen to you."

Kliman? Too implausible. You smell, you smell, old man, and then he calls up and, without even apologizing, asks me for my help? After I've told him I will do everything to destroy him? Is he this audaciously manipulative, or is he just this messy, or is Kliman one of those people who attach themselves to someone they can't let go of? One of those whom, no matter what you say to rebuff them, you can't drive away. No matter what you do, they will not give up trying to get from you what they want. And whatever they do, no matter what horrifying things they say, the habit of their lives is never to recognize that they have irredeemably crossed the line. Yes, a big, virile, handsome boy with the certitude of his good looks, quite unafraid to give offense and then come back as though nothing happened.

Or was there further contact between us that I've forgotten? But when? "Maybe she'd listen to you." But why does he imagine that Amy Bellette would listen to me when he knows that we met only once? And does he know even that? As far as Kliman is concerned, we never met. Unless I told him. Maybe she told him. She must have—she must have told him that too!

I put Amy's number beside the phone and dialed it. When she answered, I addressed to her words something like those that I'd wanted to address to Jamie Logan. "I want to come to see you. I'd like to come to see you now."

"Where were you?" she asked.

"I went to the wrong restaurant. I'm sorry. Tell me where you live. I want to talk to you."

"I live in a terrible place," she said.

"Tell me where you are, please."

She did, and I left by taxi for her First Avenue address because I had to find out whether what they were saying about
Lonoff was true. Don't ask why I had to. I didn't know. And
the nonsensical character of my quest didn't stop me. Nothing
that was nonsensical was stopping me. An aging man, his battles behind him, who suddenly feels the urge . . . to what?
Once around with the passions wasn't enough? Once around
with the unknowable wasn't enough? Into the mutability *again*?

It wasn't as bad as I'd been imagining on the way there, though
it seemed hardly right for such a woman, the surviving consort
of this brilliant writer, to be calling this building her home.
There was a spaghetti joint at street level and beside that an
Irish bar and no lock on the building's entry door or the inside
door leading to the stairwell. Heavily dented metal garbage
cans were shoved into a dark alcove beneath the first flight of
stairs. When I'd rung her bell, alongside the bank of mailboxes,
I saw that one of the boxes was missing its lock and its slotted
door hung ajar. I wasn't sure that the bell I pressed worked
and was surprised when, from above, I heard Amy's voice calling to me, "Careful. Loose treads on the stairs."
    A few naked bulbs screwed into ceiling fixtures lit the stair-
way well enough, but the hallways leading off it were dark.
The odor permeating the interior passages of the building
could have been from the urine of cats or rats or from both.
    She was waiting on the third landing, her half-shaved head
and her single gray braid the first I saw of this old woman, who
was now even more pitiful to behold in a long, shapeless lemon-
colored dress meant to exude gaiety than in the hospital gown
she'd redesigned for her street wear. Yet she looked to be
oblivious of her appearance and almost childishly happy to see
me. She extended a hand for me to shake, but instead I found
myself kissing her on both cheeks, a delight I would have devoted a strenuous effort to winning back in 1956. Everything
about kissing her seemed a miracle, the greatest being that,
despite the physical evidence to the contrary, she was, alas,
herself and no impostor. That she had survived all her ordeals
to meet me in these dismal surroundings—that was a grave
miracle, almost making it seem as though my seeing her, my
completing a meeting, a moment with a young woman who

had held such a strong attraction for me almost fifty years ago, was my unknown reason for coming to New York, why I'd come and why I'd impetuously decided to stay. Coming back to someone after that span of time, and after I've had cancer and she's had cancer, our clever young brains both the worse for wear—maybe that's why I was close to trembling and why she had donned a long yellow dress in fashion, if ever, half a century before. Each of us so in need of this figure from the past. Time—the power and the force of time—and that old yellow dress over her defenseless frame overshadowed by death! Suppose I were to turn now and see Lonoff himself walking up the stairs? What would I say to him? "I still admire you"? "I just reread you"? "I'm once again a boy with you"? What he would say—I could hear him saying it—was "Look after her. The prospect of her suffering is unendurable." In death he was more corpulent than in life. He'd put on weight in the grave. "I understand," he continued, quickly adopting a tone of benign sarcasm, "that you are no longer such a great lover. That should make it easier."

"Physical failings," I replied, "make nothing easier. I will do what I can." I had several hundred dollars in my billfold that I could leave for her now, and at the hotel I'd write a check to mail off in the morning, though I'd have to remember, on leaving, to be sure that hers wasn't the mailbox with no lock. If it was, I'd see that she received the funds another way.

"Thank you," said Lonoff as I followed the yellow dress into the apartment, a narrow railroad flat whose two interior rooms —a study and, behind an arched entryway, a kitchen—were windowless. At the front, above the First Avenue traffic and the restaurant, was a small living room with two gated windows, and at the back a still smaller room with but one gated window, the room itself big enough for just a night table and a narrow bed. Three windows. In the Lonoff Berkshire farmhouse there must have been two dozen that you never had to lock.

The bedroom looked out on an air shaft and down to a tiny back alley, where the restaurant's garbage cans were stored. A toilet, I discovered, was in a closet-sized room on the other side of a door beside the kitchen sink. A smallish bathtub raised on claw feet rested on the kitchen floor, fitted with barely inches to spare between the refrigerator and the stove. Since the front of the apartment was noisy because of the buses, trucks, and cars barreling up First Avenue, and the back of the apartment was noisy because of the incessant racket from the restaurant kitchen, whose rear door remained open for ventilation year round, Amy took us to sit in the relative quiet of her dark study, amid piles of papers and books that crammed the shelves lining the walls and sat stacked around the base of the Formica-topped kitchen table that doubled as a desk. The lamp on the desk furnished the room's only light. It was a wide, tall, semi-transparent brownish bottle wired for a bulb and topped by a shade ridged like a fan and shaped like a broad sun hat. I'd last seen it forty-eight years ago. It was Lonoff's homely desk lamp. Off to the side I saw another relic from his study, the large, dull brown horsehair easy chair, molded over the decades to the contour of his substantial torso—and, it seemed to me, to the imprint of his thought and the shape of his stoicism—the same timeworn chair from which he'd first intimidated me with the simplest questions about my youthful pursuits. I thought, "What! Are *you* here?" and then remembered where that very line appears in Eliot's "Little Gidding," at the point where the poet, walking the streets before dawn, meets the "compound ghost," who tells him what pain he will encounter. "For last year's words belong to last year's language / And next year's words await another voice." How does Eliot's ghost begin? Sardonically. "Let me disclose the gifts reserved for age." Reserved for age. Reserved for age. Beyond that I cannot go. A frightful prophecy follows that I don't remember. I'll look it up when I get home.

Silently, I addressed an observation to Lonoff that had only just come to me: "You are no longer my senior by thirty-odd years. I am yours now by ten."

"Did you eat anything?" she asked.

"I'm not hungry," I told her. "I'm too startled by being with you." I was so affected by a visitation so unimaginable that I could say no more. However imprecise or elusive my thinking could become these days, my recollection of Amy, whom I'd met but once long ago, was still sharp and marked by the sense I had in 1956 that she was somebody of unusual importance. Back then, I'd gone so far as to work out an elaborately detailed scenario that endowed her with the horrific data of the European biography of Anne Frank, but an Anne Frank who, for my purposes, had survived Europe and the Second World War to re-create herself, pseudonymously, as an orphaned college girl in New England, a foreign student from Holland, a pupil and then a lover of E. I. Lonoff, to whom one day, in her twenty-second year—after she'd gone off by herself to Manhattan to see the first production of *The Diary of Anne Frank*—she had confided her true identity. Of course I had none of the young man's motives to continue to elaborate that flamboyant fiction. The feelings that had exploited my imagination to that end in my mid-twenties had long since disappeared, along with the moral imperatives pressed upon me then by eminent elders of the Jewish community. Their denunciation of my first published stories as sinister manifestations of "Jewish self-hatred" had not been without its sting despite the galling righteousness of their Jewish self-love, which I opposed with all my loathing—and opposed by transforming Lonoff's Amy into the martyred Anne, whom, with only an ounce of irony, I imagined myself wanting to marry. As the sprightly, youthful Jewish saint, Amy became my fictional fortification against the excoriating indictment.

"Would you like a drink?" she asked. "Would you like a beer?"

I wouldn't have minded something stiffer, but I no longer took more than a glass of wine with dinner because alcohol intensified my mental lapses. "No, I'm fine. Did *you* get something to eat?"

"I don't eat," she said. *I don't.* That had become a great refrain of mine as well.

"Are you all right?" I asked.

"I was. I was fine for months. But they just told me the damn thing's returned. That's what happens—destiny's behind your back and one day pops out and cries 'Boo!' When I had the first tumor, before I even knew I had it, I did things I wouldn't like to repeat. Kicked my neighbor's dog. Little dog, out in the hallway yapping all the time and nipping at your shoes, pain-in-the-ass dog who shouldn't be out there anyway, and I reared back and gave it a good kick. I began writing to *The New York Times*. I had a fit at the public library. I went completely nuts.

I went to the library to see an exhibit about E. E. Cummings. I loved his poetry when I first came here as a student: 'i sing of Olaf glad and big.' When I left the Cummings exhibit, I saw that in the corridor, arranged along the walls, there was a much bigger, more dramatic exhibit called Landmarks of Modern Literature. Large portrait photographs hanging above glass cases displaying first editions in their original jackets, and it was all terribly stupid politically correct crap. Ordinarily, I would have kept walking, and on the subway home talked to Manny about it. He was the firebrand of tact—tact, wit, patience. The human folly never surprised him. Even dead, he soothes me so."

"After forty years? Was there no one else in forty years who became important enough to soothe you?"

"Could there have been?"

"Could there not have been?"

"After *him*?"

"You were thirty when he died. To have your entire life defined by one episode . . . You were still a young woman." I stopped myself from saying "Was everything that followed crushed by those few years?" because the answer was obvious by now. Everything, every last thing.

"Inconsequential" was her reply to what I did say.

"So what have you done, then?"

"Done? What a word. Done. I've translated books: from Norwegian into English, from English into Norwegian, from Swedish into English, from English into Swedish. That's what I've done. But mostly what I do is drift. I've just drifted and drifted and now I'm seventy-five. That's how I got to be seventy-five: continually drifting. But you haven't drifted. Your life has been an arrow. You've worked."

"And that's how I got to be seventy-one. This way or that, arrow or drifter, you still reach the end. Did you never go to that villa in Florence with someone else?"

"How do you know about the villa in Florence?"

"Because he talked about it with me that night. Abstractly, only as something he'd thought about. And then," I confessed, "I overheard the two of you. I took the liberty of overhearing your conversation with him that night."

"How did you manage that?"

"I was sleeping just below you. You wouldn't remember that.

He'd made up the day bed in his study for me. I stood on his desk and put my ear to the ceiling. You said, 'Oh, Manny, we could be so happy in Florence.'"

Learning this made her enormously happy. "Oh, my. You were such a bad boy. What else? What else? To have a witness to something so long gone—what a gift! Tell me what you heard, bad boy! Tell me everything!"

Tell me, she was saying to me, tell me, please, about this intimate moment with this irreplaceable person I love who is dead, tell me on the day I've learned of the return of the tumor that is hurtling me toward my own death and in celebration of which I've donned my yellow dress!

"I wish I could," I said. "But I don't remember much more. I remember Florence because he had talked about it too—the villa in Florence and the young woman there with him who would make life beautiful and new."

"'Beautiful and new'—he said that?"

"I think so. Did you ever go to Florence?"

"We two? Never. I went myself. I went there and I stayed there after he died. I cut the flowers for his vase. I wrote in my journal. I took the walks. I rented a car and took the drives. For several years, each June, I'd go to a *pensione* there and take my translation work with me, and perform all the rites."

"And you never dared it with someone else."

"Why would I?"

"How can one live so long in a memory?"

"It's never been that. I speak to him all the time."

"And he to you?"

"Oh, yes. We've circumvented very nicely the predicament of his being extinct. We're so unlike everyone else now and so like each other."

The emotional impact of hearing this made me look at her probingly to see if she had said what she intended to say or was deliberately being immoderate or if her words had been spoken, as it were, accidentally by the brain that was missing a piece. All I saw was someone unprotected by anyone. All I saw was what Kliman saw.

"What would he think of your living like this?" I asked her. "Wouldn't he have wanted you to find someone? What would

he have thought of your living alone all these years?" Then I
added, "What does he tell you about it?"

"He never mentions it."

"What does he think of your living here, now, in this place?"

"Oh, we don't bother about that."

"What then?"

"Books I read. We talk about books."

"Nothing else?"

"Things that happen. I told him about the library."

"What did he say?"

"He said what he always said. He laughed. He said, 'You take
such matters too seriously.'"

"What does he say about the brain tumor?"

"I mustn't be frightened. It's not good, but I mustn't be
frightened."

"You believe what he tells you?"

"When we talk, there's no more pain for a while."

"Just the love."

"Yes. Absolutely."

"So what did you tell him about the library? Tell me the rest
about the library."

"Oh, I stormed up and down that corridor, fuming at the
photographs of these writers who'd written the great landmarks
of modern literature. I lost my temper. I began to shout. Two
guards rushed up, and in no time I was out on the library steps.
They must have thought I was a madwoman who'd strayed in
off the street. I thought so too. A mad, evil woman with her evil
thoughts. That's when I was beginning to talk a mile a minute.
I still do. I do it even when I'm by myself. I didn't know yet
about the tumor, you see. I said that already. But it was already
there at the back of my head, turning me inside out. All my life,
whenever I couldn't find my way, I've always been able to ask
myself, What would Manny do? What would Manny do with
this ridiculous state of affairs? All my life he's been here to guide
me. I was in love with a great man. That lasts. But then came the
tumor, and I couldn't hear him, not above the incessant roar."

"There are noises?"

"No. I should have said 'a cloud.' It's a cloud. In your head
you have a thundercloud."

"What was the terribly stupid politically correct crap?"

She laughed, the face, finely wrinkled and without a vestige of the beauty once inscribed there—the face laughed, but because of the half-shaved skull with the new-grown fuzz and that demonic scar, the laugh itself was shot through with all the wrong meanings. "You can guess. They had Gertrude Stein in the exhibit but not Ernest Hemingway. They had Edna St. Vincent Millay but not William Carlos Williams or Wallace Stevens or Robert Lowell. Just nonsense. It started in the colleges and now it's everywhere. Richard Wright, Ralph Ellison, and Toni Morrison, but not Faulkner."

"What did you shout?" I asked.

"I shouted, 'Where is E. I. Lonoff? How dare you leave out E. I. Lonoff!' I'd intended to say, 'How dare you leave out William Faulkner!' but Manny's was the name that came out. I drew quite a crowd."

"And how did you discover the tumor was there?"

"I was getting headaches. Headaches so terrible they made me vomit. You'll help me get rid of this Kliman, won't you?"

"I will try."

"The thing's come back. Did I tell you that?"

"Yes," I said.

"Somebody has to protect Manny from this man. Any biography he writes will be the resentment of an inferior person writ large. The Nietzschean prophecy come true: art killed by resentment. Before I knew I had the tumor, he paid me a visit. It was just after the library fiasco. I was already talking a mile a minute. I served him tea and he was so proper and he seemed, to my tumor, to speak so brilliantly about Manny's stories—to my tumor, he seemed a purely literary being, an earnest, Harvard-educated young man who wanted nothing more than to restore Manny's reputation. My tumor found Kliman *winning*."

"Well, you should have found the dog winning and kicked Kliman. How did you get a diagnosis?" I asked.

"I passed out. I was putting the kettle on the stove one day, and I switched on the gas, and the next thing I knew there were two policemen standing over me in the emergency room of Lenox Hill Hospital. The super smelled the gas, and he found me there"—she pointed behind us to the kitchen with the bathtub in it—"on the floor, and they thought I'd tried to kill myself. *That* made me angry. *Everything* made me angry. I was once a nice, sweet girl, was I not?"

"You seemed well behaved to me."

"Well, I really gave it to those cops."

It occurred to me for the first time since I'd been waiting for her at Pierluigi's that it wasn't I who had gone to the wrong restaurant; it was Amy. The tumor that had come back was turning her inside out again—the tumor that had come back that had induced a state of mind that did not seem to allow for her to be terrified by its return. Twice she had told me it was back, and not as though she had come to this evening off of this momentous day, but each time as though she were talking about little more than a check that had not cleared because she'd overdrawn her account.

Out of the silence we'd been sitting through for several minutes, she said, "I have his shoes."

"I don't follow you."

"Eventually I got rid of all his clothes, but I couldn't part with his shoes."

"Where are they?"

"In my bedroom closet."

"May I see them?" I asked only because it seemed that she wanted me to ask.

"Would you like to?"

"Sure."

The bedroom was tiny and the door to the closet opened only partway before bumping into one side of the bed. A string with a frayed end hung down inside the closet, and when she pulled it a low-wattage bulb went on. The first thing I noticed hanging amid the dozen or so garments there was the dress she'd made of a hospital gown. Then, lined up on the floor, I saw Lonoff's shoes. Four pairs, all pointed forward, all black, all well worn. Four pairs of a dead man's shoes.

"They're just as he left them," she told me.

"You see them every day," I said.

"Every morning. Every night. Sometimes more."

"Is it ever eerie to see them there?"

"To the contrary, no. What could be more comforting than his shoes?"

"He had no brown shoes?" I asked.

"He never wore brown shoes."

"Do you ever put them on?" I asked. "Do you ever stand in them?"

"How did you know?"

"It's only human. That's human life."

"They are my treasures," she said.

"I would treasure them too."

"Would you like a pair, Nathan?"

"You've had them a long time. You shouldn't give them up."

"I wouldn't be giving them up. I'd be passing them on. If I should die of this tumor, I don't want everything to be lost."

"I think you should keep them. You never know how things are going to turn out. You may have them here to look at for years to come."

"I will probably die, Nathan, this time round."

"You keep all the shoes, Amy. Keep them for him right where they are."

She pulled the string that turned off the light and closed the closet door, and we passed through the kitchen and returned to her study. I felt the fatigue of one who'd just run ten miles at top speed.

"Do you remember what you talked about with Kliman?" I asked her, now that I had seen the shoes. "Do you remember what you told him, the time you met?"

"I don't think I told him anything."

"Nothing about Manny, nothing about you?"

"I don't know. I don't positively know."

"Did you give him anything?"

"Why? Does he say I did?"

"He says he has a photocopy of half the manuscript of Manny's novel. He says you promised him the rest."

"I never would have done that. I couldn't have."

"Might the tumor have done it?"

"Oh, dear. Oh, God. Oh, no."

There were some loose pages atop the table, and in her agitation she began to fiddle with them. "Are those from the novel?" I asked.

"No."

"Is the novel here?"

"I have the original in a safe-deposit box in Boston. I have a copy here, yes."

"He couldn't write it because of the subject."

She looked alarmed. "How do you know that?"

"You said so."

"Did I? I don't know what I'm doing. I don't know what's going on. I wish everyone would let me be about that book." Then she looked at the pages in her hand and, laughing brightly, she said, "This is a brilliant letter to the *Times*. It's so brilliant they never printed it. Oh, I don't care."

"When did you write it?" I asked.

"A few days ago. A week ago. They had an article about Hemingway. Maybe it was a year ago. Maybe five years ago. I don't know. The article is around somewhere. I clipped it out, and the other night I found it, and it got me so worked up I sat down and wrote the letter. A reporter went to Michigan to try to hunt down the real-life models for Hemingway's Upper Peninsula stories. So I wrote and told them what I thought about that."

"Looks long for a letter to a paper."

"I've got them even longer."

"May I read it?" I asked her.

"Oh, it's just a nutty old woman rambling on. The excrescence of the excrescence." Abruptly she went into the kitchen to turn on the kettle and make something for us to eat, leaving me alone with the letter. It was written with a ballpoint pen. At first I thought it must have been composed not in one night but bit by bit over a period of days, weeks, or months because the color of the ink changed a couple of times at least on every page. Then I thought she *had* written it in a single sitting—a response to an article perhaps five years old—and the various colors of ink attested only to the pervasiveness of her confusion. Yet the sentences themselves were coherent, and the way of thinking was anything but the excrescence of her brain's excrescence.

> To the Editor:
>   There was a time when intelligent people used literature to think. That time is coming to an end. During the decades of the Cold War, in the Soviet Union and its Eastern European satellites, it was the serious writers who were expelled from

literature; now, in America, it is literature that has been expelled as a serious influence on how life is perceived. The predominant uses to which literature is now put in the culture pages of the enlightened newspapers and in university English departments are so destructively at odds with the aims of imaginative writing, as well as with the rewards that literature affords an open-minded reader, that it would be better if literature were no longer put to any public use.

Your paper's cultural journalism—the more of it there is, the worse it gets. As soon as one enters into the ideological simplifications and biographical reductivism of cultural journalism, the essence of the artifact is lost. Your cultural journalism is tabloid gossip disguised as an interest in "the arts," and everything that it touches is contracted into what it is not. Who is the celebrity, what is the price, what is the scandal? What transgression has the writer committed, and not against the exigencies of literary aesthetics but against his or her daughter, son, mother, father, spouse, lover, friend, publisher, or pet? Without the least idea of what is innately transgressive about the literary imagination, cultural journalism is ever mindful of phony ethical issues: "Does the writer have the right to blah-blah-blah?" It is hypersensitive to the invasion of privacy perpetrated by literature over the millennia, while maniacally dedicated to exposing in print, unfictionalized, whose privacy has been invaded and how. One is struck by the regard cultural journalists have for the barriers of privacy when it comes to the novel.

Hemingway's early stories are set in Michigan's Upper Peninsula, so your cultural journalist goes to the Upper Peninsula and finds out the names of the locals who are said to have been models for the characters in the early stories. Surprise of surprises, they or their descendants feel badly served by Ernest Hemingway. These feelings, unwarranted or childish or downright imaginary as they may be, are taken more seriously than the fiction because they're easier for your cultural journalist to talk about than the fiction. The integrity of the journalist's informant is never questioned—only the integrity of the writer. The writer works alone for years on end, stakes his or her everything on the writing, pores over every sentence sixty-two times, and yet is without any sort of overriding literary consciousness, understanding, or goal. Everything the writer builds, meticulously, phrase by phrase and detail by detail, is a ruse and a lie. The writer is without literary motive. Any interest in depicting reality is nil. The writer's guiding motives are always personal and generally low.

And this knowledge comes as a comfort, for it turns out that not only are these writers not superior to the rest of us, as they pretend to be—they are worse than the rest of us. Those terrible geniuses!

The way in which serious fiction eludes paraphrase and description—hence requiring *thought*—is a nuisance to your cultural journalist. Only its imagined sources are to be taken seriously, only *that* fiction, the lazy journalist's fiction. The original nature of the imagination in those early Hemingway stories (an imagination that in a handful of pages transformed the short story and American prose) is incomprehensible to your cultural journalist, whose own writing turns our honest English words into nonsense. If you told a cultural journalist, "Look inward at the story only," he wouldn't have a thing to say. Imagination? There is no imagination. Literature? There is no literature. All the exquisite parts—even the not so exquisite parts—disappear, and there are only these people whose feelings are hurt because of what Hemingway did to them. Did Hemingway have the right . . . ? Does any author have the right . . . ? Sensationalist cultural vandalism masquerading as a responsible newspaper's devotion to "the arts."

If I had something like Stalin's power, I would not squander it on silencing the imaginative writers. I would silence those who write about the imaginative writers. I'd forbid all public discussion of literature in newspapers, magazines, and scholarly periodicals. I'd forbid all instruction in literature in every grade school, high school, college, and university in the country. I'd outlaw reading groups and Internet book chatter, and police the bookstores to be certain that no clerk ever spoke to a customer about a book and that the customers did not dare to speak to one another. I'd leave the readers alone with the books, to make of them what they would on their own. I'd do this for as many centuries as are required to detoxify the society of your poisonous nonsense.

Amy Bellette

Had I read these pages without knowing Amy, I would have taken the argument at face value and received the outburst not without some sympathy, though my putting myself out of range of what Amy called "cultural journalism" relieved me of ever having to think about it or to speak of it as she did, which was no small boon. Under the circumstances, however, the key to the letter's intention and its interest for me seemed to lie in a couple of sentences in the second paragraph, which I reread while Amy continued in the kitchen to prepare our snack of toast and jam and tea. "What transgression has the writer committed, and not against the exigencies of literary aesthetics but against his or her daughter, son, mother, father, spouse, lover, friend, publisher, or pet?" Could it be that "half-sister" didn't appear in the list of those transgressed against because she was not fully aware of what was driving her indignation, or was it because she knew very well and monitored her own composition, line by line, to be certain "half-sister" wasn't furtively smuggled in by the tumor?

It seemed to me that the letter to the Times had mainly to do with Richard Kliman.

When she came out of the kitchen, carrying our food on a tray, I said, "And what grade did Manny give you for sentences so cogent and biting?"

"He didn't give me a grade."

"Why not?"

"Because I didn't write it."

"Who did?"

"He did."

"Did he? You told me before these were the words of a nutty old woman rambling on."

"That wasn't entirely true."

"How so?"

"He dictated it. They're his words. He said, 'Reading/writing people, we are finished, we are ghosts witnessing the end of the literary era—take this down.' I did as he told me."

I was there listening to her until well after midnight. I said hardly anything, heard a lot, and tended to believe most of it and to be able to make sense of it. There was never a deliberate attempt to mislead, as far as I could tell. Rather the rapid divulging of a massive backlog of information caused the particulars of her many stories to become so intertwined that at times it appeared that she was wholly at the mercy of the tumor. Or that the tumor simply overturned the obstacles ordinarily established by inhibition and convention. Or that she was just a desperately ill and lonely woman drinking in a man's interest after all the years of doing without, a woman who, five decades earlier, had lived for four precious years with a brilliant loved one whose integrity, which to her was the key to his majesty as both a writer and a man, was now threatened with demolition by the inexplicable "resentment of an inferior person" who'd anointed himself the loved one's biographer. Maybe the flood of words revealed nothing more than how old and deep her suffering was and how long she'd been without him.

It was curious to watch a mind being compressed and distended all at once. And sometimes alarmingly misfiring, as when, after several hours of holding forth, she looked at me wearily and, perhaps with more wit than I could discern, asked, "Was I ever married to you?"

I laughed and said, "I don't think so. I thought about it, however."

"Our being married?"

"Yes, when I was a boy, when we first met at the Lonoffs'. I thought it would be marvelous to be married to you. You were something to behold."

"I was, was I?"

"Yes, you looked tamed and well behaved, but obviously you were unusual."

"I had no idea what I was doing."

"Then?"

"Then, now, always. I had no idea of the risk I was taking with this man so much older than me. But he was irresistible. *He* was something. I was so proud of myself for inspiring his love. How had I done it? I was so proud of not being afraid of him. And all the while I was terrified: terrified of Hope and what she'd do, and terrified of what I was doing to her. And I hadn't any idea of the wound that I was marking *him* with. I *should* have married you. But Hope undid the marriage, and I ran off with E. I. Lonoff. Too naive to understand anything, thinking I was taking a great, bold womanly risk, I returned to my childhood, Nathan. The truth is, I've never left it. I'll die a child."

A child because she was with someone who was so much older? Because she stayed in his shadow, always looking up adoringly at him? Why was this harrowing union that must have destroyed many of her illusions a force that kept her in her childhood? "Which isn't to say that you were childish," I said.

"It isn't, no."

"I don't understand, then, about your being a child."

"Then tell you I must, mustn't I?"

And here the legendary biography with which I had invested her in 1956 was replaced by the genuine biography, which, if less inflated with the moral significance my own invention held for me back then, was factually contiguous with what I'd come up with. It had to be, for everything had happened on the same doomed continent to a member of the same doomed generation of the same doomed enemy of the master race. Transforming herself out of what I'd transformed her into did not permit erasing the fate by which her family had been no less besieged than the Franks. That was a disaster whose dimensions no mind could rewrite and no imagination undo and whose memory even the tumor wouldn't displace, until it had killed her.

This was how I learned Amy was not from the Netherlands, where I had hidden her in the sealed-off attic above a warehouse on an Amsterdam canal that would later become a martyr's shrine, but from Norway—from Norway, from Sweden, from New England, from New York—which is to say, by now from nowhere, like any number of other Jewish children of her era born in Europe instead of in America, who'd miraculously escaped death during World War Two, though their youths had coincided with Hitler's maturity. This was how I learned of the circumstances of that suffering whose reality never ceases to arouse, along with rage, incredulity. In the listener. In the narrator there was no heat. And certainly no disbelief. The deeper into her misfortune she proceeded, the more deceptively matter-of-fact she became. As if all this loss could ever lose its hold.

"My grandmother came from Lithuania. On my father's side they came from Poland."

"What got them to Oslo, of all places?"

"My grandparents were on their way to America from Lithuania. When they came to Oslo they were stopped, and my grandfather was forced to stay there. American officials stopped him, and he didn't get the papers. My mother and my uncle were born in Oslo. My father had been in America, almost as a youthful adventure. He was on his way back to Poland when the First World War broke out. He was in England at that time, and he didn't want to go back and go into the army. So he stopped in Norway. 1915. And he met my mother. Jews hadn't been allowed in Norway. But there was a well-known Norwegian writer, and he campaigned for the Jews, and in 1905 Jews began to be admitted. My parents married in 1915. We were five, four brothers and me."

"And everybody was saved," I asked, making the hopeful assumption, "mother, father, your four brothers?"

"Not my mother and not my father and not my oldest brother."

And so I asked, "What happened?"

"In 1940, when the Germans came, they didn't do anything. Everything was normal-seeming. But in October 1942 they arrested all the Jewish men eighteen and up."

"The Germans or the Norwegians?"

"The Germans gave the orders, but it was Norwegian Nazis, the Quislings. Five o'clock in the morning they appeared at the door. My mother said, 'Oh, I thought you were the ambulance coming. I just called the doctor. My husband had a heart attack. He's in bed. You can't touch him.' And we younger children were crying."

"She made this story up?" I asked.

"Yes. My mother was very smart. She begged them and she begged them, and so they said okay, we'll be back at ten and see if he's gone. So she called the doctor, and my father was taken to the hospital. In the hospital he planned his escape to Sweden. But he was afraid that when they found out he'd escaped, they would come and take us. So he waited almost a month, and one morning the hospital called us and said the Gestapo was there. There was shouting that you could hear even over the phone. We didn't live far from the hospital, so my mother and my brothers and I ran to the hospital. I was thirteen. My father was lying on a stretcher. We begged them not to take him."

"Was he ill?"

"No, he wasn't ill. It wouldn't have mattered anyway. They took him away. We went home, and it was November, and we got warm clothes for him and went back to Nazi headquarters. We tried to talk to people and we cried, we told them he was

sick, he had nothing to wear but his hospital gown, but nothing helped. We said we would go home and would come back
again tomorrow, but they told us, 'You can't go home, you're
arrested.' My mother said no. My mother was strong and said,
'We are Norwegians like everyone else, and we are not going
to be arrested.' There was a great argument but after a while
they let us go home. Outside it was dark. Everything was black.
My mother said we could not go home—she was sure that if
we went home they would come for us in the morning.

"So there we were, out in the dark street, and just then there
was an air raid. In the confusion of the air raid one of my older
brothers disappeared, and my oldest brother, who had just got
married, went into hiding with his wife's family. That left my
mother, two younger brothers, and me. When the air raid was
over, I said to my mother, 'The lady in the flower store is nice
to me. I know she's not a Nazi sympathizer.' My mother said
to call her. So we found a phone and I called her, and I said,
'Can we come up and have a party?' She understood, and she
said yes. 'Try to be careful when you come,' she said. And so
we went there and she let us stay. But we couldn't walk on the
floors—we all had to sit squeezed together on the couch. She
was friendly with her neighbors across the hall, and the next
morning she went to see them. They had a connection with
the Resistance. They were non-Jewish Norwegians, he was a
taxi driver, and he told us that they were rounding up all the
Jews and taking them away. That night he came back with two
other men, and they took my two younger brothers, twelve
and eleven. They said the rest of us would have to wait. They
would come back for us. That was my mother and me. But
when they came back, they said they could take only one of us
at a time. I said to my mother, 'If I go, will you come?' 'Absolutely,' she said. 'I would never let you down.' I learned afterward that later that evening, she was picked up in a taxi, men
with guns, Resistance fighters who, on the way out of Oslo,
picked up another woman and a boy, a mother with her son,
whom my mother knew by name. Oslo was a small community.
Most Jews knew one another. Anyway, they drove out of Oslo
and were never seen again. Meanwhile, they had taken me and
put me on a train. There was a Nazi officer on the train with a
swastika armband. I was told that when he got off, he would

give me a wink, and I should follow him. I was sure that I was
falling into a trap. He got off close to the border with Sweden,
and I got off, and then another man took over and we began
to walk. Through the woods. We walked and we walked. The
one who takes you knows the markings on the trees. It's a long
walk, five, six miles. We walked to Sweden. Through the woods
to the farmlands. And my brother who got lost the night of
the air raid—he was the one who met me. He thought he had
lost his whole family. Then my two younger brothers turned
up, and after them, me. But that was all. We waited for my
mother and my married brother, but they never came."

When she finished, I said, "Now I understand."

"Tell me, please. You understand what?"

"For most people, to say I've stayed in my childhood my
whole life would mean I've stayed innocent and it's all been
pretty. For you to say I stayed in my childhood my whole life
means I stayed in this terrible story—life remained a terrible
story. It means that I had so much pain in my youth that, one
way or another, I stayed in it forever."

"More or less," she replied.

Late as it was when I got back to the hotel, I immediately set
to work to record all I could manage to remember Amy's having told me about her escape from occupied Norway to neutral
Sweden and about the years with Lonoff and about the novel
he'd failed to finish while they lived together in Cambridge,
then Oslo, then back in Cambridge, where he died. Three or
four years back, I could still have carried the bulk of her mono-
logue in my head for days on end—my memory had been a
strong resource since earliest childhood and gave ballast to one
who, for professional reasons, always had to write everything
down. But now, less than an hour after leaving Amy, I had to
wait patiently on my recollections in order to piece together
as best I could what she'd confided in me. It was a struggle at
first, and I often felt helpless and wondered why I persisted in
attempting what I clearly could no longer do. Yet I was too
stimulated by her and her predicament not to, and too habituated to free myself from the task, too dependent on the force
that guided my mind and made my mind mine. By three A.M.
I had filled fifteen pages of hotel stationery, front and back,

with all I could manage to recall of Amy's ordeal, wondering, as I wrote, which of these stories she had told to Kliman and how, full of his own intentions, he would transform them, garble them, distort them, misinterpret and misunderstand them, wondering what could be done to deliver her from him before he made use of her to turn everything into a sham and a shambles. I wondered which of these stories she had herself transformed, garbled, distorted, misinterpreted, and misunderstood.

"He began to write totally unlike himself," she had told me. "Before, he'd tried to see how much he could leave out. Now it was how much he could put in. He saw his laconic style as a barrier, and yet he hated what he was doing instead. He said, 'It's boring. It's endless. It has no shape. No design.' I said, 'None that you can impose. It will impose its own design.' 'When? When I'm dead?' He became so bitter and cutting—the man and the writer both, so completely changed. But he had to give some meaning to the upheaval in his life, and so he wrote his novel and got stuck for weeks, and he said, 'I can't ever publish this. Nobody needs this from me. My children hate me enough without this.' And always I was sure he regretted going off with me. Hope had shown him the door because of me. His children had turned on him because of me. I should never have stayed. Yet how could I go when this was what I'd wanted for so long? He even told me to go. But I couldn't. He could never have survived alone. And then he didn't anyway."

The evening's climax came with the plea Amy made to me when I was at the door, ready to leave. Earlier, I had asked her for an envelope, a mailing envelope, and into it I had put all my cash, except for what I'd need for a taxi to the hotel. I thought it would be easier for her to accept the money that way. I handed her the envelope and said, "Take this. In a few days I'll send you a check. I want you to cash it." I had written my Berkshires address and phone number on the face of the envelope. "I don't know what I can do about Kliman, but I am able to help you financially, and I want to. Manny Lonoff treated me like a man when I was nothing but a boy with a couple of published short stories. That invitation to his house was worth a thousand times what's in this envelope."

She did not offer the resistance I was prepared for but simply reached out and accepted the envelope, and then, for the first time, began to cry. "Nathan," she said, "won't *you* be Manny's biographer?"

"Oh, Amy, I wouldn't know where to begin. I'm not a biographer. I'm a novelist."

"But is that terrible Kliman a biographer? He's an impostor. He'll blemish everything and everyone, and pass it off as the truth. It's Manny's integrity he wants to destroy—and he doesn't even want that. It's just the way it's done now—to expose the writer to censure. To compose the definitive reckoning of every last misdoing. Destroying reputations is how these little nobodies make their little mark. People's values and obligations and virtues and rules are nothing but a cover, camouflage only to hide the disgusting slime underneath. Is it because of their powers that everyone's so fascinated by their faults? Is it some sort of hypocrisy on their part that they're made of flesh and blood? Oh, Nathan, I had that damn tumor, and I made mistakes in judgment. I made mistakes with him that were unforgivable even *with* the tumor. And now I can't get rid of him. *Manny* can't get rid of him. It won't be that there was once a free and unique imagination loosed upon the world that went by the name of E. I. Lonoff—everything will be seen through the lens of the incest. With that he'll dispose of Manny's every book, of every wonderful word he wrote, and no one will ever have the faintest idea of all this man was and how hard he worked and with what precise workmanship he worked and what he worked for and why. Instead he will turn a man who was upright and dutiful and self-supervising to a fault, who wanted only to produce strong works of enduring fiction, into nothing more than a pariah. That will be the sum of Manny's achievement on earth—the sole fragment of him to be remembered! To be *reviled*! Everything will be crushed beneath *that*!"

"That" being incest.

"Shall I stay a while longer?" I asked. "May I come back in?" And we returned to her study, where she sat back down at her desk and stunned me by saying right off—and now without a single tear being shed—"Manny had an incestuous affair with his sister."

"Lasting how long?"

"Three years."

"How did they conceal it for three years?"

"I don't know. With the cunning that lovers have. With luck. They concealed it with the same excitement that they pulled it off. It was not accompanied by any torment. I fell in love with him—why shouldn't she? I was his student, less than half his age—he let that happen. Well, he let this happen too."

So there was the subject of the novel he couldn't write and the reason he couldn't write it and why he said he could never publish it. So long as he was married to Hope, Amy told me, he never mentioned to anyone having had a sister, let alone written a word about their illicit adolescent lust. After they were discovered together by a family friend and the scandal was revealed to their Roxbury neighbors, Frieda was spirited away by their parents to begin life anew with them in the morally pure atmosphere of pioneering Zionist Palestine. Manny was judged the guilty party, denounced as a demon, the corrupter of his older sister and author of the family's disgrace, and purged—left behind in Boston to fend for himself at seventeen. Had he stayed in his marriage to Hope, he would have kept writing his brilliant, elliptical short stories and never have had to come anywhere near exposing the hidden shame. "But when he became an outcast to his family again by living with a younger woman," Amy explained, "when chaos struck Manny's discipline for the second time, everything came undone. When he was abandoned by his family in Boston he was only seventeen, penniless and an anathema. Yet cruel as that expulsion was, he was strong and he survived and he made himself into everything that *wasn't* an anathema. But the second time, when it was he who abandoned his family, he was over fifty and he never recovered."

"Now this is what he wrote about his being seventeen," I said to her, "but this is not what he told you about his life at seventeen."

My assertion flustered her. "Why would I lie to you?"

"I only wonder if you're confused. You're telling me that he told you this about himself and that you knew about it before he began writing the book."

"I only knew about it when the book began to drive him

crazy. No, I never knew about it before. No one in his adult life knew."

"I don't understand, then, why he told you, why he didn't just say to you, 'It's driving me crazy because it's something I cannot fathom. It's driving me crazy because I have set myself to imagining what I cannot imagine.' He tried to be equal to a task he could not perform. He was imagining not what he did do but what he could never do. He wasn't the first."

"I know what he said to me, Nathan."

"Do you? Describe to me the circumstances in which Manny told you that the book he was writing, unlike anything he had ever written before, was drawn wholly from his personal history. Remember for me the time and the place. Remember the words that were spoken."

"This was all a hundred years ago. How can I possibly remember those things?"

"But if this was his biggest secret, and if it had preyed on his mind for so long—or even if it had been repressed for so long—then the articulation of it would have been like Raskolnikov's making his confession to Sonia. After all those years of his muffling the family explosion, his confession would have been unforgettable. Tell me, then. Tell me what his confession was like."

"Why do you attack me like this?"

"Amy, you're not under attack, certainly not by me. Listen, please," and this time when I sat, I chose deliberately to settle into Lonoff's easy chair ("What! Are *you* here?") and speak to her from it. "The source for Manny's tale of incest wasn't his life. It couldn't have been. The source was the life of Nathaniel Hawthorne."

"What?" she said loudly, as though I'd startled her from sleep. "Have I missed something? Who's talking about Hawthorne?"

"I am. With good reason."

"You're confusing me hopelessly."

"I don't mean to. Listen to me. You won't be confused. I mean to make everything clear to you."

"Oh, would my tumor love that."

"Listen, please," I said. "I cannot write Manny's biography, but I can write the biography of that book. So can you. And that's what we're going to do. You know the fluctuations of a novelist's mind. He puts everything in motion. He makes everything shift and slide. It couldn't be clearer how this book came about. Manny was deeply read in the lives of writers, of the New England writers, particularly, on whose terrain he'd lived with Hope for over thirty years. Had he been born and reared in the Berkshires a hundred years earlier, Hawthorne and Melville would have been his neighbors. He was a student of their work. He read their correspondence so often, he knew portions by heart. Of course he knew what Melville had said of his friend Hawthorne. That Hawthorne had lived with a 'great secret.' And he knew what renegade scholars had drawn from that remark, and from others made by family and friends, about Hawthorne's reticence. Manny knew the cunning, scholarly, unprovable conjectures about Hawthorne and his sister Elizabeth, and so in searching for a story to encapsulate his own improbabilities—to examine all the surprising new emotions that had transformed him, as you say, into a man so utterly unlike himself—he laid claim to these conjectures about Hawthorne and his beautiful, enchanting older sister. For this wholly unautobiographical writer, blessed with his genius for complete transformation, the choice was almost inevitable. It's what opened his predicament out for him and enabled him to leave the personal behind. Fiction for him was never representation. It was rumination in narrative form. He thought, I'll make this my reality." While, in fact, I was thinking in much the same vein: I'll make this reality mine, Amy's, Kliman's, everyone's. And for the next hour I proceeded to, effulgently arguing its logic until I had come to believe it myself.

4

My Brain

HE

Why would a woman like you marry anyone at twenty-five or twenty-four? In my era, it went without saying that you would have had a child by twenty-four or twenty-five—or twenty-two. But now . . . tell me . . . I don't know anything you know. I haven't been around.

SHE

Well, besides the obvious of having met someone I fell in love with, and who fell crazily in love with me, and someone who . . . anyway, besides all that obvious stuff, if anything for exactly the opposite reason—because nobody would do such a thing in my era. If everyone did it when you were my age, I was the only person I knew from my college class, the only person among my friends who moved to New York after Harvard who (*laughing*)—who got married when she was twenty-five. It seemed kind of a wild adventure we'd go on together.

HE

(*Not quite believing her*) Is this true?

SHE

It is true. (*Laughing again*) Why would I lie about it?

HE

What did your friends make of it when you did it?

SHE

People were . . . no one was shocked. People were happy. But I was the first to do it. Daring to settle in. I like being a first.

HE

Yet you haven't any children.

SHE

No, not yet. Not now, anyway. I think we both want to establish ourselves a bit more before that happens.

HE

As writers.

SHE

Yes. Yes. That's part of the idea of going up there. We'll just work and work.

HE

As opposed to?

SHE

As opposed to working and being here and being confined in a city apartment, and running up against each other all the time, and seeing our friends all the time. I've been so nervous recently, I can't sit still. I can't work. I can't do anything. So I think if we can deal with that, I'll have a better shot at getting something done.

HE

But why did you choose this young man to marry? Is he the most exciting person you could find? You say you wanted an adventure. I've met him. I like him, he's been extremely considerate toward me in just these last twenty-four hours, but I would have thought Kliman would be more of an adventure. He was your lover in college—correct?

SHE

It would be impossible being married to Richard Kliman. He's a live wire. He's better in other capacities. Why Billy? He's smart, he was interesting, we could talk for hours, he didn't bore me. He's nice, and there seems to be an idea that a nice person can't be interesting. Of course I know all that he's not: he's not intense, he's not a fireball. But who wants a fireball? He can be gentle, he can be charming, and he adores me. He absolutely adores me.

HE

Do you adore him?

SHE

I love him very much. But he adores me in another way. He's moving to Massachusetts for a year because I want to. He doesn't want to. I probably wouldn't do that for him.

HE

But you have the money. Of course he does it for you. You two are living on your money, aren't you?

SHE

(*She looks startled by his bluntness.*) What makes you think that?

HE

Well, you've published one story in *The New Yorker*, and as yet he's published nothing in a commercial magazine. Who's paying the rent? Your family is.

SHE

Well, it's my money now. It comes from my family but it's my money now.

HE

So he's living off your money.

SHE

You're saying that's why he's going off with me to Massachusetts?

HE

No, no. I'm saying that in an important way he is beholden to you.

SHE

I suppose.

HE

Don't you feel a certain advantage because you have the money and he doesn't?

SHE

I suppose, yes. A lot of men would be very uncomfortable with that.

HE

And a lot of them would be very comfortable with it.

SHE

Yes, a lot of them would love it. (*Laughing*) And he's not either of those.

HE

Is there a lot of money?

SHE

Money's not a problem.

HE

Lucky girl.

SHE

(*Almost with wonderment, as though she is amazed whenever she remembers*) Yes. Very.

HE

Is this oil money?

SHE

Yes.

HE

Is your father a friend of George Bush's father?

SHE

Not friends. The elder Bush is somewhat older. There's business to be done. (*Emphatically*) They're not friends.

HE

They voted for them.

SHE

(*Laughing*) If Bush's friends were the only ones who voted for him, we'd be much better off. Wouldn't we? It's that world. It's the same world. My father—and (*she confesses*) I suppose I—have the same financial interests as Bush and his father. But they're not friends—I wouldn't say that.

HE

They don't socialize?

SHE

There are parties both go to.

HE

The country club?

SHE

Yeah. Houston Country Club.

HE

Is that the club for the bluebloods?

SHE

Yes. For the nineteenth-century bluebloods. The older Houstonians. A lot of debutante balls take place there. They're put on parade. There's a swirl of white. And the rest is dancing and drinking and puking.

HE

Did you go swimming at that country club when you were a girl?

SHE

I spent every day of the summer there swimming and playing tennis, except on Mondays, when it was closed. My friend and I helped the Australian pro pick up balls when he was giving a lesson. I was fourteen. My friend was two years older and far sassier, and she slept with him. The assistant pro was the cute son of one of the club members. He was captain of the tennis team at Tulane. I didn't sleep with him, but we did all the other stuff. A cold fish. I didn't enjoy it. Adolescent sex is awful. You don't understand it, and mostly you're trying to see if you can even do it, and it's not enjoyable at all. Once I threw up, fortunately all over him, when he kept thrusting himself too far down my throat.

HE

And you were still only a girl.

SHE

Girls weren't like this in the 1940s?

HE

Nothing like this. Louisa May Alcott would have been at home in my high school. Did you come out? Were you a debutante?

SHE

Oh, you're getting into my dirty secrets. (*Laughing heartily*)
Yes, yes, yes. I did. It was awful. I hated every second of it. My
mom was so bent on it. We fought through the entire thing.
We fought through high school. But I did it for her. (*Laughs
more gently now—the range of her laughter is considerable, yet
another indication of how at ease she is in her skin.*) And she
appreciated it. She did. It was probably the right thing. When
I went off to college the first year, my Savannah-born mother
told me, "Be nice to the eastern girls, Jamie Hallie."

HE

And did you fall in with the other debutantes at Harvard?

SHE

People hide their debutante luster at Harvard.

HE

Yes?

SHE

Yes. One doesn't talk about that. You keep your sordid secret
to yourself. (*Both laugh*)

HE

So you fell in with the other rich girls at Harvard.

SHE

Some of them.

HE

And? What was that like?

SHE

What do you want to know?

HE

I don't know anything. I went to another school in another
era.

SHE

Honestly, I don't know what to say. They were my friends.

HE

Were they like Billy—interesting and never boring?

SHE

No. They were pretty, very well dressed, very superior. So they —we—thought.

HE

Superior to whom?

SHE

To the stringy-haired, not terribly well-dressed girls from Wisconsin who were great at science. (*Laughs*)

HE

What were you great at? Where did you get the idea that you wanted to be a writer?

SHE

Early. I think I knew that back in high school. Plugged away at it.

HE

Are you any good?

SHE

I hope so. I always thought I was. I haven't had all that much luck.

HE

The *New Yorker* story.

SHE

That was great. I thought I'd jumped on, and then—(*trajectory gesture with one hand*) phooo . . .

HE

How long ago was that?

SHE

That was five years ago. A time of delight. I got married. I got my first story published in *The New Yorker*. But I've lost confidence, and I can't concentrate anymore. As you know, concentration is everything, or a large part of it. And that has made me feel desperate, which makes me less able to concentrate and gives me less confidence. I feel I've moved away from being a person who could do something.

HE

That's why you're talking to me.

SHE

How do you put the two together?

HE

Maybe you haven't lost as much confidence as you think. You don't appear to be without confidence.

SHE

I'm not without confidence with men. I'm not without confidence with people in general. I have less and less confidence with my computer.

HE

And when you're in my house, across from the swamp, with only the tall reeds and the heron for company out the window . . .

SHE

That's part of the idea. Then I won't have men, I won't have people, I won't have parties, I won't be able to gather what I need from any of those sources, and I won't be so worked up, hopefully, and I won't be so frayed, hopefully, and I won't be in such a state, hopefully, and I figure—

HE

You misuse "hopefully."

SHE

(*She laughs. Shyly—to his surprise—she asks*) Am I? Do I?

HE

"I hope" would do. You could try "with any luck." In the old days, before well-brought-up adolescent girls had their faces fucked forcefully, you never heard "hopefully" misused like that. The vulgate "in hopes of" was sometimes substituted for "in the hope of," but that was as bad as things got when I was your age and wanted to be a writer.

SHE

Don't do that. You did it yesterday. Don't do it again.

HE

I was only correcting a little English usage.

SHE

I know. Don't do that. If you want to talk, we should talk. If I ever were to give you something that I wrote, that I would want you to read, then please correct my English. But if we're speaking—it's not an exam. If I start to think it's an exam, then I won't speak as freely. So please don't do that. (*Pause*) But yes, the thought is that if I can't draw my confidence from my social life, then I'll return the effort to my work, and hopefully the confidence will follow that. Stop laughing at me.

HE

I'm laughing because you, who were so superior to the stringy-haired girls from Wisconsin, haven't corrected yourself. Won't correct yourself.

SHE

Because I got interested in my thought and wasn't thinking about whether you'd approve of me or whether you'd approve of my wording or not.

HE

Why am I doing this to you, do you think?

SHE

To assert *your* superiority?

HE

With "hopefully"? How stupid of me.

SHE

Yes, (*laughs*) how stupid of you.

HE

I guess I'm afraid of you.

SHE

(*Long pause*) I'm a little afraid of you.

HE

Did it ever occur to you that I might be afraid of you?

SHE

No, I didn't think you'd be afraid of me. It occurred to me that you might enjoy me, that you might like to be in my presence, but it didn't occur to me that you might be afraid of me.

HE

I am.

SHE

Why?

HE

Why do you think? You're the writer. Hopefully.

SHE

(*Laughs*) So are you. (*Pause*) The only thing I can think is that I'm young and I'm female and I'm good-looking. But I won't be young forever, and then the female part won't matter so much, and the good looks—what does that have to do with anything? But maybe there are other reasons that I don't know about. Why do you think?

HE

I haven't had a chance to figure it out.

SHE

If you think of any other reasons, I'd love to know them. If you come up with just those three, you don't need to tell me. But if you think of anything else, you might help me out a lot by telling me, so please do.

HE

You exude confidence. The way you sit with your arms crossed over your head like that and holding your hair up with your hands like that so that I can see that you're no less beautiful that way too. All of you is in that pose. You exude confidence when you smile. You exude confidence with your shape, with your body. That must give you confidence.

SHE

It does. But it won't give me confidence with the swamp and the heron. Then I'll have to find my confidence here. (*She tilts her head.*)

HE

In your brain rather than in your breasts.

SHE

Yes.

HE

Do your breasts give you confidence?

SHE

Yes.

HE

Tell me about that.

SHE

About my breasts giving me confidence? I know I have something people will like, people will be jealous of, people will want. To have the confidence that you will be wanted—that's what confidence is. Confidence that you will be approved of, thought well of, desired. If you know that, then you're confident. I know that anything that has to do with these—

HE

Your breasts.

SHE

My breasts. I can do well.

HE

You're an original, Jamie. There aren't a million copies of you.

SHE

You figure out what people want, you figure out what will impress people, and you give them what will impress them, and you get what you want.

HE

So, what will impress me? What will I want? Or do you not care to impress me?

SHE

Oh, I'd like very much to impress you. I look up to you. You're a great mystery, you know. You're a source of great fascination.

HE

Why of fascination?

SHE

Because except for that heron out your window, nobody knows
anything about you. Anyone who's famous, everyone knows
everything about them—so they think. But with you, you've
written these things that make you famous among a certain
group of people. You're no Tom Cruise. (*Laughs*)

HE

Who's Tom Cruise?

SHE

He's somebody so famous that you don't even know who he is.
That's who Tom Cruise is. If you read all the star magazine
stuff about someone day in and day out, of course you don't
know anything about them, but you can imagine that you do.
But no one can imagine they know anything about you.

HE

They think they know everything each time I publish a book.

SHE

Those are the idiots. You're a mystery.

HE

You want to impress a mystery.

SHE

Yes. Yes, I want to impress you. So what will impress you?

HE

Your breasts impress me.

SHE

Tell me something I don't know.

HE

All of you impresses me.

SHE

What else?

HE

Your brain. I know I'm supposed to say that under the rules of 2004, but I don't live by those rules.

SHE

So is it or isn't it true that my brain impresses you?

HE

So far so good.

SHE

Anything else?

HE

Your beauty. Your charm. Your gracefulness. Your candor.

SHE

Well, there you have it.

HE

Billy has it.

SHE

He does.

HE

What do you mean when you say Billy adores you? What's the adoration like?

SHE

When we go to Texas he wants to see where I played as a child. He wants to sit on the swing where my nanny would swing me and the seesaw where she sat on one end and I on the other when I was four. He has me take him out to my school, Kinkaid, so he can see the third-grade classroom where we churned butter and the fourth-grade classroom where we did a science experiment with a petri dish. I took him to the library because I'd belonged to the Library Club, a special club for the best students, and at the window, he gazed out at the lush grounds of the school like the romantic poet beholding his rainbow. He had to see the big playing field where I was in the stilt race on Field Day in the fourth grade, and it was so like a medieval pageant, with purple and gold flags fluttering everywhere, that

I got so excited I fell, fell on my face ten feet from the starting line, though I was the speedy one slated to win. We had to drive from our house in River Oaks and follow exactly my route to school so he could see the lawns and the trees and the shrubs and the houses that the chauffeur had to drive by to get me the five miles out to Kinkaid. In Houston he'll only jog along the path I used when I was fifteen. It's unending with Billy. My me-ness is his magnetic pole. When I have dreams that I'm having sex, the sort of dreams that everyone has, male or female, he's jealous of my dreams. When I go to the bathroom, he's jealous of the bathroom. He's jealous of my toothbrush. He's jealous of my barrette. He's jealous of my underwear. Pieces of my underwear are in all of his pants pockets. I find them when I take his clothes to the cleaner. More, or will that suffice?

HE

So adoration means he's in love not merely with you—he's in love with your life.

SHE

Yes, my biography's a wonder to him. Rhapsodic words of love are all I hear. When I dress or I undress it's like being just behind a window that his face is pressed against.

HE

The curves no less hypnotic than the seesaw.

SHE

His praise for my silhouette is unstinting when I'm backlit in the bedroom. When I'm in my underpants in the kitchen making the morning coffee and he comes up behind me to hold my breasts and lick my ears, he recites Keats: "There's a sigh for yes, and a sigh for no, / And a sigh for I can't bear it! / O what can be done, shall we stay or run? / O cut the sweet apple and share it!"

HE

Well, quoting from memory a love poem by Keats makes Billy a rare member of his generation.

SHE

It does. He is. He quotes me reams of Keats.

HE

Does he quote the letters? Has he quoted from Keats's last letter? He wrote it when he was five years younger than you and gravely ill. Only months later he was dead. "I have an habitual feeling of my real life having past," he said, "and that I am leading a posthumous existence."

SHE

No, I don't know his letters. As for a posthumous existence, it's not come up.

HE

Tell me, how does the object of such uxorious worship find the strength to endure it?

SHE

Oh, (*tenderly laughing*) I know how to behave.

HE

You have all this sexual attention. Yet you're restless and desperate.

SHE

We have plenty of sex. But sex is not always the source of tremendous excitement for one partner that it is for the other. It often is at the beginning.

HE

I remember that.

SHE

When was the last time you had an affair with a woman?

HE

When you were a debutante.

SHE

Has it been hard not to have an affair with a woman for that long? Have you not had sex for that long?

HE

I haven't.

SHE

Has that been hard?

HE

Everything is hard at a certain point.

SHE

But particularly hard. (*Their voices are faint now, barely able to be heard when a car passes beneath the window.*)

HE

It's among the things that are particularly hard.

SHE

Why? I know you live in the country, in the middle of nowhere, but there must be . . . well, you say there's a college nearby. I know your age, but there must be girls there that read your books and would be quite impressed. Why? Why did you decide to give that up, too, along with the city?

HE

It decided to give me up.

SHE

What do you mean?

HE

Just that.

SHE

I don't understand.

HE

And you won't.

SHE

Not if you won't tell me, I won't. Would you ever change your mind about giving that up too?

HE

I'm changing it. That's why I'm still here.

SHE

Well . . . I'm flattered. If it's true that it's been years and years, I'm extremely flattered.

HE

Jamie. Jamie Logan. Jamie Hallie Logan. Do you speak any languages, Jamie?

SHE

Not well.

HE

You speak English well. I like your Texas accent.

SHE

(*Laughs*) I worked hard to get rid of my Texas accent when I got to college.

HE

Is that right?

SHE

I did, yes.

HE

I would have thought you'd have exploited it.

SHE

It was one and the same as not telling anyone about the debutante. As not telling anyone that I went to the same country club as both George Bushes.

HE

But it's still there.

SHE

Well, I try not to have one. Except for ironic purposes. I did go off to Harvard with my "y'all" intact but I dropped it quickly enough.

HE

Too bad.

SHE

Oh, I didn't know anyone, I was just eighteen, and I turned up at Wigglesworth and everyone looked at me and I said, "Hi, y'all." They thought I was the biggest hick. I never said it again. I was quite naive compared to a lot of the freshmen there. Compared to the kids who'd gone to prep schools in Manhattan, I *was* a hick. They were terrifying. If I have it today it's because I'm unhinged today. Perhaps it's there a bit more than usual. When I get unhinged, it comes out.

HE
You don't miss a trick. You have a reason for everything.

SHE
Well, I know myself. Quite well. I think.

HE
That's three things. I know myself. Quite well. I think.

SHE
You know who does that? Conrad.

HE
Triplets.

SHE
Yeah. Conrad's triplets. Have you noticed? (*She shows him the paperback book that's been lying out of sight beneath a magazine on the glass-topped coffee table.*) I got *The Shadow-Line.* You mentioned it, so I went to Barnes and Noble and got it. The passage you recited for me you got exactly right. You have a good memory.

HE
For books, for books. You move quickly.

SHE
Listen to this. The triplets, the drama of the triplets. Page 35, he's just gotten his first command, and he's ecstatic. "I floated down the staircase. I floated out of the official and imposing portal. I went on floating along." Page 47, still in the grip of the ecstasy. "I thought of my unknown ship. It was amusement enough, torment enough, occupation enough." Page 53, describing the sea. "An immensity that receives no impress, preserves no memories, and keeps no reckoning of lives." He does it all the time, and near the end especially. Page 131. " 'But I'll tell you, Captain Giles, how I feel. I feel old. And I must be.' " Page 130. "He looked like a frightful and elaborate scarecrow, set up on the poop of a death-stricken ship, to keep the seabirds from the corpses." Page 129. "Life was a boon to him—this precarious hard life—and he was thoroughly alarmed about himself. " Page 125. "Mr. Burns wrung his hands, and cried out suddenly." Then one: " 'How will the ship get into harbour,

sir, without men to handle her?' " Next paragraph, two: "And I couldn't tell him." Next paragraph, three: "Well—it did get done about forty hours afterwards." Then all over again. Still page 125. "I shall never forget the last night, dark, windy, and starry. I steered." The paragraph goes on. Then the next paragraph begins, "And I steered . . ."

HE

(*Everything is a flirtation, including quoting Conrad.*) Read the whole thing to me.

SHE

"And I steered, too tired for anxiety, too tired for connected thought. I had moments of grim exultation and then my heart would sink awfully at the thought of that forecastle at the other end of the dark deck, full of fever stricken men—some of them dying. By my fault. But never mind. Remorse must wait. I had to steer." I could read more. (*Sets the book down*) I enjoy reading to you. Billy doesn't like to be read to.

HE

Steer. I had to steer. Have you read any other Conrad?

SHE

I used to. Quite a bit.

HE

What did you like best?

SHE

Have you ever read a story called "Youth"? Quite wonderful.

HE

"Typhoon"?

SHE

Great.

HE

When you were down there in Texas, and you were at the pool of the country club in your bikini with all the other oil millionaires' daughters, did you read?

SHE

Funny you should mention that.

HE

Were you the only one who read?

SHE

Yes. It's true. You know, when I was younger, when I was really young, at a certain point it got ridiculous. One day I was caught, and it was so embarrassing that I stopped. I used to take my books and fold them inside *Seventeen* magazine so no one could see what I was reading. But I got over that. The embarrassment, if caught, was so much greater than if I just read the book, so I stopped doing that.

HE

Which books would you hide inside *Seventeen*?

SHE

The time I was caught I was thirteen and I was reading *Lady Chatterley's Lover* inside *Seventeen*. They made fun of me, but if they'd started to read it, they would have realized it was much juicier than *Seventeen*.

HE

Did you like *Lady Chatterley's Lover*?

SHE

I like Lawrence a lot. *Lady Chatterley's Lover* wasn't my favorite. I hate to disappoint you, but I didn't quite get it at that age. I read *Anna Karenina* when I was fifteen. Luckily I reread that later. I was always reading books I wasn't ready for. (*Laughing*) But it did me no harm. Yes, it's a good question, what did I read when I was fourteen. Hardy. I read Hardy.

HE

Which books?

SHE

I remember *Tess of the D'Urbervilles*. I remember . . . what's the other one? It's funny. Not *Jude the Obscure*. What's the other one?

HE

You mean the one with the reddler in it? Not *Far from the Madding Crowd*.

SHE

Yeah. *Far from the Madding Crowd.*

HE

There's also the one with the reddler in it, the reddleman. What's that book called? And the heroine, the tragic heroine. Oh, my memory. (*But she does not hear his three-word lament. She is too busy remembering her fourteenth year. And with such ease.*)

SHE

Wuthering Heights. I loved *Wuthering Heights.* I was a little younger, maybe twelve or thirteen. Got there through *Jane Eyre.*

HE

Now men.

SHE

(*Yawning a little, quite familiar now*) Are you interviewing me for a job?

HE

Yes, I'm interviewing you for a job.

SHE

What job?

HE

The job of leaving the husband who adores you and coming to live instead with a man you can read aloud to.

SHE

Well—you must be crazy.

HE

I am, but so what? I'm crazy to be here. I'm crazy to be in New York. The reason I came to New York was crazy. Sitting here and talking to you is crazy. Sitting here and being unable to leave you is crazy. I can't leave you today, I couldn't leave you yesterday, and so I'm interviewing you for the job of your leaving your young husband and coming to live a posthumous existence with a seventy-one-year-old. Let's continue. Let's continue with the interview. Tell me about men.

SHE

(*Softly now, almost as if in a trance*) What do you want to know?

HE

(*Just as softly*) I want to die of jealousy. Tell me about all the men you've had. I've heard about the boy from the Tulane tennis team who thrust his cock so far down your throat in the summer of your fourteenth year that you threw up all over him. But though that was sufficiently difficult to take, I seem to want to hear more. Yes, tell me more. Tell me everything.

SHE

Well, there was the first. The first lover. He was my teacher. In high school. It was my senior year of high school. He was twenty-four. And he was—he seduced me.

HE

How old were you then?

SHE

It was three years later. I was seventeen.

HE

Nothing to report between fourteen and seventeen?

SHE

Yes, there were further adolescent mishaps.

HE

All of them mishaps? None were exciting?

SHE

Some were exciting. It was exciting when a grown man pulled up my T-shirt at the staid old Houston Country Club and sucked on my nipples. I was dumbstruck. I didn't tell anyone. I waited for him to come back and do it again. But he must have frightened himself because when I saw him next he acted as though nothing had ever happened between us. He was a friend of my older sister's. In his early thirties. He had just gotten engaged to my sister's most beautiful friend. I cried and cried. I believed he didn't come back because there was something wrong with me.

HE

How old were you?

SHE

That was earlier. I was thirteen.

HE

Go on. Your teacher.

SHE

He was completely his own person. He wasn't trying to impress anyone. (*Laughing*) But then, he wasn't a high school senior. He was older. That was impressive enough.

HE

To *you* much older, I would think. Tell me, does twenty-four seem older to a seventeen-year-old girl than seventy-one seems to a thirty-year-old woman? Does thirty seem older to a thirteen-year-old girl than seventy-one seems to a thirty-year-old woman? We must get to those questions sooner or later.

SHE

(*Long pause*) Yes, the teacher seemed much, much older. He was from Maine. Maine seemed exotic to me. It seemed wonderfully exotic. He wasn't from Texas and he had no money. Which was why he was doing this job. He was committed to teaching. He'd done Teach for America for two years after college. Where you make no money.

HE

What's Teach for America?

SHE

Oh dear, you *are* out of it. It's a program where college graduates volunteer two years of their time in the most deprived schools in America, in what they call "underprivileged"—

HE

"Underprivileged" bothers you.

SHE

(*Laughing heartily*) I don't like that word.

HE

Why?

SHE

Well, what does it mean? Under privileged. Either you do have privilege or you don't have privilege. If you are underprivileged, you just don't have privilege. Privilege in and of itself is something above the mean. I hate that word.

HE

You were yourself so privileged. One might even say overprivileged.

SHE

Okay. Is that to punish me for not being Louisa May Alcott? Is that for sucking off my young tennis player when I was fourteen or for the man who excited me by sucking my nipples when I was thirteen?

HE

I was only asking if that's what makes the word unnerving.

SHE

I just think it's bad usage. Bad English usage. Like "hopefully."

HE

You're charming this man to death. Torturing him and charming him both.

SHE

By telling you about my first love? You want to be charmed to death?

HE

Yes.

SHE

A good way to go. In any case, that's what Teach for America is—a domestic equivalent of the Peace Corps. So he'd done that, this young idealist, but he needed to pay off some school loans, and he didn't want to stop teaching and go off and be a banker, so he went to teach at a rich school in Houston, where you got paid a decent salary. That's all he was doing there—he had nothing to do with that social world. He was unimpressed by it. In fact, he was quite disgusted by it. In the parking lot, there were the BMWs that the students drove to school, and then there were the faculty cars, the Hondas and such, and then there was his—a twelve-year-old rusting something-or-other that had Maine plates and a rope to shut the back door because the handle was missing. Completely his own person—like no one I'd ever met before. He didn't give a damn about the Kinkaid caste system. He was my history teacher. Ours was the only section in the school that had a unit that did work in current events.

HE

How did it start?

SHE

How it started? I would just go for my weekly meeting to his office. He opened up a world of thought that I had no idea existed. I'd go and we would talk and we would talk and we would talk, and I had such feeling for him, and despite the early experiences that so perplex you—and whether you know it or not, that are by now all but universal—I was still a girl, only a girl, and I had no idea it was sexual feeling. (*Smiles*) But he knew. It was wonderful. So that was the first.

HE

How long did it go on?

SHE

Through the whole year. When I left for college, we had a plan to stay together. And I was heartbroken when we didn't. I cried through much of my first semester of college. But I wasn't thirteen anymore. This time I got myself *up* and *out*. I met these girls and I met their guys and I got myself back together. I had fun. Yeah, I got to college, and he stopped returning my calls, and I had fun.

HE

The young idealist must have had another seventeen-year-old.

SHE

You don't like him any more than you like the tennis player.

HE

That shouldn't be hard to figure out for a girl who went to Kinkaid from kindergarten through grade twelve.

SHE

He wrote me a letter a year later, when I'd finally gotten over it. Said he'd done it because he thought that's what was best for me, and he had been so confused . . . But you're probably right.

HE

I don't think I can take more of this.

SHE

Why not? (*A light laugh*) I've only told you about one.

HE

You've only told me about three. But I get the idea. You were appealing very early.

SHE

Does that surprise you?

HE

No, it just kills me.

SHE

Why?

HE

Oh, Jamie.

SHE

You don't want to say it?

HE

Say what?

SHE

Say why it kills you.

HE

Because I'm crazy about you.

SHE

Well . . . I just wanted to hear it.

HE

(*Long pause, pain more on his side than hers; curiosity reigns on hers*) So. That concludes our interview for the job of she-who-leaves-her-husband-for-the-much-much-older-man. I'll call you.

SHE

You'll call me?

HE

I'll call you and let you know how you did.

SHE

Okay.

HE

Are you free for the job?

SHE

If the job gets offered to me, I'll have to figure out whether or not I can arrange my life so that I can do the job well. Then *I'll* get back to *you*.

HE

This isn't fair. I've lost my authority.

SHE

How does it feel?

HE

I came here with so much authority. I'm leaving with none.

SHE

Does it feel good?

HE

A man disoriented by everything that once he knew so very well is now a lost man to boot. I'm going.

SHE

It never gets better for you alone with me.

HE

It can't.

SHE

The better it gets, the worse it gets.

HE

That's the situation. Yes.

*

(He gets up and he leaves. Outside, on the steps of her apartment building and looking across to the church, he remembers something: The Return of the Native, *the title of the Hardy novel with the reddleman in it. He has a good memory for books? No, not even for books. Only now does he recall the tragic heroine's name that had always beguiled him: Eustacia Vye. He does not move for the street, yet works strongly to suppress the desire to turn back and lift his hand to ring the bell and tell her, "The Return of the Native,* Eustacia Vye," *and in that way get back upstairs alone with her. They never kiss, he never touches her, nothing: this is his last love scene. His memory failed him only that once. During all that conversation, only once. Twice: when she asked how long he'd been alone. Or had she asked that question the day before? Or hadn't she asked that question at all? Well, she needn't know any more of the forgetfulness than what she'd seen so far. So they never kiss and he never touches her—so what? He takes that hard? So what? His last love scene? Let it be. Never mind. Remorse must wait.)*

5

Rash Moments

I WAS awakened by the phone ringing. I had fallen asleep on the bed, clothed and with my underlined copy of *The Shadow-Line* beside me. I thought, "Amy, Jamie, Billy, Rob," but failed to include Kliman in the list of those who might find reason to call me at the hotel. Having spent until almost five A.M. at the desk writing, I felt like a man after a night of too much drinking. And I'd had a dream, I now remembered, a very small dream airy with childish hopefulness. I am on the phone to my mother. "Ma, can you do me a favor?" She laughs at my naiveté. "Sweetheart, there's nothing I wouldn't do for you. What is it, darling?" she asks. "Can we have incest?" "Oh, Nathan," she says, laughing again, "I'm a rotting old corpse. I'm in the grave." "Still, I'd like to commit incest with you. You're my mother. My only mother." "Whatever you want, darling." Then she is in front of me, and she is not a corpse in a grave. Her presence thrills me. She's the slender, pretty, vivacious twenty-three-year-old brunette my father married, she has the lightness of a young girl and that soft voice that is never severe, while I am the age I am now—and *I* am the one in the ground forever. She takes my hand as though I'm still a little boy with the most innocent aims and goals, we leave the cemetery for my bedroom, and the dream ends with my desire gaining strength and the room of large bare windows flooded with light. The last triumphant words she says are "My dear one, my dear one—birth! birth! birth!" Was there ever a mother more tender and kind?

"Hi," Kliman said. "Shall I wait down here?" "For what?" "Lunch." "What are you talking about?" "Today. At noon. You said I could take you to lunch today at noon." "I said no such thing." "You certainly did, Mr. Zuckerman. You wanted me to tell you about George Plimpton's memorial service." "George Plimpton is dead?" "Yes. We talked about this." "George died? When did he die?" "Just over a year ago." "He was how old?"

627

"He was seventy-six. He had a fatal heart attack in his sleep."
"And you told me this when?" "On the phone," Kliman said.

No need to report that I remembered no such phone call.
Yet to have forgotten it seemed impossible—as impossible as
George's dying. I'd met George Plimpton in the late 1950s
when, after my discharge from the army, I first came to New
York to live, for seventy bucks a month, in a two-room subter-
ranean apartment and began publishing in his new literary
quarterly the stories that I'd been writing at night while I was
in the service; till then they'd been turned down everywhere
I'd submitted them. I was twenty-four when George invited
me to lunch to meet the *The Paris Review*'s other editors, young
men in their late twenties and early thirties, for the most part,
like him mainly from wealthy, old-line families who'd sent their
sons to exclusive preparatory schools and then on to Harvard,
which, in those early postwar years, as in prior decades, was
mainly a bastion for educating the offspring of the socially
elite. There they'd all got to know one another, if they hadn't
met previously during the summer on the tennis courts or at
the yacht clubs of Newport or Southampton or Edgartown.
My familiarity with their world or the world of their immediate
forebears was limited to the fiction I'd read by Henry James
and Edith Wharton as a student at the University of Chicago,
books I'd been taught to admire but that had for me as little
bearing on American life as *Pilgrim's Progress* or *Paradise Lost*.
Before meeting George and his colleagues I'd no idea what
such people looked like or sounded like other than from hearing FDR over the radio and in the newsreels as a child—and to
such a child, the son of a Jewish podiatrist educated in night
school, FDR was not a representative of either class or caste
but rather a politician and statesman unique unto himself, a
democratic hero perceived by the preponderance of America's
Jews, including my large extended family, as a blessing and a
gift. George's unlikely manner of speaking might have seemed
to me a comical exaggeration of a swell's, one perhaps even
outright preposterous if encountered in a less forthright,
gifted, intelligent, and graceful young man, steeped as it was in
the Anglified enunciation and cadences of the monied Protestant hierarchy that had reigned over Boston and New York
society while my own poor ancestors were being ruled by rab-

bis in the ghettos of Eastern Europe. George afforded my first glimpse of privilege and its vast rewards—he seemingly had nothing to escape, no flaw to hide or injustice to defy or defect to compensate for or weakness to overcome or obstacle to circumvent, appearing instead to have learned everything and to be open to everything altogether effortlessly. I'd never imagined getting anywhere without the unstinting persistence in which my hardworking family had diligently schooled me; George would have known from the outset all he was automatically destined for.

At parties at his comfortable East 72nd Street apartment, I met virtually every other young writer in New York and some of the famous established ones, and gazed longingly at the limbs of the glamorous young women who flocked around him, American debutantes, European models, and princesses whose families had been exiled in Paris since the Treaty of Versailles. In the early days I saw more of a few lesser associates of the magazine, whose writing worries and love struggles disclosed an undercurrent of hardship I could better understand, those like me for whom Difficulty had the status of a god. Yet I was there at Stillman's seedy Eighth Avenue gym to marvel at his courage on that afternoon he dared to go the three short, vigorous rounds with boxing's then light-heavyweight champion of the world, Archie Moore, a bout that left him with a broken, bloodied nose and the material for an account in *Sports Illustrated*. And I was a guest at a friend's apartment on Central Park South where George married for the first time, in the 1960s, and for several summers I sat with a hundred or so others on the dark, wide beach at Water Mill, Long Island, when George presided over his lavish annual Fourth of July fireworks display, thereby remaining a daredevil of a boy even as he pursued the interests of a playful, debonair, deeply inquisitive man of the world, a journalist, editor, and occasional film and television performer. It was little more than a year earlier (and, I now realized, only weeks before he died) that George had phoned me and, speaking nearly as formally to me as to someone he'd never met, and yet, as was his nature, as warmly as if we'd had dinner together only the night before—and by then we hadn't seen each other for a decade at least—asked if I'd come down to New York to make some introductory remarks

at a fundraising gala for *The Paris Review*. I could remember
that phone conversation perfectly, not only because of the good
feeling exchanged but because it launched me into spending
my evenings over the next couple of weeks rereading his famous works of "participatory journalism"—the books in which
he assaults the mystery of his charmed life by recording his
mishaps and failures as a bumbling amateur athlete up against
the mighty pros—and the several collections of shorter pieces,
in which he wrote as himself, as the urbane, witty gentleman of
easy intelligence and aristocratic bearing that made him anything but a bumbler to anyone who knew him.

There, his charm (as in the accounts of taking his nine-year-
old daughter to a Harvard-Yale game or the poet Marianne
Moore to Yankee Stadium), his lyricism (as in the evocative
hymn to fireworks), his filial gravity (as in the eulogy to his
father) attest to the skills of an elegant essayist able to write
rings around the disadvantaged George Plimpton he concocted
for the sports books, where, repeatedly cast by his ineptness in
the role of the virginal victim, he goes to the most extreme
lengths to acquire the semblance of humiliation and is able
fleetingly to relish the masochistic ignominy of being out of
his league. In his parody of Truman Capote writing of his face-
lift in the style of Ernest Hemingway he was the equal of Mark
Twain in his lambasting satire of James Fenimore Cooper; indeed, watching others perform foolishly rather than purportedly watching himself perform foolishly, he was at his subtle
best. Yes, I remembered the good feeling permeating our call
that night a year before and the pleasure I'd had rereading his
books afterward, but I could not remember any call from Kliman about having lunch to discuss George's death.

Nor could I believe in George's death. The idea was excessive in every way that George wasn't, and incongruent with his
curiosity's robust engagement with the "great variety of life"—
a phrase he used when he was happily imagining himself as an
African riverbird eyeing everything with wings and paws and
hooves and feathers and scales and hide that was drawn to the
rushing waters. Kliman must have meant to say something else
about George Plimpton, because if I had been asked, "Who
among your contemporaries will be the last to die? Who among
your contemporaries is least likely to die? Who among your

contemporaries will not only elude death but write with wit, precision, and modesty of his amused bafflement at successfully pulling off eternal life?" the only answer possible would have been "George Plimpton." Like the ninety-four-year-old count in *A Farewell to Arms* with whom Frederic Henry plays a game of billiards—to whom Frederic Henry, on parting, says, "I hope you live forever," and who replies, "I have"—George Plimpton was on his way to living forever from the time he was born. George had no more intention of dying than, say, Tom Sawyer; his not-dying was an assumption inseparable from his competitive encounters with the greatest of athletes. I am pitching against the New York Yankees, I am running plays for the Detroit Lions, I am in the ring with Archie Moore in order to report with authority what it is to survive everything that is superior to you and lined up to crush you.

There was more underlying those books, of course, and George was never more graciously attentive than the evening many years ago when I speculated over dinner with him on his hidden motives. It was the issue of social class that seemed to me the deepest inspiration for his writing so singularly about sports, cagily venturing into situations where he plays at being bereft of his class advantages (except for the upper-crust manners, which, in a world wholly alien, if not hostile, to good breeding, he knowingly employs for the comic effect of their unsuitability). "Me" is his self-mocking double—the working journalist—unburdened of the privileged George that he inescapably was, that he masterfully was and so enjoyed being. To be sure, his advantages—as embodied in what he modestly called his "Eastern Seaboard cosmopolitan accent" but which was more the accent of the Eastern Seaboard's disappearing ruling class—made him the butt of the jokes of the professional athletes with whom he competed as an amateur. Yet he did not attempt in *Paper Lion* or in *Out of My League* anything like what the modern era's first astonishingly percipient "participatory journalist"—the other George with a gentleman's accent, who missed not a one of the social differences, gross or minute, that he saw everywhere he went—painstakingly describes himself doing in *Down and Out in Paris and London*. Like Orwell, Plimpton tried to look straight at the thing and describe plainly what he saw and how it worked and so grasp hold of it for the reader. He did not, however, take on the lowliest jobs in the dirty, overheated restaurant kitchens of Paris, to be reduced in those turbulent pigsties to the status of a brutalized slave and to learn an object lesson in poverty, nor did he attempt, as Orwell subsequently did when he went on the road as a tramp in England, to see what it was to touch bottom. Instead, he entered a world no less glamorous than his own, the world of the ruling class of America's transcendent popular culture, the world of professional sports. *Down and Out in the Major Leagues. Down and Out in the NFL. Down and Out in the NBA.* Courting embarrassment and losing his dignity and flaunting his inadequacies with the pros, George in fact succeeded in maximizing his glamour rather than repudiating it, a ploy for which I admired him and that was at the heart of my enjoyment of the books. Books advertised as pitting the ungainly amateur against the impregnable professional were in actuality about a well-coordinated, excellently equipped athlete born into America's oldest elite playing at being a bumbler of an athlete with the majestically equipped athletes of America's newest elite, the superstars of sports. In *Out of My League* the easygoing master of self-possession goes so far as to envy the poise of the Yankee batboy; in *Paper Lion* he pretends that he hardly knew how to hold a football when he was quarterbacking the Detroit Lions, though I clearly remember touch football games on the Westchester lawn of one of his closest friends, in which George threw spirals as accurate as any a pass receiver could hope for in *any* league. Hemingway had it wrong when he described George's adventures with professional athletes as "the dark side of the moon of Walter Mitty." It was the bright side of being born George Plimpton, who uniquely managed to make a tremendously enjoyable vocation of leaving his old world of glamorous privilege to partake vicariously of the new world of glamorous privilege, the only American world that could possibly equal his own in the prestige his once had. Therein lay George's true brilliance, his ability to move across the class line of scrimmage, making himself, as he put it, "a laughingstock," without becoming, like George Orwell barely surviving among "the dregs" as an abject Paris dishwasher and a hungry, penniless London tramp, punishingly and horribly—and in deadly earnest—a déclassé. George escaped his glamour without losing his glamour, only further enhancing it in autobiographical books seemingly driven by self-deprecation. Climbing into the ring with Archie Moore he was simply practicing noblesse oblige in its most exquisite form—a form, moreover, that he had invented. When people say to themselves "I want to be happy," they could as well be saying "I want to be George Plimpton": one achieves, one is productive, and there's pleasure and ease in all of it.

Nobody on such casual good terms with the mighty and the accomplished and the renowned, nobody so in love with the excitement of deeds and words, for whom the suffering that is mortality seemed so remote, nobody with as many admirers as George had, with as many attributes as George had, nobody who could speak to anyone and everyone as easily as George did . . . On I went, thinking that the closest George would ever come to dying would be to simulate it in an article for *Sports Illustrated*.

I got up from the bed and, on the desk where I'd been writing for most of the night, found my chore book and began to leaf backward through the pages, looking for a notation about an appointment with Kliman and meanwhile telling him, "I can't go to lunch with you."

"But I have it. I brought it with me. You're welcome to see it."

"See what?"

"The first half of the novel. Lonoff's manuscript."

"I'm not interested."

"But you're the one who told me to bring it with me."

"I did no such thing. Goodbye."

The hotel stationery covered on both sides with recollections of my evening with Amy and the pages of repartee from *He and She*—all that writing I'd done between getting back from Amy's and falling asleep fully clothed and dreaming about my mother—was still there on the desk. In the five minutes before Kliman called again, I was able to review my notes to find out what I'd said to Amy about Kliman and the biography. I'd promised her I'd stop him from writing it. I'd impressed upon her that Lonoff's inspiration for his novel had been taken not from his own life but from highly dubious scholarly speculation about the life of Nathaniel Hawthorne. I'd given her some money . . . I read over what I'd said and done but was not immediately clear about my overall intention, if I'd even had one.

When Kliman rang from the lobby, I wondered if it could have been he who'd sent those death threats to me and to the reviewer eleven years back. His doing that then was wholly unlikely—and yet what if it were so? What if the malicious prank of a college freshman with a craving for mischief had launched me into how and where I've lived during the past decade? Ridiculous if true, and for the moment I couldn't help but be convinced it *was* true, because of its absurdity. The ludicrousness of that decision to go out to the country and never return—as ludicrous as my belief that Richard Kliman was the one who'd pushed me to make it.

"I'll be down in a few minutes," I told him, "and we'll go to lunch." And I'll frustrate your every ambition. I'll ruin you.

I thought this because I had to. I couldn't just talk about it, I couldn't just write about it—before I left Manhattan for home, I had to master Kliman, if nothing else. Mastering him was my last obligation to literature.

How could George be dead? I kept coming back to that. George's having died a year ago made everything absurd. How could that happen to *him*? And how did what happened happen to me for these past eleven years? Never to see George again—never to see anyone again! I did this because of that? I did that because of this? I defined my life around that accident or that person or that ridiculously minor event? How outlandish I seemed, and all because, without my knowing it, George Plimpton had died. Suddenly my way of being had no justification, and George was my—what is the word I'm looking for? The antonym of doppelgänger. Suddenly George Plimpton stood for all that I had squandered by removing myself as forcefully as I had and retreating onto Lonoff's mountain, to seek asylum there from the great variety of life. "It's our time," George said to me, his singular voice ringing with its spirited confidence. "It's our humanity. We have to be a part of it too."

Kliman took me to a coffee shop just down the street on Sixth Avenue, and no sooner had we ordered than he began telling me about George's memorial service. Used to systematically regulating my day's routine and apportioning every hour as I saw fit, I now found myself—in clothes I hadn't removed for almost thirty hours and, I realized, wearing a pad inside my plastic briefs that I hadn't changed since the night before— seated at lunch across from an unpredictable force bent on dominating me. Wasn't that why I was getting the full brunt before I'd even gotten my orange juice—to have demonstrated to me that, contrary to my warning and threats, I was not his equal, let alone his superior, and that he was beyond my control and attached to no restraints? I thought, The Jews can't stop making these. Eddie Cantor. Jerry Lewis. Abbie Hoffman. Lenny Bruce. The Jew at his most buoyant, capable of a calm relationship with nothing and no one. I would have supposed the type had all but disappeared from his generation and that mild, reasonable Billy Davidoff was closer to the current norm —and for all I knew, Kliman *was* the last of the agitators and affronters. I had been out of contact with anyone like him for a long time. I had been out of contact with a lot of things for a long time, and not just with the resistance of vital beings but with having either to endlessly enact the role of myself or to parry fantasies of the author extrapolated from fiction by the most naive readers—a stale labor from whose tedium I had also disengaged. For I had been something of an affronter once too. It was the affronter whom George Plimpton had first published when no one else would. But nothing like that now, I thought. No, it's not watching George in the ring at Stillman's Gym with Archie Moore in 1959, but me in the ring of an unknown Manhattan with this club-fisted kid in 2004.

"It was just about a year ago, last November," Kliman said. "At Saint John the Divine. Huge place and it's jammed—every seat taken. Two thousand people. Maybe more. Begins with a gospel group. George had seen them somewhere and loved them, and so there they were. Leader very tall, good-looking black guy, groovin' on the pomp and circumstance, and as soon as they start in singing, he starts his shouting. 'It's a celebration! It's a celebration!' and I thought, Oh Christ, here we go, somebody dies and it's a celebration. 'It's a celebration! Everybody say it's a celebration. Tell your neighbor it's a celebration!' So all the white folk begin to nod their heads out of time with the music, and, I tell you, it doesn't look too good

for George. Then the minister gives the minister speech, and
the speakers step up one by one. First George's sister talks
about the museum he made of his room in the house on Long
Island, where he kept all his animal skins and dead birds, and
how passionate a boy he was about all these things, and the
delivery is stunning. Totally affectless she is, has that strange
absolute absence of strangeness that only the purest-bred old-
fashioned Wasp can pull off. Then a guy from Texas named
Victor Emanuel, probably in his fifties, maybe a little older, an
authority on birds, he and George fast friends through their
powerful interest in birds. Knew all the birds. This guy talks
very plainly, about birding with George and the birding trips
they took together, and all of it being uttered in the house
of the Lord—though the only ones who care to mention the
Lord are the minister and the gospel singers. On that subject
everybody else is mum, man, like it has nothing to do with
them. They just happen to *be* there. Then Norman Mailer.
Overwhelming. I'd never seen Norman Mailer off the screen
before. Guy's eighty now, both knees shot, walks with two
canes, can't take a stride of more than six inches alone, but he
refuses help going up to the pulpit, won't even use one of the
canes. Climbs this tall pulpit all by himself. Everybody pulling
for him step by step. The conquistador is here and the high
drama begins. The Twilight of the Gods. He surveys the assemblage. Looks down the length of the nave and out to Amsterdam Avenue and across the U.S. to the Pacific. Reminds
me of Father Mapple in *Moby-Dick*. I expected him to begin
"Shipmates!" and preach upon the lesson Jonah teaches. But
no, he too speaks very simply about George. This is no longer
the Mailer in quest of a quarrel, yet his thumbprint is on every
word. He speaks about a friendship with George that flourished only in recent years—tells us how the two of them and
their wives had traveled together to wherever they were performing in a play they'd written together, and of how close the
two couples had become, and I'm thinking, Well, it's been a
long time coming, America, but there on the pulpit is Norman
Mailer speaking as a husband in praise of coupledom. Funda-
mentalist creeps, you have met your match."

There was no stopping him. What had happened between us

so far he had set out to obliterate with a big performance designed to quell me, and it was doing its job: I felt myself—despite myself—growing progressively smaller the more flamboyant the display of Kliman's self-delight. Mailer is no longer in quest of a quarrel and can barely walk. Amy is no longer beautiful or in possession of all of her brain. I no longer have the totality of my mental functions or my virility or my continence. George Plimpton is no longer alive. E. I. Lonoff no longer has his great secret, if such a secret there ever was. All of us are now "no-longers" while the excited mind of Richard Kliman believes that his heart, his knees, his cerebrum, his prostate, his bladder sphincter, his *everything* is indestructible and that he, and he alone, is not in the hands of his cells. Believing this is no soaring achievement for those who are twenty-eight, certainly not if they know themselves to be beckoned by greatness. They are not "no-longers," losing faculties, losing control, shamefully dispossessed from themselves, marked by deprivation and experiencing the organic rebellion staged by the body against the elderly; they are "not-yets," with no idea how quickly things turn out another way.

He had a battered briefcase at his feet that I believed contained the half of Lonoff's manuscript. Maybe it contained as well the photographs that Amy had given him while under the influence of the tumor. No, extricating Amy wasn't going to be simple. Any effort at persuasion wasn't going to discourage Kliman; it would only further validate his significance to himself. I tried to figure out if a lawyer might help or if money might help or a combination of both—threatening him with legal action and then paying him off. Maybe he could be blackmailed. Maybe, it occurred to me, Jamie wasn't fleeing bin Laden—maybe she was fleeing him.

SHE

Richard, I'm married.

HE

I know that. Billy's the guy to marry and I'm the guy to fuck. You tell me why all the time. "It's so thick. The base is so thick. The head is so beautiful. This is just the kind I like."

SHE

Leave me alone. You have to leave me alone. This has to be over.

HE

You don't want to come anymore? You don't want the intense sensations anymore? You don't want that ever again?

SHE

We're not going to have this discussion. We don't talk to each other like this anymore.

HE

You want to come now, right now?

SHE

No. You stop it. It's over. If you ever talk to me like this again, we won't talk ever again.

HE

I'm talking to you now. I want you to suck the beautiful head.

SHE

Get the fuck away from me. Get out of my apartment.

HE

The brutal lover makes you come and the obedient lover does not.

SHE

That's not what we're talking about. I'm married to Billy. I'm not with you. Billy's my husband. You and I are over. What you're saying doesn't matter.

HE

Yield.

SHE

No. You yield. Leave.

HE

That's not the way it works between us.

SHE

That's the way it works now.

HE

You love to yield.

SHE

Shut the fuck up. Stop it. Just stop it.

HE

I thought you were so articulate. You are when we play our games. You say all kinds of devilish things when we play call girl and client. You make all sorts of delicious sounds when we play at Jamie being taken by force. Is this all you can say now— "Shut the fuck up" and "Stop it"?

SHE

I'm telling you this is over, and it's over. Leave my house.

HE

I'm not leaving.

SHE

Then I'm leaving.

HE

Where are you going?

SHE

Away.

HE

Come on, sweetie. You've got the prettiest cunt in the world. Let's play the strange games. Say the devilish things.

SHE

Get away from me. Get out of here right now. Billy's coming home. Get out. Get out of my house or I'll call the police.

HE

Wait'll the police see you in just that top and those shorts. They won't leave either. You've got the prettiest cunt and the basest instincts.

SHE

Whatever I say you're just going to talk about my cunt? You try to say something to someone and they don't hear you.

HE

This makes me hot.

SHE

This makes me angry. I'm leaving this house right now.

HE

Here. Look.

SHE

No!
(*But he doesn't stop, and so she flees.*)

People in the coffee shop might easily have thought Kliman
was my son from the way I let him go on in his self-delighted
and domineering way, and also because, at strategic moments,
he reached out to touch me—my arm, my hand, my shoulder
—in order to drive home his point.

"Nobody let you down that day," he told me. "Most interesting of all was a journalist named McDonell. He said something like, 'I'm dedicated to being lighthearted, because it's the
only way I can keep myself together up here.' Told many illus-
trative stories about George. Spoke out of real love. I don't
mean the others didn't speak with love. But you felt from Mc-
Donell an intense male love. And admiration. And the understanding of what George was. I think he was the one who told
the story about George and his T-shirt, though maybe it was
the bird guy. Anyway, they went to look for some bird in Arizona. They went out into the desert around dusk. That's when
this bird is supposed to be around. They couldn't find it. Suddenly George pulled off his T-shirt and threw it high in the air.
And bats swooped in and swarmed the T-shirt and followed it
all the way down to the ground. So George began to toss it up
in the air, over and over, as high as he could. And more and
more bats swarmed around it, and George cried, 'They think
it's a giant moth!' It reminded me of *Henderson the Rain King*,
at the end, where Henderson gets off the plane in Labrador or
Newfoundland, I forget which, and he begins to dance around
on this ice cap with all his African rain king exuberance, with
that rare strain of privileged, wealthy, Wasp exuberance that
you see in one out of ten thousand of them. And that was

George's triumph. It's what George *was*. The Exuberant Wasp.
I wish I could remember more of what this wonderful guy said,
because he was the one who carried the message. But then that
damn singing started up again. 'Oh magnify the Lord! Magnify
the Lord!' and every time I heard 'magnify the Lord,' under my
breath I said, 'He's not here, and everyone knows he's not here
except you. Here is the *last* place he'd be.' Every size and shape
of black woman was in that singing group. The ones with the
enormous cans, and the little balding gnarled ones looking a
hundred years old, and the thinnish, longish, elegant, pretty
girls, shy girls some of them, the ones who, when you see them,
you know what terror there was in the fields when the master
came around looking for his fun. And the big ones who are
confident and the big ones who are angry, and about half a
dozen sleek black guys singing along too, and I kept thinking
of slavery, Mr. Zuckerman. I don't think I've ever thought of
slavery so much when I've been with blacks before. Because it
was so white an assemblage they were entertaining, it seemed
like minstrelsy to me. I saw the last faint remnants of slavery
there in that Christianity. Back of them at the head of the apse
there was a gold cross huge enough to crucify King Kong. And
I have to tell you—two things I hate most about America are
slavery and the cross, especially the way they were intertwined
and the slave owners justified owning their Negroes by what
God told them in their holy book. But that's extraneous, my
hating that shit. The speakers started up again. Nine in all."

Lunch had arrived, and he took a moment to drink half his
coffee but I remained silent, determined to ask no questions
and just wait to see what he came up with next to steamroll me
into believing he was a twenty-eight-year-old titan of literature
and I should get out of his way.

"You're wondering how I met George," he said. "I met him
when he came up to Harvard for a party at the *Lampoon*. He
danced on a table with my girlfriend. She was the sexiest, so
he picked her out. He was great. Gave a great speech. George
Plimpton was a great man. People said that even dying he
managed gracefully. Bullshit to that. He just didn't have a
chance to put up a fight. He was a competitor. If it had happened to him during the day, he'd have had a shot at beating
it. But at night, asleep? Blindsided."

I remembered then that in one of his books George had set himself to interviewing his literary friends about what he called their "death fantasies." When I got back home to my library I discovered that the book was *Shadow Box*, which opens with his description of his adventure in the ring with Archie Moore in 1959 and ends in 1974 in Zaire, where George had gone to cover the heavyweight championship fight between Muhammad Ali and George Foreman for *Sports Illustrated*. Plimpton was fifty when *Shadow Box* was published, in 1977, and probably somewhere in his late forties when he was researching and writing it, and so it must have seemed a lark of an assignment to ask other writers to tell him how they imagined themselves meeting death—scenarios that, as he recounts them, were invariably comical or dramatic or bizarre. The columnist Art Buchwald told him that he "fancied himself dropping dead on the center court at Wimbledon during the men's final—at the age of ninety-three." In the bar of Kinshasa's Intercontinental Hotel a young Englishwoman who described herself as a "free-lance poet" informed George that "it would be terrific to be electrocuted while playing a bass guitar in a rock group." Mailer was also in Kinshasa to write about the championship fight, and he seemed fondest of the idea of being killed by an animal—if on land, a lion; if at sea, a whale. As for George, he saw himself dying at Yankee Stadium, "sometimes as a batter beaned by a villainous man with a beard, occasionally as an outfielder running into the monuments that once stood in deep center field."

Humorously and unusually—that's how George and his friends imagined themselves dying back before they believed they would, back when dying was just another idea to have fun with. "Oh, there's death too!" But the death of George Plimpton was neither humorous nor unusual. It was no fantasy either. He died not in pinstripes at Yankee Stadium but in pajamas in his sleep. He died as we all do: as a rank amateur.

I couldn't bear him. I couldn't bear his outsized boy's energy and smug self-certainty and the pride he took in being an enthusiast and a raconteur. The crushing immediacy of him—surely George couldn't have borne it either. But if I intended to do whatever could be done to prevent Kliman from becoming Lonoff's biographer, I would have to suppress that ebbing and flowing inclination to get my car and go back to the Berkshires. I would have to wait to see what he came up with next that he imagined would advance his interests. Having, in recent years, all but forgotten how to negotiate antagonism head-on, I instructed myself not to underestimate an opponent's shrewdness because he masquerades as a garrulous geyser.

When he'd finished a second cup of coffee, he said abruptly, "Lonoff and his sister changes things, does it not?"

So Jamie had told him she'd told me. Yet another unsettling facet of Jamie. What, if anything, should I make of her serving as the conduit between Kliman and me? "It's nonsense," I said.

He reached down to slap the side of the briefcase.

"A novel is not evidence," I said, "a novel's a novel," and resumed eating.

Smiling, he reached down again, and this time he opened the briefcase, removed a thin manila envelope, unclasped it, and poured its contents out onto our table, in the midst of our dishes. We were sitting in the window of the luncheonette and could see people walking by on the street. At the moment I looked up, every one of them was talking on a cell phone. Why did those phones seem like the embodiment of everything I had to escape? They were an inevitable technological development, and yet, in their abundance, I saw the measure of how far I had fallen away from the community of contemporary souls. I don't belong here anymore, I thought. My membership has lapsed. Go.

I picked up the photos. There were four faded pictures of a tall, skinny Lonoff and a tall, skinny girl who Kliman would have me believe was his half-sister, Frieda. In one they were standing on the sidewalk in front of a nondescript wooden house on a street that looked to be baking in the sun. Frieda wore a thin white dress and her hair was in long, heavy braids. Lonoff leaned on her shoulder, feigning heat exhaustion, and Frieda was smiling broadly, a big-jawed girl showing the large teeth that gave her a sturdy livestock look. He was a handsome boy with a dark pompadour and a cast to his lean face that might have enabled him to pass for a young desert dweller, half Muslim, half Jew. In another picture the two were gazing up from a picnic blanket laughing at something indistinguishable that

Lonoff was pointing to on one of the plates. In a third they were several years older. Lonoff was holding one arm high in the air, and Frieda, who had grown stouter, was pretending to be a dog, begging with her paws. Lonoff looked stern, giving her his command. In the fourth she must have been twenty and no longer the willing handmaid to her half-brother's whimsy but a tall, heavy-set, unsmiling young woman; by contrast, at seventeen, Lonoff looked ethereal and beyond the lure of temptation by anything other than the harmless muse of juvenilia. A case could be made that the photographs revealed nothing unusual other than to a mind as eager to be inflamed as Kliman's, and that the most one could reasonably conclude was that half-sister and half-brother enjoyed each other, were devoted to each other, appeared to understand each other, and, in the first quarter of the twentieth century, were sometimes photographed together by a parent or a neighbor or a friend.

"These pictures," I said. "There's nothing in these pictures."

"In the novel," he said, "Lonoff makes Frieda the instigator."

"There is no Lonoff and no Frieda in a novel."

"Spare me the lecture about the impenetrable line dividing fiction from reality. This is something Lonoff lived through. This is a tormented confession disguised as a novel."

"Unless it's a novel disguised as a tormented confession."

"Then why did it shatter him to write it?"

"Because writers can be shattered by writing. The primacy of the imaginative life can do that, and more."

"I've shown you the photographs," he said, as though what I'd seen were a set of filthy pictures, "and now I'll show you the manuscript, and then you dare to tell me that writing about a possibility that *wasn't* a reality was the force that drove this book."

"Look, you're coming off badly, Kliman. This news can't register wholly as a surprise on a *littérateur* like yourself."

Here he extracted the manuscript from his briefcase and placed it on the table, atop the photographs—between two and three hundred pages held together by a thick elastic band.

What a disaster. This reckless, hard-driving, shameless, opportunistic young man, whose way of absorbing a work of fiction was absolutely antithetical to Lonoff's, in possession of the first part of a novel that Lonoff never finished, felt he'd bungled, and might well never have published had he lived to complete it.

"Did Amy Bellette give this to you? Or did you take it from her?" I asked. "Did you steal it from under the poor woman's nose?"

His answer was just to push it toward me. "It's a photocopy. I had it run off especially for you."

He remained intent on gathering me in. I could be useful to him. Just to say he'd given me a copy could perhaps be useful to him. I wondered how feeble he thought I was, then wondered how feeble I had become up in my cabin on my own. Why was I even here at this table? None of what he told me had taken place between the two of us had really taken place—not the phone call, not the date for lunch, not the request to hear about Plimpton's memorial service, not the request to see the Lonoff manuscript. I remembered now precisely what *had* happened. *You smell bad, old man, you smell like death.* And I smelled again, the odor rising from my lap, very like the odor I'd encountered in the interior passages of Amy's building—and all the while he who had shouted those insults at me continued calmly finishing off his sandwich only a few feet from where I ate mine. That I had allowed this meeting to occur left me feeling without any more protection than Amy, porous, diluted, weaker mentally than I could ever have imagined becoming.

And Kliman knew that. Kliman had fostered that. Kliman had gauged my condition right off: Who would have thought that Nathan Zuckerman couldn't take it? Yet he can't, he's kaput, a tiny isolated little being, an exhausted escapee now from the coarse-grained world, eviscerated by impotence and in the worst state of his life. Just keep him confused, don't temper the battering, and down the doddering old fucker will go. Reread *The Master Builder*, Zuckerman: make way for the young!

I watched him, up on his pinnacle, move in on me for the kill. And suddenly I saw him not as a person but as a door. I see a heavy wooden door where Kliman is sitting. Meaning what? A door to what? A door between what? Clarity and confusion? That could be. I never know whether he is telling the truth or I have forgotten something or he is making things up. A door between clarity and confusion, a door between Amy and Jamie, a door to George Plimpton's death, a door swinging open and shut just inches from my face. Is there more to him than that? All I know is the door.

"With your imprimatur," he told me, "I could do a lot for Lonoff."

I laughed at him. "You've callously preyed on a grievously ill woman with brain cancer. You've stolen these pages from her, by one means or another."

"I did no such thing."

"Of course you did. She wouldn't have given you just the first half. If she wanted you to have the book, she would have given you the whole thing. You stole what you were able to lay your hands on. The other half was out of sight or somewhere in the apartment where you couldn't grab it. Of course you stole it—who gives somebody half of a novel? And now," I said, before he could answer, "now you want to impose on a specimen like me?"

Unfazed, he said, "You can take care of yourself. You've written lots of books. You've had your share of adventures. And you can be ruthless too."

"I can," I said, hoping that was still true.

"George always spoke of you with great admiration, Mr. Zuckerman. He admired the fortitude that fired the talent. I share that admiration."

Simply as I could, I said, "Good. Then don't go anywhere near her, and don't try in any way to contact me." I laid some cash on the table to cover the cost of the meal and headed for the door.

It took seconds for Kliman to pack his things and come racing after me. "This is censorship. You, yourself a writer, are trying to block the publication of another writer's work."

"Not assisting you with this spurious book is not blocking you in any way. If anything, by crawling into my hole to die, I'm getting out of your way."

"But it's not spurious. Amy Bellette herself recognizes the incest. It's she who first *told* me about it."

"Amy Bellette has had half of her brain removed."

"But she hadn't when I spoke to her. This is *before* the surgery. She hadn't been operated on then. She hadn't even been diagnosed with the tumor."

"But the tumor was there, was it not? She had a head full of cancer, did she not? Undiagnosed, to be sure, but she had that tumor invading her brain. Her *brain*, Kliman. She was passing out and she was vomiting and she was blinded by headaches and she was blinded by fear and the woman didn't know what she was saying to *anyone*. At that point she was *truly* out of her mind."

"But it's *obvious* that this is what happened."

"Obvious to no one but you."

"I cannot believe this!" he cried, walking beside me and showing me the baffled face of his fury. He was no longer in a mood to enjoy my contempt, and so down came the defenses against my judgment, and the rancorous beggar beneath the presumptuous bully at last made his entrance—unless that too was an act of guile and, from beginning to end, I was there only to play his old fool. "You of all people! The man had a penis, Mr. Zuckerman. His penis made them criminals in their world for over three years. Then came the scandal, and he hid from it for the next forty years. Then at the end he wrote this book. This book that is his masterpiece! Art arising from the tormented conscience! The aesthetic triumph over shame! *He* didn't know it—he was too frightened and miserable to know it. And Amy was too frightened by his misery to know it. But how can *you* be frightened? You who know what makes people insatiable! You who know the howling hunger for more! Here is a great writer's reckoning with the crime that intimidated him every day of his life. Lonoff's final struggle with his impurity. His long-delayed effort to let in the repellent. You know all about that. Let the repellent in! That's your achievement, Mr. Zuckerman. Well, this is his. His effort to lift this burden is too heroic for you to turn your back on now. The portrait of himself is not a flattering one, believe me. The young boy rising from a forty-year sleep! It's extraordinary. This is Lonoff's *Scarlet Letter*. It's *Lolita* without Quilty and the stupid jokes. It's what Thomas Mann would have written if he'd been someone other than Thomas Mann. Hear me out! *Help* me out! At some point you must take seriously the incest! Your hiding from it makes no sense and does you no credit! Antagonism to me is blinding you to the truth, sir! Which is simply this: that it took his giving up the home with Hope and going through his hell with Amy for him to release from captivity the sorrows of young Lonoff. I beseech you: read the amazing result!"

He was now in front of me, walking rapidly backward, thrusting the photocopy of the manuscript into my chest. I stopped where I was, hands at my sides and my mouth shut. I should have greeted him with silence from the start. I should—thought I for the hundredth time—never have left home in the first place. The years I'd been gone, the fort I'd constructed against the intruders drawn to my work, the armored layers of suspicion—and yet here I was, looking into those beautiful eyes aglitter with their rabid gray sheen. A literary lunatic. Another one. Like me, like Lonoff, like all whose most violent passion is for a book. Why couldn't it have been gentle Billy Davidoff wanting to write the Lonoff biography? Why couldn't deeply disrespectful, ardent Kliman be gentle Billy, and gentle Billy be deeply disrespectful, ardent Kliman, and why couldn't Jamie Logan, instead of being theirs, be mine? Why did I have to get cancer of the prostate? Why did I have to get those death threats? Why must strength's abatement be so quick and cruel? Oh, to wish what is into what is not, other than on the page!

Suddenly, his exasperation reached its crescendo, but rather than hurling the manuscript at my head—as I fully expected, instinctively raising my arms to protect my face—he dropped it onto the pavement, onto the New York sidewalk only inches in front of my feet, and fled into the traffic, darting between the streaming cars that I could only hope to see shatter the rampaging would-be biographer to bits.

At the hotel, after discarding my urine-soaked underclothes and washing myself at the sink, I phoned Amy. I wanted to know where Kliman's manuscript had come from. I had it in the room with me. I had picked it up and taken it with me. I had waited till Kliman was out of sight and then snatched it off the pavement and carried it back to the hotel. What else could I do? I had no interest in reading it. I could participate no further in this frenzy. I'd survived frenzy enough back when I was younger and clearheaded and a lot more wily and resilient than I was now. I didn't want to know what Lonoff had made of himself and his sister and their great misadventure, or to continue to argue what I still believed—that no such misadventure had ever occurred. However much the man had fascinated me when I was first starting out—and even though just the other day I had gone off to buy all his books, copies of books that I'd owned for decades—I wanted to be rid of the manuscript and completely free of Richard Kliman and everything about him that I could not assess and that was alien to everything I took seriously. Even if the forceful exertions all somehow looked like an act, like the reckless, loathsome, boyish stunt of someone superficial pretending to have a mind and a reverence for letters, he seemed to me no less my nemesis than Lonoff's. I foresaw only defeat should I persist in colliding with this impostor's aims and the vitality and ambition and tenacity and anger that fueled them. After I spoke with Amy and arranged to get those pages back into her hands, I'd phone Jamie and Billy and tell them the deal was off. And I'd leave New York without returning to the urologist. I hadn't that fortitude Kliman so admired, at least not for any further interventions. The urologist could change nothing, as I could change nothing. I may have accumulated over four decades the prestige of writing book after book, but I had reached the end of my effectiveness nonetheless. I had reached the end of my protectiveness as well, and had known as much when I ceased being able to protect myself other than by disappearing. I couldn't stop that kid, even by taking Amy back to the Berkshires or posting a guard at her door.

Nor could I stop him, when he was finished with Lonoff, from turning his blazing attention on me. Once I was dead, who could protect the story of my life from Richard Kliman? Wasn't Lonoff his literary steppingstone to me? And what would my "incest" be? How will I have failed to be the model human being? *My* great, unseemly secret. Surely there was one. Surely there was more than one. An astonishing thing it is, too, that one's prowess and achievement, such as they have been, should find their consummation in the retribution of biographical inquisition. The man in control of the words, the man making up the stories all his life, winds up, after death, remembered, if at all, for a story made up about him, his covert brand of baseness discovered and described with uncompromising candor, clarity, self-certainty, with grave concern for the most delicate issues of morality, and with no small measure of delight.

So I was next. Why had it taken till now to realize the obvious? Unless I had realized it all along.

There was no answer at Amy's apartment. I phoned Jamie and Billy. The machine picked up after only one ring. I said, "This is Nathan Zuckerman. I'm calling from my hotel. The number—"

Here Jamie herself answered. I should have hung up. I shouldn't have phoned. I should do this and I shouldn't have done that and now I should do the other thing! But I had no control over my thoughts once I was accosted by the stimulus of her voice. Instead of proceeding to extricate myself from the disaster of believing I could alter my condition—the condition of having been unalterably altered—I did the opposite, my thoughts rooted not in what I was but in what I was not: the thoughts of one still capable of making an onslaught on life.

"I'd like to talk to you," I said.

"Yes."

"I'd like to talk to you here."

During the pause that followed, I dealt as best I could with the ridiculous words the past was pressing me to speak.

"I don't think I can do that," she said.

"I was hoping that you could," I said.

"It's an interesting idea, Mr. Zuckerman, but no."

What could I, an exhausted "no-longer" with neither the confidence for the seduction nor the capacity for the performance, say to make her waver? All I had left were the instincts: to want, to crave, to have. And the stupid strengthening of my determination to act. At last, to act!

"Come to my hotel," I said.

"I'm quite thrown," she said. "I never expected this call."

"I didn't either."

"Why did you make it?" she asked.

"Something has got into me since we were together at your place."

"But it's something that I can't satisfy, I'm afraid."

"Please come."

"Please stop. It doesn't take much to make me go off the rails. You think I'm combative? Bristling Jamie? Aggressive Jamie? I'm a combative bundle of nerves. You think Richard Kliman is my lover? You think that still? That I would have nothing to do with him sexually should be abundantly clear to you by now. You've imagined a woman who isn't me. Can't you realize what a relief it was when I met Billy and someone wasn't screaming all the time when I didn't accede to his wishes?"

What could I say to draw her on? What could I possibly say that she would be susceptible to?

"Are you alone?" I asked.

"No."

"Who is there?"

"Richard. He's in the other room. He's been telling me what happened with you. That's all we're doing here. He's talking. I'm listening. That's it. The rest is your illusion. What a wounded person you are to imagine otherwise."

"Please, Jamie, come." Out of all the resources of language, those words were the richest I could light upon to repeat.

"I'm foolish," she said, "so please stop."

I saw myself, heard myself, was appropriately sardonic about myself and disgusted with myself and revolted by the degree of my desperation, but years ago the sexual union with women had been broken so abruptly by the prostate surgery that now, with Jamie, I could not prevent myself from pretending otherwise and acting in behalf of an ego I no longer possessed.

"I phoned you," I said, "to say something else entirely. I did not call with this in mind. I thought I had freed myself of all this."

"Is that possible?" She sounded as if she were asking not about me but about herself.

"Come, Jamie. I feel you can teach me something that it's too late for me to learn."

"That's a hallucination. It all is. No, I can't come, Mr. Zuckerman." And then, to be kind, or merely to get herself off the hook, or even perhaps because a part of her meant it, she added, "Another time," as though I had all the days that she did to hang around and wait.

*

And so I fled the forces that once had sustained my own force
and challenged my strength and aroused my enthusiasms and
my passions and my power of resistance and my need to take
everything, big or small, to heart and to make everything of
significance. I did not stay and fight as of old but fled Lonoff's
manuscript and all the emotion it had stirred up, and all the
emotion it *would* stir up when I came upon Kliman's notes in
the margin and found there the deadly literal-mindedness and
vulgarity that attributes everything to its source in a wholly
stupid way. I could not meet contention's demands, wanted no
part of its perplexities, and—as if this were work by a writer I
had been indifferent to all my life—I dumped the manuscript
unread into the hotel room wastebasket, got the car, and was
home just after dark. In flight you hurriedly make a choice of
what you take with you, and I chose to leave behind not only
the manuscript but the six Lonoff books I'd got at the Strand.
The set I had at home, bought fifty years earlier, was sufficient
to see me through the rest of my life.

The upheaval of New York had taken little more than a week.
There is no more worldly in-the-world place than New York,
full of all those people on their cell phones going to restaurants,
having affairs, getting jobs, reading the news, being consumed
with political emotion, and I'd thought to come back in from
where I'd been, to resume residence there reembodied, to take
on all the things I'd decided to relinquish—love, desire, quar-
rels, professional conflict, the whole messy legacy of the past—
and instead, as in a speeded-up old movie, I passed through for
the briefest moment, only to pull out to come back here. All
that happened is that things almost happened, yet I returned
as though from some massive happening. I attempted nothing
really, for a few days just stood there, replete with frustration,
buffeted by the merciless encounter between the no-longers
and the not-yets. That was humbling enough.

Now I was back where I needed never be in collision with
anyone or be coveting anything or go about being someone,
convincing people of this or that and seeking a role in the
drama of my times. Kliman would pursue Lonoff's secret with
all his crude intensity, and Amy Bellette would be as powerless
to stop him as she'd been as a girl to prevent the murder of her

mother, her father, and her brother, or to stop the tumor from killing her now. I would send her a check that very day and another on the first of every month, but she would be dead within the year anyhow. Kliman would persist and perhaps make himself of literary importance for a few months by writing the superfluous exposé revealing Lonoff's alleged wrongdoing as the key to everything. He might even steal Jamie away from Billy, if she was sufficiently troubled or deluded or bored to seek her escape in his obnoxious swagger. And along the way, like Amy, like Lonoff, like Plimpton, like everyone in the cemetery who had braved the feat and the task, I would die too, though not before I sat down at the desk by the window, looking out through the gray light of a November morning, across a snow-dusted road onto the silent, wind-flurried waters of the swamp, already icing up at the edge of the foundering stalks of the skeletal bed of plumeless reeds, and, from that safe haven, with all of them in New York having vanished from sight—and before my ebbing memory receded completely —wrote the final scene of *He and She*.

HE

Billy's still probably two hours away. Why don't you come to my hotel? I'm at the Hilton. Room 1418.

SHE

(*Lightly laughing*) When you left her, you said it was killing you and you didn't want to see her again.

HE

Now I do want to see her.

SHE

What changed?

HE

The degree of desperation changed. I'm more desperate. Are you?

SHE

I . . . I . . . I'm feeling less. Why are you more desperate?

HE

Go ask desperation why it's more desperate.

SHE

I have to come clean with you. I think I know why you're more desperate. And I don't think that my coming to your hotel room is going to help. I have Richard here. He came over and told me about your meeting earlier. I have to tell you that I think you're making a big mistake. Richard's only trying to do his work as you do your work. He's extremely upset. You're obviously extremely upset. You're calling and inviting something into your life you don't want to invite—

HE

I'm inviting you to my room. To come to me here in my hotel room. Kliman is your lover.

SHE

No.

HE

He is.

SHE

(*Emphatically*) No.

HE

You said as much the other day.

SHE

I didn't. You either misunderstood or heard incorrectly. You've got it all wrong.

HE

So you can lie too. Well, good. I'm glad you can lie.

SHE

What makes you think I'm lying? You're saying because I was his lover in college, I must be his lover now?

HE

I said I was jealous of your lover. I took him for your lover. You're telling me he's not your lover.

SHE

No, he's not.

HE

So someone else is your lover. I don't know whether that's worse or better.

SHE

I'd prefer not to discuss my lover. You want to be my lover—is that what you're saying to me?

HE

Yes.

SHE

You want me to come over now, six o'clock. I'd be there by six thirty. I can come home with some groceries as late as nine and say I was out shopping. I'd have to pick up some groceries or you can go grocery shopping for me now—we can have a few more minutes together.

HE

What time are you coming?

SHE

I'm just working it out. You could go grocery shopping now. I could get Richard out of here. Get in a cab. I could be at your place by six thirty. I'd have to leave by eight thirty. We'd have two hours together. Does that sound like a good idea to you?

HE

Yes.

SHE

And then what?

HE

We'd have had two hours together.

SHE

I'm insane today, you know. (*Laughing*) You're taking advantage of an insane woman.

HE

I'm reaping the harvest of the election.

SHE

(*Laughing*) Yes, you are.

HE
They stole Ohio—I'm going to steal you.

SHE
I could use a little strong medicine today.

HE
Once upon a time, I sold strong medicine door-to-door.

SHE
This all makes me think of the bayous.

HE
What are you saying?

SHE
The bayous in Houston. We'd get to them by cutting through somebody's property and we'd find a rope swing and jump in. Swimming in that mysterious chocolate-milk-colored water filled with dead old trees, where you couldn't see your hand in the water it was so opaque, moss hanging from the trees and the water this muddy color—I don't know how I did it, except that it was one of the things my parents wouldn't have wanted me to be doing. My older sister took me along with her my first time. She was the daredevil, not me. She was the one driven totally crazy by my mother's staggering concern for appearances. She was the one not even my admonishing father could control, let alone my mom. I married Billy. The worst he was was Jewish.

HE
That's the worst I am, too.

SHE
Is it?

HE
Come, Jamie. Come to me.

SHE
(*Lightly, quickly*) Okay. Where are you again?

HE
The Hilton. Room 1418.

SHE

Where's the Hilton? I don't know New York hotels.

HE

The Hilton is on Sixth Avenue, between 53rd and 54th. Across from the CBS building. Diagonally across from the Warwick Hotel.

SHE

It's that huge hotel that's not very beautiful.

HE

That's it. I thought I was going to be here only a few days. I came down to see my friend who's ill.

SHE

I know about your friend who's ill. We won't discuss any of that.

HE

What did Kliman tell you about her? Do you know what he's doing to a woman who's dying of brain cancer?

SHE

He's trying to get her story. Not even her story. The story of a person she loved whose work has been lost, whose reputation has vanished. Look, Richard, unfortunately, is his own bad press. But you oughtn't to be misled by that. Here is an energetic, compulsive, dedicated, interested person who has fastened onto this now very obscure writer who nobody reads anymore. He's compelled by him, he's excited by him, he thinks he's got some secret about him that could be instructive and interesting rather than simply scandalous. Yes, he has the insane rapaciousness of the biographical drive. Yes, he has the ruthless desire to get what he wants. Yes, he'll do anything. But if he's serious, why should he not? He's trying to restore this person to his true place in American literature, and he wants her help —to tell a story that hurts no one. No one. The people it involves have been dead for years and years.

HE

He has three living children. What about them? How would you like to find this out about your father?

SHE

When he was seventeen he had an affair with his half-sister—he was younger, he was fourteen when it began. If anything, he was the innocent, he was the younger child. There's no shame in that.

HE

You're so generous. Do you think your father and mother will be so generous when they read about Lonoff's youth?

SHE

My father and mother voted for George Bush on Tuesday. So the answer is no. (*Laughing*) If you worked for their approval, you'd never publish anything that my father and mother would look kindly on. None of your books would have been published, my friend.

HE

What about you? Would you look kindly on your father if you found this out about him?

SHE

It wouldn't be easy.

HE

Do you have an aunt?

SHE

I don't have an aunt. But I have a brother. I don't have children. But if I did, it's not something I would want my children to know about if that happened between my brother and me. But I think there are some things that are more important than—

HE

Please. Not art.

SHE

What have you given up your life for, then?

HE

I didn't know I was giving it up. I did what I did, and I didn't know. Do you understand what the papers will do with this? Do you understand what the reviewers will do with this? This has nothing to do with art and less with truth or even with comprehending transgression. It has to do with titillation. Lonoff, if he were around, would be sorry he ever wrote a word.

SHE

He's dead. He won't be sorry.

HE

He'll just be maligned. For no good reason, maliciously maligned by the moralist prigs, by the feminist scolds, by the sickening superiority of the lice of literature. A lot of the reviewers who are nice people will consider his a great sexual crime. What are you laughing at now?

SHE

The condescension. You think if it hadn't been for the "feminist scolds" I'd even be considering coming to your hotel room in twenty minutes? Do you think a girl brought up like me would begin to have the guts to do such a thing? So you're reaping the benefits of the election *and* the feminists. George Bush *and* Betty Friedan. (*Speaking tough, suddenly, like a moll in a movie*) Listen, do you want me to come over—is that what you want? Or do you want to talk about Richard Kliman on the phone?

HE

I don't believe you. I don't believe you about Kliman. That's all I'm saying.

SHE

Fine. Fine. Does that matter for our two hours together? You can believe me or not believe me, and if you don't believe me and you don't want me to come over, that's fine. If you don't believe me and you do want me to come over, that's fine. If you believe me and you want me to come over, that's fine too. You tell me what you want.

HE

Are you all so extremely self-possessed these days, all you thirty-year-old young women, or is there only so long that the performance can be maintained?

SHE

Neither.

HE

So is it just the thirty-year-old women with literary aspirations?

SHE

No.

HE

Is it the thirty-year-old women who grew up in oil-rich Houston families? Is it the superprivileged young women?

SHE

No, it's *me*. You're talking to *me*.

HE

I adore you.

SHE

You don't know me.

HE

I adore you.

SHE

You're madly attracted to me.

HE

I adore you.

SHE

You don't adore me. You can't. It's impossible. The words are meaningless. You strike me as a person who was spoiling for adventure but didn't know it. You, who spurned all experience for eleven years, who closed himself off to everything other than writing and thinking—you who'd held his existence so very close to his vest, you had no idea. Only when he finds himself back in the big city does he discover that he wants to be back in life and that the only way to get there is through his unreasoned, unconsidered . . . well, himself at the mercy of a completely unreasonable drive. I'm talking to a virtually inhumanly disciplined, rational person who has lost all sense of proportion and entered into a desperate story of unreasonable wishes. Yet that is what it is to be in life, isn't it? What it is to *forge* a life. You know your reason can reassert itself at any time—and if it does, there goes life and the instability that *is* life. Everyone's lot: instability. The only other possible motive you could have to think you adore me is that at the moment you're a writer without a book. Start another book and get into it and we'll see how much you adore Jamie Logan. Anyway, I'll be right over.

HE

Your agreeing to come to my hotel suggests to me that you're in big trouble yourself. Rash moments. This is yours.

SHE

Rash moments that lead to rash encounters. Rash moments that lead to perilous choices. You might not want to remind me of that too forcefully.

HE

I think I can rely on you to remind yourself all the way here in the taxicab.

SHE

Well, I've told you you're taking advantage of the election returns. So yes, you're right.

HE

You're crossing Conrad's shadow-line, first from childhood into maturity, then from maturity into something else.

SHE

Into insanity. I'll be there shortly.

HE

Good. Hurry. Into insanity. Off with your clothes and into the bayous. (*He hangs up.*) Into the chocolate-milk-colored water filled with dead old trees.

(*Thus, with only a moment's more insanity on his part—a moment of insane excitement—he throws everything into his bag—except the unread manuscript and the used Lonoff books—and gets out as fast as he can. How can he not [as he likes to say]? He disintegrates. She's on her way and he leaves. Gone for good.*)

CHRONOLOGY

NOTE ON THE TEXTS

NOTES

Chronology

1933
Born Philip Roth on March 19 in Newark, New Jersey, second child of Herman Roth and Bess Finkel. (Bess Finkel, the second child of five, was born in 1904 in Elizabeth, New Jersey, to Philip and Dora Finkel, Jewish immigrants from near Kiev. Herman Roth was born in 1901 in Newark, New Jersey, the middle child of seven born to Sender and Bertha Roth, Jewish immigrants from Polish Galicia. They were married in Newark on February 21, 1926, and shortly afterward opened a small family-run shoe store. Their son Sanford ["Sandy"] was born December 26, 1927. Following the bankruptcy of the shoe store and a briefly held position as city marshal, Herman Roth took a job as agent with the Newark district office of the Metropolitan Life Insurance Company, and would remain with the company until his retirement as district manager in 1966.) Family moves into second-floor flat of two-and-a-half-family house (with five-room apartments on each of the first two floors and a three-room apartment on the top floor) at 81 Summit Avenue in Newark. Summit Avenue was a lower-middle-class residential street in the Weequahic section, a twenty-minute bus ride from commercial downtown Newark and less than a block from Chancellor Avenue School and from Weequahic High School, then considered the state's best academic public high school. These were the two schools that Sandy and Philip attended. Between 1910 and 1920, Weequahic had been developed as a new city neighborhood at the southwest corner of Newark, some three miles from the edge of industrial Newark and from the international shipping facilities at Port Newark on Newark Bay. In the first half of the twentieth century Newark was a prosperous working-class city of approximately 420,000, the majority of its citizens of German, Italian, Slavic, and Irish extraction. Blacks and Jews composed two of the smallest groups in the city. From the 1930s to the 1950s, the Jews lived mainly in the predominantly Jewish Weequahic section.

1938   Philip enters kindergarten at Chancellor Avenue School in January.

1942   Roth family moves to second-floor flat of two-and-a-half-family house at 359 Leslie Street, three blocks west of Summit Avenue, still within the Weequahic neighborhood but nearer to semi-industrial boundary with Irvington.

1946   Philip graduates from elementary school in January, having skipped a year. Brother graduates from high school and chooses to enter U.S. Navy for two years rather than be drafted into the peacetime army.

1947   Family moves to first-floor flat of two-and-a-half-family house at 385 Leslie Street, just a few doors from commercial Chancellor Avenue, the neighborhood's main artery. Philip turns from reading sports fiction by John R. Tunis and adventure fiction by Howard Pease to reading the left-leaning historical novels of Howard Fast.

1948   Brother is discharged from navy and, with the aid of G.I. Bill, enrolls as commercial art student at Pratt Institute, Brooklyn. Philip takes strong interest in politics during the four-way U.S. presidential election in which the Republican Dewey loses to the Democrat Truman despite a segregationist Dixiecrat Party and a left-wing Progressive Party drawing away traditionally Democratic voters.

1950   Graduates from high school in January. Works as stock clerk at S. Klein department store in downtown Newark. Reads Thomas Wolfe; discovers Sherwood Anderson, Ring Lardner, Erskine Caldwell, and Theodore Dreiser. In September enters Newark College of Rutgers as pre-law student while continuing to live at home. (Newark Rutgers was at this time a newly formed college housed in two small converted downtown buildings, one formerly a bank, the other formerly a brewery.)

1951   Still a pre-law student, transfers in September to Bucknell University in Lewisburg, Pennsylvania. Brother graduates from Pratt Institute and moves to New York City to work for advertising agency. Parents move to Moorestown, New Jersey, approximately seventy miles southwest of Newark; father takes job as manager of Metropolitan Life's south Jersey district after having previously managed several north Jersey district offices.

1952   Roth decides to study English literature. With two friends, founds Bucknell literary magazine, *Et Cetera*, and becomes its first editor. Writes first short stories. Strongly influenced in his literary studies by English professor Mildred Martin, under whose tutelage he reads extensively, and with whom he will maintain lifelong friendship.

1954   Is elected to Phi Beta Kappa and graduates from Bucknell magna cum laude in English. Accepts scholarship to study English at the University of Chicago graduate school, beginning in September. Reads Saul Bellow's *The Adventures of Augie March*, and under its influence explores Chicago.

1955   In June receives M.A. with Honors in English. In September, rather than wait to be drafted, enlists in U.S. Army for two years. Suffers spinal injury during basic training at Fort Dix. In November, is assigned to Public Information Office at Walter Reed Army Hospital, Washington, D.C. Begins to write short stories "The Conversion of the Jews" and "Epstein." *Epoch*, a Cornell University literary quarterly, publishes "The Contest for Aaron Gold," which is reprinted in Martha Foley's *Best American Short Stories 1956*.

1956   Is hospitalized in June for complications from spinal injury. After two-month hospital stay receives honorable discharge for medical reasons and a disability pension. In September returns to University of Chicago as instructor in the liberal arts college, teaching freshman composition. Begins course work for Ph.D. but drops out after one term. Meets Ted Solotaroff, who is also a graduate student, and they become friends.

1957   Publishes in *Commentary* "You Can't Tell a Man by the Song He Sings." Writes novella "Goodbye, Columbus." Meets Saul Bellow at University of Chicago when Bellow is a classroom guest of Roth's friend and colleague, the writer Richard Stern. Begins to review movies and television for *The New Republic* after magazine publishes "Positive Thinking on Pennsylvania Avenue," a humor piece satirizing President Eisenhower's religious beliefs.

1958   Publishes "The Conversion of the Jews" and "Epstein" in *The Paris Review*; "Epstein" wins *Paris Review* Aga Khan Prize, presented to Roth in Paris in July. Spends first summer abroad, mainly in Paris. Houghton Mifflin awards Roth the Houghton Mifflin Literary Fellowship to publish the novella and five stories in one volume; George Starbuck, a poet and friend from Chicago, is his editor. Resigns from teaching position at University of Chicago. Moves to two-room basement apartment on Manhattan's Lower East Side. Becomes friendly with *Paris Review* editors George Plimpton and Robert Silvers and *Commentary* editor Martin Greenberg.

1959   Marries Margaret Martinson Williams. Publishes "Defender of the Faith" in *The New Yorker*, causing consternation among Jewish organizations and rabbis who attack magazine and condemn author as anti-Semitic; story collected in *Goodbye, Columbus* and included in *Best American Short Stories 1960* and *Prize Stories 1960: The O. Henry Awards*, where it wins second prize. *Goodbye, Columbus* is published in May. Roth receives Guggenheim fellowship and award from the American Academy of Arts and Letters. *Goodbye, Columbus* gains highly favorable reviews from Bellow, Alfred Kazin, Leslie Fiedler, and Irving Howe; influential rabbis denounce Roth in their sermons as "a self-hating Jew." Roth and wife leave U.S. to spend seven months in Italy, where he works on his first novel, *Letting Go*; he meets William Styron, who is living in Rome and who becomes a lifelong friend. Styron introduces Roth to his publisher, Donald Klopfer of Random House; when George Starbuck leaves Houghton Mifflin, Roth moves to Random House.

1960   *Goodbye, Columbus and Five Short Stories* wins National Book Award. The collection also wins Daroff Award of the Jewish Book Council of America. Roth returns to America to teach at the Writers' Workshop of the University of Iowa, Iowa City. Meets drama professor Howard Stein (later dean of the Columbia University Drama School), who becomes lifelong friend. Continues working on *Letting Go*. Travels in Midwest. Participates in *Esquire* magazine symposium at Stanford University; his speech "Writing American Fiction," published in *Commentary* in March 1961, is widely discussed. After a speaking engagement in Oregon, meets Bernard Malamud, whose fiction he admires.

1962   After two years at Iowa, accepts two-year position as writer-in-residence at Princeton. Separates from Margaret Roth. Moves to New York City and commutes to Princeton classes. (Lives at various Manhattan locations until 1970.) Meets Princeton sociologist Melvin Tumin, a Newark native who becomes a friend. Random House publishes *Letting Go*.

1963   Receives Ford Foundation grant to write plays in affiliation with American Place Theater in New York. Is legally separated from Margaret Roth. Becomes close friend of Aaron Asher, a University of Chicago graduate and editor at Meridian Books, original paperback publisher of *Goodbye, Columbus*. In June takes part in American Jewish Congress symposium in Tel Aviv, Israel, along with American writers Leslie Fiedler, Max Lerner, and literary critic David Boroff. Travels in Israel for a month.

1964   Teaches at State University of New York at Stony Brook, Long Island. Reviews plays by James Baldwin, LeRoi Jones, and Edward Albee for newly founded *New York Review of Books*. Spends a month at Yaddo, writers' retreat in Saratoga Springs, New York, that provides free room and board. (Will work at Yaddo for several months at a time throughout the 1960s.) Meets and establishes friendships there with novelist Alison Lurie and painter Julius Goldstein.

1965   Begins to teach comparative literature at University of Pennsylvania one semester each year more or less annually until the mid-1970s. Meets professor Joel Conarroe, who becomes a close friend. Begins work on *When She Was Good* after abandoning another novel, begun in 1962.

1966   Publishes section of *When She Was Good* in *Harper's*. Is increasingly troubled by Vietnam War and in ensuing years takes part in marches and demonstrations against it.

1967   Publishes *When She Was Good*. Begins work on *Portnoy's Complaint*, of which he publishes excerpts in *Esquire, Partisan Review*, and *New American Review*, where Ted Solotaroff is editor.

1968   Margaret Roth dies in an automobile accident. Roth spends two months at Yaddo completing *Portnoy's Complaint*.

1969   *Portnoy's Complaint* published in February. Within weeks
        becomes number-one fiction best seller and a widely dis-
        cussed cultural phenomenon. Roth makes no public ap-
        pearances and retreats for several months to Yaddo. Rents
        house in Woodstock, New York, and meets the painter
        Philip Guston, who lives nearby. They remain close friends
        and see each other regularly until Guston's death in 1980.
        Renews friendship with Bernard Malamud, who like Roth
        is serving as a member of The Corporation of Yaddo.

1970   Spends March traveling in Thailand, Burma, Cambodia,
        and Hong Kong. Begins work on *My Life as a Man* and
        publishes excerpt in *Modern Occasions*. Is elected to Na-
        tional Institute of Arts and Letters and is its youngest
        member. Commutes to his classes at University of Penn-
        sylvania and lives mainly in Woodstock until 1972.

1971   Excerpts of *Our Gang*, satire of the Nixon administration,
        appear in *New York Review of Books* and *Modern Occa-
        sions*; the book is published by Random House in the fall.
        Continues work on *My Life as a Man*; writes *The Breast*
        and *The Great American Novel*. Begins teaching a Kafka
        course at University of Pennsylvania.

1972   *The Breast*, first book of three featuring protagonist David
        Kepesh, published by Holt, Rinehart, Winston, where
        Aaron Asher is his editor. Roth buys old farmhouse and
        forty acres in northwest Connecticut, one hundred miles
        from New York City, and moves there from Woodstock.
        In May travels to Venice, Vienna, and, for the first time,
        Prague. Meets his translators there, Luba and Rudolph
        Pilar, and they describe to him the impact of the political
        situation on Czech writers. In U.S., arranges to meet
        exiled Czech editor Antonin Liehm in New York; attends
        Liehm's weekly classes in Czech history, literature, and
        film at College of Staten Island, City University of New
        York. Through friendship with Liehm meets numerous
        Czech exiles, including film directors Ivan Passer and Jiří
        Weiss, who become friends. Is elected to the American
        Academy of Arts and Sciences.

1973   Publishes *The Great American Novel* and the essay
        "Looking at Kafka" in *New American Review*. Returns to
        Prague and meets novelists Milan Kundera, Ivan Klíma,
        Ludvik Vaculik, the poet Miroslav Holub, and other
        writers blacklisted and persecuted by the Soviet-backed

Communist regime; becomes friendly with Rita Klímová, a blacklisted translator and academic, who will serve as Czechoslovakia's first ambassador to U.S. following the 1989 "Velvet Revolution." (Will make annual spring trips to Prague to visit his writer friends until he is denied an entry visa in 1977.) Writes "Country Report" on Czechoslovakia for American PEN. Proposes paperback series, "Writers from the Other Europe," to Penguin Books USA; becomes general editor of the series, selecting titles, commissioning introductions, and overseeing publication of Eastern European writers relatively unknown to American readers. Beginning in 1974, series publishes fiction by Polish writers Jerzy Andrzejewski, Tadeusz Borowski, Tadeusz Konwicki, Witold Gombrowicz, and Bruno Schulz; Hungarian writers György Konrád and Géza Csáth; Yugoslav writer Danilo Kiš; and Czech writers Bohumil Hrabal, Milan Kundera, and Ludvik Vaculik; series ends in 1989. "Watergate Edition" of *Our Gang* published, which includes a new preface by Roth.

1974   Roth publishes *My Life as a Man*. Visits Budapest as well as Prague and meets Budapest writers through Hungarian PEN and the *Hungarian Quarterly*. In Prague meets Vaclav Havel. Through friend Professor Zdenek Strybyrny, visits and becomes friend of the niece of Franz Kafka, Vera Saudkova, who shows him Kafka family photographs and family belongings; subsequently becomes friendly in London with Marianne Steiner, daughter of Kafka's sister Valli. Also through Strybyrny meets the widow of Jiří Weil; upon his return to America arranges for translation and publication of Weil's novel *Life with a Star* as well as publication of several Weil short stories in *American Poetry Review*, for which he provides an introduction. In Princeton meets Joanna Rostropowicz Clark, wife of friend Blair Clark; she becomes close friend and introduces Roth to contemporary Polish writing and to Polish writers visiting America, including Konwicki and Kazimierz Brandys. Publishes "Imagining Jews" in *New York Review of Books*; essay prompts letter from university professor, editor, writer, and former Jesuit Jack Miles. Correspondence ensues and the two establish a lasting intellectual friendship. In New York, meets teacher, editor, author, and journalist Bernard Avishai; they quickly establish a strong intellectual bond and become lifelong friends.

1975   Aaron Asher leaves Holt and becomes editor in chief at
         Farrar, Straus and Giroux; Roth moves to FSG with Asher
         for publication of *Reading Myself and Others*, a collection
         of interviews and critical essays. Meets British actress Claire
         Bloom.

1976   Interviews Isaac Bashevis Singer about Bruno Schulz for
         New York Times Book Review article to coincide with pub-
         lication of Schulz's *Street of Crocodiles* in "Writers from
         the Other Europe" series. Moves with Claire Bloom to
         London, where they live six to seven months a year for
         the next twelve years. Spends the remaining months in
         Connecticut, where Bloom joins him when she is not act-
         ing in films, television, or stage productions. In London
         resumes an old friendship with British critic A. Alvarez
         and, a few years later, begins a friendship with American
         writer Michael Herr (author of *Dispatches*, which Roth
         admires) and with the American painter R. B. Kitaj. Also
         meets critic and biographer Hermione Lee, who becomes
         a friend, as does novelist Edna O'Brien. Begins regular
         visits to France to see Milan Kundera and another new
         friend, French writer-critic Alain Finkielkraut. Visits Israel
         for the first time since 1963 and returns there regularly,
         keeping a journal that eventually provides ideas and ma-
         terial for novels *The Counterlife* and *Operation Shylock*.
         Meets the writer Aharon Appelfeld in Jerusalem and they
         become close friends.

1977   Publishes *The Professor of Desire*, second book of Kepesh
         trilogy. Beginning in 1977 and continuing over the next
         few years, writes series of TV dramas for Claire Bloom:
         adaptations of *The Name-Day Party*, a short story by
         Chekhov; *Journey into the Whirlwind*, the gulag autobi-
         ography of Eugenia Ginzburg; and, with David Plante,
         It Isn't Fair, Plante's memoir of Jean Rhys. At request
         of Chichester Festival director, modernizes the David
         Magarshack translation of Chekhov's *The Cherry Orchard*
         for Claire Bloom's 1981 performance at the festival as
         Madame Ranyevskaya.

1979   *The Ghost Writer*, first novel featuring novelist Nathan
         Zuckerman as protagonist, is published in its entirety in
         The New Yorker, then published by Farrar, Straus and Gi-
         roux. Bucknell awards Roth his first honorary degree;
         eventually receives honorary degrees from Amherst,

Brown, Columbia, Dartmouth, Harvard, Pennsylvania, and Rutgers, among others.

1980   *A Philip Roth Reader* published, edited by Martin Green. Milan and Vera Kundera visit Connecticut on first trip to U.S.; Roth introduces Kundera to friend and *New Yorker* editor Veronica Geng, who also becomes Kundera's editor at the magazine. Conversation with Milan Kundera, in London and Connecticut, published in *New York Times Book Review*.

1981   Mother dies of a sudden heart attack in Elizabeth, New Jersey. *Zuckerman Unbound* published.

1982   Corresponds with Judith Thurman after reading her biography of Isak Dinesen, and they begin a friendship.

1983   Roth's physician and Litchfield County neighbor, Dr. C. H. Huvelle, retires from his Connecticut practice and the two become close friends.

1984   *The Anatomy Lesson* published. Aaron Asher leaves FSG and David Rieff becomes Roth's editor; the two soon become close friends. Conversation with Edna O'Brien in London published in *New York Times Book Review*. With BBC director Tristram Powell, adapts *The Ghost Writer* for television drama, featuring Claire Bloom; program is aired in U.S. and U.K. Meets University of Connecticut professor Ross Miller and the two forge strong literary friendship.

1985   *Zuckerman Bound*, a compilation of *The Ghost Writer*, *Zuckerman Unbound*, *The Anatomy Lesson*, with epilogue *The Prague Orgy*, published. Adapts *The Prague Orgy* for a British television production that is never realized.

1986   Spends several days in Turin with Primo Levi. Conversation with Levi published in *New York Times Book Review*, which also asks that Roth write a memoir about Bernard Malamud upon Malamud's death at age seventy-two. *The Counterlife* published; wins National Book Critics Circle Award for fiction that year.

1987   Corresponds with exiled Romanian writer Norman Manea, who is living in Berlin, and encourages him to come to live in U.S.; Manea arrives the next year, and the two become close friends.

1988   *The Facts* published. Travels to Jerusalem for Aharon Appelfeld interview, which is published in *New York Times Book Review*. In Jerusalem, attends daily the trial of Ivan Demjanjuk, the alleged Treblinka guard "Ivan the Terrible." Returns to America to live year-round. Becomes Distinguished Professor of Literature at Hunter College of the City University of New York, where he will teach one semester each year until 1991.

1989   Father dies of brain tumor after yearlong illness. David Rieff leaves Farrar, Straus. For the first time since 1970, acquires a literary agent, Andrew Wylie of Wylie, Aitken, and Stone. Leaves FSG for Simon and Schuster. Writes a memoir of Philip Guston, which is published in *Vanity Fair* and subsequently reprinted in Guston catalogs.

1990   Travels to post-Communist Prague for conversation with Ivan Klíma, published in *New York Review of Books*. *Deception* published by Simon and Schuster. Roth marries Claire Bloom in New York.

1991   *Patrimony* published; wins National Book Critics Circle Award for biography. Renews strong friendship with Saul Bellow.

1992   Reads from *Patrimony* for nationwide reading tour, extending into 1993. Publishes brief profile of Norman Manea in *New York Times Book Review*.

1993   *Operation Shylock* published; wins PEN/Faulkner Award for fiction. Separates from Claire Bloom. Writes *Dr. Huvelle: A Biographical Sketch*, which he publishes privately as a thirty-four-page booklet for local distribution.

1994   Divorces Claire Bloom.

1995   Returns to Houghton Mifflin, where John Sterling is his editor. *Sabbath's Theater* is published and wins National Book Award for fiction.

1997   John Sterling leaves Houghton Mifflin and Wendy Strothman becomes Roth's editor. *American Pastoral*, first book of the "American Trilogy," is published and wins Pulitzer Prize for fiction.

1998   *I Married a Communist*, the second book of the trilogy, is published and wins Ambassador Book Award of the English-Speaking Union. In October Roth attends three-day international literary program honoring his work in Aix-en-Provence. In November receives National Medal of Arts at the White House.

2000   Publishes *The Human Stain*, final book of American trilogy, which wins PEN/Faulkner Award in U.S., the W. H. Smith Award in the U.K., and the Prix Medicis for the best foreign book of the year in France. Publishes "Rereading Saul Bellow" in *The New Yorker*.

2001   Publishes *The Dying Animal*, final book of the Kepesh trilogy, and *Shop Talk*, a collection of interviews with and essays on Primo Levi, Aharon Appelfeld, I. B. Singer, Edna O'Brien, Milan Kundera, Ivan Klíma, Philip Guston, Bernard Malamud, and Saul Bellow, and an exchange with Mary McCarthy. Receives highest award of the American Academy of Arts and Letters, the Gold Medal in fiction, given every six years "for the entire work of the recipient," previously awarded to Willa Cather, Edith Wharton, John Dos Passos, William Faulkner, Saul Bellow, and Isaac Bashevis Singer, among others. Is awarded the Edward McDowell Medal; William Styron, chair of the selection committee, remarks at the presentation ceremony that Roth "has caused to be lodged in our collective consciousness a small, select company of human beings who are as arrestingly alive and as fully realized as any in modern fiction."

2002   Wins the National Book Foundation's Medal for Distinguished Contribution to American Letters.

2003   Receives honorary degrees at Harvard University and University of Pennsylvania. Roth's work now appears in 31 languages.

2004   Publishes novel *The Plot Against America*, which becomes a best seller and wins the W. H. Smith Award for best book of the year in the U.K.; Roth is the first writer in the forty-six-year history of the prize to win it twice.

2005   *The Plot Against America* wins the Society of American Historians' James Fenimore Cooper Prize as the outstanding historical novel on an American theme for 2003–04. On October 23, Roth's childhood home at 81 Summit Avenue in Newark is marked with a plaque as a historic landmark and the nearby intersection is named Philip Roth Plaza.

2006   Publishes *Everyman* in May. Becomes fourth recipient of
            PEN's highest writing honor, the PEN/Nabokov Award.
            Receives Power of the Press Award from the New Jersey
            Library Association for Newark *Star-Ledger* eulogy to
            his close friend, Newark librarian and city historian
            Charles Cummings.

2007   Receives PEN/Faulkner Award for *Everyman*, the first
            author to be given the award three times. Wins the inau-
            gural PEN/Saul Bellow Award for Achievement in Ameri-
            can Fiction and Italy's first Grinzane-Masters Award, an
            award dedicated to the grand masters of literature. *Exit
            Ghost* is published.

2008   Roth's seventy-fifth birthday is marked by a celebration of
            his life and work at Columbia University. *Indignation* is
            published.

2009   Honored in program at Queens College, "A 50th An-
            niversary Celebration of the Work of Philip Roth." Re-
            ceives the Charles Cummings Award from the Newark
            Preservation and Landmarks Committee, the sponsor of
            semi-annual tours of "Philip Roth's Newark." Publishes
            The Humbling. Wins the annual literary prize of the Ger-
            man newspaper *Die Welt*.

2010   Receives *Paris Review*'s Hadada Award in April. Publishes
            Nemesis in September.

2011   In March receives the National Humanities Medal at the
            White House. Wins the Man Booker International Prize.

2012   Receives Library of Congress Creative Achievement Award.
            In October, wins Spain's Prince of Asturias Award for
            Literature.

Note on the Texts

This volume contains three novels by Philip Roth: *The Dying Animal* (2001), *The Plot Against America* (2004), and *Exit Ghost* (2007). At the author's request, and because corrections were made to the texts of the novels when brought out in paperback, this volume prints the versions published under Random House's Vintage International imprint.

The Dying Animal, the third and final novel with David Kepesh as a protagonist, was published in New York by Houghton Mifflin and in London by Jonathan Cape in 2001. The text printed here is taken from the Vintage paperback edition, published in July 2002.

The Plot Against America was published in New York by Houghton Mifflin and in London by Jonathan Cape in 2004. The Vintage paperback edition, published in September 2005, contains the text of *The Plot Against America* printed here.

Exit Ghost, the ninth and last of the "Zuckerman Books" (as Roth has called them), was published in New York by Houghton Mifflin and in London by Jonathan Cape in 2007. The text printed here is taken from the Vintage paperback edition, published in November 2008.

This volume presents the texts of the original printings chosen for inclusion here, but it does not attempt to reproduce nontextual features of their typographic design. The texts are presented without change, except for the correction of typographical errors. Spelling, punctuation, and capitalization are often expressive features and are not altered, even when inconsistent or irregular. The following is a list of typographical errors corrected and an author emendation cited by page and line number: 12.15, must a; 34.39, Bernadine; 117.20, Above; 138.35, became; 174.6, reserves which; 318.9, full time; 342.38, Couglin's; 373.39, Uncle; 382.26, launch of an; 393.8, Peron; 406.34, 18; 417.38, who; 435.38, far eastern; 436.29, swearing in; 440.25, address Depression suffering [emendation by Philip Roth]; 578.4, recreate; 616.30, must be.".

Notes

In the notes below, the reference numbers denote page and line of this volume (the line count includes chapter headings). Biblical quotations are keyed to the King James Version. Quotations from Shakespeare are keyed to *The Riverside Shakespeare*, ed. G. Blakemore Evans (Boston: Houghton Mifflin, 1974).

THE DYING ANIMAL

1.1   DYING ANIMAL] See "Sailing to Byzantium" (1928) by Irish poet William Butler Yeats (1865–1939): "Consume my heart away; sick with desire / And fastened to a dying animal / It knows not what it is; and gather me / Into the artifice of eternity."

3.3   EDNA O'BRIEN] Irish novelist and short-story writer (b. 1930); the quote is taken from a 1984 conversation between Philip Roth and O'Brien in London, later included in Roth's *Shop Talk: A Writer and His Colleagues and Their Work* (2001).

5.7–8   NPR . . . Thirteen] National Public Radio; New York public-television channel WNET.

5.20   Mark Twain story] In *Roughing It* (1872), ch. 7.

6.9   Brancusi] Romanian-born French sculptor Constantin Brancusi (1876–1957), renowned for his sensual abstract sculptures.

7.14   in loco parentis] Latin: in place of a parent, the notion that the university serves a parental role for its students.

8.9–10   goat . . . hide] In "The Wolf and the Seven Little Kids," German fairy tale collected by the Brothers Grimm, a wolf devours six of seven young goats; the seventh avoids being eaten by hiding inside a grandfather clock.

8.12–13   Prospero's daughter . . . Miranda] In Shakespeare's *The Tempest*.

8.23   transgressive Balthus virgin] French artist Balthasar Klossowski (1908–2001) is known for his sexualized paintings of adolescent girls.

12.17   Velázquez, *The Maids of Honor*] *Las Meninas* (1656) by Spanish artist Diego Velázquez (1599–1660), painting of the artist at work on a group portrait of the Infanta Margarita and her maids of honor while her royal parents, visible in a mirror on the back wall, look on.

14.23   the Algonquin, the Carlyle]   Manhattan hotels catering to literary and café society.

14.35   Page Six of the *Post*.]   Gossip column of the tabloid *New York Post*.

15.5   the *Musical Offering*]   Collection (1747) of thirteen works by German composer Johann Sebastian Bach (1685–1750), comprising fugues, canons, and a trio sonata based on a theme by Frederick the Great.

15.10   Bernstein]   American conductor and composer Leonard Bernstein (1918–1990).

15.36–37   *Moments Musicaux*]   Six lyrical pieces for piano, op. 94, D. 780 by Austrian composer Franz Schubert (1797–1828), called "Musical Moments" by his publisher upon their first publication in 1828.

23.2   Byron's *Don Juan*]   Unfinished satirical mock-epic (1818–24) by George Gordon, Lord Byron (1788–1824).

25.5   Practical Criticism]   Title of influential book (1929) by English critic I. A. Richards (1893–1979). The method of "close reading" advocated by Richards and other New Critics became the dominant mode of literary criticism taught at American universities from the 1950s through the early 1980s.

25.5   PBS]   Public Broadcasting System.

29.32–33   *El Diario* and the *Bergen Record*]   New York's most popular Spanish-language daily; New Jersey's daily with the second-largest circulation, after the Newark *Star-Ledger*.

31.5–6   Abbie Hoffman]   American political activist and prankster (1936–1989).

33.1   Parietal regulations.]   Visitation rules for members of the opposite sex in college dormitories.

33.7   what Hawthorne called "the limit-loving class."]   In Nathaniel Hawthorne's novel *The House of the Seven Gables* (1851), ch. 8, the character Phoebe Pyncheon is said to belong to "the trim, orderly, and limit-loving class."

34.18–19   Amy Fisher . . . mechanic]   Dubbed the "Long Island Lolita" by the tabloids, Amy Fisher (b. 1974) began having a sexual relationship at the age of sixteen with Joey Buttafuoco (b. 1956), owner of an auto body shop in Baldwin, New York. According to Fisher, during their affair Buttafuoco arranged for her employment as a prostitute. Fisher shot Buttafuoco's wife, Mary Jo, in the head on May 19, 1992. She later pled guilty to a charge of first-degree assault and served six years in prison.

34.28   Dr. Spock . . . tools of disobedience]   American pediatrician and left-wing political activist Benjamin Spock (1903–1998), author of the best-selling *Baby and Child Care* (1946).

34.32   Little Richard] Stage name of the rock-and-roll singer and song-writer Richard Wayne Penniman (b. 1932).

34.36   Lord of the Flies U] *Lord of the Flies* (1954), novel by the English writer William Golding (1911–1993), about the descent into barbarism of a group of British schoolboys left on a deserted island.

34.38–39   revolutionary cell . . . Boudin.] Dohrn (b. 1942) and Boudin (b. 1943) were members of Weatherman (later called the Weather Under-ground), a violent splinter faction of the leftist Students for a Democratic Society (SDS).

34.39–40   the Betty Friedans] Writer and activist Betty Friedan (1921–2006), author of *The Feminine Mystique* (1963), a widely influential book of feminist social criticism, and the first president of the National Organization for Women.

35.5–7   communal righteousness . . . Thoreau.] Henry David Thoreau's essay "Resistance to Civil Government" (1849), commonly known by the posthumous title "Civil Disobedience," was an influence on the nonviolent activism practiced by Martin Luther King and others in the civil rights move-ment.

35.13–14   Twist and shout, work it on out] Lyrics from "Twist and Shout" (1961), written by Phil Medley (1916–1997) and Bert Russell (1929–1967), a hit single for the Isley Brothers as well as the Beatles.

35.14   the "Internationale,"] Poem by Eugène Pottier (1816–1887), a member of the Paris Commune, set to music in 1888 by Pierre de Geyter (1848–1932). It was the anthem of the international socialist movement, and was later adopted by the Communists.

35.18   Glenn Miller] Big Band conductor and trombonist (1904–1944).

35.19   Tin Pan Alley] American popular music of the late nineteenth and first half of the twentieth century, named for an area of Manhattan (between Broadway and Sixth Avenue, around 28th Street) where music publishers had their offices.

35.30–31   Janis Joplin . . . whiteface] Soulful rock singer Janis Joplin (1943–1970); blues singer Bessie Smith (1894–1937).

35.32   Judy Garland] American film actress and singer (1922–1969), best known for her starring roles in the musicals *The Wizard of Oz* (1939), *Meet Me in St. Louis* (1944), and *A Star Is Born* (1954).

35.32–33   Jimi Hendrix . . . guitar] Rock guitarist Jimi Hendrix (1942–1970), whose virtuosity and compositional innovations are comparable to those of jazz saxophonist Charlie Parker (1920–1955).

36.35–36   Hawthorne based a story] "The Maypole of Merry Mount" (1837), the source for the quotation at 37.1–2 in this volume.

38.11–12   unexpurgated, as Henry Miller] American novelist Henry Miller (1891–1980) wrote candidly about sex in novels such as *Tropic of Cancer* (1934), one of several of his books that were banned in the United States for decades. An obscenity decision by the Supreme Court in 1964 ended the threat of litigation against Miller and his publishers.

42.25–26   his tracts on divorce] John Milton (1608–1674) wrote several tracts about divorce from 1643 to 1645; the quote at 42.28–30 is from *The Doctrine and Discipline of Divorce* (1643).

43.14   Gaston Lachaise] French-born American sculptor (1882–1935), best known for his large bronze sculptures of broad-hipped, voluptuous women.

44.12   Mantegna's Saint Sebastian] Italian Renaissance artist Andrea Mantegna (c. 1431–1506) completed at least three paintings of Saint Sebastian bound to a column and pierced by a volley of Roman arrows.

47.37   Karamazov father] Cruel, dissipated patriarch in *The Brothers Karamazov* (1880), novel by Russian writer Fyodor Dostoyevsky (1821–1881).

50.1–2   'men . . . sieve'] Cf. Alexis de Tocqueville, *Democracy in America* (1835–40), vol. 2, pt. 3, ch.19: "From hatred of privilege and embarrassment in choosing, all men, whatever their capacities, are finally forced through the same sieve, and all without discrimination are made to pass a host of petty preliminary tests, wasting their youth and suffocating their imagination. So they come to despair of ever fully enjoying the good things proffered, and when at last they reach a position in which they could do something out of the ordinary, the taste for it has left them." (Translation by George Lawrence.)

50.19   Conceived in liberty] From the first sentence of Abraham Lincoln's Gettysburg Address, delivered November 19, 1863: "Four score and seven years ago our fathers brought forth on this continent, a new nation conceived in liberty, and dedicated to the proposition that all men are created equal."

53.36–37   rouge . . . Aschenbach] In the novella *Death in Venice* (1912) by German author Thomas Mann (1875–1955), Gustave von Aschenbach, a dying writer, rouges his cheeks in a vain attempt to make himself attractive to Tadzio, a beautiful youth with whom he is obsessed.

58.18–19   Modigliani nude] *Reclining Nude* (c. 1919) by Italian artist Amedeo Modigliani (1884–1920).

60.10   Joseph Conrad . . . lost] Spoken by protagonist Axel Heyst in *Victory* (1915), novel by Polish-born English writer Joseph Conrad (1857–1924).

60.34   "K. 457."] Every Mozart composition can be identified by its Köchel number, as assigned in the catalogue of his works (1862) prepared by Austrian botanist and music bibliographer Ludwig Ritter von Köchel (1800–1877). K. 457 is Piano Sonata No. 14 in C minor.

61.19   Isn't that Yeats?] See note 1.1.

62.3   Schiele . . . paint it] In his erotic paintings and drawings, Austrian Expressionist artist Egon Schiele (1890–1918) often blatantly emphasized the genitals.

62.23   Telemachus] Son of Odysseus and his wife Penelope in Homer's *Odyssey*. Telemachus and Penelope wait twenty years in Ithaka for Odysseus' return from the Trojan War.

62.32   Ionesco's] Romanian-born French playwright Eugène Ionesco (1909–1994), author of absurdist plays such as *The Bald Soprano* (1950), *The Lesson* (1951), and *Rhinoceros* (1959).

66.2–3   Give me liberty or give me death] From a speech delivered by American Revolutionary leader Patrick Henry (1736–1799), March 23, 1775.

73.31   a Maillol] A sculpture made by French artist Aristide Maillol (1861–1944); most of his sculptures depicted the female body.

74.7   White Whale] I.e., Moby-Dick, in Herman Melville's novel (1851).

75.32   that plane to Paris.] TWA Flight 800, en route from New York to Paris, accidentally exploded and crashed into the Atlantic Ocean off eastern Long Island shortly after taking off from John F. Kennedy Airport on July 17, 1996.

78.14   Leica] German camera manufacturer, whose 35mm cameras have been widely used and admired among professional photographers.

78.21   Mata Hari] Dutch exotic dancer and legendary femme fatale Mata Hari, born Margaretha Geertruida Zelle (1876–1917), was executed by the French on charges (which many now believe to be false) of being a German spy during World War I.

82.39   *Death and the Maiden*] String Quartet No. 14 in D minor (1824), by Austrian composer Franz Schubert, named for its doleful second movement based on a theme from a song the composer wrote in 1817.

83.40–84.1   There's a painting . . . Tate] *Double Nude Portrait: The Artist and His Second Wife* (1937), also known as the "Leg of Mutton Nude," by English painter Sir Stanley Spencer (1891–1959), currently in the collection of the Tate Modern museum in London.

84.32   none ignited by bin Laden.] Thwarted attacks linked to the Al Qaeda terrorist network led by Osama bin Laden (1957–2011), including the bombings of Los Angeles International Airport and several sites in Jordan, were set to take place on or near January 1, 2000.

84.33–34   London . . . The Blitz] The Luftwaffe began its bombing campaign against London with a daylight raid on September 7, 1940, and continued night raids against the city through May 16, 1941.

84.36–37   Wernher von Braun . . . arsenal] German rocket engineer and scientist Wernher von Braun (1912–1977) designed the V-2 missile for the Nazis during World War II, then immigrated to the United States, where he became a central figure in the American space program.

85.2–3   August 6, 1945] Date of the American atomic bomb attack on Hiroshima, Japan.

85.13–14   The Triumph of the Surface] A play on the title of *Triumph of the Will* (1935), Nazi propaganda film by director Leni Riefenstahl (1902–2003).

85.14   Barbara Walters] Television journalist and personality (b. 1929).

86.14   Batista corruption] Cuban general and president Fulgencio Batista (1901–1973) ruled Cuba from 1933 to 1944 and 1952 to 1959, when he was deposed by the revolution led by Fidel Castro; under Batista's regime, American organized crime syndicates controlled much of the gambling and prostitution on the island.

87.36   *The MacNeil-Lehrer NewsHour*] Public television news program, named for its co-anchors Robert MacNeil (b. 1931) and Jim Lehrer (b. 1934).

88.38–39   *Buena Vista Social Club*] Documentary film (1999) by German director Wim Wenders (b. 1945), about aging Cuban musicians whose careers had begun in Havana before the revolution and were later revived by an internationally acclaimed recording of the same name, released in 1997.

THE PLOT AGAINST AMERICA

93.1   THE PLOT AGAINST AMERICA] Roth provides his own annotation for the novel in his Postscript, pp. 431–58 in this volume; the notes provided here explain only those references not treated there.

100.25   Decoration Day] Now called Memorial Day.

101.7–8   Soviet poster art] Stylized propaganda posters featuring industrial workers, farmers, and soldiers doing the work of the state.

104.22–23   infantile paralysis . . . Roosevelt's birthday] Infantile paralysis was the common name for polio (poliomyelitis). Beginning in 1934, annual balls were organized around the country and held on the birthday of President Roosevelt (himself stricken with a paralytic illness in 1921, diagnosed as polio) to raise money for the Georgia Warm Springs Foundation, a polio research organization named for the resort that he had bought and transformed into a facility to treat polio patients, and later the National Foundation for Infantile Paralysis, founded in 1938 by Roosevelt and attorney Basil O'Connor (1892–1972). The phrase "March of Dimes," used for the foundation's dances and other fundraising efforts, was coined in 1937 by singer and comedian Eddie Cantor (1892–1964), who asked Americans to send their dimes to the White House to help fight the disease.

105.24–25   German-American Bund] See Roth's entry on Fritz Kuhn, p. 449 in this volume.

108.5–6   pressure Roosevelt . . . embargo] The Neutrality Act of 1935, extended in 1936 and superseded by the Neutrality Act of 1937, prohibited arms shipments to nations at war. On September 21, 1939, three weeks after Germany invaded Poland, Roosevelt convened a special session of Congress to consider changes to the law, and on November 4 he signed legislation allowing the Allies to purchase munitions with cash and transport them in their own shipping.

112.32   Kishinev . . . 1903] Government-supported anti-Jewish riots in 1903 in Chişinău (now the capital of Moldova) in Russia.

113.12-13   Tom Meany and Joe Cummiskey] Sportswriters Tom Meany (1903–1964), who was on the staff of *PM* from 1940 to 1948, and Joe Cummiskey, *PM*'s sports editor.

115.13   L'il Abner] Comic strip, 1934–77, by Al Capp (1909–1979).

117.23   Aladdin's lamp] From the story "Aladdin and the Magic Lamp" in *One Thousand and One Nights*, traditional stories compiled in Arabic from Middle Eastern and South Asian sources dating back to the ninth century.

117.29   Flying Jenny] The Curtiss JN-4, developed in 1916 as a training plane for the U.S. Army, and often flown in barnstorming exhibitions after World War I when thousands of surplus planes were put on the market.

117.30–31   Pan-American Exposition] World's Fair, May 1–November 2, 1901, in Buffalo, New York.

117.35–39   Horace Mann . . . Negro] Educational reformer Horace Mann (1796–1859), member of the U.S. House of Representatives, 1848–53; educator Mark Hopkins (1802–1887), president of Williams College, 1836–72; academic Charles William Eliot (1834–1926), Harvard University's longest-serving president, 1869–1909; educator, temperance advocate, and suffragist Frances E. Willard (1839–1898); educator and civil rights leader Booker T. Washington (1856–1915), author of *Up from Slavery* (1901).

127.36   Mayor Raymond] Thomas Lynch Raymond (1875–1928), mayor of Newark, 1915–17, 1925–28.

134.15   Glen Gray Casa Loma Orchestra] Popular jazz dance band, 1927–63, led by saxophonist Glen Gray (1900–1963).

134.26–27   "Gotta Be This or That"] Popular song (1945) written by Sunny Skylar (1913–2009).

142.21   No mañana] Spanish: no tomorrow.

148.10   Quentin Reynolds and William L. Shirer] American journalists Quentin Reynolds (1902 1965), columnist for *Collier's* magazine, 1933–45, and William L. Shirer (1904–1993), author of *Berlin Diary: The Journal of a Foreign Correspondent, 1934–1941* (1941).

148.13   *Barnaby*] Syndicated comic strip, 1942–52, 1960–62, that debuted in *PM*, created by cartoonist and children's author Crockett Johnson, pseudonym of David Johnson Leisk (1906–1975).

164.5   *Information Please*] Radio quiz show, 1938–51, moderated by book critic Clifton Fadiman (1904–1999).

182.24   dip sheep] Sheep dip is a bath of soapy water treated with fungicides and insecticides to protect the herd against parasites.

197.15–16   understanding . . . keep it?] British prime minister Neville Chamberlain (1869–1940) agreed to cede the Sudetenland region of Czechoslovakia to Nazi Germany at negotiations in Munich in September 1938, declaring upon his return to England that the agreement would ensure "peace in our time." Germany invaded the rest of Czechoslovakia in March 1939, ending Chamberlain's policy of appeasement.

198.35   Nazi Brown Shirts] The Sturmabteilung (SA), a Nazi paramilitary organization whose members were often called "brown shirts" because of the color of their uniforms. It lost power to the SS after many of its leaders were executed in Hitler's "Night of the Long Knives" purge, June 30–July 2, 1934.

205.40   Military Park] Six-acre park in downtown Newark.

210.24   *machers*] Yiddish: big shots.

220.8   Lenni Lenapes] American Indian inhabitants of present-day northern New Jersey (and elsewhere in the mid-Atlantic region) when the first European settlers arrived.

225.3–7   Hades . . . Pluto] In Greek mythology, Cerberus was the three-headed dog who guarded the gates to the underworld, called Hades after the god who ruled over it. The River Styx separated earth and underworld. Pluto was the Roman name for the god Hades.

229.18   kickoff for old Notre Dame.] From "Notre Dame Victory March," fight song for college football powerhouse Notre Dame.

248.3–4   "Omaha" and "Whirlaway," . . . Derby winners] In 1935 and 1941, respectively.

248.10   beyond the pale.] Phrase referring to the Pale of Settlement, area in the Russian Empire where Jews were allowed permanent residency, established in 1791.

248.26–27   persecuted socialist hero Eugene V. Debs] American union leader (1855–1926), five-time Socialist Party candidate for president, twice imprisoned for his political views.

248.35   *Gangbusters*]   Radio drama, 1935–57, involving the FBI and based on actual criminal cases.

261.12–14   "The only thing . . . a first inaugural—]   From Roosevelt's Inaugural Address, March 4, 1933: "Let me assert my firm belief that the only thing we have to fear is fear itself."

261.25   Quisling blueprint]   During the German occupation of Norway, 1940–45, the Nazis installed a puppet regime led by fascist politician and former military officer Vidkun Quisling (1887–1945).

263.7   "The March of Time"]   Series of short films, 1935–51, that combined documentary footage with dramatic reenactments of current events.

263.19–22   Tojo. Pétain. Batista . . . Pope Pius]   Japanese general Hideki Tojo (1884–1948), prime minister of Japan, 1941–44; French soldier and politician Henri-Phillipe Pétain (1856–1951), head of state, 1940–44, of the French government at Vichy, which collaborated with the Nazis; Batista, see note 86.14; Irish revolutionary and statesman Éamon de Valera (1882–1975), prime minister of Ireland, 1937–48, 1951–54, 1957–59; autocratic Panamanian politician Arnulfo Arias (1901–1988), president of Panama, 1940–41, 1949–51, 1968; Filipino statesman Manuel Luis Quezon (1878–1944), first Filipino president of the Commonwealth of the Philippines, 1935–44; Mexican general and politician Manuel Ávila Camacho (1897–1955), president of Mexico, 1940–46; Soviet politician and diplomat Maxim Litvinov (1876–1951), Soviet foreign minister, 1930–39, and ambassador to the U.S., 1941–43; Soviet military commander Georgi Zhukov (1896–1974), the most successful Red Army leader during World War II; American politician Cordell Hull (1871–1955), secretary of state, 1933–44; American diplomat Sumner Welles (1892–1961), undersecretary of state, 1937–43; American industrialist, politician, and diplomat W. Averell Harriman (1891–1986), U.S. ambassador to the Soviet Union, 1943–45; Texas congressman Martin Dies (1900–1972), chairman, 1938–45, of the House Special Committee to Investigate Un-American Activities; SS leader Reinhard Heydrich (1904–1942), who as head of the RHSA (Reich Security Main Office) played a crucial role in planning and implementing the Holocaust; French socialist politician Léon Blum (1872–1950), French premier, 1936–37 and 1938, imprisoned by Vichy government and by the Nazis, 1940–45; Quisling, see note 261.25; German Field Marshal Erwin Rommel (1891–1944), commander of the Axis army in North Africa, 1941–43; British admiral and statesman Lord Louis Mountbatten (1900–1979), appointed chief of combined operations in 1941; George VI (1895–1952), king of the United Kingdom, 1936–52; Francisco Franco (1892–1975), fascist dictator of Spain, 1936–75; Eugenio Pacelli (1876–1958), Pope Pius XII, 1939–58.

264.20   Lowell Thomas]   American journalist and broadcaster (1892–1981).

264.21   Bill Stern]   American sports broadcaster (1907–1971).

269.34–35   Abbott and Costello movie.] American comedy duo Bud Abbott (1895–1974) and Lou Costello (1906–1959), veterans of burlesque and vaudeville, made thirty-six movies together, starting with *One Night in the Tropics* (1940).

274.5–6   Chamberlain . . . treaty] See note 197.15–16.

274.14   Hess] Rudolf Hess (1894–1987), deputy leader of the Nazi Party, who flew alone to Scotland on May 10, 1941, in a personal attempt to negotiate Britain's surrender, and was arrested and later sentenced to life imprisonment by the postwar Nuremberg tribunal.

274.19–20   Danzig . . . what happened to it?] The Baltic port of Danzig (now Gdańsk, Poland) was made a free city under League of Nations supervision by the Treaty of Versailles in 1919. Poland was given free use of the city's port and railways and control of its foreign relations, while its internal affairs were conducted by a government elected by Danzig's majority German population. The Nazis gained control of the city's legislative assembly parliament in 1933, and Jews became the targets of violence and official discriminatory measures. Hitler demanded Danzig's "return to the Reich" in October 1938, and the city was annexed to Nazi Germany following the German invasion of Poland in September 1939.

281.37–38   "Intermezzo," . . . *Isolde.*] Song (1940) with music by Heinz Provost (c. 1890–1959) and words by Robert Henning, after the violin theme in David O. Selznick's film *Intermezzo* (1939), starring Leslie Howard and Ingrid Bergman; its melody is derived from a leitmotif in Richard Wagner's opera *Tristan und Isolde* (1865).

295.17   Thumbelina] Tiny heroine of a fairy tale (1835) by Danish author Hans Christian Andersen (1805–1875).

299.8   *The Fred Allen Show*] Popular radio comedy program, 1932–49 (until 1939 called *Town Hall Tonight*), hosted by comedian Fred Allen (1894–1956).

299.25   the shiva] From the Hebrew word *sheva* (seven): a weeklong period of mourning held at the home of the deceased.

308.16–17   last of the Mohicans] I.e., last of a kind, phrase derived from James Fenimore Cooper's (1789–1851) novel *The Last of the Mohicans* (1826).

308.31–32   Oswald Mosley's British fascist party] British Union of Fascists, party founded and led, 1932–40, by British politician Oswald Mosley (1896–1980).

309.5   Ben Grauer] American broadcast journalist (1908–1977), announcer for Winchell's radio program, 1932–48.

328.37   schmegeggy] Yiddish: idiot.

342.12–13   John Gunther]   American journalist (1901–1970), foreign correspondent and author of *Inside Europe* (1936) and *Inside Asia* (1939).

344.25   Silver Shirts]   Silver Legion of America, extreme right-wing group modeled on the Nazi Brown Shirts (see note 198.35), founded by journalist and occultist William Dudley Pelley (1890–1965).

344.26   Black Legion]   A midwestern splinter group of the Ku Klux Klan, formed in Ohio in 1931, whose members committed several murders during the 1930s.

360.22–24   Mr. Davis . . . Mr. Smith]   John W. Davis (1873–1955), Democratic candidate for president in 1924; Al Smith (1873–1944), Democratic candidate for president in 1928.

360.32   Mr. Landon]   Alf Landon (1887–1987), Republican candidate for president in 1936.

363.39–40   Beau Jack . . . Larkin]   American boxer Sidney Walker (1921–2000), known as "Beau Jack," won the lightweight title with a third-round knockout of Tippy Larkin (born Anthony Pilleteri, 1917–1991), December 18, 1942.

370.27–28   Pearl Buck or Fannie Hurst or Edna Ferber]   American novelist Pearl Buck (1892–1973), best known for *The Good Earth* (1931); American novelist Fannie Hurst (1889–1968), author of *Imitation of Life* (1933); American novelist and playwright Edna Ferber (1885–1968), whose best-selling works include the play *Show Boat* (1926).

376.40   anti-Tammany]   The Tammany Society (1789–1961), known as Tammany Hall after its headquarters on 14th Street, was the political machine that controlled Democratic Party politics in New York City through the 1930s, when its influence waned due to the reforms of La Guardia and its loss of federal patronage.

377.1   Fusion]   A candidate endorsed by more than one political party.

378.1   Sherman Billingsley]   Businessman (1897–1966), former bootlegger and owner of the Stork Club, nightclub on East 53rd Street off Fifth Avenue.

378.3   'noble experiment,']   In his speech accepting the Republican nomination for president, August 11, 1928, Herbert Hoover (1874–1964) referred to Prohibition as "a great social and economic experiment, noble in motive and far-reaching in purpose."

378.23–25   Dieses and the Bilbos . . . United States Congress]   Martin Dies, see note 263.19–22; Theodore G. Bilbo (1877–1947), U.S. senator from Mississippi, 1935–47, an advocate for white supremacy; J. Parnell Thomas (1895–1970), Republican congressman from New Jersey, 1937–50, later chairman of the House Committee on Un American Activities (HUAC), 1947–49, who pleaded no contest in 1949 to corruption charges involving the use of his congressional office payroll and served nine months in federal prison.

379.9   Hopkins]   Harry Hopkins (1890–1946), administrator of several New Deal agencies, secretary of commerce, 1938–40, and a close advisor to President Franklin D. Roosevelt.

379.9   Farley]   James A. Farley (1888–1976), Roosevelt's campaign manager in 1932 and 1936; Postmaster General, 1933–40.

379.9   Berle]   Adolf A. Berle Jr. (1895–1971), lawyer who was a member of Roosevelt's "brains trust" circle of advisors; assistant secretary of state, 1938 44.

383.37   Rabbi Stephen Wise]   Prominent American Reform rabbi (1874–1949).

411.2   Alien and Sedition Acts of 1798]   Four laws passed in June–July 1798 by the Federalist-controlled Fifth Congress: the Naturalization Act, the Alien Act, the Alien Enemies Act, and the Sedition Act. These laws extended the period required for naturalization from five to fourteen years, gave the president the power to expel or, in wartime, imprison dangerous aliens, and made publication of writing attacking the government a crime punishable by two years in prison.

411.2–3   what Jefferson called the Federalist "reign of witches,"]   In a letter to John Taylor, June 4, 1798.

425.33–35   defending their lands . . . the great Tecumseh]   Shawnee chief (c. 1768–1813), leader of a confederation of tribes that resisted the encroachment of white settlers.

EXIT GHOST

459.1   EXIT GHOST]   Stage direction given several times in Shakespeare's tragedies, including *Hamlet* and *Macbeth*.

464.31   *The Shadow-Line*]   Novella, serialized in 1916–17 and published as a book in 1917, by Polish-born English novelist Joseph Conrad (1857–1924).

465.20   Tanglewood]   Summer home of the Boston Symphony Orchestra.

466.20   GI Bill]   Officially called the Servicemen's Readjustment Act (1944), the G.I. Bill guaranteed access to college education and provided tuition funding for veterans.

472.8   Rip Van Winkle's]   Protagonist of the eponymous short story (1819) by Washington Irving (1783–1859).

475.38   Pascal] French mathematician and philosopher Blaise Pascal (1623–1662).

480.37   David Levine] American artist and illustrator (1926–2009), whose caricatures were a long-running feature of *The New York Review of Books*.

484.37   *Four Last Songs*] *Four Last Songs* (1948) for soprano and orchestra by German composer Richard Strauss (1864–1949).

485.6–7   *Rosenkavalier. . . . Arabella. . . . The Egyptian Helen.*] Richard Strauss operas premiering in 1911, 1933, and 1928, respectively.

493.25   The wound and the bow.] In *The Wound and the Bow: Seven Studies in Literature* (1941), American critic Edmund Wilson (1895–1972) used the story in Homer's *Iliad* of Philoctetes, an Athenian warrior waylaid by a serpent's bite on his way to Troy, to illustrate the dynamic between trauma (wound) and insight (bow) in literature.

493.27–28   it's been argued . . . secret too] Critic Philip Young, in *Hawthorne's Secret: An Untold Tale* (1984), argued that Hawthorne's preoccupation with ancestral guilt in much of his work was rooted in a concealed incestuous relationship with his sister Elizabeth.

493.31   Hawthorne's son wrote] In Julian Hawthorne's *Hawthorne and His Circle* (1903).

501.21   Bartók quartet.] Hungarian composer Béla Bartók (1881–1945) wrote six string quartets.

508.19–20   "great communicator"] Name given to President Ronald Reagan (1911–2004) by his admirers.

511.7   Duncan] King of Scotland, murdered by Macbeth in *Macbeth*.

515.31   Broncos] Make of popular sport utility vehicle manufactured by Ford.

515.32   UT] University of Texas at Austin.

516.7   Lou Gehrig's disease] The degenerative disease amyotrophic lateral sclerosis (ALS), named for New York Yankees first baseman Lou Gehrig (1903–1941).

519.29   There was Nader] Ralph Nader (b. 1934), consumer advocate and political activist, ran for president as the Green Party candidate in 2000. Although he received less than 3 percent of the popular vote, he probably swayed the outcome of the election by receiving votes that would otherwise have been cast for Al Gore.

520.6–7   Kent State students were shot.] Thirteen unarmed students at Kent State University were shot, four of them fatally, by members of the Ohio National Guard on May 4, 1970, during a protest against the Vietnam War.

525.23   Rehnquist will be dead by tomorrow.] William Rehnquist (1924–2005), chief justice of the U.S. Supreme Court since 1986, had undergone surgery for thyroid cancer and had begun chemotherapy shortly before the 2004 presidential election.

529.29–31   *Partisan Review . . . Commentary . . . The New Leader . . . Dissent*] Influential American literary journals prominent in the 1950s and 1960s.

530.11–12   Singer is, with three volumes of stories.] A three-volume edition of the stories of Polish-born Yiddish writer Isaac Bashevis Singer (1902–1991) was published by The Library of America in 2004.

534.2   Wolfowitz] Paul Wolfowitz (b. 1943), deputy secretary of defense under Donald Rumsfeld, 2001–5.

534.3   That Rice woman] Condoleezza Rice (b. 1954), national security adviser, 2001–5, and secretary of state, 2005–9.

536.5–6   Eames chairs] Elegant bentwood lounge chair on a swivel steel base with a matching ottoman by the American furniture and industrial designer Charles Eames (1907–1978).

541.39   Jewish Pale] See note 248.10.

542.2   pre-Mandate Palestine.] Mandate Palestine refers to the period of British rule over Palestine, 1922–48, as established by a League of Nations mandate after the breakup of the Ottoman Empire.

546.6   the case of Salman Rushdie] Iran's Supreme Leader, the Ayatollah Ruhollah Khomeini (1900–1989), declared in a 1989 fatwa that British author Salman Rushdie (b. 1947) should be put to death because of alleged blasphemy in his novel *The Satanic Verses* (1988).

561.1   A Doll's House] Play (1879) by Norwegian playwright Henrik Ibsen (1828–1906).

561.23–24   *"The center of gravity . . . he and she"*] See the letter of May 10, 1886, by Anton Chekhov (1860–1904) to his eldest brother, Alexander: "Shun all descriptions of the characters' spiritual state. You must try to have that state emerge clearly from their actions. Don't try for too many characters. The center of gravity should reside in two: he and she."

564.38–565.4   Primo Levi . . . *Drowned and the Saved.*] Italian chemist and novelist Primo Levi (1919–1987), a survivor of the Auschwitz concentration camp. *The Drowned and the Saved* (1986) was his final book.

567.24   Lady Sneerwells] Lady Sneerwell, character in the comic play *The School for Scandal* (1777) by Richard Brinsley Sheridan (1751–1816).

577.21   "Little Gidding,"] Fourth poem of *Four Quartets* (1943) by American poet T. S. Eliot (1888–1965).

578.8   first production of *The Diary of Anne Frank*]   Broadway stage adaptation (1955) by Frances Goodrich and Albert Hackett of Anne Frank's *Diary*, first published in the Netherlands in 1947.

585.17–18   Hemingway's Upper Peninsula stories.]   "Big Two-Hearted River," story from *In Our Time* (1925) by Ernest Hemingway (1899–1961), is set on Michigan's Upper Peninsula; other Hemingway stories about his fictional alter ego Nick Adams take place in northern Michigan.

591.4–5   a well-known Norwegian writer . . . Jews]   Norwegian poet and playwright Henrik Wergeland (1808–1845), whose civil rights advocacy led to the 1851 revision of the "Jewish paragraph" of Norway's 1814 constitution, which had prohibited Jews from entering the country.

597.19–20   Raskolnikov's . . . Sonia]   The protagonist of Fyodor Dostoyevsky's *Crime and Punishment* (1866) confesses his murders to his girlfriend Sonia in part 5, ch. 4, of the novel.

612.29–32   There's a sigh . . . share it!"]   From "Sharing Eve's Apple" (1818), st. 5, by English poet John Keats (1795–1821).

613.4–6   "I have an habitual feeling . . . posthumous existence."]   From Keats's letter to Charles Brown, November 30, 1820.

618.14–15   *Lady Chatterley's Lover*]   Novel (1928) by English writer D. H. Lawrence (1885–1930) about a woman's affair with her estate's gamekeeper, banned in the United States as an obscene book until 1959.

618.23   *Anna Karenina*]   Novel (1878) by Russian writer Leo Tolstoy (1828–1910).

618.26   Hardy]   English poet and novelist Thomas Hardy (1840–1928), whose novels include *Far from the Madding Crowd* (1874), *The Return of the Native* (1878), *Tess of the d'Urbervilles* (1891), and *Jude the Obscure* (1895).

619.10–12   *Wuthering Heights . . . Jane Eyre*]   Novels published in 1847 by English novelists Emily Brontë (1818–1848) and Charlotte Brontë (1816–1855).

628.12   *The Paris Review*'s other editors]   George Plimpton (1927–2003) founded *The Paris Review* in 1953 with the writers Harold L. Humes (1926–1992) and Peter Matthiessen (b. 1927).

630.23–24   Mark Twain in his lambasting satire]   "Fenimore Cooper's Literary Offenses" (1895).

631.5   *A Farewell to Arms*]   Novel (1929) by Ernest Hemingway.

632.27–29   Hemingway had it wrong . . . Mitty."]   In a blurb for Plimpton's *Out of My League* (1961), Walter Mitty is the daydreaming protagonist of "The Secret Life of Walter Mitty," a short story by American cartoonist and humorist James Thurber (1894–1961) first published in *The New Yorker* on March 18, 1939.

635.10–12 The Jews . . . Bruce.] Vaudeville comedian, singer, and radio personality Eddie Cantor (1892–1964); comedian Jerry Lewis (b. 1926), half of the popular nightclub act Martin and Lewis and star of films including *The Bellboy* (1960) and *The Nutty Professor* (1963); Abbie Hoffman, see note 31.5–6; comedian Lenny Bruce (1925–1966), arrested numerous times on obscenity charges.

636.9 Victor Emanuel] American naturalist whom Plimpton first wrote about in *Audubon* magazine in 1972, when he joined Emanuel on a bird-watching tour.

636.24 The Twilight of the Gods.] In Norse mythology a series of events resulting in the death of the gods, dramatized in Richard Wagner's opera *Götterdammerung* (1876).

636.27–28 Father Mapple . . . lesson Jonah teaches] See ch. 9 in Melville's *Moby-Dick* (1851).

640.16 journalist named McDonell] Terry McDonell (b. 1944), journalist and editor at *Rolling Stone*, *Esquire*, *Sports Illustrated*, and other magazines.

640.32 *Henderson the Rain King*] Novel (1959) by American writer Saul Bellow (1915–2005).

641.33 *Lampoon*] *The Harvard Lampoon*, satirical undergraduate humor magazine.

642.14–15 Art Buchwald] Popular American syndicated columnist and humorist (1925–2007).

645.33–34 *The Master Builder*] Play (1892) by Ibsen.

647.36 Quilty] Clare Quilty, rival of protagonist Humbert Humbert for the love of the pubescent girl Dolores Haze in *Lolita* (1955), novel by Vladimir Nabokov (1899–1977).

659.19 Betty Friedan] See note 34.39–40.

THE LIBRARY OF AMERICA SERIES

The Library of America fosters appreciation and pride in America's literary heritage by publishing, and keeping permanently in print, authoritative editions of America's best and most significant writing. An independent nonprofit organization, it was founded in 1979 with seed funding from the National Endowment for the Humanities and the Ford Foundation.

To subscribe to the series or to order individual copies, please visit www.loa.org or call (800) 964.5778.

This book is set in 10 point ITC Galliard Pro,
a face designed for digital composition by Matthew Carter
and based on the sixteenth-century face Granjon. The paper
is acid-free lightweight opaque and meets the requirements
for permanence of the American National Standards Institute.
The binding material is Brillianta, a woven rayon cloth made
by Van Heek-Scholco Textielfabrieken, Holland. Compo-
sition by Dedicated Book Services. Printing and
binding by Edwards Brothers Malloy, Ann Arbor.
Designed by Bruce Campbell.

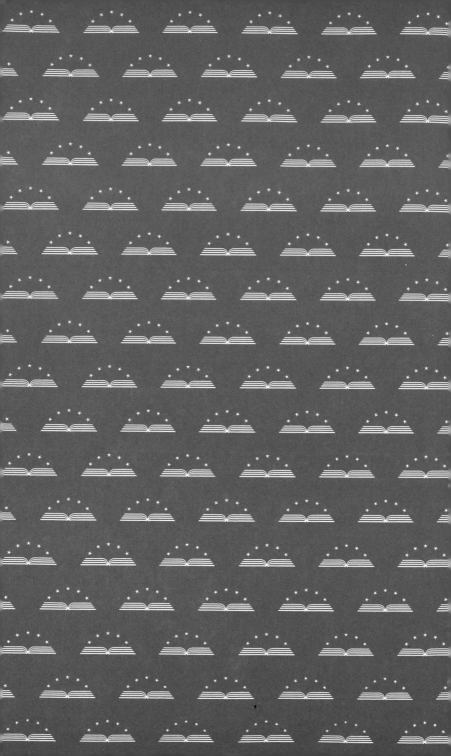